M000278255

The Editor

Jacqueline Goldsby is Professor of English and African American Studies at Yale University. She is the author of *A Spectacular Secret: Lynching in American Life and Literature*, winner of the Modern Language Association's William S. Scarborough Prize, and author of the forthcoming *In the Flow: African American Literary Culture of the 1940s and 1950s*. A digital humanities project she directed, *Mapping the Stacks: A Guide to Black Chicago's Archives*, can be accessed at www.mts.lib.uchicago.edu.

NORTON CRITICAL EDITIONS
Modernist & Contemporary Eras

ANDERSON, Winesburg, Ohio
AZUELA, The Underdogs
BABEL, Isaac Babel's Selected Writings
BURGESS, A Clockwork Orange
CATHER, My Ántonia
CATHER, O Pioneers!
CONRAD, Heart of Darkness
CONRAD, Lord Jim
Eight Modern Plays
ELIOT, The Waste Land
FAULKNER, As I Lay Dying
FAULKNER, The Sound and the Fury
FORD, The Good Soldier
FORSTER, Howards End
FRIEDAN, The Feminine Mystique
JOHNSON, The Autobiography of an Ex-Colored Man
JOYCE, Dubliners
JOYCE, A Portrait of the Artist as a Young Man
KAFKA, Kafka's Selected Stories
LARSEN, Passing
LEACOCK, Sunshine Sketches of a Little Town
MANN, Death in Venice
MANSFIELD, Katherine Mansfield's Selected Stories
Modern African Drama
Modern and Contemporary Irish Drama
PROUST, Swann's Way
RHYS, Wide Sargasso Sea
RICH, Adrienne Rich's Poetry and Prose
SHAW, George Bernard Shaw's Plays
SOYINKA, Death and the King's Horseman
STEIN, Three Lives and Q.E.D.
TOOMER, Cane
WATSON, The Double Helix
WHARTON, The Age of Innocence
WHARTON, Ethan Frome
WHARTON, The House of Mirth
WOOLF, Jacob's Room
YEATS, Yeats's Poetry, Drama, and Prose

For a complete list of Norton Critical Editions, visit
wwnorton.com/nortoncriticals

A NORTON CRITICAL EDITION

James Weldon Johnson

THE AUTOBIOGRAPHY OF AN EX-COLORED MAN

AUTHORITATIVE TEXT
BACKGROUNDS AND SOURCES
CRITICISM

Edited by
JACQUELINE GOLDSBY
YALE UNIVERSITY

W • W • NORTON & COMPANY • *New York* • *London*

W. W. Norton & Company has been independent since its founding in 1923, when William Warder Norton and Mary D. Herter Norton first published lectures delivered at the People's Institute, the adult education division of New York City's Cooper Union. The firm soon expanded its program beyond the Institute, publishing books by celebrated academics from America and abroad. By midcentury, the two major pillars of Norton's publishing program—trade books and college texts—were firmly established. In the 1950s, the Norton family transferred control of the company to its employees, and today—with a staff of four hundred and a comparable number of trade, college, and professional titles published each year—W. W. Norton & Company stands as the largest and oldest publishing house owned wholly by its employees.

Printed in the United States of America
First Edition

Library of Congress Cataloging-in-Publication Data

Johnson, James Weldon, 1871–1938.
The autobiography of an ex-colored man : authoritative text, backgrounds and sources, criticism / James Weldon Johnson ; edited by Jacqueline Goldsby.
pages cm.—(A Norton critical edition)
Includes bibliographical references and index.
ISBN 978-0-393-97286-3 (pbk. : alk. paper)
1. African American men—Fiction. I. Goldsby, Jacqueline Denise, editor. II. Title.
PS3519.O2625A95 2015
813'.52—dc23

2014041925

W. W. Norton & Company, Inc., 500 Fifth Avenue, New York, NY 10110
wwnorton.com

W. W. Norton & Company Ltd., 15 Carlisle Street, London W1D 3BS
5 6 7 8 9 0

Contents

Introduction: "Giving the Country Something New and Unknown": James Weldon Johnson's *The Autobiography of an Ex-Colored Man* ix

Acknowledgments lvii
Note on the Text lix

The Text of *The Autobiography of an Ex-Colored Man* 1
Appendix A: Revisions to Chapter X 111
Appendix B: Original Conclusion 115
Appendix C: Carl Van Vechten, Introduction to Mr. Knopf's New Edition 121
Appendix D: Introduction to the 1928 German Edition 124

Backgrounds and Sources 129
ON THE LIFE OF JAMES WELDON JOHNSON 131
James Weldon Johnson • *From* Along This Way 131
Eugene Levy • *From* James Weldon Johnson: Black Leader, Black Voice 158
Obituaries of J. Douglas Wetmore 172
Obituary of Dr. Thomas Osmond Summers 176
ON THE CULTURAL HISTORY AND MILIEU OF *THE AUTOBIOGRAPHY OF AN EX-COLORED MAN* 179
W. E. B. Du Bois • *From* The Souls of Black Folk 179
James Weldon Johnson • *From* Black Manhattan 197
Edward A. Berlin • *From* Ragtime: A Musical and Cultural History 205
COMPOSITION AND PUBLICATION CORRESPONDENCE: 1912 EDITION 221
James Weldon Johnson to Brander Matthews, [ca. November 1908] 221
James Weldon Johnson to Sherman, French & Company, February 17, 1912 222

James Weldon Johnson to Grace Nail Johnson, May 24, [1912] 224
James Weldon Johnson to John E. Nail, May 26, 1912 226
James Weldon Johnson to Grace Nail Johnson, June 26, 1912 226
George A. Towns to James Weldon Johnson, July 1, 1912 228
James Weldon Johnson to Grace Nail Johnson, September 11, [1912] 230
Charles A. Stephens to James Weldon Johnson, September 24, 1912 232
James Weldon Johnson to George A. Towns, February 4, 1913 233
Sherman, French & Co. to James Weldon Johnson, April 24, 1914 233
COMPOSITION AND PUBLICATION CORRESPONDENCE: 1927 EDITION 235
James Weldon Johnson to Carl Van Doren, December 28, 1922 235
James Weldon Johnson to Heywood Broun, May 2, 1924 236
Carl Van Vechten to James Weldon Johnson, March 23, 1925 236
James Weldon Johnson to Carl Van Vechten, March 25, 1925 237
James Weldon Johnson to Blanche W. Knopf, March 8, 1926 238
Blanche W. Knopf to James Weldon Johnson, March 31, 1926 239
Blanche W. Knopf to James Weldon Johnson, April 20, 1926 239
James Weldon Johnson to Blanche W. Knopf, April 29, 1926 240
James Weldon Johnson to Carl Van Vechten, [March 6, 1927] 240
Aaron Douglas to James Weldon Johnson, June 6, 1927 241
Carl Van Vechten to James Weldon Johnson, October 16, 1927 242
Blanche W. Knopf to James Weldon Johnson, February 15, 1929 243
Blue Jade Library Advertising Copy (1927) 243
COMPOSITION AND PUBLICATION CORRESPONDENCE: 1948 EDITION 245
Victor Weybright to Joseph G. Lesser, May 2, 1946 245
Victor Weybright to Joseph G. Lesser, January 12, 1948 246
Victor Weybright to Charles S. Johnson, January 30, 1948 247

Cecile Fishbein to New American Library, [ca. October 1948] 248
Arabel J. Porter to Cecile Fishbein, October 25, 1948 249
Ellen Tarry to "Friend," June 7, 1948 250
Arabel J. Porter to Joseph C. Lesser, June 21, 1951 251
Arabel J. Porter to Joseph C. Lesser, July 5, 1951 252
Joseph C. Lesser to Arabel J. Porter, July 10, 1951 252
RELATED WRITINGS BY JAMES WELDON JOHNSON 253
Art (ca. 1910–12) 253
Dilemma of the Poets (ca. 1910–12) 254
Words and Clothes (1911) 255
Dilemma of the Negro Author (1928) 258
ILLUSTRATIONS 266
Portrait of James Weldon Johnson (1906) 266
James Weldon Johnson's Writing Desk, Puerto Cabello, Venezuela (1907–09) 267
Sales Flyer for 1912 Edition of *Ex-Colored Man* 268
Front Cover of 1912 Edition of *Ex-Colored Man* 269
Front Cover of 1927 Edition of *Ex-Colored Man* 270
Front Cover of 1948 Edition of *Ex-Colored Man* 271
CONTEMPORARY REVIEWS: 1912 273
St. Louis (MO) *Globe-Democrat*, May 11, 1912 273
Springfield (MA) *Republican*, May 19, 1912 274
New York Times, May 26, 1912 279
Crimson and Gray (Atlanta University), June 1912 281
New York American, June 8, 1912 281
Cleveland Gazette, June 15, 1912 282
Springfield (MA) *Union*, June 15, 1912 282
Detroit Saturday Night, June 22, 1912 284
Nashville Tennessean, June 23, 1912 285
Chicago Record-Herald, July 1, 1912 286
Chicago Defender, July 3, 1912 286
New Orleans Picayune, July 12, 1927 287
Christian Advocate (NYC), July 18, 1912 287
Boston Guardian, July 20, 1912 288
Louisville Courier–Journal, July 27, 1912 288
Washington (DC) *Bee*, August 3, 1912 289
Living Age (Boston), August 17, 1912 290
Philadelphia Telegraph, August 21, 1912 290
Portland (ME) *Express*, September 14, 1912 291
Chicago Standard, October 12, 1912 293
Jessie Fauset • What to Read, *The Crisis*, November 1912 293
Brander Matthews • American Character in American Fiction, *Munsey's Magazine*, August 1913 294

CONTEMPORARY REVIEWS: 1927 303
Baltimore Afro-American, August 13, 1927 303
New York Amsterdam News, August 24, 1927 303
Chicago Daily News, August 17, 1927 304
New York World, August 23, 1927 305
Alice Dunbar-Nelson • "As in a Looking Glass," *Washington* (DC) *Eagle*, September 2, 1927 308
New Yorker, September 3, 1927 309
Chicago Defender, September 17, 1927 309
Springfield (MA) *Union*, September 21, 1927 312
The Independent, September 24, 1927 314
New York Herald Tribune, October 2, 1927 320
New York Times, October 16, 1927 321
Alice Dunbar-Nelson • "Our Bookshelf," *Opportunity*, November 1927 324
Survey Graphic, November 1, 1927 327
New York American, November 9, 1927 328
New Republic, February 1, 1928 330
Times Literary Supplement (London), March 22, 1928 331
CONTEMPORARY REVIEWS: 1948 333
Baltimore Afro-American, April 3, 1948 333
Atlanta Daily World, June 22, 1948 335
Pittsburgh Courier, September 4, 1948 335
Baltimore Afro-American, March 12, 1949 341

Criticism 339
Robert B. Stepto • Lost in a Quest: James Weldon Johnson's *The Autobiography of an Ex-Colored Man* 341
M. Giulia Fabi • The Mark Within: Parody in James Weldon Johnson's *The Autobiography of an Ex-Coloured Man* 370
Siobhan B. Somerville • Double Lives on the Color Line: "Perverse" Desire in *The Autobiography of an Ex-Colored Man* 388
Cristina L. Ruotolo • James Weldon Johnson and the Autobiography of an Ex-Colored Musician 406

James Weldon Johnson's Life and Times: A Chronology 429
Selected Bibliography 435

Introduction

"Giving the Country Something New and Unknown": James Weldon Johnson's *The Autobiography of an Ex-Colored Man*

> The problem before the novelist at present . . . is to contrive the means of being free to set down what he chooses. He has to have the courage to say that what interests him is no longer 'this' but 'that': out of 'that' alone must he construct his work. For the moderns 'that,' the point of interest, lies very likely in the dark places of psychology. At once, therefore, the accent falls a little differently; the emphasis is upon something hitherto ignored; at once a different outline of form becomes necessary, difficult for us to grasp, incomprehensible to our predecessors.
>
> —Virginia Woolf, "Modern Fiction" (1919)

> You are so passive, so unassertive, so cold; how can I sum up what seems to be your fault of character? I might say your negativeness—
>
> What you term my negativeness has cost me years of struggle to attain.
>
> —James Weldon Johnson, "The Red Book"
> (Notebook 4, ca. 1910)

A Different Outline of Form

The students enrolled in Creative Writing I, The Modern Novel, at Fisk University during spring term 1932 must have been thrilled—and intimidated—by the topic for their seventeenth meeting. That day, their professor, James Weldon Johnson, announced the books he wanted class members to discuss. Included among the modern novels they would analyze was Johnson's first and only work of prose fiction, *The Autobiography of an Ex-Colored Man* (*ECM*).[1] This would be a class to write home about.

1. James Weldon Johnson (JWJ), Fisk University Lectures, Creative Literature and Writing (1932), JWJ MSS Johnson (J.W.), Manuscripts, Box 193–224, Folders 220–22, James Weldon Johnson and Grace Nail Johnson Papers, Yale Collection of American Literature, Beinecke Rare Book and Manuscript Library (hereafter abbreviated as Beinecke). Fisk University was founded in 1866, in Nashville, Tennessee, to educate African Americans. For JWJ's account of his years teaching at Fisk, see *Along This Way* in

Just five years earlier in 1927, *ECM* had been reissued with high fanfare by the New York publisher Alfred A. Knopf. Released at the peak of the New Negro, or Harlem Renaissance, of the 1920s, the novel helped rekindle Johnson's artistic career. In the early 1900s Johnson enjoyed success as a poet, first with *Fifty Years and Other Poems* (1917), a volume that earned editorial page notice in the *New York Times*.[2] Poetry lent itself to song lyric writing, at which Johnson excelled, too. He penned an enduring hit when, in 1901, he and his brother, Rosamond, composed "Lift Every Voice and Sing," known as the Negro National Anthem. The brothers' renown burgeoned once they teamed with Bob Cole to form Johnson Brothers and Cole. The song-writing trio gained fast fame for revamping racist stereotypes promoted by the still-popular minstrel show and its repertoire of "coon songs."[3] Shuffling, pop-eyed, wide-grinning, speech-mangling, criminal characters appear nowhere in the tunes the group composed, like "Nobody's Lookin' but de Owl and de Moon" (1901), "Under the Bamboo Tree" (1903), and "Congo Love Song" (1903).[4] Remarkably, middle-class white Americans bought Johnson Brothers and Cole's sheet music by the hundreds of thousands, ranking the group among the country's most lucratively paid composers at the start of the twentieth century.[5]

At the same time that his poetry and music career thrived, Johnson worked full time in politics. Between 1916 and 1930 he served as field secretary and then executive secretary of the National Association for the Advancement of Colored People (NAACP), leading that civil rights organization's antilynching campaign for more than two decades.[6] Though absorbed by his political activism, Johnson

---

James Weldon Johnson: Writings (New York: Library of America, 2005), 591–93. Hereafter cited as *Along This Way*.

2. JWJ completed *Fifty Years* at the same time he composed *ECM*. Thematically, the poems critically celebrate the meaning of Emancipation on its half-century anniversary. JWJ's literary mentor, Columbia University professor Brander Matthews, was so impressed by the collection he persuaded his contacts at the *New York Times* to publish the title poem, "Fifty Years," on its editorial page (January 1, 1913).
3. A form of comic theater, minstrelsy featured white actors who used makeup to darken their skin and perform skits and songs that traded on racist stereotypes of African Americans. According to music historian Edward A. Berlin, coon songs made "the basest appeals to racial bigotry, using caricatured, stereotyped ridicule and brutally coarse language." See *Ragtime: A Musical and Cultural History* (Berkeley: University of California Press, 1980), 33. Minstrelsy's popularity has endured from its start in the 1830s to the present day.
4. JWJ's discussion of the trio's song-writing innovations can be found in his autobiography, *Along This Way*, chaps. 13–14, 16–20. "Under the Bamboo Tree" proved so irresistible that Yale undergraduates adapted it to compose the school's fight song, "Boola, Boola." More consequentially, T. S. Eliot wove a piece of the song lyric into his 1927 poem "Fragment of an Agon."
5. For sales data on the group's sheet music, see Eugene Levy, "Ragtime and Race Pride: The Career of James Weldon Johnson," *Phylon* 1.4 (Spring 1968): 368, n. 23.
6. For more on JWJ's career with the NAACP and his role in its antilynching drive in particular, see Charles Flint Kellogg, *NAACP: A History of the National Association for the Advancement of Colored People*, Vol. 1, *1909–1920* (Baltimore: Johns Hopkins

kept producing literary works throughout the 1920s. He edited what scholars now recognize as landmark anthologies, *The Book of American Negro Poetry* (1922) and *The Book of American Negro Spirituals* (1925). In 1927 he released *God's Trombones*, a poetry collection that adapted African American dialect and sermonic style into verse form. As if these literary landmarks were not enough, Johnson mentored younger writers who became the stars of the Harlem Renaissance. Johnson mobilized his formidable social networks to help authors Langston Hughes, Zora Neale Hurston, Claude McKay, and Countee Cullen secure day jobs, writing fellowships, travel visas, and publishing contacts that fostered their careers.[7]

With three decades of extraordinary achievement preceding him to Fisk University, Johnson sat before his students as a luminary in Harlem's literary circles, a politician of national renown, and the first-ever African American named to an endowed professorship in a U.S. college or university.[8] Hobnobbing with a celebrity like Johnson would have been awe-inspiring enough; analyzing Johnson's literary work—and in his company, no less—must have been a daunting prospect for the students, given the issues Johnson raised for the group's discussion.

According to his seminar notebook, Johnson spent at least three sessions discussing his novel and its "technical and psychological aspects."[9] As he explained, *ECM* did not employ a common style of narration in which "a character in the story becomes the narrator," or "by which the author assumes omniscience or omnipresence."[1] Instead, like the two texts Johnson assigned the class to read along with his own (*The Autobiography of Benvenuto Cellini* and *Robinson Crusoe*), *ECM*'s point of view aimed to produce a specific literary effect.[2] "The author becomes the narrator," Johnson declared. After this point in his teaching notebook, a blank space appears

University Press, 1980); Jacqueline Goldsby, *A Spectacular Secret: Lynching in American Life and Literature* (Chicago: University of Chicago Press, 2006), 170–82.

7. An insightful but critical account of Johnson's role as a literary gatekeeper can be found in David Levering Lewis, *When Harlem Was in Vogue* (New York: Penguin, 1997, 1979), 143–49. A similarly complex critique can be gleaned from Michael North's characterization of Johnson's poetic theories in *Dialect of Modernism: Race, Language, and Twentieth-Century Literature* (New York: Oxford University Press, 1998). Zora Neale Hurston offers a humorous parody of Johnson's cultural clout in her 1942 memoir, *Dust Tracks on a Road* (New York: Harper Perennial Modern Classics, 2010), 238.
8. Before to JWJ's appointment at Fisk, no African American scholar or artist ever held an endowed professorship at a U.S. college or university.
9. JWJ, Fisk University Lecture, Creative Literature and Writing (1932). Lecture 19, April 5, 1932, Beinecke.
1. JWJ, Fisk University Lecture, Creative Literature and Writing (1932). Lecture 17, March 29, 1932. Beinecke.
2. Ibid. Daniel Defoe's eighteenth-century classic is a suggestive antecedent to *ECM*; see Alice Dunbar Nelson's 1927 review on p. 325, in this volume. Italian sculptor Benvenuto Cellini's scandalous exposé of his career in Renaissance art and court circles was first translated into English in 1887 by John Addington Symonds.

suggestively, implying Johnson meant for his students to discuss this technique.[3] Because according to the next talking point enumerated in his notes, Johnson proposed, "so far as I know *ECM* is the only piece of fiction of Negro life . . . written according to this method."[4]

How did the Fisk undergraduates respond to their professor's claim? We cannot know because there are no classroom transcripts or other archival records documenting their responses. Johnson's course notebooks still exist, though, and together with the background reading he tackled to plan his classes, we can glean more insights into why he wanted to teach his novel as a modern work of fiction.

His teaching assignments at Fisk occurred at the same time that American scholars and critics were fiercely debating whether contemporary fiction was worthy of college-level study. This culture war, which started in the 1890s, kept "modern" fiction from finding a secure niche in college English departments until the 1930s.[5] To navigate his way through those conflicts, Johnson relied on V. L. Parrington's highly regarded (and best-selling) *Main Currents of American Thought* (1927) to develop his Fisk courses.[6] Following Parrington's paradigm, Johnson organized a lecture survey, "American Literature, 1880–1930," using the rubrics of historical romance, realism, and naturalism.[7] For his seminar "The Modern Novel," he turned to a different critical reference because Parrington's literary genealogy stopped around World War I. E. M. Forster's *Aspects of the Novel* (1927) clearly resonated with Johnson's understanding of modern fiction's formal developments, given how consistently he relied on Forster's typologies to organize his creative writing class discussions. For instance, Johnson's notebook lays out queries and examples that distinguish between story and plot, flat and round characters, pattern and rhythm, as Forster does in his study.[8] More

3. Ibid.
4. Ibid.
5. Gerald Graff, *Professing Literature: An Institutional History* (Chicago: University of Chicago Press, 2007, 1987), chaps. 7–8.
6. Now considered to be a founding work in American Studies, Parrington's book won the Pulitzer Prize in 1928. See Graff, *Professing Literature*, 215–16. JWJ's correspondents Carl Van Doren and Joel E. Spingarn recommended Parrington and Forster to read. See JWJ to Carl Van Doren, October 3, 1932, and Joel E. Spingarn to JWJ, October 19, 1933, Beinecke. Importantly, both Van Doren and Spingarn taught at Columbia University, a key site where the modern fiction curricular wars were fought. Spingarn—a comparative literature scholar who was also president of the NAACP—was a leading proponent of modernist literary studies. On Spingarn's literary career, see Graff, *Professing Literature*, 126–28.
7. See JWJ, Fisk University Lectures, "Contemporary American Literature, 1933," Beinecke
8. According to his seminar notebook, JWJ did not cover two aspects Forster termed "fantasy" and "prophesy." See JWJ, Fisk University Lectures, Creative Literature & Writing, Beinecke. However, JWJ's survey lecture incorporated Forster's typology more

interesting, Johnson's choice of novels demonstrates how thoroughly he absorbed Forster's theory of literary movements and periods, an approach that explains *ECM*'s inclusion in Johnson's syllabus.

Forster insists that the novel's literary history knows no national boundaries. In fact, *Aspects of the Novel* begins by rejecting the dominance of the British canon altogether. "An unpleasant and unpatriotic truth has here to be faced," Forster advises, "the English novel is nowhere near as accomplished as the Russian or French novel. . . . Before these triumphs we must pause."[9] In Forster's thinking, linear chronologies did not demarcate the novel's history either, because artistic progress cannot always be gauged through forward-leaning momentum; novels from earlier times could instruct contemporary writers. Thus Forster declares, "this idea of a period of a development in time, with its consequent emphasis on influences and schools, happens to be exactly what I am hoping to avoid during our brief survey. . . . Time, all the way through, is to be our enemy" (8). Instead, the history of modern novel writing was, in Forster's view, temporally fluid, socially communal, and aesthetically flexible, as this astonishing mise-en-scène suggests:

> We are to visualize the English novelists not as flowing down that stream which bears its sons away unless they are careful, but as seated together in a room, a circular room, a sort of British Museum reading-room—all writing their novels simultaneously. They do not, as they sit there, think "I live under Queen Victoria, I under Anne, I carry on the tradition of Trollope, I am reacting against Aldous Huxley." The fact that their pens are in their hands is far more vivid to them. They are half-mesmerized, their sorrows and joys are pouring through their ink, they are approximated by the act of creation (8–9).

Encountering this argument as he planned his Fisk courses, Johnson was likely inspired by Forster's claims. A de-emphasis on the British canon's taste-shaping power enabled him to see *ECM*'s achievements in a more expansive matrix. Using Forster's framework, Johnson could place his novel in conversation with other texts and locate it in a global literary practice. Moreover, *Aspects of the Novel* reoriented the timeline by which Johnson could evaluate his own creative effort. If novel writing happened "simultaneously," as Forster insisted, then *ECM* could be read alongside both the novels of Johnson's contemporaries and also works that preceded his own. With the field of novel writing desegregated in this way, literary alliances, resemblances, and affinities—what novelist Ralph Ellison would later call "literary

---

extensively into his argument's scheme. See JWJ, Fisk University Lectures, "Contemporary American Literature, 1933," Beinecke.

9. E. M. Forster, *Aspects of the Novel* (Orlando, FL: Harcourt Brace Books, 1927), 7.

ancestry" and literary theorists "intertextuality"—could be claimed and asserted as first principles of understanding and not merely after the fact.[1] Put another way, *Aspects of the Novel* taught Johnson that it was not too late for him to claim the novel he first published in 1912 as modern literature in 1932.

And indeed, Johnson wrote a novel that so thoroughly transformed the depiction of character, consciousness, time, and plot that the American reading public was utterly confounded when *ECM* was released in 1912. Based on the novel's first edition (rather than its 1927 reprint), this Norton Critical Edition (NCE) aims to reconstruct *ECM*'s modernity in the literary histories of its own and our times. Bringing together a wealth of previously unpublished archival materials and a rich range of secondary sources that explicate the novel's narrative innovations and intricacies, this volume approaches *ECM* as an early experiment in literary modernism whose aesthetic innovations and cultural history established African American novel writing in a global literary-historical scheme.[2] This introduction presents the following lines of analysis to develop this claim.

First, the essay considers *ECM*'s entry into the African American literary canon. What was at stake in Johnson's choice to fictionalize the autobiography mode? How did that experiment reorient African American life and fiction writing in the late-nineteenth and early-twentieth centuries? Second, because *ECM*'s aesthetic developments coincide with and sometimes anticipate key features that define modern Anglo-American novel writing, the essay considers how *ECM* links to such works as Virginia Woolf's *Jacob's Room* (1919), Jean Toomer's *Cane* (1923), F. Scott Fitzgerald's *The Great Gatsby* (1925), Nella Larsen's *Quicksand* (1928), and Gertrude Stein's *The Autobiography of Alice B. Toklas* (1933). What does it mean that *ECM*'s stylistic features resonate so powerfully with these works' signature narrative designs? Third, the essay details how the novel's physical form symbolizes key developments in U.S. publishing. Why does *ECM*'s history as a book make it modernist? Finally, the essay surveys the critical reception of *ECM* to chart how, over time, the public's response to the

1. Ellison introduces this famous concept in his essay "The Hidden Name and the Complex Fate" (1964). See *Shadow and Act* (New York: Vintage, 1995, 1964), 162.
2. Two other editions of *ECM* stress the novel's modernist sensibilities. See the introductions by Henry Louis Gates Jr. and William L. Andrews to the Vintage (1989) and Penguin (1990) volumes, respectively. This NCE differs from those in two respects: it places *ECM* in a comparative context beyond the African American and U.S. canons; and it provides unprecedented access to archival sources that allow readers to explore the novel's modernist ambitions directly for themselves. For these reasons, this essay builds upon but differs from the analysis of *ECM* that I offer in *A Spectacular Secret: Lynching in American Life and Literature* (Chicago: University of Chicago Press, 2006), chap. 4. There, I argue that the novel's experimental energies are vested in challenging the norms of literary realism as adequate to the task of depicting the violence of lynching. Here, I place emphasis on the modernist innovations that *ECM*'s defiance of realism made possible.

novel reflected what Johnson famously called "the dilemma of the Negro artist": what challenges did *ECM* surmount to be read by racially segregated audiences? Confronting this task required levels of ingenuity from Johnson that could not have been fully named in the moment of *ECM's* making, given how tenuous the literary field was for black novels in the first decades of the twentieth century. However, in 1932 Johnson and his Fisk students could take a first view to see how transformative *ECM* was in and across its times. From the vantage point this Norton Critical Edition provides, today's readers can judge for themselves how "modern" the novel still proves to be.

A New Black "I": ECM's *Revision of African American Autobiography*

The Autobiography of an Ex-Colored Man reads as the *bildungsroman* (or coming-of-age) narrative that its title suggests. Born in Georgia "a few years after the close of the Civil War" (5),[3] the narrator is "the child of [the] unsanctioned love" (25) between a prosperous white Southern businessman and an African American woman. For reasons that are not explicitly stated (but are no doubt influenced by the South's prohibitions against interracial marriage), the narrator's mother relocates to Connecticut. Supported by a stipend from his wealthy father and his mother's earnings as a seamstress, the narrator enjoys a comfortable upbringing that depends on two crucial presumptions: the narrator believes he is rich and white. His sense of privilege shatters when, in a humiliating scene at school, the narrator learns he is "a nigger" (12). He then endures a second blow: the death of his beloved mother. Orphaned and uncertain about his identity, the narrator begins a tumultuous journey that makes up the core of the novel.

Migrating up and down America's southeastern coast, his ambiguous racial appearance allows him to live as black or white at will. He mixes and mingles among African American college students in Atlanta; Cuban refugee nationalists in Jacksonville, Florida; and gamblers, nightclub musicians, and socialites of all racial and cultural backgrounds in Manhattan. A musical prodigy, the narrator develops his piano-playing talents to rise in the world of ragtime music, where he rapidly builds a fan base. He soon wins financial backing from the moody "Millionaire," who sponsors the narrator's travels abroad to Europe. Performing at this white patron's parties in London, Berlin, and Paris, the narrator gains a reputation for "ragging the classics"—adapting classical music into ragtime piano's signature

3. *ECM* page numbers refer to this Norton Critical Edition.

sounds and cadence. However, when a German pianist performs ragtime music to sound classical itself, the narrator adopts this method as his own and returns to America to pursue his career by presenting himself as an African American archivist and performer of black folk music.

The novel's climax occurs with the grim destruction of the narrator's plan. While conducting fieldwork in Georgia to collect Negro spirituals, the narrator witnesses a brutal lynching of a black man. This horrific event spurs him to "neither disclaim the black race nor claim the white race; but [to] change my name, raise a moustache, and let the world take me for what it would" (99). The novel concludes with the pyrrhic victories the narrator enjoys living in his self-defined limbo as an "ex-colored man." Emulating his white male role models, he becomes a businessman like his Southern father and aims to earn millions like his former musical patron by dealing real estate in New York City. His wealth and supposed whiteness allow him to socialize with other white elites, a network that leads him to the white woman he decides to marry. The couple's courtship thrives until the narrator reveals his biracial identity to his fiancée. At first, the woman breaks off their engagement. She eventually relents and marries the narrator, though their union comes at a high price: she dies giving birth to their second child. Left to raise their daughter and infant son on his own, bereft and confused about his life's purpose, the narrator closes his narrative with this sobering confession to himself and the reader:

> . . . when I sometimes open a little box in which I still keep my fast yellowing manuscripts [i.e., his sheet music compositions], the only tangible remnants of a vanished dream, a dead ambition, a sacrificed talent, I cannot repress the thought that, after all, I have chosen the lesser part, that I have sold my birthright for a mess of pottage. (110)

To call this story an "autobiography" was a heretical act on Johnson's part, given that genre's legacy in African American literature.[4] Before the Civil War—particularly during the 1830s, 1840s, and 1850s—"narratives of the life" were vigorously promoted by the antislavery movement. Under the aegis of abolitionist newspapers and book printers, fugitive slaves' lectures were published as print narratives to further the political campaign for black emancipation. Widely read in the United States, England, and across Europe,

4. For comprehensive analyses of the genre's development across the nineteenth century, see William L. Andrews, *To Tell a Free Story: The First Century of Afro-American Autobiography, 1760–1865* (Urbana: University of Illinois Press, 1988); Frances Smith Foster, *Written by Herself: Literary Production by African American Women, 1746–1892* (Bloomington: Indiana University Press, 1993); and Henry Louis Gates Jr. and Charles T. Davis, eds., *The Slave's Narrative* (New York: Oxford University Press, 1991).

works by Frederick Douglass, William Wells Brown, William and Ellen Craft, and Henry "Box" Brown commanded the field of African American writing before Emancipation.

After the Civil War, African American autobiographies evolved in two distinct ways that reflected the political climate of the postbellum era, known as the "nadir." The rise of Jim Crow segregation laws, the exploitation of black laborers under the sharecropping and convict lease systems in the South, the political disenfranchisement of the Southern black electorate, and the rise of lynching and rape as means to terrorize black communities to comply with these new forms of white supremacy gave fresh purpose and meaning to African American autobiography from the 1870s to the early 1900s. Freedwomen and freedmen needed role models whose courageous, exemplary conduct could inspire them to "uplift the race," as the motto went, despite the repression raging against them.[5] Unlike antebellum narratives, which aimed to persuade a predominantly white readership to support the antislavery movement, postbellum autobiographies widened their purview to encourage African American readers to realize their potential for self-help. Crucially, because emancipation fostered the development of black-owned printing firms, African American autobiographers were liberated from the editorial control of white abolitionists, freeing them to exercise more authority over the stories they told.[6] Though narratives extolling the lives and achievements of black "masterminds" abounded in the African American periodical press, two works towered above them all: Booker T. Washington's *Up from Slavery* (1901) and W. E. B. Du Bois's *The Souls of Black Folk* (1903).

At key moments, Johnson's narrator makes explicit allusions to Washington's self-help credo and Du Bois's famous narrative. For instance, the novel concludes at a rally in New York City, where the Wizard of Tuskegee (as Washington was known) delivers a lecture at Carnegie Hall exhorting his listeners with "so much earnestness

5. Insightful accounts of postbellum autobiographies include, Henry Louis Gates Jr., "The Trope of the New Negro and the Reconstruction of the Image of the Black," *Representations* 24 (Autumn 1988): 129–55; and P. Gabrielle Foreman's helpful concept, "histotextuality," in *Activist Sentiments: Reading Black Women in the Nineteenth Century* (Urbana: University of Illinois Press, 2009).

6. African Americans owned and operated printing presses before the Civil War as well. However, those proprietors were limited to free blacks in the urban North. Though white-owned firms continued to publish postbellum autobiographies (for instance, Du Bois's *Souls of Black Folk* and Washington's *Up from Slavery*), after 1865 the ranks of black-owned and managed printing presses increased and spread across the nation, including the Deep South. On this shift see Donald Franklin Joyce, *Gatekeepers of Black Culture: Black-Owned Book Publishing in the United States, 1817–1981* (Westport, CT: Greenwood Press, 1983); Arthur and Abby Johnson, *Propaganda and Aesthetics: the Literary Politics of African American Magazines in the Twentieth Century* (Amherst: University of Massachusetts Press, 1991).

and faith" (110).[7] In several passages across the text, the narrator mulls over Du Bois's concept of "double consciousness," suggesting that *Souls of Black Folk* serves as a touchstone referent for the character, if not Johnson himself. Allusions such as these have prompted scholars to explore *ECM*'s literary echoes of *Up from Slavery* and *Souls*.[8] However, Johnson's homage is not so straightforward. Though he had read both works, he disliked those authors to the point where he chafed at the thought of following in either Washington's or Du Bois's literary footsteps. "B.T. Wash ought to have been a field hand. Du Bois a house servant," Johnson wrote in one of the several diaries he kept while drafting *ECM*.[9] In fact, a literary rivalry emerged between Johnson and Du Bois once *ECM* was published. Johnson fumed that Du Bois ignored his work by suppressing news of its release in the magazine he edited: "So *The Crisis* has not reviewed my book," Johnson complained to his wife, Grace. "It will be a test of just how big minded a man he is."[1] Du Bois's literary ego did take precedence, as his novel *The Quest of the Silver Fleece* (1911) received constant publicity and a much longer review than *ECM*.[2] A close reading of the ex-colored man's plan to popularize African American spirituals might explain why Du Bois gave short shrift to Johnson's novel: does the ex-colored man affirm or defy Du Bois's veneration of the "sorrow songs"? NCE readers can explore both possibilities by comparing Johnson's depiction of his protagonist's outlook (Chapter X) with the excerpt included from *Souls of Black Folk* in this volume.

A more likely influence on Johnson's reconception of the autobiographical canon is *The Life and Times of Frederick Douglass* (1881). That work, which Johnson read and deeply admired, is remarkable because with it, Douglass abandons the moral aim of his antebellum accounts.[3] Where the 1845 and 1855 narratives situated Douglass's plight in communal contexts and his journey to literacy and freedom as exemplary, *Life and Times* stresses

7. The novel indicates that the rally was held on behalf of the Hampton Institute, a historically black college in Virginia. However, the incident the narrator describes exactly fits news reports of Washington's 1906 speech at Carnegie Hall, which was a fundraiser/celebration of Tuskegee's fiftieth anniversary. See *New York Tribune*, January 28, 1906, 1, chroniclingamerica.loc.gov/lccn/sn83030214/1906-01-28/ed-1/seq-15.
8. See the essay by Robert Stepto on in this volume.
9. JWJ, Notebook #3, 7, Beinecke. JWJ's acerbic views tempered with time. After a decade of political collaboration through the NAACP, JWJ publicly praised Du Bois's *Souls* as the most significant work by a black author between the Civil War and World War I.
1. JWJ to Grace Nail Johnson, August 31 [1912]. Beinecke.
2. Along with the lengthier review (December 1911), the *Crisis* promoted Du Bois's novel aggressively, showcasing multiple listings of its display ads for a full year after the novel's release.
3. JWJ won a copy of Douglass's *Life and Times* as a prize in high school. Shortly afterward, the two met in 1895. See *Along This Way*, 201.

Douglass's achievements to have been won by a singular, self-made man. Presenting himself to be exceptional rather than representative, Douglass's revision of the slave narrative tradition is more akin to the skeptical spirit that suffuses *ECM*. Unlike *Up from Slavery* or *The Souls of Black Folk*, Johnson's novel parodies how autobiography's protocols racialized the genre to narrow, rather than liberate, the channels through which African American voices and experiences could be heard.

For instance, *ECM* broke rank with a key authorial norm that shaped antebellum slave narratives by insisting on the protagonist's invisibility.[4] To begin with, he elected not to title the novel with this explicitly fictive phrase, "The Chameleon."[5] He also rejected this awkward version: "The Autobiography of a (Formerly) Colored Man (or) of an Ex-Colored Man."[6] Shortened to "The Autobiography of an Ex-Colored Man," the title renders the idea of literary categories indistinct, a critique that extends to a second authorial norm that Johnson breaks: erasing direct references to the book's author. Notably, the narrator refuses to disclose his name to the reader; he only identifies himself as an "ex-colored man" and remains anonymous. Where antebellum autobiographers sat for frontispiece portraits and published their names on their book covers and title pages to assert the subjectivity and identity that slavery denied them, Johnson's narrator refuses to do so. In fact, his physical descriptions echo his name because those verbal self-portraits render him functionally invisible—they appear only twice. By contrast, declaiming the author's name was typically emphasized in black-authored antebellum autobiographies, as that gesture archived one of enslavement's special cruelties. Birthplaces, birthdates, and parentage mark embittered memory lapses in slave narratives because narrators are often overwhelmed to detail the economic exploitation and sexual violence that defined their family trees.

Johnson's novel draws this pattern to a close when the narrator describes meeting his father for the first time (19–21). The clear pain the protagonist feels greeting his estranged parent with "the

4. In "Irony and Symbolic Action in James Weldon Johnson's *The Autobiography of an Ex-Colored Man*," *American Quarterly* 32.5 (Winter 1980): 540–58, critic Joseph T. Skerrett, Jr., deploys the phrase *authorial norms* to delineate the innovations of Johnson's novel. Later in this discussion, I characterize the novel's aimless, seemingly shapeless course as evidence of its modernist techniques; for a different take on the novel's plotlessness, see Simone Vauthier's "The Interplay of Narrative Modes in James Weldon Johnson's *The Autobiography of an Ex-Colored Man*," *Jarbuch fur Amkerikastudien* 18 (1973): 173–81, which links *ECM* to the tradition of the pícaresque novels in Spanish-language literatures. Vauthier's interpretation underscores the novel's transnational lineages that JWJ, fluent in Hispanophone literatures and drafting the book in Latin America, undoubtedly brought to bear on his novel writing.
5. JWJ's brother, Rosamond, suggested this title; see *Along This Way*, 394.
6. JWJ, Notebook #3 (c. 1910), Beinecke.

word which had been . . . a source of doubt and perplexity" (20) is held at bay by the cool detachment which the narrator summons to recall the scene:

> My mother stood at my side with one hand on my shoulder almost pushing me forward, but I did not move. I can well remember the look of disappointment, even pain, in her face; and I can now understand that she could not expect nothing else but that at the name "father" I should throw myself into his arms. But I could not rise to this dramatic or, better, melodramatic climax. (20)

Here, the narrator rejects white patriarchy's claim to omnipotence, together with the slave narrative's formal norm of moral power: the open expression of emotion. Though he terms it *melodrama,* the narrator derides the literary codes of nineteenth-century sentimentalism, which held that the thoughts and actions of characters should be perfectly transparent to readers who, in turn, would find such narratives credible or true because of the mirrored response the story would evoke. Crying (and sympathy's visible marker, tears) symbolized sentimentalism's literary power best, as weeping over a character's fate demonstrated readers' sincere investment in the narrative's action. However, in this scene from Johnson's novel, tears are nowhere to be seen; cries are soundless. Only "the look of disappointment, even pain" crosses the mother's face. The narrator's dispassionate tone refuses to "rise" and reveal the ex-colored man's emotional state. Consequently, the reader finds herself able to "expect nothing else" from her own reaction as well. Though scholars argue powerfully that this anti-sentimentalism links the ex-colored man to a later literary figure like Ralph Ellison's invisible man,[7] it is important to consider how, as early as 1912, Johnson revised antebellum autobiography's rhetoric of protest to escape the racial codes that would delimit his authorial identity and ambition as a black writer working in the early twentieth century.

ECM's Preface unsettles a third authorial norm that defined African American autobiography across the ante- and postbellum eras. At a first glance, the 1912 edition appears to rehearse the antislavery movement's tactic of offering white-authored testimony to guarantee the black-authored narrative as legitimate. And indeed, "The Publishers" of *ECM* offer an enthusiastic endorsement of the work. However, no one at Sherman & French Company—Johnson's 1912 publisher—wrote the copy. Johnson's correspondence confirms that he composed the Preface to the 1912 edition, which NCE readers have direct access to for the first time.

7. For one example, see the essay by Stepto on p. 347 in this volume.

The novel's Preface, given Johnson's authorship of it, stages multiple acts of forgery. He composed the statement on behalf of his white publisher, pretending to be the anonymous ex-colored man who is the book's supposed author. Read in this way, the Preface decidedly rejects the idea of white sponsors legitimating black writing, a publication practice that slave narratives promoted.[8] Consequently, NCE readers should parse the Preface's claims carefully, as its statements encode how Johnson's novel dislodges the racial politics underpinning autobiography's nineteenth-century form.[9]

ECM unsettled yet a fourth racial contract informing nineteenth- and early-twentieth-century African American autobiography. Antebellum narratives placed a premium on depicting arduous physical experience because the brutalities meted out during enslavement and the terrors endured to escape North to freedom piqued white readers' interest most. Consequently, descriptions of black bodies in pain abound in fugitive slave narratives.[1] These corporeal-focused accounts were often entwined with a companion plot: the narrator's journey toward attaining literacy. Because, in the United States, literacy was forbidden to slaves and often punished by physical torture, learning to read and write was often depicted as profoundly moral and, indeed, spiritual acts that involved great suffering.[2] However, literacy and its signature tropes—like the black-body-in-pain's value as a sign of autobiographical authenticity—come under critical revision in *ECM*.

Growing up well-funded by his Southern white father in liberal New England, the ex-colored man did not have to steal his education the way that Frederick Douglass famously describes across all of his narratives. However, the narrator's relationship to reading and writing begs for close analysis given the ways he flaunts his

8. On this practice, see Robert B. Stepto, *From behind the Veil: A Study of Afro-American Narrative* (Urbana: University of Illinois Press, 1991, 1979), chap. 1; and John Sekora, "Black Message/White Envelope: Genre, Authenticity, and Authority in the Antebellum Slave Narrative," *Callaloo* 32 (Summer 1987): 482–515.
9. Many critics have described the novel's generic hybridity as a formal expression of its thematic concern with racial passing. For exemplary critical works in this vein, see the essays by Stepto and M. Gulia Fabi on p. 370 in this volume. However, such arguments depend on knowing the novel is, in fact, a work of fiction, an interpretation Johnson labored assiduously to thwart in 1912.
1. The most compelling compendium of this pornography of pain can be found in Theodore Weld's *American Slavery As It Is* (1838), but most—if not all—slave narratives feature it. Ephraim Peabody's 1849 review, "Narratives of Fugitive Slaves," frets over this reading taste. Scholarship on this poetics of cruelty is quite extensive. Saidiya Hartman offers the most thorough critique of the limitations of this narrative-historical convention; see *Scenes of Subjection: Terror, Slavery, and Self-Making in Nineteenth-Century America* (New York: Oxford University Press, 1997).
2. Perhaps the most vivid example of this trope occurs in Frederick Douglass's 1845 *Narrative*, where he describes the end of a day's labor on Colonel Lloyd's plantation: "I sle[pt] on the cold, damp floor, with my head and feet out [of a burlap bag]. My feet have been so cracked by the frost, that the pen with which I am writing might be laid in its gashes." See *Narrative of the Life of Frederick Douglass, An American Slave, Written by Himself*, eds. William L. Andrews and William S. McFeely (New York: Norton, 1997), 26.

literacy skills throughout the text. Despite his unlimited access to books, his constant allusions to what he reads, and his unrelenting boasts about his superior reading talents, the narrator uses these privileges to avoid any social responsibility toward the black communities he encounters.[3] Perhaps the most heretical instance of his intellectual narcissism occurs when, in Jacksonville, Florida, the narrator works as a *lector*, reading Spanish novels and newspapers to the Cuban factory laborers who make cigars. The narrator unabashedly admits he accepts the post for its cultural prestige—the *lector*, he tells us, "must have a reputation among the men for intelligence, for being well-adjusted, and having in his head a stock of varied information" (40). Then, in a remarkable show of hubris, he openly declares he sought the work to avoid the bodily toil and economic hardships faced by his fellow workers. "My position as a 'reader' not only released me from the rather monotonous work of rolling cigars, and gave me something more in accordance with my tastes, [it] also added considerably to my income. I was now earning about twenty-five dollars a week," the narrator drolly recalls (40).

Read with twenty-first-century sensibilities, the ex-colored man's fluency in Spanish not only recalls Johnson's own foreign language skills, but the character's linguistic prowess also beckons us to question the predominance of English as America's national language.[4] At the same time, the ex-colored man's crass confession refuses the moral imperative of collective uplift that energized scenes of reading and education in both antebellum slave narratives and postbellum autobiographies. This plot point reveals *ECM*'s most heretical challenge to those genres: Johnson's antiheroic depiction of the narrator. How, for instance, should NCE readers respond when the ex-colored man jilts the schoolteacher he all but promised to marry in Jacksonville (45, 48)? His "gaslight life" (48) in New York City's Tenderloin district borders on scandal and deliberately so; the narrator's wayward choices are meant to flout bourgeois codes of propriety. Such carelessness leads the ex-colored man to flee situations that other black autobiographers risked their lives to protest—most famously, the lynching that makes up the novel's climax. That critics have never stopped debating the narrator's flight from that scene suggests how unusual the ex-colored man remains

3. Gayle F. Wald explicates this tendency brilliantly; see "The Satire of Race in James Weldon Johnson's *Autobiography of an Ex-Colored Man*," in *Cross-Addressing: Resistance Literature and Cultural Borders*, ed. John C. Harley (Albany: State University of New York Press, 1996), 139–55.

4. In *Along This Way*, JWJ proudly recounts his lifelong fluency in Spanish. Given its explicit contest to English language's hegemony, *ECM* stages an important rebuttal to his mentor Brander Matthews's philosophy of linguistic nationalism, which implies JWJ may not have been the literary conservative Michael North presents in *The Dialect of Modernism*.

in the African American canon. While some scholars explain this irreverence (or cowardice) as a sign of the protagonist's Africanist trickster sensibility and others proclaim it as early evidence of his skeptical relation to a black cultural identity, the range of emotions the ex-colored man feels in breaking the rules of racial respectability for their own sake merits close study.[5] For that reason, NCE readers should track the instances of the ECM's racial heresies (especially his exposés of the "freemasonry of the race") and ponder why Johnson felt compelled to undermine autobiography's modes of narration so thoroughly. Why could that genre not adequately address the varied ways in which African American identity and solidarity might be imagined?

Another Country: ECM's *Revolt against "Race" Novels*

Johnson could push the boundaries of African American life writing to these limits because *ECM* was—and is—a work for fiction. However, the novel's success depended on Johnson concealing its fictive origins from his reading public. Indeed, for his parody of autobiography to work its full narrative effect when it was first published in 1912, Johnson did not openly avow that *ECM* was a novel at all. This NCE provides examples from Johnson's private correspondence in which he orchestrates his campaign to publicize the novel as an authentic autobiography rather than the novel it was. In one such letter, Johnson explained to his wife, Grace:

> the absolute secrecy of the authorship must be maintained. . . . [As] soon as it is known that the author is a colored man who could not be the character in the book, interest in it will fall. There must always be in the reader's mind the thought that, at least, it may be true.[6]

Johnson's success at this ruse helps explain why in most accounts of what scholars call Afro-modernism, *ECM* is often not named as a landmark work in that canon. More often than not, Jean Toomer's *Cane* (1923) receives that critical acclaim.[7] If, however, we position

5. For instance, see the essays by Fabi and Stepto on in this volume.
6. JWJ to Grace Nail Johnson, June 26, 1912, Beinecke. For an analysis of JWJ's publicity campaign, see Jacqueline Goldsby, "Keeping the Secret of Authorship: A Critical Look at the 1912 Publication of James Weldon Johnson's *The Autobiography of an Ex-Colored Man*," in *Print Culture in a Diverse America*, eds. James P. Danky and Wayne A. Wiegand (Urbana: University of Illinois Press, 1998), 244–71.
7. Arguably, ECM epitomizes black modernism's signature style as defined by Houston A. Baker Jr.—demonstrating the "mastery of form" in order to "de-form" racial constructs of mastery. However, the novel's not highlighted in Baker's *Modernism and the Harlem Renaissance* (Chicago: University of Chicago Press, 1987). Nor is it featured in Craig Werner's *Playing the Changes: From Afro-Modernism to the Jazz Impulse* (Urbana: University of Illinois Press, 1994). More recently, James Smethurst analyzes the ex-colored man's angst-ridden relationship to his racial identity as evidence of the "dualism" that

ECM back to its first edition's release in 1912, capping off the decades when African American novel writing emerges as a full-fledged aesthetic movement, what might our understanding of Johnson's contribution be?

Before the Civil War, only three book-length works of fiction by African American authors made it to print, and all of those appeared during the 1850s.[8] After Reconstruction, black novel writing boomed during the 1890s and early 1900s.[9] The African American novel's rise followed this uneven development for complex, but logical reasons. First, the antislavery movement's global networks of lecture venues, newspapers, printing firms, editors, and readers could have supported African American fiction writing; after all, the literacy skills required to invent (rather than to document) social worlds could have served as equally compelling proof of African Americans' intelligence, humanity, and right to freedom as well. However, the African American novel did not earn that favor precisely because the genre's appeal lay entirely in its authors' and readers' imaginative capacities. In fiction, African American writers could depict characters, conflicts, and setting without reference to social history because, unlike autobiography, a novel's story need not be empirically accurate to be true.

Furthermore, to persuade readers to suspend belief in their own real worlds subverted the social order of things; inhabiting milieu invented by the black text they held in their hands, readers subjected themselves to the imaginative powers of African American writers. This dynamic granted fiction writers intellectual authority that American society otherwise denied black people. These status quo–breaking tendencies of novel writing and novel reading explain why antebellum Northern newspapers managed by free blacks regularly published prose fiction (short stories and serialized novels) by African American and Anglo-American writers alike. As literary historian Elizabeth McHenry points out, this publishing practice "advanced the unprecedented idea of . . . creative parity" on behalf

---

would preoccupy Anglo-American modernism after World War I; see *The African American Roots of Modernism: From Reconstruction of the Harlem Renaissance* (Chapel Hill: University of North Carolina Press, 2011), pp. 61–64, as do the introductions by Gates and Andrews to the Vintage and Penguin editions of *ECM*. Nicole Morrissette provides a rich, extensive analysis of *ECM*'s modernism by tracing how Johnson's experiments with music infused and transformed his approach to prose fiction. See *James Weldon Johnson's Modern Soundscapes* (Iowa City: University of Iowa Press, 2013).

8. The novels included William Wells Brown, *Clotel* (1853); Hannah Craft, *The Bondswoman's Narrative* (1853–1861); Frank J. Webb, *The Garies and Their Friends* (1857); Martin Delany, *Blake* (1859); and Harriet Wilson, *Our Nig* (1859). I exclude serialized novels from this tally.
9. On this shift, see Dickson D. Bruce Jr., *Black American Writing from the Nadir: The Evolution of a Tradition, 1877–1915* (Baton Rouge: Louisiana State University Press, 1989), chaps. 1, 3, 4.

of "reclaim[ing] imagination as a feature of African American literature."[1] However, as McHenry also documents, antebellum black print media encompassed a broad band of sources as "literature"—newspapers, pamphlets, convention proceedings, and letters all rivaled book-length fiction as a valued conduit for reading material.[2] No more—or no less—important than any other medium, the novel occupied a liminal space in pre–Civil War black writing.

The approximately sixty-five novels published between the Civil War's end and the start of World War I found their way into print because of the same developments that shaped postbellum autobiography's popularity: the emergence of a nationally networked, black-owned publishing industry; the interests of a white reading audience that eagerly consumed black fiction; and the rise of a literate black readership anxious for stories that modeled how to resist racism's self-denying power in their daily lives. Unlike real-life narratives, though, "race novels" (as they were called) relied on an aesthetics of hyperbole—allegory and melodrama—to liberate their readers' perceptions of the world's racial arrangements and how racism's modes of domination could be undone. Staging elaborate, crisis-ridden stories whose resolutions typically entailed black characters struggling to triumph over American racism, allegory and melodrama endowed black authors degrees of narrative power that were mirrored in the reading experience itself. For their part, readers of race allegories (such as Frances E. W. Harper's *Iola Leroy* [1892] or Pauline Hopkins's *Contending Forces* [1900]) had to be savvy to note and interpret the webs of allusions and foreshadows that hinged panoramic plots together. Race melodramas (like Charles W. Chesnutt's *The Marrow of Tradition* [1901]), on the other hand, demanded a different order of literary labor from readers. Starkly drawn doppelgängers who could be readily typed as good and evil, unbelievable coincidences that organized the plots, angled by sharply drawn climaxes and denouements that rewarded and punished accordingly pulled readers into these novels through the cumulative effects of such exaggerations.[3]

Johnson's novel breached allegory's and melodrama's narrative norms in clear, decisive ways. For instance, *ECM*'s tone has always been its most-studied formal innovation. Upon its release in 1912,

1. Elizabeth McHenry, *Forgotten Readers: Recovering the Lost History of African American Literary Societies* (Durham, NC: Duke University Press, 2002), pp. 124, 120.
2. Ibid., chaps. 1–2.
3. Claudia Tate's *Domestic Allegories of Political Desire: The Black Heroine's Text at the Turn of the Century* (New York: Oxford University Press, 1996), P. Gabrielle Foreman's *Activist Sentiments*, and Susan Gillman's *Blood Talk: American Race Melodrama and the Cult of the Occult* (Chicago: University of Chicago Press, 2003) offer the clearest analyses of this trend in postbellum African American novel writing. M. Giulia Fabi analyzes *ECM*'s parodic relation to this phase of black novel writing; that essay is on p. 370 in this volume.

for instance, the *Portland* (Maine) *Express* found the narrator's "dispassionate self-analysis" absorbing, while the *Chicago Record-Herald* enthusiastically applauded the work's "unbiased discussion of the negro problem."[4] Scholars have since interpreted what the novel's early reviewers called objectivity as irony, contending that the ex-colored man's racial masquerade demands his constant discernment of reality from appearance.[5] When read alongside race allegories and melodramas, though, the ex-colored man's tone reverberates with a sound all its own. Consider this passage, where the narrator recounts his private piano recitals for his patron, the Millionaire:

> The man's powers of endurance in listening often exceeded mine in performing—yet I am not sure that he was always listening. At times I became so oppressed with fatigue and sleepiness that it took almost superhuman effort to keep my fingers going; in fact, I believe I sometimes did so while dozing. During such moments, this man sitting there so mysteriously silent, almost hid in a cloud of heavy-scented smoke, filled me with a sort of unearthly terror. He seemed to be some grim, mute, but relentless tyrant, possessing over me a supernatural power which he used to drive me mercilessly to exhaustion. But these feelings came very rarely; besides, he paid me so liberally I could forget much. (64)

The ex-colored man draws on both registers of the race novel to evoke this scene: the Millionaire looms villainously; a "grim, mute, . . . relentless tyrant," provoking "unearthly terror" in the narrator-victim, as effective melodrama should. The overstrong hint that slavery has not ended allegorizes an argument likening artistic production and patronage to bondage, the allusion suggesting that the antebellum's economy of exploitation persists in the making of modern art.

However, readers' identification with these political critiques gets aborted with this passage's final line. To learn that the narrator "very rarely" felt oppressed and that his salary bribed him into "forget[ting] much" blunts our mounting concern because of the phrasing's flattened mood. Why does the narrator push us away from empathizing with his plight? The moral threat of this passage stems not only from the Millionaire's predatory listening, it follows from the ex-colored man's affectless tone as well, which estranges readers from the text.

4. *Portland* (Maine) *Express*, September 14, 1912; *Chicago Record-Herald*, July 1, 1912.
5. Robert E. Fleming launched this line of analysis in "Irony as Key to Johnson's *Autobiography of an Ex-Colored Man*," *American Literature* 43.1 (March 1971): 83–96.

Norton Critical Edition readers can truly appreciate the literary effort Johnson expended to distance the novel from allegory's and melodrama's poetics of excess by studying the drafts of *ECM*'s final chapters. Johnson revised material in Chapters X and XI substantially. This volume makes the text-copy of the 1908–10 manuscript available to readers for the first time. Contrasting the draft to the 1912 edition makes for remarkable discoveries about Johnson's style. For instance, note how the lynching scene in draft form evolves to the published edition at the level of the sentence; how does Johnson use punctuation to articulate the ex-colored man's unbearable shame at witnessing the mob murder? Most starkly, the draft manuscript's conclusion is entirely different from that of the 1912 print volume. Readers of the Norton Critical Edition can see first hand how Johnson fretted over ending the novel by examining his correspondence with Brander Matthews, to whom Johnson confided this frustration. Then there is the novel's conclusion itself. Which one makes for a more satisfying finish to the novel? Why? If one ends more bleakly than the other, on what bases do we make that judgment?[6]

Refusing the intimacy and trust that race allegories and melodramas cultivated to realize novel writing's libratory potential, *ECM* anticipates Nella Larsen's advice to an aspiring novelist in the 1920s instead.[7] Black writers, the author of *Quicksand* and *Passing* observed, needed to adopt a "sardonic tone" to succeed in the Jazz Age's literary milieu.[8] Remarkably, writing a generation sooner, James Weldon Johnson made that tonal turn and did so alone.

Narrating "the hidden life" of characters was an aspect of modern fiction that E. M. Forster defined as a signature "specialty," and *ECM* explores interiority in ways that African American novels published before it did not attempt.[9] "Studying" and "analyzing" his actions and motives constantly, the ex-colored man's inward gaze contrasts sharply to fictional protagonists of race fiction. The protagonists of, for instance, any of Sutton Griggs's novels, Harper's

6. For my own view on this debate, see my discussion of the novel's revised ending in *A Spectacular Secret*, 208–11.
7. Carla L. Peterson, "Black Gotham," Lecture, New York University, March 22, 2011.
8. That Jessie Fauset's *Plum Bun* (1928) billed its story of passing as a "novel without a moral" and Claude McKay's *Banjo* (1933) announced it was a "novel without a plot" arguably find precedent in *ECM's* refusal of those narrative and ethical frameworks.
9. See Forster, *Aspects*, 45, 83–84. For instance, *Our Nig* (1853) begins to pry into its secondary figures' mental worlds, but author Harriet Wilson does not sustain that exploration beyond the book's first chapter, keeping her omniscient narrator at a far remove from the protagonist Frado's inner thoughts. Madison Washington, the central figure of Frederick Douglass's *The Heroic Slave* (1852) and Henrico Blaccus of Martin Delany's *Blake* (1859) are highly cerebral figures who think a lot, as do the free urbanites in Frank J. Webb's *The Garies and Their Friends* (1859). However, these characters' intellectual acuities and emotions are described by omniscient narrators, too, leaving the geographies of their characters' interiorities unmapped for readers to fathom.

Iola Leroy, or Du Bois's *The Quest for the Silver Fleece* (1911), are strong willed and vividly drawn, but those characters tend to read "flat" rather than "round," to recall E. M. Forster's typology of modern fiction's characters.[1] While Chesnutt's *Marrow of Tradition*, Hopkins's *Contending Forces*, and Paul Laurence Dunbar's *The Sport of the Gods* (1902) feature characters whose inner thoughts are accessible to the reader in complex ways, that access is mediated through the focalizing voice of a third-person omniscient narrator exterior to the protagonists themselves. In *ECM*, Johnson narrates from the inside out; readers see the world only through the ex-colored man's first-person perspective. Constructing interiority such that distances between surface and depth collapse, Johnson created the literary scaffolding that Jean Toomer would build on to create a character like Kabnis in *Cane*, while the ex-colored man's impersonality anticipates the likes of Nella Larsen's Helga Crane and Irene Redfield. Indeed, later novels like Zora Neale Hurston's *Their Eyes Were Watching God* (1937), Ann Petry's *The Street* (1946), Ralph Ellison's *Invisible Man* (1952), and James Baldwin's *Giovanni's Room* (1956) would extend Johnson's experiment with interiority to the mode called "free indirect discourse," a narrative technique that transformed African American novel writing during the mid-twentieth century.[2]

ECM's multiple urban settings (Atlanta, Manhattan, Berlin, London, and Paris) distinguish it from city novels of the 1900s, such as Hopkins's *Contending Forces* (set in Boston) or Dunbar's *The Sport of the Gods* (set in New York City).[3] The ex-colored man's nomadic journeys among these locales modernized the city as a trope in African American fiction by making migration and urbanization central to the novel's plot in advance of a novel like Claude McKay's *Home to Harlem* (1928).[4] However, read through the lens of the 1927 edition, the novel's descriptions of Manhattan may trick readers into supposing that Harlem is the site of the narrator's journey when it is not. Rather, in the early 1900s the novel mainly

1. Forster, *Aspects of the Novel*, 67–78. For an illuminating analysis of early African American novels' character development, see Richard Yarborough, "The First Person in Afro-American Fiction," in *Afro-American Literary Study in the 1990s*, ed. Houston A. Baker Jr. and Patricia Redmond (Chicago: University of Chicago Press, 1992).
2. Free indirect discourse entails merging the perspective and voice of an omniscient, externalized narrator with the inner thoughts and voice of a character.
3. Indeed, as early as the 1940s, scholars noted that the novel's cityscapes marked an unprecedented shift in African American novel writing because of its urban settings. See the works by Hugh M. Gloster, Sterling A. Brown, and Robert Bone listed in the selected bibliography at the end of this volume.
4. Insightful discussions of this trope include Farah J. Griffin, *Who Set You Flowin'?: The African American Migration Narrative* (New York: Oxford University Press, 1996), and Thomas Morgan, "The City As Refuge: Constructing Urban Blackness in Paul Laurence Dunbar's *Sport of the Gods* and James Weldon Johnson's *ECM*," *African American Review* 38.2 (Summer 2004): 213–37.

takes place in the district known as San Juan Hill on Manhattan's West Side.[5] While this amorphous mapping of space reflects Manhattan's special tendency toward "creative destruction" (as the city planner Robert Moses would later define), it also points toward one of the novel's more daring literary experiments. Johnson's prose renders cityscapes into eerie, fantastical forms that call the very idea of setting into question. In *ECM*, descriptive language dissolves the solidity of the built environment as the narrator perceives it, making geographic space a projection of the narrator's state of mind. Consider this passage, in which Manhattan and the Statue of Liberty transform into specters of death:

> We steamed up into New York harbor late one afternoon in the spring. The last efforts of the sun were being put forth in the turning waters of the bay to glistening gold, the green islands on either side, in spite of their warlike mountings, looked calm and peaceful; the buildings of the town shone out in a reflected light which gave the city an air of enchantment; and, truly it is an enchanted spot. New York City is the most fatally fascinating thing in America. She sits like a great white witch at the gate of the country, showing her alluring white face and hiding her crooked hands and her feet under the folds of her white garments,—constantly enticing thousands from within, and tempting those who come from across the seas to go no farther. All these become the victims of her caprice. Some she at once crushes beneath her cruel feet; others she condemns to a fate like that of galley slaves; a few she favors and fondles, riding them high on the bubbles of fortune; then with a sudden breath she blows the bubbles out and laughs mockingly as she watches them fall (48–49).

Though it begins with a bucolic vision of New York's harbor (the "glistening gold" sunset illuminating the "green islands" of Manhattan and Brooklyn), this passage descends into the despair that grips the narrator throughout the novel.[6] Hence the description morphs the Statue of Liberty into a lethal siren out of Homer's *Odyssey*. Like the muddied streets and confidence men that sink

5. This neighborhood spanned a narrow band of blocks in mid-Manhattan, from 59th to 65th Streets (south to north), between Amsterdam and 11th Avenues (east to west). For more on San Juan Hill's history as the city's "black belt," see the excerpts from Johnson's *Black Manhattan* reprinted in this volume. Other useful sources include Marcy S. Sacks, *Before Harlem: The Black Experience in New York City before World War I* (Philadelphia: University of Pennsylvania Press, 2006), and Robert M. Dowling, "A Marginal Man in Black Bohemia: James Weldon Johnson in the New York Tenderloin," in *Post-Bellum, Pre-Harlem: African American Literature and Culture*, eds. Barbara McCaskill and Caroline Gebhard (New York: New York University Press, 2006), 117–32.

6. *ECM*'s description of the Statue of Liberty becomes the title and text of JWJ's 1917 poem, "The White Witch."

and suck him of hope and money in Atlanta, the cruel totem of national citizenship reflects the narrator's unmoored bearings after his mother's death. When not terrifying, national space becomes inchoate and permeable: Georgia melds into Connecticut; Connecticut into Georgia; Georgia into Florida; Florida into New York. What does this fluidity reveal about the narrator's state of mind? But what of Europe's capital cities—London, Berlin, Paris—how do these cities' narrative topographies read against the novel's map of America? What might those differences teach us about the uses of city space to define the novel's concerns?

Just as the geographies of black migration and city life modernize the novel's social and formal interests, so does the sonic landscape of early-twentieth-century America. *ECM* can and has been read by musicologists as a primer on the history of ragtime music and the performance of spirituals in early-twentieth-century American culture, given Johnson's personal success in those fields.[7] And indeed, the modernity of ragtime's style—its skipping, staccato-paced tempo; its intricately woven chord structures; its movement across America's largest urban centers (New Orleans to Chicago to New York); and its celebration of prodigal talents and geniuses—infuses the novel with such precise allusions to the U.S. music industry that Norton readers can analyze the novel's aural range and aspects (together with its prose stylings), to debate how hierarchies of taste, the fate of black folk culture, and the rise of intellectual property rights under commodity (and now, information-age) capitalism shape its formal and cultural concerns.[8]

The cultural flux that music both embodies and activates—like the narrator's migrations across the country and around the world—finds yet another source in *ECM*'s theme of racial passing. Late-nineteenth- and early-twentieth-century race allegories and melodramas often feature biracial characters (pejoratively called "tragic mulattos") whose ambiguous physical appearance expose the fallibility of racial categories.[9] For this reason, it may seem that *ECM*'s treatment of passing breaks no new ground, but it does, in two genre-defining ways.

7. See the essays by Berlin and Ruotolo at pp. 205 and 406. For other important examinations of this approach, see Morrissette, *James Weldon Johnson's Modern Soundscapes*; Eric J. Sundquist, "These Old Slave Songs: *The Autobiography of an Ex-Colored Man*," from *The Hammers of Creation: Folk Culture in Modern African American Fiction* (Athens: University of Georgia Press, 1992), 1–48; and Katherine Biers, "Syncope Fever: James Weldon Johnson and the Black Voice," *Representations* 96 (Fall 2006): 99–125.
8. Johnson addressed early versions of these concerns in his preface to *The Book of American Negro Poetry* (New York: Harcourt Brace & Co., 1922). Importantly, this later essay draws passages directly from *ECM* for key claims in its argument.
9. For an excellent genealogy of this literary type, see Carla Kaplan, "Nella Larsen's Erotics of Race," in *Passing*, ed. Carla Kaplan (New York: Norton, 2007). Also see the essay by Fabi and Somerville on pp. 370 and 388 in this volume.

First, the narrator's canny strategy of acting white then acting black to advance his self-interests suggest that racial identity as such is performed, premised on scripts that can be learned (or forgotten) at will. Passing becomes modern in Johnson's novel because of the self-conscious calculations by which the narrator positions himself in the world. Moreover, assessing the material gains that this practice of racial masquerade provides, the ex-colored man economizes race into a rational (rather than moral) choice, undermining ideologies that held race and identity to be a natural or biological construct.[1] Second, the narrator's disembodied presence in the text turns his acts of passing into feats of language. When Johnson's ex-colored man crosses the color line, he rarely describes himself at all. The narrator's body is barely visible in language *as* text, suggesting that words do not possess the energy to depict life forms. To appreciate this strategy's innovative force, readers might compare *ECM* to the 1928 novel *Quicksand* and author Nella Larsen's descriptions of her biracial protagonist.

Though Helga Crane's racial appearance defies easy categorization, her body gets recounted in luxurious detail. Put another way, the substance of Helga Crane's subjectivity depends of language's vitality, unlike the ex-colored man's persona, which drains words of their energizing force. Nowhere is this dynamic more powerful than in *ECM*'s lynching scene. Though the most copiously described event in the novel, the lynching extracts linguistic life from both its silent, nameless victim and the narrator, whose prolific protest on the page paradoxically creates a void: not only does he resolve to pass for white and, so, disappears from social view; he declares himself to be an "ex-colored man." This new name is no name at all. With it, the narrator negates his own humanity through the rules of writing. The suffix *ex-* doubles for the letter *x*, crossing and canceling him out as if he did not exist, linking grammar and spelling to forms of death. No African American novel before 1912 used the trope of passing to contemplate not simply the arbitrariness of racial categories but to confront the entropy of language itself. Thus the question becomes; What drove Johnson to conceive his novel in these radicalizing ways?

Beyond a Boundary: ECM *and Anglo-American Modernism*

Johnson's preface to the 1922 edition of *The Book of American Negro Poetry* sheds useful light on *ECM*'s experimental ambition.

1. NCE readers can debate whether the ex-colored man's gender allows him this fluidity compared to the women who predominate African American novels' genealogy of the "tragic mulatta." See the essay by Somerville in this volume.

Assessing the record of black verse-writing around the world, Johnson lamented that the U.S. canon lagged behind poetry published elsewhere because "the Negro in the United States is consuming all of his intellectual energy in [the] grueling race-struggle."[2] Freed from "this lamentable conflict," black writers in Latin America could focus their energies on aesthetics and craftsmanship, Johnson believed. Consequently, the works of Cuba's Plácido and Juan Manzano, Brazil's Machado de Assis, Haiti's Damocles Vieux and Oswald Durand, and Martinique's Léon Laviaux surpassed that of African American writers because "the colored poet in the United States labors . . . is always on the defensive or the offensive. The pressure upon him to be propagandistic is well nigh irresistible. These conditions are suffocating to breadth and real art in poetry."[3] Johnson sought to free himself of U.S. racism's "lamentable conflicts" in three ways that bore directly upon *ECM*'s "breadth and real art."

First, Johnson drafted the novel while he was a student at Columbia University in New York City, with Brander Matthews, a leading critic in American literary studies whose modern novel course was the first to be taught in an American university. Thus Johnson initially conceived *ECM* while being exposed to the newest examples of the genre's form.[4]

At the same time, Johnson's professional networks in Manhattan's performing arts community taught him invaluable lessons that no doubt shaped his approach to prose fiction writing. Thanks to his songwriting success, Johnson gained access to artistic circles where African American culture-makers attended each other's performances and discussed their aesthetic practices. These encounters surely seeped into Johnson's musings about his novel.[5] Moreover, as critic Noelle Morrissette importantly observes, Johnson's success at songwriting de-romanticized his concept of authorship; collectively composing tunes with his brother and Bob Cole was no less (but differently) meaningful than a single-authored project. In which case, publishing anonymously opened new possibilities for Johnson to envision the form his novel might take.[6] Second, Johnson worked most intensively on the novel in his idealized writing space: Latin

2. JWJ, Preface to *The Book of American Negro Poetry*, Rev. ed. (San Diego: Harcourt Brace Jovanovich, 1931 [1922]), 38–39.
3. Ibid., pp. 14–15. To be sure, Johnson romanticizes the histories of race and racism in the Caribbean and Latin America with claims such as these.
4. A proponent of Anglophone literary nationalism, an author of the earliest American literature survey textbooks, and a founding president of the Modern Language Association, Matthews occupied a prime position to introduce Johnson to a broad band of reading.
5. For Johnson's descriptions of "Black Bohemia" and its artistic salons, see the selections from *Black Manhattan* reprinted in this volume at pp. 197–205.
6. Morrissette discusses these intersections of Johnson's career with great insight in *James Weldon Johnson's Modern Soundscapes*, 37–40.

America. Through Booker T. Washington's influence, Johnson won a diplomatic post with the U.S. State Department.[7] Stationed first at Puerto Cabello, Venezuela (1906–10) then at Corinto, Nicaragua (1910–12), Johnson used these opportunities to focus on his literary projects. As he confided to his best friend from college, George A. Towns:

> I have lots of leisure time for reading . . . I brought down about 50 selected books. It is an ideal sort of life for a man of any mental resources. . . . In these four months of quiet thought [during which] I seem to have obtained my first perspective of life. I am gaining how to adjust the various experiences of my whole life to their relative places of importance.
>
> I am doing some writing [?] not poetry, however; a man must write prose now if he wishes to get an audience.[8]

Today, critics are increasingly interested in Johnson's career as a diplomat, and NCE readers might consider how writing from what scholars now call the Global South influenced Johnson's ideas about racial categories and his depictions of the narrator's biracial identity and strategic uses of passing.[9] What, though, about those "50 selected books" and Johnson's decision to "write prose now . . . to get an audience": how did reading those works abroad shape the formal experimentalism of *ECM*?

In a diary he kept while revising the novel, Johnson noted some of the novels he read. Notably, black-authored race fiction does not appear in his bibliography. Instead, works by Frank Norris, William Dean Howells, and Mark Twain dominate the list. Three titles stand out: Henry James's *What Maisie Knew* (1897), Stephen Crane's *The Red Badge of Courage* (1893), and Thomas Hardy's *Jude the Obscure* (1895).[1] Johnson's interest in what scholars agree to be Anglo-American modernism's "transitional" texts invites us to speculate about the literary directions Johnson intended *ECM* to explore. For instance, did *What Maisie Knew* stir Johnson's thinking about constructing limited consciousness? How might Henry James's use of point of view be reimagined from a naïve girl-child to

7. Impressed with Johnson's musical career and political potential, Washington used his patronage networks to secure this post for him. For a detailed account of this favor, see Goldsby "Keeping the Secret of Authorship."
8. JWJ to George A. Towns, October 19, 19[08?], Papers of George A. Towns, Special Collections Library, Atlanta University.
9. See Morrissette, *James Weldon Johnson's Modern Soundscapes*, Chap. 2; Brian Russell Roberts, "Passing into Diplomacy: U.S. Consul James Weldon Johnson and *The Autobiography of an Ex-Colored Man*," *Modern Fiction Studies* 56.2 (Summer 2010): 290–316; and Harilaos Stecopoulos, *Reconstructing the World: Southern Fictions and U.S. Imperialisms, 1898–1976* (Ithaca: Cornell University Press, 2008), chap. 2.
1. For a list of novels JWJ likely read, see the back cover of Notebook #4, Beinecke. Grace Johnson regularly mailed additional reading material to JWJ but did not consistently produce lists of the books and magazines she sent.

a world-weary adult like the ex-colored man? Likewise, did Henry Fleming's chance breakthroughs in *The Red Badge of Courage* lead Johnson to think differently about history and causality for his protagonist? Perhaps Johnson wanted his novel to scandalize the U.S. reading public the way Thomas Hardy's Jude Fawley and Sue Bridehead unnerved British readers when *Jude the Obscure* was released; if so, to what ends would the ex-colored man shock American readers?

As these comparisons suggest, writing *The Autobiography of an Ex-Colored Man* away from the United States allowed Johnson to think about the novel form beyond the "grueling struggles" white supremacy imposed on African American authors. Writing from a distance also allowed Johnson to consider the systems and structures through which modern novel writing asserted its place in the cultural field. Readers of this Norton Critical Edition can explore Johnson's musings on these issues in unpublished "essayettes" that he wrote between 1910 and 1912: "Art," "Dilemma of the Poets," and "Words and Clothes." Decoding those writings—together with the novels he was reading as he drafted his own—readers can trace *ECM*'s intriguing affiliations with classic principles and texts of Anglo American modernism.

For instance, read alongside James, Crane, and Hardy, Johnson's experiments with nonlinear conceptions of time, consciousness, and point of view become easier to grasp. Though the ex-colored man drops enough cues to date his life story after the Civil War and into the throes of America's Gilded Age, that historical backdrop remains hazy and indistinct. Time surges and fades without concern for pegging events into legible temporal grids. Consider this passage where the ex-colored man recalls an early romantic attraction:

> There was just the proper setting to produce the effect upon a boy such as I was; the half dim church, the air of devotion on the part of the listeners, the heaving tremor of the organ under the clear wail of the violin, and she, her eyes almost closing, the escaping strands of her dark hair wildly framing her pale face, and her slender body swaying to the tones she called forth, all combined to fire my imagination and my heart with a passion though boyish, yet strong and somehow, lasting. I have tried to describe the scene; if I have succeeded it is only a half success, for words can only partially express what I would wish to convey. Always in recalling that Sunday afternoon I am subconscious of a faint but distinct fragrance which, like some old memory-awakening perfume, rises and suffuses my whole imagination, inducing a state of reverie so airy as to just evade the powers of expression. (18)

This Sunday reverie endures across time, suffusing the narrator's "whole imagination," precisely because of the "subconscious" forces of a recalled smell—the scent of the girl's perfume brings him to a linguistic abyss. "Words can only partially express what I wish to convey," the narrator admits. Both in the moment and recalling that time, his experience "just evade[s] the powers of expression." If the "memory-awakening" perfume brings to mind Marcel Proust's madeleine cookie from *The Remembrance of Things Past* (1927), that may be because *ECM* enacts, in its own ways, the theory of temporality that shaped Proust's novel, Henri Bergson's *Matter and Memory* (1911). "Durational flow," according to Bergson, extended events from their present into the future as well as from the past. In this passage, chronology moves in multiple directions at once: the "half dim church" and its "air of devotion" not only link themselves to the narrator's romantic crush but, eerily, anticipate the later scene of the lynching, which happens under the shadows of nightfall as if the mob murder is a sacred rite. If the girl's perfume calls forth memories of love that disturbingly evoke the rancid fumes of the lynch victim being burned at the pyre, that is because ideals of love and racial hate sear the narrator's mind in equally potent ways. As time and causation get loosened from their conventional linear anchors in *ECM,* the novel's plotlessness captures how that fluidity exacts a social price upon the lives of black people, especially in the lynching scene. Thus, in its own way, Johnson's novel runs parallel to but clarifies how race and racism structure Bergson's idea of durational flow.[2]

Featuring a protagonist-narrator whose interiorized perspective ebbs into and out of clear view, concealing as much as he reveals, Johnson's novel swam in the stream of consciousness that defined Anglo-American modernism in the early twentieth century. Though this technique was not coined as a literary concept until 1918, William James articulated a foundational version of it in his *Principles of Psychology* (1890). If Johnson encountered this work at Columbia University, he would know that James argued that the tensions between "mind wandering" and "selective attention" organized the human thoughts and individual consciousness. Since, for James, "whatever excites and stimulates our interest is real," humans were free to define what things are for themselves. On the one hand, James's call for spontaneity characterized Johnson's own experience writing *ECM*:

> The story developed in my mind more rapidly than I expected it would; at times, outrunning my speed at getting it down. The use of prose as a creative medium was new to me; and its

2. For a compelling study of this dynamic, see Daylanne K. English, *Each Hour Redeem: Time and Justice in African American Literature* (Minneapolis: University of Minnesota Press, 2013).

> latitude, its flexibility, its comprehensiveness, the variety of approaches it afforded me for surmounting technical difficulties gave me a feeling of exhilaration, exhilaration similar to that which goes with freedom of motion.[3]

On the other hand, in the novel Johnson presents a different view of mind wandering as a narrative principle. Voiced by the ex-colored man:

> In the life of every one there is a limited number of unhappy experiences which are not written upon the memory, but stamped there with a die; and in long years after they can be called up in detail, and every emotion that was stirred by them can be lived through anew; these are the tragedies of life. (13)

This is a key passage, because it outlines the logic of the novel's plot. Here, Johnson's narrator states that stream of consciousness needs limits. Not every experience should be retained in memory; only tragedies merit recollection. Furthermore, memory's record must be fixed—"stamped with a die," says the ex-colored man. This notion contradicts William James's point that writing allows fluidity: "only as a reflection becomes developed do we become aware of an inner world at all," James argued.[4] Committed to the proposition that "the unhappy experiences" define reality most acutely, *ECM* issues a bleak promise. Only crisis makes interior life knowable and legible. By this logic, the lynching scene's copious and specific details suggest it is the greatest tragedy the narrator endures, stamping racial violence as the historical crisis that shapes modern consciousness most of all.

With its extensions of time, stream of consciousness, and point of view clearly convergent with the modern novel's development globally speaking, *ECM*'s formal kinships to other works published with and after it become possible to trace. For instance, Virginia Woolf's *Jacob's Room* (1922) echoes *ECM* in several rich ways.[5] First, the novels' protagonists and stories closely resemble each other. Like the ex-colored man, Jacob Flanders is in search of himself and his vocation. Both are handsome, intelligent aesthetes; where Jacob aspires to be a writer-critic, the ex-colored man strives to become a world-renowned musician. Second, both men live in a

3. Johnson, *Along This Way*, 393–94.
4. James, *Principles of Psychology*, 679, cited in at *Stanford Encyclopedia of Philosophy*, available at plato.stanford.edu/entries/james/#3.
5. Virginia Woolf, *Jacob's Room* (San Diego: Harcourt, 1960, 1922), 138. *Mrs. Dalloway* (1925) and *To the Lighthouse* (1927) are cited as Woolf's modernist masterpieces, but *Jacob's Room* helped sharpen Woolf's methods of representing interior states and narrating temporality to function as epistemological and ethical standpoints. JWJ clearly followed Woolf's writings on modernism, copying quotes from her famous essay "Modern Fiction" in a diary entry dated February 16, 1919. Interestingly, this is the same journal he kept while drafting *ECM*. See JWJ Notebook #3, Beinecke.

"gloom, this surrender to dark waters which lap us about" (Woolf, 138), their melancholia incited once their dreams of grandeur get cut short by history. Jacob is summoned from his comfortable bourgeois life in Edwardian England to fight and die in World War I; the ex-colored man's migrations from his New England home (during America's Gilded Age) leads him to Georgia's backwoods, where the lynching he witnesses culminates in his social death.[6] These wounded, maimed men; the dead and walking dead: the modernist antihero gains expressive force from *ECM* to *Jacob's Room* because the novels' redefinition of character clarify each other's efforts across the decade that separates them.

Another character trait of the ex-colored man—his caginess—links Johnson's novel to F. Scott Fitzgerald's *The Great Gatsby* (1925). The 1927 edition of *ECM* places it after Fitzgerald's most famous work, but when we recall *ECM* appeared more than a decade ahead of *Gatsby*, the resonances between them raise the stakes of both novels' aesthetic and cultural politics. Read together, the historical arc of the Jazz Age extends from Long Island's East and West Eggs back to the 1900s Manhattan neighborhood where *ECM* is largely set. Indeed, the Club where the ex-colored man performs ragtime music draws the predecessors of Tom and Daisy Buchanan, Jay Gatsby, and Nick Carraway into the city like moths to the flame—that is to say, Johnson's novel foreshadows *Gatsby*'s world of self-made elites, spectacular wealth-making schemes, and frenzied materialism (thus the parties thrown by the ex-colored man's Millionaire patron are not foils but complements to the reckless soirées staged by Jay Gatsby). However, the novels' cultural commentaries demand and sustain readers' attention because of the formal innovation that Johnson and Fitzgerald each deploy so shrewdly: unleashing an unreliable narrator to depict the social worlds of their texts.

Like the ex-colored man, Nick Carraway is a detached observer of his social milieu: "I was within and without, simultaneously enchanted and repelled by the inexhaustible variety of life," Nick remarks.[7] Nick gains access to this otherwise closed world, passing in and out of its domains at will, thanks to the cultural capital of his class credentials and whiteness. His familial connection to Daisy and Tom Buchanan, together with the Ivy League education that lands him a job on Wall Street, function comparably to the

6. In Freudian terms, writing functions therapeutically, urging Johnson's narrator from the depths of melancholy toward the healthier state of mourning. *ECM*'s modernity invites psychoanalytic interpretations, an approach JWJ would have endorsed given his long-standing interest in Freud's new science (which is well documented in *Along This Way*).
7. F. Scott Fitzgerald, *The Great Gatsby* (New York: Scribner's, 2004, [1925]), 35.

ex-colored man's wealth and racially ambiguous appearance. Standing apart from the West and East Egg cultures, disdainful of wealth and yet powerfully attracted to it, Nick's isolation mirrors that of Johnson's narrator.

Given these resonances, we might be tempted to say Nick lives behind his own veil of double consciousness. However, because he shares the ex-colored man's fantasy of self-contained mastery, both men resist acknowledging that his perspective might be deficient or incomplete. Presenting themselves as the sole measure by which it is not only possible but desirable to know the worlds they inhabit, Nick's and the ex-colored man's narratives offer totalizing visions that eclipse other points of view that might rival their perspectives and power. Though a key difference between the men is that Nick reports on Gatsby's life (and his own), whereas the ex-colored man is both observer and actor on the story's main stage.[8] Alongside *Gatsby*, then, Johnson's use of first-person narration lays bare the "technical difficulty" (as Johnson called it) involved in sustaining a fictionalized "I": how to maintain interest in a narrator whose narcissism and unreliability make his point of view discomfiting to the reader?

Johnson's solution anticipates Fitzgerald's. In both novels, the project of writing is central to the action of the text. Narrated retrospectively, *ECM* exposes the seams of its construction unapologetically, directing the reader's attention to the composition process itself from the novel's start:

> I know that in writing the following pages I am divulging the great secret of my life, the secret which for some years I have guarded far more carefully than any of my earthly possessions; and it is a curious study to me to analyze the motives which prompt me to do it. I feel that I am led by the same impulse which forces the unfound-out criminal to take somebody in his confidence, although he knows that the act is liable, even almost certain, to lead to his undoing. I know that I am playing with fire, and I feel the thrill which accompanies that most fascinating pasttime; and back of it all, I think I find a sort of savage and diabolical desire to gather up all the little tragedies of my life, and turn them into a practical joke on society. (5)

Here, note how the ex-colored man defines narration: it is transgressive (stemming from an "impulse"; offered by an "unfound-out criminal"); destructive ("playing with fire"); barbarous and cruel (a "savage and diabolical desire" turns narrative "into a practical joke on society"). Like *The Great Gatsby*'s self-reflexive narration, *ECM*

8. My thanks to Richard Yarborough for this insight.

suggests that in modern fiction, the methods of writing constitute a story's subject as much as anything else. In this regard, Johnson's and Fitzgerald's efforts would be taken to their logical extreme in Gertrude Stein's *The Autobiography of Alice B. Toklas* (1933). Arguably, though, Stein could pen this work under her own name (but as a screen behind which she could openly flirt with the principles of authenticity that first-person narration supposedly safeguards) because of the precedents that Johnson and Fitzgerald helped set with their novels. The role of scribe, which Fitzgerald has Nick dodge and Johnson felt compelled to disavow, Stein was free to promote as her own invention and not simply because her famous ego prompted her to do so. Rather, by 1933 modernism's unreliable narrators were sufficiently numerous, understood, and appreciated in ways that Johnson could not openly enjoy in 1912.[9]

"Facts Do Not Make Fiction": ECM *and the Life of James Weldon Johnson*

According to African American literary history, the future of black writing was shaped by authors like Richard Wright, whose "Blueprint for Negro Literature" (1937) and *Native Son* (1940) advanced social realism to the fore of mid-twentieth-century African American novel writing; or by Langston Hughes and Zora Neale Hurston, who channeled black folk culture into every literary medium—poetry, drama, short fiction, novels, journalism—as the expressive and professional need arose; or by Jean Toomer, who embodied a new idea of black authorship given his resistance to racial categorization. "I do not see things in terms of Negro, Anglo-Saxon, Jewish, and so on," Toomer explained to Johnson in 1930. "I see myself as an American, simply American. As regards art, I particularly hold this view. I see our art and literature as primarily American art and literature. I do not see it as Negro, Anglo-Saxon, and so on."[1]

That Johnson actually shared Toomer's view—"in most of my writings I have stressed the truth that the work done by colored creative artist[s] is a part of our common, national culture," he

9. JWJ and Stein made each other's acquaintance and read the other's work, 1933–38 thanks to Carl Van Vechten who arranged for these exchanges to occur. In his correspondence, JWJ named what he'd read of Stein's: *Three Lives* and *The Autobiography of Alice B. Toklas*. See JWJ to Carl Van Vechten, October 8. 1933; October 15, 1933; and November 9, 1933, in JWJ/Van Vechten, Letters from Blacks, Box JOHN, Folder 1933–38, Beinecke. Stein was cagier, not detailing which books she read that Van Vechten had sent. See Van Vechten to Stein, October 23, [1933] in Edward Burns, ed., *The Letters of Gertrude Stein to Carl van Vechten*, vol. I (New York: Columbia University Press, 1986), 281–82.

1. Jean Toomer to JWJ, July 26, 1930, Beinecke. This exchange arose when JWJ sought Toomer's permission to include his work in the 1931 edition of *The Book of American Negro Poetry*.

insisted—is easy to forget if, by relying on the 1927 edition, we presume *ECM* followed in *Cane*'s wake. Read from the contexts of its initial release in 1912, the literary future that *ECM* exemplified for modern novel writing can be traced back to three life influences that shaped the novel's making: Johnson's racial upbringing in Jacksonville; his embrace of literary secularism at Atlanta University; and his song-writing career for the Broadway stage.[2]

Born in Jacksonville, Florida, in 1871, Johnson entered the world legally free. Crucially, his parents enabled his psychic emancipation as well. Having started their married life together in the British-ruled (but antislavery) Bahamas during the 1860s, Helen Dillet and James Johnson Sr. migrated to America with "no adequate conception" of their "'place'" as black people in the U.S. South.[3] Used to her social privilege as the fair-skinned daughter of a successful politician in Nassau, Johnson's schoolteacher mother reared her children as cultural elites. A shrewd, industrious entrepreneur, Johnson's father used his higher-end wages as headwaiter at the St. James Hotel to fund real estate deals across the city. During these "plastic years," as their eldest son, James, called them, "neither my father nor mother . . . taught me directly anything about race."[4] On the contrary, watching their parents prosper, James and his brother, Rosamond, grew up believing that being black placed no limits on what they, as human beings, could aspire to be and do.[5] The boys were reared by Irish women hired by their working mother, whose white physician called her "Queen," after Britain's monarch, Victoria. Their father's sterling reputation as head waiter at the St. James and successful property broker filled James with indescribable pride.[6] Encouraged by their parents' worldliness, James and Rosamond excelled at school, reading widely in popular fiction and poetry. James befriended and learned the language of Spanish-speaking friends from nearby Cuba, and his music-minded mother cultivated her sons' prodigious talents at piano playing and singing.

2. The Chronology on p. 429 in this volume outlines the long arc of JWJ's life and career. For detailed accounts of Johnson's life, see his memoir, *Along This Way*, Eugene Levy's authoritative biography, *Black Leader, Black Voice*, and Sondra Kathryn Wilson's introductions to Johnson's *Selected Writings* (New York: Oxford University Press, 1995).
3. JWJ details his parents' courtship and early marriage in *Along This Way*, chaps. 1–2. The quoted phrases occur at 142.
4. JWJ, *Along This Way*, pp. 152, 167.
5. Johnson's recollections of his hometown recalls Zora Neale Hurston's memories of growing up in another all-black Florida town, Eatonville. Interestingly, Hurston depicts Jacksonville as the antithesis to Eatonville's harmony. See *Dust Tracks on a Road*, chap. 4.
6. Throughout the Florida chapters in *Along This Way*, JWJ attributes his habits of self-restraint to his father's economic rationalism and credits his mother for encouraging his aesthetic experimentalism.

Though Johnson rued the fact that by the 1930s, the "rise to power of the poor whites" turned Jacksonville into a "one hundred percent Cracker town," during his youth in the 1870s to 1890s, the city was a place where Johnson experienced his identity beyond race, an outlook that decidedly informs the ex-colored man's worldview. In these decades, James forged two friendships that fostered his fluid understanding of race and directly influenced *ECM*'s development. J. Douglas Wetmore was a boyhood friend whom Johnson identifies as the inspiration for the ex-colored man. A brilliant social climber who used his light-skinned appearance to pass for white, Wetmore has remained understudied as a source for interpreting *ECM*. This NCE provides revealing information on Wetmore's personal history (obituaries detailing his career and tragic suicide), along with Johnson's recollections of his friend's racial masquerades. Another cultural rebel who found his way into Johnson's life and the pages of *ECM* was Dr. T. O. Summers. This white surgeon, for whom Johnson worked as an office assistant before he went to college, was "[a]n extraordinary man . . . of great culture." A "cosmopolite," Summers shared his vast knowledge of literature, art, and travel with young James without regard for their racial or generational difference. As Johnson recalled, Summers "neither condescended nor patronized; in fact, he treated me as an intellectual equal." But Summers was also "careless" with his money and, according to Johnson, partook of cocaine. This "brooding" man no doubt inspired the Millionaire. To trace these resonances, NCE readers can examine Johnson's writings about his relationship with Summers along with biographical information on the surgeon. These documents can be found in the same sections as the Wetmore material.[7]

In college (1893–97), Johnson experienced strong challenges to his racial upbringing in Jacksonville which, in turn, decisively shaped his own and his novel's sensibility. On the one hand, Atlanta University mirrored the richness of Johnson's life in Jacksonville.[8] The all-black campus sat atop the tallest hill in the New South's capital city. Black undergraduates studied the liberal arts with a distinguished faculty in august, stately classroom buildings. Johnson's

7. See Skerrett for an insightful analysis of Wetmore's and Summers' influence on *ECM*. A third role model that Skerrett does not consider and who may have influenced JWJ's invention of "Shiny," the ex-colored man's erudite schoolmate is the unnamed "West Indian teacher" who tutored JWJ in 1888, when a yellow fever outbreak shut down Jacksonville's schools. By trade a cobbler, this man was a "fine scholar" who taught JWJ Roman history, politics, and Latin. For JWJ's account of this mentor, see *Along This Way*, 234–36.
8. JWJ attended two divisions at Atlanta University. Between 1888 and 1889, he enrolled in its "prepatory division," a finishing school that prepared students for baccalaureate-level work. In 1890, JWJ matriculated as a college student, earning his bachelor's degree in 1894.

social life thrived. On the other hand, the university's stern codes of conduct bordered on an asceticism that frustrated him. As he recalled, "we were never allowed to entertain any thought of being educated as 'go-getters.' . . . The ideal constantly held up to so was of education as a means of living, not of making a living. . . . An odd, old-fashioned, naïve conception? Rather."[9]

Crucially, Johnson bristled against the school's religious outlook. "I doubt not that there were students who enjoyed . . . prayer meetings and were spiritually benefitted [by them], but I believe the main effect was to put a premium on hypocrisy or, almost as bad, to substitute for religion a lazy and stupid conformity."[1] Stifling students' questions about faith only intensified the university's prescriptive views on race, as Johnson experienced them. Because in Jacksonville racial hierarchies did not organize or dominate his social life before college, Johnson claimed he had to "learn" what it meant to be Negro, and he received his education in what he dubbed the "arcana of race" at Atlanta University. "[I]t was simply in the spirit of the institution; the atmosphere of the place was charged with it. Students talked 'race,'" Johnson recalled, sounding exasperated forty years later. "It was the subject of essays, orations, and debates. Nearly all that was acquired, mental and moral, was destined to be fitted into a particular system of which 'race' was the center".[2] A summer spent working in rural Georgia among the black working class tempered Johnson's individualism. Nonetheless, his resistance to the university's codes of conduct regarding race and religion reveals a secularist worldview. This distinctly anti-Victorian temperament would inform *ECM*'s heretical outlook and tone.

Atlanta University's liberal arts curriculum sharpened Johnson's secularist edge in other crucial ways as well. First, he met English major George A. Towns, who would become a pivotal confidant as Johnson drafted *ECM* in its early stages.[3] Norton readers can review their correspondence not only to trace how Towns spurred Johnson's thinking about *ECM*'s impact on the reading public in 1912 but also to debate: could Towns have been a model for Shiny,

9. *Along This Way*, 268–69.
1. JWJ, *Along This Way*, 228. For an equally impertinent critique, see the Preface to *The Book of American Negro Spirituals* (New York: Viking Press, 1925), 20. JWJ's skepticism toward institutionalized religion did not mean he lived without a spiritual code. He explains his personal theology in *Along This Way*, 597–98.
2. *Along This Way*, 207. JWJ would go on to place race work at the center of his life. After college he returned to Jacksonville where he taught at the Stanton School and served as its principal; published a black newspaper, *The Daily American*; and was the first African American to pass the Florida State bar exam. His twenty-year career with the NAACP epitomized this commitment.
3. JWJ describes his friendship with Towns in *Along This Way*, 246. For their exchanges during *ECM*'s development, see Miles M. Jackson, "Letters to a Friend: Correspondence from James Weldon Johnson to George A. Towns," *Phylon* 29.2 (1968): 182–98. Also see their correspondence reprinted in this volume.

the scholarly character who serves as the ex-colored man's moral foil? Second, during his junior year, Johnson worked as an apprentice in Atlanta University's printing office. This work not only prepared him to manage his own newspaper once he graduated but the job also exposed Johnson to the protocols of small publishing firms, knowledge that would prove key to *ECM*'s 1912 edition.[4] Finally, he read more broadly in college.[5] The novels he encountered—by Charles Dickens, George Eliot, William Thackeray, and Richard Blackmore Doddridge—eschewed "divine revelation and Christian dogma," Johnson recalled, relieved that "bald moral purpose" did not weigh down their plots. Immersed in the social worlds of these novels, Johnson found his inner self deeply engaged: he "began . . . to think of life not only as it touched [him] from without but also as it moved [him] from within." These lessons in novelistic interiority and literary secularism were important teachings that Johnson tapped into when writing *ECM* a decade later.

Perhaps the most devastating event that shaped Johnson's life and *ECM*'s composition was his near-death at the hands of a lynch mob in Jacksonville.[6] That incident, which occurred in 1901, traumatized Johnson profoundly, fueled his later activism with the NAACP, and inspired him to cast that incident as the turning point of the ex-colored man's life.[7] This NCE includes Johnson's recollections of this awful event (in "Backgrounds and Sources"). However, another cultural history is ingrained in that violent episode, one that sheds crucial light on the novel's making and meaning as a physical book.

Like so many African Americans who migrated out of the South before World War I, Johnson left Jacksonville permanently after his near-lynching, relocating North, in New York City. That circumstance reunited him with his brother, Rosamond, and the siblings formed Johnson Brothers and Cole (the vaudeville song-writing and performing team described earlier in this essay). However, before he left Florida, Johnson composed a poem, "Lift Every Voice and Sing," a lyric meant to commemorate Abraham Lincoln's birthday. Inspired by its rich feeling, Rosamond set the verse to music. Quickly completing the song, the brothers had the score printed cheaply by their New York publisher, to distribute to the mass choir they had assembled for the holiday performance. The song was an immediate hit with its black singers, who began sharing mimeographed copies of the score and passing on the tune by word of mouth.

4. On JWJ's printer's apprenticeship, see *Along This Way*, 244.
5. JWJ recounts his college reading lists and revelations in *Along This Way*, 220.
6. JWJ details a harrowing account of this event in *Along This Way*, which is reprinted on pp. 139–44 in this volume.
7. See Goldsby, *A Spectacular Secret*, chap. 4, for a detailed analysis of this scene.

Though their publisher filed for the song's copyright, the Johnson brothers let "Lift Every Voice and Sing" circulate freely in the public domain. Doing so, black churches, schools, and organizations absorbed the song into their repertoires, spreading the tune that much more broadly and deeply.[8] This route to popularity and fame no doubt taught Johnson a valuable lesson that informed *ECM*'s conception: literary success could be gauged by impact as much as by profit. Mass-manufactured "hits" and limited edition "underground" works could leverage different but comparable influences on popular culture. Grasping literature's potential reach through music publishing's terms, Johnson would (as I will explain in the next section) craft *ECM* to exploit—and, so, explore—the tensions intrinsic to the making of books as art and commodity objects.

To be sure, these turns in Johnson's personal life shaped *ECM* central concerns and plot. This critical approach—tracking the "novelization" of Johnson's biography into fiction—has steered fruitful analyses of the novel, and the archival materials assembled in this volume allow NCE readers to engage that line of analysis as well. For instance, it should be clear that Johnson drew on his privileged upbringing to depict the ex-colored man's elitist outlook. The character's fluency in Spanish echoes Johnson's own, as does the trajectory of the narrator's musical career: Johnson Brothers and Cole's worldwide travels and fame lend verisimilitude to Chapters VI–IX of the novel, which trace the narrator's piano-playing gigs in Manhattan and across Europe. The ex-colored man, the Millionaire, and Shiny arguably reincarnate Johnson's friendships with J. Douglas Wetmore, T. O. Summers, and George A. Towns; and, as noted earlier, Johnson's harrowing experience at the hands of a lynch mob charges the intensity of the lynching scene that makes up the novel's climax.

However, at what point do biographical facts cede their analytic authority to the demands of art? Is it necessary to know that Wetmore inspired Johnson to invent the ex-colored man's character? Could Johnson have created the lynching scene if he had not been nearly killed by a mob himself? How, then, should we interpret Johnson's choice to make the ex-colored man a spectator in that scene—what narrative effects and ethical consequences follow from placing the narrator in a bystander's position? Johnson adored Manhattan, but in the novel the Tenderloin's "gaslight life" exerts a menacing force that bears little resemblance to Johnson's personal enthusiasm for the city. Given how it revises the facts of Johnson's

8. JWJ traces the history of the song's composition and circulation in *Along This Way*, 301–03.

life, how should readers understand the novel's transformation of biography into literary material? This volume reprints selections from Johnson's memoir, *Along This Way*, so that readers can engage these questions directly themselves.

Before Emancipation, the idea of "life writing" was a near contradiction in terms for African American autobiographers, because the lives slavery forced black people to lead were so fantastic the actual details bordered on being fictive. Not until *ECM* did an African American writer pressure narrative's capacities to its logical ends in order to explore this distinction. Liberating notions of the self from claims that would root identity exclusively to ascertainable, empirical sources, *ECM* can be read alongside (as I suggested earlier) Stein's *The Autobiography of Alice B. Toklas* and other modernist autobiographies like W. E. B. Du Bois's *The Souls of Black Folk*, Henry Adams's *The Education of Henry Adams* (1903), James Joyce's *The Portrait of an Artist as a Young Man* (1916), Virginia Woolf's *Orlando* (1928) or Djuna Barnes's *Nightwood* (1936).[9] Collapsing the distinctions between autobiography and fiction so flagrantly, *ECM* requires us to think about how the idea of "fictiveness" comes into its own within U.S. literary history's canon formation. For, as Johnson reminded himself in a work diary he kept while drafting *ECM*, "facts do not make fiction."[1]

Judging a Book by Its Covers: The Publication History of ECM

Though Johnson understood the difference between the facts of his life and his novelization of it in *ECM*, readers often confused the author with his fictive creation. "I continue to receive letters from persons who have read the book inquiring about this or that phase of my life as told in it," Johnson marveled in his own memoir, *Along This Way* (1933), which he wrote in part "to inform the reader that the [novel's] story was not the story of my life."[2] The inclination to regard *ECM* as Johnson's actual life history (rather than a parody of both autobiography's and fiction's truth claims) is historically significant, because the mix-up uncovers how the novel's publication constituted its own experiments in modern novel writing. From its initial appearance in 1912 to its major reprintings in 1927 and 1948, the novel's physical form as a book—or, more precisely, its malleability as a market commodity—parallels the modernization

9. John Paul Riquelme shared this insight with me via e-mail, February 28, 2012, as did Maryemma Graham, in a personal conversation at MLA 2011 in Seattle.
1. JWJ, Notebook #4, 101, Beinecke.
2. JWJ, *Along This Way*, 394.

of the U.S. publishing industry across the first half of the twentieth century. Judging *ECM*'s covers over time (reprinted in this volume's "Illustrations" section) clarifies why *ECM*'s status as a modern novel was so tenuous for Johnson to claim.

The front cover to the 1912 edition is starkly plain but elegant. Its hard cloth boards are bound in maroon leather with gold lettering on the front cover and side spine. Readers should ask, how does this cover design further Johnson's ruse to present the novel as an anonymously authored autobiography? This question is important to explore, because it pinpoints Johnson's clever and deliberate effort to game the system of early twentieth-century book publishing.[3]

An important vector to trace runs back to Johnson's decision to publish the 1912 edition with Sherman, French & Company. With his success at selling his song lyrics through New York City's leading sheet music publishers, Johnson knew full well where the centers of power existed in American print culture. Nevertheless, he chose this small, obscure firm in Boston, which was not equipped to make *ECM* a mass hit. The company could print only a limited run of the novel; moreover, it lacked the funds to mount an national publicity campaign. Johnson never even met his publisher face to face.[4] Why constrain the book's market potential in this way? NCE readers can examine Johnson's correspondence with Sherman French & Company (together with his frank letters to his wife) to debate Johnson's aims in placing his novel with this small-market publisher instead of one of the emerging firms that transformed publishing into a decidedly profit-driven system. Why did Johnson reject the book industry's "modern" model in this way?

The 1912 edition's limited print run has led scholars to assert that the book was ignored when it was first released. As the contemporary reviews reprinted in this volume make clear, that was not the case. However, by 1915 the novel was out of print. A short-lived revival occurred when the African American women's magazine *Half-Century* serialized the novel between November 1919 and November 1920.[5] However, the 1927 reprinting of *ECM* by Alfred A. Knopf contributes to its standing as a modernist text for reasons that would eclipse the innovations of the plainer-looking 1912 edition.

First, it was an enormous coup for Johnson to land the book with this prestigious publishing firm. Unlike Sherman French, Knopf was not a "gentleman's" firm on the decline but a "businessman's" house on the rise for its then growing reputation as a champion of

3. For a detailed examination of Johnson's manipulation of the publishing industry with the 1912 edition, see my essay "Keeping the Secret of Authorship."
4. JWJ, *Along This Way*, 394.
5. According to Noelle Morrissette, the novel was serialized in the *Chicago Defender* newspaper in 1919; see *James Weldon Johnson's Modern Soundscapes*, p. 104. However, the only Chicago-based reprint I can trace (via print, microfilm, and digital database sources) is the series published in the *Half-Century*.

experimental fiction.[6] Second—again in vivid contrast to the 1912 edition—the Knopf reprint trumpets the book's physical form as its own work of art. Knopf specialized in graphic design, packaging books to be seen as aesthetic objects in their own right. Under the firm's direction, dust jackets became integral to the meaning and promotion of a book.[7] Sparing no expense, Knopf hired Aaron Douglas, then the most acclaimed African American painter in the United States, to design *ECM*'s cover.[8] Douglas's response to this assignment is both moving and revealing for its account of the novel's experimentalism.

Douglas's illustration dazzles the eye, with its acute rendering of the modern world envisioned in the novel's text. Against a burnt orange background (as if the world is aflame), a shadowed, black figure—masculine, lean—emerges tentatively out of the tall grass of a rural countryside. The man looks toward the horizon, also cast as dark shadow. Before him, a row of factories and skyscrapers (drawn, too, in silhouette) cuts a jagged line from the dust jacket's midpoint to its right edge. Though he faces this urban scene, the man's viewpoint is drawn in profile; the slit that marks where his eyes would be is filled with orange light. Thus, what the man sees in this landscape is open to question. Is he awakened or blinded by the view? Douglas's sensitivity to the novel's ambiguities is heightened by the appearance of Johnson's name on Knopf's dust jacket. In 1927, unlike 1912, the reading public would know that the "autobiography" was a work of fiction. And yet, as the press reviews from that year clearly demonstrate (a point discussed in the next section), *ECM* was not received as a novel. Why was that misreading possible?

The reviews anthologized in this NCE allow readers to track this curious response through the thorny questions of white patronage that emerge in the correspondence surrounding the Knopf publication. The letters between Johnson and Carl Van Vechten are key to such discussions.[9] Scholars have rightly pointed out that Van Vechten was

6. On Knopf's standing in the field of modernist publishing, see Clare Badaracco, "ECM by James Weldon Johnson: the 1927 Knopf Edition," *Papers of the Bibliographic Society of America* 96.2 (2002): 279–87. As William L. Andrews points out in the Library of America edition of the novel, Johnson made slight, not substantive, changes to the novel's text. The most conspicuous revision to the 1912 edition is the Anglicized spelling of "coloured" in the title. For details about the 1927 edition, see Andrews, "Note on the Text," in *James Weldon Johnson: Writings* (New York: Library of America, 2004), 892–93.
7. Ibid.
8. Caroline Groesser, *Picturing the New Negro: Harlem Renaissance Print Culture and Modern Black Identity* (Lawrence: University Press of Kansas, 2007), 45–47.
9. From his post as culture critic of *Vanity Fair* magazine, Carl Van Vechten championed the new arts of modernism, ranging from the photographs of Edward Steiglitz to the Cubist narratives of Gertrude Stein and the blues shouts of Ma Rainey and Bessie Smith. Van Vechten's affinities for African American art and his friendships with black artists inspired him to pen his own novel, *Nigger Heaven* (1928), whose *success de scandale* increased his influence as a talent scout for white publishers interested in new black writers. Van Vechten's controversial career is insightfully explained by Emily Bernard; see *Carl Van Vechten and the Harlem Renaissance* (New Haven, CT: Yale University Press, 2012).

instrumental in securing Johnson's publishing contract with Knopf, but NCE readers should query Van Vechten's justifications for republishing *ECM*. Likewise, extra scrutiny needs to be paid to Van Vechten's introduction to the Knopf edition, which asserts that *ECM*'s aesthetic contribution lay chiefly in its utility as a "documentary sourcebook." Is this praise for or a disavowal of *ECM* as a work of modern fiction? Given the polemical force of that claim (which readers can gauge by tracking how the phrase echoes across press reviews of the 1927 edition), Van Vechten's essay is included in this volume as a contextual document rather than as a preface to the text itself.

The politics of patronage, race, and modern publishing can also be explored through Johnson's exchanges with Blanche W. Knopf, wife of Alfred. Blanche's letters to Johnson reveal her to be a shrewd acquisitions editor in her own right. She not only approved the novel's republication with great enthusiasm, she secured its reprinting in England and Germany as well.[1] Indeed, the German-language edition's preface is translated and reprinted in this volume for the first time. However, what does it mean that Blanche Knopf reissued *ECM* as part of the firm's Blue Jade Series? NCE readers can examine this plan through the publicity descriptions of that editorial series and judge how Johnson's novel was presented to the reading public in 1927. Could it be regarded as "new" or "modern" in that line of books? How, then, does Blanche Knopf's judgment (as well as that of Van Vechten's) compare to Aaron Douglas's letter to Johnson, which marvels at the persistence of *ECM*'s prescience? These documents (together with the novel's reception, which I outline next) suggest why the novel's standing as a fictive work was so unstable during the 1920s.

Knopf kept the novel in print for several decades, printing six editions between 1927 and 1961. That track record brought the novel to the attention of New American Library (NAL), whose mission remapped the landscape of American book publishing after World War II, a transformation that depended on the firm's acquisition of *ECM*.[2]

First established as a U.S. subsidiary of Britain's Penguin Books, NAL reprinted popular works originally issued by trade hardback publishing firms. Using cheaper paper for both the cover and inside

1. While discussions ensued between Knopf and JWJ to publish a Francophone edition, that volume never materialized. Instead, Knopf secured rights with the German publisher, Frankfurter-Societas Druckerai, which released *Der Weisse Neger* (*The White Negro*), in 1928. A translation of the German-language preface is reprinted here for the first time. I thank Moira Weigel for preparing that text.
2. On NAL and the mass-market paperback publishing trade, see John Tebbel, *Between Covers: The Rise and Transformation of American Book Publishing* (New York: Oxford University Press, 1987), chap. 15.

leaves of its books—known in the book trade as "pulp"—NAL published editions in the hundreds of thousands and priced volumes for quick, affordable sales, twenty-five to fifty cents per book. NAL and its pulp fiction competitors (such as Avon, Ballantine, Bantam, Dell, and Fawcett) commissioned artists to design bold, racy covers topped with headline banners that sensationalized the books' contents—even for texts as restrained and complex as *ECM*. However, unlike its competitors, NAL set itself apart as a purveyor of mass-market literature by focusing on works that were intellectually and aesthetically challenging. Its corporate motto, "Good Books for the Millions," merged the ethos of gentleman and businessman publishing that distinguished nineteenth- from twentieth- century print culture production. In the words of NAL President Victor Weybright, "our interest [lies] in the educational responsibilities of popular publishing."[3]

In 1948 NAL decided it wanted to develop an African American readership for its books, and the firm selected *ECM* to launch that effort. This would be a posthumous edition, since Johnson had died in a tragic car accident in 1938. As one of its first African American–authored mass-marketed paperbacks, NAL implicitly ratified the novel's enduring literary powers—or did it? NCE readers can track the firm's editorial process through the correspondence that documents its acquisition of *ECM* from Knopf and the publishing rights from Johnson's widow, Grace Nail Johnson. Also important to study are the internal staff memos that detail NAL's publicity campaign. These archival sources must be read in tandem with the book's cover, whose pulp stylings beg for attention and analysis.

Lurking amid the eye-popping scheme and titillating cover copy ("The Vivid Story of a Negro Who Crossed the Colour Line") is a shadowed face. As if called on cue, this figure moves to the cover's foreground and thrusts itself from behind a curtain of color (three diagonal strips of brown and mustard yellow hues) into clear view. A strikingly handsome illustration of James Weldon Johnson appears before our eyes, dominating the cover's foreground. Crucially, though, his name occupies a liminal space. Cutting across the folds of the colored veil, the words boldly pronounce themselves—or are they graphically trapped within the binary structures of racial categories? "James" appears in black font, "Weldon Johnson" in white. Given these visual teasers and tensions, how are readers to assess these juxtapositions of images and text? Do they complement or compromise the novel's standing as literary fiction? The small sample of press and public opinion documented in the Reviews and

3. Victor Weybright to Charles G. Boste, April 30, 1946. New American Library Archives, MSS 070, Fales Library and Special Collections, New York University.

Correspondence sections of this volume invites readers' investigations into these questions. More profoundly, because there are significantly fewer newspaper or magazine reviews of *ECM*'s 1948 edition—and given NAL's sincere efforts to acquire and market the novel—how can the novel's lackluster reception be explained? After all, the year before was a banner year for American novels about racial passing: in 1947 Sinclair Lewis's *Kingsblood Royal* and Willard Savoy's *Alien Land* racked up sufficient critical praise and strong sales numbers to warrant reprinting as cheap mass-market fiction.[4] Moreover, films like *Pinky* (1949) and *Lost Boundaries* (1949) drew millions to movie theaters to see passing narratives on screen. In this milieu, why did *ECM*'s account of racial passing not resonate with the American reading public in the late 1940s? Given the brutalities of post–World War II Jim Crow segregation, why did the novel not find an audience?

The Dilemma of the Modern Negro Novel: The Popular Reception of ECM

ECM's eclipse by the mid-twentieth century underscores a critical truism: the reception of literary works changes over time, depending on how the texts resonate with the cultural mores and politics of a given historical moment. Just as its cover designs embed a literary history of its making and meanings, press reviews track the novel's strange career in the public's imagination as well.

When *ECM*'s first edition appeared during the week of May 18, 1912, the book was widely reviewed, in all regions of the country.[5] This is remarkable when we consider the historical moment: at the nadir of racial repression in the early twentieth century, *ECM* was openly discussed from Pasadena, California, to Portland, Maine; from Detroit, Michigan, to New Orleans, Louisiana; from New York City to St. Louis, Missouri. Consequently, NCE readers can analyze the run of 1912 reviews reprinted in this volume to track comparisons along any number of axes. For instance, the first edition's critics expressed open curiosity about the book's claims to be a genuine autobiography. Indeed, many questioned if *ECM* was, in fact, a novel. On what textual grounds did reviewers base their suspicions? In 1912 Southern critics complained that *ECM*

4. Lewis's scabrous satire was first published by Random House and then reprinted by Bantam Books. Savoy's haunting novel was originally published by E. P. Dutton and reissued by NAL.

5. I have compiled this archive by relying on JWJ's scrapbooks. For both the 1912 and 1927 editions, he subscribed to a news clipping service (not unlike Google Alerts), which supplied him with copies of the novel's reviews. However, because those firms did not collect items from the African American press, I conducted a separate survey of the black press to complete this archive.

was an uncredible autobiography because the narrator-author's experiences as a mixed-race man simply could not be believed. Nevertheless, Southern reviewers did not sound the sensationalist alarm they could have—and that we might have expected—to *ECM*'s frank treatment of passing's scandalous nature. Though these critics' language about the "unpleasing" and "evil" consequences of interracial contact cannot be ignored or condoned, such discourse deserves scrutiny given the era's race-baiting tendencies. Thus NCE readers should compare the reviews' both across and within regional lines. What factors explain the absence of racial hysteria? In addition to passing, what issues raised critics' racial concerns in 1912?

The lack of hyperbole in the 1912 reviews perhaps reflects the novel's formal achievement because nearly all of the reviews praise the first edition for its "dispassionate" point of view. NCE readers should track the range of reasons why reviewers appreciated the novel's tone and question whether those reasons follow regional patterns or not. Comparative analyses between the black press reception and the white mainstream media's reviews can yield fascinating patterns too. For instance, is the novel's tonal restraint understood similarly across the color line? In the white press reviews, the narrator-author's "objectivity" earns praise for defusing the usual intensities around discussing the "race question." Black reviewers point out how the narrator-author's restraint places racism's indignities in a more abhorrent light. What issues and scenes did these accounts highlight? To make what points about the novel's cultural critique and formal achievements?

The sheer number of news clippings in Johnson's archives suggest that the 1927 edition of *ECM* enjoyed a wider response, with reviews ranging across the United States and abroad to the United Kingdom. Five trends emerge in the 1927 reviews that NCE readers should bear in mind. First, as critics Alice Dunbar Nelson and Mary White Ovington report, the novel sparked much literary gossip when it first appeared in 1912.[6] Though that public "furore" never made it to print, NCE readers can read Dunbar Nelson's and Ovington's accounts to consider how literary ephemera shapes our reading of texts and assess the time-bending effects that undocumented and unarchived opinions provide.

Second, the biggest "furore" of them all—the revelation of Johnson's identity as *ECM*'s author—did not change how most critics approached the book. Though there are exceptions, instead of

6. Dunbar Nelson and Ovington report one rumor that held that the novel's anonymous author was "a prominent Chicago publisher" who had been identified as Negro upon his death. The *Chicago Defender* editorial notice (July 13, 1912) reprinted at p. 286 hints at who this literary impostor might be.

assessing it as a work of fiction 1927 reviewers persisted in reading it as autobiography. Why refuse to call it a novel? The resistance to engage *ECM*'s fictive form gets underscored by the third theme across the 1927 reviews: critics' conflation of Harlem—by then the contemporary node of African American cultural production—with the novel's Tenderloin setting. As Harry Salpeter argues in the *New York World*, "There was no Harlem in those days" of the early 1900s; thus *ECM* envisions a world that was to come. Echoing Salpeter's point, nearly every book review in 1927 comments effusively on *ECM*'s capacity to foretell the cultural future that would take root in New York's New Negro art scene during the 1920s. As Ben Ray Redman confidently declares in the *New York Herald Tribune* (October 2, 1927): "First published in 1912, it must have come to a shock to many white readers who found described in it phases of colored society of whose existence they had never dreamed. To-day it holds no revelations for anyone who has even the slightest acquaintance with Negro life and literature."

Reviewers in the African American press decoded Harlem's site in the novel differently, giving voice to the fourth trend that distinguishes the 1927 edition: what historical time is being narrated by the novel, the past, present, or future? Are those periods linked as a continuum, or do they stand apart as distinct temporal divides? The final and, perhaps, single most important influence on the novel's reception in 1927 was Carl Van Vechten's introduction to the book. As I noted earlier, the critical terms that Van Vechten deployed to explain the novel's importance—*ECM* was "prophetic," a "documentary sourcebook," and a "composite autobiography"—reverberated through both the mainstream and African American press. Tracking how this terminology permeates the 1927 reviews (itself a case study of newspaper wire services' consolidation in the 1920s), NCE readers can assess Alice Dunbar-Nelson's review of the novel in a clearer light. Reprinted in its entirety, Dunbar-Nelson's essay is, perhaps, the very best review the novel ever earned. Dunbar-Nelson's focus on the novel's formal achievements starkly contrasts to Van Vechten's introduction. Read together with Johnson's critique of American literature's segregated readerships, his 1928 essay "The Dilemma of the Negro Author" (on p. 258 in this volume), Dunbar-Nelson's shrewd case for *ECM*'s aesthetic power demonstrates the "fused" intelligence that Johnson's essay sought to inculcate. Precisely because she was a renowned race fiction writer of the 1890s, Dunbar-Nelson's review also reminds us how the literary categories of "old" and "new," "black" and "modern" were upset by Johnson's novel and its innovations to the genre's form.

"Breaking the Narrow Limits of Tradition": Scholarly Assessments of ECM

Based on the absence of popular press reviews, the 1948 edition of *ECM* did not stir the reading public's interest. However, the 1940s mark the moment when scholarly criticism of the novel gathers momentum. If the popular press resisted seeing the novel's innovations as modern, the academy embraced that idea, albeit in a dispersed way.

Scholars of the late 1930s and 1940s recognized *ECM*'s themes as groundbreaking developments. Writing in 1937, Sterling A. Brown stressed how the figure of the "aristocratic mulatto" presented the "problem of passing" with newfound verve. Likewise, Hugh Gloster concurred that Johnson treated miscegenation differently, "with no bitterness." Where Brown praised Johnson's recovery of African American folk materials for effective descriptive use, Gloster emphasized the novel's focus on urban life as the hallmark innovative change. And while these early assessments disagree about Johnson's exploration of the "freemasonry of the race"—for Sterling Brown, those passages overburden the novel and cause its technical failure; for Gloster, these passages are valuable instances of "frank self-expression"—these readers do call *ECM* by its rightful name, a "novel." This acknowledgment constitutes a breakthrough all its own because the popular press reception of the 1910s and 1920s refused to classify the work by its proper literary genre at all.[7]

Perhaps the most decisive early assessment remains Robert Bone's revised edition of *The Negro Novel in America* (1965), which put *ECM* on the literary map in an aggressive way. Praising Johnson as "*the only true artist* among the early Negro novelists" and lauding the novel with this polarizing pronouncement—"*ECM*, simply by virtue of its form, demanded a discipline and restraint hitherto unknown in the Negro author"—Bone's discussion caps off these assertions with this stunning polemic: the novel succeeds as a work of art because the novel "subordinat[es] racial protest to artistic considerations" (48). With these claims, Bone set aesthetic form above theme as the criteria for the *ECM*'s modernizing force.

Though Bone issued these pronouncements at the height of the civil rights movement, it would be a mistake to borrow conventional political markers to periodize the novel's scholarly reception because that approach conceals a remarkable paradox. When black arts production is at its most politically charged during the nationalist-separatist decades of the 1970s and early 1980s, analyses of *ECM*

7. See the selected bibliography for full citations of these early works.

adopt highly formalist approaches.[8] For instance, Robert Fleming proffers a sustained analysis of how irony undergirds the novel's structure without concern to define *ECM*'s mode as modernist. Simone Vauthier, Robert Stepto, and Houston A. Baker Jr. trace *ECM*'s literary genealogy to the picaresque novel (Vauthier), black autobiography and *The Souls of Black Folk* (Stepto), and a "forgotten prototype" to the racial alienation dramatized in Ellison's *Invisible Man* (Baker). And Joseph T. Skerrett Jr. considers the "symbolic action" by which Johnson novelized elements of his own life into *ECM*'s fictive form. However, these critics do not shy away from the novel's politicized themes. The novel's urban setting, the narrator's strategies of passing and relation to black folk culture generate varied opinions among these scholars, particularly around the novel's skepticism toward race and authenticity.[9]

Recent criticism (from the 1980s to the present) addresses the novel's modernity as a function of its cultural critique. For instance, the novel's account of ragtime's rise has led critics to focus on *ECM*'s skeptical outlook toward black culture's claims to authenticity.[1] Then there is the matter of the book's matter; as I suggest earlier in this essay, the novel's physical form as a material object encodes a cultural history of modern book publishing in the United States that poses a far-reaching institutional critique of literary value, origins, and originality. While the novel's depiction of racial passing calls those same concepts into question, more recent analyses of those issues stake out new directions in what the body politics of *ECM* may mean. Where earlier scholarship posited the ex-colored man's biracial identifications as a fundamentally alienating condition, contemporary critics have shifted toward a more flexible view of the character's identity politics. Multiplicity, not binaries; plurality, not singularity, become the frames through which racial identity symbolizes modernity in these accounts.[2] Likewise, Siobhan B. Somerville explains, the ex-colored man's apparent ease in the company of other men discloses the homoerotic energies that organize the novel's concerns and logic.[3] Precisely because its name could

8. One important exception would be Addison Gayle's analysis of the novel. See *The Way of the New World: The Black Novel in America* (Garden City, NY: Doubleday, 1975), 91–111.
9. See selected bibliography for full citations of works by Fleming, Vauthier, Baker, and Skerrett. Stepto's analysis is reprinted in this volume.
1. For exemplary arguments of this sort, see works by Ruotolo (reprinted in this volume), Biers, and Morrissette.
2. For an illuminating analysis that interprets racial passing in these ways, see M. Giulia Fabi's essay reprinted in this volume.
3. Further proof that supports a queer theory of the novel can be found in *Along This Way*. JWJ's experience in the "man's world" (400) of Venezuela and Nicaragua crucially restored his sense of self following his near-lynching in Florida. Thus a further question can be asked: how might Latin American cultures of machísmo and homosociality (ca. 1906–12) have shaped JWJ's characterization of the ex-colored man?

not be spoken explicitly in the text, the illegibility of the ex-colored man's sexuality makes his predicament modern, not unlike his racially ambiguous appearance, both of which unseat normative definitions of identity and subjectivity, queer theorists contend.[4]

By no means do the critical essays reprinted in this volume exhaust the range of approaches to defining *ECM's* literary history as a modern novel. The bibliography prepared for this volume provides a comprehensive list of publications dating from 1937 to 2013. Urged on by this critical archive, NCE readers can discover more terrains and approaches to interpret this complex text.

A Novel (Un)like Others

As the histories of its composition, publication, and reception attest, Johnson "[gave] the country something new and unknown" with *ECM*. However, Johnson's reluctance to call himself and his novel modernist is important to recall. Making original art forms was not easy in 1912 (and remains so to this day) because recognition of those creative labors is hard earned, if it ever comes at all, especially for African American innovators. Johnson could have been writing about himself when he lamented this burden in one of his most famous poems, "O Black and Unknown Bards" (1908):

> What merely living clod, what captive thing,
> Could up toward God through all its darkness grope,
> And find within its deadened heart to sing
> These songs of sorrow, love, and faith, and hope?
> How did it catch *that subtle undertone,*
> *That note in music not heard with the ears*?
> How sound *the elusive reed, so seldom blown,*
> Which stirs the soul or melts the heart to tears?
>
> (lines 17–24; emphasis added)

"That subtle undertone," "'that note in music not heard with ears," "the elusive reed, so seldom blown"—writing his novel at a time when literary critical terms were in flux was challenging enough. Historicizing his strategies required vocabularies that Johnson could not have named in advance, given how tenuous the literary field was for black novel writers and novel writing in the first decades of the twentieth century.

4. For instance, see Cheryl Clarke, "Race, Homosocial Desire, and 'Mammon' in *Autobiography of an Ex-Coloured Man*," in *Professions of Desire: Lesbian and Gay Studies in Literature*, eds. George E. Haggerty and Bonnie Zimmerman (New York: Modern Language Association of America, 1995), 84–97; Philip Brian Harper, *Are We Not Men?: Masculine Anxiety and the Problem of African American Identity* (New York: Oxford University Press, 1998), chap. 5; and Darieck Scott, *Extravagant Abjection: Blackness, Power, and Sexuality in the Literary Imagination* (New York: New York University Press, 2010), chap. 2.

To be sure, Johnson knew full well that literary criticism routinely excluded African American literature from its analytic categories. Before World War I—when he drafted and first published *ECM*—black-authored texts rarely attained paradigmatic examination (let alone mention) in histories of literary practices and forms.[5] Indeed, he turned to anthologizing Negro spirituals and poetry in part to contest that practice of cultural segregation. Uncollected, unhistoricized, and unconceptualized, African American sacred singing and verse would have been lost had Johnson not collated them into books for future study.

However, as a creative writer himself—more precisely, as a novelist—Johnson no doubt agreed with E. M. Forster's insistence on the primacy of the imagination, the "act of creation," as the critical standard by which periodization and schools of writing should be defined. If Johnson borrowed from *Aspects of the Novel* to codify *ECM*'s "creative act" he did so not because he could not grasp the workings of his own novel's form. Rather, Johnson needed nearly twenty years to find a critical discourse that illuminated and explained his novel's ambitions because literary criticism and the work of creative writing did then, and still do, enrich the other. Johnson's wait need not be our own, though, because this Norton Critical Edition provides readers with archival and critical sources to discover how *The Autobiography of an Ex-Colored Man* contributed to the history of modernism's future.

5. Interestingly, E. M. Forster does cite one black text in his survey, Rene Maran's prize-winning *Batuoala* (1925), as an example of primitivism's new influence in the construction of character. See *Aspects*, 43–44.

Acknowledgments

While this volume focuses on James Weldon Johnson's achievement as a novelist, editing it has led me to appreciate the particular skills and talents he must have possessed as an anthologist. This project has made me keenly aware of the responsibilities assembling a critical edition entails. Tracking down, assembling, and—then, the truly humbling task—selecting evidence of *The Autobiography of an Ex-Colored Man*'s composition, publication, and reception has been an adventure and joy, thanks to the individuals and institutions I salute here.

James Weldon Johnson himself deserves credit for leaving such a well-detailed archive of his novel's history. Yale University's Beinecke Rare Book and Manuscript Library, which holds the main bulk of Johnson's papers, provided extraordinary support to this project. In particular, curator Nancy Kuhl generously provided me copies of key archival documents that are included in this volume and has been a great conversation partner as I worked out the organizing rubrics for this edition. I'm grateful for her engagement and enthusiasm for what this volume aims to accomplish.

Likewise, I am grateful to the James Weldon Johnson estate and its executor, Jill Rosenberg Jones, for granting me permission to cite and reprint the archival materials assembled in this volume. The late Dr. Sondra Kathryn Wilson's scholarship on James Weldon Johnson's career has been invaluable to my research. I am glad we shared the goal of creating an edition of *Ex-Colored Man* that allows readers and critics to grapple with the novel's multilayered literary history.

Librarians and archivists at repositories around the country dug deep into their holdings to locate materials that fleshed out the novel's composition history. I am grateful for the labors of: Trashinda Wright and Karen Jefferson at the Robert W. Woodruff Library of the Atlanta University Center, Dominique Daniel of the University of Michigan's Bentley Historical Library, Mary H. Teloh of the Eskind Biomedical Library at Vanderbilt University, Stephen Yates at the State Archives of Florida, Marvin Taylor at New York University Library's Fales Collection, and Sarah Elliston Weiner of Columbia University's Miriam and Ira D. Wallach Art Gallery. Early trips to the Beinecke Library and the Harry Ransom Center at the University of Texas, Austin, were funded by a research fellowship from the Bibliographic Society of America; I am grateful for that support.

This project has traveled with me across these middle years of my career; at each turn, the schools where I worked funded the research for this project. To Dean Martha Roth at the University of Chicago, (former) Provost Richard Foley of NYU, Deputy Provost Emily Bakemeier and Faculty of Arts and Sciences dean Tamar Gendler at Yale University—thank you for supporting this project.

Importantly, my research funds allowed me to hire excellent graduate research assistants whose labors made this volume possible. Summer McDonald at the University of Chicago showed remarkable creativity and diligence in her key assignments: pursuing rare evidence like the obituaries of J. Douglas Wetmore and researching the annotations to the novel's text. Chloe Flower at New York University immersed herself in a welter of bibliographic sources that needed to be identified, copied, and organized for this volume. At Yale, Anusha Alles filled final gaps that poked open with thorough, precise fact checking and document gathering. Moira Weigel came recommended to me by my colleague Katie Trumpener as an excellent, capacious student of early-twentieth-century German literary history. Moira lived up to that endorsement by preparing an excellent translation of the introduction and preface to *Der Weise Neger*, the 1928 German edition of *Ex-Colored Man*.

Defining the intellectual design of this volume presented its own challenges and pleasures, too. The conversations I have had with archivists, librarians, and research assistants shaped my thinking and planning, to be sure. So did the provocations raised by audiences where I presented the central rubrics of this volume, as a lecture (at Boston University) and the focus of a graduate seminar (the Americanist Colloquium at Tufts University). I'm grateful to Gene Jarrett (at BU) and Christina Sharpe and Virginia Jackson (at Tufts) for those opportunities.

However, I owe a special debt to two colleagues—Joan Bryant and P. Gabrielle Foreman—for the ongoing, in-depth discussions and debates we've about the novel over these years. Their moral support has meant the world to me. Likewise, once I committed my ideas to the page, Joan Bryant and Sherry Wolf (who role-played as my target undergraduate reader) offered insightful critiques of the introductory essay, as did Richard Yarborough, whose provocations demanded the utmost clarity from me. I hope I measured up to their those expectations.

This project came into my hands because of the most generous suggestion I have ever received—from Philip Brian Harper, who recommended me to Carol Bemis at W. W. Norton to edit this volume. Carol, in turn, has been the most considerate, committed editor I could ever hope for. Words cannot do justice to the gratitude I feel toward them both for trusting me with this work.

For all the good counsel and financial and material support I have received in the course of this project, I am thankful. Whatever errors of fact or omission emerge in this volume are mine, and mine alone.

A Note on the Text

The text of this edition is based on the 1912 publication of *The Autobiography of an Ex-Colored Man*, issued by Sherman, French & Company of Boston. Johnson's original spelling and punctuation have been retained throughout.

The concluding chapters (X and XI) differ significantly from the extant draft manuscripts of 1908 and 1910. However, both chapters are published as they appeared in the 1912 edition. The unpublished versions can be found on pp. 111 and 115 of this volume.

The Text of
THE AUTOBIOGRAPHY OF AN EX-COLORED MAN

Preface[1]

This vivid and startlingly new picture of conditions brought about by the race question in the United States makes no special plea for the Negro, but shows in a dispassionate, though sympathetic, manner conditions as they actually exist between the whites and blacks to-day. Special pleas have already been made for and against the Negro in hundreds of books, but in these books either his virtues or his vices have been exaggerated. This is because writers, in nearly every instance, have treated the colored American as a *whole;* each has taken some one group of the race to prove his case. Not before has a composite and proportionate presentation of the entire race, embracing all of its various groups and elements, showing their relations with each other and to the whites, been made.

It is very likely that the Negroes of the United States have a fairly correct idea of what the white people of the country think of them, for that opinion has for a long time been and is still being constantly stated; but they are themselves more or less a sphinx to the whites. It is curiously interesting and even vitally important to know what are the thoughts of ten millions of them concerning the people among whom they live. In these pages it is as though a veil had been drawn aside: the reader is given a view of the inner life of the Negro in America, is initiated into the "freemasonry," as it were, of the race.

These pages also reveal the unsuspected fact that prejudice against the Negro is exerting a pressure, which, in New York and other large cities where the opportunity is open, is actually and constantly forcing an unascertainable number of fair-complexioned colored people over into the white race.

In this book the reader is given a glimpse behind the scenes of this race-drama which is being here enacted,—he is taken upon an elevation where he can catch a bird's-eye view of the conflict which is being waged.

THE PUBLISHERS.

1. This statement was drafted by James Weldon Johnson himself, not "the publishers" whose title appears at the preface's end. This volume reprints the letter (dated Feb. 17, 1912) in which Johnson sketches out these ideas to Sherman, French & Company. See pp. 222–24.

The Autobiography of an Ex-Colored Man

Chapter I

I know that in writing the following pages I am divulging the great secret of my life, the secret which for some years I have guarded far more carefully than any of my earthly possessions; and it is a curious study to me to analyze the motives which prompt me to do it. I feel that I am led by the same impulse which forces the unfound-out criminal to take somebody into his confidence, although he knows that the act is liable, even almost certain, to lead to his undoing. I know that I am playing with fire, and I feel the thrill which accompanies that most fascinating pastime; and, back of it all, I think I find a sort of savage and diabolical desire to gather up all the little tragedies of my life, and turn them into a practical joke on society.

And, too, I suffer a vague feeling of unsatisfaction, of regret, of almost remorse from which I am seeking relief, and of which I shall speak in the last paragraph of this account.

I was born in a little town of Georgia a few years after the close of the Civil War. I shall not mention the name of the town, because there are people still living there who could be connected with this narrative. I have only a faint recollection of the place of my birth. At times I can close my eyes, and call up in a dream-like way things that seem to have happened ages ago in some other world. I can see in this half vision a little house,—I am quite sure it was not a large one;—I can remember that flowers grew in the front yard, and that around each bed of flowers was a hedge of vari-colored glass bottles[2] stuck in the ground neck down. I remember that once, while playing around in the sand, I became curious to know whether or not the bottles grew as the flowers did, and I proceeded to dig them

2. Before and after Emancipation, African Americans who kept subsistence gardens used bottles to protect crops and flowers from rabbits and moles, because the sound of wind blowing against the glass frightened such pests away. This folkway probably stemmed from an African (Kongo) tradition of tying bottles to tree limbs. The sounds created by this arrangement were thought to ward off evil spirits and thieves.

up to find out; the investigation brought me a terrific spanking which indelibly fixed the incident in my mind. I can remember, too, that behind the house was a shed under which stood two or three wooden wash-tubs. These tubs were the earliest aversion of my life, for regularly on certain evenings I was plunged into one of them, and scrubbed until my skin ached. I can remember to this day the pain caused by the strong, rank soap getting into my eyes.

Back from the house a vegetable garden ran, perhaps, seventy-five or one hundred feet; but to my childish fancy it was an endless territory. I can still recall the thrill of joy, excitement and wonder it gave me to go on an exploring expedition through it, to find the blackberries, both ripe and green, that grew along the edge of the fence.

I remember with what pleasure I used to arrive at, and stand before, a little enclosure in which stood a patient cow chewing her cud, how I would occasionally offer her through the bars a piece of my bread and molasses, and how I would jerk back my hand in half fright if she made any motion to accept my offer.

I have a dim recollection of several people who moved in and about this little house, but I have a distinct mental image of only two; one, my mother, and the other, a tall man with a small, dark mustache. I remember that his shoes or boots were always shiny, and that he wore a gold chain and a great gold watch with which he was always willing to let me play. My admiration was almost equally divided between the watch and chain and the shoes. He used to come to the house evenings, perhaps two or three times a week; and it became my appointed duty whenever he came to bring him a pair of slippers, and to put the shiny shoes in a particular corner; he often gave me in return for this service a bright coin which my mother taught me to promptly drop in a little tin bank. I remember distinctly the last time this tall man came to the little house in Georgia; that evening before I went to bed he took me up in his arms, and squeezed me very tightly; my mother stood behind his chair wiping tears from her eyes. I remember how I sat upon his knee, and watched him laboriously drill a hole through a ten-dollar gold piece, and then tie the coin around my neck with a string. I have worn that gold piece around my neck the greater part of my life, and still possess it, but more than once I have wished that some other way had been found of attaching it to me besides putting a hole through it.

On the day after the coin was put around my neck my mother and I started on what seemed to me an endless journey. I knelt on the seat and watched through the train window the corn and cotton fields pass swiftly by until I fell asleep. When I fully awoke we were being driven through the streets of a large city—Savannah. I sat up and blinked at the bright lights. At Savannah we boarded a steamer which finally landed us in New York. From New York we went to a town in Connecticut, which became the home of my boyhood.

My mother and I lived together in a little cottage which seemed to me to be fitted up almost luxuriously; there were horse-hair covered chairs in the parlor, and a little square piano; there was a stairway with red carpet on it leading to a half second story; there were pictures on the walls, and a few books in a glass-doored case. My mother dressed me very neatly, and I developed that pride which well-dressed boys generally have. She was careful about my associates, and I myself was quite particular. As I look back now I can see that I was a perfect little aristocrat. My mother rarely went to anyone's house, but she did sewing, and there were a great many ladies coming to our cottage. If I were around they would generally call me, and ask me my name and age and tell my mother what a pretty boy I was. Some of them would pat me on the head and kiss me.

My mother was kept very busy with her sewing; sometimes she would have another woman helping her. I think she must have derived a fair income from her work. I know, too, that at least once each month she received a letter; I used to watch for the postman, get the letter, and run to her with it; whether she was busy or not she would take it and instantly thrust it into her bosom. I never saw her read one of them. I knew later that these letters contained money and, what was to her, more than money. As busy as she generally was she, however, found time to teach me my letters and figures and how to spell a number of easy words. Always on Sunday evenings she opened the little square piano, and picked out hymns. I can recall now that whenever she played hymns from the book her tempos were always decidedly largo.[3] Sometimes on other evenings when she was not sewing she would play simple accompaniments to some old southern songs which she sang. In these songs she was freer, because she played them by ear. Those evenings on which she opened the little piano were the happiest hours of my childhood. Whenever she started toward the instrument I used to follow her with all the interest and irrepressible joy that a pampered pet dog shows when a package is opened in which he knows there is a sweet bit for him. I used to stand by her side, and often interrupt and annoy her by chiming in with strange harmonies which I found either on the high keys of the treble or low keys of the bass. I remember that I had a particular fondness for the black keys. Always on such evenings, when the music was over, my mother would sit with me in her arms often for a very long time. She would

3. Very slow and deliberate.

hold me close, softly crooning some old melody without words, all the while gently stroking her face against my head; many and many a night I thus fell asleep. I can see her now, her great dark eyes looking into the fire, to where? No one knew but she. The memory of that picture has more than once kept me from straying too far from the place of purity and safety in which her arms held me.

At a very early age I began to thump on the piano alone, and it was not long before I was able to pick out a few tunes. When I was seven years old I could play by ear all of the hymns and songs that my mother knew. I had also learned the names of the notes in both clefs, but I preferred not to be hampered by notes. About this time several ladies for whom my mother sewed heard me play, and they persuaded her that I should at once be put under a teacher; so arrangements were made for me to study the piano with a lady who was a fairly good musician; at the same time arrangements were made for me to study my books with this lady's daughter. My music teacher had no small difficulty at first in pinning me down to the notes. If she played my lesson over for me I invariably attempted to reproduce the required sounds without the slightest recourse to the written characters. Her daughter, my other teacher, also had her worries. She found that, in reading, whenever I came to words that were, difficult or unfamiliar I was prone to bring my imagination to the rescue and read from the picture. She has laughingly told me, since then, that I would sometimes substitute whole sentences and even paragraphs from what meaning I thought the illustrations conveyed. She said she sometimes was not only amused at the fresh treatment I would give an author's subject, but that when I gave some new and sudden turn to the plot of the story she often grew interested and even excited in listening to hear what kind of a denouement I would bring about. But I am sure this was not due to dullness, for I made rapid progress in both my music and my books.

And so, for a couple of years my life was divided between my music and my school books. Music took up the greater part of my time. I had no playmates, but amused myself with games—some of them my own invention—which could be played alone. I knew a few boys whom I had met at the church which I attended with my mother, but I had formed no close friendships with any of them. Then, when I was nine years old, my mother decided to enter me in the public school, so all at once I found myself thrown among a crowd of boys of all sizes and kinds; some of them seemed to me like savages. I shall never forget the bewilderment, the pain, the heart-sickness of that first day at school. I seemed to be the only stranger in the place; every other boy seemed to know every other boy. I was fortunate enough, however, to be assigned to a teacher who knew me; my mother made her dresses. She was one of the ladies who used to pat me on the head and kiss me. She had the tact to address a few words directly to me; this gave me a certain sort of standing in the class, and put me somewhat at ease.

Within a few days I had made one staunch friend, and was on fairly good terms with most of the boys. I was shy of the girls, and remained so; even now, a word or look from a pretty woman sets me all a-tremble. This friend I bound to me with hooks of steel in a very simple way. He was a big awkward boy with a face full of freckles and a head full of very red hair. He was perhaps fourteen years of age; that is, four or five years older than any other boy in the class. This seniority was due to the fact that he had spent twice the required amount of time in several of the preceding classes. I had not been at school many hours before I felt that "Red Head"—as I involuntarily called him—and I were to be friends. I do not doubt that this feeling was strengthened, by the fact that I had been quick enough to see that a big, strong boy was a friend to be desired at a public school; and, perhaps, in spite of his dullness, "Red Head" had been able to discern that I could be of service to him. At any rate there was a simultaneous mutual attraction.

The teacher had strung the class promiscuously round the walls of the room for a sort of trial heat for places of rank; when the line was straightened out I found that by skillful maneuvering I had placed myself, third, and had piloted "Red Head" to the place next to me. The teacher began by giving us to spell the words corresponding to our order in the line. "Spell first." "Spell second." "Spell third." I rattled off, "t-h-i-r-d, third," in a way which said, "Why don't you give us something hard?" As the words went down the line I could see how lucky I had been to get a good place together with an easy word. As young as I was I felt impressed with the unfairness of the whole proceeding when I saw the tailenders going down before "twelfth" and "twentieth," and I felt sorry for those who had to spell such words in order to hold a low position. "Spell fourth." "Red Head," with his hands clutched tightly behind his back, began bravely, "f-o-r-t-h." Like a flash a score of hands went up, and the teacher began saying, "No snapping of fingers, no snapping of fingers." This was the first word missed, and it seemed to me that some of the scholars were about to lose their senses; some were dancing up and down on one foot with a hand above their heads, the fingers working furiously, and joy beaming all over their faces; others stood still, their hands raised not so high, their fingers working less rapidly, and their faces expressing not quite so much happiness; there were still others who did not move nor raise their hands, but stood with great wrinkles on their foreheads, looking very thoughtful.

The whole thing was new to me, and I did not raise my hand, but slyly whispered the letter "u" to "Red Head" several times. "Second chance," said the teacher. The hands went down and the class became quiet. "Red Head," his face now red, after looking beseechingly at the ceiling, then pitiably at the floor, began very haltingly, "f-u." Immediately an impulse to raise hands went through the class, but the teacher checked it, and poor "Red Head," though he knew that each letter he added only took him farther out of the way, went doggedly on and finished, "r-t-h." The hand raising was now repeated with more hubbub and excitement than at first. Those who before had not moved a finger were now waving their hands above their heads. "Red Head" felt that he was lost. He looked very big and foolish, and some of the scholars began to snicker. His helpless condition went straight to my heart, and gripped my sympathies. I felt that if he failed it would in some way be my failure. I raised my hand, and under cover of the excitement and the teacher's attempts to regain order, I hurriedly shot up into his ear twice, quite distinctly, "f-o-u-r-t-h," "f-o-u-r-t-h." The teacher tapped on her desk and said, "Third and last chance." The hands came down, the silence became oppressive. "Red Head" began, "f"— Since that day I have waited anxiously for many a turn of the wheel of fortune, but never under greater tension than I watched for the order in which those letters would fall from "Red's" lips—"o-u-r-t-h." A sigh of relief and disappointment went up from the class. Afterwards, through all our school days, "Red Head" shared my wit and quickness and I benefited by his strength and dogged faithfulness.

There were some black and brown boys and girls in the school, and several of them were in my class. One of the boys strongly attracted my attention from the first day I saw him. His face was as black as night, but shone as though it was polished; he had sparkling eyes, and when he opened his mouth he displayed glistening white teeth. It struck me at once as appropriate to call him "Shiny face," or "Shiny eyes," or "Shiny teeth," and I spoke of him often by one of these names to the other boys. These terms were finally merged into "Shiny," and to that name he answered good naturedly during the balance of his public school days.

"Shiny" was considered without question to be the best speller, the best reader, the best penman, in a word, the best scholar, in the class. He was very quick to catch anything; but, nevertheless, studied hard; thus he possessed two powers very rarely combined in one boy. I saw him year after year, on up into the high school, win the majority of the prizes for punctuality, deportment, essay writing and declamation. Yet it did not take me long to discover that, in spite of his standing as a scholar, he was in some way looked down upon.

The other black boys and girls were still more looked down upon. Some of the boys often spoke of them as "niggers." Sometimes on the way home from school a crowd would walk behind them repeating:

"Nigger, nigger, never die,
Black face and shiny eye."

On one such afternoon one of the black boys turned suddenly on his tormentors, and hurled a slate; it struck one of the white boys in the mouth, cutting a slight gash in his lip. At sight of the blood the boy who had thrown the slate ran, and his companions quickly followed. We ran after them pelting them with stones until they separated in several directions. I was very much wrought up over the affair, and went home and told my mother how one of the "niggers" had struck a boy with a slate. I shall never forget how she turned on me. "Don't you ever use that word again," she said, "and don't you ever bother the colored children at school. You ought to be ashamed of yourself." I did hang my head in shame, but not because she had convinced me that I had done wrong, but because I was hurt by the first sharp word she had ever given me.

My school days ran along very pleasantly. I stood well in my studies, not always so well with regard to my behavior. I was never guilty of any serious misconduct, but my love of fun sometimes got me into trouble. I remember, however, that my sense of humor was so sly that most of the trouble usually fell on the head of the other fellow. My ability to play on the piano at school exercises was looked upon as little short of marvelous in a boy of my age. I was not chummy with many of my mates, but, on the whole, was about as popular as it is good for a boy to be.

One day near the end of my second term at school the principal came into our room, and after talking to the teacher, for some reason said, "I wish all of the white scholars to stand for a moment." I rose with the others. The teacher looked at me, and calling my name said, "You sit down for the present, and rise with the others." I did not quite understand her, and questioned, "Ma'm?" She repeated with a softer tone in her voice, "You sit down now, and rise with the others." I sat down dazed. I saw and heard nothing. When the others were asked to rise I did not know it. When school was dismissed I went out in a kind of stupor. A few of the white boys jeered me, saying, "Oh, you're a nigger too." I heard some black children say, "We knew he was colored." "Shiny" said to them, "Come along, don't tease him," and thereby won my undying gratitude.

I hurried on as fast as I could, and had gone some distance before I perceived that "Red Head" was walking by my side. After a while he said to me, "Le' me carry your books." I gave him my strap without being able to answer. When we got to my gate he said as he handed me my books, "Say, you know my big red agate?[4] I can't shoot with it any more. I'm going to bring it to school for you tomorrow." I took my books and ran into the house. As I passed through the hallway I saw that my mother was busy with one of her customers; I rushed up into my own little room, shut the door, and went quickly to where my looking-glass hung on the wall. For an instant I was afraid to look, but when I did I looked long and earnestly. I had often heard people say to my mother, "What a pretty boy you have." I was accustomed to hear remarks about my beauty; but, now, for the first time, I became conscious of it, and recognized it. I noticed the ivory whiteness of my skin, the beauty of my mouth, the size and liquid darkness of my eyes, and how the long black lashes that fringed and shaded them produced an effect that was strangely fascinating even to me. I noticed the softness and glossiness of my dark hair that fell in waves over my temples, making my forehead appear whiter than it really was. How long I stood there gazing at my image I do not know. When I came out and reached the head of the stairs, I heard the lady who had been with my mother going out. I ran downstairs, and rushed to where my mother was sitting with a piece of work in her hands. I buried my head in her lap and blurted out, "Mother, mother, tell me, am I a nigger?" I could not see her face, but I knew the piece of work dropped to the floor, and I felt her hands on my head. I looked up into her face and repeated, "Tell me, mother, am I a nigger?" There were tears in her eyes, and I could see that she was suffering for me. And then it was that I looked at her critically for the first time. I had thought of her in a childish way only as the most beautiful woman in the world; now I looked at her searching for defects. I could see that her skin was almost brown, that her hair was not so soft as mine, and that she did differ in some way from the other ladies who came to the house; yet, even so, I could see that she was very beautiful, more beautiful than any of them. She must have felt that I was examining her, for she hid her face in my hair, and said with difficulty, "No, my darling, you are not a nigger." She went on, "You are as good as anybody; if anyone calls you a nigger don't notice them." But the more she talked the less was I reassured, and I stopped her by asking, "Well, mother, am I white? Are you white?" She answered tremblingly, "No, I am not white, but you—your father is one of the greatest men in the country—the best blood of the South is in you—" This suddenly opened up in my heart a fresh chasm of misgiving and fear, and I almost fiercely demanded, "Who is my father? Where is

4. A glass playing marble that closely resembles the semiprecious stone after which it is named.

he?" She stroked my hair and said, "I'll tell you about him some day." I sobbed, "I want to know now." She answered, "No, not now."

Perhaps it had to be done, but I have never forgiven the woman who did it so cruelly. It may be that she never knew that she gave me a sword-thrust that day in school which was years in healing.

Chapter II

Since I have grown older I have often gone back and tried to analyze the change that came into my life after that fateful day in school. There did come a radical change, and, young as I was, I felt fully conscious of it, though I did not fully comprehend it. Like my first spanking, it is one of the few incidents in my life that I can remember clearly. In the life of every one there is a limited number of unhappy experiences which are not written upon the memory, but stamped there with a die; and in long years after they can be called up in detail, and every emotion that was stirred by them can be lived through anew; these are the tragedies of life. We may grow to include some of them among the trivial incidents of childhood—a broken toy, a promise made to us which was not kept, a harsh, heart-piercing word—but these, too, as well as the bitter experiences and disappointments of mature years, are the tragedies of life.

And so I have often lived through that hour, that day, that week in which was wrought the miracle of my transition from one world into another; for I did indeed pass into another world. From that time I looked out through other eyes, my thoughts were colored, my words dictated, my actions limited by one dominating, all-pervading idea which constantly increased in force and weight until I finally realized in it a great, tangible fact.

And this is the dwarfing, warping, distorting influence which operates upon each colored man in the United States. He is forced to take his outlook on all things, not from the viewpoint of a citizen, or a man, nor even a human being, but from the viewpoint of a *colored* man. It is wonderful to me that the race has progressed so broadly as it has, since most of its thought and all of its activity must run through the narrow neck of one funnel.

And it is this, too, which makes the colored people of this country, in reality, a mystery to the whites. It is a difficult thing for a white man to learn what a colored man really thinks; because, generally, with the latter an additional and different light must be brought to bear on what he thinks; and his thoughts are often influenced by considerations so delicate and subtle that it would be impossible for him to confess or explain them to one of the opposite race. This gives to every colored man, in proportion to his intellectuality, a sort of dual personality; there is one phase of him which is disclosed only in the freemasonry[5] of his own race. I have often watched with interest and sometimes with amazement even ignorant colored men under cover of broad grins and minstrel[6] antics maintain this dualism in the presence of white men.

I believe it to be a fact that the colored people of this country know and understand the white people better than the white people know and understand them.

I now think that this change which came into my life was at first more subjective than objective. I do not think my friends at school changed so much toward me as I did toward them. I grew reserved, I might say suspicious. I grew constantly more and more afraid of laying myself open to some injury to my feelings or my pride. I frequently saw or fancied some slight where, I am sure, none was intended. On the other hand, my friends and teachers were, if anything different, more considerate of me; but I can remember that it was against this very attitude in particular that my sensitiveness revolted. "Red" was the only one who did not so wound me; up to this day I recall with a swelling heart his clumsy efforts to make me understand that nothing could change his love for me.

I am sure that at this time the majority of my white schoolmates did not understand or appreciate any differences between me and themselves; but there were a few who had evidently received instructions at home on the matter, and more than once they displayed their knowledge in word and action. As the years passed I noticed that the most innocent and ignorant among the others grew in wisdom.

I, myself, would not have so clearly understood this difference had it not been for the presence of the other colored children at

5. A fraternal organization that emerged in mid-17th century England and spread across Europe and the United States. Known for their secret membership rolls and organizational rituals, freemasons promote charitable social work and the moral rectitude of lodge members. Excluded or discouraged from joining white Masonic lodges, African American men organized their own cells as early as 1775. Consisting of free-born middle-class African Americans, Prince Hall Freemasons (so named after the first black man to join a U.S. lodge) were an exclusive group. They regarded themselves as exceptional, natural-born leaders who embodied the moral and civic ideals to which members of the race should aspire.

6. Historically refers to nomadic street performers in early modern Europe who roamed from town to town performing songs and ballads for local communities and elites. In the 19th-century United States, the term referred to theatrical stage performers—often white men—who made an art form out of mocking African American cultural practices. "Blacking up," as the masquerade was known, minstrels would paint their faces with burnt cork or greasepaint and invent comedic song and dance acts that became the most popular form of entertainment in the United States during the 1850s, particularly among the white working class in Northern cities as well as in the South. Minstrelsy's repertoire of racial caricatures—blacks as lazy, ne'er do-well country bumpkins; ostentatious, malapropism-speaking urban dandies; overweight, desexed mammies; always-contrite, never-assertive Uncle Toms (see p. 24, n. 6)—reinforced negative stereotypes then circulating about African Americans that still persist.

school; I had learned what their status was, and now I learned that theirs was mine. I had had no particular like or dislike for these black and brown boys and girls; in fact, with the exception of "Shiny," they had occupied very little of my thought, but I do know that when the blow fell I had a very strong aversion to being classed with them. So I became something of a solitary. "Red" and I remained inseparable, and there was between "Shiny" and me a sort of sympathetic bond, but my intercourse with the others was never entirely free from a feeling of constraint. But I must add that this feeling was confined almost entirely to my intercourse with boys and girls of about my own age; I did not experience it with my seniors. And when I grew to manhood I found myself freer with elderly white people than with those near my own age.

I was now about eleven years old, but these emotions and impressions which I have just described could not have been stronger or more distinct at an older age. There were two immediate results of my forced loneliness; I began to find company in books, and greater pleasure in music. I made the former discovery through a big, gilt-bound, illustrated copy of the Bible, which used to lie in splendid neglect on the center table in our little parlor. On top of the Bible lay a photograph album. I had often looked at the pictures in the album, and one day after taking the larger book down, and opening it on the floor, I was overjoyed to find that it contained what seemed to be an inexhaustible supply of pictures. I looked at these pictures many times; in fact, so often that I knew the story of each one without having to read the subject, and then, somehow, I picked up the thread of history on which is strung the trials and tribulations of the Hebrew children; this I followed with feverish interest and excitement. For a long time King David, with Samson a close second, stood at the head of my list of heroes; he was not displaced until I came to know Robert the Bruce.[7] I read a good portion of the Old Testament, all that part treating of wars and rumors of wars, and then started in on the New. I became interested in the life of Christ, but became impatient and disappointed when I found that, notwithstanding the great power he possessed, he did not make use of it when, in my judgment, he most needed to do so. And so my first general impression of the Bible was what my later impression

7. Renowned warrior (1274–1329), who led Scotland during its wars of independence against England (in the late 13th and 14th centuries) and rose to serve as king of Scotland from 1306 until his death. King David, prominent Old Testament figure and second king of Israel, who as a young boy killed the Philistine giant Goliath by throwing a rock at him with his sling, proving that size was not a prerequisite for physical might. Samson, an Old Testament figure known for his gift of incredible strength, which he would lose should he cut his hair. He fell in love with the temptress Delilah, who uncovered the secret to his strength and ordered a servant to cut Samson's hair as he slept, therefore weakening him.

has been of a number of modern books, that the authors put their best work in the first part, and grew either exhausted or careless toward the end.

After reading the Bible, or those parts which held my attention, I began to explore the glass-doored book-case which I have already mentioned. I found there "Pilgrim's Progress," "Peter Parley's History of the United States," Grimm's "Household Stories," "Tales of a Grandfather," a bound volume of an old English publication, I think it was called "The Mirror," a little volume called "Familiar Science," and somebody's "Natural Theology,"[8] which latter, of course, I could not read, but which, nevertheless, I tackled, with the result of gaining a permanent dislike for all kinds of theology. There were several other books of no particular name or merit, such as agents sell to people who know nothing of buying books. How my mother came by this little library which, considering all things, was so well suited to me, I never sought to know. But she was far from being an ignorant woman, and had herself, very likely, read the majority of these books, though I do not remember ever having seen her with a book in her hand, with the exception of the Episcopal Prayer-book. At any rate she encouraged in me the habit of reading, and when I had about exhausted those books in the little library which interested me, she began to buy books for me. She also regularly gave me money to buy a weekly paper which was then very popular for boys.

At this time I went in for music with an earnestness worthy of maturer years; a change of teachers was largely responsible for this. I began now to take lessons of the organist of the church which I attended with my mother; he was a good teacher and quite a thorough musician. He was so skillful in his instruction, and filled me with such enthusiasm that my progress—these are his words—was marvelous. I remember that when I was barely twelve years old I

8. The narrator rightfully cannot recall the author of this work because its title was so ubiquitous across the 17th and 19th centuries. *Pilgrim's Progress*: a Christian allegory published by John Bunyan in 1678. The text figures prominently in Harriet Beecher Stowe's antislavery novel, *Uncle Tom's Cabin* (see p. 24, n. 5) and was widely read in the United States during the 18th and 19th centuries. *History of the United States*:—Under the pseudonym Peter Parley, Samuel Griswold Goodrich (1793–1860) published a popular series of children's books on various subjects, including history, science, and geography. The books sold nearly 7 million copies and spawned several Peter Parley imitators. The volume here is most likely *A Pictorial History of the United States*, published in 1846. *Household Stories*: popularly known as Grimm's fairy tales; brothers Jacob and Wilhelm Grimm published the first volume of their collection in Germany in 1812. Written for children, the Grimms' stories include such legendary tales as "Snow White" and "Hansel and Gretel." *The Mirror*: a Scottish periodical published by novelist Henry Mackenzie (1745–1831) from January 1779 to May 1780. A once-, then twice-weekly periodical, it was the product of the Mirror Club, a small literary society for of young Scottish men. The bound copy referred to here was originally published in 1781. *Familiar Science*: probably *Peterson's Familiar Science*, edited by Robert Evans Peterson and originally published in 1851. This work sought to explain the science of commonplace phenomena in layman's terms.

appeared on a program with a number of adults at an entertainment given for some charitable purpose, and carried off the honors. I did more, I brought upon myself through the local newspapers the handicapping title of "Infant prodigy."

I can believe that I did astonish my audience, for I never played the piano like a child, that is, in the "one-two-three" style with accelerated motion. Neither did I depend upon mere brilliancy of technic, a trick by which children often surprise their listeners, but I always tried to interpret a piece of music; I always played with feeling. Very early I acquired that knack of using the pedals which makes the piano a sympathetic, singing instrument; quite a different thing from the source of hard or blurred sounds it so generally is. I think this was due not entirely to natural artistic temperament, but largely to the fact that I did not begin to learn the piano by counting out exercises, but by trying to reproduce the quaint songs which my mother used to sing, with all their pathetic turns and cadences.

Even at a tender age, in playing, I helped to express what I felt by some of the mannerisms which I afterwards observed in great performers; I had not copied them. I have often heard people speak of the mannerisms of musicians as affectations adopted for mere effect; in some cases this may be so; but a true artist can no more play upon the piano or violin without putting his whole body in accord with the emotions he is striving to express than a swallow can fly without being graceful. Often when playing I could not keep the tears which formed in my eyes from rolling down my cheeks. Sometimes at the end or even in the midst of a composition, as big a boy as I was, I would jump from the piano, and throw myself sobbing into my mother's arms. She, by her caresses and often her tears, only encouraged these fits of sentimental hysteria. Of course, to counteract this tendency to temperamental excesses I should have been out playing ball or in swimming with other boys of my age; but my mother didn't know that. There was only once when she was really firm with me, making me do what she considered was best; I did not want to return to school after the unpleasant episode which I have related, and she was inflexible.

I began my third term, and the days ran along as I have already indicated. I had been promoted twice, and had managed each time to pull "Red" along with me. I think the teachers came to consider me the only hope of his ever getting through school, and I believe they secretly conspired with me to bring about the desired end. At any rate, I know it became easier in each succeeding examination for me not only to assist "Red," but absolutely to do his work. It is strange how in some things honest people can be dishonest without the slightest compunction. I knew boys at school who were too honorable to tell a fib even when one would have been just the right thing, but could not resist the temptation to assist or receive assistance in an examination. I have long considered it the highest proof of honesty in a man to hand his street-car fare to the conductor who had overlooked it.

One afternoon after school, during my third term, I rushed home in a great hurry to get my dinner, and go to my music teacher's. I was never reluctant about going there, but on this particular afternoon I was impetuous. The reason of this was, I had been asked to play the accompaniment for a young lady who was to play a violin solo at a concert given by the young people of the church, and on this afternoon we were to have our first rehearsal. At that time playing accompaniments was the only thing in music I did not enjoy; later this feeling grew into positive dislike. I have never been a really good accompanist because my ideas of interpretation were always too strongly individual. I constantly forced my accelerandos and rubatos[9] upon the soloist, often throwing the duet entirely out of gear.

Perhaps the reader has already guessed why I was so willing and anxious to play the accompaniment to this violin solo; if not,—the violinist was a girl of seventeen or eighteen whom I had first heard play a short time before on a Sunday afternoon at a special service of some kind, and who had moved me to a degree which now I can hardly think of as possible. At present I do not think it was due to her wonderful playing, though I judge she must have been a very fair performer, but there was just the proper setting to produce the effect upon a boy such as I was; the half dim church, the air of devotion on the part of the listeners, the heaving tremor of the organ under the clear wail of the violin, and she, her eyes almost closing, the escaping strands of her dark hair wildly framing her pale face, and her slender body swaying to the tones she called forth, all combined to fire my imagination and my heart with a passion though boyish, yet strong and, somehow, lasting. I have tried to describe the scene; if I have succeeded it is only half success, for words can only partially express what I would wish to convey. Always in recalling that Sunday afternoon I am subconscious of a faint but distinct fragrance which, like some old memory-awakening perfume, rises and suffuses my whole imagination, inducing a state of reverie so airy as to just evade the powers of expression.

She was my first love, and I loved her as only a boy loves. I dreamed of her, I built air castles for her, she was the incarnation of each beautiful heroine I knew; when I played the piano it was to her, not even did music furnish an adequate outlet for my passion; I bought a new note-book, and, to sing her praises, made my first and last attempts at poetry. I remember one day at school, after

9. Changes in the music's cadence. *Accelerandos*: increases in the tempo of music.

having given in our note-books to have some exercises corrected, the teacher called me to her desk and said, "I couldn't correct your exercises because I found nothing in your book but a rhapsody on somebody's brown eyes." I had passed in the wrong note-book. I don't think I have felt greater embarrassment in my whole life than I did at that moment. I was not only ashamed that my teacher should see this nakedness of my heart, but that she should find out that I had any knowledge of such affairs. It did not then occur to me to be ashamed of the kind of poetry I had written.

Of course, the reader must know that all of this adoration was in secret; next to my great love for this young lady was the dread that in some way she would find it out. I did not know what some men never find out, that the woman who cannot discern when she is loved has never lived. It makes me laugh to think how successful I was in concealing it all; within a short time after our duet all of the friends of my dear one were referring to me as her "little sweetheart," or her "little beau," and she laughingly encouraged it. This did not entirely satisfy me; I wanted to be taken seriously. I had definitely made up my mind that I should never love another woman, and that if she deceived me I should do something desperate—the great difficulty was to think of something sufficiently desperate—and the heartless jade, how she led me on!

So I hurried home that afternoon, humming snatches of the violin part of the duet, my heart beating with pleasurable excitement over the fact that I was going to be near her, to have her attention placed directly upon me; that I was going to be of service to her, and in a way in which I could show myself to advantage—this last consideration has much to do with cheerful service.—The anticipation produced in me a sensation somewhat between bliss and fear. I rushed through the gate, took the three steps to the house at one bound, threw open the door, and was about to hang my cap on its accustomed peg of the hall rack when I noticed that that particular peg was occupied by a black derby hat. I stopped suddenly, and gazed at this hat as though I had never seen an object of its description. I was still looking at it in open-eyed wonder when my mother, coming out of the parlor into the hallway, called me, and said there was someone inside who wanted to see me. Feeling that I was being made a party to some kind of mystery I went in with her, and there I saw a man standing leaning with one elbow on the mantel, his back partly turned toward the door. As I entered he turned, and I saw a tall, handsome, well dressed gentleman of perhaps thirty-five; he advanced a step toward me with a smile on his face. I stopped and looked at him with the same feelings with which I had looked at the derby hat, except that they were greatly magnified. I looked at him from head to foot, but he was an absolute blank to me until my eyes rested on his slender, elegant, polished shoes; then it seemed that indistinct and partly obliterated films of memory began at first slowly then rapidly to unroll, forming a vague panorama of my childhood days in Georgia.

My mother broke the spell by calling me by name, and saying, "This is your father."

"Father, Father," that was the word which had been to me a source of doubt and perplexity ever since the interview with my mother on the subject. How often I had wondered about my father, who he was, what he was like, whether alive or dead, and above all, why she would not tell me about him. More than once I had been on the point of recalling to her the promise she had made me, but I instinctively felt that she was happier for not telling me and that I was happier for not being told; yet I had not the slightest idea what the real truth was. And here he stood before me, just the kind of looking father I had wishfully pictured him to be; but I made no advance toward him; I stood there feeling embarrassed and foolish, not knowing what to say or do. I am not sure but that he felt pretty much the same. My mother stood at my side with one hand on my shoulder almost pushing me forward, but I did not move. I can well remember the look of disappointment, even pain, on her face; and I can now understand that she could expect nothing else but that at the name "father" I should throw myself into his arms. But I could not rise to this dramatic or, better, melodramatic climax. Somehow I could not arouse any considerable feeling of need for a father. He broke the awkward tableau by saying, "Well, boy, aren't you glad to see me?" He evidently meant the words kindly enough, but I don't know what he could have said that would have had a worse effect; however, my good breeding came to my rescue, and I answered, "Yes, sir," and went to him and offered him my hand. He took my hand into one of his, and, with the other, stroked my head saying that I had grown into a fine youngster. He asked me how old I was; which, of course, he must have done merely to say something more, or perhaps he did so as a test of my intelligence. I replied, "Twelve, sir." He then made the trite observation about the flight of time, and we lapsed into another awkward pause.

My mother was all in smiles; I believe that was one of the happiest moments of her life. Either to put me more at ease or to show me off, she asked me to play something for my father. There is only one thing in the world that can make music, at all times and under all circumstances, up to its general standard, that is a hand-organ, or one of its variations. I went to the piano and played something in a listless, halfhearted way. I simply was not in the mood. I was wondering, while playing, when my mother would dismiss me and let me go; but my father was so enthusiastic in his praise that he touched my vanity—which was great—and more than that; he displayed that sincere appreciation which always arouses an artist to his best effort, and, too, in an unexplainable manner, makes him feel like shedding tears. I showed my gratitude by playing for him a Chopin[1] waltz with all the feeling that was in me. When I had finished my mother's eyes were glistening with tears; my father stepped across the room, seized me in his arms, and squeezed me to his breast. I am certain that for that moment he was proud to be my father. He sat and held me standing between his knees while he talked to my mother. I, in the meantime, examined him with more curiosity, perhaps, than politeness. I interrupted the conversation by asking, "Mother, is he going to stay with us now?" I found it impossible to frame the word "father"; it was too new to me; so I asked the question through my mother. Without waiting for her to speak, my father answered, "I've got to go back to New York this afternoon, but I'm coming to see you again." I turned abruptly and went over to my mother, and almost in a whisper reminded her that I had an appointment which I should not miss; to my pleasant surprise she said that she would give me something to eat at once so that I might go. She went out of the room, and I began to gather from off the piano the music I needed. When I had finished, my father, who had been watching me, asked, "Are you going?" I replied, "Yes, sir, I've got to go to practice for a concert." He spoke some words of advice to me about being a good boy and taking care of my mother when I grew up, and added that he was going to send me something nice from New York. My mother called, and I said good-by to him, and went out. I saw him only once after that.

I quickly swallowed down what my mother had put on the table for me, seized my cap and music, and hurried off to my teacher's house. On the way I could think of nothing but this new father, where he came from, where he had been, why he was here, and why he would not stay. In my mind I ran over the whole list of fathers I had become acquainted with in my reading, but I could not classify him. The thought did not cross my mind that he was different from me, and even if it had the mystery would not thereby have been explained; for notwithstanding my changed relations with most of my schoolmates, I had only a faint knowledge of prejudice and no idea at all how it ramified and affected the entire social organism. I felt, however, that there was something about the whole affair which had to be hid.

1. Frédéric Chopin (1810–1849) wrote eighteen waltzes, nine of which were published during his lifetime. Like most of his music, Chopin's waltzes were written for piano and geared toward the smaller, more intimate setting of the salon, as opposed to the ballroom, where the waltz—a dance form originating in the 18th century but reaching its peak in the late 19th—was generally performed.

When I arrived I found that she of the brown eyes had been rehearsing with my teacher, and was on the point of leaving. My teacher with some expressions of surprise asked why I was late, and I stammered out the first deliberate lie of which I have any recollection. I told him that when I reached home from school I found my mother quite sick, and that I had stayed with her a while before coming. Then unnecessarily and gratuitously, to give my words force of conviction, I suppose, I added, "I don't think she'll be with us very long." In speaking these words I must have been comical; for I noticed that my teacher, instead of showing signs of anxiety or sorrow, half hid a smile. But how little did I know that in that lie I was speaking a prophecy.

She of the brown eyes unpacked her violin, and we went through the duet several times. I was soon lost to all other thoughts in the delights of music and love. I say delights of love without reservation; for at no time of life is love so pure, so delicious, so poetic, so romantic, as it is in boyhood. A great deal has been said about the heart of a girl when she stands "where the brook and river meet," but what she feels is negative; more interesting is the heart of a boy when just at the budding dawn of manhood he stands looking wide-eyed into the long vistas opening before him; when he first becomes conscious of the awakening and quickening of strange desires and unknown powers; when what he sees and feels is still shadowy and mystical enough to be intangible, and, so, more beautiful; when his imagination is unsullied, and his faith new and whole—then it is that love wears a halo—the man who has not loved before he was fourteen has missed a fore-taste of Elysium.[2]

When I reached home it was quite dark, and I found my mother without a light, sitting rocking in a chair as she so often used to do in my childhood days, looking into the fire and singing softly to herself. I nestled close to her, and with her arms around me she haltingly told me who my father was,—a great man, a fine gentleman,—he loved me and loved her very much; he was going to make a great man of me. All she said was so limited by reserve and so colored by her feelings that it was but half truth; and so, I did not yet fully understand.

Chapter III

Perhaps I ought not pass on this narrative without mentioning that the duet was a great success; so great that we were obliged to

2. In Greek mythology the place in the afterworld where those blessed with immortality are sent to dwell.

respond with two encores. It seemed to me that life could hold no greater joy than it contained when I took her hand and we stepped down to the front of the stage bowing to our enthusiastic audience. When we reached the little dressing-room, where the other performers were applauding as wildly as the audience, she impulsively threw both her arms around me, and kissed me, while I struggled to get away.

One day a couple of weeks after my father had been to see us, a wagon drove up to our cottage loaded with a big box. I was about to tell the man on the wagon that they had made a mistake, when my mother, acting darkly wise, told them to bring their load in; she had them to unpack the box, and quickly there was evolved from the boards, paper and other packing material, a beautiful, brand new, upright piano. Then she informed me that it was a present to me from my father. I at once sat down and ran my fingers over the keys; the full, mellow tone of the instrument was ravishing. I thought, almost remorsefully, of how I had left my father; but, even so, there momentarily crossed my mind a feeling of disappointment that the piano was not a grand. The new instrument greatly increased the pleasure of my hours of study and practice at home.

Shortly after this I was made a member of the boys' choir, it being found that I possessed a clear, strong soprano[3] voice. I enjoyed the singing very much. About a year later I began the study of the pipe organ and the theory of music; and before I finished the grammar school I had written out several simple preludes[4] for organ which won the admiration of my teacher, and which he did me the honor to play at services.

The older I grew the more thought I gave to the question of my and my mother's position, and what was our exact relation to the world in general. My idea of the whole matter was rather hazy. My study of United States history had been confined to those periods which were designated in my book as "Discovery," "Colonial," "Revolutionary," and "Constitutional." I now began to study about the Civil War, but the story was told in such a condensed and skipping style that I gained from it very little real information. It is a marvel how children ever learn any history out of books of that sort. And, too, I began now to read the newspapers; I often saw articles which aroused my curiosity, but did not enlighten me. But, one day, I drew from the circulating library a book that cleared the whole mystery, a book that I read with the same feverish intensity with which I had

3. The highest vocal range, generally sung by females and boys.
4. Pieces that introduce longer musical works, establishing the key and melody of the complete composition.

read the old Bible stories, a book that gave me my first perspective of the life I was entering; that book was "Uncle Tom's Cabin."[5]

This work of Harriet Beecher Stowe has been the object of much unfavorable criticism. It has been assailed, not only as fiction of the most imaginative sort, but as being a direct misrepresentation. Several successful attempts have lately been made to displace the book from northern school libraries. Its critics would brush it aside with the remark that there never was a Negro as good as Uncle Tom,[6] nor a slave-holder as bad as Lagree.[7] For my part, I was never an admirer of Uncle Tom, nor of his type of goodness; but I believe that there were lots of old Negroes as foolishly good as he; the proof of which is that they knowingly stayed and worked the plantations that furnished sinews for the army which was fighting to keep them enslaved. But, in these later years, several cases have come to my personal knowledge in which old Negroes have died and left what was a considerable fortune to the descendants of their former masters. I do not think it takes any great stretch of the imagination to believe there was a fairly large class of slave holders typified in Lagree. And we must also remember that the author depicted a number of worthless if not vicious Negroes, and a slave holder who was as much of a Christian and a gentleman as it was possible for one in his position to be; that she pictured the happy, singing, shuffling darkey as well as the mother waiting for her child sold "down river."

I do not think it is claiming too much to say that "Uncle Tom's Cabin" was a fair and truthful panorama of slavery; however that may be, it opened my eyes as to who and what I was and what my country considered me; in fact, it gave me my bearing. But there was no shock; I took the whole revelation in a kind of stoical way. One of the greatest benefits I derived from reading the book was that I could afterwards talk frankly with my mother on all the questions which had been vaguely troubling my mind. As a result, she was entirely freed from reserve, and often herself brought up the subject, talking of things directly touching her life and mine and of things which had come down to her through the "old folks." What she told me interested and even fascinated me; and, what may seem strange, kindled in me a strong desire to see the South. She spoke to me quite frankly about herself, my father and myself; she, the sewing girl of my father's mother; he, an impetuous young man home from college; I, the child

5. *Uncle Tom's Cabin, or, Life Among the Lowly* (1852), by Harriet Beecher Stowe. This best-selling antislavery novel not only stirred controversy in the abolitionist movement but it also influenced African American novel writing well into the 20th century by serving as one model of social protest fiction.

6. The main character in Stowe's novel, known for his Christ-like qualities despite the cruelties he experienced as a slave.

7. I.e., Simon Legree, the prototypically cruel slave master from Stowe's *Uncle Tom's Cabin*.

of this unsanctioned love. She told me even the principal reason for our coming North. My father was about to be married to a young lady of another great Southern family. She did not neglect to add that another reason for our being in Connecticut was that he intended to give me an education, and make a man of me. In none of her talks did she ever utter one word of complaint against my father. She always endeavored to impress upon me how good he had been and still was, and that he was all to us that custom and the law would allow. She loved him; more, she worshiped him, and she died firmly believing that he loved her more than any other woman in the world. Perhaps she was right. Who knows?

All of these newly awakened ideas and thoughts took the form of a definite aspiration on the day I graduated from the grammar school. And what a day that was! The girls in white dresess with fresh ribbons in their hair; the boys in new suits and creaky shoes; the great crowd of parents and friends, the flowers, the prizes and congratulations, made the day seem to me one of the greatest importance. I was on the programme, and played a piano solo which was received by the audience with that amount of applause which I had come to look upon as being only the just due to my talent.

But the real enthusiasm was aroused by "Shiny." He was the principal speaker of the day, and well did he measure up to the honor. He made a striking picture, that thin little black boy standing on the platform, dressed in clothes that did not fit him any too well, his eyes burning with excitement, his shrill, musical voice vibrating in tones of appealing defiance, and his black face alight with such great intelligence and earnestness as to be positively handsome. What were his thoughts when he stepped forward and looked into that crowd of faces, all white with the exception of a score or so that were lost to view. I do not know, but I fancy he felt his loneliness. I think there must have rushed over him a feeling akin to that of a gladiator tossed into the arena and bade to fight for his life. I think that solitary little black figure standing there felt that for the particular time and place he bore the weight and responsibility of his race; that for him to fail meant general defeat; but he won, and nobly. His oration was Wendell Phillips' "Toussant L'Ouverture,"[8] a speech which may now be classed as rhetorical, even, perhaps, bombastic; but as the words fell from "Shiny's" lips their effect was magical. How so young an orator could stir so great enthusiasm was to be wondered at. When in the famous

8. Phillips was a Harvard-educated lawyer and white antislavery activist (1811–1884) whose 1861 lecture "Toussaint L'Ouverture" chronicled the life of the Haitian revolution's leader and held that blacks were not inferior but should in fact be regarded as equal to whites.

peroration, his voice trembling with suppressed emotion rose higher and higher and then rested on the name Toussant L'Ouverture, it was like touching an electric button which loosed the pent-up feelings of his listeners. They actually rose to him.

I have since known of colored men who have been chosen as class orators in our leading universities, of others who have played on the 'Varsity foot-ball and base-ball teams, of colored speakers who have addressed great white audiences. In each of these instances I believe the men were stirred by the same emotions which actuated "Shiny" on the day of his graduation; and, too, in each case where the efforts have reached any high standard of excellence they have been followed by the same phenomenon of enthusiasm. I think the explanation of the latter lies in what is a basic, though often dormant, principle of the Anglo-Saxon heart, love of fair play. "Shiny," it is true, was what is so common in his race, a natural orator; but I doubt that any white boy of equal talent could have wrought the same effect. The sight of that boy gallantly waging with puny, black arms, so unequal a battle, touched the deep springs in the hearts of his audience, and they were swept by a wave of sympathy and admiration.

But the effect upon me of "Shiny's" speech was double; I not only shared the enthusiasm of his audience, but he imparted to me some of his own enthusiasm. I felt leap within me pride that I was colored; and I began to form wild dreams of bringing glory and honor to the Negro race. For days I could talk of nothing else with my mother except my ambitions to be a great man, a great colored man, to reflect credit on the race, and gain fame for myself. It was not until years after that I formulated a definite and feasible plan for realizing my dreams.

I entered the high school with my class, and still continued my study of the piano, the pipe organ and the theory of music. I had to drop out of the boys' choir on account of a changing voice; this I regretted very much. As I grew older my love for reading grew stronger. I read with studious interest everything I could find relating to colored men who had gained prominence. My heroes had been King David, then Robert the Bruce; now Frederick Douglass[9] was enshrined in the place of honor. When I learned that Alexander Dumas was a colored man, I re-read "Monte Cristo" and "The Three Guardsmen"[1] with magnified pleasure. I lived between

9. The 19th century's most important African American abolitionist (1818–1895); escaped from slavery to become an orator, author, and newspaper editor and publisher.

1. Two novels by Dumas, père (1802–1870), a French novelist noted for his historical and adventure fiction. His paternal grandmother was of African Caribbean descent. *The Count of Monte Cristo* (1844) is one of his most enduring works. *The Three Guardsmen* (1902) was the sequel to his *The Adventures of the Three Musketeers* (1844).

my music and books, on the whole a rather unwholesome life for a boy to lead. I dwelt in a world of imagination, of dreams and air castles,—the kind of atmosphere that sometimes nourishes a genius, more often men unfitted for the practical struggles of life. I never played a game of ball, never went fishing or learned to swim; in fact, the only outdoor exercise in which I took any interest was skating. Nevertheless, though slender, I grew well-formed and in perfect health. After I entered the high school I began to notice the change in my mother's health, which I suppose had been going on for some years. She began to complain a little and to cough a great deal; she tried several remedies, and finally went to see a doctor; but though she was failing in health she kept her spirits up. She still did a great deal of sewing, and in the busy seasons hired two women to help her. The purpose she had formed of having me go through college without financial worries kept her at work when she was not fit for it. I was so fortunate as to be able to organize a class of eight or ten beginners on the piano, and so start a separate little fund of my own. As the time for my graduation from the high school grew nearer, the plans for my college career became the chief subject of our talks. I sent for catalogues of all the prominent schools in the East, and eagerly gathered all the information I could concerning them from different sources. My mother told me that my father wanted me to go to Harvard or Yale; she herself had a half desire for me to go to Atlanta University,[2] and even had me write for a catalogue of that school. There were two reasons, however, that inclined her to my father's choice: the first, that at Harvard or Yale I should be near her; the second, that my father had promised to pay a part of my college education.

Both "Shiny" and "Red" came to my house quite often of evenings, and we used to talk over our plans and prospects for the future. Sometimes I would play for them, and they seemed to enjoy the music very much. My mother often prepared sundry southern dishes for them, which I am not sure but that they enjoyed more. "Shiny" had an uncle in Amherst, Mass., and he expected to live with him and work his way through Amherst College. "Red" declared that he had enough of school and that after he got his high school diploma he would get a position in a bank. It was his ambition to become a banker, and he felt sure of getting the opportunity through certain members of his family.

My mother barely had strength to attend the closing exercises of the high school when I graduated; and after that day she was

2. A historically African American university located in Atlanta, Georgia, and founded in 1865 by the American Missionary Association. Johnson graduated from the school in 1894.

seldom out of bed. She could no longer direct her work, and under the expense of medicines, doctors, and someone to look after her, our college fund began to diminish rapidly. Many of her customers and some of the neighbors were very kind, and frequently brought her nourishment of one kind or another. My mother realized what I did not, that she was mortally ill, and she had me write a long letter to my father. For some time past she had heard from him only at irregular intervals; we never received an answer. In those last days I often sat at her bedside and read to her until she fell asleep. Sometimes I would leave the parlor door open and play on the piano, just loud enough for the music to reach her. This she always enjoyed.

One night, near the end of July, after I had been watching beside her for some hours, I went into the parlor, and throwing myself into the big arm chair dozed off into a fitful sleep. I was suddenly aroused by one of the neighbors, who had come in to sit with her that night. She said, "Come to your mother at once." I hurried upstairs, and at the bedroom door met the woman who was acting as nurse. I noted with a dissolving heart the strange look of awe on her face. From my first glance at my mother, I discerned the light of death upon her countenance. I fell upon my knees beside the bed, and burying my face in the sheets sobbed convulsively. She died with the fingers of her left hand entwined in my hair.

I will not rake over this, one of the two sacred sorrows of my life; nor could I describe the feeling of unutterable loneliness that fell upon me. After the funeral I went to the house of my music teacher; he had kindly offered me the hospitality of his home for so long as I might need it. A few days later I moved my trunk, piano, my music and most of my books to his home; the rest of my books I divided between "Shiny" and "Red." Some of the household effects I gave to "Shiny's" mother and to two or three of the neighbors who had been kind to us during my mother's illness; the others I sold. After settling up my little estate I found that besides a good supply of clothes, a piano, some books and other trinkets, I had about two hundred dollars in cash.

The question of what I was to do now confronted me. My teacher suggested a concert tour; but both of us realized that I was too old to be exploited as an infant prodigy and too young and inexperienced to go before the public as a finished artist. He, however, insisted that the people of the town would generously patronize a benefit concert, so took up the matter, and made arrangements for such an entertainment. A more than sufficient number of people with musical and elocutionary talent volunteered their services to make a programme. Among these was my brown-eyed violinist. But our relations were not the same as they were when we had played our first duet together. A year or so after that time she had dealt me a crushing blow by getting married. I was partially avenged, however, by the fact that, though she was growing more beautiful, she was losing her ability to play the violin.

I was down on the programme for one number. My selection might have appeared at that particular time as a bit of affectation, but I considered it deeply appropriate; I played Beethoven's "Sonata Pathétique."[3] When I sat down at the piano, and glanced into the faces of the several hundreds of people who were there solely on account of love or sympathy for me, emotions swelled in my heart which enabled me to play the "Pathétique" as I could never again play it. When the last tone died away the few who began to applaud were hushed by the silence of the others; and for once I played without receiving an encore.

The benefit yielded me a little more than two hundred dollars, thus raising my cash capital to about four hundred dollars. I still held to my determination of going to college; so it was now a question of trying to squeeze through a year at Harvard or going to Atlanta where the money I had would pay my actual expenses for at least two years. The peculiar fascination which the South held over my imagination and my limited capital decided me in favor of Atlanta University; so about the last of September I bade farewell to the friends and scenes of my boyhood, and boarded a train for the South.

Chapter IV

The farther I got below Washington the more disappointed I became in the appearance of the country. I peered through the car windows, looking in vain for the luxuriant semi-tropical scenery which I had pictured in my mind. I did not find the grass so green, nor the woods so beautiful, nor the flowers so plentiful, as they were in Connecticut. Instead, the red earth partly covered by tough, scrawny grass, the muddy straggling roads, the cottages of unpainted pine boards, and the clay daubed huts imparted a "burnt up" impression. Occasionally we ran through a little white and green village that was like an oasis in a desert.

When I reached Atlanta my steadily increasing disappointment was not lessened. I found it a big, dull, red town. This dull red color of that part of the South I was then seeing had much, I think, to do

3. Probably the most popular of Beethoven's early works. Published in 1799, it consists of three parts and features a melancholy mood.

with the extreme depression of my spirits—no public squares, no fountains, dingy street-cars and, with the exception of three or four principal thoroughfares, unpaved streets. It was raining when I arrived and some of these unpaved streets were absolutely impassable. Wheels sank to the hubs in red mire, and I actually stood for an hour and watched four or five men work to save a mule, which had stepped into a deep sink, from drowning, or, rather, suffocating in the mud. The Atlanta of to-day is a new city.

On the train I had talked with one of the Pullman car porters,[4] a bright young fellow who was himself a student, and told him that I was going to Atlanta to attend school. I had also asked him to tell me where I might stop for a day or two until the University opened. He said I might go with him to the place where he stopped during his "layovers" in Atlanta. I gladly accepted his offer, and went with him along one of those muddy streets until we came to a rather rickety looking frame house, which we entered. The proprietor of the house was a big, fat, greasy looking brown-skinned man. When I asked him if he could give me accommodation he wanted to know how long I would stay. I told him perhaps two days, not more than three. In reply he said, "Oh, dat's all right den," at the same time leading the way up a pair of creaky stairs. I followed him and the porter to a room, the door of which the proprietor opened while continuing, it seemed, his remark, "Oh, dat's all right den," by adding, "You kin sleep in dat cot in de corner der. Fifty cents please." The porter interrupted by saying, "You needn't collect from him now, he's got a trunk." This seemed to satisfy the man, and he went down leaving me and my porter friend in the room. I glanced around the apartment and saw that it contained a double bed and two cots, two washstands, three chairs, and a time-worn bureau with a looking-glass that would have made Adonis[5] appear hideous. I looked at the cot in which I was to sleep and suspected, not without good reasons, that I should not be the first to use the sheets and pillow-case since they had last come from the wash. When I thought of the clean, tidy, comfortable surroundings in which I had been reared, a wave of homesickness swept over me that made me feel faint. Had it not been for the presence of my companion, and that I knew this much of his history,—that he was not yet quite twenty, just three years older than myself, and that he had been fighting his own way in the world, earning his own living and providing for his

4. African American men hired by the Pullman Palace Car Company of Chicago to assist passengers with baggage and other personal duties on its trains, functionally serving as butlers to white patrons. Though demeaning in many ways, the position paid better than most jobs for African Americans at the time and was therefore highly sought after.

5. From Greek mythology, a remarkably beautiful man.

own education since he was fourteen, I should not have been able to stop the tears that were welling up in my eyes.

I asked him why it was that the proprietor of the house seemed unwilling to accommodate me for more than a couple of days. He informed me that the man ran a lodging house especially for Pullman porters, and as their stays in town were not longer than one or two nights it would interfere with his arrangements to have anyone stay longer. He went on to say, "You see this room is fixed up to accommodate four men at a time. Well, by keeping a sort of table of trips, in and out, of the men, and working them like checkers, he can accommodate fifteen or sixteen in each week, and generally avoid having an empty bed. You happen to catch a bed that would have been empty for a couple of nights." I asked him where he was going to sleep. He answered, "I sleep in that other cot to-night; to-morrow night I go out." He went on to tell me that the man who kept the house did not serve meals, and that if I was hungry we would go out and get something to eat.

We went into the street, and in passing the railroad station I hired a wagon to take my trunk to my lodging place. We passed along until, finally, we turned into a street that stretched away, up and down hill, for a mile or two; and here I caught my first sight of colored people in large numbers. I had seen little squads around the railroad stations on my way south; but here I saw a street crowded with them. They filled the shops and thronged the sidewalks and lined the curb. I asked my companion if all the colored people in Atlanta lived in this street. He said they did not, and assured me that the ones I saw were of the lower class. I felt relieved, in spite of the size of the lower class. The unkempt appearance, the shambling, slouching gait and loud talk and laughter of these people aroused in me a feeling of almost repulsion. Only one thing about them awoke a feeling of interest; that was their dialect. I had read some Negro dialect and had heard snatches of it on my journey down from Washington; but here I heard it in all of its fullness and freedom. I was particularly struck by the way in which it was punctuated by such exclamatory phrases as "Lawd a mussy!" "G'wan man!" "Bless ma soul!" "Look heah chile!" These people talked and laughed without restraint. In fact, they talked straight from their lungs, and laughed from the pits of their stomachs. And this hearty laughter was often justified by the droll humor of some remark. I paused long enough to hear one man say to another, "W'at's de mattah wid you an' yo' fr'en' Sam?" and the other came back like a flash, "Ma fr'en? He ma fr'en? Man! I'd go to his funeral jes de same as I'd go to a minstrel show." I have since learned that this ability to laugh heartily is, in part, the salvation of the American Negro; it does much to keep him from going the way of the Indian.

The business places of the street along which we were passing consisted chiefly of low bars, cheap dry-goods and notion stores, barber shops, and fish and bread restaurants. We, at length, turned down a pair of stairs that led to a basement, and I found myself in an eating-house somewhat better than those I had seen in passing; but that did not mean much for its excellence. The place was smoky, the tables were covered with oilcloth, the floor covered with sawdust, and from the kitchen came a rancid odor of fish fried over several times, which almost nauseated me. I asked my companion if this were the place where we were to eat. He informed me that it was the best place in town where a colored man could get a meal. I then wanted to know why somebody didn't open a place where respectable colored people who had money could be accommodated. He answered, "It wouldn't pay; all the respectable colored people eat at home, and the few who travel generally have friends in the towns to which they go, who entertain them." He added, "Of course, you could go in any place in the city; they wouldn't know you from white."

I sat down with the porter at one of the tables, but was not hungry enough to eat with any relish what was put before me. The food was not badly cooked; but the iron knives and forks needed to be scrubbed, the plates and dishes and glasses needed to be washed and well dried. I minced over what I took on my plate while my companion ate. When we finished we paid the waiter twenty cents each and went out. We walked around until the lights of the city were lit. Then the porter said that he must get to bed and have some rest, as he had not had six hours' sleep since he left Jersey City. I went back to our lodging-house with him.

When I awoke in the morning there were, besides my new found friend, two other men in the room, asleep in the double bed. I got up and dressed myself very quietly, so as not to awake anyone. I then drew from under the pillow my precious roll of greenbacks,[6] took out a ten dollar bill, and very softly unlocking my trunk, put the remainder, about three hundred dollars, in the inside pocket of a coat near the bottom; glad of the opportunity to put it unobserved in a place of safety. When I had carefully locked my trunk, I tiptoed toward the door with the intention of going out to look for a decent restaurant where I might get something fit to eat. As I was easing the door open, my porter friend said with a yawn, "Hello! You're going out?" I answered him, "Yes." "Oh!" he yawned again, "I guess I've had enough sleep; wait a minute, I'll go with you." For the instant his friendship bored and embarrassed me. I had visions of

6. U.S. paper currency (slang). Also used to refer to paper money issued by the federal government beginning in 1862.

another meal in the greasy restaurant of the day before. He must have divined my thoughts; for he went on to say, "I know a woman across town who takes a few boarders; I think we can go over there and get a good breakfast." With a feeling of mingled fears and doubts regarding what the breakfast might be, I waited until he had dressed himself.

When I saw the neat appearance of the cottage we entered my fears vanished, and when I saw the woman who kept it my doubts followed the same course. Scrupulously clean, in a spotless white apron and colored head handkerchief, her round face beaming with motherly kindness, she was picturesquely beautiful. She impressed me as one broad expanse of happiness and good nature. In a, few minutes she was addressing me as "chile" and "honey." She made me feel as though I should like to lay my head on her capacious bosom and go to sleep.

And the breakfast, simple as it was, I could not have had at any restaurant in Atlanta at any price. There was fried chicken, as it is fried only in the South, hominy[7] boiled to the consistency where it could be eaten with a fork, and biscuits so light and flaky that a fellow with any appetite at all would have no difficulty in disposing of eight or ten. When I had finished I felt that I had experienced the realization of, at least, one of my dreams of Southern life.

During the meal we found out from our hostess, who had two boys in school, that Atlanta University opened on that very day. I had somehow mixed my dates. My friend the porter suggested that I go out to the University at once and offered to walk over and show me the way. We had to walk because, although the University was not more than twenty minutes distance from the center of the city, there were no street-cars running in that direction. My first sight of the school grounds made me feel that I was not far from home; here the red hills had been terraced and covered with green grass; clean gravel walks, well shaded, lead up to the buildings; indeed, it was a bit of New England transplanted. At the gate my companion said he would bid me good-by, because it was likely that he would not see me again before his car went out. He told me that he would make two more trips to Atlanta, and that he would come out and see me; that after his second trip he would leave the Pullman service for the winter and return to school in Nashville. We shook hands, I thanked him for all his kindness, and we said good-by.

I walked up to a group of students and made some inquiries. They directed me to the president's office in the main building. The president gave me a cordial welcome; it was more than cordial; he

7. A kind of porridge prepared from boiled corn kernels, also known as hominy grits or grits; the dish is quite common throughout the U.S. South.

talked to me, not as the official head of a college, but as though he were adopting me into what was his large family, to personally look after my general welfare as well as my education. He seemed especially pleased with the fact that I had come to them all the way from the North. He told me that I could have come to the school as soon as I had reached the city, and that I had better move my trunk out at once. I gladly promised him that I would do so. He then called a boy and directed him to take me to the matron, and to show me around afterwards. I found the matron even more motherly than the president was fatherly. She had me to register, which was in effect to sign a pledge to abstain from the use of intoxicating beverages, tobacco, and profane language, while I was a student in the school. This act caused me no sacrifice; as, up to that time, I was free from either habit. The boy who was with me then showed me about the grounds. I was especially interested in the industrial building.

The sounding of a bell, he told me, was the signal for the students to gather in the general assembly hall, and he asked me if I would go. Of course I would. There were between three and four hundred students and perhaps all of the teachers gathered in the room. I noticed that several of the latter were colored. The president gave a talk addressed principally to new comers; but I scarcely heard what he said, I was so much occupied in looking at those around me. They were of all types and colors, the more intelligent types predominating. The colors ranged from jet black to pure white, with light hair and eyes. Among the girls especially there were many so fair that it was difficult to believe that they had Negro blood in them. And, too, I could not help but notice that many of the girls, particularly those of the delicate brown shades, with black eyes and wavy dark hair, were decidedly pretty. Among the boys, many of the blackest were fine specimens of young manhood, tall, straight, and muscular, with magnificent heads; these were the kind of boys who developed into the patriarchal "uncles" of the old slave régime.

When I left the University it was with the determination to get my trunk, and move out to the school before night. I walked back across the city with a light step and a light heart. I felt perfectly satisfied with life for the first time since my mother's death. In passing the railroad station I hired a wagon and rode with the driver as far as my stopping place. I settled with my landlord and went upstairs to put away several articles I had left out. As soon as I opened my trunk a dart of suspicion shot through my heart; the arrangement of things did not look familiar. I began to dig down excitedly to the bottom till I reached the coat in which I had concealed my treasure. My money was gone! Every single bill of it. I knew it was useless to do so, but I searched through every other coat, every pair of trousers, every vest, and even into each pair of socks. When I had finished my fruitless search I sat down dazed and heartsick. I called the landlord up, and informed him of my loss; he comforted me by saying that I ought to have better sense than to keep money in a trunk, and that he was not responsible for his lodgers' personal effects. His cooling words brought me enough to my senses to cause me to look and see if anything else was missing. Several small articles were gone, among them a black and gray necktie of odd design upon which my heart was set; almost as much as the loss of my money, I felt the loss of my tie.

After thinking for awhile as best I could, I wisely decided to go at once back to the University and lay my troubles before the president. I rushed breathlessly back to the school. As I neared the grounds the thought came across me, would not my story sound fishy? Would it not place me in the position of an impostor or beggar? What right had I to worry these busy people with the results of my carelessness? If the money could not be recovered, and I doubted that it could, what good would it do to tell them about it. The shame and embarrassment which the whole situation gave me caused me to stop at the gate. I paused, undecided, for a moment; then turned and slowly retraced my steps, and so changed the whole course of my life.

If the reader has never been in a strange city without money or friends, it is useless to try to describe what my feelings were; he could not understand. If he has been, it is equally useless, for he understands more than words could convey. When I reached my lodgings I found in the room one of the porters who had slept there the night before. When he heard what misfortune had befallen me he offered many words of sympathy and advice. He asked me how much money I had left, I told him that I had ten or twelve dollars in my pocket. He said, "That won't last you very long here, and you will hardly be able to find anything to do in Atlanta. I'll tell you what you do, go down to Jacksonville and you won't have any trouble to get a job in one of the big hotels there, or in St. Augustine."[8] I thanked him, but intimated my doubts of being able to get to Jacksonville on the money I had. He reassured me by saying, "Oh, that's all right. You express your trunk on through, and I'll take you down in my closet." I thanked him again, not knowing then, what it was to travel in a Pullman porter's closet. He put me under a deeper debt of gratitude by lending me fifteen dollars, which he said I could pay back after I had secured work. His generosity brought tears to my eyes, and I concluded that, after all, there were some kind hearts in the world.

8. Cities on the eastern coast of Florida that were popular winter resort towns.

I now forgot my troubles in the hurry and excitement of getting my trunk off in time to catch the train, which went out at seven o'clock. I even forgot that I hadn't eaten anything since morning. We got a wagon—the porter went with me—and took my trunk to the express office. My new friend then told me to come to the station at about a quarter of seven, and walk straight to the car where I should see him standing, and not to lose my nerve. I found my rôle not so difficult to play as I thought it would be, because the train did not leave from the central station, but from a smaller one, where there were no gates and guards to pass. I followed directions, and the porter took me on his car, and locked me in his closet. In a few minutes the train pulled out for Jacksonville.

I may live to be a hundred years old, but I shall never forget the agonies I suffered that night. I spent twelve hours doubled up in the porter's basket for soiled linen, not being able to straighten up on account of the shelves for clean linen just over my head. The air was hot and suffocating and the smell of damp towels and used linen was sickening. At each lurch of the car over the none too smooth track, I was bumped and bruised against the narrow walls of my narrow compartment. I became acutely conscious of the fact that I had not eaten for hours. Then nausea took possession of me, and at one time I had grave doubts about reaching my destination alive. If I had the trip to make again, I should prefer to walk.

Chapter V

The next morning I got out of the car at Jacksonville with a stiff and aching body. I determined to ask no more porters, not even my benefactor, about stopping places; so I found myself on the street not knowing where to go. I walked along listlessly until I met a colored man who had the appearance of a preacher. I asked him if he could direct me to a respectable boarding-house for colored people. He said that if I walked along with him in the direction he was going he would show me such a place. I turned and walked at his side. He proved to be a minister, and asked me a great many direct questions about myself. I answered as many as I saw fit to answer; the others I evaded or ignored. At length we stopped in front of a frame house, and my guide informed me that it was the place. A woman was standing in the doorway, and he called to her saying that he had brought her a new boarder. I thanked him for his trouble, and after he had urged upon me to attend his church while I was in the city, he went on his way.

I went in and found the house neat and not uncomfortable. The parlor was furnished with cane-bottomed chairs, each of which was adorned with a white crocheted tidy. The mantel over the fireplace had a white crocheted cover; a marble-topped center table held a lamp, a photograph album and several trinkets, each of which was set upon a white crocheted mat. There was a cottage organ in a corner of the room, and I noted that the lamp-racks upon it were covered with white crocheted mats. There was a matting on the floor, but a white crocheted carpet would not have been out of keeping. I made arrangements with the landlady for my board and lodging; the amount was, I think, three dollars and a half a week. She was a rather fine looking, stout, brown-skinned woman of about forty years of age. Her husband was a light colored Cuban, a man about one half her size, and one whose age could not be guessed from his appearance. He was small in size, but a handsome black mustache and typical Spanish eyes redeemed him from insignificance.

I was in time for breakfast, and at the table I had the opportunity to see my fellow-boarders. There were eight or ten of them. Two, as I afterwards learned, were colored Americans. All of them were cigar makers and worked in one of the large factories—cigar making is the one trade in which the color-line is not drawn. The conversation was carried on entirely in Spanish, and my ignorance of the language subjected me more to alarm than embarrassment. I had never heard such uproarious conversation; everybody talked at once, loud exclamations, rolling "*carambas*,"[9] menacing gesticulations with knives, forks, and spoons. I looked every moment for the clash of blows. One man was emphasizing his remarks by flourishing a cup in his hand, seemingly forgetful of the fact that it was nearly full of hot coffee. He ended by emptying it over what was, relatively, the only quiet man at the table excepting myself, bringing from him a volley of language which made the others appear dumb by comparison. I soon learned that in all of this clatter of voices and table utensils they were discussing purely ordinary affairs and arguing about mere trifles, and that not the least ill-feeling was aroused. It was not long before I enjoyed the spirited chatter and badinage at the table as much as I did my meals,—and the meals were not bad.

I spent the afternoon in looking around the town. The streets were sandy, but were well shaded by fine oak trees, and far preferable to the clay roads of Atlanta. One or two public squares with green grass and trees gave the city a touch of freshness. That night after supper I spoke to my landlady and her husband about my intentions. They told me that the big winter hotels would not open within two months. It can easily be imagined what effect this news

9. Spanish exclamations of surprise or outrage.

had on me. I spoke to them frankly about my financial condition and related the main fact of my misfortune in Atlanta. I modestly mentioned my ability to teach music and asked if there was any likelihood of my being able to get some scholars. My landlady suggested that I speak to the preacher who had shown me her house; she felt sure that through his influence I should be able to get up a class in piano. She added, however, that the colored people were poor, and that the general price for music lessons was only twenty-five cents. I noticed that the thought of my teaching white pupils did not even remotely enter her mind. None of this information made my prospects look much brighter.

The husband, who up to this time had allowed the woman to do most of the talking, gave me the first bit of tangible hope; he said that he could get me a job as a "stripper" in the factory where he worked, and that if I succeeded in getting some music pupils I could teach a couple of them every night, and so make a living until something better turned up. He went on to say that it would not be a bad thing for me to stay at the factory and learn my trade as a cigar maker,[1] and impressed on me that, for a young man knocking about the country, a trade was a handy thing to have. I determined to accept his offer and thanked him heartily. In fact, I became enthusiastic, not only because I saw a way out of my financial troubles, but also because I was eager and curious over the new experience I was about to enter. I wanted to know all about the cigar making business. This narrowed the conversation down to the husband and myself, so the wife went in and left us talking.

He was what is called a *regaliá* workman, and earned from thirty-five to forty dollars a week. He generally worked a sixty dollar job; that is, he made cigars for which he was paid at the rate of sixty dollars per thousand. It was impossible for him to make a thousand in a week because he had to work very carefully and slowly. Each cigar was made entirely by hand. Each piece of filler and each wrapper had to be selected with care. He was able to make a bundle of one hundred cigars in a day, not one of which could be told from the others by any difference in size or shape, or even by any appreciable difference in weight. This was the acme of artistic skill in cigar making. Workmen of this class were rare, never more than three or four of them in one factory, and it was never necessary for them to remain out of work. There were men who made two, three, and four hundred cigars of the cheaper grades in a day; they had to be very fast in order to make decent week's wages. Cigar making

1. Florida became a center of cigar manufacture in the 1830s, reaching its production peaks after the Civil War. The trade was characterized by its Cuban-owned factories and largely Spanish-speaking labor force from Cuba and other parts of Latin America.

was a rather independent trade; the men went to work when they pleased and knocked off when they felt like doing so. As a class the workmen were careless and improvident; some very rapid makers would not work more than three or four days out of the week, and there were others who never showed up at the factory on Mondays. "Strippers" were the boys who pulled the long stems from the tobacco leaves. After they had served at that work for a certain time they were given tables as apprentices.

All of this was interesting to me; and we drifted along in conversation until my companion struck the subject nearest his heart, the independence of Cuba.[2] He was an exile from the island, and a prominent member of the Jacksonville *Junta*.[3] Every week sums of money were collected from *juntas* all over the country. This money went to buy arms and ammunition for the insurgents. As the man sat there nervously smoking his long, "green" cigar, and telling me of the Gomezes, both the white one and the black one, of Macco and Bandera,[4] he grew positively eloquent. He also showed that he was a man of considerable education and reading. He spoke English excellently, and frequently surprised me by using words one would hardly expect from a foreigner. The first one of this class of words he employed almost shocked me, and I never forgot it, 'twas "ramify." We sat on the piazza until after ten o'clock. When we arose to go in to bed it was with the understanding that I should start in the factory on the next day.

I began work the next morning seated at a barrel with another boy, who showed me how to strip the stems from the leaves, to smooth out each half leaf, and to put the "rights" together in one pile, and the "lefts" together in another pile on the edge of the barrel. My fingers, strong and sensitive from their long training, were well adapted to this kind of work; and within two weeks I was accounted the fastest "stripper" in the factory. At first the heavy odor of the tobacco almost sickened me; but when I became accustomed to it I liked the smell. I was now earning four dollars a week, and was soon able to pick up a couple more by teaching a few scholars at night, whom I had secured through the good offices of the preacher I had met on my first morning in Jacksonville.

2. From ca. 1868 to 1898, citizens of Cuba fought three wars to free themselves from colonial rule of the Spanish, who had controlled the island for over four hundred years. The War of Independence (1895–98) saw Cuba achieve autonomy from Spain only to be annexed by its one-time ally, the United States.
3. Committee (Spanish); a group that provided financial backing and other material support for the Cuban rebels and promoted the idea of Cuban independence throughout the United States.
4. Máximo Gómez y Báez (1836–1905); Gomez's son, Francisco Gomez Toro (1876–1896), Antonio de la Caridad Maceo y Grajales (1845–1896), and Jose Quintino Bandera (1834–1906), and served as military commanders for Cuba during the Cuban War of Independence against Spain.

At the end of about three months, through my skill as a "stripper" and the influence of my landlord, I was advanced to a table, and began to learn my trade; in fact, more than my trade; for I learned not only to make cigars, but also to smoke, to swear, and to speak Spanish. I discovered that I had a talent for languages as well as for music. The rapidity and ease with which I acquired Spanish astonished my associates. In a short time I was able not only to understand most of what was said at the table during meals, but to join in the conversation. I bought a method for learning the Spanish language, and with the aid of my landlord, as a teacher, by constant practice with my fellow workmen, and by regularly reading the Cuban newspapers, and finally some books of standard Spanish literature which were at the house, I was able in less than a year to speak like a native. In fact, it was my pride that I spoke better Spanish than many of the Cuban workmen at the factory.

After I had been in the factory a little over a year, I was repaid for all the effort I had put forth to learn Spanish by being selected as "reader." The "reader" is quite an institution in all cigar factories which employ Spanish-speaking workmen. He sits in the center of the large room in which the cigar makers work and reads to them for a certain number of hours each day all the important news from the papers and whatever else he may consider would be interesting. He often selects an exciting novel, and reads it in daily installments. He must, of course, have a good voice, but he must also have a reputation among the men for intelligence, for being well posted and having in his head a stock of varied information. He is generally the final authority on all arguments which arise; and, in a cigar factory, these arguments are many and frequent, ranging from discussions on the respective and relative merits of rival baseball clubs to the duration of the sun's light and energy—cigar-making is a trade in which talk does not interfere with work. My position as "reader" not only released me from the rather monotonous work of rolling cigars, and gave me something more in accord with my tastes, but also added considerably to my income. I was now earning about twenty-five dollars a week, and was able to give up my peripatetic method of giving music lessons. I hired a piano and taught only those who could arrange to take their lessons where I lived. I finally gave up teaching entirely; as what I made scarcely paid for my time and trouble. I kept the piano, however, in order to keep up my own studies, and occasionally I played at some church concert or other charitable entertainment.

Through my music teaching and my not absolutely irregular attendance at church I became acquainted with the best class of colored people in Jacksonville. This was really my entrance into the race. It was my initiation into what I have termed the freemasonry of the race. I had formulated a theory of what it was to be colored, now I was getting the practice. The novelty of my position caused me to observe and consider things which, I think, entirely escaped the young men I associated with; or, at least, were so commonplace to them as not to attract their attention. And of many of the impressions which came to me then I have realized the full import only within the past few years, since I have had a broader knowledge of men and history, and a fuller comprehension of the tremendous struggle which is going on between the races in the South.

It is a struggle; for though the black man fights passively he nevertheless fights; and his passive resistance is more effective at present than active resistance could possibly be. He bears the fury of the storm as does the willow tree.

It is a struggle; for though the white man of the South may be too proud to admit it, he is, nevertheless, using in the contest his best energies; he is devoting to it the greater part of his thought and much of his endeavor. The South to-day stands panting and almost breathless from its exertions.

And how the scene of the struggle has shifted! The battle was first waged over the right of the Negro to be classed as a human being with a soul; later, as to whether he had sufficient intellect to master even the rudiments of learning; and to-day it is being fought out over his social recognition.

I said somewhere in the early part of this narrative that because the colored man looked at everything through the prism of his relationship to society as a *colored* man, and because most of his mental efforts ran through the narrow channel bounded by his rights and his wrongs, it was to be wondered at that he has progressed so broadly as he has. The same thing may be said of the white man of the South; most of his mental efforts run through one narrow channel; his life as a man and a citizen, many of his financial activities and all of his political activities are impassably limited by the ever present "Negro question." I am sure it would be safe to wager that no group of Southern white men could get together and talk for sixty minutes without bringing up the "race question." If a Northern white man happened to be in the group the time could be safely cut to thirty minutes. In this respect I consider the condition of the whites more to be deplored than that of the blacks. Here, a truly great people, a people that produced a majority of the great historic Americans from Washington to Lincoln now forced to use up its energies in a conflict as lamentable as it is violent.

I shall give the observations I made in Jacksonville as seen through the light of after years; and they apply generally to every Southern community. The colored people may be said to be roughly divided into three classes, not so much in respect to themselves as in respect to their relations with the whites. There are those constituting what might be called the desperate class,—the men who work in the lumber and turpentine camps,[5] the ex-convicts, the barroom loafers are all in this class. These men conform to the requirements of civilization much as a trained lion with low muttered growls goes through his stunts under the crack of the trainer's whip. They cherish a sullen hatred for all white men, and they value life as cheap. I have heard more than one of them say, "I'll go to hell for the first white man that bothers me." Many who have expressed that sentiment have kept their word; and it is that fact which gives such prominence to this class; for in numbers it is but a small proportion of the colored people, but it often dominates public opinion concerning the whole race. Happily, this class represents the black people of the South far below their normal physical and moral condition, but in its increase lies the possibility of grave dangers. I am sure there is no more urgent work before the white South, not only for its present happiness, but its future safety, than the decreasing of this class of blacks. And it is not at all a hopeless class; for these men are but the creatures of conditions, as much so as the slum and criminal elements of all the great cities of the world are creatures of conditions. Decreasing their number by shooting and burning them off will not be successful; for these men are truly desperate, and thoughts of death, however terrible, have little effect in deterring them from acts the result of hatred or degeneracy. This class of blacks hate everything covered by a white skin, and in return they are loathed by the whites. The whites regard them just about as a man would a vicious mule, a thing to be worked, driven and beaten, and killed for kicking.

The second class, as regards the relation between blacks and whites, comprises the servants, the washer-women, the waiters, the cooks, the coachmen, and all who are connected with the whites by domestic service. These may be generally characterized as simple, kindhearted and faithful; not over fine in their moral deductions, but intensely religious, and relatively,—such matters can be judged only relatively,—about as honest and wholesome in their lives as any other grade of society. Any white person is "good" who treats them kindly, and they love them for that kindness. In return, the white people with whom they have to do regard them with indulgent affection. They come into close daily contact with the whites, and may be called the connecting link between whites and blacks;

5. In parts of the post–Civil War South, black laborers were freed from farm-based labor to do the grueling, low-wage work of axing trees for the lumber industry and turpentine companies. Florida was notorious for allowing especially harsh labor conditions, from substandard living quarters to corporal punishment. African American piano players could often find work at these camps playing for the laborers.

in fact, it is through them that the whites know the rest of their colored neighbors. Between this class of the blacks and the whites there is little or no friction.

The third class is composed of the independent workmen and tradesmen, and of the well-to-do and educated colored people; and, strange to say, for a directly opposite reason they are as far removed from the whites as the members of the first class I mentioned. These people live in a little world of their own; in fact, I concluded that if a colored man wanted to separate himself from his white neighbors he had but to acquire some money, education and culture, and to live in accordance. For example, the proudest and fairest lady in the South could with propriety—and it is what she would most likely do—go to the cabin of Aunt Mary, her cook, if Aunt Mary were sick, and minister to her comfort with her own hands; but if Mary's daughter, Eliza, a girl who used to run around my lady's kitchen, but who has received an education and married a prosperous young colored man, were at death's door, my lady would no more think of crossing the threshold of Eliza's cottage than she would of going into a bar-room for a drink.

I was walking down the street one day with a young man who was born in Jacksonville, but had been away to prepare himself for a professional life. We passed a young white man, and my companion said to me, "You see that young man? We grew up together, we have played, hunted, and fished together, we have even eaten and slept together, and now since I have come back home he barely speaks to me." The fact that the whites of the South despise and ill-treat the desperate class of blacks is not only explainable according to the ancient laws of human nature, but it is not nearly so serious or important as the fact that as the progressive colored people advance they constantly widen the gulf between themselves and their white neighbors. I think that the white people somehow feel that colored people who have education and money, who wear good clothes and live in comfortable houses, are "putting on airs," that they do these things for the sole purpose of "spiting the white folks," or are, at best, going through a sort of monkey-like imitation. Of course, such feelings can only cause irritation or breed disgust. It seems that the whites have not yet been able to realize and understand that these people in striving to better their physical and social surroundings in accordance with their financial and intellectual progress are simply obeying an impulse which is common to human nature the world over. I am in grave doubt as to whether the greater part of the friction in the South is caused by the whites having a natural antipathy to Negroes as a race, or an acquired antipathy to Negroes in certain relations to themselves. However that may be, there is to my mind no more pathetic side of this many sided question than the isolated position into which arc forced the very colored people who most need and who could best appreciate sympathetic coöperation; and their position grows tragic when the effort is made to couple them, whether or no, with the Negroes of the first class I mentioned.

This latter class of colored people are well disposed towards the whites, and always willing to meet them more than half way. They, however, feel keenly any injustice or gross discrimination, and generally show their resentment. The effort is sometimes made to convey the impression that the better class of colored people fight against riding in "jim crow" cars[6] because they want to ride with white people or object to being with humbler members of their own race. The truth is they object to the humiliation of being forced to ride in a *particular* car, aside from the fact that that car is distinctly inferior, and that they are required to pay full first-class fare. To say that the whites are forced to ride in the superior car is less than a joke. And, too, odd as it may sound, refined colored people get no more pleasure out of riding with offensive Negroes than anybody else would get.

I can realize more fully than I could years ago that the position of the advanced element of the colored race is often very trying. They are the ones among the blacks who carry the entire weight of the race question; it worries the others very little, and I believe the only thing which at times sustains them is that they know that they are in the right. On the other hand, this class of colored people get a good deal of pleasure out of life; their existence is far from being one long groan about their condition. Out of a chaos of ignorance and poverty they have evolved a social life of which they need not be ashamed. In cities where the professional and well-to-do class is large, they have formed society,—society as discriminating as the actual conditions will allow it to be; I should say, perhaps, society possessing discriminating tendencies which become rules as fast as actual conditions allow. This statement will, I know, sound preposterous, even ridiculous, to some persons but as this class of colored people is the least known of the race it is not surprising. These social circles are connected throughout the country, and a person in good standing in one city is readily accepted in another. One who is on the outside will often find it a difficult matter to get in. I know of one case personally in which money to the extent of thirty

6. To maintain legally sanctioned racial segregation on trains, African American passengers were required to ride in specially designated "colored" cars, whether or not they had purchased first-class seats. The cars were of inferior quality and often lacked the amenities reserved for white passengers (e.g., dining cars and food service, or bathrooms). This discriminatory practice lasted almost a century, starting in the 1870s and continuing until the Civil Rights Act was passed in 1964.

or forty thousand dollars and a fine house, not backed up by a good reputation, after several years of repeated effort, failed to gain entry for the possessor. These people have their dances and dinners and card parties, their musicals and their literary societies. The women attend social affairs dressed in good taste, and the men in evening dress-suits which they own; and the reader will make a mistake to confound these entertainments with the "Bellman's Balls" and "Whitewashers' Picnics" and "Lime Kiln Clubs" with which the humorous press of the country illustrates "Cullud Sassiety."

Jacksonville, when I was there, was a small town, and the number of educated and well-to-do colored people was few; so this society phase of life did not equal what I have since seen in Boston, Washington, Richmond, and Nashville; and it is upon what I have more recently seen in these cities that I have made the observations just above. However, there were many comfortable and pleasant homes in Jacksonville to which I was often invited. I belonged to the literary society—at which we generally discussed the race question—and attended all of the church festivals and other charitable entertainments. In this way I passed three years which were not at all the least enjoyable of my life. In fact, my joy took such an exuberant turn that I fell in love with a young school teacher and began to have dreams of matrimonial bliss; but another turn in the course of my life brought these dreams to an end.

I do not wish to mislead my readers into thinking that I led a life in Jacksonville which would make copy as the hero of a Sunday School library book. I was a hale fellow well met with all of the workmen at the factory, most of whom knew little and cared less about social distinctions. From their example I learned to be careless about money; and for that reason I constantly postponed and finally abandoned returning to Atlanta University. It seemed impossible for me to save as much as two hundred dollars. Several of the men at the factory were my intimate friends, and I frequently joined them in their pleasures. During the summer months we went almost every Monday on an excursion to a seaside resort called Pablo Beach.[7] These excursions were always crowded. There was a dancing pavilion, a great deal of drinking and generally a fight or two to add to the excitement. I also contracted the cigar-maker's habit of riding around in a hack on Sunday afternoons. I sometimes went with my cigar-maker friends to public balls that were given at a large hall on one of the main streets. I learned to take a drink occasionally and paid for quite a number that my friends took; but strong liquors never appealed to my appetite. I drank them only when the company I was

7. A small city near Jacksonville, known as Jacksonville Beach since 1925.

in required it, and suffered for it afterwards. On the whole, though I was a bit wild, I can't remember that I ever did anything disgraceful, or, as the usual standard for young men goes, anything to forfeit my claim to respectability.

At one of the first public balls I attended I saw the Pullman car porter who had so kindly assisted me in getting to Jacksonville. I went immediately to one of my factory friends and borrowed fifteen dollars with which to repay the loan my benefactor had made me. After I had given him the money, and was thanking him, I noticed that he wore what was, at least, an exact duplicate of my lamented black and gray tie. It was somewhat worn, but distinct enough for me to trace the same odd design which had first attracted my eye. This was enough to arouse my strongest suspicions, but whether it was sufficient for the law to take cognizance of I did not consider. My astonishment and the ironical humor of the situation drove everything else out of my mind.

These balls were attended by a great variety of people. They were generally given by the waiters of some one of the big hotels, and were often patronized by a number of hotel guests who came to "see the sights." The crowd was always noisy, but good-natured; there was much quadrille[8] dancing, and a strong-lunged man called figures in a voice which did not confine itself to the limits of the hall. It is not worth the while for me to describe in detail how these people acted; they conducted themselves in about the same manner as I have seen other people at similar balls conduct themselves. When one has seen something of the world and human nature he must conclude, after all, that between people in like stations of life there is very little difference the world over.

However, it was at one of these balls that I first saw the cake-walk.[9] There was a contest for a gold watch, to be awarded to the hotel head-waiter receiving the greatest number of votes. There was some dancing while the votes were being counted. Then the floor was cleared for the cake-walk. A half-dozen guests from some of the hotels took seats on the stage to act as judges, and twelve or fourteen couples began to walk for a "sure enough" highly decorated cake, which was in plain evidence. The spectators crowded about the space reserved for the contestants and watched them with interest and excitement.

8. An 18th-century French ballroom dance later transplanted to England and the rest of Europe; performed by four couples tracing intricate steps in box-shaped formations, it is a predecessor to the American square dance.

9. A 19th-century dance that originated among African American slaves in which they would satirically imitate the ballroom dances of their white owners. After Emancipation, its high-energy movement contributed to the maturation of ragtime. The dance was a competitive art form, requiring physical agility and sartorial finesse; though the exaggerated movements and were often caricatured by minstrels, the dance was an eloquent expression of physical prowess.

The couples did not walk around in a circle, but in a square, with the men on the inside. The fine points to be considered were the bearing of the men, the precision with which they turned the corners, the grace of the women, and the ease with which they swung around the pivots. The men walked with stately and soldierly step, and the women with considerable grace. The judges arrived at their decision by a process of elimination. The music and the walk continued for some minutes; then both were stopped while the judges conferred, when the walk began again several couples were left out. In this way the contest was finally narrowed down to three or four couples. Then the excitement became intense; there was much partisan cheering as one couple or another would execute a turn in extra elegant style. When the cake was finally awarded the spectators were about evenly divided between those who cheered the winners and those who muttered about the unfairness of the judges. This was the cake-walk in its original form, and it is what the colored performers on the theatrical stage developed into the prancing movements now known all over the world, and which some Parisian critics pronounced the acme of poetic motion.

There are a great many colored people who are ashamed of the cake-walk, but I think they ought to be proud of it. It is my opinion that the colored people of this country have done four things which refute the oft advanced theory that they are an absolutely inferior race, which demonstrate that they have originality and artistic conception; and, what is more, the power of creating that which can influence and appeal universally. The first two of these are the Uncle Remus stories, collected by Joel Chandler Harris, and the Jubilee songs,[1] to which the Fisk singers made the public and the skilled musicians of both America and Europe listen. The other two are ragtime[2] music and the cake-walk. No one who has traveled can question the world-conquering influence of ragtime; and I do not think

1. American Negro spirituals or sacred music, popularized in the 1870s by the Fisk Jubilee Singers, who were sponsored by Fisk University (see p. 81, n. 4). Before the Fisk vocalists toured the United States and Europe, spirituals were mostly unknown to the larger white public. Harris (1848–1908), a Georgia journalist who authored one of the most important short story collections in the plantation school literary movement of the 1870s and 1880s. His Uncle Remus stories, were based on African American folktales collected from ex-slaves. Read literally, the animal fables recount the humorous mishaps of a powerful fox trying to snare a wily rabbit for his daily meal. Interpreted as allegory, the stories envision black slaves (Br'er Rabbit) overturning the domination of white masters (Br'er Fox); the subversive possibilities were muted, however, by the role of his chief narrator, Uncle Remus, who openly longs for the "good old days" of enslavement and recounts the stories to white children while speaking in slave dialect.
2. A progenitor of jazz that revolutionized American popular music around the turn of the twentieth century. Its quick-fingered syncopation and hyperfast tempos broke away from the stately paced time signatures and melodies of march and parade music (best exemplified by John Philip Sousa's bands). At first performed by orchestras with vocal accompaniment, ragtime became even more popular once its instrumentation spotlighted the piano and solo vocals. Pared back to these elements, fans could enjoy and play ragtime on their own by purchasing sheet music. Pioneer artists and songs

it would be an exaggeration to say that in Europe the United States is popularly known better by ragtime than by anything else it has produced in a generation. In Paris they call it American music. The newspapers have already told how the practice of intricate cake walk steps has taken up the time of European royalty and nobility. These are lower forms of art, but they give evidence of a power that will some day be applied to the higher forms. In this measure, at least, and aside from the number of prominent individuals the colored people of the United States have produced, the race has been a world influence; and all of the Indians between Alaska and Patagonia[3] haven't done as much.

Just when I was beginning to look upon Jacksonville as my permanent home, and was beginning to plan about marrying the young school teacher, raising a family, and working in a cigar factory the rest of my life, for some reason, which I do not now remember, the factory at which I worked was indefinitely shut down. Some of the men got work in other factories in town, some decided to go to Key West and Tampa, others made up their minds to go to New York for work. All at once a desire like a fever seized me to see the North again, and I cast my lot with those bound for New York.

Chapter VI

We steamed up into New York harbor late one afternoon in spring. The last efforts of the sun were being put forth in turning the waters of the bay to glistening gold; the green islands on either side, in spite of their warlike mountings, looked calm and peaceful; the buildings of the town shone out in a reflected light which gave the city an air of enchantment; and, truly, it is an enchanted spot. New York City is the most fatally fascinating thing in America. She sits like a great witch[4] at the gate of the country, showing her alluring white face, and hiding her crooked hands and feet under the folds of her wide garments,—constantly enticing thousands from far within, and tempting those who come from across the seas to go no farther. And all these become the victims of her caprice. Some she at once crushes beneath her cruel feet; others she condemns to a fate like that of galley slaves; a few she favors and fondles, riding them high

include Thomas "Blind Tom" Greene Wiggins's "Grand March Resurrection" (1901), Scott Joplin's "Maple Leaf Rag" (1903), Irving Berlin's "Alexander's Ragtime Band" (1911), and W. C. Handy's "Memphis Blues" (1912). Notably, Johnson (along with his brother, Rosamond, and their songwriting partner, Bob Cole) composed several hits in ragtime's early canon, including their best-seller "Under the Bamboo Tree" (1903).

3. The southern tip of South America, including parts of Argentina and Chile.
4. Allusion to Johnson's poem "The White Witch," published in *Fifty Years and Other Poems* (1917). ,

on the bubbles of fortune; then with a sudden breath she blows the bubbles out and laughs mockingly as she watches them fall.

Twice I had passed through it; but this was really my first visit to New York; and as I walked about that evening I began to feel the dread power of the city; the crowds, the lights, the excitement, the gayety and all its subtler stimulating influences began to take effect upon me. My blood ran quicker, and I felt that I was just beginning to live. To some natures this stimulant of life in a great city becomes a thing as binding and necessary as opium is to one addicted to the habit. It becomes their breath of life; they cannot exist outside of it; rather than be deprived of it they are content to suffer hunger, want, pain and misery; they would not exchange even a ragged and wretched condition among the great crowd for any degree of comfort away from it.

As soon as we landed, four of us went directly to a lodging-house in 27th Street, just west of Sixth Avenue.[5] The house was run by a short, stout mulatto man, who was exceedingly talkative and inquisitive. In fifteen minutes he not only knew the history of the past life of each one of us, but had a clearer idea of what we intended to do in the future than we ourselves. He sought this information so much with an air of being very particular as to whom he admitted into his house that we tremblingly answered every question that he asked. When we had become located we went out and got supper; then walked around until about ten o'clock. At that hour we met a couple of young fellows who lived in New York and were known to one of the members of our party. It was suggested we go to a certain place which was known by the proprietor's name. We turned into one of the cross streets and mounted the stoop of a house in about the middle of a block between Sixth and Seventh Avenues. One of the young men whom we had met rang a bell, and a man on the inside cracked the door a couple of inches; then opened it and let us in. We found ourselves in the hallway of what had once been a residence. The front parlor had been converted into a bar, and a half dozen or so of well dressed men were in the room. We went in, and after a general introduction had several rounds of beer. In the back parlor a crowd was sitting and standing around the walls of the room watching an exciting and noisy game of pool. I walked back and joined this crowd to watch the game, and principally to get away from the drinking party. The game was really interesting, the players being quite expert, and the excitement was heightened by the bets which were being made on the result. At times

5. In Negro Bohemia, where African American artists, musicians, and others lived and worked in the early 1900s. The district initially encompassed the west side's 24th to 42nd Streets, bounded by 5th and 7th Avenues. Johnson and his brother lived in this area when they composed music for the Broadway stage. For more background on this district and its growth, see selections by Levy and JWJ in "Background and Sources."

the antics and remarks of both players and spectators were amusing. When, at a critical point, a player missed a shot he was deluged by those financially interested in his making it with a flood of epithets synonymous to "chump"; while from the others he would be jeered by such remarks as "Nigger, dat cue ain't no hoe-handle." I noticed that among this class of colored men the word "nigger" was freely used in about the same sense as the word "fellow," and sometimes as a term of almost endearment; but I soon learned that its use was positively and absolutely prohibited to white men.

I stood watching this pool game until I was called by my friends, who were still in the barroom, to go upstairs. On the second floor there were two large rooms. From the hall I looked into the one on the front. There was a large, round table in the center, at which five or six men were seated playing poker. The air and conduct here were greatly in contrast to what I had just seen in the pool-room; these men were evidently the aristocrats of the place; they were well, perhaps a bit flashily, dressed and spoke in low modulated voices, frequently using the word "gentlemen"; in fact, they seemed to be practicing a sort of Chester-fieldian[6] politeness towards each other. I was watching these men with a great deal of interest and some degree of admiration, when I was again called by the members of our party, and I followed them on to the back room. There was a doorkeeper at this room, and we were admitted only after inspection. When we got inside I saw a crowd of men of all ages and kinds grouped about an old billiard table, regarding some of whom, in supposing them to be white, I made no mistake. At first I did not know what these men were doing; they were using terms that were strange to me. I could hear only a confusion of voices exclaiming, "Shoot the two!" "Shoot the four!" "Fate me!" "Fate me!" "I've got you fated!" "Twenty-five cents he don't turn!" This was the ancient and terribly fascinating game of dice, popularly known as "craps." I, myself, had played pool in Jacksonville; it is a favorite game among cigar-makers, and I had seen others play cards; but here was something new. I edged my way in to the table and stood between one of my new-found New York friends and a tall, slender, black fellow, who was making side bets while the dice were at the other end of the table. My companion explained to me the principles of the game; and they are so simple that they hardly need to be explained twice. The dice came around the table until they reached the man on the other side of the tall, black fellow. He lost, and the latter said, "Gimme the bones." He threw a dollar on the table and said, "Shoot

6. Polite, polished, or sophisticated; derived from Philip Dormer Stanhope, fourth Earl of Chesterfield (1694–1773), who served in the British Parliament and as an ambassador to Holland and who also wrote on manners.

the dollar." His style of play was so strenuous that he had to be allowed plenty of room. He shook the dice high above his head, and each time he threw them on the table he emitted a grunt such as men give when they are putting forth physical exertion with a rhythmic regularity. He frequently whirled completely around on his heels, throwing the dice the entire length of the table, and talking to them as though they were trained animals. He appealed to them in short singsong phrases. "Come dice," he would say. "Little Phoebe," "Little Joe," "'Way down yonder in the cornfield." Whether these mystic incantations were efficacious or not I could not say, but, at any rate, his luck was great, and he had what gamblers term "nerve." "Shoot the dollar!" "Shoot the two!" "Shoot the four!" "Shoot the eight!" came from his lips as quickly as the dice turned to his advantage. My companion asked me if I had ever played. I told him no. He said that I ought to try my luck; that everybody won at first. The tall man at my side was waving his arms in the air exclaiming "Shoot the sixteen!" "Shoot the sixteen!" "Fate me!" Whether it was my companion's suggestion or some latent dare-devil strain in my blood which suddenly sprang into activity I do not know; but with a thrill of excitement which went through my whole body I threw a twenty dollar bill on the table and said in a trembling voice, "I fate you."

I could feel that I had gained the attention and respect of everybody in the room, every eye was fixed on me, and the widespread question, "Who is he?" went around. This was gratifying to a certain sense of vanity of which I have never been able to rid myself, and I felt that it was worth the money even if I lost. The tall man with a whirl on his heels and a double grunt threw the dice; four was the number which turned up. This is considered as a hard "point" to make. He redoubled his contortions and his grunts and his pleadings to the dice; but on his third or fourth throw the fateful seven turned up, and I had won. My companion and all my friends shouted to me to follow up my luck. The fever was on me. I seized the dice. My hands were so hot that the bits of bone felt like pieces of ice. I shouted as loudly as I could, "Shoot it all!" but the blood was tingling so about my ears that I could not hear my own voice. I was soon "fated." I threw the dice—seven—I had won. "Shoot it all!" I cried again. There was a pause; the stake was more than one man cared to or could cover. I was finally "fated" by several men taking "a part" of it. I then threw the dice again. Seven. I had won. "Shoot it all!" I shouted excitedly. After a short delay I was "fated." Again I rolled the dice. Eleven. Again I had won. My friends now surrounded me and, much against my inclination, forced me to take down all of the money except five dollars. I tried my luck once more, and threw some small "Point" which I failed to make, and the dice passed on to the next man.

In less than three minutes I had won more than two hundred dollars, a sum which afterwards cost me dearly. I was the hero of the moment, and was soon surrounded by a group of men who expressed admiration for my "nerve" and predicted for me a brilliant future as a gambler. Although at the time I had no thought of becoming a gambler I felt proud of my success. I felt a bit ashamed, too, that I had allowed my friends to persuade me to take down my money so soon. Another set of men also got around me, and begged me for twenty-five or fifty cents to put them back into the game. I gave each of them something. I saw that several of them had on linen dusters, and as I looked about I noticed that there were perhaps a dozen men in the room similarly clad. I asked the fellow who had been my prompter at the dice table why they dressed in such a manner. He told me that men who had lost all the money and jewelry they possessed, frequently, in an effort to recoup their losses, would gamble away all their outer clothing and even their shoes; and that the proprietor kept on hand a supply of linen dusters for all who were so unfortunate. My informant went on to say that sometimes a fellow would become almost completely dressed and then, by a turn of the dice, would be thrown back into a state of semi-nakedness. Some of them were virtually prisoners and unable to get into the streets for days at a time. They ate at the lunch counter, where their credit was good so long as they were fair gamblers and did not attempt to jump their debts, and they slept around in chairs. They importuned friends and winners to put them back in the game, and kept at it until fortune again smiled on them. I laughed heartily at this, not thinking the day was coming which would find me in the same ludicrous predicament.

On passing downstairs I was told that the third and top floor of the house was occupied by the proprietor. When we passed through the bar I treated everybody in the room,—and that was no small number, for eight or ten had followed us down. Then our party went out. It was now about half-past twelve, but my nerves were at such a tension that I could not endure the mere thought of going to bed. I asked if there was no other place to which we could go; our guides said yes, and suggested that we go to the "Club."[7] We went to Sixth Avenue, walked two blocks, and turned to the west into another street. We stopped in front of a house with three stories and a basement. In the basement was a Chinese Chopsuey restaurant. There was a red lantern at the iron gate to the areaway, inside of which

7. Probably based on Ike Hines's Club. Nightlife spots like this one were popular in New York City's Negro Bohemia during the early 1900s. For Johnson's description of this haunt for "professionals," see *Along This Way*, 323–24. For more on these venues, see related material by Johnson (from *Black Manhattan*), and Levy in Background and Sources.

the Chinaman's name was printed. We went up the steps of the stoop, rang the bell, and were admitted without any delay. From the outside the house bore a rather gloomy aspect, the windows being absolutely dark, but within it was a veritable house of mirth. When we had passed through a small vestibule and reached the hallway we heard mingled sounds of music and laughter, the clink of glasses and the pop of bottles. We went into the main room, and I was little prepared for what I saw. The brilliancy of the place, the display of diamond rings, scarf-pins, ear-rings and breast-pins, the big rolls of money that were brought into evidence when drinks were paid for, and the air of gayety that pervaded, all completely dazzled and dazed me. I felt positively giddy, and it was several minutes before I was able to make any clear and definite observations.

We at length secured places at a table in a corner of the room, and as soon as we could attract the attention of one of the busy waiters ordered a round of drinks. When I had somewhat collected my senses I realized that in a large back room into which the main room opened, there was a young fellow singing a song, accompanied on the piano by a short, thick-set, dark man. Between each verse he did some dance steps, which brought forth great applause and a shower of small coins at his feet. After the singer had responded to a rousing encore, the stout man at the piano began to run his fingers up and down the keyboard. This he did in a manner which indicated that he was master of a good deal of technic. Then he began to play; and such playing! I stopped talking to listen. It was music of a kind I had never heard before. It was music that demanded physical response, patting of the feet, drumming of the fingers, or nodding of the head in time with the beat. The barbaric harmonies, the audacious resolutions often consisting of an abrupt jump from one key to another, the intricate rhythms in which the accents fell in the most unexpected places, but in which the beat was never lost, produced a most curious effect. And, too, the player,—the dexterity of his left hand in making rapid octave runs and jumps was little short of marvelous; and, with his right hand, he frequently swept half the keyboard with clean cut chromatics[8] which he fitted in so nicely as never to fail to arouse in his listeners a sort of pleasant surprise at the accomplishment of the feat.

This was ragtime music, then a novelty in New York, and just growing to be a rage which has not yet subsided. It was originated in the questionable resorts about Memphis and St. Louis by Negro piano players, who knew no more of the theory of music than they

8. A musical technique in which a performer plays notes that are not part of a song's musical key (or that sound dissonant or off-key) to tease forth the sound of the song's melody.

did of the theory of the universe, but were guided by natural musical instinct and talent. It made its way to Chicago, where it was popular some time before it reached New York. These players often improvised crude and, at times, vulgar words to fit the melodies. This was the beginning of the ragtime song. Several of these improvisations were taken down by white men, the words slightly altered, and published under the names of the arrangers. They sprang into immediate popularity and earned small fortunes, of which the Negro originators got only a few dollars. But I have learned that since that time a number of colored men, of not only musical talent, but training, are writing out their own melodies and words and reaping the reward of their work. I have learned also that they have a large number of white imitators and adulterators.

American musicians, instead of investigating ragtime, attempt to ignore it or dismiss it with a contemptuous word. But that has always been the course of scholasticism in every branch of art. Whatever new thing the *people* like is pooh-poohed; whatever is *popular* is spoken of as not worth the while. The fact is, nothing great or enduring, especially in music, has ever sprung full-fledged and unprecedented from the brain of any master; the best that he gives to the world he gathers from the hearts of the people, and runs it through the alembic of his genius. In spite of the bans which musicians and music teachers have placed upon it, the people still demand and enjoy ragtime. One thing cannot be denied; it is music which possesses at least one strong element of greatness; it appeals universally; not only the American, but the English, the French, and even the German people, find delight in it. In fact, there is not a corner of the civilized world in which it is not known, and this proves its originality; for if it were an imitation, the people of Europe, anyhow, would not have found it a novelty. Anyone who doubts that there is a peculiar heel-tickling, smile-provoking, joy-awakening charm in ragtime needs only to hear a skillful performer play the genuine article to be convinced. I believe that it has its place as well as the music which draws from us sighs and tears.

I became so interested in both the music and the player that I left the table where I was sitting, and made my way through the hall into the back room, where I could see as well as hear. I talked to the piano player between the musical numbers, and found out that he was just a natural musician, never having taken a lesson in his life. Not only could he play almost anything he heard, but could accompany singers in songs he had never heard. He had by ear alone, composed some pieces, several of which he played over for me; each of them was properly proportioned and balanced. I began to wonder what this man with such a lavish natural endowment would have done had he been trained. Perhaps he wouldn't have done anything at all; he might have become, at best, a mediocre imitator of the great masters in what they have already done to a finish, or one of the modern innovators who strive after originality by seeing how cleverly they can dodge about through the rules of harmony, and at the same time avoid melody. It is certain that he would not have been so delightful as he was in ragtime.

I sat by watching and listening to this man until I was dragged away by my friends. The place was now almost deserted; only a few stragglers hung on, and they were all the worse for drink. My friends were well up in this class. We passed into the street; the lamps were pale against the sky; day was just breaking. We went home and got into bed. I fell into a fitful sort of sleep with ragtime music ringing continually in my ears.

Chapter VII

I shall take advantage of this pause in my narrative to more closely describe the "Club" spoken of in the latter part of the preceding chapter,—to describe it, as I afterwards came to know it, as an habitue. I shall do this, not only because of the direct influence it had on my life, but also because it was at that time the most famous place of its kind in New York, and was well known to both white and colored people of certain classes.

I have already stated that in the basement of the house there was a Chinese restaurant. The Chinaman who kept it did an exceptionally good business; for chop-suey was a favorite dish among the frequenters of the place. It is a food that, somehow, has the power of absorbing alcoholic liquors that have been taken into the stomach. I have heard men claim that they could sober up on chop-suey. Perhaps that accounted, in some degree, for its popularity. On the main floor there were two large rooms, a parlor about thirty feet in length and a large square back room into which the parlor opened. The floor of the parlor was carpeted; small tables and chairs were arranged about the room; the windows were draped with lace curtains, and the walls were literally covered with photographs or lithographs[9] of every colored man in America who had ever "done anything." There were pictures of Frederick Douglass and of Peter Jackson,[1] of all the lesser lights of the prizefighting ring, of all the

9. Prints made by an intricate technique discovered in 18th-century Germany. Lithographs were handmade by drawing on a smooth surface with utensils that bond with oil, rather than engraving into the surface and filling those carved lines with ink. Once this process was mechanized in the mid-1800s, lithography became a relatively inexpensive way to decorate homes with "fine" art.

1. A West Indian–born black boxer from Australia (1861–1901), known as the "Black Prince," who won the Australian heavyweight championship in 1886.

famous jockeys and the stage celebrities, down to the newest song and dance team. The most of these photographs were autographed and, in a sense, made a really valuable collection. In the back room there was a piano; and tables were placed around the wall. The floor was bare and the center was left vacant for singers, dancers and others who entertained the patrons. In a closet in this room which jutted out into the hall the proprietor kept his buffet. There was no open bar, because the place had no liquor license. In this back room the tables were sometimes pushed aside, and the floor given over to general dancing. The front room on the next floor was a sort of private party room; a back room on the same floor contained no furniture, and was devoted to the use of new and ambitions performers. In this room song and dance teams practiced their steps, acrobatic teams practiced their tumbles, and many other kinds of "acts" rehearsed their "turns." The other rooms of the house were used as sleeping apartments.

No gambling was allowed, and the conduct of the place was surprisingly orderly. It was, in short, a center of colored bohemians and sports. Here the great prize fighters were wont to come, the famous jockeys, the noted minstrels, whose names and faces were familiar on every bill-board in the country; and these drew a multitude of those who love to dwell in the shadow of greatness. There were then no organizations giving performances of such order as are now given by several colored companies; that was because no manager could imagine that audiences would pay to see Negro performers in any other rôle than that of Mississippi River roustabouts; but there was lots of talent and ambition. I often heard the younger and brighter men discussing the time when they would compel the public to recognize that they could do something more than grin and cut pigeon wings.

Sometimes one or two of the visiting stage professionals, after being sufficiently urged, would go into the back room, and take the places of the regular amateur entertainers, but they were very sparing with these favors, and the patrons regarded them as special treats. There was one man, a minstrel, who, whenever he responded to a request to "do something," never essayed anything below a reading from Shakespeare. How well he read I do not know, but he greatly impressed me; and I can, at least, say that he had a voice which strangely stirred those who heard it. Here was a man who made people laugh at the size of his mouth, while he carried in his heart a burning ambition to be a tragedian; and so after all he did play a part in a tragedy.

These notables of the ring, the turf and the stage, drew to the place crowds of admirers, both white and colored. Whenever one of them came in there were awe-inspired whispers from those who knew him by sight, in which they enlightened those around them as to his identity, and hinted darkly at their great intimacy with the noted one. Those who were on terms of approach immediately showed their privilege over others less fortunate by gathering around their divinity. I was, at first, among those who dwelt in darkness. Most of these celebrities I had never heard of. This made me an object of pity among many of my new associates. I, however, soon learned to fake a knowledge for the benefit of those who were greener than I; and, finally, I became personally acquainted with the majority of the famous personages who came to the "Club."

A great deal of money was spent here; so many of the patrons were men who earned large sums. I remember one night a dapper little brown-skinned fellow was pointed out to me, and I was told that he was the most popular jockey of the day, and that he earned $12,000 a year. This latter statement I couldn't doubt, for with my own eyes I saw him spending at about that rate. For his friends and those who were introduced to him he bought nothing but wine;—in the sporting circles, "wine" means champagne—and paid for it at five dollars a quart. He sent a quart to every table in the place with his compliments; and on the table at which he and his party were seated there were more than a dozen bottles. It was the custom at the "Club" for the waiter not to remove the bottles when champagne was being drunk until the party had finished. There were reasons for this; it advertised the brand of wine, it advertised that the party was drinking wine, and advertised how much they had bought. This jockey had won a great race that day, and he was rewarding his admirers for the homage they paid him, all of which he accepted with a fine air of condescension.

Besides the people I have just been describing there was at the place almost every night one or two parties of white people, men and women, who were out sight-seeing, or slumming.[2] They generally came in cabs; some of them would stay only for a few minutes, while others sometimes stayed until morning. There was also another set of white people who came frequently; it was made up of variety performers and others who delineated darky characters; they came to get their imitatations first hand from the Negro entertainers they saw there.

There was still another set of white patrons, composed of women; these were not occasional visitors, but five or six of them were regular habitues. When I first saw them I was not sure that they were white. In the first place, among the many colored women who came to the "Club" there were several just as fair; and, secondly, I always

2. Visiting areas or establishments below one's socioeconomic class purely for the sake of diversion. The slang term emerged in public discourse around the 1880s.

saw these women in company with colored men. They were all good-looking and well dressed, and seemed to be women of some education. One of these in particular attracted my attention; she was an exceedingly beautiful woman of perhaps thirty-five; she had glistening copper-colored hair, very white skin and eyes very much like Du Maurier's conception of Trilby's "twin gray stars."[3] When I came to know her I found that she was a woman of considerable culture; she had traveled in Europe, spoke French, and played the piano well. She was always dressed elegantly, but in absolute good taste. She always came to the "Club" in a cab, and was soon joined by a well set up, very black young fellow. He was always faultlessly dressed; one of the most exclusive tailors in New York made his clothes, and he wore a number of diamonds in about as good taste as they could be worn by a man. I learned that she paid for his clothes and his diamonds. I learned, too, that he was not the only one of his kind. More that I learned would be better suited to a book on social phenomena than to a narrative of my life.

This woman was known at the "Club" as the rich widow. She went by a very aristocratic sounding name, which corresponded to her appearance. I shall never forget how hard it was for me to get over my feelings of surprise, perhaps more than surprise, at seeing her with her black companion; somehow I never exactly enjoyed the sight. I have devoted so much time to this pair the "widow" and her companion, because it was through them that another decided turn was brought about in my life.

Chapter VIII

On the day following our night at the "Club" we slept until late in the afternoon; so late that beginning of search for work was entirely out of the question. This did not cause me much worry, for I had more than three hundred dollars, and New York had impressed me as a place where there was lots of money and not much difficulty in getting it. It is needless to inform my readers that I did not long hold this opinion. We got out of the house about dark, went round to a restaurant on Sixth Avenue and ate something, then walked around for a couple of hours. I finally suggested that we visit the same places we had been in the night before. Following my suggestion we started first to the gambling house. The man on the door let us in without any question; I accredited this to my success of the night before. We went straight to the "crap" room, and I at once

3. In George du Maurier's Gothic novel, *Trilby* (1894), the namesake heroine has stunning eyes, which du Maurier likens to "twin gray stars."

made my way to a table, where I was rather flattered by the murmur of recognition which went around. I played in up and down luck for three or four hours; then, worn with nervous excitement, quit, having lost about fifty dollars. But I was so strongly possessed with the thought that I would make up my losses the next time I played that I left the place with a light heart.

When we got into the street our party was divided against itself; two were for going home at once and getting to bed. They gave as a reason that we were to get up early and look for jobs. I think the real reason was that they had each lost several dollars in the game. I lived to learn that in the world of sport all men win alike but lose differently; and so gamblers are rated, not by the way in which they win, but by the way in which they lose. Some men lose with a careless smile, recognizing that losing is a part of the game; others curse their luck and rail at fortune; and others, still, lose sadly; after each such experience they are swept by a wave of reform; they resolve to stop gambling and be good. When in this frame of mind it would take very little persuasion to lead them into a prayer-meeting. Those in the first class are looked upon with admiration; those in the second class are merely commonplace; while those in the third are regarded with contempt. I believe these distinctions hold good in all the ventures of life. After some minutes one of my friends and I succeeded in convincing the other two that a while at the "Club" would put us all in better spirits; and they consented to go on our promise not to stay longer than an hour. We found the place crowded, and the same sort of thing going on which we had seen the night before. I took a seat at once by the side of the piano player, and was soon lost to everything else except the novel charm of the music. I watched the performer with the idea of catching the trick; and, during one of his intermissions, I took his place at the piano and made an attempt to imitate him, but even my quick ear and ready fingers were unequal to the task on first trial.

We did not stay at the "Club" very long, but went home to bed in order to be up early the next day. We had no difficulty in finding work, and my third morning in New York found me at a table rolling cigars. I worked steadily for some weeks, at the same time spending my earnings between the "crap" game and the "Club." Making cigars became more and more irksome to me; perhaps my more congenial work as a "reader" had unfitted me for work at the table. And, too, the late hours I was keeping made such a sedentary occupation almost beyond the powers of will and endurance. I often found it hard to keep my eyes open and sometimes had to get up and move around to keep from falling asleep. I began to miss whole days from the factory, days on which I was compelled to stay at home and sleep.

My luck at the gambling table was varied; sometimes I was fifty to a hundred dollars ahead, and at other times I had to borrow money from my fellow workmen to settle my room rent and pay for my meals. Each night after leaving the dice game I went to the "Club" to hear the music and watch the gayety. If I had won, this was in accord with my mood; if I had lost, it made me forget. I at last realized that making cigars for a living and gambling for a living could not both be carried on at the same time, and I resolved to give up the cigar-making. This resolution led me into a life which held me bound more than a year. During that period my regular time for going to bed was somewhere between four and six o'clock in the mornings. I got up late in the afternoons, walked about a little, then went to the gambling house or the "Club." My New York was limited to ten blocks; the boundaries were Sixth Avenue from Twenty-third to Thirty-third Streets, with the cross streets one block to the west. Central Park[4] was a distant forest, and the lower part of the city a foreign land. I look back upon the life I then led with a shudder when I think what would have been had I not escaped it. But had I not escaped it, I would have been no more unfortunate than are many young colored men who come to New York. During that dark period I became acquainted with a score of bright, intelligent young fellows who had come up to the great city with high hopes and ambitions, and who had fallen under the spell of this under life, a spell they could not throw off. There was one popularly known as "the doctor"; he had had two years in the Harvard Medical School; but here he was, living this gas-light life, his will and moral sense so enervated and deadened that it was impossible for him to break away. I do not doubt that the same thing is going on now, but I have rather sympathy than censure for these victims, for I know how easy it is to slip into a slough from which it takes a herculean effort to leap.

I regret that I cannot contrast my views of life among colored people of New York; but the truth is, during my entire stay in this city I did not become acquainted with a single respectable family. I knew that there were several colored men worth a hundred or so thousand dollars each, and some families who proudly dated their free ancestry back a half-dozen generations. I also learned that in Brooklyn there lived quite a large colony in comfortable homes,

4. A large park, completed in 1873, located in Manhattan, bordered on the east and west by 5th and 8th Avenues and on the north and south by 110th and 59th streets and designed by landscape architect and "City Beautiful" advocate Frederick Law Olmstead. Notably, the park's construction required the razing of Seneca Village, one of the first African American communities in New York City.

most of which they owned; but at no point did my life come in contact with theirs.

In my gambling experiences I passed through all the states and conditions that a gambler is heir to. Some days found me able to peel ten and twenty dollar bills from a roll, and others found me clad in a linen duster and carpet slippers. I finally caught up another method of earning money, and so did not have to depend entirely upon the caprices of fortune at the gaming table. Through continually listening to the music at the "Club," and through my own previous training, my natural talent and perseverance, I developed into a remarkable player of ragtime; indeed, I had the name at that time of being the best ragtime player in New York. I brought all my knowledge of classic music to bear and, in so doing, achieved some novelties which pleased and even astonished my listeners. It was I who first made ragtime transcriptions of familiar classic selections. I used to play Mendelssohn's "Wedding March"[5] in a manner that never failed to arouse enthusiasm among the patrons of the "Club." Very few nights passed during which I was not asked to play it. It was no secret that the great increase in slumming visitors was due to my playing. By mastering ragtime I gained several things; first of all, I gained the title of professor. I was known as the "professor" as long as I remained in that world. Then, too, I gained the means of earning a rather fair livelihood. This work took up much of my time and kept me almost entirely away from the gambling table. Through it I also gained a friend who was the means by which I escaped from this lower world. And, finally, I secured a wedge which has opened to me more doors and made me a welcome guest than my playing of Beethoven and Chopin could ever have done.

The greater part of the money I now began to earn came through the friend to whom I alluded in the foregoing paragraph. Among the other white "slummers" there came into the "Club" one night a clean cut, slender, but athletic looking man, who would have been taken for a youth had it not been for the tinge of gray about his temples. He was clean shaven, had regular features, and all of his movements bore the indefinable but unmistakable stamp of culture. He spoke to no one, but sat languidly puffing cigarettes and sipping a glass of beer. He was the center of a great deal of attention, all of the old timers were wondering who he was. When I had finished playing he called a waiter and by him sent me a five dollar bill. For about a month after that he was at the "Club" one or two nights each week, and each time after I had played he gave me five dollars.

5. Originally written in 1842 as music for Shakespeare's *A Midsummer's Night's Dream* by Felix Mendelssohn (1809–1847), it is often used and recognized as the recessional music for marriage ceremonies.

One night he sent for me to come to his table; he asked me several questions about myself; then told me that he had an engagement which he wanted me to fill. He gave me a card containing his address and asked me to be there on a certain night.

I was on hand promptly, and found that he was giving a dinner in his own apartments to a party of ladies and gentlemen, and that I was expected to furnish the musical entertainment. When the grave, dignified man at the door let me in, the place struck me as being almost dark, my eyes had been so accustomed to the garish light of the "Club." He took my coat and hat, bade me take a seat, and went to tell his master that I had come. When my eyes were adjusted to the soft light I saw that I was in the midst of elegance and luxury in such a degree as I had never seen; but not the elegance which makes one ill at ease. As I sank into a great chair the subdued tone, the delicately sensuous harmony of my surroundings drew from me a deep sigh of relief and comfort. How long the man was gone I do not know; but I was startled by a voice saying, "Come this way, if you please, sir," and I saw him standing by my chair. I had been asleep; and I awoke very much confused and a little ashamed, because I did not know how many times he may have called me. I followed him through into the dining-room, where the butler was putting the finishing touches to a table which already looked like a big jewel. The doorman turned me over to the butler, and I passed with the butler on back to where several waiters were busy polishing and assorting table utensils. Without being asked whether I was hungry or not, I was placed at a table and given something to eat. Before I had finished eating I heard the laughter and talk of the guests who were arriving. Soon afterwards I was called in to begin my work.

I passed in to where the company was gathered, and went directly to the piano. According to a suggestion from the host I began with classic music. During the first number there was absolute quiet and appreciative attention, and when I had finished I was given a round of generous applause. After that the talk and the laughter began to grow until the music was only an accompaniment to the chatter. This, however, did not disconcert me as it once would have done, for I had become accustomed to playing in the midst of uproarious noise. As the guests began to pay less attention to me I was enabled to pay more to them. There were about a dozen of them. The men ranged in appearance from a girlish looking youth to a big grizzled man whom everybody addressed as "Judge." None of the women appeared to be under thirty, but each of them struck me as being handsome. I was not long in finding out that they were all decidedly blasé. Several of the women smoked cigarettes, and with a careless grace which showed they were used to the habit. Occasionally a "damn it!" escaped from the lips of some one of them, but in such a charming way as to rob it of all vulgarity. The most notable thing which I observed was that the reserve of the host increased in direct proportion with the hilarity of his guests. I thought that there was something going wrong which displeased him. I afterwards learned that it was his habitual manner on such occasions. He seemed to take cynical delight in watching and studying others indulging in excess. His guests were evidently accustomed to his rather non-participating attitude, for it did not seem in any degree to dampen their spirits.

When dinner was served the piano was moved and the door left open, so that the company might hear the music while eating. At a word from the host I struck up one of my liveliest ragtime pieces. The effect was perhaps surprising, even to the host; the ragtime music came very near spoiling the party so far as eating the dinner was concerned. As soon as I began the conversation stopped suddenly. It was a pleasure to me to watch the expression of astonishment and delight that grew on the faces of everybody. These were people,—and they represented a large class,—who were ever expecting to find happiness in novelty, each day restlessly exploring and exhausting every resource of this great city that might possibly furnish a new sensation or awaken a fresh emotion, and who were always grateful to anyone who aided them in their quest. Several of the women left the table and gathered about the piano. They watched my fingers, asked what kind of music it was that I was playing, where I had learned it and a host of other questions. It was only by being repeatedly called back to the table that they were induced to finish their dinner. When the guests arose I struck up my ragtime transcription of Mendelssohn's "Wedding March," playing it with terrific chromatic octave runs in the base.[6] This raised everybody's spirits to the highest point of gayety, and the whole company involuntarily and unconsciously did an impromptu cake-walk. From that time on until the time of leaving they kept me so busy that my arms ached. I obtained a little respite when the girlish looking youth and one or two of the ladies sang several songs, but after each of these it was, "back to ragtime."

In leaving, the guests were enthusiastic in telling the host that he had furnished them the most unique entertainment they had "ever" enjoyed. When they had gone, my millionaire friend,—for he was reported to be a millionaire,—said to me with a smile, "Well, I have given them something they've never had before." After I had put on my coat and was ready to leave he made me take a glass of wine; he then gave me a cigar and twenty dollars in bills. He told me that he

6. Embellishing a song by rapidly playing the lower-tone notes that all belong to the same key.

would give me lots of work, his only stipulation being that I should not play any engagements such as I had just filled for him, except by his instructions. I readily accepted the proposition, for I was sure that I could not be the loser by such a contract.

I afterwards played for him at many dinners and parties of one kind or another. Occasionally he "loaned" me to some of his friends. And, too, I often played for him alone at his apartments. At such times he was quite a puzzle to me until I became accustomed to his manners. He would sometimes sit for three or four hours hearing me play, his eyes almost closed, making scarcely a motion except to light a fresh cigarette, and never commenting one way or another on the music. At first, I used sometimes to think that he had fallen asleep and would pause in playing. The stopping of the music always aroused him enough to tell me to play this or that; and I soon learned that my task was not to he considered finished until he got up from his chair and said, "That will do." The man's powers of endurance in listening often exceeded mine in performing—yet I am not sure that he was always listening. At times I became so oppressed with fatigue and sleepiness that it took almost superhuman effort to keep my fingers going; in fact, I believe I sometimes did so while dozing. During such moments, this man sitting there so mysteriously silent, almost hid in a cloud of heavy-scented smoke, filled me with a sort of unearthly terror. He seemed to be some grim, mute, but relentless tyrant, possessing over me a supernatural power which he used to drive me on mercilessly to exhaustion. But these feelings came very rarely; besides, he paid me so liberally I could forget much. There at length grew between us a familiar and warm relationship; and I am sure he had a decided personal liking for me. On my part, I looked upon him at that time as about all a man could wish to be.

The "Club" still remained my headquarters, and when I was not playing for my good patron I was generally to be found there. However, I no longer depended on playing at the "Club" to earn my living; I rather took rank with the visiting celebrities and, occasionally, after being sufficiently urged, would favor my old and new admirers with a number or two. I say, without any egotistic pride, that among my admirers were several of the best looking women who frequented the place, and who made no secret of the fact that they admired me as much as they did my playing. Among these was the "widow"; indeed, her attentions became so marked that one of my friends warned me to beware of her black companion, who was generally known as a "bad man." He said there was much more reason to be careful because the pair had lately quarreled, and had not been together at the "Club" for some nights. This warning greatly impressed me and I resolved to stop the affair before it should go any further; but the woman was so beautiful that my native gallantry and delicacy would not allow me to repulse her; my finer feelings entirely overcame my judgment. The warning also opened my eyes sufficiently to see that though my artistic temperament and skill made me interesting and attractive to the woman, she was, after all, using me only to excite the jealousy of her companion and revenge herself upon him. It was this surly black despot who held sway over her deepest emotions.

One night, shortly afterwards, I went into the "Club" and saw the "widow" sitting at a table in company with another woman. She at once beckoned for me to come to her. I went, knowing that I was committing worse than folly. She ordered a quart of champagne and insisted that I sit down and drink with her. I took a chair on the opposite side of the table and began to sip a glass of the wine. Suddenly I noticed by an expression on the "widow's" face that something had occurred. I instinctively glanced around and saw that her companion had just entered. His ugly look completely frightened me. My back was turned to him, but by watching the "widow's" eyes I judged that he was pacing back and forth across the room. My feelings were far from being comfortable; I expected every moment to feel a blow on my head. She, too, was very nervous; she was trying hard to appear unconcerned, but could not succeed in hiding her real feelings. I decided that it was best to get out of such a predicament even at the expense of appearing cowardly, and I made a motion to rise. Just as I partly turned in my chair, I saw the black fellow approaching; he walked directly to our table and leaned over. The "Widow" evidently feared he was going to strike her, and she threw back her head. Instead of striking her he whipped out a revolver and fired; the first shot went straight into her throat. There were other shots fired, but how many I do not know; for the first knowledge I had of my surroundings and actions was that I was rushing through the chop-suey restaurant into the street. Just which streets I followed when I got outside I do not know, but I think I must have gone towards Eighth Avenue, then down towards Twenty-third Street and across towards Fifth Avenue. I traveled not by sight, but instinctively. I felt like one fleeing in a horrible nightmare.

How long and far I walked I cannot tell; but on Fifth Avenue, under a light, I passed a cab containing a solitary occupant, who called to me, and I recognized the voice and face of my millionaire friend. He stopped the cab and asked, "What on earth are you doing strolling in this part of the town?" For answer I got into the cab and related to him all that had happened. He reassured me by saying that no charge of any kind could be brought against me; then added, "But, of course, you don't want to be mixed up in such an affair." He directed the driver to turn around and go into the park, and then went on to say, "I decided last night that I'd go to Europe to-morrow. I think I'll take you along instead of Walter." Walter was his valet. It was settled that I should go to his apartments for the rest of the night and sail with him in the morning.

We drove around through the park, exchanging only an occasional word. The cool air somewhat calmed my nerves and I lay back and closed my eyes; but still I could see that beautiful white throat with the ugly wound. The jet of blood pulsing from it had placed an indelible red stain on my memory.

Chapter IX

I did not feel at ease until the ship was well out of New York harbor; and, notwithstanding the repeated reassurances of my millionaire friend and my own knowledge of the facts in the case, I somehow could not rid myself of the sentiment that I was, in a great degree, responsible for the widow's tragic end. We had brought most of the morning papers aboard with us, but my great fear of seeing my name in connection with the killing would not permit me to read the accounts, although, in one of the papers, I did look at the picture of the victim, which did not in the least resemble her. This morbid state of mind, together with seasickness, kept me miserable for three or four days. At the end of that time my spirits began to revive, and I took an interest in the ship, my fellow passengers, and the voyage in general. On the second or third day out we passed several spouting whales; but I could not arouse myself to make the effort to go to the other side of the ship to see them. A little later we ran in close proximity to a large iceberg. I was curious enough to get up and look at it, and I was fully repaid for my pains. The sun was shining full upon it, and it glistened like a mammoth diamond, cut with a million facets. As we passed it constantly changed its shape; at each different angle of vision it assumed new and astonishing forms of beauty. I watched it through a pair of glasses, seeking to verify my early conception of an iceberg—in the geographies of my grammar-school days the pictures of icebergs always included a stranded polar bear, standing desolately upon one of the snowy crags. I looked for the bear, but if he was there he refused to put himself on exhibition.

It was not, however, until the morning that we entered the harbor of Havre[7] that I was able to shake off my gloom. Then the strange sights, the chatter in an unfamiliar tongue and the excitement of

7. A port city in northwest France.

landing and passing the customs officials caused me to forget completely the events of a few days before. Indeed, I grew so light-hearted that when I caught my first sight of the train which was to take us to Paris, I enjoyed a hearty laugh. The toy-looking engine, the stuffy little compartment cars with tiny, old-fashioned wheels, struck me as being extremely funny. But before we reached Paris my respect for our train rose considerably. I found that the "tiny" engine made remarkably fast time, and that the old-fashioned wheels ran very smoothly. I even began to appreciate the "stuffy" cars for their privacy. As I watched the passing scenery from the car window it seemed too beautiful to be real. The bright-colored houses against the green background impressed me as the work of some idealistic painter. Before we arrived in Paris there was awakened in my heart a love for France which continued to grow stronger, a love which today makes that country for me the one above all others to be desired.

We rolled into the station Saint Lazare about four o'clock in the afternoon, and drove immediately to the Hotel Continental.[8] My benefactor, humoring my curiosity and enthusiasm, which seemed to please him very much, suggested that we take a short walk before dinner. We stepped out of the hotel and turned to the right into the Rue de Rivoli.[9] When the vista of the Place de la Concorde and the Champs Elysées[1] suddenly burst on me I could hardly credit my own eyes. I shall attempt no such superogatory task as a description of Paris. I wish only to give briefly the impressions which that wonderful city made upon me. It impressed me as the perfect and perfectly beautiful city; and even after I had been there for some time, and seen not only its avenues and palaces, but its most squalid alleys and hovels, this impression was not weakened. Paris became for me a charmed spot, and whenever I have returned there I have fallen under the spell, a spell which compels admiration for all of its manners and customs and justification of even its follies and sins.

We walked a short distance up the Champs Elysées and sat for a while in chairs along the sidewalk, watching the passing crowds on foot and in carriages. It was with reluctance that I went back to the hotel for dinner. After dinner we went to one of the summer theaters, and after the performance my friend took me to a large café on one of the grand boulevards. Here it was that I had my first

8. One of the most extravagant Paris hotels at the time of its opening in 1878. *Station Saint Lazare:* one of the busiest trains stations in Paris.
9. A major street of commerce that cuts between the Louvre Museum and the Tuleries Gardens in Paris; named after Napoleon's victory against Austria in the Battle of Rivoli (1797).
1. The city's showiest boulevard. The long, broad street is renowned for its luxurious retail shops, ample greenery, and historical monuments. *Place de la Concorde*: octagon shaped and the largest square in Paris; located along the Seine River between the Champ Elysées and Tuilerie Gardens.

glimpse of the French life of popular literature, so different from real French life. There were several hundred people, men and women, in the place drinking, smoking, talking, and listening to the music. My millionaire friend and I took seats at a table where we sat smoking and watching the crowd. It was not long before we were joined by two or three good-looking, well-dressed young women. My friend talked to them in French and bought drinks for the whole party. I tried to recall my high school French, but the effort availed me little. I could stammer out a few phrases, but, very naturally, could not understand a word that was said to me. We stayed at the café a couple of hours, then went back to the hotel. The next day we spent several hours in the shops and at the tailors. I had no clothes except what I had been able to gather together at my benefactor's apartments the night before we sailed. He bought me the same kind of clothes which he himself wore, and that was the best; and he treated me in every way as he dressed me, as an equal, not as a servant. In fact, I don't think anyone could have guessed that such a relation existed. My duties were light and few, and he was a man full of life and vigor, who rather enjoyed doing things for himself. He kept me supplied with money far beyond what ordinary wages would have amounted to. For the first two weeks we were together almost constantly, seeing the sights, sights old to him, but from which he seemed to get new pleasure in showing them to me. During the day we took in the places of interest, and at night the theaters and cafés. This sort of life appealed to me as ideal, and I asked him one day how long he intended to stay in Paris. He answered, "Oh, until I get tired of it." I could not understand how that could ever happen. As it was, including several short trips to the Mediterranean, to Spain, to Brussels, and to Ostend,[2] we did remain there fourteen or fifteen months. We stayed at the Hotel Continental about two months of this time. Then my millionaire took apartments, hired a piano, and lived almost the same life he lived in New York. He entertained a great deal, some of the parties being a good deal more blasé than the New York ones. I played for the guests at all of them with an effect which to relate would be but a tiresome repetition to the reader. I played not only for the guests, but continued, as I used to do in New York, to play often for the host when he was alone. This man of the world, who grew weary of everything, and was always searching for something new, appeared never to grow tired of my music; he seemed to take it as a drug. He fell into a habit which caused me no little annoyance; sometimes he would come in during the early hours of the morning, and finding me in bed asleep, would wake me up and ask me to play something. This,

2. A city in northwest Belgium.

so far as I can remember, was my only hardship during my whole stay with him in Europe.

After the first few weeks spent in sight-seeing, I had a great deal of time left to myself; my friend was often I did not know where. When not with him I spent the day nosing about all the curious nooks and corners of Paris; of this I never grew tired. At night I usually went to some theater, but always ended up at the big café on the Grand Boulevards.[3] I wish the reader to know that it was not alone the gayety which drew me there; aside from that I had a laudable purpose. I had purchased an English-French conversational dictionary, and I went there every night to take a language lesson. I used to get three or four of the young women who frequented the place at a table and buy beer and cigarettes for them. In return I received my lesson. I got more than my money's worth; for they actually compelled me to speak the language. This, together with reading the papers every day, enabled me within a few months to express myself fairly well, and, before I left Paris, to have more than an ordinary command of French. Of course, every person who goes to Paris could not dare to learn French in this manner, but I can think of no easier or quicker way of doing it. The acquiring of another foreign language awoke me to the fact that with a little effort I could secure an added accomplishment as fine and as valuable as music; so I determined to make myself as much of a linguist as possible. I bought a Spanish newspaper every day in order to freshen my memory on that language, and, for French, devised what was, so far as I knew, an original system of study. I compiled a list which I termed "Three hundred necessary words." These I thoroughly committed to memory, also the conjugation of the verbs which were included in the list. I studied these words over and over, much like children of a couple of generations ago studied the alphabet. I also practiced a set of phrases like the following: "How?" "What did you say?" "What does the word —— mean?" "I understand all you say except ——." "Please repeat." "What do you call ——?" "How do you say ——?" These I called my working sentences. In an astonishingly short time I reached the point where the language taught itself,—where I learned to speak merely by speaking. This point is the place which students taught foreign languages in our schools and colleges find great difficulty in reaching. I think the main trouble is that they learn too much of a language at a time. A French child with a vocabulary of two hundred words can express more spoken ideas than a student of French can with a knowledge of two thousand. A small vocabulary, the smaller the better, which

3. Probably Le Grand Café, which opened in 1875 and was located near the Grand Opera; a popular destination for French café society.

embraces the common, everyday-used ideas, thoroughly mastered, is the key to a language. When that much is acquired the vocabulary can be increased simply by talking. And it is easy. Who cannot commit three hundred words to memory? Later I tried my method, if I may so term it, with German, and found that it worked in the same way.

I spent a good many evenings at the Grand Opera.[4] The music there made me strangely reminiscent of my life in Connecticut, it was an atmosphere in which I caught a fresh breath of my boyhood days and early youth. Generally, in the morning, after I had attended a performance, I would sit at the piano and for a couple of hours play the music which I used to play in my mother's little parlor.

One night I went to hear "Faust."[5] I got into my seat just as the lights went down for the first act. At the end of the act I noticed that my neighbor on the left was a young girl. I cannot describe her either as to feature, color of her hair, or of her eyes; she was so young, so fair, so ethereal, that I felt to stare at her would be a violation; yet I was distinctly conscious of her beauty. During the intermission she spoke English in a low voice to a gentleman and a lady who sat in the seats to her left, addressing them as father and mother. I held my programme as though studying it, but listened to catch every sound of her voice. Her observations on the performance and the audience were so fresh and naïve as to be almost amusing. I gathered that she was just out of school, and that this was her first trip to Paris. I occasionally stole a glance at her, and each time I did so my heart leaped into my throat. Once I glanced beyond to the gentleman who sat next to her. My glance immediately turned into a stare. Yes, there he was, unmistakably, my father! looking hardly a day older than when I had seen him some ten years before. What a strange coincidence! What should I say to him? What would he say to me? Before I had recovered from my first surprise there came another shock in the realization that the beautiful, tender girl at my side was my sister. Then all the springs of affection in my heart, stopped since my mother's death, burst out in fresh and terrible torrents, and I could have fallen at her feet and worshiped her. They were singing the second act, but I did not hear the music. Slowly the desolate loneliness of my position became clear to me. I knew that I could not speak, but I would have given a part of my life to touch her hand with mine and call her sister. I sat through the opera until I could stand it no longer. I felt that I was suffocating.

4. Also known as the Paris Opéra or Palais Garnier (after its architect Charles Garnier), this elite cultural site opened in 1875.
5. Charles Gounod's (1818–1893) 1859 opera about an aging and suicidal scholar, Dr. Faust, who gives his soul to the devil, Mephistopheles, in exchange for youth and romance.

Valentine's love seemed like mockery, and I felt an almost uncontrollable impulse to rise up and scream to the audience, "Here, here in your very midst, is a tragedy, a real tragedy!" This impulse grew so strong that I became afraid of myself, and in the darkness of one of the scenes I stumbled out of the theater. I walked aimlessly about for an hour or so, my feelings divided between a desire to weep and a desire to curse. I finally took a cab and went from café to café, and for one of the very few times in my life drank myself into a stupor.

It was unwelcome news for me when my benefactor—I could not think of him as employer—informed me that he was at last tired of Paris. This news gave me, I think, a passing doubt as to his sanity. I had enjoyed life in Paris, and, taking all things into consideration, enjoyed it wholesomely. One thing which greatly contributed to my enjoyment was the fact that I was an American. Americans are immensely popular in Paris; and this is not due solely to the fact that they spend lots of money there; for they spend just as much or more in London, and in the latter city they are merely tolerated because they do spend. The Londoner seems to think that Americans are people whose only claim to be classed as civilized is that they have money, and the regrettable thing about that is that the money is not English. But the French are more logical and freer from prejudices than the British; so the difference of attitude is easily explained. Only once in Paris did I have cause to blush for my American citizenship. I had become quite friendly with a young man from Luxembourg[6] whom I had met at the big café. He was a stolid, slow-witted fellow, but, as we say, with a heart of gold. He and I grew attached to each other and were together frequently. He was a great admirer of the United States and never grew tired of talking to me about the country and asking for information. It was his intention to try his fortune there some day. One night he asked me in a tone of voice which indicated that he expected an authoritative denial of an ugly rumor, "Did they really burn a man alive in the United States?" I never knew what I stammered out to him as an answer. I should have felt relieved if I could even have said to him, "Well, only one."

When we arrived in London my sadness at leaving Paris was turned into despair. After my long stay in the French capital, huge, ponderous, massive London seemed to me as ugly a thing as man could contrive to make. I thought of Paris as a beauty spot on the face of the earth, and of London as a big freckle. But soon London's massiveness, I might say its very ugliness, began to impress me. I began to experience that sense of grandeur which one feels when

6. A small country just north of France, southeast of Germany, and southwest of Belgium.

he looks at a great mountain or a mighty river. Beside London Paris becomes a toy, a pretty plaything. And I must own that before I left the world's metropolis I discovered much there that was beautiful. The beauty in and about London is entirely different from that in and about Paris; and I could not but admit that the beauty of the French city seemed hand-made, artificial, as though set up for the photographer's camera, everything nicely adjusted so as not to spoil the picture; while that of the English city was rugged, natural and fresh.

How these two cities typify the two peoples who built them! Even the sound of their names express a certain racial difference. Paris is the concrete expression of the gayety, regard for symmetry, love of art and, I might well add, of the morality of the French people. London stands for the conservatism, the solidarity, the utilitarianism and, I might well add, the hypocrisy of the Anglo-Saxon. It may sound odd to speak of the morality of the French, if not of the hypocrisy of the English; but this seeming paradox impressed me as a deep truth. I saw many things in Paris which were immoral according to English standards, but the absence of hypocrisy, the absence of the spirit to do the thing if it might only be done in secret, robbed these very immoralities of the damning influence of the same evils in London. I have walked along the terrace cafés of Paris and seen hundreds of men and women sipping their wine and beer, without observing a sign of drunkenness. As they drank, they chatted and laughed and watched the passing crowds; the drinking seemed to be a secondary thing. This I have witnessed, not only in the cafés along the Grand Boulevards, but in the out-of-way places patronized by the working classes. In London I have seen in the "Pubs" men and women crowded in stuffy little compartments, drinking seemingly only for the pleasure of swallowing as much as they could hold. I have seen there women from eighteen to eighty, some in tatters, and some clutching babes in their arms, drinking the heavy English ales and whiskies served to them by women. In the whole scene, not one ray of brightness, not one flash of gayety, only maudlin joviality or grim despair. And I have thought, if some men and women will drink—and it is certain that some will—is it not better that they do so under the open sky, in the fresh air, than huddled together in some close, smoky room? There is a sort of frankness about the evils of Paris which robs them of much of the seductiveness of things forbidden, and with that frankness goes a certain cleanliness of thought belonging to things not hidden. London will do whatever Paris does, provided exterior morals are not shocked. As a result, Paris has the appearance only of being the more immoral city. The difference may be summed up in this: Paris practices its sins as lightly as it does its religion, while London practices both very seriously.

I should not neglect to mention what impressed me most forcibly during my stay in London. It was not St. Paul's nor the British Museum nor Westminster Abbey.[7] It was nothing more or less than the simple phrase "Thank you," or sometimes more elaborated, "Thank you very kindly, sir." I was continually surprised by the varied uses to which it was put; and, strange to say, its use as an expression of politeness seemed more limited than any other. One night I was in a cheap music hall and accidentally bumped into a waiter who was carrying a tray-load of beer, almost bringing him to several shillings' worth of grief. To my amazement he righted himself and said, "Thank ye, sir," and left me wondering whether he meant that he thanked me for not completely spilling his beer, or that he would thank me for keeping out of his way.

I also found cause to wonder upon what ground the English accuse Americans of corrupting the language by introducing slang words. I think I heard more and more different kinds of slang during my few weeks' stay in London than in my whole "tenderloin"[8] life in New York. But I suppose the English feel that the language is theirs, and that they may do with it as they please without at the same time allowing that privilege to others.

My "millionaire" was not so long in growing tired of London as of Paris. After a stay of six or eight weeks we went across into Holland. Amsterdam was a great surprise to me. I had always thought of Venice as the city of canals; but it had never entered my mind that I should find similar conditions in a Dutch town. I don't suppose the comparison goes far beyond the fact that there are canals in both cities—I have never seen Venice—but Amsterdam struck me as being extremely picturesque. From Holland we went to Germany, where we spent five or six months, most of the time in Berlin. I found Berlin more to my taste than London, and occasionally I had to admit that in some things it was superior to Paris.

In Berlin I especially enjoyed the orchestral concerts, and I attended a large number of them. I formed the acquaintance of a good many musicians, several of whom spoke of my playing in high terms. It was in Berlin that my inspiration was renewed. One night my "millionaire" entertained a party of men composed of artists, musicians, writers and, for aught I know, a count or two. They drank and smoked a great deal, talked art and music, and discussed, it

7. St. Paul's Cathedral and Westminster Abbey are two of London's most culturally significant churches. St. Paul's was destroyed in the Great Fire of 1666 and rebuilt in 1710. By the early 1900s, St. Paul's was a central post of Anglican worship and, like Westminster Abbey, a place for public memorials. Westminster Abbey sits adjacent to the Houses of Parliament and is the site of royal coronations, christenings, and burials.

8. A term coined in the 1870s to describe neighborhoods in large cities where poverty hits hardest.

seemed to me, everything that ever entered man's mind. I could only follow the general drift of what they were saying. When they discussed music it was more interesting to me; for then some fellow would run excitedly to the piano and give a demonstration of his opinions, and another would follow quickly doing the same. In this way, I learned that, regardless of what his specialty might be, every man in the party was a musician. I was at the same time impressed with the falsity of the general idea that Frenchmen are excitable and emotional, and that Germans are calm and phlegmatic. Frenchmen are merely gay and never overwhelmed by their emotions. When they talk loud and fast it is merely talk, while Germans get worked up and red in the face when sustaining an opinion; and in heated discussions are likely to allow their emotions to sweep them off their feet.

My "millionaire" planned, in the midst of the discussion on music, to have me play the "new American music" and astonish everybody present. The result was that I was more astonished than anyone else. I went to the piano and played the most intricate ragtime piece I knew. Before there was time for anybody to express an opinion on what I had done, a big be-spectacled, bushy-headed man rushed over, and, shoving me out of the chair, exclaimed, "Get up! Get up!" He seated himself at the piano, and taking the theme of my ragtime, played it through first in straight chords;[9] then varied and developed it through every known musical form. I sat amazed. I had been turning classic music into ragtime, a comparatively easy task; and this man had taken ragtime and made it classic. The thought came across me like a flash.—It can be done, why can't I do it? From that moment my mind was made up. I clearly saw the way of carrying out the ambition I had formed when a boy.

I now lost interest in our trip. I thought, here I am a man, no longer a boy, and what am I doing but wasting my time and abusing my talent. What use am I making of my gifts? What future have I before me following my present course? These thoughts made me feel remorseful, and put me in a fever to get to work, to begin to do something. Of course I know now that I was not wasting time; that there was nothing I could have done at that age which would have benefited me more than going to Europe as I did. The desire to begin work grew stronger each day. I could think of nothing else. I made up my mind to go back into the very heart of the South, to live among the people, and drink in my inspiration first-hand. I gloated over the immense amount of material I had to work with, not only modern ragtime, but also the old slave songs,—material which no one had yet touched.

9. Basic, nonembellished three-note chords.

The more decided and anxious I became to return to the United States, the more I dreaded the ordeal of breaking with my "millionaire." Between this peculiar man and me there had grown a very strong bond of affection, backed up by a debt which each owed to the other. He had taken me from a terrible life in New York and by giving me the opportunity of traveling and of coming in contact with the people with whom he associated, had made me a polished man of the world. On the other hand, I was his chief means of disposing of the thing which seemed to sum up all in life that he dreaded—Time. As I remember him now, I can see that time was what he was always endeavoring to escape, to bridge over, to blot out; and it is not strange that some years later he did escape it forever, by leaping into eternity.

For some weeks I waited for just the right moment in which to tell my patron of my decision. Those weeks were a trying time to me. I felt that I was playing the part of a traitor to my best friend. At length, one day, he said to me, "Well, get ready for a long trip; we are going to Egypt, and then to Japan." The temptation was for an instant almost overwhelming, but I summoned determination enough to say, "I don't think I want to go." "What!" he exclaimed, "you want to go back to your dear Paris? You still think that the only spot on earth? Wait until you see Cairo and Tokio, you may change your mind." "No," I stammered, "it is not because I want to go back to Paris. I want to go back to the United States." He wished to know my reason, and I told him, as best I could, my dreams, my ambition, and my decision. While I was talking he watched me with a curious, almost cynical, smile growing on his lips. When I had finished he put his hand on my shoulder.—This was the first physical expression of tender regard he had ever shown me—and looking at me in a big-brotherly way, said, "My boy, you are by blood, by appearance, by education and by tastes, a white man. Now why do you want to throw your life away amidst the poverty and ignorance, in the hopeless struggle of the black people of the United States? Then look at the terrible handicap yon are placing on yourself by going home and working as a Negro composer; you can never be able to get the hearing for your work which it might deserve. I doubt that even a white musician of recognized ability could succeed there by working on the theory that American music should be based on Negro themes. Music is a universal art; anybody's music belongs to everybody; you can't limit it to race or country. Now, if you want to become a composer, why not stay right here in Europe? I will put you under the best teachers on the continent. Then if you want to write music on Negro themes, why, go ahead and do it."

We talked for some time on music and the race question. On the latter subject I had never before heard him express any opinion.

Between him and me no suggestion of racial differences had ever come up. I found that he was a man entirely free from prejudice, but he recognized that prejudice was a big stubborn entity which had to be taken into account. He went on to say, "This idea you have of making a Negro out of yourself is nothing more than a sentiment; and you do not realize the fearful import of what you intend to do. What kind of a Negro would you make now, especially in the South? If you had remained there, or perhaps even in your club in New York, you might have succeeded very well; but now you would be miserable. I can imagine no more dissatisfied human being than an educated, cultured and refined colored man in the United States. I have given more study to the race question in the United States than you may suppose, and I sympathize with the Negroes there; but what's the use? I can't right their wrongs, and neither can you; they must do that themselves. They are unfortunate in having wrongs to right, and you would be foolish to unnecessarily take their wrongs on your shoulders. Perhaps some day, through study and observation, you will come to see that evil is a force and, like the physical and chemical forces, we cannot annihilate it; we may only change its form. We light upon one evil and hit it with all the might of our civilization, but only succeed in scattering it into a dozen of other forms. We hit slavery through a great civil war. Did we destroy it? No, we only changed it into hatred between sections of the country: in the South, into political corruption and chicanery, the degradation of the blacks through peonage, unjust laws, unfair and cruel treatment; and the degradation of the whites by their resorting to these practices; the paralyzation of the public conscience, and the ever overhanging dread of what the future may bring. Modern civilization hit ignorance of the masses through the means of popular education. What has it done but turn ignorance into anarchy, socialism, strikes, hatred between poor and rich, and universal discontent. In like manner, modern philanthropy hit at suffering and disease through asylums and hospitals; it prolongs the sufferers' lives, it is true; but is, at the same time, sending down strains of insanity and weakness into future generations. My philosophy of life is this: make yourself as happy as possible, and try to make those happy whose lives come into touch with yours; but to attempt to right the wrongs and ease the sufferings of the world in general, is a waste of effort. You had just as well try to bale the Atlantic by pouring the water into the Pacific."

This tremendous flow of serious talk from a man I was accustomed to see either gay or taciturn so surprised and overwhelmed me that I could not frame a reply. He left me thinking over what he had said. Whatever was the soundness of his logic or the moral tone of his philosophy, his argument greatly impressed me. I could see, in spite of the absolute selfishness upon which it was based, that there was reason and common sense in it. I began to analyze my own motives, and found that they, too, were very largely mixed with selfishness. Was it more a desire to help those I considered my people or more a desire to distinguish myself, which was leading me back to the United States? That is a question I have never definitely answered.

For several weeks longer I was in a troubled state of mind. Added to the fact that I was loath to leave my good friend, was the weight of the question he had aroused in my mind, whether I was not making a fatal mistake. I suffered more than one sleepless night during that time. Finally, I settled the question on purely selfish grounds, in accordance with my "millionaire's" philosophy. I argued that music offered me a better future than anything else I had any knowledge of, and, in opposition to my friend's opinion, that I should have greater chances of attracting attention as a colored composer than as a white one. But I must own that I also felt stirred by an unselfish desire to voice all the joys and sorrows, the hopes and ambitions, of the American Negro, in classic musical form.

When my mind was fully made up I told my friend. He asked me when I intended to start. I replied that I would do so at once. He then asked me how much money I had. I told him that I had saved several hundred dollars out of sums he had given me. He gave me a check for $500, told me to write to him care of his Paris bankers if I ever needed his help, wished me good luck, and bade me good-by. All this he did almost coldly; and I often wondered whether he was in a hurry to get rid of what he considered a fool, or whether he was striving to hide deeper feelings of sorrow.

And so I separated from the man who was, all in all, the best friend I ever had, except my mother, the man who exerted the greatest influence ever brought into my life, except that exerted by my mother. My affection for him was so strong, my recollections of him are so distinct; he was such a peculiar and striking character, that I could easily fill several chapters with reminiscences of him; but for fear of tiring the reader I shall go on with my narration.

I decided to go to Liverpool[1] and take ship for Boston. I still had an uneasy feeling about returning to New York; and in a few days I found myself aboard ship headed for home.

1. A major port city in northwestern England that played a prominent role in the transatlantic slave trade, serving both as a way station for human cargo and as a distributor of cotton-based textiles manufactured in the United States.

Chapter X

Among the first of my fellow passengers of whom I took any particular notice, was a tall, broad-shouldered, almost gigantic, colored man. His dark-brown face was clean shaven; he was well dressed and bore a decidedly distinguished air. In fact, if he was not handsome, he at least compelled admiration for his fine physical proportions. He attracted general attention as he strode the deck in a sort of majestic loneliness. I became curious to know who he was and determined to strike up an acquaintance with him at the first opportune moment. The chance came a day or two later. He was sitting in the smoking-room, with a cigar in his mouth which had gone out, reading a novel. I sat down beside him and, offering him a fresh cigar, said, "You don't mind my telling you something unpleasant, do you?" He looked at me with a smile, accepted the proffered cigar, and replied in a voice which comported perfectly with his size and appearance, "I think my curiosity overcomes any objections I might have." "Well," I said, "have you noticed that the man who sat at your right in the saloon during the first meal has not sat there since?" He frowned slightly without answering my question. "Well," I continued, "he asked the steward to remove him; and not only that, he attempted to persuade a number of the passengers to protest against your presence in the dining-saloon." The big man at my side took a long draw from his cigar, threw his head back and slowly blew a great cloud of smoke toward the ceiling. Then turning to me he said, "Do you know, I don't object to anyone having prejudices so long as those prejudices don't interfere with my personal liberty. Now, the man you are speaking of had a perfect right to change his seat if I in any way interfered with his appetite or his digestion. I would have no reason to complain if he removed to the farthest corner of the saloon, or even if he got off the ship; but when his prejudice attempts to move *me* one foot, one inch, out of the place where I am comfortably located, then I object." On the word "object" he brought his great fist down on the table in front of us with such a crash that everyone in the room turned to look. We both covered up the slight embarrassment with a laugh, and strolled out on the deck.

We walked the deck for an hour or more, discussing different phases of the Negro question. I, in referring to the race, used the personal pronoun "we"; my companion made no comment about it, nor evinced any surprise, except to slightly raise his eyebrows the first time he caught the significance of the word. He was the broadest minded colored man I have ever talked with on the Negro question. He even went so far as to sympathize with and offer excuses for some white Southern points of view. I asked him what were his main reasons for being so hopeful. He replied, "In spite of all that is written, said and done, this great, big, incontrovertible fact stands out,—the Negro is progressing, and that disproves all the arguments in the world that he is incapable of progress. I was born in slavery, and at emancipation was set adrift a ragged, penniless bit of humanity. I have seen the Negro in every grade, and I know what I am talking about. Our detractors point to the increase of crime as evidence against us; certainly we have progressed in crime as in other things; what less could be expected? And yet, in this respect, we are far from the point which has been reached by the more highly civilized white race. As we continue to progress, crime among us will gradually lose much of its brutal, vulgar, I might say healthy, aspect, and become more delicate, refined and subtile. Then it will be less shocking and noticeable, although more dangerous to society." Then dropping his tone of irony, he continued with some show of eloquence, "But, above all, when I am discouraged and disheartened, I have this to fall back on: if there is a principle of right in the world, which finally prevails, and I believe that there is; if there is a merciful but justice-loving God in heaven, and I believe that there is, we shall win; for we have right on our side; while those who oppose us can defend themselves by nothing in the moral law, nor even by anything in the enlightened thought of the present age."

For several days, together with other topics, we discussed the race problem, not only of the United States, but the race problem as it affected native Africans and Jews. Finally, before we reached Boston, our conversation had grown familiar and personal. I had told him something of my past and much about my intentions for the future. I learned that he was a physician, a graduate of Howard University,[2] Washington, and had done post-graduate work in Philadelphia; and this was his second trip abroad to attend professional courses. He had practiced for some years in the city of Washington, and though he did not say so, I gathered that his practice was a lucrative one. Before we left the ship he had made me promise that I would stop two or three days in Washington before going on South.

We put up at a hotel in Boston for a couple of days, and visited several of my new friend's acquaintances; they were all people of education and culture and, apparently, of means. I could not but help being struck by the great difference between them and the

2. Founded in 1867, a historically African American university located in Washington D.C., dubbed by Zora Neale Hurston as the "Black Harvard." Many notable African Americans were students, alumni, or faculty, e.g., poets Paul Laurence Dunbar and Sterling A. Brown, philosopher and critic Alain Locke, legal scholar Charles Hamilton Houston, Supreme Court Justice Thurgood Marshall, and novelists Hurston and Toni Morrison.

same class of colored people in the South. In speech and thought they were genuine Yankees.[3] The difference was especially noticeable in their speech. There was none of that heavy-tongued enunciation which characterizes even the best educated colored people of the South. It is remarkable, after all, what an adaptable creature the Negro is. I have seen the black West India gentleman in London, and he is in speech and manners a perfect Englishman. I have seen natives of Haiti and Martinique in Paris, and they are more Frenchy than a Frenchman. I have no doubt that the Negro would make a good Chinaman, with exception of the pigtail.

My stay in Washington, instead of being two or three days, was two or three weeks. This was my first visit to the National Capital, and I was, of course, interested in seeing the public buildings and something of the working of the government; but most of my time I spent with the doctor among his friends and acquaintances. The social phase of life among colored people, which I spoke of in an earlier chapter, is more developed in Washington than in any other city in the country. This is on account of the large number of individuals earning good salaries and having a reasonable amount of leisure time to be drawn from. There are dozens of physicians and lawyers, scores of school teachers and hundreds of clerks in the departments. As to the colored department clerks, I think it fair to say that in educational equipment they average above the white clerks of the same grade; for, whereas a colored college graduate will seek such a job, the white university man goes into one of the many higher vocations which are open to him.

In a previous chapter I spoke of social life among colored people; so there is no need to take it up again here. But there is one thing I did not mention: among Negroes themselves there is the peculiar inconsistency of a color question. Its existence is rarely admitted and hardly ever mentioned; it may not be too strong a statement to say that the greater portion of the race is unconscious of its influence; yet this influence, though silent, is constant. It is evidenced most plainly in marriage selection; thus the black men generally marry women fairer than themselves; while, on the other hand, the dark women of stronger mental endowment are very often married to light-complexioned men; the effect is a tendency toward lighter complexions, especially among the more active elements in the race. Some might claim that this is a tacit admission of colored people among themselves of their own inferiority judged by the color line. I do not think so. What I have termed an inconsistency

3. Northerners; before the Civil War, the term referred to only New Englanders as a regional nickname. With the war's onset, the term designated national loyalties as it was applied more broadly—and pejoratively, by supporters of the Confederacy—to Americans supporting the Union and living north of the Mason-Dixon Line.

is, after all, most natural; it is, in fact, a tendency in accordance with what might be called an economic necessity. So far as racial differences go, the United States puts a greater premium on color, or better, lack of color, than upon anything else in the world. To paraphrase, "Have a white skin, and all things else may be added unto you." I have seen advertisements in newspapers for waiters, bell boys or elevator men, which read, "Light colored man wanted." It is this tremendous pressure which the sentiment of the country exerts that is operating on the race. There is involved not only the question of higher opportunity, but often the question of earning a livelihood; and so I say it is not strange, but a natural tendency. Nor is it any more a sacrifice of self respect that a black man should give to his children every advantage he can which complexion of the skin carries, than that the new or vulgar rich should purchase for their children the advantages which ancestry, aristocracy, and social position carry. I once heard a colored man sum it up in these words, "It's no disgrace to be black, but it's often very inconvenient."

Washington shows the Negro not only at his best, but also at his worst. As I drove around with the doctor, he commented rather harshly on those of the latter class which we saw. He remarked: "You see those lazy, loafing, good-for-nothing darkies, they're not worth digging graves for; yet they are the ones who create impressions of the race for the casual observer. It's because they are always in evidence on the street corners, while the rest of us are hard at work, and you know a dozen loafing darkies make a bigger crowd and a worse impression in this country than fifty white men of the same class. But they ought not to represent the race. We are the race, and the race ought to be judged by us, not by them. Every race and every nation is judged by the best it has been able to produce, not by the worst."

The recollection of my stay in Washington is a pleasure to me now. In company with the doctor I visited Howard University, the public schools, the excellent colored hospital, with which he was in some way connected, if I remember correctly, and many comfortable and even elegant homes. It was with some reluctance that I continued my journey south. The doctor was very kind in giving me letters to people in Richmond and Nashville when I told him that I intended to stop in both of these cities. In Richmond a man who was then editing a very creditable colored newspaper, gave me a great deal of his time, and made my stay there of three or four days very pleasant. In Nashville I spent a whole day at Fisk University,[4] the home of the "Jubilee Singers," and was more than repaid for my

4. A historically African American university in Nashville, Tennessee, founded in 1866 by the American Missionary Association.

time. Among my letters of introduction was one to a very prosperous physician. He drove me about the city and introduced me to a number of people. From Nashville I went to Atlanta, where I stayed long enough to gratify an old desire to see Atlanta University again. I then continued my journey to Macon.

During the trip from Nashville to Atlanta I went into the smoking compartment of the car to smoke a cigar. I was traveling in a Pullman,[5] not because of an abundance of funds, but because through my experience with my "millionaire," a certain amount of comfort and luxury had become a necessity to me whenever it was obtainable. When I entered the car I found only a couple of men there; but in a half hour there were half a dozen or more. From the general conversation I learned that a fat Jewish looking man was a cigar manufacturer, and was experimenting in growing Havana tobacco in Florida; that a slender be-spectacled young man was from Ohio and a professor in some State institution in Alabama; that a white-mustached, well dressed man was an old Union soldier[6] who had fought through the Civil War; and that a tall, rawboned, red-faced man, who seemed bent on leaving nobody in ignorance of the fact that he was from Texas, was a cotton planter.

In the North men may ride together for hours in a "smoker" and unless they are acquainted with each other never exchange a word; in the South, men thrown together in such manner are friends in fifteen minutes. There is always present a warm-hearted cordiality which will melt down the most frigid reserve. It may be because Southerners are very much like Frenchmen in that they must talk; and not only must they talk, but they must express their opinions.

The talk in the car was for a while miscellaneous,—on the weather, crops, business prospects—the old Union soldier had invested capital in Atlanta, and he predicted that that city would soon be one of the greatest in the country—finally the conversation drifted to politics; then, as a natural sequence, turned upon the Negro question.

In the discussion of the race question, the diplomacy of the Jew was something to be admired; he had the faculty of agreeing with everybody without losing his allegiance to any side. He knew that to sanction Negro oppression would be to sanction Jewish oppression, and would expose him to a shot along that line from the old soldier, who stood firmly on the ground of equal rights and opportunity to all men; yet long traditions and business instincts told him, when in Rome to act as a Roman. Altogether his position was a delicate one, and I gave him credit for the skill he displayed in maintaining it. The young professor was apologetic. He had had the

5. An expensive sleeping car. See also p. 30, n. 4.
6. A soldier who fought for the North in the American Civil War.

same views as the G. A. R.[7] man; but a year in the South had opened his eyes, and he had to confess that the problem could hardly be handled any better than it was being handled by the Southern whites. To which the G. A. R. man responded somewhat rudely that he had spent ten times as many years in the South as his young friend, and that he could easily understand how holding a position in a State institution in Alabama would bring about a change of views. The professor turned very red and had very little more to say. The Texan was fierce, eloquent and profane in his argument and, in a lower sense, there was a direct logic in what he said, which was convincing; it was only by taking higher ground, by dealing in what Southerners call "theories" that he could be combatted. Occasionally some one of the several other men in the "smoker" would throw in a remark to reinforce what he said, but he really didn't need any help; he was sufficient in himself.

In the course of a short time the controversy narrowed itself down to an argument between the old soldier and the Texan. The latter maintained hotly that the Civil War was a criminal mistake on the part of the North, and that the humiliation which the South suffered during Reconstruction[8] could never be forgotten. The Union man retorted just as hotly that the South was responsible for the war, and that the spirit of unforgetfulness on its part was the greatest cause of present friction; that it seemed to be the one great aim of the South to convince the North that the latter made a mistake in fighting to preserve the Union and liberate the slaves. "Can you imagine," he went on to say, "what would have been the condition of things eventually if there had been no war, and the South had been allowed to follow its course? Instead of one great, prosperous country with nothing before it but the conquests of peace, a score of petty republics, as in Central and South America, wasting their energies in war with each other or in revolutions."

7. Grand Army of the Republic; a social organization of Union veterans formed in 1866, which after the Civil War and Emancipation, exercised considerable influence in electoral politics, especially within the Republican Party.
8. The immediate post–Civil War period (1865–77). During these years the Confederate states were readmitted back into the Union, conditional on the enfranchisement of newly freed African Americans. Empowered with the right to vote, protected by the Congressionally approved Civil Rights Acts of 1866 and 1875 (together with the constitutional guarantees of the Thirteenth through Fifteenth Amendments), and supported by white allies in the Republican Party, African Americans participated actively in postwar public life, running for (and winning) political posts across the South. Crucially, the presence of federal troops in the former Confederate states underscored the nation's commitment to this recovery process. In 1877, President Rutherford B. Hayes ended this show of unity, which ushered in the collapse of Reconstruction's achievements. The aftermath of Hayes's compromise, often called the "nadir" by historians, brought with it the implementation of segregation, the disenfranchisement of African American voters, and other forms of terrorism directed against blacks, including lynching.

"Well," replied the Texan, "anything—no country at all is better than having niggers over you. But anyhow, the war was fought and the niggers were freed; for it's no use beating around the bush, the niggers, and not the Union, was the cause of it; and now do you believe that all the niggers on earth are worth the good white blood that was spilt? You freed the nigger and you gave him the ballot, but you couldn't make a citizen out of him. He don't know what he's voting for, and we buy 'em like so many hogs. You're giving 'em education, but that only makes slick rascals out of 'em."

"Don't fancy for a moment," said, the Northern man, "that you have any monopoly in buying ignorant votes. The same thing is done on a larger scale in New York and Boston, and in Chicago and San Francisco; and they are not black votes either. As to education making the Negro worse, you had just as well tell me that religion does the same thing. And, by the way, how many educated colored men do you know personally?"

The Texan admitted that he knew only one, and added that he was in the penitentiary. "But," he said, "do you mean to claim, ballot or no ballot, education or no education, that niggers are the equals of white men?"

"That's not the question," answered the other, "but if the Negro is so distinctly inferior, it is a strange thing to me that it takes such tremendous effort on the part of the white man to make him realize it, and to keep him in the same place into which inferior men naturally fall. However, let us grant for sake of argument that the Negro is inferior in every respect to the white man; that fact only increases our moral responsibility in regard to our actions toward him. Inequalities of numbers, wealth and power, even of intelligence and morals, should make no difference in the essential rights of men."

"If he's inferior and weaker, and is shoved to the wall, that's his own look out," said the Texan. "That's the law of nature; and he's bound to go to the wall; for no race in the world has ever been able to stand competition with the Anglo-Saxon. The Anglo-Saxon race has always been and always will be the masters of the world, and the niggers in the South ain't going to change all the records of history."

"My friend," said the old soldier slowly, "if you have studied history, will you tell me, as confidentially between white men, what the Anglo-Saxon has ever done?"

The Texan was too much astonished by the question to venture any reply.

His opponent continued, "Can you name a single one of the great fundamental and original intellectual achievements which have raised man in the scale of civilization that may be credited to the Anglo-Saxon? The art of letters, of poetry, of music, of sculpture, of painting, of the drama, of architecture; the science of mathematics, of astronomy, of philosophy, of logic, of physics, of chemistry, the use of the metals and the principles of mechanics, were all invented or discovered by darker and what we now call inferior races and nations. We have carried many of these to their highest point of perfection, but the foundation was laid by others. Do you know the only original contribution to civilization we can claim is what we have done in steam and electricity and in making implements of war more deadly; and there we worked largely on principles which we did not discover. Why, we didn't even originate the religion we use. We are a great race, the greatest in the world to-day, but we ought to remember that we are standing on a pile of past races, and enjoy our position with a little less show of arrogance. We are simply having our turn at the game, and we were a long time getting to it. After all, racial supremacy is merely a matter of dates in history. The man here who belongs to what is, all in all, the greatest race the world ever produced, is almost ashamed to own it. If the Anglo-Saxon is the source of everything good and great in the human race from the beginning, why wasn't the German forest the birthplace of civilization?"

The Texan was somewhat disconcerted, for the argument had passed a little beyond his limits, but he swung it back to where he was sure of his ground by saying, "All that may be true, but it hasn't got much to do with us and the niggers here in the South. We've got 'em here, and we've got 'em to live with, and it's a question of white man or nigger, no middle ground. You want us to treat niggers as equals. Do you want to see 'em sitting around in our parlors? Do you want to see a mulatto South? To bring it right home to you, would you let your daughter marry a nigger?"

"No, I wouldn't consent to my daughter's marrying a nigger, but that doesn't prevent my treating a black man fairly. And I don't see what fair treatment has to do with niggers sitting around in your parlors; they can't come there unless they're invited. Out of all the white men I know, only a hundred or so have the privilege of sitting around in my parlor. As to the mulatto South, if you Southerners have one boast that is stronger than another, it is your women; you put them on a pinnacle of purity and virtue and bow down in a chivalric worship before them; yet you talk and act as though, should you treat the Negro fairly and take the anti-intermarriage laws off your statute books, these same women would rush into the arms of black lovers and husbands. It's a wonder to me that they don't rise up and resent the insult."

"Colonel," said the Texan, as he reached into his handbag and brought out a large flask of whiskey, "you might argue from now until hell freezes over, and you might convince me that you're right, but you'll never convince me that I'm wrong. All you say sounds very good, but it's got nothing to do with facts. You can say what men ought to be, but they ain't that; so there you are. Down here in the South we're up against facts, and we're meeting 'em like facts. We don't believe the nigger is or ever will be the equal of the white man, and we ain't going to treat him as an equal; I'll be damned if we will. Have a drink." Everybody, except the professor, partook of the generous Texan's flask, and the argument closed in a general laugh and good feeling.

I went back into the main part of the car with the conversation on my mind. Here I had before me the bald, raw, naked aspects of the race question in the South; and, in consideration of the step I was just taking, it was far from encouraging. The sentiments of the Texan—and he expressed the sentiments of the South—fell upon me like a chill. I was sick at heart. Yet, I must confess that underneath it all I felt a certain sort of admiration for the man who could not be swayed from what he held as his principles. Contrasted with him, the young Ohio professor was indeed a pitiable character. And all along, in spite of myself, I have been compelled to accord the same kind of admiration to the Southern white man for the manner in which he defends not only his virtues but his vices. He knows, that judged by a high standard, he is narrow and prejudiced, that he is guilty of unfairness, oppression and cruelty, but this he defends as stoutly as he would his better qualities. This same spirit obtains in a great degree among the blacks; they, too, defend their faults and failings. This spirit carries them so far at times as to make them sympathizers with members of their race who are perpetrators of crime. And, yet, among themselves they are their own most merciless critics. I have never heard the race so terribly arraigned as I have by colored speakers to strictly colored audiences. It is the spirit of the South to defend everything belonging to it. The North is too cosmopolitan and tolerant for such a spirit. If you should say to an Easterner that Paris is a gayer city than New York he would be likely to agree with you, or at least to let you have your way; but to suggest to a South Carolinian that Boston is a nicer city to live in than Charleston would be to stir his greatest depths of argument and eloquence.

But, to-day, as I think over that smoking-car argument, I can see it in a different light. The Texan's position does not render things so hopeless, for it indicates that the main difficulty of the race question does not lie so much in the actual condition of the blacks as it does in the mental attitude of the whites; and a mental attitude, especially one not based on truth, can be changed more easily than actual conditions. That is to say, the burden of the question is not that the whites are struggling to save ten million despondent and moribund people from sinking into a hopeless slough of ignorance, poverty and barbarity in their very midst, but that they are unwilling to open certain doors of opportunity and to accord certain treatment to ten million aspiring, education-and-property-acquiring people. In a word, the difficulty of the problem is not so much due to the facts presented, as to the hypothesis assumed for its solution. In this it is similar to the problem of the Solar System. By a complex, confusing and almost contradictory mathematical process, by the use of zigzags instead of straight lines, the earth can be proven to be the center of things celestial; but by an operation so simple that it can be comprehended by a schoolboy, its position can be verified among the other worlds which revolve about the sun, and its movements harmonized with the laws of the universe. So, when the white race assumes as a hypothesis that it is the main object of creation, and that all things else are merely subsidiary to its well being, sophism, subterfuge, perversion of conscience, arrogance, injustice, oppression, cruelty, sacrifice of human blood, all are required to maintain the position, and its dealings with other races become indeed a problem, a problem which, if based on a hypothesis of common humanity, could be solved by the simple rules of justice.

When I reached Macon I decided to leave my trunk and all my surplus belongings, to pack my bag, and strike out into the interior. This I did; and by train, by mule and ox-cart, I traveled through many counties. This was my first real experience among rural colored people, and all that I saw was interesting to me; but there was a great deal which does not require description at my hands; for log cabins and plantations and dialect-speaking darkies are perhaps better known in American literature than any other single picture of our national life. Indeed, they form an ideal and exclusive literary concept of the American Negro to such an extent that it is almost impossible to get the reading public to recognize him in any other setting; but I shall endeavor to avoid giving the reader any already overworked and hackneyed descriptions. This generally accepted literary ideal of the American Negro constitutes what is really an obstacle in the way of the thoughtful and progressive clement of the race. His character has been established as a happy-go-lucky, laughing, shuffling, banjo-picking being, and the reading public has not yet been prevailed upon to take him seriously. His efforts to elevate himself socially are looked upon as a sort of absurd caricature of "white civilization." A novel dealing with colored people who lived in respectable homes and amidst a fair degree of culture and who naturally acted "just like white folks" would be taken in a comic opera[9] sense. In this respect the Negro is much in the

9. Written for broad appeal, comic operas feature working-class protagonists instead of royalty or social elites and often stress spoken dialogue, as opposed to singing, to advance the action. Notably, around 1899 Johnson and his brother, Rosamond, composed

position of a great comedian who gives up the lighter rôles to play tragedy. No matter how well he may portray the deeper passions, the public is loth to give him up in his old character; they even conspire to make him a failure in serious work, in order to force him back into comedy. In the same respect, the public is not too much to be blamed, for great comedians are far more scarce than mediocre tragedians; every amateur actor is a tragedian. However, this very fact constitutes the opportunity of the future Negro novelist and poet to give the country something new and unknown, in depicting the life, the ambitions, the struggles and the passions of those of their race who are striving to break the narrow limits of traditions. A beginning has already been made in that remarkable book by Dr. Du Bois, "The Souls of Black Folk."[1]

Much, too, that I saw while on this trip, in spite of my enthusiasm, was disheartening. Often I thought of what my "millionaire" had said to me, and wished myself back in Europe. The houses in which I had to stay were generally uncomfortable, sometimes worse. I often had to sleep in a division or compartment with several other people. Once or twice I was not so fortunate as to find divisions; everybody slept on pallets on the floor. Frequently I was able to lie down and contemplate the stars which were in their zenith. The food was at times so distasteful and poorly cooked that I could not eat it. I remember that once I lived for a week or more on buttermilk, on account of not being able to stomach the fat bacon, the rank turnip tops and the heavy damp mixture of meal, salt and water, which was called corn bread. It was only my ambition to do the work which I had planned that kept me steadfast to my purpose. Occasionally I would meet with some signs of progress and uplift in even one of these backwood settlements—houses built

their own comic opera. *Tolosa, or the Royal Document* treated America's annexation of the Philippines, but the work was never staged.

1. William Edward Burghardt Du Bois, known as W. E. B. Du Bois (1868–1963), one of the great intellectuals and political activists in 20th century U.S. history; a Harvard-trained sociologist, historian, essayist, editor, and novelist who also helped found the National Association of Colored People. Over the course of his lifetime, Du Bois published more than thirty books, but *The Souls of Black Folk* (1903) remains the most famous. Weaving together sociological and historical essays, meditative memoir, lyric poetry, short fiction, and empirical analysis, it analyzes U.S. race relations from multiple vantage points that still resonate today. The book's critique of Booker T. Washington's educational philosophy (see p. 109, n. 5)—Du Bois dared to attack the Tuskegee University chancellor for renouncing liberal education over vocational training as the best means to uplift blacks economically, politically, and culturally—defined debates about the role of vanguard leadership (the class Du Bois dubbed the "Talented Tenth") in black politics. *Souls* also formulated two frameworks that are fundamental to African American cultural studies and twentieth-century humanist theory. "Double consciousness" explicates the two-pronged awareness that racial minorities possess to measure themselves in their relation to the dominant culture, and "the veil" symbolizes how racial segregation would dominate American and world politics as "the problem of the Twentieth Century."

of boards, with windows, and divided into rooms, decent food and a fair standard of living. This condition was due to the fact that there was in the community some exceptionally capable Negro farmer whose thrift served as an example. As I went about among these dull, simple people, the great majority of them hard working; in their relations with the whites, submissive, faithful, and often affectionate, negatively content with their lot, and contrasted them with those of the race who had been quickened by the forces of thought, I could not but appreciate the logic of the position held by those Southern leaders who have been bold enough to proclaim against the education of the Negro. They are consistent in their public speech with Southern sentiment and desires. Those public men of the South who have not been daring or heedless enough to defy the ideals of twentieth century civilization and of modern humanitarianism and philanthropy, find themselves in the embarrassing situation of preaching one thing and praying for another. They are in the position of the fashionable woman who is compelled by the laws of polite society to say to her dearest enemy, "How happy I am to see you."

And yet in this respect how perplexing is Southern character; for in opposition to the above, it may be said that the claim of the Southern whites that they love the Negro better than the Northern whites do, is in a manner true. Northern white people love the Negro in a sort of abstract way, as a race; through a sense of justice, charity and philanthropy, they will liberally assist in his elevation. A number of them have heroically spent their lives in this effort (and just here I wish to say that when the colored people reach the monument building stage, they should not forget the men and women who went South after the war and founded schools for them). Yet, generally speaking, they have no particular liking for individuals of the race. Southern white people despise the Negro as a race, and will do nothing to aid in his elevation as such; but for certain individuals they have a strong affection, and are helpful to them in many ways. With these individual members of the race they live on terms of the greatest intimacy; they intrust to them their children, their family treasures and their family secrets; in trouble they often go to them for comfort and counsel; in sickness they often rely upon their care. This affectionate relation between the Southern whites and those blacks who come into close touch with them has not been overdrawn even in fiction.

This perplexity of Southern character extends even to the mixture of the races. That is spoken of as though it were dreaded worse than smallpox, leprosy or the plague. Yet, when I was in Jacksonville I knew several prominent families there with large colored branches, which went by the same name and were known and acknowledged as blood relatives. And what is more, there seemed to exist between these black brothers and sisters and uncles and aunts a decided friendly feeling.

I said above that Southern whites would do nothing for the Negro as a race. I know the South claims that it has spent millions for the education of the blacks, and that it has of its own free will shouldered this awful burden. It seems to be forgetful of the fact that these millions have been taken from the public tax funds for education, and that the law of political economy which recognizes the land owner as the one who really pays the taxes is not tenable. It would be just as reasonable for the relatively few landowners of Manhattan to complain that they had to stand the financial burden of the education of the thousands and thousands of children whose parents pay rent for tenements and flats. Let the millions of producing and consuming Negroes be taken out of the South, and it would be quickly seen how much less of public funds there would be to appropriate for education or any other purpose.

In thus traveling about through the country, I was sometimes amused on arriving at some little railroad-station town to be taken for and treated as a white man, and six hours later, when it was learned that I was stopping at the house of the colored preacher or school teacher, to note the attitude of the whole town change. At times this led even to embarrassment. Yet it cannot be so embarrassing for a colored man to be taken for white as for a white man to be taken for colored; and I have heard of several cases of the latter kind.

All this while I was gathering material for work, jotting down in my note-book themes and melodies, and trying to catch the spirit of the Negro in his relatively primitive state. I began to feel the necessity of hurrying so that I might get back to some city like Nashville to begin my compositions, and at the same time earn at least a living by teaching and performing before my funds gave out. At the last settlement in which I stopped I found a mine of material. This was due to the fact that "big meeting" was in progress. "Big meeting" is an institution something like camp-meeting; the difference being that it is held in a permanent church, and not in a temporary structure. All the churches of some one denomination—of course, either Methodist or Baptist—in a county or, perhaps, in several adjoining counties, are closed, and the congregations unite at some centrally located church for a series of meetings lasting a week. It is really a social as well as a religious function. The people come in great numbers, making the trip, according to their financial status, in buggies drawn by sleek, fleet-footed mules, in ox-teams, or on foot. It was amusing to see some of the latter class trudging down the hot and dusty road with their shoes, which were brand new, strung across their shoulders. When they got near the church they sat on the side of the road and, with many grimaces, tenderly packed their feet into those instruments of torture.

This furnished, indeed, a trying test of their religion. The famous preachers come from near and far, and take turns in warning sinners of the day of wrath. Food, in the form of those two Southern luxuries, fried chicken and roast pork, is plentiful, and no one need go hungry. On the opening Sunday the women are immaculate in starched stiff white dresses adorned with ribbons either red or blue. Even a great many of the men wear streamers of vari-colored ribbons in the button-holes of their coats. A few of them carefully cultivate a fore lock of hair by wrapping it in twine, and on such festive occasions decorate it with a narrow ribbon streamer. Big meetings afford a fine opportunity to the younger people to meet each other dressed in their Sunday clothes, and much rustic courting, which is as enjoyable as any other kind, is indulged in.

This big meeting which I was lucky enough to catch was particularly well attended; the extra large attendance was due principally to two attractions, a man by name of John Brown,[2] who was renowned as the most powerful preacher for miles around; and a wonderful leader of singing, who was known as "Singing Johnson." These two men were a study and a revelation to me. They caused me to reflect upon how great an influence their types have been in the development of the Negro in America. Both these types are now looked upon generally with condescension or contempt by the progressive clement among the colored people; but it should never be forgotten that it was they who led the race from paganism, and kept it steadfast to Christianity through all the long, dark years of slavery.

John Brown was a jet black man of medium size, with a strikingly intelligent head and face, and a voice like an organ peal. He preached each night after several lesser lights successively held the pulpit during an hour or so. As far as subject matter is concerned, all of the sermons were alike; each began with the fall of man, ran through various trials and tribulations of the Hebrew children, on to the redemption by Christ, and ended with a fervid picture of the judgment day and the fate of the damned. But John Brown possessed magnetism and an imagination so free and daring that he was able to carry through what the other preachers would not attempt. He knew all the arts and tricks of oratory, the modulation of the voice to almost a whisper, the pause for effect, the rise through light, rapid fire sentences to the terrific, thundering outburst of an electrifying climax. In addition, he had the intuition of a born theatrical manager. Night after night this man held me fascinated. He convinced me that, after

2. Also the name of the radical white abolitionist (1800–1859) who advocated violent revolt against slavery. In 1859 Brown and twenty-one followers raided a federal arsenal at Harpers Ferry, Virginia. Their goal was to confiscate weapons to arm a slave rebellion. Brown's plot was defeated by U.S. troops led by General Robert E. Lee. Brown was tried, sentenced, and executed (by hanging) for treason.

all, eloquence consists more in the manner of saying than in what is said. It is largely a matter of tone pictures.

The most striking example of John Brown's magnetism and imagination was his "heavenly march";[3] I shall never forget how it impressed me when I heard it. He opened his sermon in the usual way; then proclaiming to his listeners that he was going to take them on the heavenly march, he seized the Bible under his arm and began to pace up and down the pulpit platform. The congregation immediately began with their feet a tramp, tramp, tramp, in time with the preacher's march in the pulpit, all the while singing in an undertone a hymn about marching to Zion.[4] Suddenly he cried, "Halt!" Every foot stopped with the precision of a company of well drilled soldiers, and the singing ceased. The morning star had been reached. Here the preacher described the beauties of that celestial body. Then the march, the tramp, tramp, tramp, and the singing was again taken up. Another "Halt!" They had reached the evening star. And so on, past the sun and the moon—the intensity of religious emotion all the time increasing—along the milky way, on up to the gates of heaven. Here the halt was longer, and the preacher described at length the gates and walls of the New Jerusalem.[5] Then he took his hearers through the pearly gates, along the golden streets, pointing out the glories of the City, pausing occasionally to greet some patriarchal members of the church, well known to most of his listeners in life, who had had "the tears wiped from their eyes, were clad in robes of spotless white, with crowns of gold upon their heads and harps within their hands," and ended his march before the great white throne. To the reader this may sound ridiculous, but listened to under the circumstances, it was highly and effectively dramatic. I was a more or less sophisticated and non-religious man of the world, but the torrent of the preacher's words, moving with the rhythm and glowing with the eloquence of primitive poetry swept me along, and I, too, felt like joining in the shouts of "Amen! Hallelujah!"

John Brown's powers in describing the delights of heaven were no greater than those in depicting the horrors of hell. I saw great, strapping fellows, trembling and weeping like children at the "mourners' bench."[6] His warnings to sinners were truly terrible. I shall never forget one expression that he used, which for originality

3. A popular sermon theme in early twentieth-century African American liturgy. As Johnson described it in the preface to *God's Trombones* (1927), this sermon "gave in detail the journey of the faithful from earth, on up through the pearly gates to the great white throne."
4. Israel, or the Promised Land. In African American Christianity, believers have often identified with Old Testament stories of the Israelites' sufferings and migrations; thus Zion symbolizes an existential refuge.
5. I.e., Zion.
6. In African American evangelical liturgy, an altar or bench usually located at the front of a church where sinners were encouraged to pray publicly for penance.

and aptness could not be excelled. In my opinion, it is more graphic and, for us, far more expressive than St. Paul's "It is hard to kick against the pricks." He struck the attitude of a pugilist and thundered out, "Young man, yo' arm's too short to box wid God!"

As interesting as was John Brown to me, the other man, "Singing Johnson," was more so. He was a small, dark-brown, one-eyed man, with a clear, strong, high-pitched voice, a leader of singing, a maker of songs, a man who could improvise at the moment lines to fit the occasion. Not so striking a figure as John Brown, but, at "big meetings," equally important. It is indispensable to the success of the singing, when the congregation is a large one made up of people from different communities, to have someone with a strong voice who knows just what hymn to sing and when to sing it, who can pitch it in the right key, and who has all the leading lines committed to memory. Sometimes it devolves upon the leader to "sing down" a long-winded, or uninteresting speaker. Committing to memory the leading lines of all the Negro spiritual songs is no easy task, for they run up into the hundreds. But the accomplished leader must know them all, because the congregation sings only the refrains and repeats; every ear in the church is fixed upon him, and if he becomes mixed in his lines or forgets them, the responsibility falls directly on his shoulders.

For example, most of these hymns are constructed to be sung in the following manner:

Lender—	"Swing low, sweet chariot."
Congregation—	"Coming for to carry me home."
Leader—	"Swing low, sweet chariot."
Congregation—	"Coming for to entry me home."
Leader—	"I look over yonder, what do I see?"
Congregation—	"Coming for to carry me home."
Leader—	Two little angels coming after me."
Congregation—	"Coming for to carry me home."
—	etc., etc., etc.

The solitary and plaintive voice of the leader is answered by a sound like the roll of the sea, producing a most curious effect.[7]

In only a few of these songs do the leader and the congregation start off together. Such a song is the well known "Steal away to Jesus."

7. The spirituals mentioned here contain references to the Underground Railroad, a network of antislavery activists who helped fugitive slaves escape to freedom in the northern United States and Canada. "Swing Low, Sweet Chariot" features call and response, a rhetorical style characteristic of African American music. As the narrator observes, the congregation sings back (responds) what the performer has sung (the call). This exchange makes authorship and performance collective, as it blurs the line separating artist from audience.

The leader and the congregation begin:

"Steal away, steal away,
Steal away to Jesus;
Steal away, steal away home,
I ain't got long to stay here."

Then the leader alone:

"My Lord he calls me,
He calls me by the thunder,
The trumpet sounds within-a my soul."

Then all together:

"I ain't got long to stay here."

The leader and the congregation again take up the opening refrain; then the leader sings three more leading lines alone, and so on almost ad infinitum. It will be seen that even here most of the work falls upon the leader, for the congregation sings the same lines over and over, while his memory and ingenuity are taxed to keep the songs going.

Generally, the parts taken up by the congregation are sung in a three-part harmony, the women singing the soprano and a transposed tenor, the men with high voices singing the melody, and those with low voices, a thundering bass. In a few of these songs, however, the leading part is sung in unison by the whole congregation, down to the last line, which is harmonized. The effect of this is intensely thrilling. Such a hymn is "Go down Moses." It stirs the heart like a trumpet call.

"Singing Johnson" was an ideal leader; and his services were in great demand. He spent his time going about the country from one church to another. He received his support in much the same way as the preachers,—part of a collection, food and lodging. All of his leisure time he devoted to originating new words and melodies and new lines for old songs. He always sang with his eyes,—or to be more exact—his eye closed, indicating the tempo by swinging his head to and fro. He was a great judge of the proper hymn to sing at a particular moment; and I noticed several times, when the preacher reached a certain climax, or expressed a certain sentiment, that Johnson broke in with a line or two of some appropriate hymn. The speaker understood, and would pause until the singing ceased.

As I listened to the singing of these songs, the wonder of their production grew upon me more and more. How did the men who originated them manage to do it? The sentiments are easily accounted for; they are mostly taken from the Bible; but the melodies, where did they come from? Some of them so weirdly sweet, and others so wonderfully strong. Take, for instance, "Go down Moses." I doubt that there is a stronger theme in the whole musical literature of the world. And so many of these songs contain more than mere melody; there is sounded in them that elusive undertone, the note in music which is not heard with the ears. I sat often with the tears rolling down my checks and my heart melted within me. Any musical person who has never heard a Negro congregation under the spell of religious fervor sing these old songs, has missed one of the most thrilling emotions which the human heart may experience. Anyone who can listen to Negroes sing, "Nobody knows de trouble I see, Nobody knows but Jesus," without shedding tears, must indeed have a heart of stone.[8]

As yet, the Negroes themselves do not fully appreciate these old slave songs. The educated classes are rather ashamed of them, and prefer to sing hymns from books. This feeling is natural; they are still too close to the conditions under which the songs were produced; but the day will come when this slave music will be the most treasured heritage of the American Negro.

At the close of the "big meeting" I left the settlement where it was being held, full of enthusiasm. I was in that frame of mind which, in the artistic temperament, amounts to inspiration. I was now ready and anxious to get to some place where I might settle down to work, and give expression the ideas which were teeming in my head; but I strayed into another deviation from my path of life as I had it marked out, which led me into an entirely different road. Instead of going to the nearest and most convenient railroad station, I accepted the invitation of a young man who had been present the closing Sunday at the meeting, to drive with him some miles farther to the town in which he taught school, and there take the train. My conversation with this young man as we drove along through the country was extremely interesting. He had been a student in one of the Negro colleges,—strange coincidence, in the very college, as I learned through him, in which "Shiny" was now a professor. I was, of course, curious to hear about my boyhood friend; and had it not been vacation time, and that I was not sure that I would find him, I should have gone out of my way to pay him a visit; but I determined to write to him as soon as the school opened. My companion talked to me about his work among the people, of his hopes and his discouragements. He was tremendously in earnest; I might say, too much so. In fact, it may be said that the majority of intelligent colored people are, in some degree, too much in earnest

8. The "sorrow songs" discussed here differ from spirituals because the lyrics stress the singer's suffering. For more on this distinction, see Du Bois's essay on p. 179 in this volume.

over the race question. They assume and carry so much that their progress is at times impeded, and they are unable to see things in their proper proportions. In many instances, a slight exercise of the sense of humor would save much anxiety of soul. Anyone who marks the general tone of editorials in colored newspapers is apt to be impressed with this idea. If the mass of Negroes took their present and future as seriously as do the most of their leaders, the race would be in no mental condition to sustain the terrible pressure which it undergoes; it would sink of its own weight. Yet, it must be acknowledged that in the making of a race over-seriousness is a far lesser failing than its reverse, and even the faults resulting from it lean toward the right.

We drove into the town just before dark. As we passed a large, unpainted church, my companion pointed it out as the place where he held his school. I promised that I would go there with him the next morning and stay a while. The town was of that kind which hardly requires or deserves description; a straggling line of brick and wooden stores on one side of the railroad track and some cottages of various sizes on the other side constituted about the whole of it. The young school teacher boarded at the best house in the place owned by a colored man. It was painted, had glass windows, contained "store bought" furniture, an organ, and lamps with chimneys. The owner held a job of some kind on the railroad. After supper it was not long before everybody was sleepy. I occupied the room with the school teacher. In a few minutes after we got into the room he was in bed and asleep; but I took advantage of the unusual luxury of a lamp which gave light, and sat looking over my notes and jotting down some ideas which were still fresh in my mind. Suddenly I became conscious of that sense of alarm which is always aroused by the sound of hurrying footsteps on the silence of the night. I stopped work, and looked at my watch. It was after eleven. I listened, straining every nerve to hear above the tumult of my quickening pulse. I caught the murmur of voices, then the gallop of a horse, then of another and another. Now thoroughly alarmed, I woke my companion, and together we both listened. After a moment he put out the light, softly opened the window-blind, and we cautiously peeped out. We saw men moving in one direction, and from the mutterings we vaguely caught the rumor that some terrible crime had been committed, murder! rape! I put on my coat and hat. My friend did all in his power to dissuade me from venturing out; but it was impossible for me to remain in the house under such tense excitement. My nerves would not have stood it. Perhaps what bravery I exercised in going out was due to the fact that I felt sure my identity as a colored man had not yet become known in the town.

I went out, and, following the drift, reached the railroad station. There was gathered there a crowd of men, all white, and others were steadily arriving, seemingly from all the surrounding country. How did the news spread so quickly? I watched these men moving under the yellow glare of the kerosene lamps about the station, stern, comparatively silent, all of them armed, some of them in boots and spurs; fierce, determined men. I had come to know the type well, blond, tall and lean, with ragged mustache and beard, and glittering gray eyes. At the first suggestion of daylight they began to disperse in groups, going in several directions. There was no extra noise or excitement, no loud talking, only swift, sharp words of command given by those who seemed to be accepted as leaders by mutual understanding. In fact, the impression made upon me was that everything was being done in quite an orderly manner. In spite of so many leaving, the crowd around the station continued to grow; at sunrise there were a great many women and children. By this time I also noticed some colored people; a few seemed to be going about customary tasks, several were standing on the outskirts of the crowd; but the gathering of Negroes usually seen in such towns was missing.

Before noon they brought him in. Two horsemen rode abreast; between them, half dragged, the poor wretch made his way through the dust. His hands were tied behind him, and ropes around his body were fastened to the saddle horns of his double guard. The men who at midnight had been stern and silent were now emitting that terror instilling sound known as the "rebel yell."[9] A space was quickly cleared in the crowd, and a rope placed about his neck; when from somewhere came the suggestion, "Burn him!" It ran like an electric current. Have you ever witnessed the transformation of human beings into savage beasts? Nothing can be more terrible. A railroad tie was sunk into the ground, the rope was removed and a chain brought and securely coiled around the victim and the stake. There he stood, a man only in form and stature, every sign of degeneracy stamped upon his countenance. His eyes were dull and vacant, indicating not a single ray of thought. Evidently the realization of his fearful fate had robbed him of whatever reasoning power he had ever possessed. He was too stunned and stupefied even to tremble. Fuel was brought from everywhere, oil, the torch; the flames crouched for an instant, as though to gather strength, then leaped up as high as their victim's head. He squirmed, he writhed, strained at his chains, then gave out cries and groans that I shall

9. The battle cry of Confederate troops during battle charges. The yell's origins and sound have been traced to both Native American and Celtic sources. The high-pitched but guttural screams and whoops were meant to intimidate Confederates' opponents.

always hear. The cries and groans were choked off by the fire and smoke; but his eyes bulging from their sockets, rolled from side to side, appealing in vain for help. Some of the crowd yelled and cheered, others seemed appalled at what they had done, and there were those who turned away sickened at the sight. I was fixed to the spot where I stood, powerless to take my eyes from what I did not want to see.

It was over before I realized that time had elapsed. Before I could make myself believe that what I saw was really happening, I was looking at a scorched post, a smoldering fire, blackened bones, charred fragments sifting down through coils of chain, and the smell of burnt flesh—human flesh—was in my nostrils.

I walked a short distance away, and sat down in order to clear my dazed mind. A great wave of humiliation and shame swept over me. Shame that I belonged to a race that could be so dealt with; and shame for my country, that it, the great example of democracy to the world, should be the only civilized, if not the only state on earth, where a human being would be burned alive. My heart turned bitter within me. I could understand why Negroes are led to sympathize with even their worst criminals, and to protect them when possible. By all the impulses of normal human nature they can and should do nothing less.

Whenever I hear protests from the South that it should be left alone to deal with the Negro question, my thoughts go back to that scene of brutality and savagery. I do not see how a people that can find in its conscience any excuse whatever for slowly burning to death a human being, or to tolerate such an act, can be entrusted with the salvation of a race. Of course, there are in the South men of liberal thought who do not approve lynching; but I wonder how long they will endure the limits which are placed upon free speech. They still cower and tremble before "Southern opinion." Even so late as the recent Atlanta riot,[1] those men who were brave enough to speak a word in behalf of justice and humanity felt called upon, by way of apology, to preface what they said with a glowing rhetorical tribute to the Anglo-Saxon's superiority, and to refer to the "great and impassable gulf" between the races "fixed by the Creator at the foundation of the world." The question of the relative qualities of the two races is still an open one. The reference to the "great

1. The September 22–23, 1906, riot was ostensibly provoked by sensationalized news accounts of alleged crimes committed by blacks across the city, but two structural shifts actually triggered the violence. First, the current gubernatorial campaign saw candidate Hoke Smith stir anti-Negro sentiment among the white electorate. Second, simmering beneath the fear of black crime was white anxiety about African Americans' increased economic mobility. By the riot's end, two whites and more than twenty-five blacks had been killed.

gulf" loses force in face of the fact that there are in this country perhaps three or four million people with the blood of both races in their veins; but I fail to see the pertinency of either statement, subsequent to the beating and murdering of scores of innocent people in the streets of a civilized and Christian city.

The Southern whites are in many respects a great people. Looked at from a certain point of view, they are picturesque. If one will put himself in a romantic frame of mind, he can admire their notions of chivalry and bravery and justice. In this same frame of mind an intelligent man can go to the theater and applaud the impossible hero, who with his single sword slays everybody in the play except the equally impossible heroine. So can an ordinary peace-loving citizen sit by a comfortable fire and read with enjoyment of the bloody deeds of pirates and the fierce brutality of Vikings.[2] This is the way in which we gratify the old, underlying animal instincts and passions; but we should shudder with horror at the mere idea of such practices being realities in this day of enlightened and humanitarianized thought. The Southern whites are not yet living quite in the present age; many of their general ideas hark back to a former century, some of them to the Dark Ages.[3] In the light of other days, they are sometimes magnificent. To-day they are often ludicrous and cruel.

How long I sat with bitter thoughts running through my mind, I do not know; perhaps an hour or more. When I decided to get up and go back to the house I found that I could hardly stand on my feet. I was as weak as a man who had lost blood. However, I dragged myself along, with the central idea of a general plan well fixed in my mind. I did not find my school teacher friend at home, so did not see him again. I swallowed a few mouthfuls of food, packed my bag, and caught the afternoon train.

When I reached Macon, I stopped only long enough to get the main part of my luggage, and to buy a ticket for New York. All along the journey I was occupied in debating with myself the step which I had decided to take. I argued that to forsake one's race to better one's condition was no less worthy an action than to forsake one's country for the same purpose. I finally made up my mind that I would neither disclaim the black race nor claim the white race; but that I would change my name, raise a mustache, and let the world take me for what it would; that it was not necessary for me to go about with a label of inferiority pasted across my forehead. All the

2. Scandinavian warriors and pirates whose maritime prowess allowed them to invade and conquer wide swaths of Europe, from the eighth to eleventh centuries.
3. A period of European history (476–1000) marked by the absence of stable nation-states and the rise political chaos in the forms of intellectual backwardness, severe barbarity, and frequent warfare.

while, I understood that it was not discouragement, or fear, or search for a larger field of action and opportunity, that was driving me out of the Negro race. I knew that it was shame, unbearable shame. Shame at being identified with a people that could with impunity be treated worse than animals. For certainly the law would restrain and punish the malicious burning alive of animals.

So once again, I found myself gazing at the towers of New York, and wondering what future that city held in store for me.

Chapter XI

I have now reached that part of my narrative where I must be brief, and touch only lightly on important facts; therefore, the reader must make up his mind to pardon skips and jumps and meager details.

When I reached New York I was completely lost. I could not have felt more a stranger had I been suddenly dropped into Constantinople.[4] I knew not where to turn or how to strike out. I was so oppressed by a feeling of loneliness that the temptation to visit my old home in Connecticut was well nigh irresistible. I reasoned, however, that unless I found my old music teacher, I should be, after so many years of absence, as much of a stranger there as in New York; and, furthermore, that in view of the step which I had decided to take, such a visit would be injudicious. I remembered, too, that I had some property there in the shape of a piano and a few books, but decided that it would not be worth what it might cost me to take possession.

By reason of the fact that my living expenses in the South had been very small, I still had nearly four hundred dollars of my capital left. In contemplation of this, my natural and acquired Bohemian tastes asserted themselves, and I decided to have a couple of weeks' good time before worrying seriously about the future. I went to Coney Island[5] and the other resorts, took in the pre-season shows along Broadway, and ate at first class restaurants; but I shunned the old Sixth Avenue district as though it were pest infected. My few days of pleasure made appalling inroads upon what cash I had, and caused me to see that it required a good deal of money to live in New York as I wished to live, and that I should have to find, very soon, some more or less profitable employment. I was sure that unknown, without friends or prestige, it would be useless to try to establish

4. Now Istanbul, Turkey; was the capital of the Byzantine, Roman, and Ottoman Empires. Because of this lineage, the city's cultural history is a special allusion for the narrator to make in this moment, as it served as the seat of three fallen empires.
5. An amusement park located at the southern end of Brooklyn, New York. A summer destination for wealthy New Yorkers before the Civil War, Coney Island later became a leisure destination for the middle- and working-classes as public transportation became more affordable by the end of the 1800s. Coney Island still operates at present.

myself as a teacher of music; so I gave that means of earning a livelihood scarcely any consideration. And even had I considered it possible to secure pupils, as I then felt, I should have hesitated about taking up a work in which the chances for any considerable financial success are necessarily so small. I had made up my mind that since I was not going to be a Negro, I would avail myself of every possible opportunity to make a white man's success; and that, if it can be summed up in any one word, means "money."

I watched the "want" columns in the newspapers and answered a number of advertisements; but in each case found the positions were such as I could not fill or did not want. I also spent several dollars for "ads" which brought me no replies. In this way I came to know the hopes and disappointments of a large and pitiable class of humanity in this great city, the people who look for work through the newspapers. After some days of this sort of experience, I concluded that the main difficulty with me was that I was not prepared for what I wanted to do. I then decided upon a course which, for an artist, showed an uncommon amount of practical sense and judgment. I made up my mind to enter a business college. I took a small room, ate at lunch counters, in order to economize, and pursued my studies with the zeal that I have always been able to put into any work upon which I set my heart. Yet, in spite of all my economy, when I had been at the school for several months, my funds gave out completely. I reached the point where I could not afford sufficient food for each day. In this plight, I was glad to get, through one of the teachers, a job as an ordinary clerk in a downtown wholesale house. I did my work faithfully, and received a raise of salary before I expected it. I even managed to save a little money out of my modest earnings. In fact, I began then to contract the money fever, which later took strong possession of me. I kept my eyes open, watching for a chance to better my condition. It finally came in the form of a position with a house which was at the time establishing a South American department. My knowledge of Spanish was, of course, the principal cause of my good luck; and it did more for me; it placed me where the other clerks were practically put out of competition with me. I was not slow in taking advantage of the opportunity to make myself indispensable to the firm.

What an interesting and absorbing game is money making! After each deposit at my savings-bank, I used to sit and figure out, all over again, my principal and interest, and make calculations on what the increase would be in such and such time. Out of this I derived a great deal of pleasure. I denied myself as much as possible in order to swell my savings. Even so much as I enjoyed smoking, I limited myself to an occasional cigar, and that was generally of a variety which in my old days at the "Club" was known as a "Henry Mud." Drinking I cut out altogether, but that was no great sacrifice.

The day on which I was able to figure up $1,000.00 marked an epoch in my life. And this was not because I had never before had money. In my gambling days and while I was with my "millionaire" I handled sums running high up into the hundreds; but they had come to me like fairy god-mother's gifts, and at a time when my conception of money was that it was made only to spend. Here, on the other hand, was a thousand dollars which I had earned by days of honest and patient work, a thousand dollars which I had carefully watched grow from the first dollar; and I experienced, in owning them, a pride and satisfaction which to me was an entirely new sensation. As my capital went over the thousand dollar mark, I was puzzled to know what to do with it, how to put it to the most advantageous use. I turned down first one scheme and then another, as though they had been devised for the sole purpose of gobbling up my money. I finally listened to a friend who advised me to put all I had in New York real estate; and under his guidance I took equity in a piece of property on which stood a rickety old tenement-house. I did not regret following this friend's advice, for in something like six months I disposed of my equity for more than double my investment. From that time on I devoted myself to the study of New York real estate, and watched for opportunities to make similar investments. In spite of two or three speculations which did not turn out well, I have been remarkably successful. To-day I am the owner and part-owner of several flat-houses. I have changed my place of employment four times since returning to New York, and each change has been a decided advancement. Concerning the position which I now hold, I shall say nothing except that it pays extremely well.

As my outlook on the world grew brighter, I began to mingle in the social circles of the men with whom I came in contact; and gradually, by a process of elimination, I reached a grade of society of no small degree of culture. My appearance was always good and my ability to play on the piano, especially ragtime, which was then at the height of its vogue, made me a welcome guest. The anomaly of my social position often appealed strongly to my sense of humor. I frequently smiled inwardly at some remark not altogether complimentary to people of color; and more than once I felt like declaiming, "I am a colored man. Do I not disprove the theory that one drop of Negro blood renders a man unfit?" Many a night when I returned to my room after an enjoyable evening, I laughed heartily over what struck me as the capital joke I was playing.

Then I met her, and what I had regarded as a joke was gradually changed into the most serious question of my life.[6] I first saw her at

6. JWJ revised Chapter XI substantially. The narrative from this point to n. 3 at p. 109 did not appear in the original draft manuscript. To compare, see Appendix B, pp. 115–21.

a musical which was given one evening at a house to which I was frequently invited. I did not notice her among the other guests before she came forward and sang two sad little songs. When she began I was out in the hallway where many of the men were gathered; but with the first few notes I crowded with others into the doorway to see who the singer was. When I saw the girl, the surprise which I had felt at the first sound of her voice was heightened; she was almost tall and quite slender, with lustrous yellow hair and eyes so blue as to appear almost black. She was as white as a lily, and she was dressed in white. Indeed, she seemed to me the most dazzlingly white thing I had ever seen. But it was not her delicate beauty which attracted me most; it was her voice, a voice which made one wonder how tones of such passionate color could come from so fragile a body.

I determined that when the programme was over I would seek an introduction to her; but at the moment, instead of being the easy man of the world, I became again the bashful boy of fourteen, and my courage failed me. I contented myself with hovering as near her as politeness would permit; near enough to hear her voice, which in conversation was low, yet thrilling, like the deeper middle tones of a flute. I watched the men gather around her talking and laughing in an easy manner, and wondered how it was possible for them to do it. But destiny, my special destiny, was at work. I was standing near, talking with affected gayety to several young ladies, who, however, must have remarked my preoccupation; for my second sense of hearing was alert to what was being said by the group of which the girl in white was the center, when I heard her say, "I think his playing of Chopin is exquisite." And one of my friends in the group replied, "You haven't met him? Allow me—" then turning to me, "Old man, when you have a moment I wish you to meet Miss ——." I don't know what she said to me or what I said to her. I can remember that I tried to be clever, and experienced a growing conviction that I was making myself appear more and more idiotic. I am certain, too, that, in spite of my Italian-like complexion, I was as red as a beet.

Instead of taking the car I walked home. I needed the air and exercise as a sort of sedative. I am not sure whether my troubled condition of mind was due to the fact that I had been struck by love or to the feeling that I had made a bad impression upon her.

As the weeks went by, and when I had met her several more times, I came to know that I was seriously in love; and then began for me days of worry, for I had more than the usual doubts and fears of a young man in love to contend with.

Up to this time I had assumed and played my rôle as a white man with a certain degree of nonchalance, a carelessness as to the outcome, which made the whole thing more amusing to me than serious; but now I ceased to regard "being a white man" as a sort of practical joke. My acting had called for mere external effects. Now I began to doubt my ability to play the part. I watched her to see if she was scrutinizing me, to see if she was looking for anything in me which made me differ from the other men she knew. In place of an old inward feeling of superiority over many of my friends, I began to doubt myself. I began even to wonder if I really was like the men I associated with; if there was not, after all, an indefinable something which marked a difference.

But, in spite of my doubts and timidity, my affair progressed; and I finally felt sufficiently encouraged to decide to ask her to marry me. Then began the hardest struggle of my life, whether to ask her to marry me under false colors or to tell her the whole truth. My sense of what was exigent made me feel there was no necessity of saying anything; but my inborn sense of honor rebelled at even indirect deception in this case. But however much I moralized on the question, I found it more and more difficult to reach the point of confession. The dread that I might lose her took possession of me each time I sought to speak, and rendered it impossible for me to do so. That moral courage requires more than physical courage is no mere poetic fancy. I am sure I would have found it easier to take the place of a gladiator, no matter how fierce the Numidian[7] lion, than to tell that slender girl that I had Negro blood in my veins. The fact which I had at times wished to cry out, I now wished to hide forever.

During this time we were drawn together a great deal by the mutual bond of music. She loved to hear me play Chopin, and was herself far from being a poor performer of his compositions. I think I carried her every new song that was published which I thought suitable to her voice, and played the accompaniment for her. Over these songs we were like two innocent children with new toys. She had never been anything but innocent; but my innocence was a transformation wrought by my love for her, love which melted away my cynicism and whitened my sullied soul and gave me back the wholesome dreams of my boyhood. There is nothing better in all the world that a man can do for his moral welfare than to love a good woman.

My artistic temperament also underwent an awakening. I spent many hours at my piano, playing over old and new composers. I also wrote several little pieces in a more or less Chopinesque style, which I dedicated to her. And so the weeks and months went by. Often words of love trembled on my lips, but I dared not utter them, because I knew they would have to be followed by other words which I had not the courage to frame. There might have been some other woman in my set with whom I could have fallen in love and asked

7. A semi-nomadic tribe of the first century B.C.E. who lived in what is now Algeria, in North Africa.

to marry me without a word of explanation; but the more I knew this girl, the less could I find it in my heart to deceive her. And yet, in spite of this specter that was constantly looming up before me, I could never have believed that life held such happiness as was contained in those dream days of love.

One Saturday afternoon, in early June, I was coming up Fifth Avenue, and at the corner of Twenty-third Street I met her. She had been shopping. We stopped to chat for a moment, and I suggested that we spend half an hour at the Eden Musée.[8] We were standing leaning on the rail in front of a group of figures, more interested in what we had to say to each other than in the group, when my attention became fixed upon a man who stood at my side studying his catalogue. It took me only an instant to recognize in him my old friend "Shiny." My first impulse was to change my position at once. As quick as a flash I considered all the risks I might run in speaking to him, and most especially the delicate question of introducing him to her. I must confess that in my embarrassment and confusion I felt small and mean. But before I could decide what to do he looked around at me and, after an instant, said, "Pardon me; but isn't this ——?" The nobler part in me responded to the sound of his voice, and I took his hand in a hearty clasp. Whatever fears I had felt were quickly banished, for he seemed, at a glance, to divine my situation, and let drop no word that would have aroused suspicion as to the truth. With a slight misgiving I presented him to her, and was again relieved of fear. She received the introduction in her usual gracious manner, and without the least hesitancy or embarrassment joined in the conversation. An amusing part about the introduction was that I was upon the point of introducing him as "Shiny," and stammered a second or two before I could recall his name. We chatted for some fifteen minutes. He was spending his vacation North, with the intention of doing four or six weeks' work in one of the summer schools; he was also going to take a bride back with him in the fall. He asked me about myself, but in so diplomatic a way that I found no difficulty in answering him. The polish of his language and the unpedantic manner in which he revealed his culture greatly impressed her; and after we had left the Musée she showed it by questioning me about him. I was surprised at the amount of interest a refined black man could arouse. Even after changes in the conversation she reverted several times to the subject of "Shiny." Whether it was more than mere curiosity I could not tell; but I was convinced that she herself knew very little about prejudice.

8. A wax museum located in midtown Manhattan from 1883 to 1915.

Just why it should have done so I do not know; but somehow the "Shiny" incident gave me encouragement and confidence to cast the die of my fate; but I reasoned that since I wanted to marry her only, and since it concerned her alone, I would divulge my secret to no one else, not even her parents.

One evening, a few days afterwards, at her home, we were going over some new songs and compositions, when she asked me, as she often did, to play the "13th Nocturne."[9] When I began she drew a chair near to my right, and sat leaning with her elbow on the end of the piano, her chin resting on her hand, and her eyes reflecting the emotions which the music awoke in her. An impulse which I could not control rushed over me, a wave of exaltation, the music under my fingers sank almost to a whisper, and calling her for the first time by her Christian name, but without daring to look at her, I said, "I love you, I love you, I love you." My fingers were trembling, so that I ceased playing. I felt her hand creep to mine, and when I looked at her her eyes were glistening with tears. I understood, and could scarcely resist the longing to take her in my arms; but I remembered, remembered that which has been the sacrificial altar of so much happiness—Duty; and bending over her hand in mine, I said, "Yes, I love you; but there is something more, too, that I must tell you." Then I told her, in what words I do not know, the truth. I felt her hand grow cold, and when I looked up she was gazing at me with a wild, fixed stare as though I was some object she had never seen. Under the strange light in her eyes I felt that I was growing black and thick-featured and crimp-haired. She appeared not to have comprehended what I had said. Her lips trembled and she attempted to say something to me; but the words stuck in her throat. Then dropping her head on the piano she began to weep with great sobs that shook her frail body. I tried to console her, and blurted out incoherent words of love; but this seemed only to increase her distress, and when I left her she was still weeping.

When I got into the street I felt very much as I did the night after meeting my father and sister at the opera in Paris, even a similar desperate inclination to get drunk; but my self-control was stronger. This was the only time in my life that I ever felt absolute regret at being colored, that I cursed the drops of African blood in my veins, and wished that I were really white. When I reached my rooms I sat and smoked several cigars while I tried to think out the significance of what had occurred. I reviewed the whole history of our acquaintance, recalled each smile she had given me, each word

9. A composition for piano by French composer Gabriel Fauré (1845–1924). Regarded as one of Fauré's masterworks, it is distinguished for resolving the dissonance that resounds through the work's three major parts into an aurally continuous whole.

she had said to me that nourished my hope. I went over the scene we had just gone through, trying to draw from it what was in my favor and what was against me. I was rewarded by feeling confident that she loved me, but I could not estimate what was the effect upon her of my confession. At last, nervous and unhappy, I wrote her a letter, which I dropped into the mailbox before going to bed, in which I said:

> "I understand, understand even better than you, and so I suffer even more than you. But why should either of us suffer for what neither of us is to blame? If there is any blame, it belongs to me, and I can only make the old, yet strongest plea that can be offered, I love you; and I know that my love, my great love, infinitely overbalances that blame, and blots it out. What is it that stands in the way of our happiness? It is not what you feel or what I feel; it is not what you are or what I am. It is what others feel and are. But, oh! is that a fair price? In all the endeavors and struggles of life, in all our strivings and longings there is only one thing worth seeking, only one thing worth winning, and that is love. It is not always found; but when it is, there is nothing in all the world for which it can be profitably exchanged."

The second morning after, I received a note from her which stated briefly that she was going up in New Hampshire to spend the summer with relatives there. She made no reference to what had passed between us; nor did she say exactly when she would leave the city. The note contained no single word that gave me any clue to her feelings. I could only gather hope from the fact that she had written at all. On the same evening, with a degree of trepidation which rendered me almost frightened, I went to her house.

I met her mother, who told me that she had left for the country that very afternoon. Her mother treated me in her usual pleasant manner, which fact greatly reassured me; and I left the house with a vague sense of hope stirring in my breast, which sprang from the conviction that she had not yet divulged my secret. But that hope did not remain with me long. I waited one, two, three weeks, nervously examining my mail every day, looking for some word from her. All of the letters received by me seemed so insignificant, so worthless, because there was none from her. The slight buoyancy of spirit which I had felt gradually dissolved into gloomy heartsickness. I became preoccupied, I lost appetite, lost sleep, and lost ambition. Several of my friends intimated to me that perhaps I was working too hard.

She stayed away the whole summer. I did not go to the house, but saw her father at various times, and he was as friendly as ever. Even after I knew that she was back in town I did not go to see her. I determined to wait for some word or sign. I had finally taken refuge and comfort in my pride, pride which, I suppose, I came by naturally enough.

The first time I saw her after her return was one night at the theater. She and her mother sat in company with a young man whom I knew slightly, not many seats away from me. Never did she appear more beautiful; and yet, it may have been my fancy, she seemed a trifle paler and there was a suggestion of haggardness in her countenance. But that only heightened her beauty; the very delicacy of her charm melted down the strength of my pride. My situation made me feel weak and powerless, like a man trying with his bare hands to break the iron bars of his prison cell. When the performance was over I hurried out and placed myself where, unobserved, I could see her as she passed out. The haughtiness of spirit in which I had sought relief was all gone, and I was willing and ready to undergo any humiliation.

Shortly afterward we met at a progressive card party,[1] and during the evening we were thrown together at one of the tables as partners. This was really our first meeting since the eventful night at her house. Strangely enough, in spite of our mutual nervousness, we won every trick of the game, and one of our opponents jokingly quoted the old saw, "Lucky at cards, unlucky in love." Our eyes met, and I am sure that in the momentary glance my whole soul went out to her in one great plea. She lowered her eyes and uttered a nervous little laugh. During the rest of the game I fully merited the unexpressed and expressed abuse of my various partners; for my eyes followed her wherever she was, and I played whatever card my fingers happened to touch.

Later in the evening she went to the piano and began to play very softly, as to herself, the opening bars of the 13th Nocturne. I felt that the psychic moment of my life had come, a moment which if lost could never be called back; and, in as careless a manner as I could assume, I sauntered over to the piano and stood almost bending over her. She continued playing; but, in a voice that was almost a whisper, she called me by my Christian name and said, "I love you, I love you, I love you." I took her place at the piano and played the Nocturne in a manner that silenced the chatter of the company both in and out of the room; involuntarily closing it with the major triad.[2]

1. Also known as rotation; a method of playing cards in which participants play with multiple partners instead of just one person for the duration of a match.
2. A chord made up of only three notes, which are played together or pressed one after another.

We were married the following spring, and went to Europe for several months. It was a double joy for me to be in France again under such conditions.

First there came to us a little girl, with hair and eyes dark like mine, but who is growing to have ways like her mother. Two years later there came a boy, who has my temperament, but is fair like his mother, a little golden-headed god, a face and head that would have delighted the heart of an old Italian master. And this boy, with his mother's eyes and features, occupies an inner sanctuary of my heart; for it was for him that she gave all; and that is the second sacred sorrow of my life.

The few years of our married life were supremely happy, and, perhaps she was even happier than I; for after our marriage, in spite of all the wealth of her love which she lavished upon me, there came a new dread to haunt me, a dread which I cannot explain and which was unfounded, but one that never left me. I was in constant fear that she would discover in me some shortcoming which she would unconsciously attribute to my blood rather than to a failing of human nature. But no cloud ever came to mar our life together; her loss to me is irreparable. My children need a mother's care, but I shall never marry again. It is to my children that I have devoted my life. I no longer have the same fear for myself of my secret being found out; for since my wife's death I have gradually dropped out of social life; but there is nothing I would not suffer to keep the "brand" from being placed upon them.[3]

It is difficult for me to analyze my feelings concerning my present position in the world. Sometimes it seems to me that I have never really been a Negro, that I have been only a privileged spectator of their inner life; at other times I feel that I have been a coward, a deserter, and I am possessed by a strange longing for my mother's people.

Several years ago I attended a great meeting in the interest of Hampton Institute at Carnegie Hall.[4] The Hampton students sang the old songs and awoke memories that left me sad. Among the speakers were R. C. Ogden, Ex-Ambassador Choate, and Mark Twain; but the greatest interest of the audience was centered in Booker T. Washington;[5] and not because he so much surpassed the

3. This point marks the end of the material that JWJ added to his original draft manuscript of Chapter XI. To compare, see Appendix B, pp. 115–21.
4. A concert hall located in Manhattan at 7th Avenue between West 56th and West 57th Streets; opened in 1891, it was principally financed by its namesake, American business tycoon Andrew Carnegie. *Hampton Institute*: a historically African American university founded in 1868, in Hampton, Virginia; originally named Hampton Normal and Industrial Institute. The school's initial mission was to educate newly freed African Americans in industrial education; accordingly, its most famous alumni is Booker T. Washington.
5. An educator and powerful figure in African American politics after Reconstruction (1856–1915), although born a slave in Virginia. A proponent of industrial or vocational

others in eloquence, but because of what he represented with so much earnestness and faith. And it is this that all of that small but gallant band of colored men who are publicly fighting the cause of their race have behind them.[6] Even those who oppose them know that these men have the eternal principles of right on their side, and they will be victors even though they should go down in defeat. Beside them I feel small and selfish. I am an ordinarily successful white man who has made a little money. They are men who are making history and a race. I, too, might have taken part in a work so glorious.

My love for my children makes me glad that I am what I am, and keeps me from desiring to be otherwise; and yet, when I sometimes open a little box in which I still keep my fast yellowing manuscripts, the only tangible remnants of a vanished dream, a dead ambition, a sacrificed talent, I cannot repress the thought, that, after all, I have chosen the lesser part, that I have sold my birthright for a mess of pottage.

---

education, Washington headed the Tuskegee Institute, an African American college in Alabama. He was also renowned for his autobiography, *Up from Slavery* (1901), which chronicled his ascent to public power as Tuskegee's leader. Because of his conservative views on black voting rights and racial integration—in his most famous lecture, the "Atlanta Compromise" speech (1895), he announced his support for social segregation between the races in the South—Washington was highly criticized by other African American leaders. For that same reason, Washington was lionized by white power brokers who found his opinions to be congenial to their own visions of racial reconciliation. Mobilizing his white supporters' financial and political aid, Washington built what was known as the "Tuskegee Machine," a far-reaching network he used to distribute social and political patronage among his black supporters. Though Washington's tactics roused his critics' ire further, his approach allowed him to protest racial segregation surreptitiously through the patronage placements he was able to engineer. As executive secretary of the NAACP James Weldon Johnson would oppose the consequences of these policies. However, at the start of his career, Johnson benefited directly from Washington's political favoritism. *The Autobiography of an Ex-Colored Man* could not have been written without the Tuskegee Machine's support, because Washington endorsed Johnson's assignment to the U.S. Consular Service, a six-year post during which Johnson drafted and published his novel. Robert Curtis Ogden (1836–1913), a northern philanthropist and benefactor who, as a member of the Southern Education Conference, worked toward bettering educational facilities in the South, especially those serving African Americans. He served on the board of trustees at Hampton Institute from 1894 to 1913. Joseph Hodges Choate (1832–1917), one of New York City's most prominent attorneys at the turn of the century and a prominent member of the Republican Party. He served as ambassador to Great Britain under President McKinley. Mark Twain (1835–1910), humorist, novelist, and one of America's most prolific writers. His most famous works include *The Adventures of Tom Sawyer* (1876) and *The Adventures of Huckleberry Finn* (1885), his masterpiece examination of American slavery. Notably, throughout his literary career, Twain was an outspoken supporter of civil rights for African Americans.

6. From this point to the chapter's final paragraph, Johnson extensively revised the text. The earlier draft manuscript of the novel's concluding episode is reprinted on p. 118 in this volume.

APPENDIX A

Revisions to Chapter X†

Draft Paragraphs

Originally handwritten by Johnson sometime between 1910 and 1911, the following draft paragraphs close Chapter X. However, Johnson's subtle but important revisions of diction and punctuation distinguish this early version from the one published in the 1912 edition. See pp. 99–100 in this volume.

How long I sat with bitter thoughts running through my mind I do not know, perhaps an hour or more. When I decided to get up and go back to the house I found that I could hardly stand on my feet. I was as weak as a man who had lost blood; want of sleep and food and the energy expended in me. However, I dragged myself along with the central idea of a general plan well fixed in my mind. I did not find my school teacher friend at home, so did not see him again. I swallowed a few mouthfuls of food, found my bag, and caught the afternoon train.

When I got to Macon I stopped only long enough to get the main part of my luggage and to buy a ticket for New York. All along the journey I was occupied in debating dissenting with myself the step which I had decided to take. I argued that to forsake one's race to better one's condition was no less worthy an action than to forsake one's country for the same purpose. I finally made up my mind that I would neither disclaim the black race nor claim the white race, but that I would change my name, raise a mustache, and let the world take me for what it would, that it was not necessary for me to go around with a label of inferiority pasted across my forehead. All the while, I understood that it was not discouragement or fear or search for a larger field of action and opportunity for success that was driving me out of the Negro race; I knew that it was shame; unbearable shame; shame of being identified with a people that could with impunity be treated worse than animals, for certainly the law would restrain and punish the malicious burning alive of animals.

So, once again, I found myself gazing at the towers of New York, and wondering what future that city held in store for me.

† From James Weldon Johnson and Grace Nail Johnson Papers. Yale Collection of American Literature, Beinecke Rare Book and Manuscript Library. Reprinted by permission of the Estate of James Weldon Johnson. Page numbers in footnotes refer to this Norton Critical Edition.

The Smoking Car Scene

On the verso of the final handwritten pages of the 1910–11 manuscript of Chapter X (pp. 32–34), Johnson drafted material that would eventually make up the denouement of the "smoking car" scene. In that episode, which follows his return from Europe, the narrator travels by train from Boston to Georgia, passing as white by using the covers of his fair-skinned appearance and silence to eavesdrop as the Texan and Union veteran debate the race question. Some of this material also appears in Chapter XI. Stricken out by a large X that covers most of the page, most of the text that follows appears in the 1912 edition of the novel but in revised form.

[VERSO OF PAGE 32]

The spirit of the South has made the Southern white man a defender of his vices as well as his virtues; he knows that judged by the [great] high standard (law and morality) he is narrow and prejudiced, that he is guilty of unfairness, oppression and cruelty, but there he defends as hotly as he would the finer qualities which he, as a race, possesses. The same spirit in a very great degree obtains among the Negroes; they too defend their faults and failings. This spirit carries them so far at times as to [?] their sympathizers with numbers of their race who are perpetrators of crime. Yet, among themselves they are their [?] critics. I have never heard the race so forcibly arraigned as I have by Negro speakers to strictly colored audiences.[1]

Colored & white branches of same family
[?] Florida Florida Florida
Florida Florida Florida

A year or two ago I went to Carnegie Hall where a meeting was being held for Hampton. B. W. spoke and the Hampton students sang. The singers brought back my own ambitions, etc.[2]

[written in the left hand margin of the page] It is the spirit of the South to defend everything belonging to it; the North is too cosmopolitan and tolerant for such a spirit. If you should suggest to an Easterner that Paris is a gayer city than N.Y. he would be likely to agree with you or, at least, to let you have your way, but it would be next to impossible to have a South Carolinian admit that Boston is a nicer city to live in than Charleston.[3]

1. The revised version of this passage appears on p. 86.
2. A fuller version of this transition to the novel's concluding scene appears on p. 109.
3. An unfinished version of the narrator's reflections on the smoking car argument; see p. 86.

[VERSO OF PAGE 33]

After lynching a great wave of shame and humiliation swept over me. I felt ashamed to belong either to the Negro or the white race of the South. I felt compelled to leave the South.[4]

You, who are now reading these lines, do you not feel ———

[VERSO OF PAGE 34]

I wonder how long will Southern white men [in the South] of liberal [thought] and progressive views endure the limits which are placed upon free speech; they still cower and tremble before "Southern Opinion." Even so late as in the recent Atlanta riot, those men who were brave enough to speak a word in behalf of justice and humanity felt called upon [by way of apology] to preface what they said by [with] a glowing, rhetorical, tribute to the Anglo-Saxon's superiority of [sic] the Negro, and to refer to the "great [fixed] and impassable gulf" between the races "fixed by the Creator of the Foundation of the world." The question of the relative qualities of the two races is still an open one; the reference to the "great gulf" loses force in the face of the fact that there are in this country three perhaps [JWJ inserts copy editing mark for reversal here], four million people with [both] the blood of both races in their veins; but I fail to see the pertinency necessity (?) of either statement subsequent to the beating and murdering of scores of innocent people in the streets of a civilized and Christian city.[5]

[written in left-hand margin of page] After lynching?

Singing and Lynching Scenes

Finally, the 1910–11 draft handwritten manuscript of Chapter X contains material (recto and verso) that cuts between the revival camp singing and lynching scenes. These paragraphs appear on pages that are labeled "P 31a" on the original manuscript. Large X marks cross out these paragraphs on the page, perhaps to signal Johnson's inclusion of them in the final manuscript.

[written in left-hand margin of page] Plantation singing

One could not but wonder how these people had touched the mystery of music, how in their ignorance they had brought forth

4. A rougher-hewn version of the narrator's reaction to witnessing the lynching in Georgia and his stated reason for passing as white. Cf. to p. 98.
5. The revised and published version of this passage occurs on p. 98–99.

melodies which called up other tones now heard by the ears (Unknown Bards)[6]

[written in left-hand margin of page] After Lynching

I was as weak as a man who had lost blood[7]

[written in left-hand margin of page] Boston Mass. Boston Massachu-

Lynching scene. 'Twas superb brutality—. subliminal?) savagery

I cannot [do not] see how a people who can find in their conscience any excuse whatever for slowly burning to death a human being [or to tolerate such an act] can be entrusted with the salvation of a race.[8]

The southern whites are, from [in many respects] a certain point of view, a great people. If one will put himself in a romantic frame of mind he can admire their motives of chivalry, of honor, an of civilization. Just as an ordinary [a peace loving] man of intelligence can go to the theater and applaud the impossible hero who with his single sword slays or puts to flight every body [sic] in the play except the equally impossible heroine, or as [a peace loving man] he can sit by a comfortable fire, and read with enjoyment of the bloody deeds of pirates and of the fierce brutality of past races [Vikings]; this is the man in which we gratify the old, indulging animal instincts and passions; but he could shudder with horror at such pictures being realities in this day of enlightened and humanitarianized thought. The southern whites are not yet living quite in the present age; most of their general ideas [and be] hark back to a former century, many of them to the Dark (Middle) Ages; in the light of other days, they are magnificent, to-day they are often ludicrous and cruel.[9]

6. The sentiment—not the phrasing—of this passage takes published form in the narrator's reflections on the sorrow songs that he hears at the Georgia revival; see pp. 94–95.
7. Johnson uses this precise phrasing to describe the narrator's stupor after witnessing the lynching; see p. 99.
8. Rougher phrasing of the narrator's anger at the lynching; see p. 98.
9. This less-hemmed draft demonstrates how Johnson revised the manuscript carefully to achieve the narrator's sardonic tone. Cf. the finished version on p. 99.

APPENDIX B

Original Conclusion†

Also composed between 1910 and 1911, the denouement of Chapter XI's manuscript draft rests upon an entirely different order of events. Here, the narrator proposes to his fiancée without disclosing his racial identity to her, and the couple marries and prospers: the ex-colored man succeeds at his real estate career while his wife gives birth to their two children. However, as published in 1912, Johnson added material to develop the narrator's marriage as integral to the novel's plot: the narrator reveals his heritage to his would-be wife; a prolonged, anxiety-ridden time follows once she spurns his proposal; and, finally, the wife dies in childbirth.[1]

In addition, Johnson made careful sentence-level edits that distinguish the published version of Chapter XI from its original draft.

The material that Johnson added to change the novel's conclusion can be found at pp. 102–109 in this volume. His sentence-level revisions are indexed at the end of this Appendix.

Chapter XI

I have now reached that part of my narration where I must be brief and touch only lightly on important facts. The reader must make up his mind to pardon skips and jumps and meager details. When I reached New York I was completely lost; I could not have felt more a stranger, hand I been suddenly dropped into Constantinople. I knew not where to turn or how to strike out. The temptation to visit my old home in Connecticut was very strong.[2] I was so oppressed by a feeling sense of loneliness that the temptation to visit my old home in Connecticut was well nigh irresistible. I reasoned, however, that unless I found my old music teacher, I should be, after so many years of absence, as much of a stranger there as in New York; and furthermore, that in view of the step which I had decided to take, such a visit would be injudicious. I remembered, too, that I had some property there in the shape of a piano and a few books, but concluded that it would not be worth what it might cost me to take possession.

By reason of the fact that my living expenses in the South had been very small, I still had nearly four hundred dollars of my capital

† From James Weldon Johnson and Grace Nail Johnson Papers. Yale Collection of American Literature, Beinecke Rare Book and Manuscript Library. Reprinted by permission of the Estate of James Weldon Johnson. Page numbers in footnotes refer to this Norton Critical Edition.

1. As early as 1908 Johnson fretted over composing the novel's end; see his letter to Brander Matthews on p. 221 of this volume.
2. This sentence has a line through it.

left. In contemplation of this, my natural and acquired bohemian tastes asserted themselves, and I decided to have a couple weeks of good time before worrying seriously about the future. I went to Coney Island and the other resorts, took in the pre-season shows at the theaters along Broadway, and ate at first rate restaurants, but I shunned the old Sixth Avenue tenderloin district as though it were pest infected. My few days of pleasure made appalling inroads into what cash I had, and caused me to see that it required a good deal of money to live in New York as I wished to live, and that I should have to find very soon some more or less profitable employment. I knew that unknown, without friends or prestige it was almost useless to try to establish myself as a teacher of music; so I gave that means of earning a living scarcely any consideration. And even had I considered it possible to secure pupils, as I then felt, I should have hesitated about taking up work in which the chances for any considerable degree of financial success are necessarily so small. I had made up my mind that since I was not going to be a Negro, I would avail myself of every possible opportunity to make a white man's success; and that, if it can be summed up in any one word, means "money."

I watched the "want" columns in the newspapers and answered a number of advertisements, but in each case found they were positions which I could not fill or did not want. I also spent several dollars for "ads" which brought me no replies. In this way I came to know the hopes and disappointments of a large and futile class of humans in this great city, the people who look forever for employment through the newspapers. After some days of this sort of experience, I concluded that the main difficulty with me was that I was not prepared for what I wanted to do. I then decided upon a course which for an artist showed an uncommon amount of common sense and practical judgment. I made up my mind to enter a business college. I took a small room, ate at lunch counters in order to economize, and pursued my studies with the zeal which I have always been able to put into any work upon which I set my mind. Yet, in spite of all my economy, when I had been at the school for several months, my funds were out completely. I reached the point where I could not afford sufficient food for each day. In this plight, I was glad to get, through one of the teachers at the school, a job as an ordinary clerk in a downtown wholesale house. I did my work faithfully, and received a raise of salary before I expected it; I even managed to save a little money out of my modest salary. In fact, I began then to contract the money fever which later took strong possession of me. I kept my eyes open watching for a chance to better my position with a house that was at the time establishing a South American department. My knowledge of Spanish was of course the principal cause of my good luck; it did more for me; it placed me where the other clerks were practically put out of competition with me. I was not slow in taking advantage of the opportunity to make myself indispensable to the firm.

What an interesting and absorbing game is money making! After each deposit at my savings bank I used to sit and figure out, all over again, my principal and interest, and make calculations of what the increase would be in such and such a time. Out of this I got a great deal of pleasure. I denied myself as much as possible in order to swell my savings. As much as I enjoyed smoking I limited myself to an occasional cigar, and that was generally of a variety which was known in my old days at the "Club" as a "Henry Mud." Drinking I cut out altogether; but that was no great sacrifice.

The day on which I was able to figure up $1000 was an epoch in my life. And this was not because I had never before had money; in my old gambling days and while I was with my "millionaire" I handled sums of money running high up in the hundreds, but they had come to me like fairy godmother gifts, and at a time when my conception of money was that it was made only to spend. Here, on the other hand, was a thousand dollars which I had earned by days of honest and intelligent work, a thousand dollars which I had carefully watched grow from the first dollar, and I experienced in owning them this amount a pride and satisfaction which was entirely new. (I felt much as a father must feel who has watched his son grow from childhood into successful manhood) As my capital went over the thousand dollar mark I was puzzled to know what to do with it, how to put it to the most advantageous use. I turned down first one scheme and then another as though they had been laid for the sole purpose of gobbling up my money. I finally listened to a friend who advised me to put all I had into New York real estate; and under his guidance I took an equity and assumed a mortgage on a piece of property on which stood a rickety tenement house. I did not regret taking my this friend's advice, for in something like six months I disposed of my equity for more than double my investment. From that time on I devoted myself to the study of New York real estate, and watched for chances to make similar investments. In spite of two or three speculations which did not turn out (so) well (as I expected), I have been remarkably successful. Today I am the owner of one several flat house and part-owner of several others. I have changed my place of employment four times since I returned to New York, and each change has been a decided advancement; concerning the position which I now hold I shall say nothing except that it pays extremely well.

As my outlook on the world grew brighter, I began to mingle in the social world of the men with whom I came in contact; and gradually, by eliminating those at the bottom, I reached a grade of society of no small degree of culture. My appearance was always good; and my ability to play on the piano, especially ragtime, which was then at the height of its vogue, made me a welcome guest. The anomaly of my social position often appealed strongly to my sense of humor. I frequently smiled inwardly at some remark not altogether complimentary to people of color, and more than once I felt like declaring: "I am a colored man! Do I not disprove the theories that one drop of Negro blood [sic] Many nights when I returned to my room after an enjoyable evening, I laughed heartily over what struck me as the capital joke I was playing.

Then I met her, and loved her, and she loved me; and what I had regarded as a joke was suddenly changed into the most serious question of my life. We were married, and now have two beautiful children. How much I should like to describe them to the reader, to indulge in the pardonable foible of a father, and relate some of their clever sayings and doings; but that would be treading to near the danger line. As it is, looking over the pages of this last chapter, I am not sure that I have not gone too closely into particulars. I know that my wife loves me, and I do not believe that knowledge of the whole truth would change her, yet I prefer not to have her love put to that test. And even above that, I should dread having the "brand" placed upon my children.

It is difficult for me to analyse my feelings concerning my present position in the world. Sometimes it seems to me that I have never really been a Negro, that I have only been a privileged spectator of their inner life; at other times I feel that I have been a coward, a deserter, and I am possessed with a strange longing for my mother's people.

Several years ago I attended a great meeting in the interest of Hampton Institute and Carnegie Hall; the Hampton students sang the old songs, and awoke memories that left me sad. Among the speakers were Ex-Ambassador Choate,—Ogden and Mark Twain, but the greatest interest of the audience was centered in Booker T. Washington; and not because he surpassed the others in eloquence and intelligence, but because of what the man represented with so much earnestness and faith. It is this which all of the small, but gallant band of colored men who are publicly fighting the cause of this race have behind them. Even those who oppose them know that they have the eternal principles of Right on their side and that they will be victors conquerors even though they shall go down in defeat. Besides all these men I feel small and selfish. I am an ordinary successful white man who has made a little money, they are men who are making history and a race. I, too, might have taken part in a work so glorious.

My love for my wife and children makes me glad that I am what I am, and keeps me from desiring to be otherwise; and yet, when I sometimes open a little box in which I still keep my fast yellowing manuscripts, the only tangible remnants remains of a vanished dream, of a dead ambition, of a sacrificed talent, I cannot repress the thought that, after all, I have chosen the lesser part, that I have sold my birthright for a mess of pottage.

THE END

Index of Sentence-Level Revisions to Chapter XI Draft Manuscript

par. 1, s. 2:	"Therefore" added to begin sentence
par. 1, s. 3:	"When I reached New York" begins new paragraph in published version
par. 1, s. 5–6:	JWJ combines these two sentences
par. 1, s. 8:	changes "decided" to "concluded"
par. 2, s. 2:	capitalizes "Bohemian"
par. 2, s. 3:	cuts "at the theaters"
par. 2, s. 5:	changes "I was sure" to "I knew"
par. 2, s. 6:	cuts "degree of"
par. 3, s. 1:	revises sentence to read, ". . . advertisements; but in each case found the positions were such as I could not fill or did not want."
par. 3, s. 3:	changes "futile class of humanity" to "pitiable class of humans [. . .]." Changes "the people who look forever for employment through the newspapers" to "the people who look for work through the newspapers."
par. 3, s. 5:	adds comma to "which, for an artist,"
par. 3, s. 7:	adds comma to "ate at lunch counters, [. . .]" Changes "which I set my mind" to "which I set my heart"
par. 3, s. 8:	changes "my funds were out completely" to "my funds gave out completely"
par. 3, s. 10:	cuts "at the school"
par. 3, s. 11:	cuts semi-colon for sentence to read: "[. . .] before I expected it." Changes "salary" to "earnings" at end of sentence.
par. 3, s. 12:	adds comma to "contract the money fever,"
par. 3, s. 13:	revises sentence to read: "I kept my eyes open, watching for a chance to better my position. It

	finally came in the form of a position with a house which was at the time establishing a South American department."
par. 3, s. 14:	inserts "and" after "[. . .] it did more for me;"
par. 4, s. 2:	inserts comma to "After each deposit at my savings bank, [. . .]"
par. 4, s. 3:	changes "I got" to "I derived"
par. 4, s. 5:	changes "As much as I enjoyed" to "Even so much as I enjoyed"
par. 5, s. 1:	changes "$1000 was" to "$1000.00 marked"
par. 5, s. 2:	cuts semi-colon and adds period to close sentence at "money." Revises "in my old gambling days" to "In my gambling days [. . .]". Adds semi-colon to "high up in the hundreds; [. . .]." Changes spelling to "fairy god-mother [. . .]."
par. 5, s. 3:	changes comma to semi-colon at "grow from the first dollar;" Adds commas to the phrase "I experienced, in owning them, [. . .]." Cuts "this amount." Revises the end of the sentence to read, "[. . .] which was an entirely new sensation."
par. 5, s. 4:	cuts this parenthetical aside
par. 5, s. 5:	adds comma to read, "over the thousand dollar mark, [. . .]"
par. 5, s. 5–6:	revises to read: "[. . .] and then another, as though they had been devised for the sole purpose [. . .]."
par. 5, s. 7:	cuts "and assumed a mortgage"
par. 5, s. 9:	changes "chances" to "opportunities"
par. 5, s. 10:	cuts "(so)" and "(as I expected)"
par. 5, s. 11:	revises sentence to read, "To-day I am the owner and part-owner of several flathouses."
par. 5, s. 12:	changes "return" to "returning." Ends sentence at "advancement."
par. 6, s. 1:	changes "social world" to "social circles." Revises "by eliminating those at the bottom" to "by a process of elimination, [. . .]."
par. 6, s. 2:	removes semi-colon after "good;"
par. 6, s. 3:	changes comma to semi-colon after "people of color". Changes "declaring" to "declaiming". Completes sentence at "[sic]" as follows: "renders a man unfit?"
par. 7, s. 1:	cuts "and she loved me." The remainder of this paragraph is not in the published version of Chapter XI.
par. 9, s. 1:	cuts the semicolon and adds a period to end the sentence at "Carnegie Hall."
par. 9, s. 2:	adds "R.C. Ogden" to list of dignitaries. Changes comma to semicolon after "Mark Twain." Cuts "and

intelligence" to revise remainder of sentence to read: " [. . .] but because of what he represented with so much earnestness and faith."

par. 9, s. 3: adds "And" to begin sentence

par. 9, s. 4: changes "they" to "these men." Changes "Right" to lower case. Changes "shall go down in defeat" to "should go down in defeat"

par. 9, s. 5: changes "all these men" to "them"

par. 9, s. 6: changes "ordinary" to "ordinarily." Adds period to close sentence at "money"

par. 10, s. 1: cuts "wife and." Cuts "of" for phrases to read, "a dead ambition, a sacrificed talent."

APPENDIX C

CARL VAN VECHTEN: Introduction to Mr. Knopf's New Edition†

The Autobiography of an Ex-Coloured Man is, I am convinced, a remarkable book. I have read it three times and at each rereading I have found it more remarkable. Published in 1912, it then stood almost alone as an inclusive survey of racial accomplishments and traits, as an interpretation of the feelings of the Negro towards the white man and towards the members of his own race. Written, I believe, while Mr. James Weldon Johnson was U.S. Consul to Nicaragua, it was issued anonymously. The publishers attempted to persuade the author to sign a statement to the effect that the book was an actual human document. This he naturally refused to do. Nevertheless, the work was hailed on every side, for the most part, as an individual's true story.

The *Autobiography,* of course, in the matter of specific incident, has little enough to do with Mr. Johnson's own life, but it is imbued with his own personality and feeling, his *views* of the subjects discussed, so that to a person who has no previous knowledge of the author's own history, it reads like *real* autobiography. It would be truer, perhaps, to say that it reads like a composite autobiography of the Negro race in the United States in modern times.

It is surprising how little the book has dated in fifteen years. Very little that Mr. Johnson wrote then is not equally valid today,

† From James Weldon Johnson, *The Autobiography of an Ex-Coloured Man* (New York: Alfred A. Knopf, 1927), xxxiii–xxxviii. "Introduction,"

although in those remote times he found it necessary when he mentioned Negroes in evening clothes to add that they were not hired! On the other hand it is cheering to discover how much has been accomplished by the race in New York alone since the book was originally published. Then there was no Harlem—the Negro lived below Fifty-ninth Street. To encounter the cultured, respectable class of Negro one was obliged to visit Brooklyn. In the very few years since this epoch the great city beyond the Park has sprung into being, a city which boasts not only its own cabarets and gamblers, but also its intelligentsia, its rich and cultured group, its physicians, its attorneys, its educators, its large, respectable middle class, its churches, its hospitals, its theatres, its library, and its business houses. It would be possible to name fifty names such as those of Paul Robeson, Langston Hughes, Charles Gilpin, Walter White, Rudolph Fisher, Countée Cullen, Florence Mills, Ethel Waters, Aaron Douglas, Taylor Gordon and Jean Toomer, all of whom have made their mark in the artistic world within the past five years.

When I was writing *Nigger Heaven* I discovered the *Autobiography* to be an invaluable source-book for the study of Negro psychology. I believe it will be a long time before anybody can write about the Negro without consulting Mr. Johnson's pages to advantage. Naturally, the *Autobiography* had its precursors. Booker T. Washington's *Up from Slavery* (1900) is a splendid example of autobiography, but the limitations of his subject matter made it impossible for Dr. Washington to survey the field as broadly as Mr. Johnson, setting himself no limitations, could. Dr. Du Bois's important work, *The Souls of Black Folk* (1903) does, certainly, explore a wide territory, but these essays lack the insinuating influence of Mr. Johnson's calm, dispassionate tone, and they do not offer, in certain important respects, so revealing a portrait of Negro character. Charles W. Chesnutt, in his interesting novel, *The House Behind the Cedars* (1900), contributed to literature perhaps the first authentic study on the subject of "passing," and Paul Laurence Dunbar, in *The Sport of the Gods,* described the plight of a young outsider who comes to the larger New York Negro world to make his fortune, but who falls a victim to the sordid snares of that world, a theme I elaborated in 1926 to fit a newer and much more intricate social system.

Mr. Johnson, however, chose an all-embracing scheme. His young hero, the ostensible author, either discusses (or lives) pretty nearly every phase of Negro life, North and South and even in Europe, available to him at that period. That he "passes" the title indicates. Miscegenation in its slave and also its more modern aspects, both casual and marital, is competently treated. The ability of the Negro to mask his real feelings with a joke or a laugh in the presence of the inimical white man is here noted, for the first time in print, I should imagine. Negro adaptability, touchiness, and jealousy are referred to in an unself-conscious manner, totally novel in Negro writing at the time this book originally appeared. The hero declares: "It may be said that the majority of intelligent coloured people are, in some degree, too much in earnest over the race question. They assume and carry so much that their progress is at times impeded and they are unable to see things in their proper proportions. In many instances a slight exercise of the sense of humour would save much anxiety of soul." Jim Crow cars, crap-shooting, and the cake-walk are inimitably described. Colour snobbery within the race is freely spoken of, together with the economic pressure from without which creates this false condition. There is a fine passage devoted to the celebration of the Negro Spirituals and there is an excellent account of a Southern camp-meeting, together with a transcript of a typical oldtime Negro sermon. There is even a lynching.

But it is chiefly remarkable to find James Weldon Johnson in 1912, five or six years before the rest of us began to shout about it, singing hosannas to rag-time (jazz was unknown then). It is simply astonishing to discover in this book, issued the year after Alexander's Ragtime Band and the same year that The Memphis Blues were published, such a statement as this:

"American musicians, instead of investigating rag-time, attempt to ignore it, or dismiss it with a contemptuous word. But that has always been the course of scholasticism in every branch of art. Whatever new thing the *people* like is pooh-poohed; whatever is *popular* is spoken of as not worth the while. The fact is, nothing great or enduring, especially in music, has ever sprung full-fledged and unprecedented from the brain of any master; the best that he gives to the world he gathers from the hearts of the people, and runs it through the alembic of his genius." So the young hero of this Autobiography determines to develop the popular music of his people into a more serious form, thus foreseeing by twelve years the creation of The Rhapsody in Blue by George Gershwin.

Sherman, French and Co., published the Autobiography in Boston in 1912. When, a few years later, they retired from business it was out of print and, although constantly in demand and practically unprocurable, it has remained out of print until now when Alfred A. Knopf, justifiably, I believe, has seen fit to include it in his Blue Jade series. New readers, I am confident, will examine this book with interest: some to acquire through its mellow pages a new conception of how a coloured man lives and feels, others simply to follow the course of its fascinating story.

CARL VAN VECHTEN

NEW YORK
MARCH 1, 1927

Mr. Van Vechten's introduction was written for my first reissue of *The Autobiography*. It was then part of The Blue Jade Library, a series of minor classics in which readers of the twenties evinced a considerable interest. But most of the volumes in that series have passed again into obscurity and the series as such no longer exists, though some of the titles from it, like *The Autobiography of an Ex-Coloured Man*, are still in print and finding new readers.

A.A.K.[1]

APPENDIX D

Introduction to the 1928 German Edition[†]

The first German translation of *The Autobiography of an Ex-Colored Man* appeared in 1928, under the title *The White Negro: A Life between the Races,* with a brief accompanying essay commissioned from the British composer Frederick Delius. The English-language text was translated into German by Elisabeth von Gans.

The publisher was the Frankfurter Societäts-Druckerei, a house that remained at the center of the social democratic tradition, and of German Jewish thought, from its 1856 founding up to the Nazi era. It was best known for publishing the daily newspaper *Frankfurter Zeitung*, which counted many of the most prominent intellectuals of Weimar Germany among its contributors. Walter Benjamin, Ernst Bloch, Siegfried Kracauer, and Georg Simmel all published in its culture pages, as did Bertolt Brecht, his early collaborator Lion Feuchtwanger, Alfred Döblin, and Heinrich and Thomas Mann. In *Mein Kampf* (1925), Adolf Hitler singled out the *Frankfurter Zeitung* as a "Gorgon of the Jewish Press (*Judenpresse*)," railing against it as an organ of international Jewish conspiracy and blaming it for the German defeat in World War I. (The editors had taken an antiwar stance in 1914 and supported the Treaty of Versailles.) After the Nazis came to power in 1933, Hitler's new chief of propaganda, Joseph Goebbels, remarked that he could think of no greater pleasure than "to see the gentlemen of the Eschenheimer Gasse"—the street where the Societäts-Druckerei offices were located—"dancing to my tune." Publication halted briefly during World War II. In 1949, several former editors co-founded the *Frankfurter Allgemeine Zeitung*, which remains one of the most widely read German-language dailies to the present.

1. "A.A.K." refers to publisher Alfred A. Knopf. See the introduction, pp. xlvi–xlviii, for more on his firm and its role in reprinting the novel.

† From *Der weisse Neger: ein Leber zwischen den Rassen* (Frankfurt an Main: Frankfurter Societas-Druckerai, 1928). Translation and headnote by Moira Weigel.

Frankfurter Societäts-Druckerei's progressive political history suggests why Alfred A. Knopf would have contracted it to publish *ECM*. As fittingly, the German firm no doubt recruited Frederick Delius to write the preface because had he spent a few years near Jacksonville, Florida, James Weldon Johnson's hometown.[1] There, Delius first heard African American folk music, which proved to be a significant influence in his later compositions. Though Johnson would have been too young (thirteen) to know the then-twenty-two year-old composer in-training, Delius frequented Jacksonville's hotels to listen to black waiters and porters sing. Johnson's father was the head captain at the city's grandest hotel, the St. James. If James Johnson Sr. kept quiet at his post, Delius probably caught a glimpse of the older man while he eavesdropped on staff members performing the sacred and folk music they knew.

Publisher's Foreword

The problem of the American Negro has interested Europeans for a long time, since long before the great questions regarding race became common topics of conversation. *Uncle Tom's Cabin* was the favorite book of an entire generation. When jazz music and black singers and dancers broke the cool composure of European rhythms, a new epoch in the cultural relations of blacks and whites began. But the triumphal march of ragtime, spirituals, and tap dancing was so intoxicating to our ears and senses, so stimulating and striking that the great human problem that the Negro question entails was never properly put into words. We had yet to discover the realities of American life, which in some ways remain truly bitter. The incredible progress that Negros have made in the northern states, German authors have acknowledged more or less only in theory, in occasional essays and travel books.

Now that the question of the equal rights of white and colored citizens of the United States is really coming to a head, now that the preconditions of equal education and equal aptitude have almost been established, the Negro question is entering a phase that we can understand intimately. The question of the Negro race has moved definitively beyond the colonial phase, when ghettoization was proposed as a solution. The spread of free, colored American citizens of all professions and social classes all over North America has made it more complicated than ever before. Socially and psychologically, it has taken on the dividedness, and the tragic

1. Though Delius was born in England, his parents were German. For more about the composer (1862–1934), see http://delius.org.uk/biography.htm. Also of interest might be Noelle Morrissette, *James Weldon Johnson's Modern Soundscapes* (Iowa City: University of Iowa Press, 2013), pp. 111–14.

complexity, that we here in Europe and particularly in Germany know all too well from the Jewish question.

The book by James Weldon Johnson, published anonymously in 1912, is often regarded as a classic of Negro literature. It is written as an autobiography. Later the author made his identity known, but his own life story does not completely correspond to lives portrayed in the book. Still, it is precisely its nonsensationalizing, unusually calm but inwardly tense manner of storytelling that seems to speak for its veracity. It presents an unusual case: In general, authors strive to represent the authentic truth of their experiences to a skeptical world that would prefer to believe in poetry. Here, on the contrary, as van Vechten writes in his preface to the American edition, the author refrains from using his signature to assert "that the book was an actual human document. . . . Nevertheless, the work was hailed on every side, for the most part, as an individual's true story." His task is all the more difficult because the American reader always has the problem of the Negro right before his eyes and therefore can judge the truth or untruth of what is represented. So even after we have cleared up the author's anonymity, the question of poetry and truth has not yet been answered.

The publishers attempted to persuade the author to sign a statement to the effect that the book was an actual human document. This he naturally refused to do. Nevertheless, the work was hailed on every side, for the most part, as an individual's true story.

But perhaps it is precisely this wavering, this way of not saying yes but also not saying no, that is the destiny of the Negro—the destiny of an arriviste, who sways culturally and spiritually between the races and finds it difficult to make up his mind. Entirely apart from the question of its biographical origins, the book proceeds very directly to a social problem of the first order. In an era of the general mixing of peoples and races, the problem of nationality cries out for new solutions. This becomes particularly clear in this book about a white Negro, who can be recognized as mixed race only by marks that are at most barely visible. For the white Negro, who conceals himself in white American society, mimicry is not an honorable solution: it is a tragic one.

In any case, the life of Johnson, the author, did not come to such tragedy. He was, like the anonymous author of the autobiography, musical to his fingertips. One of the first people who understood and was able to represent the particular and original allure of black music, he revealed the undiscovered treasures of his people in his collections of songs. "Lift Every Voice and Sing," the national hymn of African Americans, comes from him. This musical aspect gives the book special significance. Even Frederick Delius, one of the great living European musicians—who, ages ago, through an unusual twist of fate came into contact with the music that is flooding into Europe in powerful, even overwhelming volumes today—writes in an essay that accompanies Johnson's book, how much the original musicality of Negroes has shaped it. How strong the walls erected between the opposing races must be, how heavy the burden of social inhibitions, how unfree must the despised Negro feel as a man, if, at least until the war, even someone with such extraordinary artistic gifts, still could not find the way to himself and to his own mastery of music.

On Johnson's Book, by Frederick Delius

When I was a very young man, I left the factory city where I was born in the north of England and spent a few years on an orange plantation in Florida. There, I lived in the greatest solitude, surrounded almost entirely by Negroes.

In the evening, when I sat on my veranda in the darkness, Negro songs echoed to me out of the distance. They seemed to meld wonderfully with the majestic landscape. Before me lay the endless span of the St. John River and all around me, the rainforest with its indescribably strange sounds of whirring insects, frogs, and nightingales.

Although I had grown up with classical music, now a whole new world opened within me. This Negro music struck me as something completely new. I experienced it at once as very natural and as very deep. I felt as if the blacks were by far the most musical people I had ever met. Their music came without artifice, unstudied, from within—expressing the soul of a people who had suffered greatly. It was almost always sad, almost always religious, and yet it always brimmed with personal experience and human warmth.

The landscape of Florida and its Negro music provided the strongest impulse toward my own musical creation. The so-called cakewalk, which a few years ago was being performed on all the variety stages of Europe, was nothing more than a wretched caricature of the real and wonderful cakewalk dances that were still performed at that time in the American South.

In my opinion the jazz music that all the American composers have seized upon and that has grown so beloved in dance halls and nightclubs across Europe is *also* only a travesty. It has been overwhelmed by too much Yankee vulgarity. In all my time there, the Negro of the Southern states was never vulgar. Primitive and childlike, certainly, but never vulgar.

The jazz that has been brought to Europe stands in roughly the same relation to real Negro music as the jargon of Polish Jews who have spent only a few years in America and claim to be 100 percent American stands to pure English.

I read James Weldon Johnson's book with the greatest interest, as a true and gripping reflection of the situation there. I believe that when America gives the world a great composer, he will have colored blood in his veins.

BACKGROUNDS AND SOURCES

On the Life of James Weldon Johnson

JAMES WELDON JOHNSON

From Along This Way†

In 1933, Johnson published his own memoir, *Along This Way*,[1] in part to quell the persistent confusion that *ECM* was his own autobiography. Though scholars have examined the connections between these works to explore how Johnson "novelized" aspects of his own life into the fictive form of *ECM*, these relays deserve continued scrutiny.[2]

Rather than offer selections from *Along This Way* to re-trace the arc of Johnson's early literary career, this volume offers excerpts that can be read for their textual potential: how do the people, events, and developments that Johnson experienced evolve into fictive constructs that test—and re-imagine—the boundaries between the literary categories of autobiography and fiction?[3]

[*"First Consciousness of Home"*]

Johnson's recollections of his childhood in Jacksonville offer clear resemblances to but equally striking differences from the ex-colored man's boyhood in Connecticut. The experience of isolation, the black mother's compromised social authority, and the white father's deliberate absence have been imagined afresh in the novel.

---

† From *James Weldon Johnson: Writings* (New York: Library of America, 2005 [1933]), ed. William L. Andrews, 140–44, 148–50, 152, 187–89, 313–18, 217–19, 233–42, 398–99, 570–72.

1. First published by New York City's Viking Press in 1933.
2. For such studies, see works by Skerrett, Kawash, Smith, and Sugimori listed in the Selected Bibliography in this volume. "Novelization" is a term coined by theorist Mikhail Bahktin, to gauge how prose fiction digests social history into fictive form.
3. Space constraints preclude a comprehensive survey. In addition to the excerpts reprinted here, readers might consider Johnson's years at Atlanta University (1887–94), his summer teaching in rural Georgia (1891), his time in New York City's "Black Bohemia" (1901–06), or his European tour with Bob Cole and Rosamond (1905).

I was born June 17, 1871, in the old house on the corner; but I have no recollection of having lived in it. Before I could be aware of such a thing my father had built a new house near the middle of his lot. In this new house was formed my first consciousness of home. My childish idea of it was that it was a great mansion. I saw nothing in the neighborhood that surpassed it in splendor. Of course, it was only a neat cottage. The house had three bedrooms, a parlor, and a kitchen. The four main rooms were situated, two on each side of a hall that ran through the center of the house. The kitchen, used also as a room in which the family ate, was at the rear of the house and opened on a porch that was an extension of the hall. On the front a broad piazza ran the width of the house. Under the roof was an attic to which a narrow set of steps in one of the back rooms gave access.

But the house was painted, and there were glass windows and green blinds. Before long there were some flowers and trees. One of the first things my father did was to plant two maple trees at the front gate and a dozen or more orange trees in the yard. The maples managed to live; the orange trees, naturally, flourished. The hallway of the house was covered with a strip of oilcloth and the floors of the rooms with matting. There were curtains at the windows and some pictures on the walls. In the parlor there were two or three dozen books and a cottage organ. When I was seven or eight years old, the organ gave way to a square piano. It was a tinkling old instrument, but a source of rapturous pleasure. It is one of the indelible impressions on my mind. I can still remember just how the name "Bacon" looked, stamped in gold letters above the keyboard. There was a center marble-top table on which rested a big, illustrated Bible and a couple of photograph albums. In a corner stood a what-not filled with bric-a-brac and knick-knacks. On a small stand was a glass-domed receptacle in which was a stuffed canary perched on a diminutive tree; on this stand there was also kept a stereoscope and an assortment of views photographed in various parts of the world. For my brother and me, in our childhood (my brother, John Rosamond, was born in the new house August 11, 1873), this room was an Aladdin's cave.[4] We used to stand before the what-not and stake out our claims to the objects on its shelves with a "that's mine" and a "that's mine." We never tired of looking at the stereoscopic scenes,[5] examining the photographs in the album, or putting the big Bible and other books on the floor and exploring for pictures. Two large conch shells[6] decorated the ends of the hearth. We greatly admired

4. From the *Arabian Nights*, a storehouse of riches and treasures.
5. Photographs of paired, identical images (mounted side-by-side on a single cardboard backing). Stereographs (a 19th-century binocular device) produce the illusion of seeing images in a three-dimensional visual field. Viewing them was a popular pastime in middle-class homes from the 1850s to 1930s.
6. Large sea shells common to the West Indies and Florida.

their pink, polished inner surface; and loved to put them to our ears to hear the "roar of the sea" from their cavernous depths. But the undiminishing thrill was derived from our experiments on the piano.

When I was born, my mother was very ill, too ill to nurse me. Then she found a friend and neighbor in an unexpected quarter. Mrs. McCleary, her white neighbor who lived a block away, had a short while before given birth to a girl baby. When this baby was christened she was named Angel. The mother of Angel, hearing of my mother's plight, took me and nursed me at her breast until my mother had recovered sufficiently to give me her own milk. So it appears that in the land of black mammies I had a white one. Between her and me there existed an affectionate relation through all my childhood; and even in after years when I had grown up and moved away I never, up to the time of her death, went back to my old home without paying her a visit and taking her some small gift.

I do not intend to boast about a white mammy, for I have perceived bad taste in those Southern white people who are continually boasting about their black mammies. I know the temptation for them to do so is very strong, because the honor point on the escutcheon of Southern aristocracy, the *sine qua non*[7] of a background of family, of good breeding and social prestige, in the South is the Black Mammy. Of course, many of the white people who boast of having had black mammies are romancing. Naturally, Negroes had black mammies, but black mammies for white people were expensive luxuries, and comparatively few white people had them.

When I was about a year old, my father made a trip to New York, taking my mother and me with him. It was during this visit that I developed from a creeping infant into a walking child. Without doubt, my mother welcomed this trip. She was, naturally, glad to see again the city and friends of her girlhood; and it is probable that she brought some pressure on my father to make another move—back to New York. If she did, it was without effect. I say she probably made some such effort because I know what a long time it took her to become reconciled to life in the South; in fact, she never did entirely. The New York of her childhood and youth was all the United States she knew.[8] Latterly she had lived in a British colony under conditions that rendered the weight of race comparatively light. During the earlier days of her life in Jacksonville she had no adequate conception of her "place."

And so it was that one Sunday morning she went to worship at St. John's Episcopal Church. As one who had been a member of the

7. Essential or indispensable (Latin).
8. JWJ's mother, Helen Dillet Johnson (1842–1919), was born in Nassau, Bahamas, but grew up in New York City.

choir of Christ Church Cathedral she went quite innocently. She went, in fact, not knowing any better. In the chanting of the service her soprano voice rang out clear and beautiful, and necks were craned to discover the singer. On leaving the church she was politely but definitely informed that the St. John's congregation would prefer to have her worship the Lord elsewhere. Certainly she never went back to St. John's nor to any other Episcopal church; she followed her mother and joined Ebenezer, the colored Methodist Episcopal Church in Jacksonville, and became the choir leader.

Racially she continued to be a nonconformist and a rebel. A decade or so after the St. John's Church incident Lemuel W. Livingston, a student at Cookman Institute, the Negro school in Jacksonville founded and maintained by the Methodist Church (North), was appointed as a cadet to West Point.[9] Livingston passed his written examinations, and the colored people were exultant. The members of Ebenezer Church gave a benefit that netted for him a purse of several hundred dollars. There was good reason for a show of pride; Livingston was a handsome, bronze-colored boy with a high reputation as a student, and appeared to be ideal material for a soldier and officer. But at the Academy he was turned down. The examining officials there stated that his eyesight was in some manner defective. The news that Livingston had been denied admission to West Point was given out at a Sunday service at Ebenezer Church. When at the same service the minister announced "America" as a hymn,[1] my mother refused to sing it.

My mother was artistic and more or less impractical and in my father's opinion had absolutely no sense about money. She was a splendid singer and she had a talent for drawing. One day when I was about fifteen years old, she revealed to me that she had written verse, and showed me a thin sheaf of poems copied out in her almost perfect handwriting. She was intelligent and possessed a quick though limited sense of humor. But the limitation of her sense of humor was quite the normal one: she had no relish for a joke whose butt was herself or her children; my father had the rarer capacity for laughing even at himself. She belonged to the type of mothers whose love completely surrounds their children and is all-pervading; mothers for whom sacrifice for the child means only an extension of love. Love of this kind often haunts the child in later years. He runs back again and again through all his memories, searching for a lapse or a lack or a falling short in that love so that he might in some degree balance his own innumerable

9. The U.S. military academy in New York State; trains officers for the U.S. Army.
1. Probably the 1831 song "My Country 'Tis of Thee," with lyrics Samuel F. French (1808–1865).

thought-lessnesses, his petty and great selfishnesses, his failures to begin to understand or value the thing that was once his like the air he breathed; and the search is vain.

The childhood memories that cluster round my mother are still intensely vivid to me; many of them are poignantly tender. I am between five and six years old. . . . In the early evening the lamp in the little parlor is lit. . . . If the weather is chilly, pine logs are sputtering and blazing in the fireplace. . . . I and my brother, who is a tot, are seated on the floor. . . . My mother takes a book and reads. . . . The book is *David Copperfield*.[2] . . . Night after night I follow the story, always hungry for the next installment. . . . Then the book is *Tales of a Grandfather*.[3] . . . Then it is a story by Samuel Lover. I laugh till the tears roll down my cheeks at the mishaps of Handy Andy.[4] And my brother laughs too, doubtless because he sees me laughing. . . . My mother's voice is beautiful; I especially enjoy it when she mimics the Irish brogue and Cockney accents. . . . My brother grows sleepy. . . . My mother closes the book and puts us both to bed—me feverish concerning the outcome of David's affairs or thrilling over the exploits of Wallace or Robert the Bruce,[5] or still laughing at Andy. She tucks us in and kisses us good-night. What a debt for a child to take on!

* * *

I cannot remember when I did not know my mother, but I can easily recall the at first hazy and then gradually more distinct notions about my father. My impressions of him began to take shape from finding under my pillow in the mornings an orange, some nuts, and raisins, and learning that he had put them there after I had gone to sleep. Shortly after my father got to Jacksonville the St. James Hotel[6] was built and opened. When it was opened he was the headwaiter, a job he held for twelve or thirteen years. Doubtless the hotel had been planned, and may even have been under construction, before he arrived; probably this was the definite prospect before him when he set out for Jacksonville. The St. James was for many years the most famous and the most fashionable of all the Florida resort hotels. A number of summers my father was the headwaiter at some mountain or seaside hotel in the North. So in my babyhood and first days of childhood I didn't see very much of him. His work

2. Novel (1850) by Charles Dickens.
3. Novel (1827) by Sir Walter Scott.
4. Lover (1797–1868) was an Anglo-Irish songwriter and novelist whose comic series "Handy Andy" first appeared in 1842 and was reprinted into the twentieth century.
5. William Wallace (1272–1305) and Robert the Bruce (1274–1329) were leaders of Scotland's Wars of Independence against Britain.
6. This resort opened in 1869 and became a leading destination in the tourism boom that drew travelers to the South following the Civil War.

at the St. James took him from home early in the mornings to see breakfast served, and he remained at the hotel until dinner was finished, by which time I had been put away in the little bed in which I slept. It was from the hotel that he brought the fruit and sweets that he put under my pillow. I remember, too, that our Sunday dinner always came from the hotel. It was brought in a hamper by one of the waiters, and the meat was usually fricasseed chicken.

I got acquainted with my father by being taken to the hotel to see him. As soon as Rosamond was big enough, he was taken too. My mother never went; one of the waiters fetched us until we were old enough to go alone. These visiting days were great days for us: the wide steps, the crowded verandas, the music, the soft, deep carpets of the lobby; this was a world of enchantment. My first definite thought about the hotel was that it belonged to my father. True, there was always around in the office a Mr. Campbell, a rather stooped man with a short reddish beard, who habitually gave me a friendly pat on the shoulder, and who evidently had something to do with the place. But just to the right, at the entrance to the big dining-room stands my father, peerless and imposing in full-dress clothes; he opens the door and takes me in; countless waiters, it seems, are standing around in groups; my father strikes a gong and the waiters spring to their stations and stand like soldiers at attention; I am struck with wonder at the endless rows of tables now revealed, the glitter of silver, china, and glass, and the array of napkins folded so that they look like many miniature white pyramids. Another gong, and the waiters relax; but one of them tucks a napkin under my chin and serves me as though I were a princeling. Then, with desires of heart and stomach satisfied and a quantity of reserves tied in a napkin, I am tucked away in a corner. Again the gong, the doors are thrown open, the guests stream in. My father snaps his fingers, waiters jump to carry out his orders, and guests smile him their thanks. He lords it over everything that falls within my ken. He is, quite obviously, the most important man in the St. James Hotel.

* * *

My father was a man of medium size, but constitutionally strong. One of the traditions of the home was that he was never sick. His color was light bronze, and so, a number of shades darker than that of my mother. She at fifty bore more than a slight resemblance to the later portraits of Queen Victoria; so much so that the family doctor christened her "Queen," a name to which she afterwards answered among her intimate friends.

The years as they pass keep revealing how the impressions made upon me as a child by my parents are constantly strengthening controls over my forms of habit, behavior, and conduct as a man. It appeared to me, starting into manhood, that I was to grow into something different from them; into something on a so much larger plan, a so much grander scale. As life tapers off I can see that in the deep and fundamental qualities I am each day more and more like them.

[*New York City*]

In 1884, Johnson visited New York City with his parents. This was a return migration of sorts for Helen and James Johnson, Sr. Helen grew up in Brooklyn during the 1840s; James Sr.—born free in Richmond, Virginia—moved north during his youth, in the 1830s; the couple began their courtship in Manhattan.[7]

As he recalls in this excerpt, New York City was exhilarating for Johnson as a young teenager. While the ex-colored man would no doubt agree that Manhattan requires "a love for cosmopolitanism" to be at peace in that metropolis, the wondrous tone with which Johnson describes this early encounter strikes different notes of understanding than the ex-colored man.

It would not have taken a psychologist to understand that I was born to be a New Yorker. In fact, I was partly a New Yorker already. Even then I had a dual sense of home. From the time that I could distinguish the meaning of words I had been hearing about New York. My parents talked about the city much in the manner that exiles or emigrants talk about the homeland; and I had long thought of New York, as well as Jacksonville, as my home. But being born for a New Yorker means being born, no matter where, with a love for cosmopolitanism; and one either is or is not. If, among other requirements for happiness, one needs neighbors; that is, feels that he must be on friendly terms with the people who live next door, and, in addition know all about them; if one must be able to talk across from front porches and chat over back fences; if one is possessed by a zeal to regulate the conduct of people who are neither neighbors nor friends—he is not born for a New Yorker.

When my uncle[8] and I got off in New York we would take a horse car and go as far as Lord and Taylor's,[9] then located in Grand Street. I had a lively time going through the big store while he bought his goods, some at one counter and some at another. When

7. The couple's courtship and marriage was a transnational affair, linking them from the Bahamas (Helen Dillet's homeland) to New York City and Jacksonville, Florida. See *Along This Way*, 137–40.
8. William H. C. Curtis, husband of Johnson's maternal aunt, Susan Dillet Smith.
9. One of the oldest department stores in the United States, founded in New York City in 1826.

he had finished, we would go down to the Grand Street ferry and take the boat back to Williamsburg.[1] I went to lots of other places in New York City, but my uncle never spent the time to take me. Yet, among the memories of all my goings about those of the excursions to Lord and Taylor's with him remain sharpest. I still love an old ferryboat because it is evocative of those days. I never board one and catch the smell from the deck planks redolent of horses that I do not recapture some of the sensations I experienced as a boy in crossing the East River and making the trip back and forth to Lord and Taylor's.

* * *

My grandmother[2] took me about with her a good deal visiting old friends she had known twenty or thirty or more years before. Most of the houses she visited were on Bleecker Street or Sullivan Street or Thompson Street or in the vicinity, then the principal Negro section of New York.[3] None of her old friends or acquaintances interested me; and hardly ever did I meet anyone near my own age. I was bored terribly by long conversations about old times and people who had died or, perhaps, done something worse; and I disliked the generally stuffy rooms in which I had to sit while the talk went on. But I loved to go on these trips because we rode endless miles, it seemed, on the horse cars and I was constantly seeing new sights. I especially enjoyed riding on the Broadway stage coaches. Only one of these old friends of my grandmother stuck in my memory. She was a gray-haired woman and quite stout, and sat all the while in a large armchair; she may have been lame. Suddenly she produced a pair of scissors and called me over to clip her finger nails. I found this job exceedingly distasteful; and, furthermore, she was very particular about how the work should be done. If I had been a modern-reared child I should have told the old lady to her face that I didn't want to and wouldn't clip her hard old nails; but to a product of the system under which I was brought up such action was unthinkable. When I had finished, she gave me a nickel, which I considered pretty poor pay. On one trip we went to Central Park, and I had the belated joy of riding in a goat wagon. And I mixed pleasure with duty by going round with a notebook industriously taking down a long list of the monuments to great men—names, dates, and deeds. I cannot imagine that this was a self-imposed duty, for I innately rebel at cataloguing statistical details. I must

1. Brooklyn, New York, neighborhood that borders the shoreline of the East River, roughly parallel to Manhattan's Lower East Side.
2. Johnson's maternal grandmother, Mary Barton.
3. The racial violence during the Draft Riots of 1863 pushed African Americans from the "Five Points" district in lower Manhattan to these streets in Greenwich Village.

have been following the admonishment of one of my teachers. Nor do I remember that the collected data were ever of any use to me. I think the time could have been better spent in the monkey house. With my grandmother I made the trip across and back over Brooklyn Bridge.[4] The great suspension bridges of New York are now commonplace; so the thrill of crossing Brooklyn Bridge when it was new cannot now be duplicated. But when I crossed, the echoes of the panic of the opening day, when the swaying of the great span under the tread of the crowd gave rise to the cry that the bridge was falling, had not quite died down; and I was far from feeling confident that it would not fall. Once we made a trip far up toward Harlem, a region then inhabited largely by squatters and goats.

[*Johnson's Near-Lynching*]

A pivotal event in Johnson's life—and in the writing and plot of *ECM*—was his near-death experience at the hands of a white mob in his hometown of Jacksonville, Florida, in 1901. While the ex-colored man is also transformed by the lynching that takes place in the rural Georgia woods (Chapter X), he endures the violence as a witness. Moreover, the murder he sees is not like the physical beating Johnson survived. If those distinctions are meaningful, what does the novel mean to imply about what counts as a racial trauma?[5]

There was a lady from New York[6] who was an occasional contributor to various papers and magazines visiting in Jacksonville at the time of the fire. A very handsome woman she was, with eyes and hair so dark that they blanched the whiteness of her face. One afternoon she came to the commissary depot where I was engaged and told me that she had written an article on the fire, dealing especially with its effects on the Negro population, which she would like to have me read over before she sent it off. I readily consented to read the article, but told her I couldn't possibly do so until after four o'clock, when the depot closed. It was a sweltering afternoon, and I was hot and tired; so I suggested that after closing time we might take a street car and ride out to Riverside Park, where we could sit and go over the article

4. Opened in 1883, just one year before the visit Johnson describes; spanning the East River from Tillary and Adams Streets in Manhattan (near City Hall) to Brooklyn Heights, the bridge connects the two boroughs' lower eastern sectors.
5. Johnson's account of teaching in rural Georgia is too long to reprint but bears importantly on his fictionalization of the ex-colored man's response to the lynching, See *Along This Way*, 250–69.
6. Victoria Earle Matthews (1861–1907), journalist and founding member of the National Association of Colored Women. Matthews travelled to Jacksonville to report on the cataclysmic fire (May 3, 1901) that destroyed much of the city, including the Stanton School, where Johnson served as principal.

leisurely and in comfort. She decided that instead of waiting around for me to close she would go out to the park and wait there.

At four o'clock I washed up and boarded a car. I had not yet been to this new Riverside Park; in fact, it was not yet quite a park. There was an old Riverside Park that I knew very well; but the city had recently acquired a large oak and pine covered tract on the bank of the river, a few miles farther out, which it was converting into a new park. I was, perhaps, more interested in seeing how this work had progressed than I was in reading the lady's article. When I reached the end of the carline, I noticed a rustic waiting-pavilion near the edge of the river. I made my way to it, expecting to find the lady there. She was not there, and I looked about but saw no sign of her. I judged that she had grown tired of waiting and had returned to the city. I walked back to the car-line. The car I had come out on was still there. The conductor and motorman were standing on the ground near the rear end. I waited until they were about ready to start, then got aboard. The car was empty, except for me, and I took a seat near the center—there were then no "Jim Crow" street car laws in Jacksonville. As I settled in my seat and glanced out of the window I saw a woman approaching across a little rustic bridge a hundred or so feet away whom I at once recognized by her dress and the black and white parasol she carried to be the lady I was to meet. I jumped off the car and walked over to join her. We went back across the bridge, then along some newly laid out paths until we came to a little clearing on the other side of which was a barbed wire fence. I helped her through the fence and followed. We then walked through the trees until we came to the bank of the river, where we found a bench and sat down. She read the article to me, and I offered one or two suggestions.

We sat talking. The sun was still bright, but was preparing for his plunge under the horizon, which he makes more precipitantly in the far south than he does in the north. At the point where we were sitting the St. Johns River is several miles wide. Across the water the sun began cutting a brilliant swath that constantly changed and deepened in color until it became a flaming road between us and the dark line of trees on the opposite bank. The scene was one of perfect semi-tropical beauty. Watching it, I became conscious of an uneasiness, an uneasiness that, no doubt, had been struggling the while to get up and through my subconscious. I became aware of noises, of growing, alarming noises; of men hallooing back and forth, and of dogs responding with the bay of bloodhounds. One thought, that they might be hunters, flashed through my mind; but even so, there was danger of a stray shot. And yet, what men would hunt with such noises, unless they were beating the bush to trap a wild, ferocious beast? I rose to go, and my companion followed. We threaded our way back. The noises grew more ominous. They seemed to be closing in. My pulse beat faster and my senses became more alert. I glanced at my companion; she showed no outward sign of alarm. Suddenly we reached the barbed wire fence. There we stopped. On the other side of the fence death was standing. Death turned and looked at me and I looked at death. In the instant I knew that the lowering of an eyelash meant the end.

Just across the fence in the little clearing were eight or ten militiamen in khaki with rifles and bayonets. The abrupt appearance of me and my companion seemed to have transfixed them. They stood as under a spell. Quick as a flash of light the series of occurrences that had taken place ran through my mind: The conductor and motorman saw me leave the street car and join the woman; they saw us go back into the park; they rushed to the city with a maddening tale of a Negro and a white woman meeting in the woods; there is no civil authority; the military have sent out a detachment of troops with guns and dogs to get me.

I lose self-control. But a deeper self springs up and takes command; I follow orders. I take my companion's parasol from her hand; I raise the loose strand of fence wire and gently pass her through; I follow and step into the group. The spell is instantly broken. They surge round me. They seize me. They tear my clothes and bruise my body; all the while calling to their comrades, "Come on, we've got 'im! Come on, we've got 'im!" And from all directions these comrades rush, shouting, "Kill the damned nigger! Kill the black son of a bitch!" I catch a glimpse of my companion; it seems that the blood, the life is gone out of her. There is the truth; but there is no chance to state it; nor would it be believed. As the rushing crowd comes yelling and cursing, I feel that death is bearing in upon me. Not death of the empty sockets, but death with the blazing eyes of a frenzied brute. And still, I am not terror-stricken, I am carrying out the chief command that has been given me, "Show no sign of fear; if you do you are lost." Among the men rushing to reach me is a slender young man clad in a white uniform. He breaks through the men who have hold of me. We look at each other; and I feel that a quivering message from intelligence to intelligence has been interchanged. He claps his hand on my shoulder and says, "You are my prisoner." I ask him, "What is the charge?" He answers, "Being out here with a white woman." I question once more, "Before whom do I answer this charge?" "Before Major B——, the provost marshal," he replies. At that, I answer nothing beyond "I am your prisoner."

The eternity between stepping through the barbed wire fence and the officer's words putting me under arrest passed, I judge, in less than sixty seconds. As soon as the lieutenant put his hand on me and declared me his prisoner, the howling mob of men became soldiers under discipline. Two lines were formed, with my companion and me between them, and marched to the street car. The soldiers filled the seats, jammed the aisle, and packed the platforms, and still some of them, with two men in civilian clothes holding the dogs in leash, were left over for the next car. As we began nearing the city my companion had the reactions natural to a sensitive woman. Both of us were now fairly confident that the danger of physical violence was passed, but it was easy to see that she was anxious; perhaps, about the probable notoriety; perhaps, about the opportunity for malicious tongues. I assured her as best I could that everything would come out all right. I said to her, "I know Major B——, the provost marshal, very well; he is a member of the Jacksonville bar." On the way in, the car stopped at the electric power house. It was met by a crowd of conductors, motormen, and other employees, who hailed our car with cries of, "Have you got 'em?" "Yes, we've got 'em," the soldiers cried back.

Before the car left the power house, the young lieutenant, whom I had hardly been able to see after we left the park, made his way to our seat. Again I felt the waves of mental affinity. In the midst of the brutishness that surrounded us I felt that between him and me there was somewhere a meeting place for reason. He leaned over and said, "I'm going to put these men off the car here and take you in myself." He ordered the men off. Of course, they obeyed, but they were openly a disappointed and disgruntled lot. The car moved across the aqueduct and into the heart of the city. I was thankful for the lieutenant's action; because, for reason or no reason, I did not want to be paraded through the streets of Jacksonville as a prisoner under guard of a company of soldiers. In my gratitude I was tempted to tell him what I did not have a chance to tell before I was put under arrest. But I was now comparatively light-hearted. I was already anticipating the burlesque finale to this melodrama—melodrama that might have been tragedy—and I disliked spoiling any of the effects. However, I did say to him, "The lady with me *is* white, but not legally so." He looked at her curiously, but made no comment; instead he said to me, "You know where the provost headquarters are, don't you?" I answered that I did. He continued, "When you get off the car you walk on ahead; I'll follow behind, and nobody will know you are under arrest." I thanked him again. We got off and walked to the provost headquarters, passing numbers of people, colored and white, who knew me. We went into the provost marshal's tent, followed by the lieutenant, who turned his prisoners over.

Major B—— showed astonishment and some embarrassment when he recognized me. I said to him, "Major, here I am. What is the charge?" He repeated the charge the lieutenant had made. "Major," I went on, "I know there is no use in discussing law or my rights on any such basis as, 'Suppose the lady *is* white?' so I tell you at once that according to the customs and, possibly, the laws of Florida, she *is not* white." In spite of appearances, he, of course, knew that I spoke the truth. He was apologetic and anxious to dismiss us and the matter. He spoke of the report that had been brought in, of his duty as commanding officer of the provost guard, of how he never even dreamed what the actual facts were. In answering, I told him that I appreciated how he felt about it personally but that that did not balance the jeopardy in which my life had been put. I added, "You know as well as I do, if I had turned my back once on that crowd or taken a single step in retreat, I'd now be a dead man." He agreed with me and said he was as glad as I that nothing of the kind had happened. At this point my companion began to speak. She spoke slowly and deliberately at first; then the words came in torrents. She laid on the Major's head the sins of his fathers and his fathers' fathers. She charged him that they were the ones responsible for what had happened. As we left, the Major was flushed and flustered. I felt relieved and satisfied, especially over the actually minor outcome of the avoidance of any notoriety for my companion. It was now dark, and I took her to her stopping place, The Boyland Home, a school for colored girls supported by Northern philanthropy.

I did not get the nervous reaction from my experience until I reached home. The quick turn taken by fate had buoyed me up. When I went into the provost marshal's tent my sense of relief had mounted almost to gayety. Now, the weight of all the circumstances in the event came down and carried me under. My brother was the only one of the family to whom I confided what had taken place. He was terrified over what might have happened; I never mentioned it to my parents. For weeks and months the episode with all of its implications preyed on my mind and disturbed me in my sleep. I would wake often in the night-time, after living through again those few frightful seconds, exhausted by the nightmare of a struggle with a band of murderous, bloodthirsty men in khaki, with loaded rifles and fixed bayonets. It was not until twenty years after, through work I was then engaged in, that I was able to liberate myself completely from this horror complex.

Through it all I discerned one clear and certain truth: in the core of the heart of the American race problem the sex factor is rooted; rooted so deeply that it is not always recognized when it shows at the surface. Other factors are obvious and are the ones we dare to deal with; but, regardless of how we deal with these, the race situation will continue to be acute as long as the sex factor persists.

Taken alone, it furnishes a sufficient mainspring for the rationalization of all the complexes of white racial superiority. It may be innate; I do not know. But I do know that it is strong and bitter; and that its strength and bitterness are magnified and intensified by the white man's perception, more or less, of the Negro complex of sexual superiority.

[*Building Characters*]

Johnson's "closest boyhood friendship," with Judson Douglas Wetmore (referred to as "D——" in *Along This Way*), provided rich, complex encounters for Johnson to mine when imagining the ex-colored man. So, too, did his mentor, Dr. T. O. Summers, a physician in Jacksonville, whose world-weary airs no doubt shaped the novel's "Millionaire." Perhaps, too, the fiercely brilliant West Indian cobbler who tutored Johnson when his high school closed may have inspired the character of "Shiny," the ex-colored man's scholarly black schoolmate who recurs as his foil throughout the novel. As compelling as these men were to Johnson personally, how does he re-invent their histories to serve the novel's purposes?

I was not long in finding my rank as a fellow student; and that is a rank not less important than the one in scholarship. It is, at any rate, a surer indicator of how the future man or woman is going to be met by the world. I found that I possessed a prestige entirely out of proportion to my age and class. Among the factors to which this could be attributed were: my prowess as a baseball pitcher, my ability to speak a foreign language,[7] and the presumable superiority in worldly wisdom that having lived in New York gave me. I think, at the time, D—— and I were the only students who could boast of first-hand knowledge of the great city. I could boast of having traveled even to a foreign country.[8] Another factor was my having a college student as my chum and roommate. D—— was only three months older than I, but he was more mature and far more sophisticated. Indeed, in his youth his face began to wear a jaded appearance; and, as a young man, he had a very low droop to the corners of his mouth. He had an unlimited self-assurance, while I was almost diffident; and he had inherited or acquired a good share of his father's roughness and coarseness. He had a racy style of speech, which I envied; but many of his choicest expressions I was unable to form in my own mouth. D—— was a *rara avis*[9] at Atlanta

7. Johnson was bilingual, speaking English and Spanish.
8. Johnson visited his mother's Caribbean homeland, Nassau Bahamas; see Chapter V in *Along This Way*.
9. Rare bird (Latin); unusual, unique.

University; nothing like him had ever before been seen in that cage. Yet he was popular with the boys and the girls, and, strange to say, even with the teachers. His very rakishness had a definite charm. And underneath his somewhat ribald manner he was tenderhearted and generous. Moreover, he was extremely good-looking, having, in fact, a sort of Byronic beauty.[1] He was short and inclined to stoutness. When he was a small Boy, he was fat. His head, large out of proportion to his height, was covered with thick, dark brown hair that set off his pale face and fine hazel eyes. The only thing that marred his looks was the frequent raising of the drooping corners of his mouth in a cynical curl. But speaking of his face as pale does not convey the full truth; for neither in color, features, nor hair could one detect that he had a single drop of Negro blood.

D—— was entirely at ease with the older boys and the young men of the College department; and in his take-it-for-granted way he made an opening with them for me. So almost from the start my closest associates were not among the boys of the Prep school but among the students of the College classes. I became the acknowledged fifth member of a combination made up of two Juniors, a Sophomore, and D——, calling themselves the "Big Four." We grouped ourselves whenever and wherever possible. We exchanged stories, information, and confidences; and we borrowed each other's money, generally for the purpose of paying for a late supper. Why a boy in boarding school can never get enough to eat will, I suppose, always remain a question. The meals in the dining room were never stinted, but we were always ready for a late, clandestine supper. There was an old man named Watson, whose job it was to tend the fine herd of cows owned by the school. He and his wife lived in a little house on the campus. We called this house "Little Delmonico"[2] because the good woman, who was also a good cook, furnished on short notice a supper of fried chicken, hot biscuits, and all the milk we could drink for fifteen cents. Whenever we had the money, we were ready to run the gantlet after lights were out for one of these suppers. Terms were cash, but we paid willingly; and without seeking to know whence came the milk—or the chickens either. We also passed many hours in the room of one or the other of us playing whist and seven-up, with shades drawn, hat over keyhole, crack under door chinked, and muffled voices; for playing cards was listed among the cardinal sins. But the greater part of our time together was spent seriously. We talked the eternal race

1. Refers to Romantic-era British poet Lord Byron (1788–1824).
2. During the mid-nineteenth and early-twentieth centuries, Delmonico's restaurant in Manhattan was famous for its luxurious setting and menus.

question over and over, yet always found something else to say on the subject. We discussed our ambitions, and speculated upon our chances of success; each one reassuring the others that they could not fail. There was established a bond of comradeship—among men, a nobler and more enduring bond than friendship.

It is not difficult for me to blot out forty-five years and sit again with these comrades of my youth. There is A——, tall, fair, slender, and elegant . . . peering near-sightedly through his heavy, gold-rimmed spectacles, but with his agile mind always balancing the possibilities and discovering the vantage. And H——, tall, too, but bronze-colored, broad-shouldered, heavy-jowled . . . in comparison with the ready, fluent A——, cumbrous of speech, using an almost Johnsonian vocabulary,[3] and, when roused, vehemently eloquent. T——, brown, short, and jolly, with gray eyes looking out quizzically from his moon-round face . . . speaking in anecdotes as wiser men had spoken in parables . . . always fresh stories, stories of black and white in the South, stories which, although we roared at them, we knew to have their points buried deep in the heart of the race question. And D——, worldly-wise, dare-devilish, self-confident, and combative . . . invincible on his own ground, but in danger when he exposed a superficial knowledge of other things to the adroitness of A——, to the honest logic and common sense of H——, to the humor of T——, before which what any one of the rest of us posited might be blown away like dust before a strong puff of breath. We talked, we argued, we nursed ambitions and dreams; but none of us could foretell. There is no way of getting a peep behind that dark curtain, which simply recedes with each step we take toward it; leaving in front all that we ever know. In truth, if some mysterious being had appeared in our midst and announced to A—— that he would rise to the highest office in the church; to H—— that he was to become the most influential and powerful Negro of his time in our national politics; to T—— that he was to have his heart's desire granted in being widely recognized as a typically brilliant Georgia country lawyer; and to D—— that he was to be one of the most prosperous colored lawyers in the country, a member of the Jacksonville city council, and an important factor in Florida politics,[4] we should all, probably, have been incredulous—but

3. Refers to British essayist and lexicographer Samuel Johnson's *Dictionary of the English Language* (1755).

4. Wetmore was admitted to the Florida bar in 1899, served on Jacksonville's City Council in 1905, and argued key racial discrimination cases before Florida's Supreme Court in 1906. However, Johnson's estimation of Wetmore's political career is quite generous. For contrasting views, see Louis R. Harlan and Raymond W. Smock, *The Booker T. Washington Papers, Vol. 8: 1904–06* (Urbana: University of Illinois Press, 1979), n. 1, 189; and Robert Cassanello, "Jim Crow: Negotiating Separate and Equal on Florida's Railroads and Streetcars," *Journal of Urban History* 34.3 (March 2008): esp. 445–53.

that is exactly what was behind the dark curtain. And it was also behind the dark curtain that before these lines would be written each of the four would have passed beyond the boundary of past, present, and, future.

D—— and I also had a great deal to talk over. I found that his father had declared emphatically that he would not spend another cent on his education.[5] He had decided, instead, to put his son to work. D——'s father was operating a small cigar factory in partnership with another colored man, who bore the wholly non-Aframerican name of Eichelberger. When I went to the factory I saw D—— working as a stripper; the first step in learning the cigarmaker's trade. He stripped the stems from the leaves of tobacco, smoothed out the "rights" and "lefts" and put them in separate piles over the edge of a barrel before which he was seated. He made no effort to disguise the fact that the job was distasteful to him. He was a diminutive Prometheus chained to a tobacco barrel.[6]

The summer promised to bring happy days; there were picnics and rides on the river and excursions to Pablo Beach[7] to look forward to—but there were other things in store. One day I found my mother lying across her bed groaning with pain. The doctor was called. She went to bed and remained there four months. When she got up she found herself crippled by rheumatism, crippled for life. This was a great blow to everyone in the house. Ever since she had been in Jacksonville she had taken a leading part in the educational and cultural activities of the colored people; and to be thus handicapped in the prime of her life, at the age of forty-six, was a great misfortune for her and not a small loss to the community. I was sent to buy a pair of crutches for her, and Rosamond and I undertook to help her learn to use them. We both had a difficult time choking back our emotions. She had been so active that to see her struggling like an infant again was almost more than we could stand. What made it all the more heart-breaking was her brave attempt to be cheerful; if she had complained and bemoaned her fate, we should not have been so keenly pierced.

In mid-summer, while my mother was lying ill, the great yellow fever epidemic broke out.[8] Some people fled at the first notice; but a rigid quarantine quickly made prisoners of the rest, prisoners in a charnel. There were efforts at escape, most of them futile, some of

5. Wetmore was expelled from Atlanta University for drinking alcohol; see *Along This Way*, 223–25.
6. For the crime of stealing fire from the Greek gods, Prometheus was chained to a rock and attacked by an eagle that ate his liver, only to have the organ grow back to be consumed again the next day.
7. A shoreline city near Jacksonville, Florida; known as Jacksonville Beach since 1925.
8. From July to November 1888, four thousand Jacksonville residents were infected and close to five hundred died.

them fatal. Business was paralyzed; the churches were closed, and all forms of assembly were restricted. Deaths reached a peak of more than a hundred a day. The county pest-house was enlarged by the addition of several temporary buildings, and patients were hurriedly taken there, unless they had behind them the advantage of strong influence. The people dreaded the pest-house as much as they did the disease; and every house upon which the yellow flag was nailed became, too, a pest-house. Many of the dead were buried in common graves; and that increased the terror. The cause of yellow fever had not yet been established; and I doubt that there were in Jacksonville in 1888 facilities for applying even the little that was then known about combating the plague. A few years later, the sure method of abolishing this disease was discovered.

But the possible was done. Money, supplies, and provisions were poured into Jacksonville from all over the country. The major part of the population was fed from commissariats. Some of the money contributed was expended in giving men work. I was given a job as time-keeper for a gang of men that was put at road building. For this I received two dollars a day. The fear, the suffering, the overhanging cloud of death, and my mother lying helpless, made this a memorable period of sadness for us. I watched my father grow more anxious and haggard as the days dragged slowly along. I went to bed for a couple of days with a temperature, and it looked as though the specter had entered our door. But we were among the fortunate; he passed us by. Expectations that medical skill and effort would stay the stalking pestilence were given up, and hearts finally clung to hope for an early frost.

The fall was ended before the fever had run its course and the quarantine was lifted. Reluctantly I resigned myself to the necessity of missing the year at school. I talked with my father and told him I wanted to keep it from being a lost year; that I wanted to go on with as many of my studies as possible—if I could find a tutor. He said that he knew a West Indian who was reputed to be a fine scholar. We went to see this man and found him in a small, dingy, cobbler's shop that he ran, pegging away at old shoes. He was a little man, very black, partially bald, with a scraggly beard, and but for bright, intelligent eyes an insignificant presence. At the sight of the surroundings my heart misgave me, and I was embarrassed both for my father and myself. I wondered if he misunderstood so much as to think that I wanted to be coached in spelling and arithmetic and geography. I was reassured when the little cobbler began to talk. He spoke English as no professor at the University could speak it. My father made arrangements, and I began to study with him every night. By a lamp that was often smoky and in an atmosphere filled with the odor of smelly old shoes I read Cæsar's *Gallic*

War[9] and Cicero's orations against Catiline.[1] I also began the study of elementary geometry. My teacher did more than correct, when necessary, the way in which I translated or construed Latin sentences; he had a considerable store of collateral knowledge, and gave me the benefit of it. He talked to me about Julius Cæsar and Cicero, and about Roman power and Roman politics in their time. So I got more than a language out of what I read; this collateral information not only made it interesting, but gave it sense and connected it up with life. Perhaps, the most common fault among teachers is the lack of collateral knowledge or the failure to make use of it. I remember that when I came to read the Greek dramatists I was plunged directly into the texts. There was no enlightenment as to how and why the plays were written or how and where they were performed. In fact, for me they were not plays at all; they were exercises in Greek grammar.

I cannot recall the name of my West Indian teacher or which of the islands he came from. Nor can I say how he was able to use this method of instruction without, apparently, any books to which to refer. I have the impression that he was a Jamaican and was educated at one of the excellent colleges there. At any rate, in the whole course of my school work the only other teacher who made a subject as interesting to me as did this little cobbler was Brander Matthews at Columbia. I wonder just what it was that kept him down on a cobbler's bench?

One day early in the winter a young man stopped at our gate. I knew him; his name was Robert Goode; he had worked for my father at the St. James; he was now cook for the family of Dr. T. O. Summers. Dr. Summers was regarded as the outstanding surgeon in Florida. He had been, I think, a professor of surgery at Vanderbilt University. Robert Goode told my father that the doctor was in need of someone to take charge of his reception room for patients; that the place had been held by a young white woman; that he had spoken to the doctor about me, and that I could get the job. He also said that the work would allow me time for my studies.

I went to see Dr. Summers. His office consisted of a suite of three rooms in one of the business blocks. He was then the only physician in Jacksonville who did no have his office in his residence. I found a man of thirty-eight or forty, very handsome, and well dressed. His features were what we term "classic," his hair and his well-trained mustache were dark, and his eyes were brooding. When I entered he was seated in a large chair, holding in one hand a small tin

9. The Roman statesman's account of the military campaign (58 to 51 B.C.E.) that secured the Republic's expansion into what is now France and Belgium.
1. The Roman philosopher, orator, and politician Cicero delivered a series of speeches that exposed his rival Catiline's plot to overthrow the Roman Republic (63 B.C.E.).

containing something that he languidly sniffed, first up one nostril, then up the other. He asked me to have a seat, then said, "I suppose you can read and write." I gave him the answer and he asked, "What else have you studied?" I named the regular grammar school studies, then went on proudly with "Latin, algebra—" I got no further. He straightened up and questioned, "Can you read Latin?" I grew dismayed, and answered with sincerely felt modesty, "I can read a little." He rose quickly from his chair, went to a bookcase, took out a volume bound in black, limp leather, with gilt lettering and edges, and handing it to me said, "Read me something from that." A glance at the title showed me that the book was one unknown to me— the *Roman Missal.*[2] I was not sure whether he wanted me to read or translate, but I proceeded as I had been taught; that is, to read the passage over first. I didn't think I should have made out so badly at translating, for the Latin did not strike me as difficult; but before I had finished reading the passage he said, "That will do," took the book from my hand and began telling me about my duties. These were the general duties of an attendant in a physician's reception room. But I had not been with him long before I took over entirely the matter of collecting his bills.

Since I have reached the point in life where the glance is more and more frequently backward, I look searching to discover the Key. I try to isolate and trace to their origins the forces that have determined the direction I have followed. This is a fascinating but inconclusive pursuit. The Key I do not find. I cannot separate the many forces that have been at work. I cannot unravel the myriad threads of influence that have drawn me here or there. The life, however simple, of every individual is far too complex for that sort of analysis. The number of forces, within and without, at work upon each one of us is infinite. Many of these forces are so subtle, so tangential that they are not even perceived. So when we set forth the manner in which we have definitely shaped the course of life, the precise steps by which certain ends have been reached, we are doing little more than rationalizing results. It is not possible to go back through the progression of causes. What more can any of us do than struggle to converge the forces at work toward some desired focus? We find some of them pliant and others stubborn. I have found many of them utterly unyielding. No intelligence or will power or industry that I possessed was able to bend or deflect them any fraction of a degree from their fixed and untoward direction. The forces at work on each individual are so manifold, so potent, so arbitrary, and often so veiled as to make fatalism a plausible philosophy.

2. The liturgical reference book that details the rituals and prayers of the Roman Catholic mass.

Nevertheless, I know that in the moment in which Dr. Summers took his *Roman Missal* out of my hand and said, "That will do," I had made contact with one of those mysterious forces that play close around us or flash to us across the void from another orbit. Dr. Summers was an extraordinary man. Of course, he was educated; but I had by now known a number of educated people. What was unprecedented for me was that in him I came into close touch with a man of great culture. He was, moreover, a cosmopolite. He had traveled a good part of the world over, through Europe, to North Africa, to Greece and Turkey. He spoke French and German, the latter, because of his student days in Germany, as fluently as he did English. He had wide knowledge of literature, and was himself a poet. His local literary reputation was very high because of the poems he sometimes contributed to the *Times-Union*.[3] He was an accomplished and brilliant talker. When alone, however, he was generally melancholy. He would sit for a long period inhaling from a small can of ether, seemingly lost in dreams. After I had learned something about ether, this habit caused me such anxiety that I spoke to him regarding it. He merely smiled sadly. I dared to speak to him about so personal a matter because from the beginning the relation between us was on a high level. It was not that of employer to employee. Less still was it that of white employer to Negro employee. Between the two of us, as individuals, "race" never showed its head. He neither condescended nor patronized; in fact, he treated me as an intellectual equal. We talked about things that only people in the same sphere may talk about. More than once, in conversation with others, he remarked that I had more sense than any of the Jacksonville doctors he knew anything about. This need not, however, be taken as extremely high praise; for his opinion with respect to the intellectuality of Jacksonville doctors in general was pretty low. In matters of money he was careless and, moreover, had the grand air. It was easy to believe what I vaguely gathered—that he had spent two fortunes, his own and his wife's. Mrs. Summers was pretty, petite, and rather demure. There were two beautiful children, "Bob" and Tom. "Bob," the elder, was about five years old, and a girl. She and I became great friends; and she never considered that I was at any time too busy to furnish her with information or entertainment.

My duties were light and gave me a good deal of the time to do things that appealed to me. I explored the books the doctor kept at his office. The number was not large but the range was wide; wider than that covered by the ten thousand books at the University library, many of those being, undoubtedly, donations from the libraries of defunct clergymen. A corner of the doctor's shelves was

3. Jacksonville's daily newspaper, created through a merger in 1883.

devoted to *erotica*; there I found the *Decameron* of Boccaccio[4] and the *Droll Stories* of Balzac.[5] It would be interesting, at least to me, if I could now determine what effect on me these forbidden books had. I can somewhat recall the glow that pervaded my body and my mind as I read some of these stories. Others of the stories struck me as very funny. I was stirred and entertained; was I damaged? The whole case for censorship is in that question. I cannot see that these books had the slightest deleterious effect. And I do not believe that any normal person is in any manner damaged by such reading. I grant that on persons of abnormal instincts or weaknesses there may not be this lack of bad effects, but those persons are anyhow bound to get at certain facts about life, and probably from sources far more contaminating than the wit and delicacy of Boccaccio and Balzac and the other masters of erotic literature. Did these books do me any good? That is a question the advocates of censorship might follow up with, but it raises a point not involved; a book may be 100 per cent "pure" and do nobody any good.

From the doctor's library I read some of Montaigne's essays, Thomas Paine's *Age of Reason*,[6] and Robert Ingersoll's *Some Mistakes of Moses* and *The Gods and other Lectures*.[7] was so much impressed with *The Age of Reason* that I carried it along with me so that I could read and reread it. One day my father summarily commanded me to "take that book out of the house and never bring it here again." I don't believe he was familiar with the book. Whether this stern action was prompted by having scanned it at the time or by "Tom" Paine's popular reputation, I do not know. Indeed, I was too much astounded by the sudden show of intolerance on my father's part to question the reason for his order. I simply obeyed it. I spent some of the time at my desk copying the text from the Greek Testament that I discovered among the doctor's book. I found this fascinating, although I did not understand a single word that I copied. My pages of Greek text drew enthusiastic praise from Dr. Summers, and he declared that I should have lived when the copying of manuscripts by hand was a fine art.

In the course of collecting the doctor's bills I made several futile efforts to get some money long due him by a Mr. Short. One day, I left a memorandum on the doctor's table about the collections I had made; reporting on Mr. Short, I scribbled this bit of doggerel:

4. Masterwork of the Italian lyric poet Boccaccio (1313–1375).
5. A trilogy of short stories published by the French novelist (1799–1850), between 1832 and 1837.
6. Eighteenth-century pamphlet by the American political theorist of revolution (1737–1809) that called for rational inquiry into spiritual matters.
7. Late nineteenth-century works that advocate agnosticism, or the unknowability of God.

Mr. Short—
As I "thort"—
Gave me not a single quarter;
And every time
I go to him
He seems to turn up shorter.

He thought this rather clever. Certainly the verses could not be as funny to anyone else as they were to him. At any rate, they led to my showing Dr. Summers all the verses I had written, and to his giving to me the first worthwhile literary criticism and encouragement I had yet received.

Dr. Summers had worked very hard during the yellow fever epidemic and had recorded his observations on the disease. He had prepared a large number of slides for microscopic study. In the spring he was asked to come to Washington to confer with Army medical officials as to his findings. He said to me at once, "Jimmie, I'm going to Washington, would you like to go?" He decided to go to New York by sea, and from there down to Washington. We left Jacksonville aboard a sailing vessel with auxiliary steam power, belonging to Louis K. Bucky, a Jacksonville lumber-mill owner. The ship did not carry passengers, but the exception was made because of Mr. Bucky's friendship for the doctor. I have traveled many thousands of miles by sea, and I love ships; but I am a bad sailor. This trip is memorable because it was so pleasant. The vessel lazed along through tranquil seas and perfect weather. We did not have to be dressed up; we did not have to make acquaintances; there were no shuffleboard players to obstruct the decks; and there were no romping, shouting children to break the sense of peace and quiet. For once I had no sensation of seasickness. I went to meals with a ravenous appetite. I ate at table with the captain and Dr. Summers—just the three of us, ordinarily the captain ate alone. The food was excellent; this captain, as do most sea captains, lived aboard like a nabob. I remember he had brought for his table a barrel of oysters which we depleted in the seven or eight days of the trip. At meals the doctor was more talkative and gay than I had ever seen him. He matched the captain with stories of travels to far, strange places. He gave a thrilling recital of his experiences during the bombardment of Alexandria, seven years before.[8] At other times he walked the small deck space alone, pausing frequently to look out broodingly on the sea, as though waiting for it to give him the answer to

8. Reference to the 1882 battle between the British navy and Egypt over sovereignty conflicts following the opening of the Suez Canal in 1869.

some question burning in his brain. Or he sat for long periods, a book in one hand, in the other his *vade mecum*,[9] a tin of ether.[1]

I am sure it was at Dr. Summer's suggestion, perhaps on his insistence, that I ate at the captain's table. He followed the same course at the hotels in New York and Washington. In each of these cities he engaged a double room in which both of us slept. We merely passed through New York, but our stay in Washington lasted a couple of weeks. I had practically nothing to do. The doctor sent me twice with communications to an official in the State, Army, and Navy Building; that is all I can remember having to do for him. He did not concern himself as to how I spent the time. I had much curiosity about Washington, which I went around satisfying. Naturally, the first sight was Pennsylvania Avenue. I was disappointed by its shabbiness, but amazed at its width. I went up and looked at the White House; I saw the Washington Monument; I visited various government buildings; but the major portion of my time I spent in the galleries of the Senate and the House of Representatives. The experience of looking at and for hours at a time listening to the leading figures on the floors of both houses did not tire me then. It was exciting, even when they discussed matters of which I had no comprehension. Of course I had no pre-knowledge that thirty-odd years later I should spend weeks and months between these same galleries, and in the offices of the leading figures on both floors, whom I should come to know well, in an effort to get them to do one particular thing.

When I returned to Atlanta University in the fall I was filled with regret at parting from Dr. Summers. The regret was mutual. He had formed a strong affection for me which he did not hide. I had made him my model of all that a man and a gentleman should be. The question rose in my mind whether I was not gaining more through contact with him than I would gain in going on in school. My father's estimate of this influence was not so high as mine. From my boastings at home he formed the opinion that the doctor was a very smart man, but visionary and impractical; in a word, without hard, common sense. My father was partially right. I myself could see that many of the things that Dr. Summers did and said were not governed by hard, common sense. But what my father did not appreciate, nor I, fully, was that that was the very point. I think he was glad that the time had come for me to return to Atlanta. The doctor did not intimate that I should do other than continue my schooling, but he urged upon me to choose medicine as a profession, and had a while before set me to the preliminary reading of a

9. An object regularly carried by a person (Latin).
1. A colorless liquid used as an anesthetic.

textbook on anatomy. Already, I had assisted him in several operations by administering the anæsthetic. When I left him I had thrown over the idea of becoming a lawyer for that of becoming a physician and surgeon, with the emphasis on the surgeon. I left him also with an older ambition clarified, strengthened, and brought into some shape—the ambition to write. We exchanged letters, and I sent him regularly whatever new things I wrote. He moved to a western city, and we continued the correspondence for several years. Then one day I was shocked to learn that Dr. Summers had committed suicide.[2] I was deeply grieved, for I had lost an understanding friend, one who was, in many ways, a kindred spirit.

* * *

When Bob and Rosamond came back to town, D—— moved out of the studio, but took another room in the Marshall, so I saw him every day.[3] I found that he had dissolved his partnership with the Brooklyn lawyer and had set up for himself, with offices downtown in Beekman Street.[4] I visited him there several times. He kept a suite of well-furnished rooms, and appeared to be building up a good practice. He was surely far from being discouraged and I was forced to admit that my advice to him not to leave Jacksonville had apparently been no sounder than his to me. From what I saw, his clientele was almost entirely white. In taking lunch or dinner downtown with him, I found that he was on terms of breezy intimacy with a number of professional and business men in his district. On one occasion when I was in his office a strikingly beautiful woman came in. She was young, about twenty-two, and her face was symmetrically perfect. She was tall and slender, but with that breadth of shoulders that presages an Amazonian air in middle life. But middle life to her was a long way off, and I recognized her beauty for what it was in the present. D—— took in the homage I silently paid her; I could see from the way he smiled that he relished it. It did not require the slight proprietary air that he assumed for my benefit to make me perceive that the young lady's visit was not that of a client to her lawyer. When she had gone, D—— proceeded to

2. See the obituary reprinted on 176.
3. This encounter with Wetmore occurs in 1908. Johnson returned to the United States for a leave from his diplomatic post in Puerto Cabello, Venezuela; Bob Cole and Rosamond Johnson's newest stage production, *Shoo Fly Regiment* (1907), had not been successful. Wetmore took over the trio's apartment space at the Marshall Hotel, the performance space in "Black Bohemia" where Johnson resided with his former songwriting partners. At this juncture, Johnson was dispirited: "New York did not seem the same to me," he writes. "Some of the shine seemed to have come off" (398).
4. When Wetmore moved from Jacksonville to New York City in 1906, he opened a law practice with African American attorney Rufus L. Perry. For more on Wetmore's fascinating legal career in New York, see Martha A. Sandweiss, *Passing Strange: A Gilded Age Tale of Love and Deception across the Color Line* (New York: Penguin, 2010), 258–63.

enlighten me fully on what I had already guessed to be the main point. The young lady was a Jewess; she belonged to a very nice family; she knew that he was colored but her family did not; he was deeply in love with her; she was in love with him. He enlarged on the last two points.

Throughout our lives, D—— in all his love affairs had sooner or later made me a sort of confessor. He frequently did something that I should rather have lost a finger than to do, he would read me most ardent letters from his lady loves; I recall, in particular, letters he received for several years from a girl he met at the University of Michigan, letters too tender, too sincere, yes, too sacred to be seen by a third pair of eyes; yet he read them to me. It may have been an injustice to him, but I always suspected that the act was not purely confidential in its nature, but was more or less mixed with vainglory. A confession about a great love from D—— had for some time since ceased to strike me as a crisis in his life; so I took no extreme heed of this latest one.

* * *

I spoke one Sunday morning for the Ethical Culture Society in New York.[5] As I sat on the platform, I noted D—— in the audience. He waited until the exercises were over to speak to me. I was glad of this because I had seen only little of him during these busy years. He introduced me to a very beautiful girl who was with him, as the young lady he was going to marry. I didn't fear that he was going to commit bigamy because I knew he had had matrimonial difficulties and that he and his wife were divorced. As soon as the young lady opened her mouth, I noted her Southern drawl. D——, always quick-eyed and mentally alert and, without a doubt, a mind reader with regard to me, promptly gave me the information that she was from Louisiana. The information surprised me in no manner. D——, in the confessions he used to make, had more than once confided to me the strange and strong attraction that Southern white women possessed for him. There was certainly nothing unnatural in his experience. A situation which combines the forbidden and the unknown close at hand could not do less than create a magnified lure. White men, where the races are thrown together, have never, for themselves, taken great pains to disguise that fact. There is no sound reason to think that this mysterious pull exerts itself only one direction across the color line, or that it confines

5. In keeping with his self-defined agnosticism, Johnson belonged to this nondenominational, nontheistic, social justice–oriented congregation that eschewed theology and embraced ethics as the basis for human belief and conduct. This encounter probably occured in or around 1927.

itself to only one of the sexes; the pull is double and inter-crossed. It is possible that Dame Nature never kicks up her heels in such ecstatic abandon as when she has succeeded in bringing a fair woman and a dark man together; and vice versa. Nor are there any facts on which to base a belief that, under comparable conditions, it would be more difficult for a colored man to win the love of a white woman (I am not here considering marriage, which is governed by a number of things aside from love) than for a white man to win the love of a colored woman. This is a thought well nigh impossible for the average white man to think; at least, with any equanimity. The primitive spirit of possessive and egotistic maleness is broad enough to embrace the women of other men, but its egotistic quality brooks no encroachment on the women of the clan. This primitive maleness is not limited to the white man, it is a masculine trait that may be traced back through many ages and among many races. The Negro, the Negro in the South possesses it; the difference being his lack of power to give it authority. In this whole situation, further complicated by the primitive antagonisms of femaleness, the sensitive nerve of the race problem in the South is embedded.

I saw D—— and his fiancée occasionally after they were married, they seemed perfectly happy. I enjoyed hearing her talk. In that delicious drawl she informed me: "I never knew that colored people had any problem till D—— told me about it. I used to see lots of them where I lived; sometimes I used to go to the quarter of the town where most of them lived, and they always seemed so happy to me." The three of us were at dinner one night at the Civic Club,[6] when she proudly told me that she was going to have a baby; that she hoped it was going to be a boy, and that he would be the first colored president of the United States. I gave her my best wishes, but added that, according to rumors that had been current, Warren Gamaliel Harding[7] had beaten her prospective heir to that distinction. The baby was a boy; and a girl followed, both of them lovely children. I did not see D—— frequently, but our old intimacy was in some measure re-established. He had made considerable money. He told me that it cost him twenty thousand dollars a year to live. He had put nearly all he could get together in the then recent Florida real estate boom and the burst of the bubble had hit him hard. One day in the summer of 1930, Grace, who was reading the *New York Times*, startled me with the cry that D—— was dead.[8] I

6. A New York City social club (at Fifth Avenue and Twelfth Street) that fostered interracial exchange among Manhattan's intellectual elite. Gatherings that shaped the Harlem Renaissance were held here in the 1920s.
7. The twenty-ninth president of the United States (1921–23).
8. Johnson may be referring to the obituary in the *New York Age* (see 175, below). The *New York Times* did not run a notice.

snatched the paper, and read that he had risen early, gone into the bathroom, and shot himself through the heart. At the hospital, where he died a few hours afterwards, his last words were that he was just tired of life.

Death has grieved me more deeply, but never has it more terribly shocked me.

EUGENE LEVY

From James Weldon Johnson: Black Leader, Black Voice†

Johnson's major biographer evokes the creative milieu in which Johnson became a professional artist in New York City between 1901 and 1906.[1]

The cosmopolitan strain in Johnson's personality, first seen in his youthful contact with Dr. Summers, expanded and developed on the New York scene. From the first, Johnson considered himself a "New Yorker," and he often proclaimed his love for the city.[2] Though preoccupied with Broadway and especially with the world of black show people, Johnson never completely committed himself either to show business or to its society. During his half-dozen years as a popular song writer he remained a careful observer, yet somewhat aloof from what many of his contemporaries considered the questionable life style generated by Broadway's lights.

James, Rosamond, and Bob Cole, the song-writing team of Cole and Johnson Brothers, lived at the Hotel Marshall, then newly established in a large brownstone at 127 West Fifty-Third Street, a few blocks from the present-day Museum of Modern Art. After the turn of the century many upper-strata members of the black theatrical group left the old Tenderloin District in the West Thirties and moved to the Fifty-Third Street neighborhood off Broadway. The Marshall soon became the principal meeting place for this increasingly

† From Eugene Levy, *James Weldon Johnson: Black Leader, Black Voice* (Chicago: University of Chicago Press, 1973), 79–97. Reprinted by permission of the University of Chicago Press.

1. Also see excerpts from Johnson's memoir, *Along This Way* (1933), 318–53, and *Black Manhattan* (1930), his cultural history of the African American performing arts-creative class. Selections from the latter are reprinted on 197–205. For insight into how Johnson's musical career influenced the themes and narrative style of *ECM*, see the essay by Ruotolo in this volume.
2. For example, he praised Manhattan in his poem "My City," *Century Magazine* 106 (1923): 716.

successful group. It also became an extremely popular spot for whites who wanted to see the latest in black entertainment, for the Marshall offered one of the first "cabaret"-style shows in the city, and in this sense anticipated the Harlem cabarets popular in the 1920s.[3]

Johnson soon began to live the role of a New York cosmopolite. Contemporary photographs show him as an impeccably dressed young man with a Van Dyke beard.[4] When the Klaw and Erlanger production of *Humpty Dumpty*, for which Cole and Johnson Brothers did a number of songs, opened November 21, 1904, the trio walked into the theater "attired in garment rich and almost rare, tailored with the sartorial effect obtained only in New York." James stood out among the three as a "suave and graceful" gentleman whose organizational ability provided the key element in the group's collaboration. At other times he played the bon vivant; the members of the Colored Republican Club were pleasantly surprised when Johnson, at that time president, supplied an after-meeting "lunch" of planked steaks, liquor, and cigars.[5]

The Broadway that Johnson worked on at the turn of the century was hesitantly making a place for Negroes to match the one Negroes had already made for themselves through their music. The black entertainer dated back to the early years of slavery, but his presence on the popular stage was a much later phenomenon. With few exceptions, Negroes first appeared in minstrel shows or in performances of *Uncle Tom's Cabin*. After the Civil War, all-black minstrel shows toured, but such groups followed the accepted minstrel pattern, even to donning the mask of burnt cork to become stage "darkies." The race also served as a major source of themes for popular songs, for this was the era of the so-called "coon song" and its companion the cakewalk. By 1900, ragtime, a musical style widely identified as Negro in origin, was becoming a national musical fad.[6]

By the late nineties, four black variety shows played in New York and on the road: the *Oriental America* show, the *Black Patti Troubadours*, and two groups known as the *Octoroons*. None of these groups broke completely with the black stereotypes they inherited from the contemporary American stage. One of the *Octoroon* shows, for example, had its variety acts tied together by a broad burlesque entitled "A Tenderloin Coon." One of the most popular numbers in the show was a fast-paced song called "No Coon Can Come too

3. *New York Sun*, January 18, 1903; *New York Age*, October 9, 1913; James Weldon Johnson, *Black Manhattan* (New York, 1930), 118–20.
4. See the photograph in *Along This Way*, facing 188.
5. R. C. Simmons, "Afro-Americans in the Musical World," *New York Age*, November 25, 1904; *New York Age*, February 15, 1906.
6. Edith Isaacs, *The Negro in the American Theatre* (New York, 1947), 19–23; Rudi Blesh and Harriet Janis, *They All Played Ragtime*, rev. ed. (New York, 1959), 128–29.

Black for Me." The *Black Patti Troubadours*, generally considered the most finished of the groups, also stayed close to the accepted pattern. Bob Cole wrote, directed and acted in much of the *Troubadours'* routine. In the central skit, "At Jolly Cooney Island," Cole and the chorus sang such songs as "Belle of Avenue A," "I'll Make dat Black Gal Mine" and "Black Four Hundred Ball."[7] Many of the numbers, especially in the *Oriental America* show and the *Troubadours*, were not coon songs but popular ballads and operatic arias. The "refined woman," one reviewer wrote of the *Octoroons*, would find "nothing from first to last to shock her modesty."[8]

The last years of the century saw blacks move into first-class vaudeville as well as Broadway musical comedy. Ernest Hogan, originally a minstrel, receiving top billing as a vaudeville comedian and song writer; he wrote one of the most popular songs of the period, "All Coons Look Alike to Me." In 1897 the comedy team of Bert Williams and George Walker made an extremely successful New York appearance at Koster and Bial's first-class vaudeville house, where Williams, as the shuffling, slow-witted, but extremely funny "darky," and Walker, as the flashy-dressed "colored sport," soon became one of the most popular comedy teams in show business.[9]

In 1898, a year before the Johnson brothers arrived in New York, blacks got onto the Broadway stage in other than vaudeville acts. The first to do so was Will Marion Cook, born of college-educated parents in Washington, D.C., where he grew up in surroundings not unlike those of Johnson. When he showed musical ability, his mother saw that he received the best training available, and at the age of eighteen he went to Berlin to study under the world-renowned violinist, Joachim. On returning to his native country, however, Cook turned to popular music. He saw artistic value in ragtime, and he realized that a black man had little chance of success in classical music.[1] Just as Rosamond urged his brother to write lyrics, in 1897 Cook urged his friend Paul Laurence Dunbar to collaborate with him on a musical skit, which emerged as *Clorindy: The Origin of the Cakewalk*.

Cook rewrote Dunbar's lyrics extensively, but they were still basically in the coon song tradition. The opening "strut song," for example, was "Hottes' Coon":

7. The description of these early Negro variety shows is based on a number of unidentified newspaper clippings in "Old Timers Book," JWJ MSS XI. Johnson obviously thought such songs were better forgotten, for he did not mention them when writing of these groups in *Black Manhattan*, 96–101. Cole's contemporaries thought of him as both versatile and brilliant; see Lofton Mitchell, *Black Drama* (New York, 1967), 46–47.
8. Unidentified newspaper clipping in "Old Timers Book," JWJ MSS XI.
9. Ann Charters, *Nobody: The Story of Bert Williams* (New York, 1970), 31–33, 70–71.
1. Richard Bardolph, *The Negro Vanguard* (New York, 1961), 236–37.

Behold the hottes' coon
Your eyes have lit on!
Velvet ain't good enough
For him to sit on.
When he walks down the street,
Folks yell like sixty,
Behold the hottes' coon in Dixie!

The combination of words and ragtime music made Cook's mother, an Oberlin graduate, exclaim, "Oh, Will! Will! I've sent you all over the world to study and become a great musician, and you return such a nigger!"[2] Still, Cook did not think he was degrading himself, for he thought it was time blacks developed the potentialities of their stage characterizations. When Ernest Hogan strutted on to the roof garden stage of Broadway's Casino Theater, his rendition of "Hottes' Coon" pleased not only Cook but the enthusiastic crowd as well.[3]

The Johnson brothers arrived in New York just as coon songs and ragtime were becoming increasingly popular. The lyrics James had written for *Tolosa*, the light opera they brought with them in hopes of finding a producer, clearly revealed his lack of contact with the latest musical trends. Unlike Cook's *Clorindy, Tolosa* had nothing to do with blacks. James had concocted a stylized plot and lyrics, with the action set on an imaginary Pacific isle, clearly derived from British comic opera.[4] *Tolosa*, at least in its original version, revolved around a devious American patent-medicine salesman (Dr. Hocus Pocus) and his efforts to wed Tolosa, daughter of the king, who in turn loved Lolos, a commoner. An American man-of-war (Captain Clarke and the jolly crew of the U.S.S. *Galore*) soon appeared and eventually revealed Hocus Pocus for the fraud he was, thus enabling Tolosa and Lolos to be united.

Johnson's lyrics, like the plot, had strong overtones of W. S. Gilbert's conventional approach. The opening chorus, for example, found the happy natives singing:

Good morning, good morning, what is the news today?
Good morning good morning, what have you new to say?
Oh tell me! Oh tell me no longer delay. . . .
We are a queer little people,
Whose isles are far out at sea;
We are a dear little people,
But curious as curious can be.

2. Will Marion Cook, "Clorindy, The Origin of the Cake-Walk," *Theatre Arts* 30 (September, 1947): 61–62.
3. Ibid., 65. Most of the major Broadway theatres of the era had gardens and theaters on the roof. There patrons could dine and watch lighter entertainment after the main attraction ended downstairs.
4. Several versions of the libretto are in JWJ MSS I.

The only mention of blacks occurred in a solo, when the fake doctor recounted among his deeds

> . . . a Zulu king so black
> He'd dim the brightest light;
> I rubbed him with my liniment,
> and now that king is white.

Johnson's original book for *Tolosa* also contained a secondary theme—the eventual annexation of the island by Captain Clarke and his men in the name of the United States. He later came to feel that this controversial theme might have deterred producers.[5] Despite the secondary theme, the *style* of the book and lyrics harkened back to English comic opera—a model which was rapidly becoming outdated on the American musical stage. By 1899 comic opera, burlesque, the minstrel show, and the variety show were merging into a new type of production—the musical comedy. The new musical comedy emphasized a vernacular style in songs, dances, and subject matter, as well as a plot with more or less consistent characterization.[6] Johnson's lyrics for *Tolosa* are like a formal exercise in the writing of a comic opera, in contrast to the sometimes crude, but always spirited, lyrics of Dunbar and Cook in *Clorindy*.

Johnson soon updated his style. "Louisiana Lize," the first Cole and Johnson Brothers tune, was a dialect love song. The three writers quickly sold it for fifty dollars to May Irwin, a well-known white singer, who promptly inserted it into her current musical comedy.[7] From that time on, Cole and the Johnsons concentrated largely, though by no means exclusively, on songs with Negro themes.

While they were still commuting between New York and Jacksonville, James and Rosamond managed to write and publish almost thirty songs, of which many were incorporated into the musical productions of such stars as Marie Cahill, May Irwin, and Virginia Earle. When May Irwin, in the summer of 1900, asked them to compose some songs for her new musical, *The Belle of Bridgeport*, it was evident that they were on the rise. One critic, even though he called *The Belle* a "stupid farce," had nothing but praise for the trio's "I Ain't Gwinter Work No Mo'" (1900) and May Irwin's rendering of its "droll bad darky philosophy."[8]

By the fall of 1902, when Johnson resigned from Stanton, the trio was close to both fame and wealth, although sheet music sales, on

5. *Along This Way*, 151.
6. Cecil Smith, *Musical Comedy in America* (New York, 1950), 21, 57.
7. *Along This Way*, p. 153. The published sheet music of "Louisiana Lize," as well as all other Cole and Johnson Brothers' songs mentioned in this chapter, is in the Johnson Papers. May Irwin helped inaugurate the coon song craze in 1896 with her rendition of the Mississippi River roustabout song, "I'm Lookin' for de Bully." Blesh and Janis, *They All Played Ragtime*, 93.
8. *New York Times*, October 30, 1900. For similar comments see the *New York Telegraph*, January 12, 1902.

which most of their future income depended, still lagged distressingly. Their big break came that fall when Marie Cahill heard one of their new songs, "Under the Bamboo Tree," and immediately inserted it into her musical comedy, *Sally in Our Alley*. Alone on the stage but assisted by a hidden chorus and orchestra, she sang "this pretty coon ballad in a manner both charming and captivating."[9] Its popularity cannot have been due solely to Miss Cahill's rendition, for by mid-1903 more than 400,000 copies of the song had been sold—another success for the trio's publisher, Joseph Stern Company, known as "The House of Hits." By 1903, wrote one out-of-town paper with only a little exaggeration, almost every Broadway musical featured one of the songs of Cole and Johnson Brothers. "Those ebony Offenbachs," as a New York critic dubbed them, had arrived.[1]

The trio's contemporary success rested firmly on songs with Negro themes. Some of their songs had nothing to do with blacks—"The Maiden with the Dreamy Eyes" became extremely popular—but they built their reputation on pieces like "Under the Bamboo Tree," "The Congo Love Song," and "Nobody's Lookin' but de Owl and de Moon."[2]

James largely assumed responsibility for the lyrics.[3] Many of these, especially in the first few years, employed common black stereotypes. "Labor is tiresome sho'," May Irwin sang in *The Belle*; "The best occupation is recreation; I ain't gwinter work no mo'." In another early song, "My Castle on the Nile" (1901), Johnson used the sport's desire for the highlife: "Inlaid diamonds on de flo', a baboon butler at my do'." "I've Got Troubles of my Own" (1900), written for May Irwin, the publisher promptly labeled as "a bit of coon philosophy." In stereotyped dialect, James and Bob Cole told the tale of a Baptist deacon who grew tired of listening to other people's troubles:

> Dis here takin' me for a free-lan-tho-fist,
> is cert'ny got to stop;
> It seems to me de darkies got it
> in der heads dat I'm a free pond shop.
> Sho'ly will inform 'em and inform 'em quick,
> dat friendship banks' done bust!
> I'm goin' ter notify dese glad-
> hand coons dat I don't intend
> to run no trouble-trust!

9. Unidentified newspaper clipping in second scrapbook, JWJ MSS II.
1. *Washington Post*, February 15, 1903; *New York Sun*, February 17, 1903.
2. Virginia Earle threatened to leave the cast when the producers of her new show refused to let her use "The Maiden with the Dreamy Eyes," *New York Telegram*, February 1, 1902.
3. Rosamond was very positive on this point in the comments he wrote on the copy of "Under the Bamboo Tree" in the Johnson Papers.

This was common coon song rhetoric, but admirers of the group expected more than the common run of lyrics, and even Cole and Johnson Brothers seemed a little unhappy about some of the lyrics they produced. They knew, as their close friend and admirer R. C. Simmons pointed out, that they had "written words for some of their music that are not in keeping with the spirit of such music."[4] Echoing Simmon's comment years later, Rosamond wrote that, when he and Bob Cole sang Hogan's phrase "all coons look alike to me," they substituted "boys" for "coons." The latter word always had a choking effect on their voices.[5]

Despite the crudity of some of their lyrics, the trio did not cater to the lowest levels of contemporary musical taste. In the hands of Cole and Johnson Brothers, coon song lyrics became noticeably more genteel. The song writers allied themselves with the movement in musical comedy away from Bowery bawdiness and toward a more or less well-mannered exuberance. When Marie Cahill sang their "Congo Love Song" in *Nancy Brown* in 1902, one reviewer correctly saw both the play and the song as part of the trend separating Broadway musicals from Tenderloin vaudeville. "Their business is not simply to grind out coon songs," a Jacksonville paper noted in analyzing the success of the hometown boys; "They have elevated that species of popular music by ridding it of obscene and vulgar doggerel." If Cole and the Johnsons were the "Musical Moses to lead the coon song into the Promised land," they led not as original creators of ragtime but rather as popularizers, fitting the songs to the more genteel demands of middle-class America.[6]

Johnson's upbringing and education equipped him well for such a role. He used several approaches. One was to choose carefully among the available stereotypes and avoid those picturing the black man as a razor-swinging rowdy (the "bully" of May Irwin's famous coon song) or as a semihuman buffoon. Perhaps influenced by Dunbar's dialect poems, Johnson emphasized the fun-loving aspect of the black stereotype. For instance in "Sambo and Dinah" (1904), he wrote of naïve love:

> Their love you hear them stammer
> Without respect to grammar,
> For this is how these dusky lovers
> bill and coo . . .

4. R. C. Simmons, "Europe's Reception to Negro Talent," *Colored American Magazine* 9 (1905): 639.
5. See Rosamond's comment on the copy of "Tell Me Dusky Maiden" in the Johnson Papers. This song, a parody of the theme song of the renowned Floradora Sextet, incorporated lines from Ernest Hogan's "All Coons Look Alike to Me."
6. For quotes see *Jacksonville Metropolis*, May 4, 1904, and unidentified newspaper clippings, all in second scrapbook, JWJ MSS II.

In "When the Jack O' Lantern Starts to Walk About" (1901), Bob Cole and Johnson made use of the Negro's supposed superstitious bent, but again, like Dunbar, they emphasized his simple innocence:

> Twixt de settin' ob de sun an' de breakin' ob de day,
> Den de Jack O' Lantern starts to walk about.
> Every pickaninny must be tucked in bed;
> Not a pickaninny should be out,
> When the Jack O' Lantern starts to walk about.

Johnson followed the same pattern in many of his other lyrics, such as those for "Run Brudder Possum Run" (1900), "No Use in Askin' 'Cause you Know the Reason Why" (1901), "Gimme de Leavin's" (1904) and "Hello Ma Lulu" (1905).

A second and more significant approach was to retain the coon song format but to break from specifically black stereotypes. In the lyrics of the trio's most popular songs, "Nobody's Lookin' but de Owl and de Moon" (1901), "Under the Bamboo Tree" (1902), and "Congo Love Song" (1903), Johnson sought an empathy with their predominently white listeners by emphasizing experiences and emotions common to the human race, and not those supposedly limited to blacks. Johnson's lyrics were not especially original, yet it was innovative to imply that both blacks and whites experienced the same romantic emotions in the same way. One of the first songs written in this manner, "Nobody's Lookin' but de Owl and de Moon," had emblazoned on the cover not "a darky croon" or "a bit of coon philosophy" but "a stirring American song."

The universality and simplicity of their lyrics account in part, at least, for the enormous popularity of "Under the Bamboo Tree" and "Congo Love Song." Of all Cole and Johnson Brothers songs, "Under the Bamboo Tree" achieved the greatest contemporary and most lasting fame. The song even crept into the Ivy League; Yale undergraduates immediately took it up, parodied the lyrics, and turned it into a football song.[7] Two decades later "Under the Bamboo Tree" remained indicative enough of the era for T. S. Eliot to make use of the lines "one live as two, two live as one, under the bamboo tree" in his poem "Fragment of Agon."

7. The Yale adaptation can be found in several unidentified newspaper clippings, second scrapbook, JWJ MSS II. The first verse of the Yale version went,

> Oh, I'd like to win,
> And you'd like to win,
> We'd both like to win the same.
> But we'd like to say
> This very day,
> Yale's going to win this game.

"Under the Bamboo Tree" was an uncomplicated song musically; its theme was a variation in ragtime of the spiritual "Nobody Knows de Trouble I See"—a fact which largely accounts for Bob Cole's name alone appearing on the published sheet music. At the time, Rosamond felt such musical antics beneath the dignity of a former student of the New England Conservatory.[8] The lyrics concerned a "maid of royal blood though dusky shade" who attracted the ardent attention of a "Zulu from Matabooloo." The Zulu offered his love in this famous proposal:

If you lak-a-me, I lak-a-you;
and we lak-a-both the same,
I lak-a-say, this very day,
I lak-a-change your name;
'Cause I love-a-you and love-a-true
And if you-alove-a-me,
One live as two, two live as one,
Under the bamboo tree.

Though the boy and girl were "Zulus," and though they crooned the refrain in mild dialect, the simple sweetness of the lyrics bore little resemblance to the average coon song of the period. Rather, they expressed their love in phrases universal enough to be sung everywhere by young people around parlor pianos.

Cole and Johnson Brothers followed with another song in the same vein—"Congo Love Song"—which Marie Cahill introduced in February 1903 in her musical comedy *Nancy Brown*. Recounting the efforts of a Kaffir chief to woo a Zulu maid, "Congo Love Song," like "Under the Bamboo Tree," spoke of love and not "nigger" love. Johnson made this universality—as well as the essentially respectable theme—explicit in the last verse, describing now the young maid

May have been perhaps a trifle cruder,
Than girls on the Hudson or the Seine;
Yet though she was a little Zulu,
She did what other artful maids do.

By 1903 Cole and Johnson Brothers had achieved considerable fame, though they were still bound by the desires of their largely white audiences. Consequently they saw themselves, and were seen by others, as important representatives of their race. The advance in the musical world of blacks like Cole and Johnson, wrote one critic, will perhaps "someday settle their status in the community."[9]

8. See Rosamond's comments on the copy of "Under the Bamboo Tree," in the Johnson Papers.
9. *Vanity Fair*, October 31, 1903.

No one had ever expected such social significance from any white man on Tin Pan Alley.

There is evidence that Johnson was conscious of the Negro's potential role in music even before he established himself in New York. Back in his *Daily American* days he had urged blacks to write both dialect poems and dialect songs.[1] In New York in the summer of 1899, Johnson read and preserved what was probably the first attempt to appreciate critically the new ragtime music—an appraisal by the future novelist Rupert Hughes. Neither the charge of crude innovation nor equally crude copying, Hughes maintained, would discredit ragtime, the new "negro music." Both Johnson brothers might have felt that Hughes addressed them personally when he wrote, "Perhaps the negroes themselves will rise to the emergency and develop the vast potential significance of their own school."[2]

Johnson, who himself took up this challenge, believed that the triumphs of black performers on Broadway demonstrated both the artistic abilities of blacks and their ability to compete successfully with white professionals. After Cole and Johnson Brothers' rise to fame, they would describe their musical goals in racial terms. Bob Cole, for example, spoke of how they tried to retain the racial traits of black music while avoiding the vulgarity of the coon song. Rosamond said much the same thing when he told of the group's efforts to "evolve a type of music that will have all that is distinctive in the old Negro music and yet which shall be sophisticated enough to appeal to the cultured musician."[3] In 1903 the three began to work on The Evolution of Ragtime, a series of songs designed to show the development of black music. The first in the series, "Lay Away Your Troubles," they patterned after the spirituals; the second, "Darkies Delight," tried to capture the spirit of the minstrel show; the third, "The Spirit of the Banjo," illustrated secular folk music; and "Lindy: A Love Song" was a ragtime song typical of Cole and Johnson.[4]

Yet there was an uncertainty in the minds of Bob Cole and the Johnson brothers about the development of specifically black music. While Bob Cole spoke of retaining the racial quality of that music, he also predicted that ragtime would be swallowed up by Spanish music. "The syncopation," he explained, "is the same."[5] Whatever the similarity between the flamenco and ragtime, Cole's statement

1. *The Daily American* scrapbook, JWJ MSS II.
2. Rupert Hughes, "A Eulogy of Rag-Time," *Musical Record*, 447 (April 1, 1899): 157–59. A copy of the Hughes article is in the second scrapbook, JWJ MSS II.
3. An undated clipping from the *Cleveland Plain Dealer*, JWJ MSS II.
4. The four songs in The Evolution of Ragtime were published in the *Ladies Home Journal:* May 1905, p. 29; June 1905, p. 31; July 1905, p. 23; August 1905, 19.
5. Unidentified newspaper clipping, second scrapbook, JWJ MSS II.

seemed to deemphasize the racial tradition within which he supposedly worked.

Jim Johnson's reaction to ragtime showed a similar ambiguity. In 1905 a national magazine asked him to write a short article on Negroes in contemporary music. In the course of the article Johnson gave his highest praise to those composers and performers whose music was least identifiably black. At the top of his list stood Samuel Coleridge-Taylor in England and Harry T. Burleigh in the United States—composers who made their reputation chiefly in conventional classical music. Following them were writers and performers of popular music: Williams and Walker, Ernest Hogan, and Cole and Johnson. Composers like Scott Joplin, James Lamb, Tom Turpin, and James Scott were well known among ragtime musicians, but their piano compositions were too complex and too different to compete in the market place with "Under the Bamboo Tree."[6]

Johnson believed that the acceptance by the American public of black music and musicians not only demonstrated the ability of the race but also encouraged racial pride. Yet, despite this belief, Johnson had had little direct contact with the black culture of which that music was an expression, and he remained firmly committed to accepted American values, musical and otherwise. Like Bob Cole, he wanted somehow to maintain the racial identity of the music he was helping to produce, and at the same time "refine" and "elevate" it, bringing it into conformity with conventional musical and moral standards. If it came to a choice, however, Johnson obviously preferred Coleridge-Taylor's mundane though successful "white" oratorios to Joplin's unconventional and largely unpopular "black" rags.

Johnson had confronted much the same problem a few years earlier in his essay in the Culp volume, which concluded that blacks could not preserve a distinctive identity and still advance themselves in American society. His own musical achievements pointed to an ultimate loss of racial identity. The lyrics for the most popular Cole and Johnson songs largely succeeded in avoiding the obnoxious racial stereotypes of the coon song, but replaced them with the equally stereotyped, though essentially nonracial, emotions of Tin Pan Alley.

Song writing did not take all of Johnson's time, nor did it satisfy all of his interests. The trio worked night and day when they were composing; at other times, especially when Bob and Rosamond were

6. Johnson, "The Negro of To-Day in Music," *Charities* 15 (October 7, 1905): 58–59. For an extensive social history of ragtime, see Rudi Blesh and Harriet Janis, *They All Played Ragtime*, esp. 14–127. For an intensive analysis of ragtime music, see Guy Waterman, "Ragtime" in Nat Hentoff and Albert McCarthy, *Jazz* (New York, 1959), 45–57.

on tour, Johnson found himself with considerable spare time. He went to the theater frequently and, as he later recalled, saw all the operas the Metropolitan had to offer. True to his upbringing, he abhorred idleness. Johnson urged upon his friends the maxim "employ your spare time," and he lived by those words while in New York City.[7]

The Fifty-Third Street district, and in particular the Hotel Marshall, carried a reputation among the city's black population as the place where "sports," theater people, and bohemians spent their time and money. Johnson moved in this circle but was not part of it. He observed carefully the fast crowd, both black and white, on Fifty-Third Street, but he never participated to an extent that would compromise his reputation. Many blacks who were neither poor nor "sports" lived in Brooklyn, or else went there for social functions. In their own homes they found security from potential racial affronts. John B. Nail, a well-informed and well-to-do black tavern keeper, pointed out in 1903 that, in their relations with white people, cultivated black families tried to be as inconspicuous as possible.[8] Johnson's cosmopolitan adaptability allowed him to move as freely among the status-sensitive Brooklyn set as he moved among the pleasure-seeking Fifty-Third Street crowd. He came to know many of these Brooklyn families, especially the younger members, and attended many of their functions. It was at one of these gatherings, an amateur theatrical, that he first met John Nail's daughter Grace, who later became his wife.

Besides recreation in Brooklyn and on Fifty-Third Street, Johnson sought more serious uses for his spare hours. Both his interest in poetry and his work in show business turned him to the study of literature, especially the literature of the theater. He decided to take advantage of the best instruction available—that of Brander Matthews, professor of dramatic literature at Columbia University. A teacher and critic who prided himself on being both "urban and urbane," Matthews then stood at the height of his influence. While his critical writings did much to introduce modern European drama, especially the works of Ibsen, to American audiences, he also took great interest in the popular theater, right down to the lowly minstrel show.[9] To Johnson's surprise, Matthews knew his musical comedy work and gave him a warm personal welcome to his classes.

7. *Along This Way*, 192; *New York Age*, May 17, 1906.
8. "New York's Rich Negroes," *New York Sun*, January 18, 1903; Charles W. Anderson to Booker T. Washington, January 12, 1906, BTW Papers; *Colored American Magazine* 10 (1906): 271–72.
9. Henry May, *The End of American Innocence* (New York, 1959), 470–71. Brander Matthews, "The Rise and Fall of Negro Minstrelsy," *Scribner's Magazine* 57 (1915): 754–59.

In the summer of 1905, Johnson's studies at Columbia were interrupted when Bob Cole and Rosamond were offered a six-week booking at the Palace Theatre in London. James was as excited as his two partners over a European trip, for it would be his first. Combining pleasure with business, the three men decided to tour the continent for a few weeks before the London engagement.

Most black Americans have been impressed by the friendliness and lack of discrimination shown them while in Europe. Frederick Douglass, during one of his early stays in England, exclaimed, "I live a new life"—a sentiment echoed many times by black Americans, though after wider travel some have had doubts about European color-blindness.[1] Johnson reacted typically, and his short stay precluded any disillusionment. For the first time in his life he felt free of the necessity to fend off either assaults on his dignity or special considerations because of his race. In Europe, he later wrote, he had escaped "the conflict within the Man-Negro duelism."[2]

Landing at Le Havre, the trio took the express train to Paris. Johnson had been prepared to dislike France but soon changed his mind. The ride in the privacy of their own compartment convinced him of the superiority of the French railways, though he managed to salvage a bit of national pride by finding the Gare Saint Lazare inferior to New York's Grand Central. During the next few weeks Johnson found many reasons to lavish Paris and Parisians with praise. On a few occasions, however, visiting white Americans who he came into contact with made it clear his presence was unwelcome. It was not enough, Johnson told his readers back home, that they persecute us in the United States; they have to export such behavior to countries yet untainted.[3]

Following their stay in Paris the trio visited Brussels, Antwerp, and Amsterdam and arrived in London in early August. There they found the name of Cole and Johnson everywhere. Never before had they seen vaudeville headliners so widely advertised; they were impressed enough to have postcards made up showing London busses with large placards advertising their coming appearance at the Palace Theatre.[4]

Bob and Rosamond, of course, had experienced many opening nights, but they were never more nervous than the night they opened in London. And James, in his orchestra seat, was as nervous as they. They were not afraid only that the audience in London's most

1. Douglass, *The Life and Times of Frederick Douglass* (New York, 1962), 243. For the experiences of later travelers see Pickens, *Bursting Bonds*, 163–64; Torrence, *The Story of John Hope*, 183; James Baldwin, *Notes of a Native Son* (Boston, 1955), 117–23.
2. *Along This Way*, 209.
3. See Johnson's letters to the *New York Age*, August 3 and 8, 1905.
4. James sent a card to Booker T. Washington, August 5, 1905, BTW Papers.

prestigious variety theater would find their talents meager. Despite Johnson's new sense of freedom from the burden of race, he was acutely aware that his brother and Bob Cole represented the black man before a white audience. He wanted them to succeed not only because they were his partners, but because they were black. Johnson's sense of racial identity, born of the American scene, burned too strongly to be extinguished by Europe's seeming indifference to color. When the Palace audience erupted in loud, sustained applause after the last notes of the "Congo Love Song," Johnson felt that Bob and his brother had demonstrated both their own ability and the ability of black Americans in general.[5]

* * *

Although none of the major events which befall the [hero of *The Autobiography of an Ex-Colored Man*] actually occurred in Johnson's life, his friends provided certain raw material. The most significant of these friends was his boyhood companion and former law partner, J. Douglass Wetmore, who had passed as a white man on a number of occasions. Shortly before Johnson left for Puerto Cabello, Wetmore moved to New York, where, after unsuccessfully attempting to court the favor of both Charles Anderson and the anti-Washington faction, he settled down to practice law. Though Wetmore did not sever his relations with his black friends, by 1908 he generally moved in white society and let himself be taken for white. At about the same time, Wetmore took a further step and married a white woman. Johnson himself acknowledged, though not in print, that Wetmore provided the initial idea for his central character.[6] None of *The Autobiography's* major episodes, apart from the hero's passing into white society, has any known parallel in Wetmore's life.

Of the other characters in the novel only the hero's white millionaire friend and patron seems to be based on a known person. In an early draft of the work Johnson identified this cynical cosmopolite with a wealthy friend of Al Johns, a black song writer.[7] Johnson probably also had in mind his friend Dr. Orville Summers, the first urbane individual he knew well. *The Autobiography's* millionaire feels such an ennui toward life that, like Dr. Summers, he ultimately commits suicide.

5. Simmons, "Europe's Reception to Negro Talent," 635–42; *New York Age*, August 31, 1905; *Along This Way*, 214.
6. *New York Age*, February 1, 8, April 26, June 21, 1906; Anderson to A. I. Vorys (copy), February 10, 1908, Frederick Hilles Papers, Historical Manuscripts Collection, Yale University Library; *Along This Way*, 252. The BTW Papers contain many letters between Anderson and Washington detailing Wetmore's machinations. Johnson acknowledges Wetmore as a model in a note with the manuscript of *Along This Way*, JWJ MSS IX.
7. See draft in JWJ MSS II.

As in many didactic works of fiction, character development and motivation is weak in *The Autobiography*. What there is was superimposed by the author rather than growing out of the character's psychological reaction to his environment. Johnson never makes it clear, for example, why his hero chooses Atlanta University and not a small white college; nor are the reasons for his leaving Atlanta convincing. Later incidents tend to be more melodramatic than dramatic. Johnson primarily uses his protagonist as a window through which he points out and interprets the American racial scene. He had two main purposes in writing *The Autobiography*. The first was to show that there are cultured, sophisticated, respectable blacks. The second was to demonstrate that, while the American racial scheme produced great injustice, blacks had endured and had made contributions of unique value to American culture. In his novel he presented these themes in greater detail and with more clarity than he ever had before.

ANONYMOUS

Obituaries of J. Douglas Wetmore

J. D. Wetmore Kills Self†

ROSE TO POWER AMONG WHITES; DEFENDED RACE

DRIVEN FROM FLORIDA HOME WHEN HE FOUGHT SEGREGATION A MEMBER OF CITY COUNCIL—MARRIED WHITE WOMEN TWICE

Judson Douglas Wetmore, brilliant attorney, who crossed the "color line" but never forgot his own people in their struggles, was cremated Saturday at Fresh Pond Crematory, Fresh Pond, L[ong] I[sland], after committing suicide Thursday in his summer home at Greenwich, Conn.

The lawyer's ashes will be borne back to Jacksonville, Fla., where he rose to power in politics thirty years ago. When he left his native city nearly three score years ago he was an exile, driven out because he was a Negro and dared to defend Negroes.

Mr. Wetmore shot himself through the left breast at his home on India Head road Thursday morning. For days—his friends say years—he has been melancholy and threatening to take his own life.

† *New York Amsterdam News*, July 30, 1930, 1. Reprinted with permission of Amsterdam News Pub. Co.

"TIRED OF LIFE"

Going to the bathroom he pointed his pistol at his left breast and fired. The bullet missed his heart and tore downward through his body, imbedding in his abdomen. Mrs. Wetmore, who is white, came to his aid and rushed him to Greenwich Hospital, where he died in the early evening. Surgeons were urged by Mr. Wetmore not to save him. He was tired of living. Half of Mr. Wetmore's life read like pages from James Weldon Johnson's "Autobiography of an Ex-Colored Man." Light enough to pass for white, Mr. Wetmore never denied his race. He was material enough to practice law in later years with white attorneys.

FIRST WIFE WHITE, ALSO

The attorney was first married to a white woman, from whom he separated. The second Mrs. Wetmore was also white. Of the latter union, two children, Frances, eight, and Judson Douglas, Jr., six, were born. The Wetmores maintained a town home on Riverside [D]rive and spent their summers in Greenwich.

Mr. Wetmore was born sixty years ago in Tallahassee, Fla., the son of George M. Wetmore, contractor and builder. He received his early education at Cookman Institute, Jacksonville, Fla.. Later he attended Atlanta University, from which he graduated.

Following completion of his college course, Mr. Wetmore returned to Jacksonville as principal of the South Jacksonville High School, a position he held for five years.

ENTERS POLITICS

While teaching in Jacksonville, Mr. Wetmore became interested in politics and was sent to Ann Arbor, Mich., to the University of Michigan, to study law, by Napoleon Browerd, governor of Florida. He received the degree of bachelor of laws from that institution in June, 1898.[1]

He again returned to his home in Jacksonville and was elected to the member of the Fire Committee. In 1903 he came to New York, where he was admitted to the bar the following year. From that time on until the time of his death he practice law successfully here.

Upon being admitted to practice in New York, Mr. Wetmore entered a partnership with Rufus Perry, scholarly and eccentric Brooklyn lawyer, who died recently. For several years, Mr. Wetmore

1. Wetmore did not receive his law degree from Michigan. He completed one year of coursework at the law school (1896–97) and then returned to Jacksonville, where he was admitted to the Florida bar in 1898. Dominique Daniel, graduate reference assistant, Bentley Historical Library, University of Michigan, personal communication, May 21, 2008.

practiced at 5 Beekman Street. Later he secured offices in the Pulitzer building on Park row. From there he went to 1440 Broadway.

LOST IN FLORIDA BOOM

Living in white districts and associating mainly with white attorneys, Mr. Wetmore was said to have made considerable money in his practice and in real estate. He headed a number of realty companies. During the Florida boom he invested heavily and was said to have lost a small fortune when the bottom dropped in the peninsula state. Mr. Wetmore bought a huge estate in northern New Jersey a few years ago, but gave up residence there after fortune failed to beam so brightly on him.

At 1440 Broadway he was the senior member of the firm Wetmore and Schwartz.

FORCED TO FLEE SOUTH

While a member of the City Council at Jacksonville the Nordic city fathers began laying their plains for complete segregation of the Negro and the denial of his constitutional rights. Mr. Wetmore entered the fight with a stout heart and opposed his white townsmen. So bitter did the battle wage that he was forced by threats to leave the city.

With segregation laws behind him, he set out to enjoy all the rights of citizenship. His old friends from Florida were not forgotten and he made many trips to Harlem to enjoy their banquets, eat in their homes, and smoke their cigars. Early this year, when Congressman Oscar De Priest[2] spoke here, he [Wetmore] agreed with the Representative's statement that Negroes needed a lobby in Washington. Immediately he made a generous donation and started a temporary committee.

One of his friends tells this story of him: A few years ago former Governor Charles Whitman was seeking election as district attorney of New York county.[3] Whitman was in Wetmore's office one day and made a statement indicating prejudice toward Negroes. Immediately Mr. Wetmore started a campaign against him in Negro districts. The situation became alarming and the former governor went to a Negro politician high in Republican councils and asked his assistance.

2. Oscar De Priest (1871–1951), civil rights activist, member of the Republican party, and skilled operator in Chicago's famed political machine; first African American to be elected to U.S. House of Representatives in the twentieth century (1928–35).
3. Charles S. Whitman (1868–1947), Republican who served as governor of New York from 1915 to 1918. The obituary refers to Whitman's 1909 run for district attorney in New York County.

Whitman was told to promise he would appoint a Negro as assistant district attorney if elected. He did so and was elected by a small margin. A Negro got the post.

Two brothers survive Mr. Wetmore. They are Dr. Ernest Wetmore, a dentist of Morristown, N. J., and George Wetmore of New York City.

"Doug" Wetmore, Prominent Lawyer, Commits Suicide by Shooting Self With Revolver at His Summer Home"†

NATIVE OF FLORIDA, HE CAME TO NEW YORK AND / BUILT UP LARGE LAW PRACTICE, MOSTLY WITH / WHITE CLIENTELE, BUT KEPT RACE CONTACTS

Judson Douglas Wetmore, former Jacksonville, Fla. lawyer, who came to New York and built up a large practice, committed suicide by shooting himself in the left breast Thursday evening, July 24. The tragedy occurred at his summer cottage, Indian Head Point, Greenwich, Conn.

"I was worried and tired of life," Mr. Wetmore told Medical Examiner Clarke just before he died at the Greenwich Hospital. Friends say his health had been failing for some time, and it is also reported that he suffered financial reverses during the current business depression.

At the request of the deceased, no formal funeral was held and the body was cremated at Fresh Pond, Long Island, on Saturday morning.

The late Mr. Wetmore was born sixty years ago in Tallahassee, Fla., but received his early education in Jacksonville. He was a classmate in public school with James Weldon Johnson, James C. Andrews, and several other former residents of Jacksonville now living in New York.

After completing the public schools of Jacksonville he attended Cookman College, and upon his graduation from this institution attended Atlanta University for a time. He also attended Harvard University but did not graduate. Instead, he went West and entered the University of Michigan Law School. Following his graduation from this school he returned to Jacksonville and began the practice of law in 1897.[1]

In 1906 he moved to New York and opened his law office in the World Building, where he remained for many years. Although he had many friends among members of the race in New York, most of his practice was among other races.

† *New York Age*, August 2, 1930, 1. Reprinted by permission of Dudley Products, Inc.

1. This obituary also mistakenly reports that Wetmore earned his law degree from the University of Michigan; see note 1 on 173 for details.

He was twice married, both wives being members of the Jewish race, and his law partner at the time of his death was a Hebrew.

Most of his law practice in recent years was along commercial and real estate lines, and he was reported to be wealthy, maintaining a fine home on Riverside Drive, the Greenwich Cottage, and a large office at 1440 Broadway.

In addition to his widow, Mr. Wetmore leaves two young children by his second wife, and a grown daughter by his first wife. He is also survived by two half-brothers, George Wetmore of 311 West 139th Street, New York City, and Dr. Ernest Wetmore, a dentist of Morristown, N.J.

ANONYMOUS

Obituary of Dr. Thomas Osmond Summers[†]

Dr. T.O., late of St. Louis, MO, well known to the profession of the South and West, is dead. He committed suicide in the lecture hall of the College of Physicians and Surgeons of St. Louis in which he was Professor of Anatomy, on the evening of June 13th, by shooting himself through the head. His death was a tragic and sensational denouement of a checquered and varied career.[1]

Dr. Summers was the son of a distinguished Methodist divine. He graduated in the University of Alabama at Greensboro, and studied for the ministry. Finding himself unsuited to that vocation, he studied medicine and graduated from the Medical Department at the University of Nashville. He taught chemistry in his alma mater in Alabama until he was, in 1875, called to the chair of anatomy in the Medical School in Nashville, from which he received his degree of M.D.[2] He won an enviable reputation as a teacher of anatomy and resigned his position in 1870. In 1878 he was among the first to volunteer his services in the yellow fever epidemic at Memphis, and more fortunate than others came out unscathed and with a reputation for skill in the treatment of that disease that was

† *Nashville Journal of Medicine and Surgery* 86.1 (July 1899): 45–47.

1. The *Milwaukee Journal*'s report sketches the more gruesome details of Summers's death, alluding to his addiction to morphine and reprinting excerpts from his farewell letters to a colleague, Dr. W. J. Donohue, and his wife. See *Milwaukee Journal*, June 20, 1899, available at news.google.com/newspapers?nid.
2. The University of Nashville's Medical Department merged with Vanderbilt University's then-newly established unit in 1875. The two operated jointly until 1898, when Vanderbilt separated to run its school independently. See R. H. Kampmeier, *Vanderbilt University School of Medicine: The Story in Pictures from Its Beginning to 1963* (Nashville: Vanderbilt University Medical College, 1990), 13–14. My thanks to Mary Teloh, special collections librarian at Vanderbilt's Eskind Biomedical Library, for providing me with this reference and Summers's obituary.

national in its extent. While in Nashville he practiced his profession and gained a large clientele. He went from here to Jacksonville, Fla., where he practiced for a number of years. He located afterwards in Chicago, and later in Waukesha [Wisconsin]. He subsequently was employed in New York by a drug house from which place he was called to St. Louis to the Chair of Anatomy in the College of Physicians and Surgeons. While in that city he was for some time the editor of the *St. Louis Clinique*. On the outbreak of the Spanish American war he was appointed Surgeon with the rank of Major in the Second Tennessee Regiment, and was commissioned to go to Cuba as a yellow fever expert. He was discharged from the army for some cause, and his efforts at reinstatement doubtless had much to do with his ending his life. To attempt to delineate the character of a man like Dr. Summers would result in failure, for his makeup was different in many particulars from that of all other men. He was a prodigy mentally, by reason of this fact earning the admiration of all with whom he was thrown in contact. His memory was colossal and his acquirements boundless. His faults were many, but these were to some extent condoned by his generosity and liberality. As a writer he was unequaled for care of expression and elegance of diction. He possessed no small powers as a poet and his last work was a revise written just before death on his approaching end. As a teacher of medicine he was unrivalled. Many of his old students in this vicinity are frequently heard to praise his ability as a teacher of his favorite branch, while his death and his mode of death caused little surprise among those who knew him, it is greatly regretted by all who knew him well. Had he been mentally balanced he would have made a great man. May he in death find the rest he had not in this life. "*De mortis nil nisi bonum*."[3]

3. Let no one speak ill of the dead (Latin).

On the Cultural History and Milieu of *The Autobiography of an Ex-Colored Man*

W. E. B. DU BOIS

From The Souls of Black Folk[†]

The first of these two chapters from *The Souls of Black Folk* presents Du Bois's formative definitions of racial "double consciousness" and its signature metaphor, the "veil." The second offers Du Bois's commanding assertion about the universal appeal of the "sorrow songs"; Negro spirituals, according to Du Bois, "stand to-day not simply as the sole American music, but as the most beautiful expression of human experience born this side of the seas." Johnson's narrator alludes to these key concepts throughout *The Autobiography of an Ex-Colored Man*.

I. Of Our Spiritual Strivings[1]

O water, voice of my heart, crying in the sand,
  All night long crying with a mournful cry,
As I lie and listen, and cannot understand
    The voice of my heart in my side or the voice of the sea,
O water, crying for rest, is it I, is it I?
    All night long the water is crying to me.

Unresting water, there shall never be rest
  Till the last moon droop and the last tide fail,
And the fire of the end begin to burn in the west;
    And the heart shall be weary and wonder and cry like the sea,

† From *The Souls of Black Folk: A Norton Critical Edition*. Edited by Henry Louis Gates, Jr., and Terri Hume Oliver (New York: Norton, 1999), 9–16, 154–64. Editorial notes © 1999 by Henry Louis Gates, Jr. and Terri Hume Oliver. Used by permission of W. W. Norton & Company, Inc.

1. Revised from "Strivings of the Negro People," *Atlantic Monthly* (August 1897): 194–98. The verses are from *The Crying of Waters* (1903) by Arthur Symons. The music quotation is from the Negro spiritual "Nobody Knows the Trouble I've Seen."

All life long crying without avail,
As the water all night long is crying to me.

ARTHUR SYMONS.

Between me and the other world there is ever an unasked question. unasked by some through feelings of delicacy; by others through the difficulty of rightly framing it. All, nevertheless, flutter round it. They approach me in a half-hesitant sort of way, eye me curiously or compassionately, and then, instead of saying directly, How does it feel to be a problem? they say, I know an excellent colored man in my town; or, I fought at Mechanicsville;[2] or, Do not these Southern outrages make your blood boil? At these I smile, or am interested, or reduce the boiling to a simmer, as the occasion may require. To the real question, How does it feel to be a problem? I answer seldom a word.

And yet, being a problem is a strange experience,—peculiar even for one who has never been anything else, save perhaps in babyhood and in Europe. It is in the early days of rollicking boyhood that the revelation first bursts upon one, all in a day, as it were. I remember well when the shadow swept across me. I was a little thing, away up in the hills of New England, where the dark Housatonic[3] winds between Hoosac and Taghkanic to the sea. In a wee wooden schoolhouse, something put it into the boys' and girls' heads to buy gorgeous visiting-cards—ten cents a package—and exchange. The exchange was merry, till one girl, a tall newcomer, refused my card,—refused it peremptorily, with a glance.[4] Then it dawned upon me with a certain suddenness that I was different from the others; or like, mayhap, in heart and life and longing, but shut out from their world by a vast veil. I had thereafter no desire to tear down that veil, to creep through; I held all beyond it in common contempt, and lived above it in a region of blue sky and great wandering shadows. That sky was bluest when I could beat my mates at examination-time, or beat them at a foot-race, or even beat their stringy heads. Alas, with the years all this fine contempt began to fade; for the worlds I longed for, and all their dazzling opportunities, were theirs, not mine. But they should not keep these prizes, I said; some, all, I, would wrest from them. Just how I would do it I could never decide: by reading law, by healing the sick, by

2. Site of a Civil War battle of June 1862, near Richmond, Virginia.
3. River that runs through Du Bois's hometown of Great Barrington, Massachusetts.
4. In *The Autobiography of W. E. B. Du Bois* (1968) he reports that this incident took place during his high-school years.

telling the wonderful tales that swam in my head,—some way. With other black boys the strife was not so fiercely sunny: their youth shrunk into tasteless sycophancy, or into silent hatred of the pale world about them and mocking distrust of everything white; or wasted itself in a bitter cry, Why did God make me an outcast and a stranger in mine own house?[5] The shades of the prison-house closed round about us all:[6] walls strait and stubborn to the whitest, but relentlessly narrow, tall, and unscalable to sons of night who must plod darkly on in resignation, or beat unavailing palms against the stone, or steadily, half hopelessly, watch the streak of blue above.

After the Egyptian and Indian, the Greek and Roman, the Teuton and Mongolian, the Negro is a sort of seventh son, born with a veil, and gifted with second-sight in this American world,[7]—a world which yields him no true self-consciousness, but only lets him see himself through the revelation of the other world. It is a peculiar sensation, this double-consciousness, this sense of always looking at one's self through the eyes of others, of measuring one's soul by the tape of a world that looks on in amused contempt and pity. One ever feels his two-ness,—an American, a Negro; two souls, two thoughts, two unreconciled strivings; two warring ideals in one dark body, whose dogged strength alone keeps it from being torn asunder.

The history of the American Negro is the history of this strife,—this longing to attain self-conscious manhood, to merge his double self into a better and truer self. In this merging he wishes neither of the older selves to be lost. He would not Africanize America, for America has too much to teach the world and Africa. He would not bleach his Negro soul in a flood of white Americanism, for he knows that Negro blood has a message for the world. He simply wishes to make it possible for a man to be both a Negro and an American, without being cursed and spit upon by his fellows, without having the doors of Opportunity closed roughly in his face.

This, then, is the end of his striving: to be a co-worker in the kingdom of culture, to escape both death and isolation, to husband and use his best powers and his latent genius. These powers of body and mind have in the past been strangely wasted, dispersed, or forgotten. The shadow of a mighty Negro past flits through the tale of Ethiopia the Shadowy and of Egypt the Sphinx. Throughout history, the powers of single black men flash here and there like falling stars, and die sometimes before the world has rightly gauged their

5. An ironic rewriting of Exodus 2.22, in which Moses declares, "I have been a stranger in a strange land."
6. Reference to William Wordsworth's ode *Intimations of Immortality from Recollections of Early Childhood*.
7. In African American folklore, seventh sons as well as those children born with a caul, a membrane that sometimes covers the head at birth, are reported to have special abilities, such as predicting the future and seeing ghosts.

brightness. Here in America, in the few days since Emancipation, the black man's turning hither and thither in hesitant and doubtful striving has often made his very strength to lose effectiveness, to seem like absence of power, like weakness. And yet it is not weakness,—it is the contradiction of double aims. The double-aimed struggle of the black artisan—on the one hand to escape white contempt for a nation of mere hewers of wood and drawers of water, and on the other hand to plough and nail and dig for a poverty-stricken horde—could only result in making him a poor craftsman, for he had but half a heart in either cause. By the poverty and ignorance of his people, the Negro minister or doctor was tempted toward quackery and demagogy; and by the criticism of the other world, toward ideals that made him ashamed of his lowly tasks. The would-be black *savant*[8] was confronted by the paradox that the knowledge his people needed was a twice-told tale to his white neighbors, while the knowledge which would teach the white world was Greek to his own flesh and blood. The innate love of harmony and beauty that set the ruder souls of his people a-dancing and a-singing raised but confusion and doubt in the soul of the black artist; for the beauty revealed to him was the soul-beauty of a race which his larger audience despised, and he could not articulate the message of another people. This waste of double aims, this seeking to satisfy two unreconciled ideals, has wrought sad havoc with the courage and faith and deeds of ten thousand thousand people,—has sent them often wooing false gods and invoking false means of salvation, and at times has even seemed about to make them ashamed of themselves.

Away back in the days of bondage they thought to see in one divine event the end of all doubt and disappointment; few men ever worshipped Freedom with half such unquestioning faith as did the American Negro for two centuries. To him, so far as he thought and dreamed, slavery was indeed the sum of all villainies, the cause of all sorrow, the root of all prejudice; Emancipation was the key to a promised land of sweeter beauty than ever stretched before the eyes of wearied Israelites.[9] In song and exhortation swelled one refrain—Liberty; in his tears and curses the God he implored had Freedom in his right hand. At last it came,—suddenly, fearfully, like a dream. With one wild carnival of blood and passion came the message in his own plaintive cadences:—

> "Shout, O children!
> Shout, you're free!
> For God has bought your liberty!"[1]

8. A learned scholar.
9. Following their Egyptian captivity, the Israelites reached Canaan, the Promised Land, after forty years of wandering in the wilderness.
1. Refrain of the freedom spiritual "Shout, O Children!"

Years have passed away since then,—ten, twenty, forty; forty years of national life, forty years of renewal and development, and yet the swarthy spectre sits in its accustomed seat at the Nation's feast. In vain do we cry to this our vastest social problem:—

> "Take any shape but that, and my firm nerves
> Shall never tremble!"[2]

The Nation has not yet found peace from its sins; the freedman has not yet found in freedom his promised land. Whatever of good may have come in these years of change, the shadow of a deep disappointment rests upon the Negro people,—a disappointment all the more bitter because the unattained ideal was unbounded save by the simple ignorance of a lowly people.

The first decade was merely a prolongation of the vain search for freedom, the boon that seemed ever barely to elude their grasp,—like a tantalizing will-o'-the-wisp,[3] maddening and misleading the headless host. The holocaust of war, the terrors of the Ku-Klux Klan,[4] the lies of carpet-baggers,[5] the disorganization of industry, and the contradictory advice of friends and foes, left the bewildered serf with no new watchword beyond the old cry for freedom. As the time flew, however, he began to grasp a new idea. The ideal of liberty demanded for its attainment powerful means, and these the Fifteenth Amendment gave him.[6] The ballot, which before he had looked upon as a visible sigh of freedom, he now regarded as the chief means of gaining and perfecting the liberty with which war had partially endowed him. And why not? Had not vote's made war and emancipated millions? Had not votes enfranchised the freedmen? Was anything impossible to a power that had done all this? A million black men started with renewed zeal to vote themselves into the kingdom. So the decade flew away, the revolution of 1876 came,[7] and left the half-free serf weary, wondering, but still inspired. Slowly but steadily, in the following years, a new vision began gradually to replace the

2. *Macbeth* 3.4.102–3. Du Bois symbolically represents the American character as guilty and blood-stained, like the central character of Shakespeare's tragedy.
3. A delusive or misleading goal.
4. Secret society formed in 1866 by Confederate veterans with the stated intent of protecting white, Protestant interests. It rapidly became a terrorist organization responsible for widespread violence against African Americans.
5. Northern politicians and businessmen who entered the South following the Civil War. Portrayed as carrying their belongings in cheap, fabric valises (carpetbags), they were seen as enriching themselves at the cost of a defeated Confederacy.
6. Ratified March 10, 1870; it granted voting rights to men regardless of "race, color, or previous condition of servitude." Although the amendment was a moderate measure and did not outlaw qualification tests for voters, it allowed Congress to enforce the law through federal sanctions.
7. The results of the presidential elections of 1876 were disputed by Louisiana, Florida, and South Carolina, three states that backed Democrat Samuel J. Tilden against Rutherford B. Hayes. Some Southern Democrats threatened a "revolution" of secession from the Union. Republicans, in their attempt to mollify the Democrats, significantly reduced their support of the freedmen.

dream of political power,—a powerful movement, the rise of another ideal to guide the unguided, another pillar of fire by night after a clouded day. It was the ideal of "book-learning"; the curiosity, born of compulsory ignorance, to know and test the power of the cabalistic[8] letters of the white man, the longing to know. Here at last seemed to have been discovered the mountain path to Canaan;[9] longer than the highway of Emancipation and law, steep and rugged, but straight, leading to heights high enough to overlook life.

Up the new path the advance guard toiled, slowly, heavily, doggedly; only those who have watched and guided the faltering feet, the misty minds, the dull understandings, of the dark pupils of these schools know how faithfully, how piteously, this people strove to learn. It was weary work. The cold statistician wrote down the inches of progress here and there, noted also where here and there a foot had slipped or some one had fallen. To the tired climbers, the horizon was ever dark, the mists were often cold, the Canaan was always dim and far away. If, however, the vistas disclosed as yet no goal, no resting-place, little but flattery and criticism, the journey at least gave leisure for reflection and self-examination; it changed the child of Emancipation to the youth with dawning self-consciousness, self-realization, self-respect. In those sombre forests of his striving his own soul rose before him, and he saw himself,—darkly as through a veil;[1] and yet he saw in himself some faint revelation of his power, of his mission. He began to have a dim feeling that, to attain his place in the world, he must be himself, and not another. For the first time he sought to analyze the burden he bore upon his back, that dead-weight of social degradation partially masked behind a half-named Negro problem. He felt his poverty; without a cent, without a home, without land, tools, or savings, he had entered into competition with rich, landed, skilled neighbors. To be a poor man is hard, but to be a poor race in a land of dollars is the very bottom of hardships. He felt the weight of his ignorance,—not simply of letters, but of life, of business, of the humanities; the accumulated sloth and shirking and awkwardness of decades and centuries shackled his hands and feet. Nor was his burden all poverty and ignorance. The red stain of bastardy, which two centuries of systematic legal defilement of Negro women had stamped upon his race, meant not only the loss of ancient African chastity, but

8. Mystical. The cabala, or Kabbalah, is a body of esoteric Jewish doctrines dealing with the manifestations of God. Written between the third and the sixteenth centuries, these books are difficult to interpret.

9. The Promised Land. Du Bois is reinforcing his identification of African Americans with the Israelites during their years of Egyptian captivity and their forty years of wandering in the wilderness.

1. Corinthians 13.12: "For now we see through a glass, darkly; but then face to face: now I know in part; but then shall I know even as also I am known."

also the hereditary weight of a mass of corruption from white adulterers, threatening almost the obliteration of the Negro home.

A people thus handicapped ought not to be asked to race with the world, but rather allowed to give all its time and thought to its own social problems. But alas! while sociologists gleefully count his bastards and his prostitutes, the very soul of the toiling, sweating black man is darkened by the shadow of a vast despair. Men call the shadow prejudice, and learnedly explain it as the natural defence of culture against barbarism, learning against ignorance, purity against crime, the "higher" against the "lower" races.[2] To which the Negro cries Amen! and swears that to so much of this strange prejudice as is founded on just homage to civilization, culture, righteousness, and progress, he humbly bows and meekly does obeisance.[3] But before that nameless prejudice that leaps beyond all this he stands helpless, dismayed, and well-nigh speechless; before that personal disrespect and mockery, the ridicule and systematic humiliation, the distortion of fact and wanton license of fancy, the cynical ignoring of the better and the boisterous welcoming of the worse, the all-pervading desire to inculcate disdain for everything black, from Toussaint[4] to the devil,—before this there rises a sickening despair that would disarm and discourage any nation save that black host to whom "discouragement" is an unwritten word.

But the facing of so vast a prejudice could not but bring the inevitable self-questioning, self-disparagement, and lowering of ideals which ever accompany repression and breed in an atmosphere of contempt and hate. Whisperings and portents came borne upon the four winds: Lo! we are diseased and dying, cried the dark hosts; we cannot write, our voting is vain; what need of education, since we must always cook and serve? And the Nation echoed and enforced this self-criticism, saying: Be content to be servants, and nothing more; what need of higher culture for half-men? Away with the black man's ballot, by force or fraud,—and behold the suicide of a race! Nevertheless, out of the evil came something of good,—the more careful adjustment of education to real life, the clearer perception of the Negroes' social responsibilities, and the sobering realization of the meaning of progress.

So dawned the time of *Sturm und Drang*:[5] storm and stress today rocks our little boat on the mad waters of the world-sea; there is

2. During the Enlightenment, philosophers such as Kant and Hume were convinced that certain races could be ranked hierarchically according to their psychological and moral characteristics as well as their bodily traits.
3. An attitude of deference or homage.
4. Toussaint L'Ouverture (1746–1803), leader of the black forces during the Haitian Revolution that overthrew French rule. After Napoleon tricked him into going willingly to France in 1800, L'Ouverture died there in 1803.
5. Literally, storm and stress (German). The term characterizes a German literary movement that valorizes emotional experience and spiritual struggle. Johann Wolfgang von Goethe, Du Bois's favorite author, was a leading figure in this movement.

within and without the sound of conflict, the burning of body and rending of soul; inspiration strives with doubt, and faith with vain questionings. The bright ideals of the past,—physical freedom, political power, the training of brains and the training of hands,—all these in turn have waxed and waned, until even the last grows, dim and overcast. Are they all wrong,—all false? No, not that, but each alone was over-simple and incomplete,—the dreams of a credulous race-childhood, or the fond imaginings of the other world which does not know and does not want to know our power. To be really true, all these ideals must be melted and welded into one. The training of the schools we need to-day more than ever,—the training of deft hands; quick eyes and ears, and above all the broader, deeper, higher culture of gifted minds and pure hearts. The power of the ballot we need in sheer self-defence,—else what shall save us from a second slavery? Freedom, too, the long-sought, we still seek,—the freedom of life and limb, the freedom to work and think, the freedom to love and aspire. Work, culture, liberty,—all these we need, not singly but together, not successively but together, each growing and aiding each, and all striving toward that vaster ideal that swims before the Negro people, the ideal of human brotherhood, gained through the unifying ideal of Race; the ideal of fostering and developing the traits and talents of the Negro, not in opposition to or contempt for other races, but rather in large conformity to the greater ideals of the American Republic, in order that some day on American soil two world-races may give each to each those characteristics both so sadly lack. We the darker ones come even now not altogether empty-handed: there are to-day no truer exponents of the pure human spirit of the Declaration of Independence than the American Negroes; there is no true American music but the wild sweet melodies of the Negro slave; the American fairy tales and folk-lore are Indian and African; and, all in all, we black men seem the sole oasis of simple faith and reverence in a dusty desert of dollars and smartness. Will America be poorer if she replace her brutal dyspeptic blundering with light-hearted but determined Negro humility? or her coarse and cruel wit with loving jovial good-humor? or her vulgar music with the soul of the Sorrow Songs?

Merely a concrete test of the underlying principles of the great republic is the Negro Problem, and the spiritual striving of the freedmen's sons is the travail of souls whose burden is almost beyond the measure of their strength, but who bear it in the name of an historic race, in the name of this the land of their fathers' fathers, and in the name of human opportunity.

And now what I have briefly sketched in large outline let me on coming pages tell again in many ways, with loving emphasis and deeper detail, that men may listen to the striving in the souls of black folk.

XIV. The Sorrow Songs[6]

I walk through the churchyard
    To lay this body down;
I know moon-rise, I know star-rise;
I walk in the moonlight, I walk in the starlight;
I'll lie in the grave and stretch out my arms,
I'll go to judgment in the evening of the day,
And my soul and thy soul shall meet that day,
    When I lay this body down.

NEGRO SONG.

They that walked in darkness sang songs in the olden days—Sorrow Songs—for they were weary at heart. And so before each thought that I have written in this book I have set a phrase, a haunting echo of these weird old songs in which the soul of the black slave spoke to men. Ever since I was a child these songs have stirred me strangely. They came out of the South unknown to me, one by one, and yet at once I knew them as of me and of mine. Then in after years when I came to Nashville I saw the great temple builded of these songs towering over the pale city. To me Jubilee Hall[7] seemed ever made of the songs themselves, and its bricks were red with the blood and dust of toil. Out of them rose for me morning, noon, and night, bursts of wonderful melody, full of the voices of my brothers and sisters, full of the voices of the past.

Little of beauty has America given the world save the rude grandeur God himself stamped on her bosom; the human spirit in this new world has expressed itself in vigor and ingenuity rather than in beauty. And so by fateful chance the Negro folk-song—the rhythmic cry of the slave—stands to-day not simply as the sole American music, but as the most beautiful expression of human experience born this side the seas. It has been neglected, it has been, and is, half

6. The verse is from the Negro spiritual "Lay This Body Down." The music quotation is from the Negro spiritual "Wrestlin' Jacob."
7. Jubilee Hall, a building at Fisk University in Nashville, was completed in 1875. The building was built with the proceeds from the Fisk Jubilee Singers' international singing tour.

despised, and above all it has been persistently mistaken and misunderstood; but notwithstanding, it still remains as the singular spiritual heritage of the nation and the greatest gift of the Negro people.

Away back in the thirties the melody of these slave songs stirred the nation, but the songs were soon half forgotten. Some, like "Near the lake where drooped the willow," passed into current airs and their source was forgotten; others were caricatured on the "minstrel" stage[8] and their memory died away. Then in war-time came the singular Port Royal experiment after the capture of Hilton Head, and perhaps for the first time the North met the Southern slave face to face and heart to heart with no third witness. The Sea Islands of the Carolinas, where they met, were filled with a black folk of primitive type, touched and moulded less by the world about them than any others outside the Black Belt. Their appearance was uncouth, their language funny, but their hearts were human and their singing stirred men with a mighty power. Thomas Wentworth Higginson hastened to tell of these songs, and Miss McKim[9] and others urged upon the world their rare beauty. But the world listened only half credulously until the Fisk Jubilee Singers[1] sang the slave songs so deeply into the world's heart that it can never wholly forget them again.

There was once a blacksmith's son born at Cadiz, New York, who in the changes of time taught school in Ohio and helped defend Cincinnati from Kirby Smith.[2] Then he fought at Chancellorsville and Gettysburg[3] and finally served in the Freedman's Bureau at Nashville. Here he formed a Sunday-school class of black children in 1866, and sang with them and taught them to sing. And then they taught him to sing, and when once the glory of the Jubilee songs passed into the soul of George L. White[4] he knew his life-work was to let those Negroes sing to the world as they had sung to him. So in 1871 the pilgrimage of the Fisk Jubilee Singers began. North to Cincinnati they rode,—four half-clothed black boys and five girl-women,—led by a man with a cause and a purpose. They stopped at Wilberforce, the oldest of Negro schools, where a black

8. A staged entertainment in which white performers in blackface sang and spoke in black dialect. Minstrels relied heavily on racial stereotypes.

9. Lucy McKim Garrison (1842–1877), daughter of an abolitionist. She collected and transcribed the lyrics of slave songs in South Carolina during the Civil War. Higginson (1823–1911) was a Union army officer who became the commander of a black regiment, The First South Carolina Volunteers. An abolitionist, he also wrote one of the first serious studies of black music. *The Spirituals* (1867).

1. Chorus organized at Fisk University in 1867. Originally only eleven members, the group sang all kinds of music, but their fame was based on their presentation of the spirituals in stylized form.

2. Edmund Kirby Smith, Confederate general, led an invasion of Kentucky in 1862 that threatened Cincinnati.

3. Town in southern Pennsylvania. One of the bloodiest and most important battles of the Civil War, fought on July 3, 1863. Chancellorsville, Virginia, was the site of another battle in 1863.

4. Vocal music teacher at Fisk University. He founded the Jubilee Singers.

bishop blessed them. Then they went, fighting cold and starvation, shut out of hotels, and cheerfully sneered at, ever northward; and ever the magic of their song kept thrilling hearts, until a burst of applause in the Congregational Council at Oberlin[5] revealed them to the world. They came to New York and Henry Ward Beecher[6] dared to welcome them, even though the metropolitan dailies sneered at his "Nigger Minstrels." So their songs conquered till they sang across the land and across the sea, before Queen and Kaiser, in Scotland and Ireland, Holland and Switzerland. Seven years they sang, and brought back a hundred and fifty thousand dollars to found Fisk University.

Since their day they have been imitated—sometimes well, by the singers of Hampton and Atlanta, sometimes ill, by straggling quartettes. Caricature has sought again to spoil the quaint beauty of the music, and has filled the air with many debased melodies which vulgar ears scarce know from the real. But the true Negro folk-song still lives in the hearts of those who have heard them truly sung and in the hearts of the Negro people.

What are these songs, and what do they mean? I know little of music and can say nothing in technical phrase,[7] but I know something of men, and knowing them, I know that these songs are the articulate message of the slave to the world. They tell us in these eager days that life was joyous to the black slave, careless and happy. I can easily believe this of some, of many. But not all the past South, though it rose from the dead, can gainsay the heart-touching witness of these songs. They are the music of an unhappy people, of the children of disappointment; they tell of death and suffering and unvoiced longing toward a truer world, of misty wanderings and hidden ways.

The songs are indeed the sittings of centuries; the music is far more ancient than the words, and in it we can trace here and there signs of development. My grandfather's grandmother[8] was seized by an evil Dutch trader two centuries ago; and coming to the valleys of the Hudson and Housatonic, black, little, and lithe, she shivered and shrank in the harsh north winds, looked longingly at the hills, and often crooned a heathen melody[9] to the child between her knees, thus:

5. On November 15, 1871, the Fisk Jubilee Singers gained renown for their performance at a meeting of the National Council of Congregational Churches at Oberlin College.
6. Abolitionist (1813–1887) and brother of Harriet Beecher Stowe, was pastor of Plymouth Church in New York. His invitation to the Jubilee Singers to sing at his church increased their popularity.
7. Although not a musicologist, Du Bois knew more than a little about music. He was a member of Fisk's Mozart Society and sang in Handel's *Messiah*.
8. Tom Burghardt, Du Bois's grandfather's grandfather, was married to the ancestor Du Bois refers to here.
9. Unidentified.

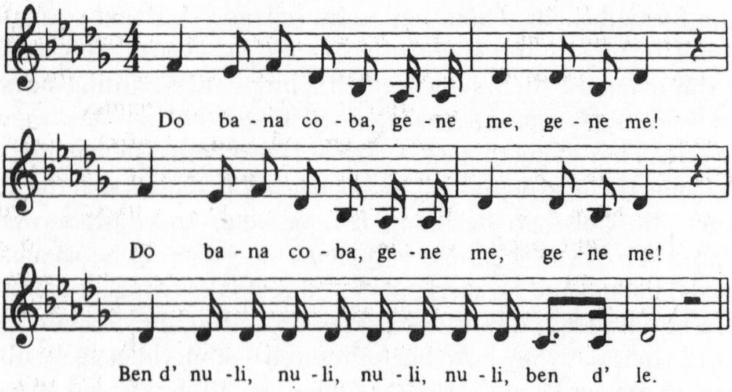
Do ba - na co - ba, ge - ne me, ge - ne me!
Do ba - na co - ba, ge - ne me, ge - ne me!
Ben d' nu - li, nu - li, nu - li, nu - li, ben d' le.

The child sang it to his children and they to their children's children, and so two hundred years it has travelled down to us and we sing it to our children, knowing as little as our fathers what its words may mean, but knowing well the meaning of its music.

This was primitive African music; it may be seen in larger form in the strange chant which heralds "The Coming of John":

> "You may bury me in the East,
> You may bury me in the West,
> But I'll hear the trumpet sound in that morning,"[1]

—the voice of exile.

Ten master songs, more or less, one may pluck from this forest of melody—songs of undoubted Negro origin and wide popular currency, and songs peculiarly characteristic of the slave. One of these I have just mentioned. Another whose strains begin this book is "Nobody knows the trouble I've seen." When, struck with a sudden poverty, the United States refused to fulfil its promises of land to the freedmen, a brigadier-general went down to the Sea Islands to carry the news. An old woman on the outskirts of the throng began singing this song; all the mass joined with her, swaying. And the soldier wept.

The third song is the cradle-song of death which all men know,—"Swing low, sweet chariot,"—whose bars begin the life story of "Alexander Crummell." Then there is the song of many waters, "Roll, Jordan, roll," a mighty chorus with minor cadences. There were many songs of the fugitive like that which opens "The Wings of Atalanta," and the more familiar "Been a-listening." The seventh is the song of the End and the Beginning—"My Lord, what a mourning! when the stars begin to fall"; a strain of this is placed before "The Dawn of Freedom." The song of groping—"My way's

1. From the Negro spiritual "You May Bury Me in the East," also called "I'll Hear the Trumpet Song."

cloudy"—begins "The Meaning of Progress"; the ninth is the song of this chapter—"Wrestlin' Jacob, the day is a-breaking,"—a pæan of hopeful strife. The last master song is the song of songs—"Steal away,"—sprung from "The Faith of the Fathers."

There are many others of the Negro folk-songs as striking and characteristic as these, as, for instance, the three strains in the third, eighth, and ninth chapters; and others I am sure could easily make a selection on more scientific principles. There are, too, songs that seem to me a step removed from the more primitive types: there is the maze-like medley, "Bright sparkles," one phrase of which heads "The Black Belt"; the Easter carol, "Dust, dust and ashes"; the dirge, "My mother's took her flight and gone home"; and that burst of melody hovering over "The Passing of the First-Born"—"I hope my mother will be there in that beautiful world on high."

These represent a third step in the development of the slave song, of which "You may bury me in the East" is the first, and songs like "March on" (chapter six) and "Steal away" are the second. The first is African music, the second Afro-American, while the third is a blending of Negro music with the music heard in the foster land. The result is still distinctively Negro and the method of blending original, but the elements are both Negro and Caucasian. One might go further and find a fourth step in this development, where the songs of white America have been distinctively influenced by the slave songs or have incorporated whole phrases of Negro melody, as "Swanee River" and "Old Black Joe."[2] Side by side, too, with the growth has gone the debasements and imitations—the Negro "minstrel" songs, many of the "gospel" hymns, and some of the contemporary "coon" songs,[3]—a mass of music in which the novice may easily lose himself and never find the real Negro melodies.

In these songs, I have said, the slave spoke to the world. Such a message is naturally veiled and half articulate. Words and music have lost each other and new and cant phrases of a dimly understood theology have displaced the older sentiment. Once in a while we catch a strange word of an unknown tongue, as the "Mighty Myo," which figures as a river of death; more often slight words or mere doggerel are joined to music of singular sweetness. Purely secular songs are few in number, partly because many of them were turned into hymns by a change of words, partly because the frolics were seldom heard by the stranger, and the music less often caught. Of nearly all the songs, however, the music is distinctly sorrowful. The ten master songs I have mentioned tell in word and music of

2. Stephen Foster (1826–1864), who wrote both of these songs, was the most famous songwriter of his day.
3. Racist songs that were used in minstrel shows. They featured a character called Zip Coon.

trouble and exile, of strife and hiding; they grope toward some unseen power and sigh for rest in the End.

The words that are left to us are not without interest, and, cleared of evident dross, they conceal much of real poetry and meaning beneath conventional theology and unmeaning rhapsody. Like all primitive folk, the slave stood near to Nature's heart. Life was a "rough and rolling sea" like the brown Atlantic of the Sea Islands; the "Wilderness" was the home of God, and the "lonesome valley" led to the way of life. "Winter'll soon be over," was the picture of life and death to a tropical imagination. The sudden wild thunderstorms of the South awed and impressed the Negroes,—at times the rumbling seemed to them "mournful," at times imperious:

"My Lord calls me,
He calls me by the thunder,
The trumpet sounds it in my soul."[4]

The monotonous toil and exposure is painted in many words. One sees the ploughmen in the hot, moist furrow, singing:

"Dere's no rain to wet you,
Dere's no sun to burn you,
Oh, push along, believer,
I want to go home."[5]

The bowed and bent old man cries, with thrice-repeated wail:

"O Lord, keep me from sinking down,"

and he rebukes the devil of doubt who can whisper:

"Jesus is dead and God's gone away."[6]

Yet the soul-hunger is there, the restlessness of the savage, the wail of the wanderer, and the plaint is put in one little phrase:[7]

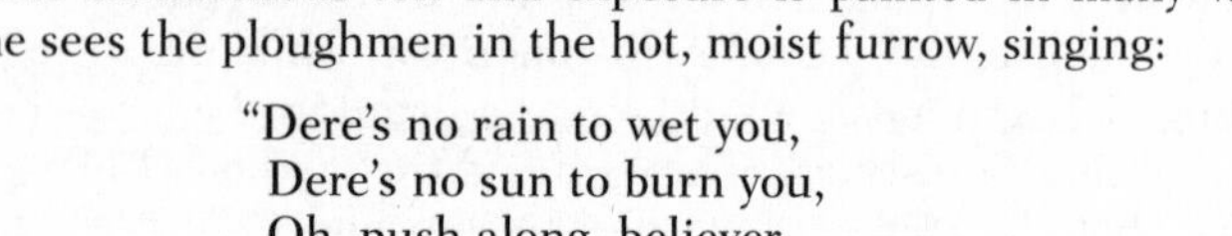

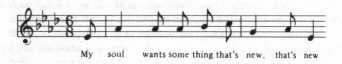

Over the inner thoughts of the slaves and their relations one with another the shadow of fear ever hung, so that we get but glimpses here and there, and also with them, eloquent omissions and silences. Mother and child are sung, but seldom father; fugitive and weary wanderer call for pity and affection, but there is little of wooing and wedding; the rocks and the mountains are well known, but home is

4. From the Negro spiritual "Steal Away."
5. From the Negro spiritual "There's No Rain to Wet You."
6. From the Negro spiritual "Keep Me from Sinking Down."
7. From the Negro spiritual "My Soul Wants Something That's New."

unknown. Strange blending of love and helplessness sings through the refrain:

"Yonder's my ole mudder,
Been waggin' at de hill so long;
'Bout time she cross over,
Git home bime-by."[8]

Elsewhere comes the cry of the "motherless" and the "Farewell, farewell, my only child."

Love-songs are scarce and fall into two categories—the frivolous and light, and the sad. Of deep successful love there is ominous silence, and in one of the oldest of these songs there is a depth of history and meaning[9]

A black woman said of the song, "It can't be sung without a full heart and a troubled sperrit." The same voice sings here that sings in the German folk-song:

"Jetz Geh i' an's brunele, trink' aber net."[1]

Of death the Negro showed little fear, but talked of it familiarly and even fondly as simply a crossing of the waters, perhaps—who knows?—back to his ancient forests again. Later days transfigured his fatalism, and amid the dust and dirt the toiler sang:

"Dust, dust and ashes, fly over my grave,
But the Lord shall bear my spirit home."[2]

The things evidently borrowed from the surrounding world undergo characteristic change when they enter the mouth of the

8. From the Negro spiritual "O'er the Crossing."
9. From the Negro spiritual "Poor Rosy."
1. From the German Folk song "Jetzt gang I ans Brunnele," "Now I'm going to the well, but I will not drink."
2. From the Negro spiritual "Dust and Ashes."

slave. Especially is this true of Bible phrases. "Weep, O captive daughter of Zion," is quaintly turned into "Zion, weep-a-low," and the wheels of Ezekiel[3] are turned every way in the mystic dreaming of the slave, till he says:

> "There's a little wheel a-turnin' in-a-my heart."[4]

As in olden time, the words of these hymns were improvised by some leading minstrel of the religious band. The circumstances of the gathering, however, the rhythm of the songs, and the limitations of allowable thought, confined the poetry for the most part to single or double lines, and they seldom were expanded to quatrains or longer tales, although there are some few examples of sustained efforts, chiefly paraphrases of the Bible. Three short series of verses have always attracted me,—the one that heads this chapter, of one line of which Thomas Wentworth Higginson has fittingly said, "Never, it seems to me, since man first lived and suffered was his infinite longing for peace uttered more plaintively." The second and third are descriptions of the Last Judgment,—the one a late improvisation, with some traces of outside influence:

> "Oh, the stars in the elements are falling,
> And the moon drips away into blood;
> And the ransomed of the Lord are returning unto God,
> Blessed be the name of the Lord."[5]

And the other earlier and homelier picture from the low coast lands:

> "Michael, haul the boat ashore,
> Then you'll hear the horn they blow,
> Then you'll hear the trumpet sound,
> Trumpet sound the world around,
> Trumpet sound for rich and poor,
> Trumpet sound the Jubilee,
> Trumpet sound for you and me."[6]

Through all the sorrow of the Sorrow Songs there breathes a hope—a faith in the ultimate justice of things. The minor cadences of despair change often to triumph and calm confidence. Sometimes it is faith in life, sometimes a faith in death, sometimes assurance of boundless justice in some fair world beyond. But whichever it is, the meaning is always clear: that sometime, somewhere, men will judge men by their souls and not by their skins. Is such a hope justified? Do the Sorrow Songs sing true?

3. See Ezekiel 1.15–28.
4. From the Negro spiritual "There's a Little Wheel a-Turnin'."
5. From the Negro spiritual "My Lord, What a Mourning!"
6. From the Negro spiritual "Michael, Row the Boat Ashore."

The silently growing assumption of this age is that the probation of races is past, and that the backward races of to-day are of proven inefficiency and not worth the saving. Such an assumption is the arrogance of peoples irreverent toward Time and ignorant of the deeds of men. A thousand years ago such an assumption easily possible, would have made it difficult for the Teuton to prove his right to life. Two thousand years ago such dogmatism, readily welcome, would have scouted the idea of blond races ever leading civilization. So wofully unorganized is sociological knowledge that the meaning of progress, the meaning of "swift" and "slow" in human doing, and the limits of human perfect-ability, are veiled, unanswered sphinxes on the shores of science. Why should Æschylus[7] have sung two thousand years before Shakespeare was born? Why has civilization flourished in Europe, and flickered, flamed, and died in Africa? So long as the world stands meekly dumb before such questions, shall this nation proclaim its ignorance and unhallowed prejudices by denying freedom of opportunity to those who brought the Sorrow Songs to the Seats of the Mighty?

Your country? How came it yours? Before the Pilgrims[8] landed we were here. Here we have brought our three gifts and mingled them with yours: a gift of story and song—soft, stirring melody in an ill-harmonized and unmelodious land; the gift of sweat and brawn to beat back the wilderness, conquer the soil, and lay the foundations of this vast economic empire two hundred years earlier than your weak hands could have done it; the third, a gift of the Spirit. Around us the history of the land has centred for thrice a hundred years; out of the nation's heart we have called all that was best to throttle and subdue all that was worst; fire and blood, prayer and sacrifice, have billowed over this people, and they have found peace only in the altars of the God of Right. Nor has our gift of the Spirit been merely passive. Actively we have woven ourselves with the very warp and woof of this nation,—we fought their battles, shared their sorrow, mingled our blood with theirs, and generation after generation have pleaded with a headstrong, careless people to despise not Justice, Mercy, and Truth, lest the nation be smitten with a curse. Our song, our toil, our cheer, and warning have been given to this nation in blood-brotherhood. Are not these gifts worth the giving? Is not this work and striving? Would America have been America without her Negro people?

Even so is the hope that sang in the songs of my fathers well sung. If somewhere in this whirl and chaos of things there dwells Eternal Good, pitiful yet masterful, then anon in His good time America

7. Ancient Greek poet and playwright (525–456 B.C.E.).
8. The pilgrims landed at Plymouth Rock, Massachusetts, in 1620. In Jamestown, Virginia, in 1619, the first Africans landed in North America. They were either slaves or indentured servants.

shall rend the Veil and the prisoned shall go free. Free, free as the sunshine trickling down the morning into these high windows of mine, free as yonder fresh young voices welling up to me from the caverns of brick and mortar below—swelling with song, instinct with life, tremulous treble and darkening bass. My children, my little children, are singing to the sunshine, and thus they sing:[9]

And the traveller girds himself, and sets his face toward the Morning, and goes his way.

9. From the Negro spiritual "Let Us Cheer the Weary Traveler."

JAMES WELDON JOHNSON

From Black Manhattan†

Johnson's historical analysis of "Black Bohemia"—the social networks and sites where artistic collaborations took shape among African American artists in early twentieth-century New York City's Tenderloin district—sheds light on three aspects of *The Autobiography of an Ex-Colored Man.*

First, *Black Manhattan* sheds light on "the Club," the venue where the narrator enters the world of ragtime music performance. Second, it clarifies that Johnson's novel was not set in Harlem but on the western edges of midtown Manhattan.* Finally, these excerpts can be read in tandem with those from Johnson's memoir *Along This Way* (see 138–58, above) for the different emphasis that each source provides: *Black Manhattan* identifies the larger, collective processes that made this artistic milieu possible; *Along This Way* reveals how Johnson experienced its organizational shifts and social relationships individually.

VIII

New York's black Bohemia constituted a part of the famous old Tenderloin; and, naturally, it nourished a number of the ever present vices; chief among them, gambling and prostitution. But it nourished other things; and one of these things was artistic effort. It is in the growth of this artistic effort that we are here interested; the rest of the manifestations were commonplaces. This black Bohemia had its physical being in a number of clubs—a dozen or more of them well established and well known. There were gambling-clubs, honky-tonks, and professional clubs. The gambling-clubs need not be explained. The honky-tonks were places with paid and volunteer entertainers where both sexes met to drink, dance, and have a good time; they were the prototype of the modern night-club. The professional clubs were particularly the rendezvous of the professionals, their satellites and admirers. Several of these clubs were famous in their day and were frequented not only by blacks, but also by whites. Among the best-known were Joe Stewart's Criterion, the Douglass Club, the Anderson Club, the Waldorf, Johnny Johnson's, Ike Hines's, and later, and a little higher up,

† From James Weldon Johnson, *Black Manhattan*, with introduction by Sondra Kathryn Wilson (New York: Da Capo Press, 1991 [1930]), 74–78, 118–25. Reprinted by permission of the Estate of James Weldon Johnson.

* For an excellent overview of African American migration and settlement patterns in Manhattan between 1865 and 1917, see Marcy S. Sacks, *Before Harlem: The Black Experience in New York City before World War I* (Philadelphia: University of Pennsylvania Press, 2006).

Barron Wilkins's Little Savoy, in West Thirty-fifth Street. The border line between the honky-tonks and some of the professional clubs was very thin. One of the latter that stood out as exclusively professional was Ike Hines's. A description of a club—really Ike Hines's—is given in *The Autobiography of an Ex-Coloured Man.*[1] That will furnish, perhaps, a fresher picture of these places and the times than anything I might now write:

> I have already stated that in the basement of the house there was a Chinese restaurant. The Chinaman who kept it did an exceptionally good business; for chop-suey was a favourite dish among the frequenters of the place. . . . On the main floor there were two large rooms: a parlour about thirty feet in length, and a large, square back room into which the parlour opened. The floor of the parlour was carpeted; small tables and chairs were arranged about the room; the windows were draped with lace curtains, and the walls were literally covered with photographs or lithographs of every coloured man in America who had ever 'done anything.' There were pictures of Frederick Douglass and of Peter Jackson, of all the lesser lights of the prize-ring, of all the famous jockeys and the stage celebrities, down to the newest song and dance team. The most of these photographs were autographed and, in a sense, made a really valuable collection. In the back room there was a piano, and tables were placed round the wall. The floor was bare and the centre was left vacant for singers, dancers, and others who entertained the patrons. In a closet in this room which jutted out into the hall the proprietor kept his buffet. There was no open bar, because the place had no liquor licence. In this back room the tables were sometimes pushed aside, and the floor given over to general dancing. The front room on the next floor was a sort of private party room; a back room on the same floor contained no furniture and was devoted to the use of new and ambitious performers. In this room song and dance teams practised their steps, acrobatic teams practised their tumbles, and many other kinds of 'acts' rehearsed their 'turns.' The other rooms of the house were used as sleeping-apartments.
>
> No gambling was allowed, and the conduct of the place was surprisingly orderly. It was, in short, a centre of coloured Bohemians and sports. Here the great prizefighters were wont to come, the famous jockeys, the noted minstrels, whose names and faces were familiar on every bill-board in the country; and these drew a multitude of those who love to dwell in the shadow

1. James Weldon Johnson: *The Autobiography of an Ex-Coloured Man.* New York, Alfred A. Knopf, 1927.

of greatness. There were then no organizations giving performances of such order as are now given by several coloured companies; that was because no manager could imagine that audiences would pay to see Negro performers in any other role than that of Mississippi River roustabouts; but there was lots of talent and ambition. I often heard the younger and brighter men discussing the time when they would compel the public to recognize that they could do something more than grin and cut pigeon-wings.

Sometimes one or two of the visiting stage-professionals, after being sufficiently urged, would go into the back room and take the places of the regular amateur entertainers, but they were very sparing with their favours, and the patrons regarded them as special treats. There was one man, a minstrel, who, whenever he responded to a request to "do something," never essayed anything below a reading from Shakspere. How well he read I do not know, but he greatly impressed me; and I can say that at least he had a voice which strangely stirred those who heard it. Here was a man who made people laugh at the size of his mouth, while he carried in his heart a burning ambition to be a tragedian; and so after all he did play a part in a tragedy.

These notables of the ring, the turf, and the stage, drew to the place crowds of admirers, both white and coloured. Whenever one of them came in, there were awe-inspired whispers from those who knew him by sight, in which they enlightened those round them as to his identity, and hinted darkly at their great intimacy with the noted one. Those who were on terms of approach showed their privilege by gathering round their divinity. . . .

A great deal of money was spent here, so many of the patrons were men who earned large sums. I remember one night a dapper little brown-skin fellow was pointed out to me and I was told that he was the most popular jockey of the day, and that he earned $12,000 a year. This latter statement I couldn't doubt, for with my own eyes I saw him spending at about thirty times that rate. For his friends and those who were introduced to him he bought nothing but wine—in sporting circles, "wine" means champagne—and paid for it at five dollars a quart. . . . This jockey had won a great race that day, and he was rewarding his admirers for the homage they paid him, all of which he accepted with a fine air of condescension.

Besides the people I have just been describing, there were at the place almost every night one or two parties of white people, men and women, who were out sight-seeing, or slumming. They generally came in cabs; some of them would stay only for a few minutes, while others sometimes stayed until morning. There was also another set of white people that came frequently; it was made up of variety performers and others who delineated "darky characters"; they came to get their imitations first-hand from the Negro entertainers they saw there.

It was in such places as this that early Negro theatrical talent created for itself a congenial atmosphere, an atmosphere of emulation and guildship. It was also an atmosphere in which new artistic ideas were born and developed.

* * *

In the midst of the period we are now considering, another shift in the Negro population took place; and by 1900 there was a new centre established in West Fifty-third Street. In this new centre there sprang up a new phase of life among coloured New Yorkers. Two well-appointed hotels, the Marshall and the Maceo, run by coloured men, were opened in the street and became the centres of a fashionable sort of life that hitherto had not existed. These hotels served dinner to music and attracted crowds of well-dressed people. On Sunday evenings the crowd became a crush; and to be sure of service one had to book a table in advance. This new centre also brought about a revolutionary change in Negro artistic life. Those engaged in artistic effort deserted almost completely the old clubs farther downtown, and the Marshall, run by Jimmie Marshall, an accomplished Boniface,[2] became famous as the headquarters of Negro talent. There gathered the actors, the musicians, the composers, the writers, and the better-paid vaudevillians; and there one went to get a close-up of Cole and Johnson, Williams and Walker, Ernest Hogan,[3] Will Marion Cook, Jim Europe, Ada Overton,[4]

2. James Marshall, the proprietor of the cabaret Marshall's Hotel, is hailed here (*boniface*) as a good host and innkeeper.
3. "Cole and Johnson": the songwriting and vaudeville trio of James Weldon Johnson, his brother, Rosamond, and Bob Cole. "Williams and Walker": best known for producing *In Dahomey* (1903), the first Broadway musical written and performed entirely by African Americans, African American performance artists Bert Williams (1874–1922) and George Walker (1872–1911) revolutionized minstrelsy by reversing its codes in two ways: donning blackface makeup themselves, and underscoring the artistry of (rather than lampooning) black folk culture and humor in their stage act. "Ernest Hogan": black vaudeville performer and composer (1865–1909), best known for his early ragtime hit "All Coons Look Alike to Me" (1896).
4. "Will Marion Cook": a formally trained violinst, Cook (1869–1944) wrote popular songs and scored musicals for the Broadway stage, often in collaboration with poet Paul Laurence Dunbar and the vaudeville team Williams and Walker. "Jim Europe": James Reese Europe (1881–1919), early jazz bandleader, arranger, composer who, in 1910, organized the transformative Clef Club (described by Johnson later in this excerpt). Europe's rhythm-driven orchestrations also won acclaim for the 369th Infantry, known as "The Hell Fighters," the black military band commissioned to perform across Europe during World War I. "Ada Overton": dancer and choreographer Overton (1880–1914) was billed as the "Queen of the Cakewalk," due to her appearances in revues led by Bert Williams and George Walker (to whom she was married), among other African American vaudeville troupes.

Abbie Mitchell, Al Johns, Theodore Drury,[5] Will Dixon, and Ford Dabney. Paul Laurence Dunbar[6] was often there. A good many white actors and musicians also frequented the Marshall, and it was no unusual thing for some among the biggest Broadway stars to run up there for an evening. So there were always present numbers of those who love to be in the light reflected from celebrities. Indeed, the Marshall for nearly ten years was one of the sights of New York, for it was gay, entertaining, and interesting. To be a visitor there, without at the same time being a rank outsider, was a distinction. The Maceo run by Benjamin F. Thomas had the more staid clientele.

In the brightest days of the Marshall the temporary blight had not yet fallen on the Negro in the theatre. Williams and Walker and Cole and Johnson were at their height; there were several good Negro road companies touring the country, and a considerable number of coloured performers were on the big time in vaudeville. In the early 1900's there came to the Marshall two young fellows, Ford Dabney and James Reese Europe, both of them from Washington, who were to play an important part in the artistic development of the Negro in a field that was, in a sense, new. It was they who first formed the coloured New York entertainers who played instruments into trained, organized bands, and thereby became not only the daddies of the Negro jazz orchestras, but the grand-daddies of the unnumbered jazz orchestras that have followed. Ford Dabney organized and directed a jazz orchestra which for a number of years was a feature of Florenz Ziegfeld's roof-garden shows.[7] Jim Europe organized the

5. "Abbie Mitchell": trained as a soprano opera singer, Mitchell (1884–1960) earned her first break in Paul Laurence Dunbar's and Will Marion Cook's musical comedy *Clorindy; or, the Origin of the Cakewalk* (1898). Her star turn in the London production of *In Dahomey* (1903) earned her international acclaim. "Al Johns": a songwriter associated with the Clef Club. "Theodore Drury": Drury (1867?–1943?) formed his own eponymously named opera company in 1889, based in New York City, for African Americans to perform opera's classical repertoire.

6. "Will Dixon": African American musician associated with the Clef Club. "Ford Dabney": composer and arranger Dabney (1883–1958) was a pianist whose 1910 hit "That's Why They Call Me Shine" (1910) helped establish the Washington, D.C. musician in New York City. Dabney also earned renown for his performances with James Reece Europe at Ziegfeld's Midnight Frolic at the New Amsterdam Theater, and he was active in The Clef Club. "Paul Laurence Dunbar": poet, novelist, and short story writer (1872–1906). In this context, Johnson refers to Dunbar's work as a song lyricist and librettist. Productions such as *Clorindy; or, the Origin of the Cakewalk* (with score by Will Marion Cook, in 1898) and *In Dahomey* (with score by Will Marion Cook and book by Jesse A. Shipp, in 1903) widened Dunbar's artistic influence as a multi-genre, crossover success in late-nineteenth- and early-twentieth-century America.

7. For nearly three decades (1907–31), Broadway impresario Ziegfeld (1867–1932) produced lavish stage revues modeled on the Folies Bergère of Paris. The roof garden shows (which ended because of Prohibition, in 1913) were testaments to sexual and architectural modernity. During the warmer weather, mixed gender crowds rode elevators to the top of the New Amsterdam Theater (at West 42nd Street, between Seventh and Eighth Avenues), where they enjoyed the vaudeville comedians, reveled at the high-stepping chorus girls, and danced to bands led by James Reece Europe (and others) in an enclosed outdoor pavilion that was air conditioned.

Clef Club.[8] Joe Jordan also became an important factor in the development of Negro bands.

How long Negro jazz bands throughout the country had been playing jazz at dances and in honky-tonks cannot be precisely stated, but the first modern jazz band ever heard on a New York stage, and probably on any other stage, was organized at the Marshall and made its début at Proctor's Twenty-third Street Theatre[9] in the early spring of 1905. It was a playing-singing-dancing orchestra, making dominant use of banjos, mandolins, guitars, saxophones, and drums in combination, and was called the Memphis Students—a very good name, overlooking the fact that the performers were not students and were not from Memphis. There was also a violin, a couple of brass instruments, and a double-bass. The band was made up of about twenty of the best performers on the instruments mentioned above that could be got together in New York. They had all been musicians and entertainers for private parties, and as such had played together in groups varying in size, according to the amount the employing host wished to spend. Will Marion Cook gave a hand in whipping them into shape for their opening. They scored an immediate success. After the Proctor engagement they went to Hammerstein's Victoria,[1] playing on the vaudeville bill in the day, and on the roof-garden at night. In the latter part of the same year they opened at Olympia in Paris; from Paris they went to the Palace Theatre in London and then to the Schumann Circus in Berlin.[2] They played all the important cities of Europe and were abroad a year.

At the opening in New York the performers who were being counted on to carry the stellar honours were: Ernest Hogan, comedian; Abbie Mitchell, soprano; and Ida Forsyne, dancer;[3] but while they made good, the band proved to be the thing. The instrumentalists were the novelty. There was one thing they did quite unconsciously; which, however, caused musicians who heard them to marvel at the feat. When the band played and sang, there were men who played one part while singing another. That is, for example,

8. Organized by bandleader James Reece Europe in 1910, the Clef Club served two aims. It was a performing group of African American musicians in New York City and a union-style contracting agency for black musicians. Johnson describes the club's founding and aims later in this excerpt.
9. Vaudeville and cinema venue in Manhattan.
1. Vaudeville hall opened in 1899 and owned by impresario Oscar Hammerstein. Located at 42nd Street and Seventh Avenue in Manhattan.
2. "Olympia Theater, Paris": music hall in the ninth *arrondissement*. "Palace Theater, London": musical theater venue in the West End. "Schumann Circus, Berlin": a venue for vaudeville reviews, light opera, and circus performances.
3. Forsyne (1883–ca. 1967) first earned fame for her cakewalk routines with the Black Patti Troubadours (1898–1904) and then in Europe, between 1905 and World War I, for her "Black Russian" numbers, in which she executed the "kazotsky"—kickouts while squatting low to the ground, with her arms folded (actually, this Cossack-Ukrainian dance move was incorrectly attributed as Russian).

some of them while playing the lead, sang bass, and some while playing an alto part sang tenor; and so on, in accordance with the instrument each man played and his natural voice. The Memphis Students deserve the credit that should go to pioneers. They were the beginners of several things that still persist as jazz-band features. They introduced the dancing conductor. Will Dixon, himself a composer of some note, conducted the band here and on its European tour. All through a number he would keep his men together by dancing out the rhythm, generally in graceful, sometimes in grotesque, steps. Often an easy shuffle would take him across the whole front of the band. This style of directing not only got the fullest possible response from the men, but kept them in just the right humour for the sort of music they were playing. Another innovation they introduced was the trick trap-drummer. "Buddy" Gilmore was the drummer with the band, and it is doubtful if he has been surpassed as a performer of juggling and acrobatic stunts while manipulating a dozen noise-making devices aside from the drums. He made this style of drumming so popular that not only was it adopted by white professionals, but many white amateurs undertook to learn it as a social accomplishment, just as they might learn to do card tricks. The whole band, with the exception, of course, of the players on wind-instruments, was a singing band; and it seems safe to say that they introduced the singing band—that is, a band singing in four-part harmony and playing at the same time.

One of the original members of the Memphis Students was Jim Europe. Afterwards he went for a season or two as the musical director with the Cole and Johnson shows; and then in the same capacity with Bert Williams's *Mr. Lode of Kole.* In 1910 he carried out an idea he had, an idea that had a business as well as an artistic reason behind it, and organized the Clef Club. He gathered all the coloured professional instrumental musicians into a chartered organization and systematized the whole business of "entertaining." The organization purchased a house in West Fifty-third Street and fitted it up as a club, and also as booking-offices. Bands of from three to thirty men could be furnished at any time, day or night. The Clef Club for quite a while held a monopoly of the business of "entertaining" private parties and furnishing music for the dance craze, which was then just beginning to sweep the country. One year the amount of business done amounted to $120,000.

The crowning artistic achievement of the Clef Club was a concert given at Carnegie Hall in May 1912. The orchestra for the occasion consisted of one hundred and twenty-five performers. It was an unorthodox combination—as is every true jazz orchestra. There were a few strings proper, the most of them being 'cellos and double-basses; the few wind-instruments consisted of cornets, saxophones, clarinets, and trombones; there was a battery of drums; but the main part of the orchestra was composed of banjos, mandolins, and guitars. On this night all these instruments were massed against a background of ten upright pianos. In certain parts the instrumentation was augmented by the voices. New York had not yet become accustomed to jazz; so when the Clef Club opened its concert with a syncopated march, playing it with a biting attack and an infectious rhythm, and on the finale bursting into singing, the effect can be imagined. The applause became a tumult. It is possible that such a band as that could produce a similar effect even today.

Later Jim Europe with his orchestra helped to make Vernon and Irene Castle famous.[4] When the World War came, he assembled the men for the band of the Fifteenth, New York's noted Negro regiment. He was with this band giving a concert in a Boston theatre, after their return from the War, when he met his tragic end.[5]

1912 was also the year in which there came up out of the South an entirely new genre of Negro songs, one that was to make an immediate and lasting effect upon American popular music; namely, the blues. These songs are as truly folk-songs as the Spirituals, or as the original plantation songs, levee songs, and rag-time songs that had already been made the foundation of our national popular music. The blues were first set down and published by William C. Handy, a coloured composer and for a while a bandleader in Memphis, Tennessee. He put out the famous "Memphis Blues" and the still more famous "St. Louis Blues" and followed them by blues of many localities and kinds. It was not long before the New York song-writers were turning out blues of every variety and every shade. Handy followed the blues to New York and has been a Harlemite ever since, where he is known as the "Father of the Blues." It is from the blues that all that may be called *American music.* derives its most distinctive characteristic.

4. During the 'teens, this husband (1887–1918)-and-wife (1893–1969) ballroom dance team popularized various forms of American vernacular dance (such as the Foxtrot) by choreographing them into more elegant, refined moves. Johnson refers here to the Castles' burnishing of ragtime dance steps like the Turkey Trot and Grizzly Bear. The couple hired James Reece Europe as their music director in 1912. Penning songs like "The Castle House Rag" (1914), Europe helped the dance team transform early twentieth-century social dance in the United States and abroad.
5. The Fifteenth New York National Guard Regiment was also known as the 369th Infantry Regiment—or, better, as the "Harlem Hellfighters." Comprised of African Americans and Puerto Ricans, this World War I unit fought both in European theaters of war and against the racial discrimination they faced from German opponents and white American soldiers. Johnson refers to the marching band that James Reece Europe organized out of the regiment; that band introduced American troops and, especially, French allies to early jazz. After the Armistice, in 1919, the Hellfighters returned to the United States for a concert tour. In Boston, Europe became embroiled in a quarrel with the band's drummer, who attacked Europe with a knife. The wound turned out to be fatal.

It was during the period we have just been discussing that the earliest attempt at rendering opera was made by Negroes in New York. Beginning in the first half of the decade 1900–10 and continuing for four or five years, the Theodore Drury Opera Company gave annually one night of grand opera at the Lexington Opera House. Among the operas sung were *Carmen, Aida*, and *Faust*. These nights of grand opera were, at least, great social affairs and were looked forward to months ahead. In September 1928 H. Lawrence Freeman, a Negro musician and the composer of six grand operas, produced his opera *Voodoo* at the Fifty-second Street Theatre. Mr. Freeman's operas are *The Martyr, The Prophecy, The Octoroon, Plantation, Vendetta,* and *Voodoo*. In the spring of the present year he presented scenes from various of his works in Steinway Hall. He was the winner of the 1929 Harmon Award and Medal[6] for musical composition.

EDWARD A. BERLIN

From Ragtime: A Musical and Cultural History[†]

In this chapter, Berlin traces ragtime music's remarkable rise and outlines what typifies its style as American and modern.

Chapter I. The Scope of Ragtime

RAGTIME AS POPULAR SONG

The earliest kind of popular song identified as ragtime is the "coon song," a Negro dialect song frequently, but not always, of an offensively denigrating nature.[1] Although the coon song had a long prior existence in the American minstrel and vaudeville traditions, in the 1890s it acquired the additional label of "ragtime."

> "Rag time" is a term applied to the peculiar, broken rhythmic features of the popular "coon song."[2]
>
> A hopper is fitted onto the press and into it are poured jerky note groups by the million, "coon poetry" by the ream, colored

6. This cultural achievement award was granted from 1926 to 1933 by the William E. Harmon Foundation to honor distinguished work by African Americans in literature, visual art, music, science, education, and industry (its race relations prize was open to civil rights activists from any racial background). The award's prestige and cash prize (up to $400) made it a desirable source of patronage during the Harlem Renaissance.

† From Edward A. Berlin, *Ragtime: A Musical and Cultural History* (Berkeley: University of California Press, 1980), 5–20,

1. Some coon-song lyrics are quoted [later in *Ragtime*].
2. "Questions and Answers," *Etude* 16 (October 1898): 285.

> inks by the ton, and out of the other end of the press comes a flood of "rag-time" abominations, that sweeps over the country.[3]

The coon songs which are cited most often (indicating a degree of popularity and currency) are Ernest Hogan's *All Coons Look Alike to Me* (1896), Joseph Howard and Ida Emerson's *Hello! Ma Baby* (1899), and Theodore Metz's *A Hot Time in the Old Town* (1896).[4]

By 1906 the popularity of the more flagrantly abusive form of coon song had faded, but popular vocal music retained the ragtime label. Some song hits, such as Lewis Muir's *Waiting for the Robert E. Lee* (1912), still presented Southern imagery, but even songs totally devoid of regional or racial implications, such as *Alexander's Ragtime Band* (1911) and *Everybody's Doin' It* (1911), fell within the scope of ragtime. This deracialization of ragtime songs was, in fact, viewed by James Weldon Johnson (1871–1938), a prominent writer on black culture, as a theft from the black man:

> The first of the so-called Ragtime songs to be published were actually Negro secular folk songs that were set down by white men, who affixed their own names as composers. In fact, before the Negro succeeded fully in establishing his title as creator of his secular music the form was taken away from him and made national instead of racial. It has been developed into the distinct musical idiom by which America expresses itself popularly, and by which it is known universally. For a long while the vocal form was almost absolutely divorced from the Negro; the separation being brought about largely through the elimination of dialect from the texts of the songs.[5]

A controversial article appearing in the London *Times* includes a rhythmic analysis of *Waiting for the Robert E. Lee* and cites as other examples of ragtime *Oh, You Beautiful Doll, Going Back to Dixie,* and *How Are You Miss Rag-Time?*[6] Although the article was widely

3. W. F. Gates, "Ethiopian Syncopation—The Decline of Ragtime," *Musician* 7 (October 1902): 341.
4. Although the well-known chorus of this last piece does not usually bear the coon-song or ragtime label today, the lyrics are in Negro dialect, the music of the verse is syncopated in the manner of ragtime, and it is referred to as ragtime in the literature of its day. See Charles R. Sherlock, "From Breakdown to Ragtime," *Cosmopolitan* (October 1901): 639; Lester Walton, "Music and the Stage: President Bans Ragtime," *New York Age*, 6 February 1908, 10; and "'A Hot Time' Is War Song," *American Musician and Art Journal* 24 (14 February 1908): 4. It is significant that these three publications concur on the categorization of *Hot Time*, for they cover a broad spectrum of opinion: *Cosmopolitan* was a general-interest magazine, *New York Age* a leading Negro newspaper, and *American Musician and Art Journal* a periodical concerned primarily with band music.
5. James Weldon Johnson, Introduction to *The Second Book of Negro Spirituals* (New York: Viking Press, 1926), 16–17.
6. "Rag-Time," *Times* (London), 8 February 1913, 11.

quoted and discussed, both in praise and criticism,[7] there was no disagreement on the choice of music cited as ragtime. Similarly, in a pair of articles by Hiram K. Moderwell, a prominent music critic, ragtime is portrayed almost exclusively in its vocal forms:

> I remember hearing a negro quartet singing "Waiting for the Robert E. Lee," in a café, and I felt my blood thumping in time, my muscles twitching to the rhythm. . . .
>
> I think of the rollicking fun of "The International Rag," the playful delicacy of "Everybody's Doing It," the bristling laziness of "Waiting for the Robert E. Lee," the sensual poignancy of "La Seduction" tango, and the tender pathos of "The Memphis Blues."[8]

In proposing that ragtime be taken out of the cafés and put into the concert halls, he writes:

> I firmly believe that a ragtime programme, well organized and well sung, would be delightful and stimulating to the best audience the community could muster.[9]

The novelist, critic, and essayist Carl Van Vechten (1880–1964), while disputing the advisability of some of Moderwell's proposals, nevertheless agrees that ragtime is vocal music.[1] And composer-educator Daniel Gregory Mason (1873–1953), who vehemently opposes most of Moderwell's views on this subject, has no qualms about accepting such songs, as *Everybody's Doin' It* and *Memphis Blues* (1912) as ragtime:

> Suppose . . . we examine in some detail a typical example of ragtime such as "The Memphis Blues" . . .[2]

As songs were the most conspicuous species of ragtime, it follows that songwriters were the most conspicuous composers. This assumption is confirmed by the literature of the time, for those named as ragtime composers were almost invariably songwriters (some exceptions will be discussed in Chapters Four and Nine). Some of the most frequently mentioned were Irving Berlin (b. 1888), George M. Cohan (1878–1942), Louis Hirsch (1887–1924), Lewis F. Muir (1884–1950),

7. Reprinted in full in *Boston Symphony Orchestra Programmes* 32 (19 February 1913): 1186–96. Quoted and discussed in "Sees National Music Created by Rag-Time," *New York Times*, 9 February 1913: 4, 5; "Ragtime as Source of National Music," *Musical America* 17 (15 February 1913): 37; "Philosophizing Rag-Time," *Literary Digest* (15 March 1913): 574–75; Francis Toye, "Ragtime: The New Tarantism," *English Review* (March 1913): 656; Daniel Gregory Mason, "Folk-Song and American Music," *Musical Quarterly* 4 (July 1918): 324–25; "Flays Rag-Time as Not Reflecting Americanism," *Musical America* 28 (20 July 1918): 22.
8. Hiram K. Moderwell, "Ragtime," *New Republic* (16 October 1915): 285.
9. Hiram K. Moderwell, "A Modest Proposal," *Seven Arts* 2 (July 1917): 371.
1. Carl Van Vechten, "Communications," *Seven Arts* 2 (September 1917): 669–70.
2. Daniel Gregory Mason, "Concerning Ragtime," *New Music Review and Church Music Review* 17 (March 1918): 114.

and Jean Schwartz (1878–1956). Irving Berlin, who did not attain prominence with his ragtime songs until 1911, even claimed a part in the genesis of ragtime:

> I believe that such songs of mine as "Alexander's Ragtime Band," "That Mysterious Rag," "Ragtime Violin," "I Want To Be in Dixie," and "Take a Little Tip from Father" virtually started the ragime mania in America.[3]

It has been suggested in recent years that the popular understanding of ragtime today is not what it was when the music was being created, but the thesis has not met with general acceptance. In a letter to the Ragtime Society newsletter in 1965, one who was apparently present during the early days of ragtime expressed his perplexity over the present trend of emphasizing a particular kind of piano ragtime and ignoring vocal ragtime:

> . . . we who were around when "Boom de Ay" was discovered in Babe Connor's place in St. Louis as the nineties started up, and when the "Hot Time" tune took words and entered the ragtime-song race . . . await enlightenment as to just what it is about a specimen of syncopation that makes it "classic ragtime," while countless of the world's favorite old ragtime numbers apparently go rejected by the modernists.[4]

Perhaps the vocal ragtime mentioned above is not on the same musical level as the best in piano ragtime. Quite possibly only a few ragtime enthusiasts today would be interested in these songs. But ignoring the fact that this music was considered ragtime conceals the historical truth and inevitably leads to serious misinterpretations. Whereas the restricted interpretation of ragtime suffices for the needs of today's entertainment, for a true historical and critical view of the subject a broader perspective must prevail.

THE RAGTIME BAND

The predominance of vocal music in early writings on ragtime is revealed not only in the relatively high proportion of articles devoted

3. Irving Berlin and Justus Dickinson, "Words and Music," *Green Book Magazine* (July 1915): 104–105.
4. Russ Cole, untitled letter, *Ragtime Society* 4 (March/April 1965): 19–20. As Cole's letter suggests, the songs *Ta-ra-ra Boom-de-ay!* (1891) and *A Hot Time in the Old Town* have been traced to Babe Connor's, a Negro brothel in St. Louis: they both appeared there around 1891. The actual origins of the songs are uncertain, as each is enmeshed in conflicting stories and claims. One version dates *Ta-ra-ra Boom-de-ay!* as far back as 1854 or even earlier—see Edward R. Winn, "'Ragging' the Popular Song-Hits," *Melody* 2 (May 1918): 8; Isaac Goldberg, *Tin Pan Alley: A Chronicle of the American Popular Music Racket*, (New York: John Day, 1930), 113–17, 165–67. The term "classic ragtime," discussed in Chapter Ten, is a designation applied to the piano rags of Scott Joplin and a few others.

exclusively to songs, but also in the frequent linking of vocal with instrumental ragtime. Although ragtime songs seem to have made their initial impact upon the musical stage, they were played as well by dance, march, and concert bands:

> Probably the majority of our readers are aware that the most popular music of the day is that known as "rag-time." . . . From New York to California and from the great lakes to the gulf ragtime music of all styles is the rage. Look at the ballroom programmes for the past season and we find rag-time and other "coon" melodies introduced into every dance where it is practicable.[5]
>
> [John Philip Sousa] was as usual liberal with his encores consisting of his own marches and ragtime ballads.[6]
>
> [In New Orleans, around 1905] many of the tunes played by the small marching bands were popular ragtime songs, not classic rags such as those composed by Joplin.[7]

Even when they were not direct adaptations of existing songs, instrumental rags were frequently thought of as derivatives of the vocal medium:

> The craze for "coon" songs, as they are familiarly known, began about three years ago, and shows little sign of abatement at the present time. Not content with "rag-time" songs, marches, two-steps, and even waltzes have been subjected to this syncopated style of treatment, in order to appease the seemingly insatiable thirst for that peculiar rhythmic effect produced by successive irregular accent.[8]

The song-to-instrument route was not one-sided; the process was also reversed as original instrumental rags such as Kerry Mills' dance hit *At a Georgia Campmeeting* (1897) were reissued in alternate versions with words. In addition, many early instrumental rag publications include a vocal chorus. Because of such developments, original instrumental pieces and adaptations from songs frequently merged into one body of ragtime literature.

An important phase of ragtime ensemble performance—important because it reflects on the origins of both ragtime and jazz—is the

5. W. H. Amstead, "'Rag-Time': The Music of the Hour," *Metronome* 15 (May 1899): 4. Amstead was the editor of *Metronome*.
6. "Sousa at the Hippodrome," *New York Times*, 15 January 1906, 9.
7. George W. Kay, "Reminiscing in Ragtime: An Interview with Roy Carew," *Jazz Journal* 17 (November 1964): 9. This is a statement by Roy Carew (1884–1967), a pioneering figure in ragtime research, recalling his experiences in New Orleans during the first decade of the twentieth century. Carew is discussed further in Chapter 9.
8. R. M. Stults, "Something about the Popular Music of Today," *Etude* 18 (March 1900): 97. Stults was a successful composer of sentimental popular songs.

improvised syncopation, or "ragging," of existing pieces. By its very nature the music is not notated, and no contemporaneous recordings have been discovered, but the style is known today through later re-creations made by musicians from the period, such as those recorded by ragtime-jazz musician Bunk Johnson (1879–1949) in the mid-1940s, and through descriptions. Johnson has related how hymns were transformed by turn-of-the-century New Orleans funeral bands,[9] and Jelly Roll Morton (1855–1941) has similarly depicted the ragging of Sousa marches,[1] a popular practice described also by black poet-song lyricist Paul Laurence Dunbar (1872–1906):

> But hit's Sousa played in ragtime, an' hit's Rastus on Parade,
> W'en de colo'd ban' comes ma'chin' down de street.[2]

Although much ensemble ragtime was published and copyrighted in piano editions, it is evident that in at least some cases the composers intended the music for band performance. On the cover of William Krell's *Mississippi Rag* (1897), the earliest identified piano score using the term "rag" in its title, is a banner proclaiming: "The First Rag-Time Two Step Ever Written, and First Played by Krell's Orchestra, Chicago." In another case, an unusual bass line in Arthur Pryor's *A Coon Band Contest* (1899) is identified as "trombone solo".

The prominence of bands in early nonvocal ragtime recordings also testifies to the importance of this medium,[3] as do the advertisements for band arrangements in some popularly oriented music magazines. One such periodical that devoted considerable space to band advertisements was *Metronome*. During 1897 *Metronome* printed numerous announcements of cakewalk marches, two-steps, schottisches, polkas, waltzes, and band arrangements of coon songs. The first advertisement in this magazine to specify "ragtime" appeared in the January 1898 issue, and by the following year such notices were commonplace. Ragtime advertisements continued to appear

9. Marshall W. Stearns, *The Story of Jazz* (London: Oxford University Press, 1956), 61.
1. Alan Lomax, *Mister Jelly Roll: The Fortunes of Jelly Roll Morton, New Orleans Creole and "Inventor of Jazz"* (New York: Duell, Sloan and Pearse, 1950; 2d ed. Berkeley, Ca.: University of California Press, 1973), 12–13.
2. Paul Laurence Dunbar, "The Colored Band" in *Lyrics of Love and Laughter* (New York: Dodd, Mead, 1903), stanza 3, lines 3–4. This poem was set to music by J. Rosamond Johnson (1873–1954) in 1901; see James Weldon Johnson, *Along This Way* (New York: Viking Press, 1933), 161.
3. The most thorough discography of ragtime recordings on 78 r.p.m. discs is David Jasen's *Recorded Ragtime, 1897–1958* (Hamden, Conn.: Archon Books, Shoe String Press, 1973). Additional ragtime recordings are listed in James R. Smart, *The Sousa Band: A Discography* (Washington, D.C.: Library of Congress, 1970), and in Allen Koenigsberg, *Edison Cylinder Records, 1889–1912; with an Illustrated History of the Phonograph* (New York: Stellar Productions, 1969).

in substantial quantities until early 1916, when the demand for this music in the ballroom was reduced. (The other dances being advertised in 1916 were one-steps, tangos, fox and turkey trots, waltzes, and maxixes.) In the November 1916 issue the category of ragtime was eliminated. Although the word "rag" continued to appear occasionally in titles, such pieces were not necessarily considered rags; Eubie Blake's *Bugle Call Rag* (1916), for instance, was labeled a fox trot.

RAGTIME FOR OTHER INSTRUMENTAL COMBINATIONS

The media for ragtime were not restricted to piano, song, and band. The instrumental diversity included some combinations which seem exotic today. The cover of the piano publication of Theodore Morse's *Coontown Capers* (1897), for instance, lists the availability of fifteen different arrangements, including orchestra; brass band; violin and piano; banjo; zither; and two mandolins, guitar, and piano. Similarly, the cover of Abe Holzmann's *Bunch o' Blackberries* (1899) advertises: "Published also for all instruments including Mandolin, Guitar, Banjo, Orchestra, Band, Etc."

Recordings of the period reveal this same diversity. While the listings in Jasen's *Recorded Ragtime* do not specify the medium, some clues to the instruments of frequently recorded artists are given on pages 7–10 of the introduction, and additional identification is occasionally supplied by the name of the performing group, such as "Murray's Ragtime Banjo Quartet."[4] Thus it is possible to detect some of the instrumental variety that was represented on recordings: two accordion performances (1914, 1915) of *Hungarian Rag*, a marimba-band version (1916) of *Dill Pickles*, three piccolo solos (1900–1902) on *Rag Time Skedaddle*, a xylophone recording (1912) of *Red Pepper.* Similarly, among the 8,000 listings in Koenigsberg's *Edison Cylinder Records*, are many of rags played on "exotic" instrumental combinations.

The relative position of piano ragtime is considered more thoroughly in Chapter Four. For the present it is sufficient to observe that with such an abundance and variety of instrumental and vocal versions of ragtime, the piano genre did not have the prominence it enjoys today.

4. Jasen, *Recorded Ragtime*, 51.

SYNCOPATION

At the core of the contemporary understanding of ragtime, regardless of medium, was syncopation. The question "What is ragtime?" was asked throughout the period, and almost invariably explanations included a statement about syncopation:

> So rag-time music is, simply, syncopated rhythm maddened into a desperate iterativeness; a rhythm overdone, to please the present public music taste.[5]

> Rag-time is merely a common form of syncopation in which the rhythm is distorted in order to produce a more or less ragged, hysterical effect.[6]

> RAG TIME. A modern term, of American origin, signifying, in the first instance, broken rhythm in melody, especially a sort of continuous syncopation.[7]

> "Rag-Time," then may be said to be a strongly syncopated melody superimposed on a strictly regular accompaniment, and it is the combination of these two rhythms that gives "rag-time" its character.[8]

> Ragtime music is chiefly a matter of rhythm and not much a matter of melody or fine harmony. It is based almost exclusively upon syncopated time.[9]

Not satisfied simply with designating syncopation as the defining feature of ragtime, Hiram Moderwell, who as a frequent contributor of music articles to *New Republic* and other periodicals should have known better, attributes an exaggerated significance to the rhythms of ragtime:

> It [ragtime] has carried the complexities of the rhythmic subdivision of the measure to a point never before reached in the history of music.[1]

Irving Berlin reverses the relationship between ragtime and syncopation as he says, not that ragtime is a form of syncopation, but that "Syncopation is nothing but another name for ragtime." From

5. C. Crozat Converse, "Rag-Time Music," *Etude* 17 (June 1899): 185. Converse (1832–1918) was a composer of religious and patriotic American music.
6. A. J. Goodrich, "Syncopated Rhythm vs. 'Rag-Time,'" *Musician* 6 (November 1901): 336. Goodrich (1847–1920) was an eminent theorist and academician.
7. *Grove's Dictionary of Music and Musicians* (New York: Macmillan, 1908), s.v. "Rag Time," by Frank Kidson.
8. "Rag-Time," *Times* (London).
9. Leo Oehmler, "'Ragtime': A Pernicious Evil and Enemy of True Art," *Musical Observer* 11 (September 1914): 14.
1. Moderwell, "Ragtime."

this false premise, he compounds his error by concluding that "the old masters" also wrote ragtime, but "in a stiff and stilted way."[2]

The implication, evident in many of these articles, that the term "ragtime" refers directly to the ragged rhythmic quality of syncopation is occasionally spelled out explicitly. An editorial referring to compositions "written *in* what is contemptuously called 'rag time'"[3] clearly designates ragtime as a rhythmic process as well as a genre. The word is also used as a synonym for syncopation: "in American slang to 'rag' a melody is to syncopate a normally regular tune."[4] "Strictly speaking, to rag a tune means to destroy its rhythm and tempo and substitute for the 2–4 or 4–4 time a syncopated rhythm."[5] An article on ragtime performance specifies that the pianist must have the ability "to syncopate (rag) the tones."[6]

The term "rag" is thus seen to be a noun, identifying a type of music; a verb, referring to the process of syncopation; and an adjective, modifying "time," that is, "ragged time." Etymologically, the hyphenated form used in the earlier articles (rag-time) and the rarer two-word form (rag time) also suggest adjectival origins.

The assumption of ragtime's being characterized primarily by a syncopated rhythm was so widespread that few writers questioned this connection. One who did was music critic and biographer Francis Toye (1883–1964). Noting the absence of syncopation in some pieces identified as ragtime, he commented:

> I do not think that rag-time can be defined as rhythm at all. True it has a characteristic rhythm and usually a syncopated one. But not invariably. The popular "Hitchy-Koo" and "Dixie," for instance, are hardly syncopated, yet it were pure pedantry not to class them as rag-time.[7]

Another writer, giving similar reasons, tried to separate the concept of ragtime from syncopation:

> Perhaps the best way to define ragtime and prove that it and syncopation are not necessarily analogous will be to go to the bottom of things and summon up some actual illustration. . . .

2. Frederick James Smith, "Irving Berlin and Modern Ragtime," *New York Dramatic Mirror,* 14 January 1914, 38.
3. "Music for Piers and Parks," *New York Times,* 29 May 1902, 8 (my emphasis).
4. "Rag-Time," *Times* (London).
5. "'To Jazz' or 'To Rag,'" *Literary Digest* (6 May 1922): 37. Quoted here is Paul Whiteman (1890–1967), a commercially successful band leader, "popularizer" of jazz, and self-acclaimed "King of Jazz."
6. Edward R. Winn, "Ragtime Piano Playing: A Practical Course of Instruction for Pianists," *Tuneful Yankee* 1 (January 1917): 42.
7. Toye, "Ragtime," 654.

> "For Me and My Gal" is typically ragtime, yet it is practically free of syncopation—to be exact, there are just three measures of syncopated melody. . . . The most striking example of ragtime music came out a few years ago in Irving Berlin's song "Alexander's Ragtime Band." . . .
>
> What made this song so popular? It was not syncopation, for there is no syncopation at all in the chorus, which is the most pleasing part of the song.[8]

These articles, however, are exceptions, and reflect the general tendency by 1911 to include in the ragtime category almost any rhythmical, popular music. At least one commentator protested against this extension of the term "ragtime," suggesting that its application be restricted to syncopated music:

> "Ragtime" . . . has become a most comprehensive word in recent years, and at least with a certain class of musicians who should know better, it means pretty nearly anything not under the head of *serious* or classical music.
>
> If the rhythmic element predominates or is at all prominent it is "ragtime," no matter whether a single instance of syncopation occurs in the music or not. . . .
>
> The writer, for one, is in favor of restricting the word ragtime to its original definition, as meaning that time or rhythm in which the dominating characteristic feature is syncopation.[9]

This protest reveals a recognition, by 1913, of the process that was already divesting ragtime of its most definitive feature. Of this process, more will be said later.

RAGTIME DANCE

From its earliest days ragtime has been associated with dancing. Performers who sang ragtime lyrics on the minstrel stage also danced to its rhythms. As the music moved to the ballroom, syncopated ragtime marches, two-steps, and cakewalks co-existed with unsyncopated versions of the same steps. In some instances the dances themselves acquired the ragtime label. Throughout the period there are references to specific steps being "rags" and to "ragging" being a style of dancing.[1] More often, though, dances were simply

8. Harold Hubbs, "What Is Ragtime?" *Outlook* (27 February 1918): 345.
9. Myron A. Bickford, "Something about Ragtime," *Cadenza* 20 (September 1913): 13.
1. Virgil Thomson, "Jazz," *American Mercury* (August 1924): 465; Rupert Hughes, "A Eulogy of Rag-Time," *Musical Record*, No. 447 (1 April 1899): 158; "Canon Newboldt's Warning," *New York Times*, 26 August 1913, 8; Ernest Ansermet, "Sur un orchestre nègre," *Revue romande* 3 (15 October 1919): 10; "The Origin of Ragtime," *New York Times*, 23 March 1924. Composer Virgil Thomson (b. 1896) and conductor Ernest Ansermet (1883–1969) are well-known figures in concert music. Rupert Hughes (1872–1956) was a novelist, a dramatist, and a respected writer on musical subjects.

associated with ragtime music without appropriating the name. While almost any duple- or quadruple-metered step could be executed to the music, some dances had an especially close affiliation with ragtime.

Ragtime sheet music, which frequently lists the "appropriate" dances, is an important source of information on ragtime ballroom styles; a year-by-year survey of the sheet music clearly reveals the gradual changes in fashions.

The dances named on the earliest ragtime sheet music are the cakewalk, march, and two-step. (As with the word "ragtime," there is no orthographical consistency; "cakewalk" and "two-step" appear also as "cake walk," "cake-walk," "two step," and "two-step.") An indication of the lack of musical distinction made between these dances is that all, or any combination, may be listed on a single piece of music: *The Rag-Time Sports. Cake Walk-March and Two Step* (1899); *Rag Time Society. Characteristic March & Two Step* (1899); or *Africana. A Rag-Time Classic. Characteristic March Two-Step and Cakewalk* (1903). Sometimes another dance, such as the polka, is also included: *The Honolulu Cake Walk. Ragtime March* (1899) "Can also be used as: Two-Step, Polka or Cake-Walk."[2]

The first of these three main dances to disappear from the sheet music was the cakewalk, which died out by 1904. The march began to decline in 1908, and the two-step in 1911; both dances, though, lingered on until the mid-1910s.

In the second decade of the century new dances were cited on ragtime sheet music, but without the persistence of the earlier steps. The turkey trot had a short life, from about 1912 to 1914; the one-step and fox trot were both prominent by 1913, the former lasting until 1917, the latter having an unmatched longevity.[3] The slow drag was mentioned throughout the entire ragtime period, but never in significant numbers.

2. The distinction between subtitle and description is also treated inconsistently. The practice in this book is to consider any dance label as part of the subtitle unless it is clearly presented as a description, in which case it will be transcribed as in the last citation.
3. The fox trot of that time, though, was not the indiscriminate shuffle commonly called "fox trot" today; note the instructions printed in *Christensen's Ragtime Review* 1 (March 1915): 8:

How To Dance the Fox Trot

The fox trot resembles the onestep, but is a slightly faster dance and is quite easy to learn. The exaggerated movements of the shoulders and arms, characteristic of the turkey trot, the things that made it capable of vulgarity, are absent from the fox trot. Here are the four figures of this dance:

Fig. 1.—Four slow steps, four running steps and four running steps turning. Repeat four times.

Fig. 2.—Two slow grapevines and four running steps. Repeat four times.

Fig. 3.—One polka step and rest: four running steps. Repeat four times.

Fig. 4.—Four wigwags, then three steps to each side.

With less consistency many other dances were associated with ragtime. The vocal version of Scott Joplin's *Ragtime Dance* is particularly interesting for its inventory of dances,[4] some of which do not appear in other sources. It is possible that these less familiar dances had a restricted circulation and were known primarily in the black communities. The dances mentioned are the "rag time dance," "cake walk prance," "slow drag," "worlds fair dance," "clean up dance," "Jennie Cooler dance," "rag two step," "back step prance," "dude walk," "stop time," and "Sedidus walk."

Despite the variety of dance names appearing in Joplin's piece, almost all of the music retains the same rhythmic character. Only the "stop time" and "Sedidus walk" use music of a different style—"stop-time" music, which appears infrequently in published ragtime.[5] It was not until the second decade of the century, with the appearance of the fox trot, that a major ragtime-related dance was again linked with music of a differentiated character. As is demonstrated in Chapter Eight, the rhythmic patterns associated with the fox trot tended to replace the accepted modes of ragtime syncopation, and this process ultimately led to the disintegration of ragtime as a distinctive musical type.

JAZZ AND THE CLOSE OF THE RAGTIME ERA

It was with the advent of the "jazz age," shortly before 1920, that the ragtime era came to a close. The end came gradually, as characteristics of ragtime were absorbed by jazz; for a while the two terms were freely interchanged. At last, supplanted by a newer wave of syncopation, ragtime ceased to be the emissary of American popular culture.

Jazz, like ragtime, originally embraced a much broader musical and social spectrum than is accorded to it by present-day thought. In publications of the late 1910s and early twenties jazz was typified not by the figures who are today considered the main exponents of that time (such as Louis Armstrong, Jelly Roll Morton, Fletcher Henderson, and Bix Beiderbecke), but by popular band leaders and songwriters (Paul Whiteman, Irving Berlin, Victor Herbert)—and by ballroom dance.

4. There are two versions of this piece, both published by Stark Music, St. Louis, Mo. The earlier publication (1902) has lyrics simulating calls as they might be heard at a country dance, and parenthetical instructions specifying when each new step is to begin. The later version (1906), subtitled a "Stop-Time Two Step," is without lyrics, and indicates only once—for the "stop-time"—where a step is to begin.

5. The main characteristics of "stop-time" are heavy accents, frequent rests, and a stereotyped cadential pattern.

Many writers used the terms ragtime and jazz almost synonymously:

> Oldtimers such as "Alexander's Ragtime Band" . . . and "Maple Leaf Rag" began to establish a conventional form for jazz. . . .
>
> For purposes of this discussion we will omit the waltz, which is not jazz, and the so-called "ballad." Just how is the typical "rag" built?[6]

A report on Roger-Ducasse's *Epithalme* discusses the composer's use of "ragtime rhythms" as "evidence of the valuable use to which the European craze for jazz can be put."[7] A discussion of jazz describes the "ragtime pianist" in terms that apply equally to the jazz pianist: "The real ragtime pianist is a composer as well as performer. That is, he can take a tune and reharmonize it if necessary, judiciously introduce innovations, alter the rhythm."[8] In describing "fly-drumming," a ballroom drum technique, one writer suggests that the distinction between jazz and ragtime is in name only: "A decade past it was called 'ragging' while today we call it 'jazzing.'"[9]

There were some who objected to the word "jazz," preferring to retain the older "ragtime": "The Rag-time movement would have been the better style, but the word 'Jazz' has passed into at least two languages."[1] Others favored the term "jazz," even applying it to music clearly falling within the ragtime era and sphere: "Ragtime was the name employed by Mason and Moderwell; jazz was the thing they were discussing."[2] While disagreeing over the more appropriate terminology, these two writers implicitly concur in assuming no substantive distinction between ragtime and jazz.

Some commentators of the time also tried to identify the characteristics of jazz, and while the intent was not necessarily to contrast it with ragtime, the descriptions and affiliations of jazz often served to differentiate it from the earlier style. One such association was with new dances, especially the fox trot:

> The latest international word seems to be "jazz." It is used almost exclusively in British papers to describe the kind of music

6. Don Knowlton, "The Anatomy of Jazz," *Harper's Magazine* (April 1926): 578–79.
7. "Ducasse Uses Ragtime in New Tone Poem," *Musical America* 37 (10 March 1923): 15.
8. William J. Morgan, "A Defense of Jazz and Ragtime," *Melody* 6 (September 1922): 5.
9. Carl E. Gardner, "Ragging and Jazzing," *Metronome* 35 (October/November 1919): 34.
1. Clive Bell, "Plus de jazz," *New Republic* (21 September 1921): 93.
2. Goldberg, *Tin Pan Alley*, 252. Critic Hiram K. Moderwell and composer Daniel Gregory Mason were on opposing sides of a heated controversy that raged over ragtime during the second decade of the century; see Chapter 3.

> dancing—particularly dancing—imported from America. . . . While society once "ragged," they now "jazz."[3]

> Jazz, in brief, is a compound of (a) the fox-trot rhythm, a four-four measure (*alla breve*) with a double accent, and (b) a syncopated melody over this rhythm.[4]

Jazz is also typified by certain unique instrumental effects:

> Jazz, strictly speaking, is instrumental effects, the principal one being the grotesque treatment of the portamento, especially in the wind instruments. The professor of jazz . . . calls these effects "smears." The writer first heard jazz performed by trombone-players in some of the marching bands. . . . Afterward the ingenious players of the popular music discovered how to produce these wailing, sliding tones on other instruments.[5]

The most common and fundamental view was that jazz was a later and more complicated phase in the development of syncopated music. While some writers continued to think of jazz and ragtime as the same phenomenon going under two labels, others considered jazz as the maturation of the earlier style:

> "Jazz" . . . is Ragtime raised to the Nth power.[6]

> Rag had been mainly a thing of rhythm, of syncopation. . . . Jazz is rag-time, plus orchestral polyphony; it is the combination, in the popular current, of melody, rhythm, harmony, and counterpoint.[7]

> Ragtime has definitely become jazz—ragtime never died, it grew up.[8]

Much of the argument seems to be reducible to a matter of semantics. What is important is that accompanying the stylistic evolution of ragtime in the late 1910s was a shift away from the term "ragtime" and toward "jazz." By 1924 it could be confidently written that jazz "is the symbol, the byword for a great many elements in the

3. "A Negro Explains Jazz," *Literary Digest* (26 April 1919): 28; reprinted in Eileen Southern, ed., *Readings in Black American Music* (New York: W. W. Norton, 1971), 224.
4. Thomson, "Jazz," p. 465. See also Aaron Copland, "Jazz Structure and Influence on Modern Music," *Modern Music* 4 (January/February 1927): 10.
5. W. J. Henderson, "Ragtime, Jazz, and High Art," *Scribner's Magazine* (February 1925): 202. Henderson (1855–1937) was a music critic for the *New York Times* and *New York Sun*, and author of many books on music. See also Thomson, "Jazz," 466, and Gilbert Seldes, *The Seven Lively Arts* (New York: Harper and Bros., 1924; rev. ed., New York: Sagamore Press, 1957), 85–96.
6. Rupert Hughes, "Will Ragtime Turn to Symphonic Poems?" *Etude* 38 (May 1920): 305.
7. Carl Engel, "Jazz: A Musical Discussion," *Atlantic Monthly* (August 1922): 186. At the time this article appeared, Engel (1883–1944) was Head of the Music Division at the Library of Congress.
8. Goldberg, *Tin Pan Alley*, 251.

spirit of the time—as far as America is concerned it is actually our characteristic expression."[9]

Contemporaneous sheet music and changes in musical style (discussed in Chapter Eight) confirm the observations made by the writers quoted above. By the late 1910s the number of compositions identified as rags had declined substantially and the stylistic traits that had previously characterized ragtime had blurred. Some aspects of ragtime were retained by later forms, but the evolution in style and terminology made it a thing of the past: the ragtime era came to a close.

9. Seldes, *Seven Lively Arts*, 83.

Composition and Publication Correspondence: 1912 Edition

James Weldon Johnson to Brander Matthews†

[ca. November 1908]

My dear Prof. Matthews:

Here is the M.S. of the last part of my book as I have rewritten in. The job has been a fearful one. I feel that I have lost the spirit of the story, and I'm afraid that what I've just written is not up to the rest. I'm also afraid that I cannot write convincingly concerning love.

I have been hindered some by the conditions of things here, between plague, fear of war and revolution, and the uncertainty of how long I should have to remain in Puerto Cabello, my mind has been far from being in a state for writing.[1]

I'd thank you very much if you would have the whole book made into a clear typewritten copy in duplicate, and send me the bill. I'll forward a check to you immediately. The duplicate copy you need not send to me; I shall have my brother or Mr. Cole[2] call and get it.

I hope that the story will get a chance. There has been an out[burst?] of literature somewhat along the same line within the past year,

† Unless otherwise indicated, all letters reprinted in this section come from the James Weldon Johnson and Grace Nail Johnson Papers, Yale Collection of American Literature, Beinecke Rare Book and Manuscript Library, and are reprinted by permission of the James Weldon Johnson Estate. Letters are reprinted exactly as the originals (i.e., without corrections).

1. Johnson wrote this letter from Puerto Cabello, Venezuela, where he was serving as Consulate for the U.S. State Department. The political crisis to which he refers most likely concerned uprisings brewing in Nicaragua, where he would be transferred just one year later, in 1909. For more background, see William E. Gibbs, "James Weldon Johnson: A Black Perspective on 'Big Stick' Diplomacy," *Diplomatic History* 8 (1984): 332–33; Eugene Levy, *James Weldon Johnson: Black Leader, Black Voice* (Chicago: University of Chicago Press, 1973), 121–47; Jacqueline Goldsby, "Keeping the Secret of Authorship," 259–262; Brian Russell Roberts, *Artistic Ambassadors: Literary and International Representation of the New Negro Era* (Charlottesville: University of Virginia Press, 2013), 42–47; and Noelle Morrissette, *James Weldon Johnson's Modern Soundscapes* (Iowa City: University of Iowa Press, 2013), 67–80.
2. Bob Cole, Johnson's songwriting partner.

Ray Stannard Baker's articles in "American Magazine," and especially several stories which appeared in "Collier's."[3]

Perhaps you saw my poem "Black Bards" in the November "Century"; I have received several letters complimenting me upon it.[4]

I am still being kept in Puerto Cabello, with no definite idea as to when I shall be able to get away. I am seriously considering a return to my old work in New York; I've been benefited by being here because during the time that I have been away, I've found myself, but I hardly think that I can gain anything more. I feel my power to do better work than before, but I also feel lack of incentive.

I hope that you are in good health and enjoying the holiday vacations. Thank you again for all your kindness. I am, yours very truly—

[James Weldon Johnson]

James Weldon Johnson to Sherman, French & Company

New York City, February 17, 1912

Dear Sirs:

I fear that I am rather a poor hand at writing advance notices; however, I am enclosing you the best effort of which I am capable. Perhaps, this statement together with my letter will furnish you with the material from which you can extract just the "notice" you desire.[1]

I wish first to say that although it cannot be stated that the story of the hero is the true life of any individual; yet, it is made up in every important fact and detail from the real experiences of several persons whom I have known, and from incidents which have come under my own observation and within my personal experience; so, in every essential particular, the biography is truth and not fiction. All of the phases given of life among the different strata of colored people throughout the country are drawn from my personal knowledge.

In advertising the book, we cannot state that it is a true human document, still it is the giving of any impression that it is fiction which I wish to avoid, or better, see avoided.

My object in writing the book was not to raise a special plea for the Negro but to present in a sympathetic yet dispassionate manner

3. Renowned muckraker (i.e., social advocacy) journalist, Baker (1870–1946), published a widely discussed series on segregation, "Following the Color Line," first in *American Magazine* (1907), then as a book with Doubleday, Page, and Company in 1908.
4. "O Black and Unknown Bards," one of Johnson's most famous poems, first appeared in the November 1908 issue of *Century*, a leading literary magazine in late-nineteenth- and early-twentieth-century American letters. The poem subsequently appeared in his debut volume of poetry, *Fifty Years and Other Poems* (1917).
1. Johnson crafts what his publishers will sign as their Preface to *The Autobiography of an Ex-Colored Man*. See 3.

a picture of conditions between the races as they actually exist to-day. Special pleas for and against the Negro have already been made in hundreds of books, and in these books his virtues or his vices have always been exaggerated. This is because writers, in nearly every instance, have treated the colored American as a *whole*; each has taken some one group from the race to prove his case. Not yet has a composite and proportionate presentation of the entire race, embracing all of its various groups, showing their relations with each other and to the whites, been made; this I have endeavored to do.

Another purpose in writing the book was to do something else which has not been done, to draw aside the curtain and give a view of the inner life of the race, an initiation into what I have termed the "freemasonry" of the race. As I have said, in the text of the book, the Negroes of the United States have a fairly correct idea of what the white people of the country think of them, for their opinions are being constantly stated, while they, themselves, are more or less a sphinx to the other race. I have been curious to know if the whites would not be interested in knowing the opinion concerning themselves held by ten million people living among them.

Another, and perhaps the main, motive in writing the book was to reveal the starting and unsuspected fact that prejudice against the Negro is exerting in New York and other large cities where the opportunity is open a pressure which is actually and constantly forcing a large but unascertainable number of fair-complexioned colored people over into the white race.

I would suggest that from the enclosed material a few paragraphs be drawn up and published with the book as a publisher's foreword, or preface.

Yours very respectfully,
[James Weldon Johnson]

(Enclosure)

"The Autobiography of an Ex-Colored Man" is a document that reads more strangely than romance. (or—stranger than fiction) But, it is more than a curious document. It presents a vivid and starting new picture of conditions brought about by the race question in the United States. And in presenting this picture it makes no special plea for the Negro but shows in a dispassionate, though sympathetic, manner conditions as they actually exist between the whites and blacks to-day. Special pleas have already been made for and against the Negro in hundreds of books, but in these books either his virtues or his vices have been exaggerated; this is because writers, in nearly every instance, have treated the colored American as a *whole*, each has taken some one group of the race to prove his case;

not before has a composite and proportionate presentation of the entire race, embracing all of its various groups and elements, showing their relations with each other and to the whites, been made. It is very likely that the Negroes of the United States have a fairly correct idea of what the white people of the country think of them, for that opinion has for a long time been and is still being constantly stated, but they are themselves more or less a sphinx to the whites. It is curiously interesting and even vitally important to know what are the thoughts of ten millions of them concerning the people among whom they live. In these pages it is as though a veil had been drawn aside, the reader is given a view of the inner life of the Negro in America, is initiated into the "freemasonry" of the race.

These pages also reveal the unsuspected fact that prejudice against the Negro is exerting a pressure which, in New York and other large cities where the opportunity is open, is actually and constantly forcing an unascertainable number of fair-complexioned colored people over into the white race.

No one can read this book without feeling that he has been given new light on the complexities of the this social problem; that he has had a glimpse behind the scenes of this race-drama which is being here enacted; that he has been taken upon an elevation and has caught a bird's-eye view of the conflict which is being waged.

I, of course, leave it to the publishers to make what statements they see fit about the literary style and quality of the book; I only wish too add that the great majority of books on the race question have been written in a dry, a complaining, a bombastic or an angry note; not yet has the entire question been comprehensively treated in an interesting story form; for the Negro has generally been introduced in fiction merely as a humorous or picturesque back-ground, or to throw into stronger relief the strength and superiorty of the white race.

James Weldon Johnson to Grace Nail Johnson

Corinto. May 24th [1912]

My dear little old darling Mudder:

I've just received your letter of the 5th and send the little note written two days later. The little love note with the pansy in it. Oh, you can *never*[1] know how much I want you. The thought of you so far away from me makes me about crazy, at times. But never mind, little girl, it will work out all right. We are *sure* to win out, and it won't be so very long before we are together again, and on our way

1. "never" was underlined twice.

to pleasanter clime. Then, we'll have a real, sure enough, regular "Three Weeks" honeymoon all over. Do you want to?

I know you and the "beautiful doll" make a stunning pair. I'm glad your new dress is pretty. I always want you to look pretty, as pretty as any body and a great deal prettier than most of them.

Dear little chicken let me know at once if you received the check which I sent the latter part of April, and also about the one I am sending—This same mail. I sealed up a big letter to you, but the ship hasn't come yet.

I should have liked very much to have been at the Clef Club affair.[2] I'm very glad you sent me the clippings.

You know, I'm afraid I've been directing some of your letters to 26 West 99th Street. I'm not sure of it, but it seems to me I've written, 26-West 99th St and at other times, 52 West 132nd St for Rosie's letter,[3] may be just a fancy, but since I've begun numbering my letters you can always tell if one is missing which you should have received.

I shall write to S.F. & Co and send the letter to Jack[4] to be forwarded on. The persons I had the books forwarded to do not know I am the author except, of course, Prof. Brander Matthews. Charlie Anderson knows I wrote the book, but I don't know whether he knows that it is published.[5] He can do a great deal to help it along without divulging the secret of the authorship. I shall write Jack a letter in which I'll outline a campaign for getting the book started. That's the main thing, as the publishers say.

I hope Rosie had his affair straightened by now. It's an awful fight, but if you've got the goods and keep at it, you're bound to win. I hope he's at work and at a fair figure.

Oh, my dear, sweet little mudder, how I do miss you. The day is long and lonely without you—and the nights are so dreary—oh so dreary. I want my little mudder, and nothing but my little mudder.

A long, long kiss, my dear little wife and sweetheart.

Your old son,
Jim

2. James Reese Europe (1881–1919) founded this African American musicians' organization in New York City in 1910. Here, Johnson probably refers to the group's historic performance at Carnegie Hall on May 2, 1912. For more on the Clef Club's functions, see Johnson's description in *Black Manhattan*, reprinted above, 203.
3. Rosamond Johnson's nickname was "Rosie."
4. Jack Nail, Grace's brother.
5. Charles W. Anderson (1866–1938) was a key confidant of and advisor to Booker T. Washington. A leader among black Republicans in New York City, Anderson chaired the Colored Republican Club, which led him to meet and recommend Johnson to Washington, who, in turn, secured Johnson's appointment to the U.S. State Department's Consular Service (1906–12).

James Weldon Johnson to John E. Nail

Corinto, Nicaragua, May 26, 1912.

Dear Jack:

I am sending you a letter enclosed which I wish you would forward to S. F. & Co. I am also sending you three lists in pencil; I wish you would please extend these as far as you may think advisable, then have them copied and sent on to the publishers with my enclosed letter. Grace and Dad may be able to make some suggestions for the lists.

I know you will do all in your power to help give the book a start. Talk it and write it to all of your friends and acquaintances without revealing your knowledge of the authorship. There will be some of our mutual friends who will suspicion that I am the author; you need not deny it, only evade a direct answer, that will all help to create interest and stir up curiosity.

I am in splendid health and getting along all right, except for the fact that I so awfully miss Grace. Working hard and still confident about my transfer. I feel sure that it will come if my case doesn't get mixed up in the political tangle. And what a tangle there is![1]

I hope business is picking up—and I also hope that we pick up a few hundreds, or better, a few thousands on the book. Kindest regards to all,

Your brother,
Jim

James Weldon Johnson to Grace Nail Johnson

June 26, 1912

My dear little "Mudder":

Were you proud to see your old son's work so highly spoken of in the Times review? Well, you have a right to be proud; for the book review of the Times is the highest and most authoritative of any daily paper in the United States. The review is a splendid one, better than I would have hoped for in the Times, which is not only "way up," but is not very sympathetic on the Negro question. I was gratified, too, to see that the book was given a place among the leading articles and included in the "contents" of the supplement, and not bunched up with many others under "Book Notes."[1]

1. Johnson refers to the U.S. State Department assignment he sought to St. Etienne, France. For more on this "tangle," see Goldsby, "Keeping the Secret of Authorship," 259–62.

1. The *New York Times* review is reprinted in this volume on 279–81.

However, what pleased me most was this: I wrote the book to be taken as a true story, and it is proven that I am sufficiently a master of the technical art of writing to make it impossible for even so keen a critic as the one on the Times to say that the story is *not* true. And it must be taken into consideration that the critic is *always* prejudiced against admitting the truth of an anonymous story; very few that have ever been written have been accepted as fact. I expect to see some critics attack the book on that ground, but I am very fully satisfied since the Times let it pass without being able to tell whether it was truth or fiction. One thing, if he has any doubts about the author, he evidently doubts his being colored; as he says that the man who wrote the book shows that he has lived on both sides.

I have been plugging away at several things, but I shall now concentrate on my poems. I must follow this book up as soon as possible with another from S.F. & Co. I have been working, but I haven't accomplished near so much as I have wished and planned. The office work has taken so much of my time and energy—I miss your help very much. If I get my poems properly launched I believe they will make a reputation for me, the kind of reputation I really want, the reputation of a writer and a thinker. Don't doubt—I'll win it—It's hard, slow work, but I know I'll succeed.

You see, for so many years I've divided my efforts an energies that I haven't done in any one line as much as I could have done by concentration. But I'm just at the right point now of knowledge and experience to do the thing I want to do. I am a great deal stronger now in intellect and character than I was five or six years ago.

I'm glad Dad[2] is taking such interest in the book; he can do a great deal to help it. And so can you and Jack and Rosie. Ask friends and acquaintances in a casual way, "Have you read The A of an Ex-Col Man?" If not, be sure to read it." You can write friends in the same way.

If Rosie goes out on the road he can do an enormous amount of advertising. But in it all, the absolute secrecy of the authorship must be maintained. You can see the importance of this from the Times' review; as soon as it is known that the author is a colored man who could not be the character in the book, interest in it will fall. There must always be in the reader's mind the thought that, at least, it may be true.

I wish you were with me now. The ship doesn't sail for another 7 or 10 days yet, so I'll scribble you a few more lines and drop them in this same envelope.

Love to all, with an ever so long kiss for you. Your old son—

Jim

2. Johnson's father-in-law, John B. Nail.

George A. Towns to James Weldon Johnson

July 1, 1912

My dear Jim,

Several week ago there came to me, ostensibly from the publisher, a copy of "The Autobiography of an Ex-Colored Man." For many good reasons which I will presently give, I have delayed thanking you until now when I must combine with this letter of thanks a letter also of condolence.

Only a few moments ago as I sat at my desk beginning this letter, I looked out of my window and saw Sidney Woodward[1] from Jacksonville who gave me the first news of the death of your dear father.[2]

I greatly regret this loss to you for I know what wise counsel you have always had from your father, and I know too that you will miss his guiding wisdom although you are growing with years into maturity of judgment yourself. It is unnecessary for me to say, I know, that you and your family have my sincere sympathy as well as that of my wife.

You will also regret to hear of the death of Mrs. M.M. Adams[3] which occurred Thursday night, June 27, after an illness of five weeks. She died in her rooms at the University. I am so glad that she had a chance to read your book along with her husband before her death. She was delighted with it and expressed the hope that it would have a wide reading and especially that it would reach the class of northern readers who needed to see "the problem" from your point of view.

For myself, I wish to express great appreciation of your story. I had not read far before I was certain that you were the author. I was gratified to see how well you had put your own personality into the story although it does not purport to be an authentic account of your own life. The ear-marks of your style convinced me of your authorship, and when I came to the story of the country preacher of Hampton, Ga. of whom we used to speak and about whom we laughed so much after your first summer as a country 'fesser—then I knew of a certainty that the author was you.[4]

1. Concert singer (1860–1924) whose international career led him back to Jacksonville in 1900. Four years earlier (1896) Woodward crossed paths with Rosamond Johnson in New York City, when both men performed with the Oriental American Company, a vaudeville troupe led by African American impresario John Isham.
2. James Johnson Senior died in June 1912.
3. Probably the wife of Myron W. Adams, a professor of Greek (and later, president, 1923–29) at Atlanta University.
4. Towns refers to Chapter X in *ECM*, where the narrator attends church revival meetings to collect Negro spirituals; see 90–95 in this volume. Towns's joke also alludes to the summer of 1891, when Johnson taught working-class blacks in rural Georgia. For Johnson's account of that important phase in his life, see *Along This Way*, Chap. XI.

Now Jim this a good story and it is unique in method and matter and if it gets a wide reading it is sure to do a great deal of good. The title is unusual and attractive—more attractive than unusual, however. If I were to criticize it, I should say that the title is not such as would make one wish to read it who is not already friendly to Negroes. It will attract all friends, but it will not invite those who are not interested in us already.

At first I thought that a more complicated plot would be better than your straightforward narrative, but upon a second reading, I have changed my mind. You have done this so effectively.

I recall that you used to say that you wanted to see *all of life*. Well, there is something to be said for that; and there is something to be said against seeing what is ugly. Despite that one point,[5] I think very much of your story. Your analysis of conditions in this country, your descriptions—that of New York, especially, your keen observations, your treatment of Negro music which is enlightening without seeming pedantic, or even "lugged" in for padding—all are strong and unusual points that ought to win a reading for the story, if one could only know beforehand that those things are in the book.

You will see in the last number of the Crimson and Gray[6] (which is late) that I did not know whether to reveal your identity or not without consulting you.

You have probably seen the two-column criticism that recently appeared in the Springfield (Mass) Republican. It was a very good criticism indeed.[7] I reviewed the story at a meeting of the teachers one Saturday night and many of them took the publisher's name to buy copies. I am talking up the book for all I am worth and I am going to send three copies to friends of mine in the north. Let me know if I should say in the next issue of the paper that you are the author. I am on the Library Committee so that I have ordered a copy for our library and I shall see that the book gets a wide reading among the students. I fear the *lure* of *the wicked* for some lads who read the book and then go to New York. They will not mean to fall, but they will, I fear.

We were very much disappointed at not seeing you and your wife here last winter. When you come again be sure to come and see how much the south has changed—except in pure cussedness. The advance of Negroes in all respects will make that cussedness a little more easily borne than formerly. You need not come without waiting to pack up, but I have three kids that *in their father's eyes* are well

5. Towns probably means the novel's lynching scene; see 96–98 in this volume.
6. Atlanta University's alumni bulletin. The article to which Towns refers is reprinted in this volume; see 281.
7. This review is reprinted on 274–79.

worth the journey from Corinto[8] to see. You remember you used to say that yours would begin speaking Latin by saying pater.[9] Well, I thought I should be different, so that mine begins with German.

Loring Palmer[1] as well as my wife joins me in good wishes to you.

Yours very sincerely,
George

James Weldon Johnson to Grace Nail Johnson

Sept. 11th [1912]

Dear little Mudder:

I received a cable from Stern & Co[1] this morning saying "come." I don't know just what is behind it, but I simply cannot leave at this time. As soon as it is possible for me to do so I intend to come. Things are gradually growing quiet here, and I don't think it will be long before I shall get away.

The railroad as now been opened as far as Chimandeya by our forces, and we are getting things to eat from there. Food has been a great problem. I have been taking my dinner quite frequently at the Mays; they are so nice. Just think of it, up to two days ago, eggs were $1.25 gold per dozen in Corinto. You remember you used to prick at $2.00 paper. You can imagine the rest. But everybody is in good spirits, when the real danger passed, the whole affair seemed like a thrilling adventure. The young officers' wives seem to really enjoy it; that is now, my! but they were frightened at first.[2]

Captain Terhume's wife and the wife of Lieutenant Lewis were around at the Consulate this morning; Mrs. Terhume wrote a note at your little desk, she saw your picture and asked if that was the picture of my wife. I told her. She said, "I think she is very pretty." I told her that I fully agreed with her opinion.

Mrs. T. is one of these quiet women through whom the culture just shines. Mrs. L is half Italiian and as scatter-brainied as she can be, but as pretty as they picture on a magazine cover. How she chatters!—Mr. Johnson, how can you get along without your wife down here? Don't you miss her? etc. etc. etc. ad infintitum

8. Port town in northwestern Nicaragua where Johnson was completing his final term as Consul for the U.S. State Department (1910–12).
9. Latin for "father."
1. A local physician (1875–1935) whose undergraduate years at Atlanta University (1888–92) overlapped with those of Towns and Johnson.
1. Johnson's sheet music publisher in New York City.
2. Nicargua's civil war (1909–12) embroiled Corinto, the port town where Johnson was stationed as U.S Consul (1910–12). This explains his references to military personnel and their wives in this letter. For more of Johnson's account, see *Along This Way*, Chaps. XXIV–XXVI.

I was out on the ship this morning to see the Admiral, in the course of our talk he said, "Mr. Johnson, I'm so glad I found a Consul like you down here I don't know what I should have done without you. We work together like two pals. If I'd found some crazy-headed Consul here I'd have had no end of trouble." Those are about his exact words, so I still have some hope on that score. I'm going to try it anyhow. I take in this strain because if I can get the kind of post I want it will suit me better than anything else I can do. And you and I can be happier and more contented if I succeed in this.

My book is creating quite a small sensation here. Judge Shoenwhich, who is a refugee here, picked it up one day and read it through without stopping; he then spoke of it to Judge Thompson, who is here, and he read it through. Judge Thompson was so enthusiastic about the book that he made almost everybody anxious to borrow it that is among the Americans. Mrs. Terhume is the last, so far, to take it up. They are all either kidding me, or they think it is a wonderful story. Judge Thompson has already written to some of his friends in the States about it.[3]

I'm sending you a few "snaps." Entirely out of film, or I could have made some dandy pictures.

My it's hot to-day. I remember how you used to suffer from this heat.

Don't get worried about what any gossips might say. You wrote in your last letter that they have take us as a topic—It isn't worth the while to worry. We know what we are doing, and we feel that we are trying to do the best thing in the best way for our own future and happiness. And, besides that, it's nobody's business, but ours. I knew they were at it. Some three months ago I received one of those meddlesome, mischievous letters which same so called friends feel they are called upon to write.

And don't get discouraged, little Mudder. Things are going to work out all right in the end. I was very blue and discouraged, and your cheerful, encouraging letters helped me a lot, but somehow, I feel that something good is coming out of it all. We just simply can't lose out; we've worked too hard, and played the game too straight to lose.

Write your old son a nice, long, sweet love letter[4], and don't forget that he is using every drop of blood in his heart and every fibre of brain in his head for you and our happiness. And we are bound to win it. Just think, you and I haven't begun yet to live, really live our lives together, to get the most out of this [?] mutually, neither

3. For an analysis of this social network's circulation of *ECM*, see Goldsby, "Keeping the Secret of Authorship," 261–62.
4. "nice, long, sweet love letter" was double underlined.

spiritually or physically—Now I'm fixing to get blue again. So, a long, long kiss.

Your old son,
Jim

Write or cable me fully about the cable from Sterns.

Charles A. Stephens to James Weldon Johnson

September 24, 1912.

My dear Mr. Johnson:—

Since writing you the other day I have received through my bookstore here "The Autobiography of an ex-Colored Man", which it was necessary to send to Boston for.[1]

I want to thank you for having suggested to me the reading of this really wonderful book. It held me from start to finish, for there is not a page that does not hold the reader. Mrs. Stephens has also read the book, and when she came to that chapter where the teacher tells the child that he is not to stand with the white children she was so affected that she cried. An author who can make his readers both laugh and weep has certainly accomplished something in a literary way.

I have become so interested in the book that I have persuaded one of the largest book dealers here, Mr. A. M. Robertson, 222 Stockton Street, to order a number of these books for his patrons, and also to bring it to the attention of the critics of the principal dailies here.

Having become interested on the subject of the Negro race, I am now reading Booker Washington's "Up from Slavery," and while it is a very interesting book, I do not regard it as interesting as "The Autobiography of an ex-Colored Man." I am curious to know the author who modestly hides his identity. Perhaps the secret you promised to tell will enlighten me.

We still read every day of the continued troubles in Nicaragua, but hope they will soon end. Let me hear from you soon, and if there is anything I can do for you here do not hesitate to ask.

Mrs. Stephens joins in sending very kindest regards. If Admiral Sutherland and Captain Halstead[2] are still in Nicaraguan waters kindly remember me to them.

Yours sincerely,
Charles A. Stephens

1. Charles A. Stephens was an official in the U.S. Custom House based in San Francisco.
2. U.S. naval personnel assigned to Corinto.

James Weldon Johnson to George A. Towns†

February Fourth Nineteen Hundred and Thirteen

My dear George:

Yours of the 28th ultimo has been received. I can't tell just when I'll be going northward, but I shall let you know in good time. About Rosie, that is another question. He is now in London, and, from all appearances, will be there indefinitely. However I am lettine [sic] him know your wishes and plans. If he gets back to this country in time I know he will be glad to come; and you may be sure that he will give you an interesting and unique entertainment.

Glad you are still working to help send my book along. It is beginning to move. There are no present prospects of its being a "best seller", but I have hopes that it will finally reach a large number of the people who ought to see it. One thing against its popular success is that it is being handled by an ultra conservative publishing house.

With kindest regards to your wife and yourself, to all my old friends among the teachers and to Loring,[1] I am,

Sincerely yours,
Jim

Sherman, French & Company to James Weldon Johnson

April twenty-fourth, Nineteen hundred and fourteen.

Dear Sir:

Since our last report to you, and up to April first, nineteen hundred and fourteen, 59 additional copies of "The Autobiography of an ex-Colored Man" have been sold, with gross proceeds therefrom amounting to $51.95. Of this amount you receive sixty per cent: namely, $31.17.

On the debit side of the account is $3.89 for author's copies sent you as per bills rendered, and $14.75 for the 2500 copies of the Brander

† From the George A. Towns Collection, Archives Research Center, Robert W. Woodruff Library at Atlanta University Center. Additional exchanges between Johnson and his longtime confidant can be found in Miles M. Jackson, "Letters to a Friend: Correspondence from James Weldon Johnson to George A. Towns," *Phylon* 29.2 (1968): 182–98.

1. Probably Loring Brainerd Palmer; see n. 1 on 230.

Mathews special circular prepared from the article in "Munsey's Magazine."

Deducting these two debits leaves a balance in your favor of $12.50, for which amount our check is enclosed.

Very truly yours,
Sherman, French & Company

Composition and Publication Correspondence: 1927 Edition

James Weldon Johnson to Carl Van Doren[†]

December 28, 1922

My dear Mr. Van Doren:[1]

I am very sorry I was unable to be present at your lecture at the One Hundred and Thirty-fifth Street Library[2] a few nights ago. A previous engagement made it impossible for me to attend.

For some time I have wanted to show you a novel of Negro life which I wrote and published some ten years ago. The book fell flat more or less, but I have sufficient egotism of the author to feel that its fate was probably due to the fact that it was published out of time and also that it was gotten out by one of those quasi publishing companies who are in fact only job printers for authors. The book also suffered by being classified as "Autobiography." I debated for some time whether to put it forth frankly as a piece of fiction under some such title as "The Chameleon," or to put it forth as a human document, and therefore, autobiography. Perhaps I made a mistake in doing the latter.

I wish you would take the time to look the book over.

I am still hoping that I may find sufficient liesure some time or other to do the story of Negro life which I believe can and ought to be written [?].

With best wishes, I am

Sincerely yours,
[James Weldon Johnson]

† Unless otherwise indicated, all letters reprinted in this section come from the James Weldon Johnson and Grace Nail Johnson Papers, Yale Collection of American Literature, Beinecke Rare Book and Manuscript Library and are reprinted by permission of the James Weldon Johnson Estate. Letters are reprinted exactly as the originals (i.e., without corrections).

1. Literary editor at *The Nation* (1919–22) and *Century Magazine* (1922–25); also taught at Columbia University (1911–30). Van Doren's editorial work on *The Cambridge History of American Literature* (1917–21) and his solo-authored *The American Novel* (1921) helped integrate U.S. literature into college-level literary studies curricula.
2. The New York Public Library's branch in Harlem; now the Schomburg Center for Research in Black Culture.

James Weldon Johnson to Heywood Broun

May 2, 1924

My dear Mr. Broun:[1]

I am sending you herewith a copy of "The Autobiography of an Ex-Colored Man," the book which we talked about on the train a couple of weeks or so ago. I published the book anonymously about fourteen years ago with a firm in Boston that went out of business during the war. I believe the book was published out of time. Fourteen years ago there was little or no interest in the Negro. In fact, we had reached the deepest depths of apathy regarding him so far as the general public is concerned.

I believe that if the book had been published ten years later it might have attracted some attention. I have sometimes thought that I might bring it down through the Great War[2] and try for another publication of it. I am not sure that it would be worth while.

The copy I am sending you is the only one I have, so I would thank you to get it back to me when you have finished with it. However, you may keep it as long as you care to.

Yours sincerely,
[James Weldon Johnson]

Carl Van Vechten to James Weldon Johnson[†]

[March 23, 1925]

Dear Mr. Johnson,

I read through The Autobiography of an Ex-Coloured Man at one sitting, and Marinoff[1] is engaged in reading it now. I shall, of course, return Mr. Nail's copy to you, but remember that I am looking for a copy for myself and that if you run into one you can do no better than present it to me! It is a remarkable book in more ways than one, but in no way more so than in the gentle irony which informs the pages from beginning to end. You have said everything there was to say and said it without passion. The book lacks, I think, sufficient narrative

1. Heywood Broun (1888–1939) was a leading journalist and syndicated columnist for New York City newspapers during the Jazz Age 1920s and Depression-era 1930s. He was also a founding member of the Algonquin Round Table (1921–29), a literary-social salon in Manhattan that was renowned for its members' razor-sharp wit. An outspoken critic of injustice and a supporter of labor unions, Broun leaned politically to the left. Broun's worldview likely prompted Johnson to seek his support for placing *ECM* with a new publisher.
2. World War I.

† From the Carl Van Vechten Papers, Yale Collection of American Literature, Beinecke Rare Book and Manuscript Library. Reprinted with permission of the Carl Van Vechten Trust.

1. Fania Marinoff (1890–1971), Carl Van Vechten's wife.

interest; the hero might have had more personal experiences, but after all you were chiefly concerned with presenting facts about Negro life in an agreeable form, through the eyes of a witness who had no reason personally to be particularly disturbed.

I was particularly interested to discover that you were apparently the first to sense the musical possibilities of ragtime and to predict for it a future as an art-form. In reviewing Woollcott's book about Irving Berlin for the New York Tribune I have found the opportunity to give you credit for this.[2]

I have not been the same person since you told me about Hayti.[3] I have discovered a passage about Christophe[4] in H.G. Wells's The Research Magnificent.[5] He refers to a book called Where Black Rules White, by Hesketh Pritchard.[6] Have you seen this? I have ordered it, but it seems to be out of print. You have not yet sent me the magazine article you referred to. I hope you won't forget this.

We shall see you Friday evening. In the meantime, will you and Mrs. Johnson, in the Victorian manner, please accept our compliments!

Carl Van Vechten

James Weldon Johnson to Carl Van Vechten

March 25, 1925

Dear Mr. Van Vechten:

I have your letter.

I am glad you like "The Autobiography," and I hope Miss Marinoff will have a good opinion of it.

You put your finger directly on the weak spot in the book so far as its character as a novel goes. To make a good novel it does lack detail in the personal experiences of the hero, but, as you yourself recognize, I was not working with the intention of writing a novel. I have sometimes since regretted that I did not frankly make the book a piece of fiction.

2. Alexander Woolcott (1887–1943) was a drama critic and columnist for New York City newspapers and then *The New Yorker* magazine during the 1920s until his death. He published *The Story of Irving Berlin* with G. P. Putnam's Sons in 1925. Importantly, Van Vechten indicates that he corrects Woolcott's claim that Berlin's tune, "Alexander's Ragtime Band" (1911) popularized ragtime music.
3. Van Vechten uses the pre-20th-century spelling of Haiti. Here, he most likely refers to Johnson's series of essays that critique U.S. policies toward the black-led republic, "Self-Determining Haiti," which appeared in *The Nation* (August–September 1920).
4. Henri Christophe (1767–1820) was a leader in the war of Haitian independence (1791–1804).
5. Wells's novel was published in London (by Macmillan), in 1915.
6. British explorer, soldier, and journalist (1876–1922) who, in 1899, visited Haiti to provide what he claimed to be the first report on the country by a white man since the end of French rule of the island in 1803. His articles first appeared in London's *Daily Express* newspaper and then were published as a book in 1900 by New York's Charles Scribner's Sons.

I appreciate that you are giving me credit in your review of Wolcott's book. I had not thought of the point, but perhaps after all I was the first to sense and to say that ragtime held possibilities of artistic development.

I must tell you some more about Haiti as soon as we have another opportunity to talk. I am sending you herewith a copy of the reprint of my four articles that appeared in *The Nation*. I had several articles in various magazines. The only one that I can put my hands on is the one which appeared in *The Crisis*, the which I am sending.[1]

I read some reviews about "Where Black Rules White" but I have never seen the book. If you succeed in getting a copy I should like to have a glance at it.

I shall remember and try and get you a copy of "The Autobiography" for yourself.

Mrs. Johnson has already done so, but I want to thank you and Miss Marinoff myself for the beautiful photograph. We both prize it very highly.

I am sending you copies of two spirituals arranged by my brother.

Looking forward to seeing you Friday evening, I am

Yours sincerely,
James W. Johnson

We should like very much to have you and Miss Marinoff go to the casino with us Friday night.[2] Won't you come by our place? We shall be leaving about 10 o'clock. You know the habits of our outside door. If you say you will come by, I'll be on the outlook for you. But in case you should find the door [?]—telephone in from the downstairs or the corner[?], and I'll come down and let you in.

James

James Weldon Johnson to Blanche W. Knopf

March 8, 1926

My dear Mrs. Knopf:[1]

I have been trying for a month to get in to see you about the book and the contract. May I come in on Wednesday or Thursday morning. Will you give me a ring on the telephone so that we might make a definite appointment.

You will remember, too, that you said you would like to read the novel which I published some twelve years ago entitled, "The

1. "The Truth about Haiti: An NAACP Investigation," *Crisis* 5 (September 1920): 217–24. For the articles Johnson refers to in *The Nation*, see n. 3., on 237.
2. This appears in JWJ's hand after his initial signature.
1. Blanche W. Knopf (1893–1966) served as director and vice president of Alfred A. Knopf, Inc., the publishing company she ran with her husband (after whom the firm was named).

Autobiography of an Ex-Colored Man." I have gotten my hands on a copy and if you still wish to see it I can bring it along with me.

I wrote you that Mrs. Johnson and I would be very glad to come on Saturday night. I guess you received my note.

Sincerely yours,
[James Weldon Johnson]

Blanche W. Knopf to James Weldon Johnson†

March 31st, 1926.

Dear James Johnson:

I am sending you another contract on Negro Life in New York[1] and I think it is now in order. If you will sign and return I will send you a copy of it for your own files with the check for the amount.

I am returning to you separately THE AUTOBIOGRAPHY OF AN EX-COLORED MAN which is exceedingly interesting, in fact, quite remarkable I think. I hear that you have arranged with the Viking Press to reissue this and I assume therefore that you will want this back at once.[2]

Yours sincerely,
Blanche
Mrs. Alfred A. Knopf.

Blanche W. Knopf to James Weldon Johnson‡

April 20, 1926.

Dear Jim,

There is no question that we want THE AUTOBIOGRAPHY OF AN EX-COLORED MAN. I have finished it now and think it is amazing. I'll send you a contract in a few days.

With regards,
Blanche
Mrs. Alfred A. Knopf

1. Perhaps an early draft title of *Black Manhattan*. However, Johnson published that work in 1930 with a different firm, Viking Press.
2. Interestingly, Knopf's suggestion that a rival publisher was prepared to reprint *ECM* is quite feasible since Viking eventually released Johnson's (then) newest work of poetry, *God's Trombones*, in April 1927. However, whatever plans Viking may have had for *ECM* did not materialize. Knopf's comment might instead reflect the impact of Johnson's efforts to lobby Carl Van Doren and Heywood Broun for help in securing a new publisher for the novel; see those queries on 235/236.

James Weldon Johnson to Blanche W. Knopf

April 29, 1926

My dear Blanche:

I am sending you herewith the contract for the Autobiography signed and witnessed. I shall, of course, assign the copyright to Knopf. If you will have the assignment drawn I will sign it at any time.

I should like very much to see the book included in the Blue Jade Library. I think it would go best there as a reprint.[1] I will talk that over with you, as well as the probable date of publication, when I see you.

I am sending you at the same time the musical setting of one of my poems called "The Creation."[2] I thought you might be interested in seeing it. The score is by Louis Gruenberg.[3] Perhaps you know him. It was published in Vienna.

Sincerely yours,
[James Weldon Johnson]

James Weldon Johnson to Carl Van Vechten†

If you have finished the introduction, pay no attention to this note. I think anyhow you have fully [?] covered the idea I have so vaguely outlined here.[1]

Sunday [March 6, 1927]

Dear Carl:

Harry Salpeter's interview of you in today's World is a good one—Thank you for mentioning me so advantageously in it.[2]

I have another point for the introduction to the Autobiography—if you think it worthwhile:

We are still on the job of getting over into the American consciousness the idea that in our cultural world the Negro is a creator as well as a receiver—that he has aesthetic values as well as values physical, economic, and otherwise. This is a vitally important job—perhaps the most important connected with the race question and prejudice. In recent years great advance has been made on it. You have done brave

1. See advertising copy for this line of books on 243–44.
2. One of the "seven Negro sermons in verse" that comprise Johnson's collection, *God's Trombones*, published by Viking in 1927.
3. Influenced by African American spirituals, ragtime, and jazz, pianist and composer Gruenberg (1884–1964) is best known for adapting Eugene O'Neill's *The Emperor Jones* for New York City's Metropolitan Opera in 1933.

† From the Carl Van Vechten Papers, Yale Collection of American Literature, Beinecke Rare Book and Manuscript Library.

1. Written in JWJ's hand across the top of the stationery.
2. Salpeter (1895–1967) was a critic and feature writer for the *New York World* newspaper.

service. And Odin [?] & Johnson[3]—Dorothy Scarborough[4] and the greatest of the Negro artists—Hayes, Robeson, etc.[5] But as I look back I believe I can claim to be a pioneer in this particular field. I have been just glancing through the Autobiography—on pages 84–85 I mention the 4 popular art creations of the Negro—and among them I place the cakewalk (the forerunner of all these modern dances). I can see now that it took courage and foresight to declare the cakewalk to be a form of art, when the Autobiography was written. You have already pointed out that the book (on page 139) foretells The Rhapsody in Blue.[6] I wonder if I've made the idea I have in mind clear. I mean in the Autobiography I started doing for ragtime and the Negro dances what you have more recently done almost single handed for The Blues—[7] to prove that they were art creations and art expressions and that their creators were in so much *artists.* And I am coming to believe that nothing can go farther to destroy race prejudice than the recognition of the Negro as a creator and a contributor to American civilization.

This is a terribly muddled note—but, Carl, you always know what I mean without explanation.

Love,
Jim

Aaron Douglas to James Weldon Johnson[†]

June 6, 1927

Dear Mr. Johnson,

It is my good fortune to have the privilege again of helping in the publication of one of your books. The publishers have asked me to design a jacket for The Autobiography of an Ex-Colored Man. I have just finished reading the book and I am carried away with amazement and admiration. Your depth of thought, breadth of vision, and

3. Most likely John "Ole" Olsen and Harold "Chic" Johnson, a white vaudeville duo from 1890s Chicago who brought their act to New York in 1918. The pair quickly earned notice for their madcap, highly physical comedy routines, which stemmed from their early interests in ragtime music.
4. Emily Dorothy Scarborough (1878–1935) was a white novelist from Texas who earned her Ph.D. (1917) and taught creative writing at Columbia University during the 1920s. Her novel *In the Land of Cotton* (1923) offered a critical view of tenant farming.
5. Internationally renowned, Roland Hayes (1887–1977) was an African American concert singer (tenor) whose repertoire spanned European classics and Negro spirituals. His peer bass-baritone Paul Robeson (1898–1976) performed from these song canons as well. Through his work as a stage and film actor (most notably in *Body and Soul* [1925], *Othello* [1930], and *The Emperor Jones* [1933]), together with his radical civil rights activism, Robeson had a global impact across the first half of the twentieth century.
6. Composed by George Gershwin (1898–1937), this work's famous clarinet opening solo launched the fusion of jazz and classical idioms that earned its billing as "an experiment in modern music" when it was first performed in 1924.
7. Here JWJ's writing crawls along the right margin of the page.

subtlety and beauty of expression awakens in me the greatest admiration. I am amazed at the gigantic effort which must have been necessary for the writing and publishing of the book at such an early date. The post-war Negro, blinded by the glare and almost sudden bursting of a new day, finds much difficulty in realizing the immense power and effort, which the pre-war Negro has made to prepare the country for what we now feel to be the 'Awakening.'

I want to thank you for allowing me to share in the making of your great book 'God's Trombones.' [*sic*][1]

Sincerely,
Aaron Douglas.

Carl Van Vechten to James Weldon Johnson†

[October 16, 1927]

Dear Jim,

That was a great review you received in the Times today.[1] Perhaps you'd be interested in a quotation from a recent letter from Hunter Stagg[2] of Richmond:

> "And I have not thanked you for Mr. Johnson's book with your preface, but I do assure you I got a great kick out of it. I somehow never thought of him as writing a novel, especially a novel like that. I had only read his prefaces to the Spiritual books,[3] you see, and the prose in the Autobiography—such beautiful prose it is, too—is so different that—well, I wish he would do some more fiction. He really ought to, in justice to the Negroes, inasmuch as he writes rings around the others. I burst out with this because, as I recall it, the writing of his prefaces was merely dignified and scholarly, not necessarily the writing of an artist, and it comes to me with the force of a discovery—not that it is possible for a Negro to write like that—you know me better than to think so—but that a Negro who can doesn't do it

1. A trained painter whose murals and canvases defined his reputation during the Harlem Renaissance, Douglas (1899–1979) worked as a graphic designer for both major publishing firms in New York and leading progressive journals aimed at African American and civil rights–minded readerships. Here, Douglas refers to his artwork for Johnson's verse collection released by Viking Press in 1927.

† From the Carl Van Vechten Papers, Yale Collection of American Literature, Beinecke Rare Books and Manuscript Library. Reprinted with permission of the Carl Van Vechten Trust.

1. See Charles Willis Thompson, "The Negro Question," *New York Times Book Review*, October 16, 1927, reprinted in this volume on 321–24.
2. Hunter Taylor Stagg (1895–1960) co-founded *The Reviewer*, a literary magazine based in Richmond, Virginia (1921–24) that helped galvanize the Southern renaissance of the 1920s. Stagg published Van Vechten's essays in *The Reviewer*; Van Vechten introduced Stagg to literary circles in New York City.
3. In 1925, Johnson published *The Book of American Negro Spirituals*, whose preface endures as a significant analysis of black sacred music's rich and complex genealogy.

more. Of course he is probably too busy doing other things more important, but I can't be expected to be broad enough to think anything more important than the writing of beautiful books by people who can."

with affection always,
Carl

Blanche W. Knopf to James Weldon Johnson†

February 15, 1929

Dear Jim,

We could not possibly have the Agence Litteraire Internationale sell the rights in THE AUTOBIOGRAPHY OF AN EX-COLOURED [*sic*] MAN on the Continent because we have our agents who handle all the Continental markets for us. We have sold the German book and serial rights to the Frankfurter Societats Druckerei and they have published the book under the title DER WEISSE NEGER.[1] I will take up with Mr. Bradley, our French agent, the offer made to you by the Agence Litteraire Internationale and see whether he can get into communication with them regarding a French edition.

Yours ever,
Blanche

Blue Jade Library Advertising Copy‡

On the Rear Cover

This book was first published, anonymously, in 1912. It was allowed to go out of print after the withdrawal from business of its publishers, and it has since been one of the rarest and most sought-after source-books on the life of the Negro in America. Many changes have come about in the intervening fifteen years, but the value of this book as a unique human document remains. The truths postulated by Mr. Johnson in 1912 still hold good in 1927, and most of his astonishing predictions have become realities. In no other book is the phenomenon of "passing," with all its attendant psychological

1. For background on this firm, see Moira Weigel's translation of the German edition's preface and foreword in this volume, 124–25.

and racial complications, treated so objectively, so sanely, and with such sympathetic understanding. *The Autobiography of an Ex-Coloured Man* has become a classic in Negro literature.

On the Back Jacket Flap[1]

The Blue Jade Library is designed to cover "the field of semi-classic, semi-curious books—books which for one reason or another have enjoyed great celebrity but little actual distribution." The plan is an excellent one and the selection made so far has been equally excellent: and it is to be hoped that both the celebrity and the distribution of these classic and curious books is being greatly widened. Their format is delightful, their price moderate, and their appeal is so intelligent.

On the Frontispiece[2]

James Weldon Johnson, *The Autobiography of an Ex-Colored Man*
James Morler, *The Adventures of Hajji Baba of Ispahan*
C. K. Scott Moncrieff, trans. *The Letters of Abelard and Heloise*
Haldane Macfall, *The Wooings of Jezebel Pettyfer*
Carlo Goldoni, *The Memoirs of Carlo Goldoni*
Richard Garnett, *The Twilight of the Gods*
Henri Boyle-Stendhal, *The Life of Henri Brulard*
Andrew Kippis, *Captain Cook's Voyages*
Frederick Baron Corvo, *Hadrian the Seventh*
Francisco de Quevedo-Villegas, *Pablo de Segovia*
Marmaduke Pickthall, *Saïd the Fisherman*
Villiers de l'Isle-Adam, *Sardonic Tales*
Morley Roberts, *Rachel Marr*
Theophile Gauthier, *A Romantic in Spain*
Pere Huc, *Travels in Tartary*
Martin A. S. Hume, *Sir Walter Raleigh*
Barbey d' Aurevilly, *The Diaboliques*
Multatuli, *Max Havelaar*

1. The text describes the publishing agenda of the Blue Jade Library, quoting a review of *Twilight of the Gods* (1903) that had appeared in the *New York Sun*.
2. The front and rear inner flaps list the books in the series. Older titles (known as the backlist) appear in the rear and current titles up front. The frontispiece page collates them all.

Composition and Publication Correspondence: 1948 Edition

Victor Weybright to Joseph G. Lesser†

May 2, 1946

Dear Mr. Lesser:[1]

I am sorry for the delay in responding to your letter of April 22nd, but I have been off on my first week's holiday in five years.

We are all very pleased by the prospect of reprinting some of the books which we discussed. Contracts are under preparation for Elizabeth Bowen's THE HOUSE IN PARIS, John Collier's DEFY THE FOUL FIEND, and David Garnett's LADY INTO FOX AND MAN IN THE ZOO. On these titles the advance royalty guarantee is $1,500, and they are to be scheduled not later than 1947. Would payments on each of $500 on the signing of the contract, $500 on publication and $500 six months after publication be satisfactory to you?

The contract for AUTOBIOGRAPHY OF AN EX-COLORED MAN by James Weldon Johnson is under preparation with an advance royalty guarantee of $1,000. Would payments of $250 on signing, $500 on publication and $250 six months after publication be satisfactory? We are also publishing during the year ahead Roi Ottley's NEW WORLD A-COMIN'.[2] We want to publish this book prior to the James Weldon Johnson book, which means that AUTOBIOGRAPHY OF AN EX-COLORED MAN will probably be issued during the

† From the New American Library Archive, MSS 070, Fales Library and Special Collections, New York University Library. Unless otherwise indicated, this and all subsequent letters regarding the 1948 reprinting of *ECM* come from this source and repository.

1. Victor Weybright (1903–1978) founded the mass paperback publishing firm, New American Library, along with Kurt Enoch in the 1940s. As treasurer of Alfred A. Knopf, Inc., Joseph C. Lesser (dates unknown) coordinated the transactions for reprinting contracts.
2. African American journalist Vincent Lushington "Roi" Ottley (1906–1960) composed this social portrait of 1920s–30s Harlem, using oral interviews collected by the Federal Writers Project in New York City during the Depression. The book was originally published by Houghton Mifflin in 1943. NAL would have wanted to reprint it, given the book's critical success and popular adaptation as a radio show.

latter half of 1947 if this scheduling meets with your approval and the approval of Mrs. Johnson.

TACY CROMWELL by Conrad Richter, unfortunately, seems to fall so far short of THE SEA OF GRASS that, much as we like Richter, we are returning it to you under separate cover. Our hope to have THE SEA OF GRASS still remains when you reach the point of releasing it.

I am terribly disappointed that D. H. Lawrence's THE VIRGIN AND THE GYPSY has gone elsewhere. I discovered that we have no reading copy in the office of MORNINGS IN MEXICO. Could you lend us one?

We look forward to reading the Stephen Crane stories, which you so kindly sent us.

Sincerely yours,
Victor Weybright

Victor Weybright to Joseph G. Lesser

January 12, 1948

Dear Mr. Lesser:

Mr. Enoch and I greatly appreciate the chance to discuss this title which we were unable to issue within the year 1947, as specified by the contract. We are distressed by this lapse, and, confirming our conversation, will definitely publish the book, in our non-fiction series, in 1948.

One of the principal reasons for postponement of publication in our reprint edition was the failure of our plan to precede the book with a more contemporary and challenging volume on a kindred racial theme—NEW WORLD A-COMING by Roi Ottley.[1] We have definitely decided not to fix the scheduling of AUTOBIOGRAPHY OF AN EX-COLORED MAN in relation to the above-mentioned book—and in view of this, I wonder if Mrs. Johnson would write, arrange for, or approve, a brief special introduction establishing the book not only as an American autobiographical classic, but making it clear to the contemporary reader that the book was written prior to the more recent developments in the field of racial relations in the United States. My preference would be for an introduction, written under our editorial guidance, subject to the approval of yourselves and the Johnson estate, of not more than 1,000 words. I would rely on the advice of our Editorial Advisory Board in this mater, and would incline toward

1. See n. 2, above.

an introduction by someone like Prof. Ralph J. Bunche,[2] who worked on the Myrdel Survey and who is now a key figure in the United Nations mission to Palestine. If Dr. Bunche would not be available, I should prefer as an alternate Dr. Alaine Locke of Howard University.[3] Failing these two candidates, I believe that an introduction by Mrs. Johnson would be peculiarly appropriate because of the underlying personal nature of the AUTOBIOGRAPHY, which in our mind ranks with Jane Addams' 20 YEARS AT HULL HOUSE as a great personal document of historical significance for American reader.[4]

In any event, we shall publish the book, but I believe the introduction would add immeasurably to appreciation of it by the present generation.

Sincerely yours,
Victor Weybright

Victor Weybright to Charles S. Johnson

January 30, 1948

Mr. dear Dr. Johnson:[1]

You may identify the writer as formerly managing editor for some years of Survey Graphic[2] and still on the board of Survey Associates.

2. Political scientist Bunche (1904–1971) worked as the lead researcher and writer (1938–40) for Swedish sociologist Gunnar Myrdal's widely influential but controversial *An American Dilemma: The Negro Problem and Modern Democracy* (1944). Bunche's career with the United Nations began with crafting its charter in 1945; the Middle East mission Weybright refers to concerns Bunche's central role in brokering a truce between the emerging state of Israel, Palestine, and neighboring Arab countries in 1949. For this work, Bunche was awarded the Nobel Peace Prize in 1950.
3. Harvard- and Oxford-trained philosopher Locke (1885–1954) organized what is considered to be the founding volume of the Harlem Renaissance, *The New Negro: An Interpretation* (1925).
4. Addams's chronicle of her life (1860–1935), in particular her establishment of the settlement house movement in early-twentieth-century Chicago. First published by Macmillan in 1910.

1. Two years before this letter, Charles S. Johnson (1893–1956) was appointed president of Fisk University, after a twenty-year career leading its sociology department. Between 1921 and 1926, he worked in New York City, where he edited the National Urban League's journal, *Opportunity*. That post brought Johnson into contact with the leading activists, writers, and intellectuals of the Harlem Renaissance. It also led him to Weybright, whose work on the magazine *Survey Graphic* (see note below) stemmed from *Opportunity*'s annual awards dinner, which Johnson organized in 1924.
2. A progressive monthly magazine published in New York City and headed by Paul U. Kellogg, *Survey Graphic* aimed to make social work issues—e.g., poverty, child labor, immigration, housing, health, and racial discrimination—accessible to a broad lay readership through a combination of strong narrative writing, reliable empirical evidence, and eye-catching illustrations. In March 1925, the magazine released an issue devoted to "Harlem: Mecca of the New Negro," which was inspired by *Opportunity* magazine's awards dinner for 1924. Philosopher Alain Locke edited the issue; leading artists and intellectuals contributed essays, poems, short fiction, and graphic art. The magazine sold out its 30,000-copy print run, leading to its publication in book form, *The New Negro: An Interpretation* (1925). This literary history is the "personal connection" to which Weybright refers.

I mention this personal connection, even though I am now writing you as editor of Penguin Books, since it may be a point in persuading you to undertake the writing of a foreword for our forthcoming paper bound edition of THE AUTOBIOGRAPHY OF AN EX-COLORED MAN. Yesterday, by good chance, I was able to discuss the popular edition of the book with Mrs. James Weldon Johnson. I feel that, even though the AUTOBIOGRAPHY stands as a great classic of American biographical writing, its significance for the contemporary reader would be enhanced by an introduction which makes it clear that the book was written prior to recent developments and recent literature in the field of racial relations in the United States. The introduction need not be long; indeed something about 1,000 words should suffice.

Would you be willing to undertake it as a labor of love—since our fee would be a modest one; $20.00

I don't believe I need outline either the scope or intention o the introduction we have in mind, since you will be more sensitive to its purpose than I could possibly define. The greatness of James Weldon Johnson, his courage in writing the book in the day and age of the first edition, and the pertinence of his prophetic qualities today can well bear re-stating.

I hope that Mrs. James Weldon Johnson will find an opportunity to discuss this with you personally during your present visit to New York. If not, you will know at any rate that the suggestion has her blessing. The deadline should be not later than February 20, and the length anywhere between 700 and 1,500 words. I know that your introduction would add immeasurably to the appreciation of THE AUTOBIOGRAPHY OF AN EX-COLOURED MAN by the present generation.

Sincerely yours,
jn/ Victor Weybright

Cecile Fishbein to New American Library

[ca. October 1948]

To whom it may concern;

I would deeply appreciate it if you could take a moment of your time to clarify one or two things about the Pelican Mentor Book—"The autobiography of an ex-colored man."

I should like to say at this time that the story by James Weldon Johnson is a marvelous piece of work. All I hold against the author is that he had this published anonymously at first.

On the back cover (about the author) there are a few things that contradict the authors [*sic*] own story:

1. Mr. Johnson said he was born in a small town in Georgia, in disaccord with what you say about his having been born in Jacksonville, Florida. (Page 1)
2. In Mr. Johson's [*sic*] story he states that he did not attend Atlanta University due to the fac that his money was taken from him that was to pay for his tuition. (Page 46) If it were not for the fact that you say he married after he received his B.A. and M.A. degrees, one might draw the conclusion that he returned to Atlanta University after he became a father.
3. He makes no mention of having had a brother.

I am genuinly [*sic*] interested in the answers to the above inquiries. Not to prove that you erred (if that is the case) but to get a fuller picture of what Mr. Johnson's life really was.

May I say in closing that this autobiography is a dynamic one which should be read by any and all of us who are interested in fighting this anti-Negro, Jew, Catholic, etc. campaign that some people insist on encouraging.

I thank you for the opportunity Pelican Mentor Books offer in the way of inexpensive pocket editions.

Very truly yours,
Cecile Fishbein

Arabel J. Porter to Cecile Fishbein

October 25, 1948

Dear Miss Fishbein:

We are pleased to learn of your pleasure in reading James Weldon Johnson's THE AUTOBIOGRAPHY OF AN EX COLOURED MAN. We are sorry, though, that we did not make sufficiently clear in the biographical sketch on the back cover, and in the note, "About This Book" that THE AUTOBIOGRAPHY OF AN EX COLOURED MAN is not Mr. Johnson's own life story, but a work of fiction. Mr. Johnson did draw on some of his own experiences for the book, but his life was actually quite different. It is described briefly and correctly on the back cover of our edition of the book, and in considerable more detail in ALONG THIS WAY, published by the Viking Press. We feel, as you do, that THE AUTOBIOGRAPHY OF AN EX COLOURED MAN is a powerful and important book.

You will perhaps like to have the enclosed folder which lists many other books that may interst you.

Sincerely yours,
Arabel J. Porter
Associate Editor

Ellen Tarry, New American Library Publicity Letter[1]

June 7, 1948

Dear Friend:

Programs to commemorate the birth of James Weldon Johnson on June 17th are being planned throughout the country. In order to help you take part in this nation-wide celebration, we are enclosing a digest of the highlights of James Weldon Johnson's life.

Furthermore, in connection with the renewed interest in the life and works of James Weldon Johnson, The New American Library is publishing in June a popular reprint edition of *The Autobiography of an Ex-Coloured Man*, was first of the "passing" books, originally published in 1912. Because of your interest in broader cultural development, we are sure you will wish to facilitate the distribution of this book among your organizational friends.

We call your attention to other books by and about the Negro published by us. Among them are Richard Wright's *Uncle Tom's Children* and Lillian Smith's *Strange Fruit* and such allied books as *Heredity, Race and Society* by L. C. Dunn and Th. Dobzhansky and *Patterns of Culture* by Ruth Benedict. These will be found on the enclosed complete list of Signet and Mentor books which also includes a wide variety of fiction and non-fiction titles to suit every mood, taste, and interest.

The wide distribution of these books not only fulfills a cultural mission but also represents a source of revenue for any group anxious to swell its treasure. Many organizations have found it profitable to stock a selection of the titles in the Signet and Mentor lines for sale in their own offices or by mail. Signet books retail for 25¢ a copy and Mentor books are sold at 35¢ a copy. *The Autobiography of an Ex-Coloured* Man is a Mentor book which will be sold to you at the educational price of 28¢ a copy net on orders of 1 to 999 copies. For 1000 copies or more the price is 27¢ a copy. On orders of Signet books (*Uncle Tom's Children, Strange Fruit*, etc.) the price is 20¢ net on orders of 1 to 999 copies and 19¢ for orders of 1000 copies or more.

1. Best-known during the 1940s for her children's books, young adult biographies, and friendship with poet-novelist Claude McKay (1889–1948), Ellen Tarry (1906–2008) moved to New York City from Birmingham, Alabama in 1929. An aspiring journalist, she made quick connections to fellow writers in Harlem and librarians at the 135th Street branch of the New York Public Library, who introduced her to James Weldon and Grace Nail Johnson. These connections, along with Tarry's membership in the James Weldon Johnson Literary Guild (established by the branch librarians in 1931), brought her to New American Library's attention as publicity coordinator for its release of *The Autobiography of an Ex-Colored Man* in 1948.

We will be happy to cooperate with you should you desire any further information. about discounts and procedures.

A newsletter listing all the James Weldon Johnson Birthday Celebrations taking place on June 17th will be sent to editors throughout the United States. If you plan a celebration which has not already been listed with us, will you please be kind enough to let us hear from you.

Sincerely,
Ellen Tarry

Arabel J. Porter to Joseph C. Lesser

June 21, 1951.

Dear Mr. Lesser:

Our records indicate that THE AUTOBIOGRAPHY OF AN EX-COLORED MAN by James Weldon Johnson, published by you in the United States, has not been issued by a British publisher. If the book is under contract to a British publisher, and if you control the British Empire rights, we would be interested in selling our edition in the Empire through an extension of the market areas of our contract dated May 29, 1946.

Would you, therefore, grant us British Empire selling rights for our edition of this book, making the license effective for three years from our first shipment to one of these areas, to be automatically extended until written notice of termination is received from you. [*sic*] On all Empire sales, our regular export royalties will apply: 1¢ net per copy sold for 25¢ books, 1.4¢ for 35¢ books, 2¢ for 50¢ books. At this time we cannot guarantee the quantity that might be sold in Empire territories but estimate an average between five and ten thousand copies per title annually.

We are currently developing a promising market for Signet and Mentor editions in British Empire territories, particularly in South Africa, India, Pakistan, New Zealand, and Australia, and may also do so in the United Kingdom as well. In South Africa, for example, our books are being sold through one of the largest distributors in the field, one who has had long experience in handling inexpensive editions through magazine outlets.

All of our books sold in British Empire areas, so far, have been enthusiastically received—in many instances because we have made literature available that has never been sold in these areas, in either hard-cover or inexpensive editions. We feel it so important that all Empire distributors be given a wide variety of titles so that the best possible cross-section of not only American literature but that of other countries can be represented.

We shall be grateful for early word from you.

Sincerely,
Arabel J. Porter,
Executive Editor

Arabel J. Porter to Joseph C. Lesser

July 5, 1951.

Dear Mr. Lesser:

RE: THE AUTOBIOGRAPHY OF AN EX-COLORED MAN
By James Weldon Johnson.

We should like very much to sell our edition of THE AUTOBIOGRAPHY OF AN EX-COLORED MAN by James Weldon Johnson in India and Indonesia, under an experimental project sponsored by the State Department.

We should, therefore, appreciate your extending our market area, as set down in our contract with you dated May 19, 1946 to include those areas, with the understanding that our sales, [*sic*] (we estimate an average of between five and ten thousand copies), will be made with the limitations of this special government-sponsored program.

Our regular export royalties will apply; in this case, 1.4¢ net per copy sold.

Sincerely,
Arabel J. Porter,
Executive Editor.

Joseph C. Lesser to Arabel J. Porter†

July 10, 1951

Dear Miss Porter:

We are agreeable to amending the agreement of May 29, 1946 to permit you to sell your edition of THE AUTOBIOGRAPHY OF AN EX-COLORED MAN by James Weldon Johnson in India and Indonesia, under an experimental project sponsored by the State Department.

You pay us your regular export royalties on such sales, which in this case is 1.4¢ net per copy sold.

Yours sincerely,
Joseph C. Lesser
Treasurer

Related Writings by James Weldon Johnson

Art†

Johnson wrote this "essayette" while drafting *The Autobiography of an Ex-Colored Man* during his tenure as U.S. Consul in Puerto Cabello, Venezuela, probably between 1908 and 1909. In this musing, he debates how authenticity might be best achieved through the studied and deliberate use of artistic techniques to depict the material world, or "life."

Art is not and should not be Life, but it should be so like Life as to excite wonder, admiration and pleasure and to stir the deeper emotions by its verisimilitude. It must always force the exclamation, "How *like* life!" It should never call up the doubt "Is this Art or Life?" In fact, the very essence of the pleasure derived from Art grows out of the wonder that Art could create such a thing so like life. If we learn that the thing really is life the wonder ceases, and with it, the greater part of the pleasure.

For example, no matter how well a person or an animal might pose, neither could produce the pleasurable wonder caused by a statue that called for the exclamation, "How like life!"

Or, if one posing should be taken for a work of Art, the pleasure would cease as soon as it was learned that it was life not art. (Living pictures—why they are not art)

The raison d'être of Art is pleasure and the essence of this pleasure is the wonder that Art can create a thing so like life. And there must never be any doubt that the creation is a work of Art and is not Life.

The emotions called up by Life and those called up by Art are distinct, and it is a mistake to confound them. And so it is a mistake for Art to attempt to call out the emotions which Life evokes. And if Art could succeed in doing so it would be the loser.

† From James Weldon Johnson and Grace Nail Johnson Papers. Yale Collection of American Literature, Beinecke Rare Book and Manuscript Library. Unless noted otherwise, subsequent essays in this section come from this source and repository. Reprinted by permission of the James Weldon Johnson Estate.

For example, the emotions called up by a sunset are entirely different from those called out by a perfect painting of a sunset. To go farther, suppose a window in a room[1] could be so framed that on entering the room we would think that we were looking at the painting of a sunset, can you not feel how our wonder, and consequently, our pleasure would be decreased as soon as we found out it was a real sunset and not a painting. Not that the real sunset would not afford no pleasure or even deeper emotions, but the pleasure derived from the wonder that art could create a thing so like life would be lost. On the other hand, suppose a painting could be so hung that on entering a room we would take it for a real sunset, can you not feel how our wonder and pleasure would be heightened on learning that it was a painting?

To turn to the drama, given two actors of equal merit, one a Chinaman and the other an American, to play a Chinese character in a play. Do you not feel that if the American played the part so that you would think him a Chinaman if you did not know him to be an American, he would produce greater pleasure that it would be possible for the Chinaman to produce. And why? Because in the American's case there would be the wonder that art could create a thing so like life. And this wonder and the consequent pleasure would depend on knowing that he was not[2] a Chinaman.

The Dilemma of the Poets

These fragmentary ideas surfaced in the same notebook where "Art" (253–54) is found. Intriguingly, Johnson not only shows interest in the linguistic boundaries between poetry and prose, but also raises complex claims about originality's relation to history. While it is unclear which "new poets" Johnson has in mind when writing this in 1908–09, the theory of literary experimentation he gestures toward might be read in tandem with such later manifestos as T. S. Eliot's "Tradition and the Individual Talent" (1922) and prose-poem works like William Carlos Williams's *Spring and All* (1923).

Not a lack of Poets but of a new language[.] The English language worn out[.] Every language has its periods of blossoms—full bloom to ~~finish~~ fruit[.] Then follow lesser blooms then decay.

There is only one full bloom[.] Poetry depends upon minted phrases—these grow smooth with use and lose the images originally imprinted.

1. Here JWJ inserted "looking out on a sunset."
2. Double underlined.

Prose—on the other hand depends on clear expression of ideas and thoughts.

The "new poets" delude themselves in thinking they [are] discoverers, originators, innovators [as?] they are not at the beginning, they are at the end. They are raking dry bones.

Words and Clothes

Written near the end of the drafting of *The Autobiography of an Ex-Colored Man*, this essay draws inspiration from Thomas Carlyle's *Sartor Resartus* (1836) and that novel's "philosophy of clothes."[1] However, where Carlyle develops the conceit of fashion into a critique of how ideas assume form as symbols, Johnson uses the trope of clothes to think about problems of economy and excess, standard and vernacular expression, representation and gender (take note of how he dodges the test case of women's apparel, even though "by reason of its more frequent variations, [it] would better illustrate [his] theme"), popularity and timing at the level of diction. One question, then, becomes: are these concerns taken to scale in Johnson's novel? If so, how?[2]

Clothes are those habiliments with which we dress our bodies; words are those habiliments with which we dress our thoughts. But the anology [*sic*] goes deeper than a mere epigram. There are certain clothes which are necessary for covering our nakedness and protecting our bodies [*sic*] these are, a breech-cloth in the tropics and a bear skin the arctics [*sic*], with modifications between these two extremes to suit the latitude and altitude. All clothes over and above these we use for dressing, or adorning ourselves, and they are regulated by style and fashion. So, there are certain words absolutely necessary for the communication and interchange of ideas; these are the words we use to express our thoughts; all words over and above these we use to dress and adorn our speech, and they, like clothes of the second class, are regulated by style and fashion.

The dress adapted to our latitude is the ordinary coat, vest and trousers; and it has remained practically the same for more than a half century. There have been variations, but this mode is the normal, the what [*sic*] is necessary for us, and the variations have all finally swung back to that normal. Of course, there have been more

1. Though Johnson does not specifically mention Carlyle in *Along This Way*, given Johnson's range of reading during his youth in Jacksonville, his apprenticeship with Dr. T. O. Summers, and his years at Atlanta University, it is quite likely that he encountered *Sartor Resartus* directly.
2. Zora Neale Hurston's formulations about vernacular culture and African Americans' "will to adorn" language in "Characteristics of Negro Expression" (1934) might suggest ways to approach this question.

or less radical changes in clothes just as there have been in speech; a change from the knickerbockers of Colonial days to long trousers, and a change from the English of Chaucer to modern American; but I am, of course dealing with an epoch. It will be noticed that I shall confine myself to men's clothes; for though the apparel of women, by reason of it's more frequent variations, would better illustrate my theme, yet in discussing it I should feel that I was treading on unknown ground or, better, exploring unknown regions where I was not sure of my bearings.

A man may depend upon it, that in sticking to the coat, vest and trousers of ordinary cut and color he can never be wrong. The charge may be brought against him that he is not up-to-date, but not that he is violating the cannons [*sic*] of good taste. But to be dressed correctly, fashionably, even elegantly is not unworthy of attention and effort. There is nothing outside of absolute mental superiority that gives the ease, the poise and the confidence that correct and fashionable clothes give. It takes a man of great intellect—or of none at all—to feel perfectly at ease when he looks around the company and perceives by comparison that his pantaloons are cut too short or his coat too narrow, or that his vest, in contra-distinction to the others, shows a stubborn aversion to coming into contact with the waistband of his trousers.

The fashion in dress is very often a wide divergence from what I have called the normal; it sometimes approaches the bizarre; but the man who devotes strict attention to dress must follow, unless it be a style so extreme as to appeal to people of vulgar tastes. Yet, whereas the normal dress may be worn at any and all times, the distinct variations can be worn only when they are in vogue. This rule is inflexible; for just as it is a sign of urbanity, of being "au courant," of having "savoir faire" to be arrayed in the latest fashion, just as surely, for one to affect these distinct variations, sometimes even the following year, is evidence of rusticity, of verdancy, of being a bumpkin. You would find few men brave enough to wear that not so long ago popular summer garment, a seersucker suit, or to go out in a pair of spring-bottom trousers, or to don for a railroad journey the once indispensable linen duster. The effect cannot be conceived which would be made by a woman going through the streets wearing hoop-skirts or one of the great bustles of a couple of decades ago.

A study of clothes and fashion shows that these variations are not permanent, but that they have a certain vogue, and that the length of their vogue is in an inverse ratio to their divergence from the normal. Thus some simple variations have endured for years, while many of the ultra effects have barely lived through a season. At times, however, there are innovations or additions made which appeal so strongly to our sense of comfort and utility that they become a permanent part of our clothes; such were garters and negligee shirts for men, and shirt-waists and tailor-made skirts for women.

Now, as there are designers in clothes who, by new cuts, colors and combinations, turn out fresh styles of dress, so there [*sic*] designers in words who, by the manipulation of adjectives and adverbs, and by coupling them to nouns and verbs with which they have not before been used, furnish new and striking phrases. These phrases follow the rule of fashion in clothes; that is, they have their vogue, and the more striking and brilliant they are, the shorter their vogue is. And, just as it gives beauty, piquancy and verve to written and spoken speech to use these phrases while they are in vogue, it imparts a dull, hackneyed and behind-date air to use them when their vogue is past. For example; "valor," "courage" and "glance" are three good, necessary and indispensable words, but when we say, "pristine valor," "lion-hearted courage" and "eagle-eyed glance" we are distinctly out of fashion. Fledgling poets, more than other persons, are prone to this fault; because Poetry is, as it were, the tailor shop for variations in phrases; and the young poet or the poet without genius or talent continues to adopt the style of a bygone day. Thus we still see in rhythmic effusions so many "silver moons" and gentle zephyrs," [*sic*] etc.

There are also words and phrases corresponding to the extreme and "outré" fashions which are avoided by people or refined and delicate tastes; these styles in speech are denominated slang, and in writing and speaking, except when one wishes to do a bit of masquerading, they are not used. Sometimes as a garment, fashionable years before, is re-introduced, so a word which has become obsolete may be again used with fresh sense and charm. Occasionally there is a man of such attractive eccentricity that he is able to make some peculiar style of dress his own [*sic*] it becomes identified with him, and to imitate his clothes would be almost as bad as to imitate his signature. Sometimes an author will coin a word or a phrase so odd, so individual, so expressive of his own personality that when others use it they must do so with quotation marks or run the risk of being indicted for plagiarism.

We have all walked through a picture gallery and admired the ruffled shirts, the lace cuffs, the silk knickerbockers, the low-cut bodices and the full flowing gowns in the portraits of past generations, and we have all admitted how much more beautiful they were then than the garb of the present day; yet, at the same time, we felt that to take them out of their gilt frames and put them to modern use would be to strip them of all their charm. In like manner it is hazardous to attempt to make current the extreme styles of those old master word coiners and phrase designers of the English language. To touch the "Heaven kissing hill" of Shakespeare is to be guilty of almost vandalism.

If one has not the knowledge and taste to keep in touch with the latest styles in phrases, and the discernment to know when they are out of vogue, it is safer for him to stick to the normal words which are never out of date.

The Dilemma of the Negro Author†

Unlike the previous writings, Johnson published this essay a year after *The Autobiography of an Ex-Colored Man*'s reprinting in 1927. The "dilemma" he describes—how African American authors navigate the conflicting expectations of racially segregated audiences—resolves itself by way of an ideal that sheds light on the novel's 1912 publication and poses a relevant question about African American literature's development across the twentieth and twenty-first centuries as well. Does the Negro artist's dilemma persist across time *and* genre? Under what conditions might the "fusion" of reception publics that Johnson calls for be possible?

The Negro author—the creative author—has arrived. He is here. He appears in the lists of the best publishers. He even breaks into the lists of the best-sellers. To the general American public he is a novelty, a strange phenomenon, a miracle straight out of the skies. Well, he *is* a novelty, but he is by no means a new thing.

The line of American Negro authors runs back for a hundred and fifty years, back to Phillis Wheatley, the poet.[1] Since Phillis Wheatley there have been several hundred Negro authors who have written books of many kinds. But in all these generations down to within the past six years only seven or eight of the hundreds have ever been heard of by the general American public or even by the specialists in American literature. As many Negro writers have gained recognition by both in the past six years as in all the generations gone before. What has happened is that efforts which have been going on for more than a century are being noticed and appreciated at last, and that this appreciation has served as a stimulus to greater effort and output. America is aware today that there are such things as Negro authors. Several converging forces have been at work to produce this state of mind. Had these forces been at work three decades ago, it is possible that we then should have had a condition similar to the one which now exists.

† From *American Mercury*, December 1928, 477–81. Reprinted with permission of the James Weldon Johnson Estate.

1. In both her first book, *Poems on Various Subjects, Religious and Moral* (1773) and her person, Wheatley (1753–1784) embodied the dilemma Johnson's essay identifies. Her neoclassical verse style defied white stereotypes about the illiteracy of enslaved blacks; her literary techniques sometimes turned black readers away from her work—a distance Johnson kept himself, judging by his commentary about Wheatley in his preface to the 1922 *Book of American Negro Poetry*.

Now that the Negro author has come into the range of vision of the American public eye, it seems to me only fair to point out some of the difficulties he finds in his way. But I wish to state emphatically that I have no intention of making an apology or asking any special allowances for him; such a plea would at once disqualify him and void the very recognition he has gained. But the Negro writer does face peculiar difficulties that ought to be taken into account when passing judgment upon him.

It is unnecessary to say that he faces every one of the difficulties common to all that crowd of demon-driven individuals who feel that they must write. But the Aframerican[2] author faces a special problem which the plain American author knows nothing about—the problem of the double audience. It is more than a double audience; it is a divided audience, an audience made up of two elements with differing and often opposite and antagonistic points of view. His audience is always both white America and black America. The moment a Negro writer takes up his pen or sits down to his typewriter he is immediately called upon to solve, consciously or unconsciously, this problem of the double audience. To whom shall he address himself, to his own black group or to white America? Many a Negro writer has fallen down, as it were, between these two stools.

It may be asked why he doesn't just go ahead and write and not bother himself about audiences. That is easier said than done. It is doubtful if anything with meaning can be written unless the writer has some definite audience in mind. His audience may be as far away as the angelic host or the rulers of darkness, but an audience he must have in mind. As soon as he selects his audience he immediately falls, whether he wills it or not, under the laws which govern the influence of the audience upon the artist, laws that operate in every branch of art.

Now, it is axiomatic that the artist achieves his best when working at his best with the materials he knows best. And it goes without saying that the material which the Negro as a creative or general writer knows best comes out of the life and experience of the colored people in America. The overwhelming bulk of the best work done by Aframerican writers has some bearing on the Negro and his relations to civilization and society in the United States. Leaving authors, white or black, writing for coteries on special and technical subjects out of the discussion, it is safe to say that the white American author, when he sits down to write, has in mind a

2. This fused term, joining "Afro" to "American," first appeared in black denominational periodicals of the 1890s, such as the *African Methodist Episcopal Church Review.* It became widespread in the black secular media by the early twentieth century. Johnson used it in print as early as his 1922 preface to the *Book of American Negro Poetry.* My thanks to Joan Bryant, P. Gabrielle Foreman, and Richard Yarborough for sharing information about this term's etymology.

white audience—and naturally. The influence of the Negro as a group on his work is infinitesimal if not zero. Even when he talks about the Negro he talks to white people. But with the Aframerican author the case is different. When he attempts to handle his best known material he is thrown upon two, indeed, if it is permissible to say so, upon three horns of a dilemma. He must intentionally or unintentionally choose a black audience or a white audience or a combination of the two; and each of them presents peculiar difficulties.

If the Negro author selects white America as his audience he is bound to run up against many long-standing artistic conceptions about the Negro; against numerous conventions and traditions which through age have become binding; in a word, against a whole row of hard-set stereotypes which are not easily broken up. White America has some firm opinions as to what the Negro is, and consequently some pretty well fixed ideas as to what should be written about him, and how.

What is the Negro in the artistic conception of white America? In the brighter light, he is a simple, indolent, docile, improvident peasant; a singing, dancing, laughing, weeping child; picturesque beside his log cabin and in the snowy fields of cotton; naïvely charming with his banjo and his songs in the moonlight along the lazy Southern rivers; a faithful, ever-smiling and genuflecting old servitor to the white folks of quality; a pathetic and pitiable figure. In a darker light, he is an impulsive, irrational, passionate savage, reluctantly wearing a thin coat of culture, sullenly hating the white man, but holding an innate and unescapable belief in the white man's superiority; an everlastingly alien and irredeemable element in the nation; a menace to Southern civilization; a threat to Nordic race purity; a figure casting a sinister shadow across the future of the country.

Ninety-nine one-hundredths of all that has been written about the Negro in the United States in three centuries and read with any degree of interest or pleasure by white America has been written in conformity to one or more of these ideas. I am not saying that they do not provide good material for literature; in fact, they make material for poetry and romance and comedy and tragedy of a high order. But I do say they have become stencils, and that the Negro author finds these stencils inadequate for the portrayal and interpretation of Negro life today. Moreover, when he does attempt to make use of them he finds himself impaled upon the second horn of his dilemma.

II

It is known that art—literature in particular, unless it be sheer fantasy—must be based on more or less well established conventions, upon ideas that have some room in the general consciousness, that are at least somewhat familiar to the public mind. It is this that gives it verisimilitude and finality. Even revolutionary literature, if it is to have any convincing power, must start from a basis of conventions, regarding of how unconventional its objective may be. These conventions are changed by slow and gradual processes—except they be changed in a flash. The conventions held by white America regarding the Negro will be changed. Actually they are being changed, but they have not yet sufficiently changed to lessen to any great extent the dilemma of the Negro author.

It would be straining the credulity of white America beyond the breaking point for a Negro writer to put out a novel dealing with the wealthy class of colored people. The idea of Negroes of wealth living in a luxurious manner is still too unfamiliar. Such a story would have to be written in a burlesque vein to make it at all plausible and acceptable. Before Florence Mills and Josephine Baker[3] implanted a new general idea in the public mind it would have been worse than a waste of time for a Negro author to write for white America the story of a Negro girl who rose in spite of all obstacles, racial and others, to a place of world success and acclaim on the musical revue stage. It would be proof of little less than supreme genius in a Negro poet for him to take one of the tragic characters in American Negro history—say Crispus Attucks or Nat Turner or Denmark Vesey[4]—, put heroic language in his mouth and have white America accept the work as authentic. American Negroes as heroes form no part of white America's concept of the race. Indeed, I question if three out of ten of the white Americans who will read these lines know anything of either Attucks, Turner or Vesey; although each of the three played a rôle in the history of the nation. The Aframerican poet might take an African chief or warrior, set him forth in heroic couplets or blank verse and present him to white America with infinitely greater chance of having his work accepted.

But these limiting conventions held by white America do not constitute the whole difficulty of the Negro author in dealing with a white audience. In addition to these conventions regarding the Negro

3. Mills's premature death (1896–1927; just one year before Johnson's essay was published) made her dance moves in *Shuffle Along* (1921) and mesmerizing vocals in the *Blackbirds* revue (1926) all the more compelling to the multitudes of fans who adored her in the United States and Europe. Baker (1906–1975) debuted in *La Revue Nègre* in 1925, tantalizing audiences in Paris with her sensual performances in dance and song. In this context, Johnson suggests that Mills's and Baker's life histories, talent, and charisma transformed the public's perception of what "Negro" art might encompass.

4. Attucks (1723–1770) was the first casualty in the colonies' war against the British Crown at the Boston Massacre in 1770. Turner (1800–1831) and Vesey (1767–1822) were condemned to die for organizing rebellions to free enslaved blacks in Southampton County, Virginia, and Charleston, South Carolina.

as a race, white America has certain definite opinions regarding the Negro as an artist, regarding the scope of his efforts. White America has a strong feeling that Negro artists should refrain from making use of white subject matter. I mean by that, subject matter which it feels belongs to the white world. In plain words, white America does not welcome seeing the Negro competing with the white man on what it considers the white man's own ground.

In many white people this feeling is dormant, but brought to the test it flares up, if only faintly. During his first season in this country after his European success a most common criticism of Roland Hayes[5] was provoked by the fact that his programme consisted of groups of English, French, German, and Italian songs, closing always with a group of Negro Spirituals. A remark frequently made was, "Why doesn't he confine himself to the Spirituals?" This in face of the fact that no tenor on the American concert stage could surpass Hayes in singing French and German songs. The truth is that white America was not quite prepared to relish the sight of a black man in a dress suit singing French and German love songs, and singing them exquisitely. The first reaction was that there was something incongruous about it. It gave a jar to the old conventions and something of a shock to the Nordic superiority complex. The years have not been many since Negro players have dared to interpolate a love duet in a musical show to be witnessed by white people. The representation of romantic lovemaking by Negroes struck the white audience as somewhat ridiculous; Negroes were supposed to mate in a more primeval manner.

White America has for a long time been annexing and appropriating Negro territory, and is prone to think of every part of the domain it now controls as originally—and aboriginally—its own. One sometimes hears the critics in reviewing a Negro musical show lament the fact that it is so much like white musical shows. But a great deal of this similarity it would be hard to avoid because of the plain fact that two out of the four chief ingredients in the present day white musical show, the music and the dancing, are directly derived from the Negro. These ideas and opinions regarding the scope of artistic effort affect the Negro author, the poet in particular. So whenever an Aframerican writer addresses himself to white America and attempts to break away from or break through these conventions and limitations he makes more than an ordinary demand upon his literary skill and power.

At this point it would appear that a most natural thing for the Negro author to do would be to say, "Damn the white audience!" and devote himself to addressing his own race exclusively. But when he

5. See n. 5 on 241.

turns from the conventions of white America he runs afoul of the taboos of black America. He has no more absolute freedom to speak as he pleases addressing black America than he has in addressing white America. There are certain phases of life that he dare not touch, certain subjects that he dare not critically discuss, certain manners of treatment that he dare not use—except at the risk of rousing bitter resentment. It is quite possible for a Negro author to do a piece of work, good from every literary point of view, and at the same time bring down on his head the wrath of the entire colored pulpit and press, and gain among the literate element of his own people the reputation of being the prostitutor of his talent and a betrayer of his race—not by any means a pleasant position to get into.

This state of mind on the part of the colored people may strike white America as stupid and intolerant, but it is not without some justification and not entirely without precedent; the white South on occasion discloses a similar sensitiveness. The colored people of the United States are anomalously situated. They are a segregated and antagonized minority in a very large nation, a minority unremittingly on the defensive. Their faults and failings are exploited to produce exaggerated effects. Consequently, they have a strong feeling against exhibiting to the world anything but their best points. They feel that other groups may afford to do otherwise but, as yet, the Negro cannot. This is not to say that they refuse to listen to criticism of themselves, for they often listen to Negro speakers excoriating the race for its faults and foibles and vices. But these criticisms are not for the printed page. They are not for the ears and eyes of white America.

A curious illustration of this defensive state of mind is found in the Negro theatres. In those wherein Negro players give Negro performances for Negro audiences all of the Negro weaknesses, real and reputed, are burlesqued and ridiculed in the most hilarious manner, and are laughed at and heartily enjoyed. But the presence of a couple of dozen white people would completely change the psychology of the audience, and the players. If some of the performances so much enjoyed by strictly Negro audiences in Negro theatres were put on, say, in a Broadway theatre, a wave of indignation would sweep Aframerica from the avenues of Harlem to the canebrakes of Louisiana. These taboos of black America are as real and binding as the conventions of white America. Conditions may excuse if not warrant them; nevertheless, it is unfortunate that they exist, for their effect is blighting. In past years they have discouraged in Negro authors the production of everything but *nice* literature; they have operated to hold their work down to literature of the defensive, exculpatory sort. They have a restraining effect at the present time, which Negro writers are compelled to reckon with.

This division of audience takes the solid ground from under the feet of the Negro writer and leaves him suspended. Either choice carries hampering and discouraging conditions. The Negro author may please one audience and at the same time rouse the resentment of the other; or he may please the other and totally fail to rouse the interest of the one. The situation, moreover, constantly subjects him to the temptation of posing and posturing for the one audience or the other; and the sincerity and soundness of his work are vitiated whether he poses for white or black.

The dilemma is not made less puzzling by the fact that practically it is an extremely difficult thing for the Negro author in the United States to address himself solely to either of these two audiences. If he analyzes what he writes he will find that on one page black America is his whole or main audience, and on the very next page white America. In fact, psychoanalysis of the Negro authors of the defensive and exculpatory literature, written in strict conformity to the taboos of black America, would reveal that they were unconsciously addressing themselves mainly to white America.

III

I have sometimes thought it would be a way out, that the Negro author would be on surer ground and truer to himself, if he could disregard white America; if he could say to white America, "What I have written, I have written. I hope you'll be interested and like it. If not, I can't help it." But it is impossible for a sane American Negro to write with total disregard for nine-tenths of the people of the United States. Situated as his own race is amidst and amongst them, their influence is irresistible.

I judge there is not a single Negro writer who is not, at least secondarily, impelled by the desire to make his work have some effect on the white world for the good of his race. It may be thought that the work of the Negro writer, on account of this last named condition, gains in pointedness what it loses in breadth. Be that as it may, the situation is for the time one in which he is inextricably placed. Of course, the Negro author can try the experiment of putting black America in the orchestra chairs, so to speak, and keeping white America in the gallery, but he is likely at any moment to find his audience shifting places on him, and sometimes without notice.

And now, instead of black America and white America as separate or alternating audiences, what about the combination of the two into one? That, I believe, is the only way out. However, there needs to be more than a combination, there needs to be a fusion. In time, I cannot say how much time, there will come a gradual and natural rapprochement of these two sections of the Negro author's audience. There will come a breaking up and remodeling of most of white America's traditional stereotypes, forced by the advancement of the Negro in the various phases of our national life. Black America will abolish many of its taboos. A sufficiently large class of colored people will progress enough and become strong enough to render a constantly sensitive and defensive attitude on the part of the race unnecessary and distasteful. In the end, the Negro author will have something close to a common audience, and will be about as free from outside limitations as other writers.

Meanwhile, the making of a common audience out of white and black America presents the Negro author with enough difficulties to constitute a third horn of his dilemma. It is a task that is a very high test for all his skill and abilities, but it can be and has been accomplished. The equipped Negro author working at his best in his best known material can achieve this end; but, standing on his racial foundation, he must fashion something that rises above race, and reaches out to the universal in truth and beauty. And so, when a Negro author does write so as to fuse white and black America into one interested and approving audience he has performed no slight feat, and has most likely done a sound piece of literary work.

James Weldon Johnson in 1906. From the James Weldon Johnson and Grace Nail Johnson Papers, Yale Collection of American Literature, Beinecke Rare Book and Manuscript Library. Reprinted by permission of the James Weldon Johnson Estate.

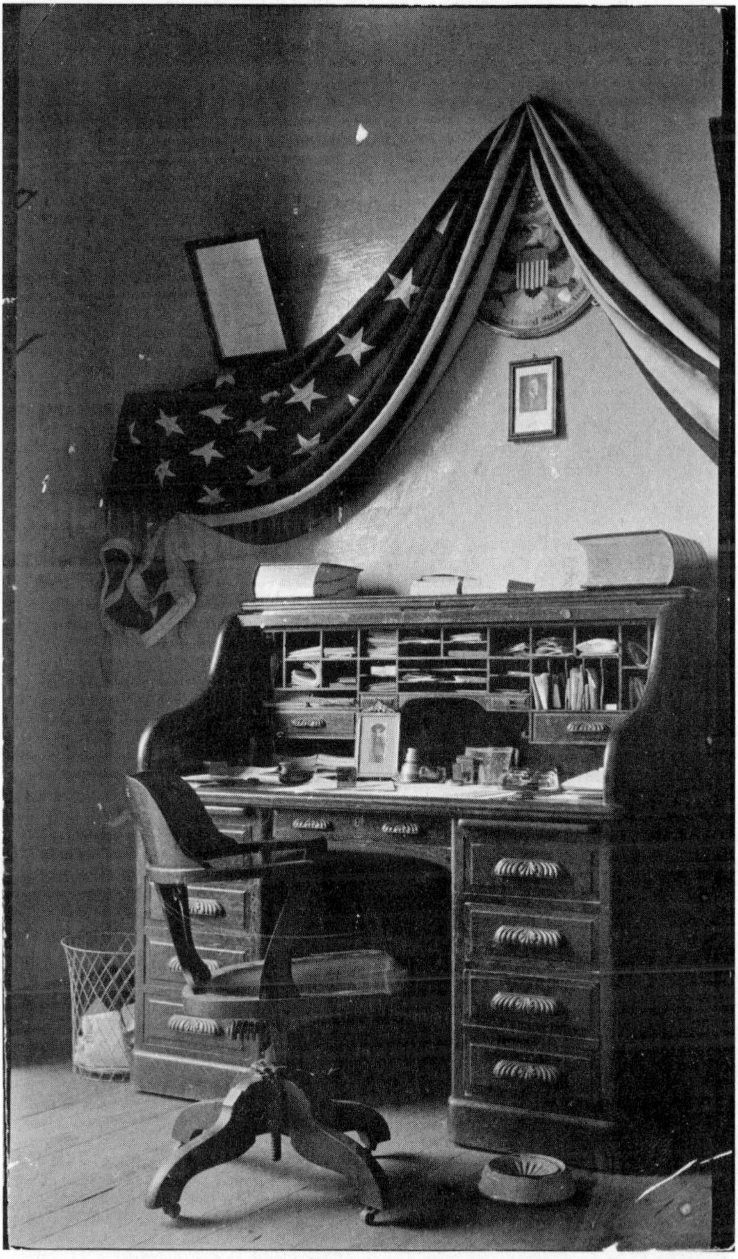

James Weldon Johnson's writing desk in Puerto Cabello, Venezuela (ca. 1907–09). From the James Weldon Johnson and Grace Nail Johnson Papers, Yale Collection of American Literature, Beinecke Rare Book and Manuscript Library. Reprinted by permission of the James Weldon Johnson Estate.

The Autobiography of an Ex-Colored Man

The autobiography of the child of a slave and her owner. Being of such complexion that he passes readily as white, as such he makes a name and place for himself in the world, socially and financially, finally marrying a white woman of refinement and wealth, to whom alone he has disclosed the secret of his birth. In his autobiography the burdensome secret of years is revealed and, incidentally, a half ironical joke is played on society.

As a document it reads more strangely than fiction. But it is more than a curious document: although intimately personal, personality is sunk in "raciality"—it might be called an initiation into the "freemasonry" of the negro race. The negroes of the United States have a pretty good idea of what white people think of them, for that opinion is being constantly stated, but the black race are somewhat of a sphinx to the white. They have been written about often, but usually the characterizations have been so influenced by the prejudices of their individual writers, who take some one group of the race to prove their point and exaggerate vices and virtues accordingly, that as characterizations they are of little value. Nevertheless, what the ten million black people living in this country think of their white neighbors is a matter of vital interest and importance.

The work has plot only in the sense that the happenings of every life form, in a way, the plot of that life. It is the personality of the writer and the composite and proportionate presentation of the entire race, embracing all its various elements and showing their relations with each other and with the white race, that give the book a peculiar interest and value.

Cloth; 8vo; $1.20 net; by mail, $1.30
SHERMAN, FRENCH & COMPANY, PUBLISHERS
6 BEACON STREET, BOSTON, MASSACHUSETTS

The Autobiography of An Ex-Colored Man

A curious and in some respects a startling tale . . . . . Whether or not it is accepted on its face value, there remains the very interesting fact that it does make an astute, dispassionate study of the race problem in the United States from the standpoint of a man who has lived on both sides of it.—***Times Saturday Review,*** New York City.

Intensely interesting.—***Informer,*** Detroit, Mich.

If the story be a true one, it is more remarkable than any piece of fiction ever written of the colored race . . . . . remarkable, vivid. . . . . The most wonderful story of self-revelation, either in fact or fiction, that has been published in many years.—***Union,*** Springfield, Mass.

To fully appreciate the worth of this remarkable book, it must be read from cover to cover. . . . . It will furnish entertainment as well as instruction. . . . . A fascinating narrative. There are bits of exquisite pathos running through it, and there is also subtle humor. . . . . There will come to you from its pages a charm and a fascination as real as the narrative is truthful.—***Southern Life Magazine,*** Atlanta, Georgia.

A book of singular power . . . . . the picture of what a negro feels and is becomes vivid and touching. . . . . graphically written.—***Living Age,*** Boston.

Gives with poignant emphasis, with humor, with pathos and fine delicacy the viewpoint of the intellectual colored man, the dual personality which these two-raced men maintain . . . . . Anyone wishing to understand the tragedy (and the triumph, too) of the bitter experience of a man with the best blood of the South running in his veins mixed with the African current, will find here a history with happenings as stirring as any romance and as thought-provoking as many a thesis on psychology.—***American,*** New York City.

Cloth; 8vo; $1.20 net; by mail, $1.30
SHERMAN, FRENCH & COMPANY, PUBLISHERS
6 BEACON STREET, BOSTON, MASSACHUSETTS

1912 sales flyer. Courtesy of the James Weldon Johnson Memorial Collection, Beinecke Rare Book and Manuscript

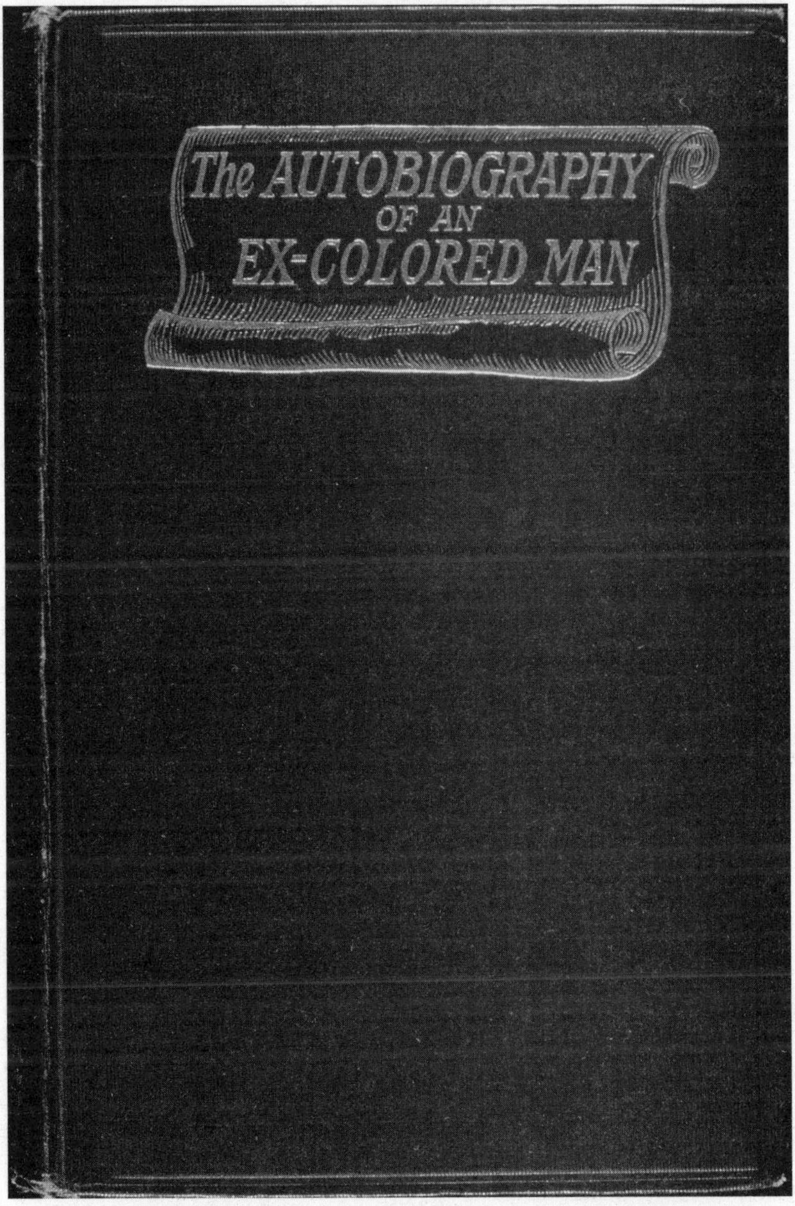

Front cover of the 1912 edition published by the Boston firm of Sherman, French & Company. Courtesy of the James Weldon Johnson Memorial Collection, Beinecke Rare Book and Manuscript Library, Yale University.

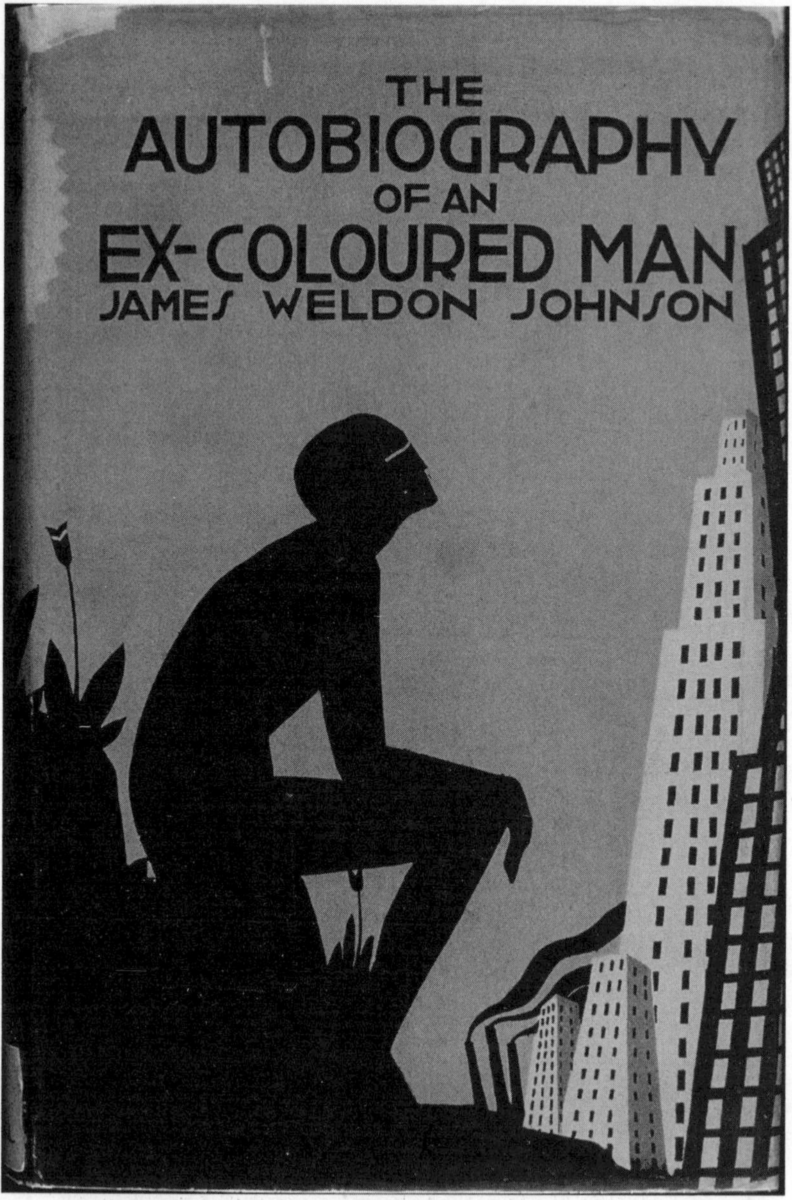

Dust jacket designed by Aaron Douglas for the 1927 edition published by Alfred A. Knopf, Inc. From the James Weldon Johnson and Grace Nail Johnson Papers, Yale Collection of American Literature, Beinecke Rare Book and Manuscript Library. Courtesy of Random House LLC.

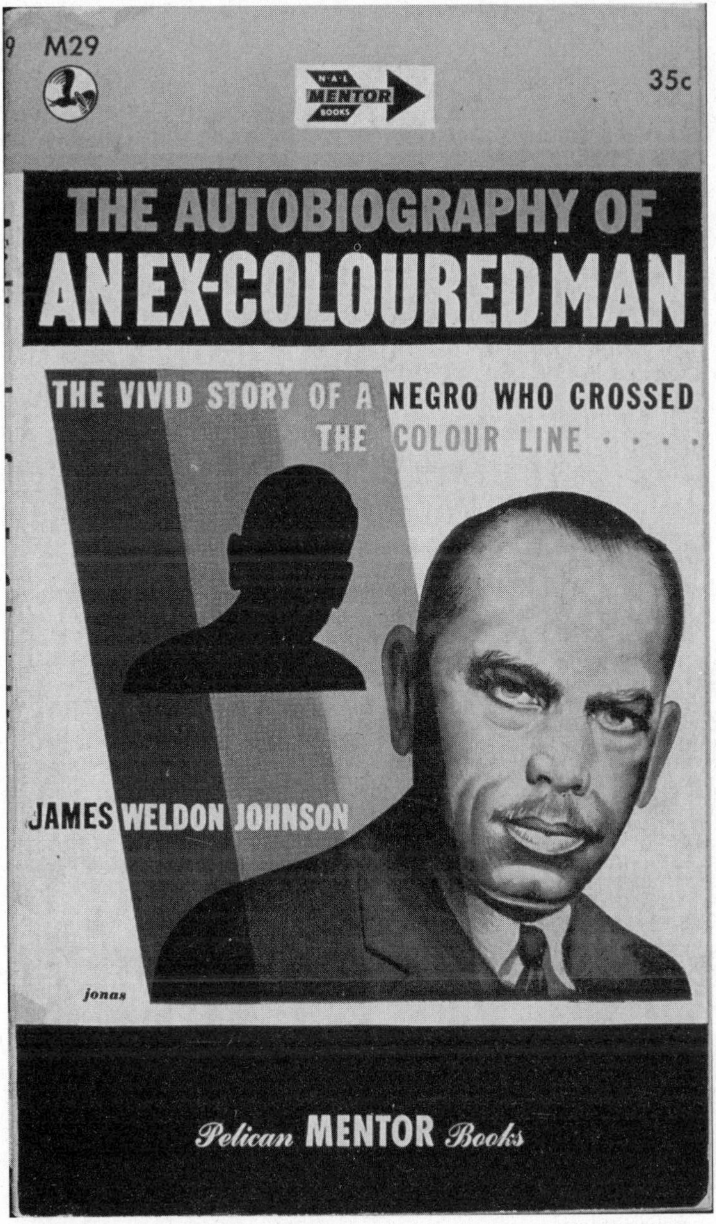

Front cover designed by James Avanti for the 1948 edition published by New American Library. From the James Weldon Johnson and Grace Nail Johnson Papers, Yale Collection of American Literature, Beinecke Rare Book and Manuscript Library.

Contemporary Reviews: 1912 Edition

Showing great foresight, Johnson subscribed to a news clipping service that collected reviews of *The Autobiography of an Ex-Colored Man* from across the United States. Johnson archived these reviews, both for the 1912 edition and for the 1927 reprinting of the novel, in two scrapbooks.

These compilations provide a comprehensive survey of *ECM*'s reception by the U.S. periodical press in 1912 and 1927. However, judging from the scrapbooks, the clipping services did not systematically monitor the African American media. To remedy this apparent gap, this Norton Critical Edition includes reviews from the black press. Because they offer intriguing and important leads for comparative reception analyses, African American sources are identified in footnotes.

Finally, the texts reprinted in this section have not been corrected for spelling or syntax errors.

A Dark Question Answered†

What is an ex-colored man? According to the nameless writer here, he is a negro who has so effectually concealed his African blood as to have deceived the white folks all his life. So this is a confession and an indictment: a confession that there are thousands upon thousands of octoroons whose African blood and characteristics are effectually hidden; and an indictment in the sense that it is these ex-negroes who alone have been able to ascertain how the white race regards them. Per contra, we have here also one of the best opportunities of finding out why the negro of the United States, after nearly three centuries of continuance on this continent, is still regarded so much of a riddle by the white man.

† From an unsigned review, *St. Louis* (MO) *Globe-Democrat*, May 11, 1912. Collected in Johnson's scrapbooks of reviews for the 1912 publication of *ECM*. James Weldon Johnson and Grace Nail Johnson Papers, Yale Collection of American Literature, Beinecke Rare Book and Manuscript Library. Unless noted otherwise, subsequent reviews of the 1912 edition are from this source.

Among the underlying causes of this want of understanding none has been stronger than that the negro in America has been treated as a whole. No allowance has been made, according to this author, for the prime fact that the class distinctions among the colored population are just as sharply defined as they are among the whites; and if this author is to be believed—even more so. It suffices to classify the negro in America by the detectable presence in his veins of all or even the smallest part of African blood.

If, therefore, the reader thinks it worth while to find out what the negro in America, and there are some 10,000,000 of him, thinks of the eighty and odd millions of whites among whom said negroes have to live, this is the book which will draw aside the veil, will initiate the reader into the freemasonry sort of way into the inherent mysteries of race attraction and repulsion. The pressure, we are told, against the negro is so strong that hundreds of those fortunate enough to possess fair skins are permitting themselves to be forced over into the white race. This is going on in a marked degree in all the large cities of the United States, especially in New York and St. Louis, says this record.

A Strange Human Document: Story of an "Ex-Colored Man"†

An Account of One Who Lived as a Negro among Negroes and a White Man among Whites[1]

Now and then appears a remarkable book of personal experiences throwing light from a new viewpoint upon some old problem and adding one more to the list of poignant human documents. Such a book is "The Autobiography of an Ex-Colored Man," which is published by Sherman, French & Co. without mention of the author's name for reasons which are soon apparent. It is the product of an unusual

† From an unsigned review, *Springfield* (MA) *Republican*, May 19, 1912.

1. This review was reprinted verbatim in the *New York Age* (June 6, 1912). This was a common practice for black newspapers such as the *Age*, for three reasons worth noting. First, reprinting (and the outright pirating of news copy) was widespread in American journalism, dating back to the eighteenth century. Second, as news-gathering, news-writing, and news-publishing evolved into the system of wire services that emerged from the mid-nineteenth into the early twentieth centuries, black newspapers often lacked the finances to pay for news feeds collated by those firms. Reprinting thus functioned as a cost-savings strategy for the cash-strapped black press. Finally, reprinting served a special political function for black newspapers. Through this approach, black editors made alliances with mainstream publications whose interests intersected with those of black readers (such as the *Springfield Republican*, a longtime advocate of black civil rights). Furthermore, black editors could select articles that were free of the racial biases that too often tainted and distorted mainstream press coverage of African American communities.

and well-equipped mind, and while in its intellectual ability it does not achieve the plane of Booker T. Washington's "Up from Slavery" or Mary Antin's "The Promised Land," it ranks near those two striking books and is possessed of a certain element which may be termed either legitimate romance or legitimate tragedy. It does not sound the note of optimism, nor is it constructive in the sense that both Dr. Washington's book and that of the young Jewish immigrant are constructive, but it tells the story of intense human interest in terms of fact and personal experience such as has been told before in weakly imaginative fiction.

The solution of the title, "The Autobiography of an Ex-Colored Man" is the one which must suggest itself to the curious reader, since there is only one. The author is the son of a white southerner and a very light mulatto, and is himself so fair that after having been identified with negroes in the South and to a certain extent in the North, he has been able to withdraw himself wholly from relations with that race and, for the sake of the children borne to him by his white wife, now dead, to class himself as a white man. So far as it concerns the practical importance of the book, it is to be found in chiefly in the warning account of the negro underworld in the big city. As for the complete identification of this kind of negro blood with the white race, the narrative may excite the fears of imaginative persons that what has happened in this case may be repeated in others to the eventual amalgamation of the races. But while it is not for a moment to be supposed that this is the only instance of its kind, those who conjure such fears may be left to deal with them.

The author was born in a little town in Georgia, which he does not name, a few years after the close of the civil war. Of his birthplace he recalls only dim recollections of a little house with flowers around it, and of various people who moved in and about it, but of two of whom he has only a distinct mental image: one his mother, and the other, a "tall man with a small, dark mustache," who, as he was later able to learn, was his father. While still a little lad, he and his mother moved North by steamer, and, after landing in New York, went to a little town in Connecticut, not named, which became his boyhood home. They lived in a small cottage, while his mother took in sewing and he went to school, fully believing himself to be a white boy, and failing to understand the intensity of his mother's reproof when he came home and told of one of the "nigger" children at school. But the day of disillusionment came. One morning the principal of the school came to the room and called upon "all the white children to stand for a moment." "I rose with the others," writes the author, and adds, "The teacher looked at me, and calling my name, said, 'You, sit down for the present, and rise with the others.'" At first he did not understand, and the light began to break in even when, as school was dismissed and he went out in a kind of stupor, a few of the white children jeered at him, saying "Oh, you're a nigger, too."

The narrative which is this introduced is told clearly and vividly, although with a touch now and then of sentimental emotion, which is the less to be wondered at as the author describes his unusual musical achievements, which suggest plainly the temperamental racial inheritance. He was 11 years old or thereabouts at the time of his discovery of the negro blood in his veins, and for some years after that he remained in the little Connecticut town, developing his musical talent and once seeing his father, who came to visit the little cottage.

On his mother's death, the boy, who would appear to have been about 16 years, went to Atlanta to enter the negro college there. Before entering the college, his hoarded money was stolen in a negro boarding-house and, ashamed of his carelessness, he did not dare to go to the college authorities, but instead taking the advice of the negro porter, who proved afterwards to have probably been the thief, he went to Jacksonville, where he obtained work in a cigar factory. With the manual dexterity, which came partly from piano playing, he soon became an expert workman, and then, with his newly discovered capacity for languages, he acquired command of Spanish, and was repaid by being selected "reader" in the cigar factory. As a regular institution in all factories which employ Spanish-speaking workmen, the "reader" is perhaps by this time familiar through frequent description; he sits in the center of the room in which the cigarmakers work, and reads to them for a certain time each day the important news from the papers and whatever else he may consider interesting, sometimes selecting a novel and reading it in daily installments.

Through his music teaching the author became acquainted with "the best class of colored people in Jacksonville," adding that "this was really" his entrance "into the race." Not only does he write strongly of the upward struggle of the negroes but in his account of conditions in Jacksonville and in other cities, he gives an unusual picture of well-to-do, well-educated negro society. As for the negroes in the South he declares that they may be roughly divided into three classes, not so much in respect to themselves, as in respect to their relations to the whites. The first class, which he describes are the lowest, that from which the criminals chiefly come. It is a class which he declares to be but a small proportion of the colored people, although unfortunately it often dominates public opinion concerning the whole race. "This class of blacks," he writes, "hate everything covered by a white skin and in regard they are loathed by the whites." The second class, as he divides them, comprises the servants, the washwomen, the waiters, the cooks, all in a word who are connected to the whites by domestic services, and between this class of the blacks and the whites he declares there to be little friction. His third class is composed of the independent workmen and tradesmen and the well-to-do and educated colored people, and he adds that for a directly opposite reason they are as far removed from the whites as are members of the first class. These people live in a little world of their own and he points out that whereas the proudest of southern women could, with propriety, and undoubtedly would, in fact, go to the cabin of Aunt Mary, her cook, if Aunt Mary was sick and would minister to comfort with her own hands, "if, on the other hand, Aunt Mary's daughter, who used to hang around the kitchen but who has received an education and married a prosperous young colored man, were at death's door, the white woman would no more think of crossing the threshold of the daughter's cottage than she would of going to a barroom for a drink."

From Jacksonville, on the closing of the cigar factory, the author drifted to New York, and the result is a description of the negro "underworld" of the metropolis such as probably been never written before. The young man with a little money in his pocket was taken about by negro friends to various resorts, including a gambling club, frequented by negro "sports" and the like, together with white persons of certain sorts. Although vivid, the description is in no sense abhorrent, although Zola[2] might, indeed, have envy of it as the basis of a picture to be filled out by his unrelenting addition of details. As it is, the reader is introduced to the clubs and restaurants where negro jockeys, flush with their winnings of the turf buy "wine" recklessly for all who sit beneath the colored celebrities from Frederick Douglass to "Jack" Johnson and the like. From this gaslight experience, as he well describes it, the author was rescued by his musical ability. In one of these resorts he had his first introduction to "ragtime" music, which was then unknown. With his classical education in music he was able to develop and adapt the negro melodies, and on the other hand to play classical music in ragtime. In the end, he became a "professor" at the piano in a negro resort, and there was taken up by a white man of wealth and leisure in search of novelty, who employed him to play at Bohemian dinners and finally took him abroad as a companion giving him opportunities in France and Germany to pick up not only the languages but more musical knowledge.

2. Emile Zola (1840–1902), French novelist who pioneered naturalist writing, a literary style defined by a focus on social underworlds; verbally dense descriptions; and a determinist understanding of causation (i.e., the belief that human character, temperament, and behavior are caused by forces beyond one's self-control). For Zola and his followers, heredity, environment, and history shape characters' destinies, not free-willed thoughts or actions.

It was at Berlin that after having played some ragtime music at a gathering of musical people, the author gained what for the time he conceived to be the inspiration for his life work. He had hardly finished his ragtime when an enthusiastic German brushed him off the stool and taking the same theme varied and developed it through every known musical form. "I had been turning classical music into ragtime, a comparatively easy task, and this man had taken ragtime and made it classical." The thought flashed into his mind that there was opportunity, that the music of America might be developed from the negro melodies. He then determined to leave his leisure loving companion and to go back to the United States to work as a negro composer. The decision made, he returned to the country and began his labors among the southern negroes in collecting their melodies and the chapter in which he tells of this work will prove of exceptional interest to any who have found an appeal in negro music. But it was while engaged in this work in a thinly settled district that he witnessed a lynching that in which the wretched victim was not merely hung but burned to death. Sick at heart, he determined, as he frankly expresses it, to forsake his race, "that I would change my name, raise a mustache, and let the world take me for what it would, that it was not necessary for me to go about with a label of inferiority pasted across my forehead. All the while I understood it was not discouragement or fear, or search for a larger field of opportunity that was driving me out of the negro race. I knew that it was shame, unbearable shame. Shame at being identified with a people that could with impunity be treated worse than animals. For certainly the law would restrain and punish alive the malicious burning alive of animals."

Returning to New York the author finally succeeded at carving out a new career for himself, being accepted without question as a white man, and by dint of perseverance taking business training in a business school and in working his way up has evidently acquired a remunerative position in some commercial establishment. For reasons which are again obvious, he is not specific in his descriptions in this part of his story. His music had been put aside a merely a diversion and as he frankly declares that he set himself to make money. After a time in the circles of white society in which he moved without question as to his race, he met a girl whom he describes with sincere feeling, and after telling her of his inheritance and living a summer worn of anxiety while she retired to the New England hills to think her problem out, they were married. With the coming of their second child, he lost her and so, as was stated at the opening, is living his life for his children, yet at the close he speaks of his position with complete frankness.

"Sometimes," he writes, it seems to me I have never really been a negro, that I have only been a privileged spectator of their inner life; at other times I feel that I have been a coward, a deserter, and I am possessed by a strange longing for my mother's people." To this he adds a reference to a meeting which he attended several years ago at Carnegie hall in the interest of the Hampton institute. "The Hampton students sang the old songs and awoke in me memories that left me sad. Among the speakers were R.C. Ogden, ex-Ambassador Choate, and Mark Twain, but the greatest interest of the audience was in Booker T. Washington, and not because he so much surpassed the others in eloquence, but because of what he represented with so much earnestness and faith. And it is this that all of that small but gallant band of colored men who are publicly fighting the cause of their race have behind them. Even those who oppose them know that these men have the eternal principles of right on their side, and they will be victors, even if they go down in defeat. Beside them, I feel small and selfish. I am an ordinarily successful white man who has made a little money. They are men who are making history and a race. I, too, might have taken part in a work so glorious. My love for my children makes me glad that I am what I am, and keeps me from desiring otherwise: and yet, when I sometimes open a little box in which I keep my fast yellowing manuscripts, the only tangible remnants of a vanished dream, a dead ambition, a sacrificed talent, I cannot repress the thought that, after all, I have chosen the lesser part, that I have sold my birthright for a mess of pottage."

An Ex-Colored Man†

A Negro Who Passed as White Tells His Life Story

A curious and in some respects a startling tale is this narration of the life experiences of a colored man who forsook his own race and joined the white. It bears some evidences of the truth. Nevertheless, it is necessary to consider the possibility that it may be merely the product of some whimsical imagination. Yet there is nothing in it that violates probability, and the book carries the publishers' assurance of good faith. And whether or not it is accepted on its face value, there remains the very interesting fact that it does make an astute, dispassionate study of the race problem in the United States from the standpoint of a man who has lived on both sides of it.

† From an unsigned review, *New York Times,* May 26, 1912.

The author describes himself as being of a complexion so white and of features so Caucasian that the slight admixture of negro blood in his veins has never been guessed except when he chooses to identify himself with his mother's race. His youth was lived in a Connecticut village, in school, where his race was known but it made no social difference. His young manhood he spent as a negro in the South in a tobacco factory, and in New York City, where he passed much time in gambling dens as a crap player and musical entertainer. An eccentric millionaire who sometimes visited the "club" which was his particular haunt, admired his piano playing because it lifted him out of the environment where he had sunk, carried him off to Europe, where they lived a long time, journeying about in leisurely fashion as friends and companions. But the author had musical ambitions, and his few drops of negro blood kept calling to him to acknowledge his race and to do something that would add to its glory. So he came back, went South again as a negro, and traveled about in rural districts gathering material for his scheme of taking up ragtime music an evolving it into a classic. Then by chance he witnessed the burning alive of a brutal negro. This so revolted him, the thought of belonging to a race that had to submit to such treatment, that he decided to throw off for all time the label of inferiority. He came again to New York, where he has lived ever since as a white man. He says that he has made money, won a good position among cultured and refined people, and married a beautiful white woman of this circle not, however, without telling her his true status. In all material ways he has succeeded. But at the end of his story he admits that when he thinks of "that small but gallant band of colored men who are publicly fighting the cause of their race," he feels "small and selfish." They are men, he says, "who are making history and a race. I, too, might have taken part in work so glorious * * * I cannot repress the thought that I have chosen the lesser part; that I have sold my birthright for a mess of pottage."

However true or untrue may be the personal side of the story, the observations upon the condition of the negro race in the South and of the attitude of the whites toward it are full of interest. He discusses, quite dispassionately, the way in which the every present 'negro question' narrows the mental, political, and financial activities of the white race, and in this respect considers "the condition of whites more to be deplored than that of the blacks." His view of "the tremendous struggle" between the two races is that of the man who has been behind the embankments on both sides and understands what each is fighting for. But his sympathies are evidently with his mother's people, though his words are calm and judicial. "The battle was first waged," he says, "over the right of the negro to be classed as a human being with a soul; later, as to whether he had sufficient intellect to master even the rudiments of learning; and to-day it is being fought out over his social recognition." The black man, he declares, fights passively, and the white man is using in the contest his best energies. "The South to-day," he concludes, "stands panting and almost breathless from its exertions."

The Autobiography of an Ex-Colored Man†

The above is the title of a novel which received a review two columns long in the Springfield (Mass.) Republican of May 23, which says it is a strong unusual novel. We are certain the book is written by a graduate of Atlanta University, although it does not bear the name of the author for reasons that are apparent. It is published by Sherman, French and Co. of Boston, Mass., and we are sure every alumnus will want to read this enjoyable story that takes one by the nose, as it were, and pulls him straight on through without stopping. We shall give a review and the name of the author in the next issue, if we are permitted.[1]

A Life Story You Will Not Forget‡

"The Autobiography of an Ex-Colored Man" purports to be the life story of a nameless man with a slight tincture of negro blood, a man who has quietly separated himself from the blacks to live as a white citizen with his two children, who are a degree lighter than himself.

The story might be fiction, so well balanced is the plot, with its artistic beginning, middle, and ending. The writer claims to be a musician of some power, and he certainly writes with ease and grace and a strong appeal to thought and emotion.

He gives with poignant emphasis, with humor, with pathos and fine delicacy the viewpoint of the intellectual colored man, the dual personality which these two-raced men maintain—one aspect for negro companions, another for the whites. Any one wishing to understand the tragedy (and the triumph, too) of the bitter experience of a man with the best blood of the South running in his veins mixed with the African current, will find here a history with

† From an unsigned review in *Crimson and Gray*, Atlanta University, June 1912. This is an African American source.

1. Johnson's college friend George A. Towns wrote this notice for their alma mater's alumni newsletter. See their exchange about the need to guard Johnson's anonymity on 228–30 in this volume.

‡ From an unsigned review, *New York American*, June 8, 1912.

happenings as stirring as any romance, and as thought-provoking as many a thesis on psychology.

A New Book†

Sherman, French & Co., publishers 6 Beacon St., Boston, Mass., announce the sale of a unique publication of surprising interest to our people. It is the autobiography of an "ex-Colored man," the child of a slave and her owner. Being of such complexion that he passes readily as white, as such he makes a name and place for himself in the world, socially and financially, finally marrying a white woman of refinement and wealth, to whom alone he disclosed the secret of his birth. In his autobiography the burdensome secret of years is revealed and, incidentally, a half ironical joke is played on society.

Review of 1912 Edition‡

"The Autobiography of an Ex-Colored Man" suggests in its title something out of the ordinary. It is a remarkable "human document," being the story of a colored man who was sufficiently light enough to pass as a white man. This is what he did after he tired of being classed as a colored man. He had some intentions of being a benefactor to his race, but his racial instincts, as he virtually confesses, held him back. Rather than face the penalties and the odium of being a colored man he renounced his race, married and to his present associates he is known as a white man though he intimates he may sometimes be mistaken for an Italian or Spaniard. He has fluent command of languages, particularly of Spanish, and could easily pass himself off as a Spainard.

If the story be a true one, it is more remarkable than any piece of fiction ever written of the colored race. Until the boy was 8 or 9 years of age he did not know that he was a colored boy. His mother was very light and his father was a white man. His mother was the sewing girl in a family of the boy's father and after the birth of the boy the mother came north, settling in Connecticut, took in sewing and gave her boy a public school education. He had a decided talent for music and became proficient on the piano. He was essentially expert as an improviser and interpreter. When it became known to him that he

† From an unsigned review, *Cleveland Gazette*, June 15, 1912.
‡ From an unsigned review, *Springfield* (MA) *Union*, June 15, 1912.

was of negro birth he kept with his kind. He grew to young manhood and decided to go to college. He had determined upon entering a college in Atlanta but his money was stolen from him. Then he drifted to Jacksonville where he learned the cigarmaking trade and finally became a "reader" for the cigarmakers. The factory closed and he went to New York. The "Tenderloin" life appealed to him and in a place he called "The Club" he became expert at playing ragtime music which was then new. A "millionaire" friend became interested in him an employed him as a valet to travel abroad with him. The young man would have extended his travels but he had a desire to get back to America and be of benefit to his race by utilizing his knowledge of music to harmonize and reconstruct negro melodies. He fell in love and though he confessed his origin to his intended bride, after the effects of the first repulsion had worn off she finally consented to marry him and the couple lived a happy life until she died in giving birth to a second child. With his marriage he renounced his race, or, as he says in his concluding sentence, "sold his birthright for a mess of pottage." He gives no clue to his present identity but it would seem to be an easy matter to trace him if the facts of his life as he records them are true.

That is just the puzzling thing about the book. It reads more like fiction than fact, yet there is a semblance of truth in it. The main elements may be true but they are embellished as the African is prone to embellish anything in which he is a participant. There is something of vainglory in the story, much of the apparently frank confession and a plausibility about the story that at times is quite convincing. The book has been written if not by a negro at least by one who has a thorough and intimate knowledge of negro traits of character. The book is in no sense an apologia, but a setting forth of the race question from the standpoint of one who openly confesses that he is of negro birth but has deliberately renounced his race. This book is of further interest because it reveals the thoughts and feelings of a negro as he is brought into relation with the white race. In a word, he puts himself so effectually in the negro's place that we see the negro as he actually is, rather than as somebody imagines he is. It is an X-ray portraiture of the soul of a negro who has gone down into the depths, redeemed himself and tried to make an honorable place for himself. A remarkable, a vivid, and, without intending to make a pun, a colorful story. The most wonderful story of self-revelation, either in fact or fiction, that as been published in many years. It ranks alongside with Booker T. Washington's life stories, but is of greater interest in that it is a revelation of a man who has not attained to such hights of intellectuality and social standing.

[Review of the 1912 Edition][†]

One of the oddest books published in some time is *The Autobiography of an Ex-Colored Man*, which, as might be judged from the title, purports to be the story of a light-complexioned "mixed-blood" who has deserted the dark race proper and joined the whites, without the latter knowing it, of course, and utterly against the accepted rule. The publishers assert that the book gives an entirely new viewpoint, in that it reveals what the Negroes think of the whites. This is true to some extent, but it nevertheless seens as if the author has in part missed his opportunity. This failure is probably due to the writer's own shortcomings, for it appears very plainly that he has not a little of the childish vanity which is characteristic of the Negro, and likewise that he lacks considerably in moral fiber. There is an instinctive feeling of repulsion for the man as he tells of his desertion of the people who had been his friends and associates, for reasons which he himself admits were purely selfish.

Some points of unquestioned interest are brought out, however. The author divides the Negroes into three classes, based on their relation to the whites: First, the desperate criminal characters who frequent saloons and dives and do as little work as possible. These hate the whites with an undying hatred, and he says he has heard many of them say they would kill the first white man who "bothered" them. This type is responsible for most of the crimes that lead to lynchings. The second class is composed of servants, who generally like the whites, at least those that are good to them. This is the largest class. The third is the more prosperous and better educated class of Negroes, who, the writer declares, are actually as far removed from the whites as the desperados. He says these people are well-disposed toward the Caucasians but are very resentful of ill-treatment. Their position is extremely trying, and they carry the entire weight of the race problem, which bothers the other classes very little.

An interesting point is the frank admission that there is a race question among colored people, the darker of both sexes, especially those of higher mentality, invariably seeking lighter-complexioned mates. The writer denies, however, that this is an admission of Negro inferiority, an attributes it to economic necessity, as it is very much harder for a black Negro to secure remunerative employment than for a lighter one. "It's no disgrace to be black," he quotes a Negro as saying, in this connection, "but it's often very inconvenient."

† From an unsigned review, *Detroit Saturday Night*, June 22, 1912.

We are inclined to wish there might have been a deeper study of the Negro attitude, and less detail of the author's experiences, though these latter, to tell the truth, are rather thrilling in spots. It is an unusual book, at any rate, and for that reason bound to attract attention.

The Autobiography of an Ex-Colored Man†

An ex-colored man will strike the reader as somewhat of a chimera, for we down here hold that there is no such thing—once a negro, always a negro. However, passing that by, let it be said that this volume is the work of a man who, with a mixture of negro blood in his veins, has succeeded in passing himself off as white, and is living as such among people of culture. This deception obviously explains the author's concealment of his identity.

That the author is drawing the long bow[1]—we are not partial to Col. Roosevelt's shorter and uglier word,[2] yet it exactly fits this case—may be seen from the outrageous statement he makes concerning the white women of the south toward the well-to-do and educated negroes. He asserts that whereas the proudest of southern women could, with propriety, and undoubtedly would, in fact, go to the cabin of Aunt Mary, her cook, if Aunt Mary was sick and minister to her comfort with her own hands, "if, on the other hand, Aunt Mary's daughter, who used to hand around the kitchen but who has received an education and married a prosperous young colored man, were at death's door, the white woman would no more think of crossing the threshold of the daughter's cottage than she would of going into a barroom for a drink."

The volume was evidently written for northern consumption, and it should have its widest circulation there. Our own opinion is that the whole yarn is the work of imagination, unhampered by respect of the verities and excited by hate or some other stimulant—a pipe-dream, in short.

† From an unsigned review, *Nashville Tennessean*, June 23, 1912.
1. A popular expression for exaggeration.
2. Even while he was U.S. president, Theodore Roosevelt (1858–1919) was popularly known as "the Colonel" because of his service in the Rough Riders unit during the Spanish-American War of 1898. Though it is unclear what "shorter and uglier word" this reviewer predicts the blunt-speaking Roosevelt might say about the ex-colored man's commentary on interracial romance, Roosevelt's racist views were well-known in his time (though the Roosevelt administration authorized James Weldon Johnson's diplomatic assignments with the U.S. State Department).

[Review of 1912 Edition][†]

This is a wonderfully interesting volume, "The Autobiography of an Ex-Colored Man." It would be difficult to find a more unbiased discussion of the negro problem as it exists in the United States today. The anonymous author does not seek to work on the sympathy of his readers; he does not uphold the attitude of either blacks or whites; he does not offer any solution for this momentous problem of the age; he merely recites facts that exist from both the viewpoint of the negro and the white man. And he is in a position to do this well, for by blood he is as much white as he is black, and far more white than black in appearance.

We are permitted to look behind the scenes, as it were, and see the negro race collectively, as well as individually, as it has been more often pictured. The attitude of the blacks toward the whites assumes quite as important proportions as does the attitude of the whites toward the blacks. This is a rather unusual presentation of the matter, and appears upon consideration to be a very important factor in the solution of the negro problem.

One of America's great men once made the statement that if he had to be a colored man he would rather be the blackest one on earth. One can understand his preference after reading this account of the continuous struggle with his own conscience fought by a man who possesses the appearance, tastes, education, culture, and refinement of a white man, and yet is always conscious of the fact that his life is a sham, small, ignoble, because he had failed to acknowledge his race and exert his efforts toward the uplifting of his people.

[Review of 1912 Edition][‡]

It is said Negroes of the United States have a pretty good idea of what white people think of them, for their opinion is being constantly stated, but the black race is somewhat of a sphinx to the white. In our race can be found those of ebony hue to the shade of the fairest lily. "The Autobiography of an Ex-Colored Man," which is just from the press, is a book that should be in the hands of both races. It is a book with a peculiar interest and value and shows the relations clearly of

† From an unsigned review, *Chicago Record-Herald*, July 1, 1912.
‡ From an unsigned review in the *Chicago Defender*, July 3, 1912. This is an African American newspaper. Used with permission of the *Chicago Defender*.

the two races. Mr. Alexander is destined to take his place as one of the foremost writers of the day.[1]

[Review of 1912 Edition]†

This is the story of a man whose white skin concealed the trace of negro blood in his veins. He tells of his early life as a member of the negro race, of his growth to manhood, of his experience with various means of earning a livelihood, of the constant difficulties of found in his way because of the prejudices of the white man against the negro, of his final decision to become a white man. The book is a study of the race problem from a new standpoint. It contains many interesting comments on this problem and some significant warnings against the dangers of race amalgamation. The outcome of the writer's change of race is not pleasing, yet it is suggestive of a new evil which may easily come from the mixing of race.

[Review of 1912 Edition]‡

There is a deep undercurrent of meaning in The Autobiography of an Ex-Colored Man. It is a book that ought to be read by all those who are indifferent to the "race question" in the United States, for it brings a new and an immediate phase of the subject into prominence. The title propounds a riddle as to how one could abandon a race so marked as the African, but the riddle will be solved upon reading the book. The author had that fatal esthetic nature common to the man of mixed birth, and his problem of life was too hard for him. In the end he is a white man hungering—as only Africans can hunger—for the

1. This attribution of the novel's authorship probably refers to African American journalist Charles Alexander (1868–1923), who edited the Boston-based *Alexander's Magazine* (1905–09). Alexander's own publishing ties to Sherman, French & Company and his political conservatism (fostered by his alliance with Booker T. Washington, who owned and directed the editorial content of the journal) most likely encouraged the *Defender*'s claim. For more on Alexander, see Cathy Packer, "Charles Alexander," in *American Magazine Journalists, 1900–1960*, First Series, ed. Sam G. Riley, (Detroit: Gale Research, 1990), 11-16; and Mark Schneider, *Boston Confronts Jim Crow, 1890–1920* (Boston: Northeastern University Press, 1997), 67–73.

In 1914, the *Defender* corrected itself by disclosing Johnson as the novel's author. See "The Hon. James W. Johnson," November 14, 1914, p. 8; Ralph W. Tyler, "Jacksonville, Fla., Its People and Industries," December 19, 1914; and "James Weldon Johnson," January 5, 1918.

Compare this early speculation to the "furore" about the novel's anonymous authorship as described by Alice Dunbar-Nelson and Mary White Ovington in 1927; see 308 and 327 in this volume.

† From an unsigned review, *New Orleans Picayune*, July 12, 1912.

‡ From an unsigned review, *Christian Advocate* (New York City), July 18, 1912.

kinship of his own people and filled with a questioning remorse as to whether he has not done ill to leave them even for the sake of his white children, for whom he has sunk his black inheritance. The book is passionately tragic, with the unconscious tragedy of fact.

A New View of the Race Problem†

The autobiography of an ex-Colored man is a powerful book. It is the production of a scvholar. His diction, conservative logic and philosophical comment stamp him as a man of a trained mind.

Unquestionably he is a college man, though he studiously avoids reference to any college training, contenting himself with reference to his failure to enter Atlanta University, as due to the fact that he was robbed of his savings by a pretended benefactor.

His experiences both in the upper and under social world indicate certainly in the latter respect, opportunities for observation afforded to but few Colored men and to those only who had ample means.

The book is bound to create a sensation as a fair presentation of the difficulties encountered by the superior Negro in his struggle for advancement.

It is not forgotten that in the last analysis, "Mr. ex-colored Man," was a coward.

It has often been lamented that educated, refined Colored men permit themselves to be absorbed in the white race when they are fair enough to escape special notice.

The white race do not need them and yet the black race by their act loses a powerful argument in favor of their inherent capacity for progress and culture and acquisitions of every character which our highly specialized civilization requires today.

[Review of the 1912 Edition]‡

The "ex-colored man," the son of an octoroon and a white man, tells the story of his life. The author represents himself as having been so nearly white that he passed as a white man and married a white woman. The assertion is one that will not be readily believed in the section of the United States most familiar with the so-called "Negro Problem," and the book rests under the suspicion of being fiction. But granting, for the sake of argument, that it is fact, it contributes nothing to the literature of the race question. The writer is a bright,

† From an unsigned review, *Boston Guardian,* July 20, 1912. This is an African American newspaper.

‡ From an unsigned review, *Louisville Courier-Journal,* July 27, 1912.

but superficial, observer who writes interestingly of his impressions during travels in America and Europe. He is, despite his boast that he is a traveled and accomplished man of the world, unable to see the race problem in its broader aspects, and his book is in the form of a diary that tells nothing more than the personal experiences of a shallow and self-centered individual.

The publisher's note stating that the book gives "a glimpse behind the scenes of the race drama" is not borne out. The publisher's assertion that the mistreatment of the negroes by white persons in America is "actually and constantly forcing an unascertainable number of fair complexioned people over into the white race" is based upon ignorance of the fact that it is not by complexion alone that race is ascertainable. Only ignorance can see any possibility of a mixture of Anglo-Saxons to distinguish between a North American mixed blood and a white person.

The Autobiography of an Ex-Colored Man†

The autobiography of the child of a slave and her owner. Being of such complexion that he passes readily as white, as such he makes a name and place for himself in the world, socially and financially, finally marrying a white woman of refinement and wealth, to whom alone he has disclosed the secret of his birth. In his autobiography the burdensome secret of years is revealed and, incidentally, a half ironical joke is played on society.

As a document it reads more strangely than fiction. But it is more than a curious document: although intimately personal, personality is sunk in "raciality"—it might be called an initiation into the "freemasonry" of the Negro race. The Negroes of the United States have a pretty good idea of what white people think of them, for that opinion is being constantly stated, but the black race are somewhat of a sphinx to the white. They have been written about often, but the characterizations have been so influenced by the prejudices of their individual writers, who take some one group of the race to prove their point and exaggerate vices and virtues accordingly, that as characterizations they are of little value. Nevertheless, what the ten million black people living in this country think of their white neighbors is a matter of vital interest and importance.

The work has plot only in the sense that the happenings of every life form, in a way, the plot of that life. It is the personality of the writer and the composite and proportionate presentation of the

† From an unsigned review, *Washington* (DC) *Bee*, August 3, 1912. This is an African American newspaper.

entire race, embracing all of its various elements and showing their relations with one another and with the white race that gives the book its peculiar interest and value. This book is especially interesting to the colored men and women of Washington for the reason that the colored people of this city furnish some of the strong incidents for the story. From cover to cover the book is a series of pathos and humor and soul-stirring incidents. No colored man or woman should fail to read it. Sherman, French & Co., 6 Beacon St., Boston, Mass., are the publishers.

[Review of the 1912 Edition]†

* * * An anonymous books of singular power, whether truth or fiction, is "The Autobiography of an Ex-Colored Man." The writer claims to be—perhaps is—the son of an octaroon sewing-girl by her mistress's college-boy son. After the birth of the author, on approach of his father's marriage to a white woman, the pair, mother and son, were sent North and landed in a small town in Connecticut where, because of his whiteness, the boy grew to a considerable age without suspecting he was of negro parentage. His father seems to have been mindful of him and for a long time remitted checks with regularity; but after the mother's death, he was thrown upon his own resources and led a wandering, exciting life, rather over-full of dramatic incidents for one ordinary existence, and landed at last in New York, travelled, educated. Here, after seeing a negro burning in the South, he decided to pose as an Anglo-Saxon, married a white girl, after confessing to her, and now lives the prosaic life of a successful Caucasian business-man in New York. The writer is self-evidently a negro, or intimately connected with that race, and the picture of what a negro feels and is becomes vivid and touching. The book is graphically written and in clever English. Sherman, French & Co.

Nocturne in Black and White‡

It would have been more appropriate to have called this "The Autobiography of an Ex-White Man." The author was a near-white mulatto whose father was "one of the greatest men in the country," and he had the "best blood of the South," in his veins as his mother declared. For years he practically posed and was accepted as a white

† From an unsigned review, *Living Age* (Boston), August 17, 1912.
‡ From an unsigned review, *Philadelphia Telegraph*, August 21, 1912.

man. He seems to have possessed most of the instinct and accomplishments of the white race and fitted himself to move in average, white society with credit, if not with distinction. He specialized in music, and became quite an accomplished interpreter of Chopin. His development of ragtime, however, to a pitch of almost syncopated hysteria, was perhaps an evidence of reversion to type on the maternal side. His acquisition of languages was facile, and his travels abroad added to his accomplishments in this direction. At about 11 years of age the author was informed of his paternity and the psychological shock changed his viewpoint in a flash. Thenceforth he had, with the rest of his race, to look out upon life "not from the viewpoint of a citizen, or a man, nor even a human being, but from the viewpoint of a colored man." It is from this viewpoint that the book is written. It is a glimpse behind the scenes of the race-drama. The questions involved in it are slowly but surely forging to the front. They will require more careful handling than any other great social question in the near future. We are here face to face with a condition more perilous to this country than any coming yellow peril, or race peril of any color whatsoever. The color peril is right at our doors. It comes from the South, not the Far East. It is not yellow, but black. We commend this book for its evident sincerity, its moderation, and for an absorbing narrative disclosed in an excellent style.

Crossing the Color Line†

A Study in the Race Question by an "Ex-Colored" Man—One of the Most Remarkable Human Documents of the Decade

Naturally, the name of the writer of "The Autobiography of an Ex-Colored Man" can never be divulged by the publishers of this remarkable document, Sherman, French and Company, Boston. That it is not fiction we are prepared to believe from the sincerity and directness of the work as well as from the fact that it would be impossible for any one to portray such a character without making a hero of the subject, if he were a colored man and it is unthinkable and impossible that a white man could every gain such an interior view of the life of a person of colored blood. As dispassionate self-analysis it will rank with the Confessions of St. Augustine[1] and as a human document it is far superior to the famous Diary of Marie

† From an unsigned review, *Portland* (ME) *Express*, September 14, 1912.
1. Considered to be the first autobiography in the Western canon (397–98 C.E.).

Bashkirsteff which electrified the world some years ago.[2] Just how far romance has entered into these confessions it is of course impossible to tell, but we have no doubt that the writer is just what he says he is and that the romance of the situation is in the least impossible. As a treatise on the psychology and sociology of the person of slight trace of Negro blood it is worthy of a place with the Souls of Black Folks by Du Boise. Along with the human interest there runs a serious discussion of the race problem without heat or prejudice and in the conversations recorded all standpoints are represented.

The book is an autobiography of the child of a slave and her aristocratic Southern owner. This child, a boy, is sent with his mother to a Connecticut village in order that the father may marry quietly a lady of his own race and station and undoubtedly with the further reason that the colored woman was truly loved and that the father desired his son to grown up as free as possible from the blight of race prejudice. Finally discovering that he was of colored blood the youth takes his place with his race and tells of his adventures he had among the colored people of the South and in New York City. He is so light in color that he easily passes for a white man and so remarkable a musician and performer on the piano that he is able to make his way in society wherever he cared to go. Finally he falls deeply in love with a white woman of refinement and wealth whom he married after disclosing to her his parentage. In the last chapter we find him with his children living the life of a white man of means in New York and determined to give his children the benefits of white society.

The book is a vivid and startling pictures of the conditions brought about by the race question in America and it shows dispassionately though sympathetically conditions as they exist both North and South. There is the special plea for the Negro and not the least rancor against the white man. But it is a revelation of the attitude of the Negro toward the white man and especially that large and interesting class that has only a small proportion of colored blood.

Some of the chapters rival in naïve humor the relation of the adventures of Gil Blas[3] and the picture of the life of the Negro in New York City is a revelation to those who think that they know something of the life in the metropolis.

2. Bashkirsteff's diary was first published in French, in 1887; she had died three years earlier. The daughter of Ukrainian elites, Bashkirsteff (b. 1859) was raised in France, where she studied painting and gained early success during the 1870s and 1880s, only to succumb to tuberculosis. Her private writings (though heavily censored by her mother) chronicle her experiences in the artistic circles and burgeoning feminist networks of later-nineteenth-century Paris. The English translation of her diary appeared the same year Johnson's novel was published, as *Marie Bashkirsteff: From Childhood to Girlhood*, trans. Mary J. Safford (New York: Dodd, Mead & Company, 1912).

3. The hero of the French novelist Alain-Rene Lesage (1668–1747)'s picaresque trilogy, *L'Histoire de Gil Blas de Santillanc* (1715–35).

In this book the reader is given an opportunity to hear a side of the race question that has never, to our knowledge, been exploited and the jaded seeker for a new sensation will have his pulses stirred. The style is unaffected and smooth, without any attempts at heroics or fine writing.

Autobiography of an Ex-Colored Man†

The writer of this very interesting self-revelation is far less Negro than man. He lived his first thirty years as a member of the black race, although his colored blood was not apparent in his appearance. Then the sight of a southern lynching so broke his racial pride that he yielded to the temptation to become a white man. The pent-up memories of youth, homesickness for his mother's people, and regrets over deserting the battles of a struggling and advancing race find outlet in the anonymous volume. He writes with the sense perception, the emotion, the humor, and the egotism essential to all vivid biography. In addition, the events of his life are of themselves various and exciting. Though secondary in interest to his personal experiences, his comments on the Negro problem make a strong impression. That the race has originality and youthful capacity for growth he asserts on the ground that, while the Indian has contributed nothing to the arts or legends of our country, from the Negro the United States has secured her national dance—the "cake walk;" her national myths—the Uncle Remus stories; and her national music—the jubilee songs and "rag-time."

JESSIE FAUSET

What to Read‡

The Autobiography of an Ex-Colored Man

"This vivid and startling new picture of conditions brought about by the race question in the United States makes no special appeal for the Negro, but shows in a dispassionate, though sympathetic,

† From an unsigned review, *Chicago Standard*, October 12, 1912.

‡ From *The Crisis*, November 1912, 38. As the official publication of the National Association for the Advancement of Colored People, this African American journal was an important venue for a review of *ECM*. This assessment is significant for two additional reasons. First, it represents an early book review by novelist Jessie Fauset (1882–1961), literary editor of *The Crisis* during the 1920s. Second, its brevity and belated appearance confirm Johnson's frustrations at what he took to be the magazine's underenthusiastic interest in *ECM*, a response he attributed to *The Crisis'* editor-in-chief, W. E. B. Du Bois. See the introduction to this volume (xvii–xviii) for further discussion of this point.

manner conditions as they actually exist between the whites and blacks to-day. Special pleas have already been made for and against the Negro in hundreds of books, but in these books either his virtues or his vices have been exaggerated. This is because writers, in nearly every instance, have treated the colored American as a whole; each has taken some one group of the race to prove his case. Not before has a composite and proportionate presentation of the entire race, embracing all of its various groups and elements, showing their relations with each other and to the whites, been made."

The preceding paragraph quoted from the opening lines of the preface to this very interesting book gives in a way a résumé of it. It is indeed an epitome of the race situation in the United States told in the form of an autobiography. The varied incidents, the numerous localities brought in, the setting forth in all its ramifications of our great and perplexing race problem, suggests a work of fiction founded on hard fact. The hero, a natural son of a Southerner of high station, begins his real life in a New England town to which his mother had migrated, runs the whole gamut of color-line experiences, and ends by going over on the other side.

The work gives a view of the race situation in New England, in New York City, in the far South, in city and country, in high and low society, with glimpses, too, of England, France and Germany. Practically every phase and complexity of the race question is presented at one time or another. The work is, as might be expected, anonymous.

BRANDER MATTHEWS

American Character in American Fiction†

Three Books Which Depict the Actualities of Present-Day Life

At the opposite poles of the art of fiction are the novels which are only stories and the novels which are only studies of character. Probably most of the permanent masterpieces of the art stand remote from either pole, although a little nearer to the latter. Certainly most of the "best-sellers" of any year stand closer to the former.

It is the story itself, with the swift sequence of its situation, with the flash and glitter of its surprising episodes, and with the rush and

† From *Munsey's Magazine* 49.5 (August 1913): 794–98. Matthews taught Johnson at Columbia University and conferred with him as he drafted *ECM*; see their correspondence on 221–22. This volume's introduction explores their literary relationship in more detail.

rattle of its adventures, which is most likely to win immediate popularity with the main mass of readers. Of course, this popularity has little hope of long life; and when once the situations have unrolled themselves, there is slight temptation to return to them in the vain hope of reviving the glitter or of recalling an echo of the rattle.

Few things fade away as irrevocably as the story which everybody is reading—to borrow the apt phrase of the advertisements. Where are the novels of yesteryear? Or, as *Hans Breitmann* asked:

"Where is the lovely golden cloud that floated on the mountain's brow?"

Who of us now can remember even the name of the writer of "The Lamplighter," a best-seller of sixty years ago, or of "Rutledge," a best-seller of fifty years ago, or of "Called Back," and "The House on the Marsh," and "Mr. Barnes of New York," best-sellers of more recent decades? And why should any of us wish to recall these vanished tales which left no palpable deposit on our memories? They are dead stories of dead seasons; they served their purpose in their day, in that they enabled us to pass away our time. They were stories which were only stories, tales more or less stuffed with adventure, and more or less empty of character. They did not really aspire to survive; they were contentedly ephemeral. Sufficient unto the day is the novel thereof.

These examples of story-telling for the sake of the story have faded away because they lacked the sole mordant which would have fixed them in our minds; they lacked one or more recognizable and unforgetable characters. They have gone, one and all, out into the night of black oblivion, simply because they were not peopled by fellow human beings whom we could take to heart.

In the same years when the ghosts of these dead and departed tales were still stalking the earth, other works of fiction achieved a popularity not so immediate, perhaps, and not so wide-spread at first, but far more durable. Mr. Howells's "Rise of Silas Lapham," Mr. James's "Daisy Miller," and Mark Twain's "Huckleberry Finn" had a vogue less spectacular because less overwhelming than that of "Mr. Barnes of New York"; and on the far side of the Atlantic, Robert Louis Stevenson's "Strange Case of Dr. Jekyll and Mr. Hyde," Mr. Hardy's "Tess of the D'Urbervilles," and Mr. Kipling's "Kim" succeeded in pleasing almost as many readers as "Called Back" and "The House on the Marsh."

"Kim" and "Huck Finn" are good stories, considered simply as stories; they are very good stories, indeed—better to my thinking merely as tales of adventure than their evanescent rivals. But they survive because they are something more than merely stories, whereas their more immediately popular competitors are now unwept, unhonored, and unsung.

The appeal of the mere story is exhausted absolutely with the single reading; we submit ourselves once to the shock of its situations, and there's an end to its potency. It has no storage battery of interest to thrill us again and to signal an invitation to return. But the appeal of the story which is also a gallery of characters is inexhaustible. I, for one, cannot count the number of times that I have entered again into friendly and familiar relation with *Silas Lapham* and *Daisy Miller*, or with that pair of sturdy young wanderers, *Huckleberry Finn* and *Kimball O'Hara*.

No doubt the author felt flattered when a casual stranger expressed a willingness to give a goodly sum if he had never read the author's masterpiece, explaining promptly that he would thus be able to buy back the pleasure of reading it for the first time. But this unexpected compliment is not quite so complimentary as it may appear at first sight, since it implies that the book needed the flavor of freshness, and that it could not well withstand the test of a second reading. And this implication is unfounded, because a narrative of adventure as rich in character as "Huck Finn" or "Kim" yields up its full savor only after repeated perusals. There is more in the books that are wealthy with humanity than can be discovered at the first reading, even if that first reading may amply disclose the story itself simply as a story.

The kind of novel which can be described as "a rattling good yarn" is inferior to the narrative in which human conduct is soberly considered; but it is not easy to spin and it is not without merits of its own. It is often despised by superior persons. Literary mandarins, dwellers in ivory towers, secure in their sole possession of the only key to all the arts, cannot help despising that which the plain people are competent to enjoy. It is natural that the aristocrats of culture should recoil from that which has the power of pleasing the ordinary reader. They prefer pound-cake to good bread, white or brown. But man cannot live by cake alone; and the more delicate our taste, the quicker we are to appreciate good bread. The broader and the deeper our culture is, the more likely we are to relish a good story for its own sake, even if the persons who carry on the tale are only the traditional figures of fiction.

Perhaps no man of our time had a wider outlook on books and on men than the late Andrew Lang. He was frank in the expression of his gratitude for any tale that would so entrance him for the moment that he forgot the world with all its insistent problems and its incessant conflicts. What he desired in a story was to find forgetfulness of trouble:

> Pour out the nepenthe, in short, and I shall not ask if the cup be gold-chased by Mr. Stevenson, or a buffalo-horn beaker brought by Mr. Haggard from Kakuanaland—the *Baron of*

> *Bradwardine's* bear or the "Cup of Hercules" of Théophile Gautier, or merely a common wine-glass of M. Fortuné du Boisgobey's or M. Xavier de Montépin's. If only the nepenthe be foaming there—the delightful draft of dear forgetfulness—the outside of the cup may take care of itself.

This is put with characteristic cleverness, but it evokes two remarks. The first is that Lang himself did not confine his reading to the exciting narratives of Xavier de Montépin and of Fortuné du Boisgobey; he continued to the end of his life to nourish his mind on the more solid food of Homer and Theocritus, Shakespeare and Molière. And the second remark is that in the long run it is as dangerous to go to a bookstore for the anodyne of dreams as it is to go to a drug-store for any other opiate. The novels that "take us out of ourselves," as the phrase is, are not wholesome as a steady diet; they do not invigorate our souls as do the novels that take us into ourselves, that make us think about ourselves and about our fellow men and our fellow women.

More than a score of years ago Mr. Howells expressed his frank opinion of the novels that "make one forget life and all its cares and duties; they are not in the least like the novels which make you think of these, and shame you into at least wishing to be a helpfuller and more wholesome creature than you are."

The Progress of the Art of Fiction

It was about as long ago that Mr. Howells startled and shocked the unthinking by the assertion that the art of fiction is a finer art now than it was in Thackeray's day. Of course, no one really familiar with the history of any art should have been shocked by this remark. The art of fiction is a finer art to-day than it was in Thackeray's time, just as it was finer in Thackeray's time than it had been in Fielding's time, and just as it was finer in Fielding's day than it had been in Cervantes's day. This is not to say that Fielding is a greater novelist than Cervantes, or that Thackeray is greater than Fielding, or that any novelist of this new century is greater than Thackeray. It is only to say that the art itself is finer, more delicate, more careful in its craftsmanship, in its planning, and in its joinery. "Don Quixote," for example, is perhaps the noblest novel ever written, but its construction is unspeakably careless.

I may be permitted to recall here a saying of the renowned Italian goldsmith and antiquary, Castellani, made to my father more than forty-five years ago. My father had asked as to the skill of Castellani's workmen; and the Italian expert promptly responded that there was a constant advance in certainty of execution, in finish of workmanship, in conscientious manual dexterity.

"My men can copy anything of Benvenuto Cellini's or of any of the other master workers in metal and in enamel; and their work will be more perfect than the original. But there's scarcely one of them capable of any original designing!"

What is true of the art of the goldsmith is true also of the art of the novelist. Whether or not the novelists of the present are as capable of originality as those of the past, they are at least better craftsmen, because the state of the art, to use the apt phrase of the engineers, has advanced; because fiction is to-day a finer art than it was a century ago, even if we happen now not to have as many giants as may have existed once upon a time.

Even in the dark ages of a score of years ago, when Mr. Howells was engaged in stirring up the critics in their cages, the true meaning of this chance remark ought not to have been misunderstood. It was misunderstood, however, and it brought a storm of abuse about Mr. Howells's head.

Some of those who did not relish his criticisms had their easy revenge in abusing his novels. It was very helpful for the more general appreciation of the little-understood art of the novelist that Mr. Howells should discuss this art and declare its principles and apply them. But his iconoclastic essays in criticism were not helpful to his own fame as a novelist. Most readers rather dislike technical analysis of the arts; they prefer to be ravished by the result of the artist's work, and they detest being taken into the workshop and made to consider the processes. As Joseph Joubert asserted long ago:

> We do not like, in the arts, to see whence our impressions arise; the Naiad should hide her urn; the Nile should conceal her sources.

The echo of Mr. Howells's critical battles of long ago is now faint; and many of his younger critics seem not to know that he also was a critic once upon a time. And I—who have delighted in Mr. Howells's novels ever since I read the earliest of them, "Their Wedding Journey," now twoscore years ago—have been greatly gratified to see the cordiality of appreciation with which his latest contribution to fiction has been received.

A Picture of American Life

His latest book is called "New Leaf Mills, a Chronicle"; and to convey to the reader of this paper any adequate impression of the mellow charm, the simple grace, the absolute sincerity of this quiet and restful portrayal of a group of very American characters in very American conditions, would demand a style as firm and as caressing as its author's own.

Mr. Howells here presents to us one episode from the existence of a dreamer who lacks the sense of reality although he has a sense of humor; who is unpractical although he has a Yankee ingenuity in his fingers; who refuses to believe in danger, and who thereby disarms the man who thinks himself his enemy; who believes against every doubt, and who fails again as he has failed before and as he will fail more than once after he has passed out of the pages of this volume. In spite of the Indian summer haze in which the book is bathed, the veracity of it is unflinching. The author is inexorable in setting before us things as they are and as they had to be because they were rooted in character and flowered out of circumstance. He does not seek to startle us with the emotions of surprise, and he is constantly rewarding us with emotions of recognition.

As we read, we feel that *Owen Powell* actually set out to establish the New Leaf Mills in a little village in the middle West sixty years ago; and that he took with him the wife who is painted for us in these pages with the utmost economy of stroke and with the utmost accuracy of color. We get to know his children and his relatives and the new neighbors at the lonely village where he makes his hopeless venture; and, best of all, we get to know him, *Owen Powell*, better and better; and we get to feel that he is well worth knowing, this dreamer, this optimistic idealist, this right American, incapable as he is of getting on in the world as other right Americans expect to do.

The likings of primitive man and of children—who are more or less in the same stage of progress as primitive man—are for tales of the impossible, filled with fairies and giants and dragons. The likings of men a little less primitive and of children of a larger growth are for tales of the improbable, with *Quentin Durward* and *D'Artagnan* passing unscathed through a heterogeny of deadly perils. Most of us who read novels nowadays have so far left childhood behind us that we prefer to have our story-tellers confine themselves to the treatment of the probable, as Thackeray does, for the most part, and as Trollope does nearly always.

Only a few novel-readers there are—although the number of them is steadily increasing—who make an insistent demand upon the story-teller to transcend the merely probable and to give us only the inevitable. This Hawthorne did in "The Scarlet Letter"; George Eliot in "Romola"—at least so far as *Tito Melema* is concerned; Turgenef in "Smoke"; Tolstoy in "Anna Karénina"; and Mr. Howells himself in "The Rise of Silas Lapham" and in "A Modern Instance."

This latest tale, "New Leaf Mills," is not plucked out of the palpitating heart of actuality; it is not up to date in its problems; it is not an elucidation of any scare-head story in the morning newspaper. But none the less does it rise to the same artistic plane; none the less does it strike the austere note of inevitability. If *Owen Powell* was the man that the author has projected before us, then the things which happen to him and to his in this story are the things which would have happened in real life, inevitably and inexorably.

Robert Herrick's New Book

In "One Woman's Life" Mr. Robert Herrick has also given us a study of the middle West, since Chicago is the scene of its more important episodes. Mr. Herrick does not impart quite the same sense of inevitability to his novel that we discover in Mr. Howells's tale; but all that he relates we instantly accept as certainly probable. And Mr. Herrick's novel is plucked out of the palpitating heart of actuality. Although its story begins a score of years ago, the career of its heroine is continued well into this new century. Again, while Mr. Howells's tale is leisurely in its telling, Mr. Herrick's is swift and almost tumultuous in its rapid unrolling. It rushes forward as if its author had accepted Thoreau's assertion that "there is more force in speed than in weight."

The title of Mr. Herrick's book is aptly chosen. What he has here to set before us is the life of one woman, *Milly Ridge*, from the day when she arrives in Chicago, an undeveloped girl of sixteen, to the day, nearly a score of years later, when she leaves Chicago, the bride of her second husband. It is to her character and to her career that the author invites our attention. *Milly Ridge* is the central planet; all the other figures, men and women alike, are only satellites, shining with light reflected from her. And *Milly* rewards the reader for the attention thus focused on her. She is put before us with unhesitating insight; she is not extenuated or apologized for; she stands on her own feet, and she speaks out of her own mouth. She is alive in every limb; and she is a type possible only here in these States—although doubtless it would not be difficult to find parallels in certain European countries.

Milly Ridge is a pretty woman, not a professional beauty, but undeniably a pretty woman; and, in fact, she is almost to be described as only a pretty woman. But she has the social gift, and this is her chief asset in her career. She is indisputably and indomitably social; she not only likes people and people of all sorts and conditions, but people like her at first sight, and they continue to like her to the end, even when they no longer have any very good reason to like her. She has charm, of course, but apparently her chief quality is not so much charm as a reciprocity of liking which leads casual acquaintances to lend her a helping hand and lures friends to make serious sacrifices for her.

It is a mark of deep understanding that Mr. Herrick does not endow her with an ardent temperament and does not lead her through any amorous misadventures. She is, as she understands herself, a "good woman"; in fact, she takes pride in what the elder Henry James would have termed her "flagrant morality." She is engaged without love, and she breaks the engagement. She is almost engaged with only a little love, and she throws this admirer over because she really has fallen in love at last. And when her husband dies, worn out by the struggle to supply her social exigencies, she marries after a decent interval the admirer she had thrown over.

She moves through life along the line of least resistance, taking whatever she can reach out for that chance may offer, feeling vaguely that she is a superior being, that society owes her not only a living, but a living adorned with purple and fine linen, and that society is under this obligation simply because she is a woman, a pretty woman and a "good woman." Probably this type of social parasite is not uncommon in America to-day; and Mr. Herrick is to be congratulated upon the skill with which he has depicted it, accurately, amply, and disinterestedly, without bias for or against, and permitting every reader to draw his or her own moral in his or her own fashion.

These two studies of American character are avowedly fiction, although they are also unmitigably veracious. They both fulfil the definition of the novel which the British historian, J. R. Green, once gave to Mr. Henry James:

"History without documents—nothing to prove it."

A Curious Phase of Life

Mr. Howells's book and Mr. Herrick's, each in its own way, is a contribution to the history of American life and manners. With them I wish to class another book not so recently issued and not so widely read, a book which purports to be an actual record of fact, but which seems to me to fall rather within Green's definition of fiction. This is an anonymous volume entitled "The Autobiography of an Ex-Colored Man."

The title is a little startling, but the book itself is not in the least sensational. It tells in detail the life of a young fellow of mixed blood, who is, in fact, almost white, and who in the end abandons his darker brethren and passes thereafter as a white man. He records his own feeling that he is a deserter to the cause of the negro, and he sets forth his high esteem for the men who are now maintaining that cause.

"Beside them I feel small and selfish—" he declares. "I am an ordinarily successful white man who has made a little money; they are men who are making history and a race."

That the story of this ex-colored man's career, from his childhood to his maturity, with its many episodes in many cities, was written by a colored man is indisputable; and it is therefore also a contribution to the history of American life and manners. It takes us into many circles, the existence of which is unknown to white readers; it gives, for example, a fleeting vision of the colored "Tenderloin" of New York. It may not be a record of actual fact, but it contains what is higher than actual fact, the essential truth. It has indisputable veracity, even if it is imagined rather than recollected.

It has significance for all of us who want to understand our fellow citizens of darker hue. It is written calmly, clearly, simply; in fact, it is composed in full accord with the principle enunciated by Taine in one of his letters—the principle "that a writer should be a psychologist, not a painter or a musician; that he should be a transmitter of ideas and of feelings, not of sensations."

Here, then, are three serious studies of American character in the form of fiction; and in no one of these three books is there any plot, so called, or any exciting situation, or anything that could be put on the stage or that suggests the stage. If Robert Louis Stevenson was right in declaring that the serious drama must deal with the great passionate crises of existence, "when duty and inclination come nobly to the grapple," then no one of these stories is really dramatic. Yet by one reader at least they have been found intensely interesting, because they are rich in human nature.

Contemporary Reviews: 1927 Edition

J. W. Johnson's Novel Appears in New Edition†

James Weldon Johnson's novel, "The Autobiography of an Ex-Colored Man", first published in 1912 and since then out of print, has just been republished in New York, by Alfred A. Knopf in the Blue Jade library series, with an introduction by Carl Van Vechten.

Mr. Van Vechten declares he has read the book three times and says "that it reads like a composite autobiography of the Negro race in the United States in modern times."

A. B.

An Old Book in New Dress‡

This is an old friend come to life again. Fifteen years ago, when it was first published, we were all hailing it as the first real Negro novel. The first novel, we said. We had Charles W. Chesnutt's stories of novel length,[1] but "The Autobiography of an Ex-Colored Man" was the first novel in the standard sense of the word. In the sense of a novel that is a story that affords a comprehensive view of social conditions.

In 1912 this book aroused enthusiasm among reading colored people and some perturbation among the whites. Its message was accentuated by the death at or about the time, of a prominent Chicago publisher and the revelation that he was a Negro. A New York paper printed an editorial wondering how many thousands or hundreds of thousands of white people were merely passing for white and how many had African blood without knowing it.

† From an unsigned review in *The Baltimore Afro-American*, August 13, 1927, 10. This is an African American newspaper. Used with permission from the Afro-American Newspapers Archives and Research Center.

‡ From the *New York Amsterdam News*, August 24, 1927, 20. Reprinted with permission of Amsterdam News Pub. Co.

1. *The Conjure Woman* (1899) and *The Wife of His Youth and Other Stories of the Color Line* (1899).

In a few years the book went out of print and the public forgot it. Now the Knopf firm has done us a good turn by republishing it. Carl Van Vechten, accepted by white people as a greater authority on Negro life than Negroes themselves, has written a laudatory introduction which is fully deserved.

In a little over two hundred pages Mr. Johnson gives the reader an enormous amount of information concerning the Negro, his relations with himself and his ideas of white people. Caucasians will be startled by the assertion that the Negro knows more about them than they know about him.

The story can be told here without spoiling the prospective reader's interest; its effectiveness depends on its theme and carrying power instead of dramatic surprise, suspense and the other tricks of fiction. A colored man decides to pass for white. As a white man he succeeds in business and in love. But in the end, in the last two paragraphs of his story, when he speaks of colored men who are working for their people, we find these words:

"Beside them I feel small and selfish. I am an ordinary white man who has made a little money. They are men who are making a history and a race—I cannot repress the thought that, after all, I have chosen the lesser part, that I have sold my birthright for a mess of pottage."

After all, it is not the fraction of black or white blood that determines a person's race; it is a cultural condition. A pure white infant reared by and among Negroes will grow up as much a Negro as a pure black one.

ROBERT O. BALLOU

Symphony Pathetique on Black and White Keys†

James Weldon Johnson Tells a Colored Man's Story Simply and Beautifully

Jazz may interest you. The life of an intelligent black man in America may interest you as a social problem. A simple story, beautifully told, in which a sensitive boy, born poor and a social outcast because of his race, groped his way upward through fear and sorrow to a place of distinction, may attract you. But whether for one or all three of these, it would not be difficult to imagine any one capable of reading a book who would not choose to read "The Autobiography

† From *Chicago Daily News*, August 17, 1927.

of an Ex-Colored Man" by James Weldon Johnson (Knopf) and sit long into the night at the reading.

The book was first published fifteen years ago in an inadequate edition which quickly went out of print. Mr. Knopf has now done it fitting honor by republication as a volume in the Blue Jade Library.

We have had pleas for the Negro from white and colored men alike. This is no plea. We have had panegyrics to the potential greatness of the black man. This is no song of praise. And we have had odd mixtures of fancy and fact in orgies of sentimentality, disgusting to white and colored men alike This book is none of these.

It is, rather, a calm recital of a quietly dramatic story, the tale of a boy, almost but not quite white, born with extraordinary talents, torn throughout his life between a desire to remain a part of his race and help it in its slow advance and the need for companionship and social standing which only the white race could give him. In the end—is there any end? The book is a record of conflict which continues while white men are white and black black while both feel that there is a difference between them.

HARRY SALPETER

"Harlem" 15 Years Ago†

Carl Van Vechten has performed a couple of graceful gestures. He has acknowledged a debt to one of the source books of "Nigger Heaven,"[1] persuaded Mr. Knopf to include it in his Blue Jade Library of reprints (although it is not, in spirit, a Blue Jade book), and contributed a laudatory introduction to it. "The Autobiography of an Ex-Colored Man" appears to-day, fifteen years after its anonymous publication, with the first acknowledgement of its author, who is James Weldon Johnson. Mr. Johnson is an acknowledged Negro.

An ex-colored man is a fair-skinned Negro who has crossed the line and passes for a white man. Somewhere in "Nigger Heaven," during a discussion of race, one of the characters observes that there are 10,000 such Negroes in New York. Walter White's "Flight"[2] is the story of a fair Negress, with French blood in her veins, who marries

† From the *New York World*, August 23, 1927.

1. Van Vechten's own novel, published in 1926 by Knopf, was controversial for its title and depiction of Harlem nightlife during the 1920s.
2. NAACP activist Walter F. White (1893–1955) published his second novel, *Flight*, with Knopf in 1926. White's physical appearance was comparable to that of the novel's heroine. His extremely fair complexion and blue eyes allowed him to pass for white, which he did during the 1920s in order to investigate lynchings in the South for the NAACP.

a wealthy white Babbitt,[3] a despiser of Negroes. Finally, hurt in what we might call ancestral pride, she leaves him and turns her face to Harlem. In "Nigger Heaven" and in this "Autobiography" white prejudice and the closing of economic opportunities to acknowledged Negroes are cited as justifications of the system of "passing."

"The Autobiography of an Ex-Colored Man" is not an autobiography in the generally understood sense. It is an autobiography mainly of Mr. Johnson's mental attitude and feeling. To Mr. Van Vechten, it reads like a "composite autobiography of the Negro race in modern times." Being no authority on the Negro I hesitate to state that I do not think so. At the time of original publication, says Mr. Van Vechten, it "stood almost alone as an inclusive survey of racial accomplishments and traits, as an interpretation of the feelings of the Negro toward the white man and toward the members of his own race.

And Mr. Johnson may also regard himself as a prophet justified during the event. In 1912 he boldly asserted that ragtime music was one of the American Negro's chief contributions, the other three being the Uncle Remus stories, collected by Joel Chandler Harris; the jubilee songs, popularized by the Fisk Singers; and the cakewalk. His hero—the ostensible autobiographer—is shown devoting himself to the collection of spirituals among the southern backwoods Negroes. He determines also to use his knowledge of classical music to bring to a higher point of development the ragtime he hears at the "Club," thus foreseeing, says Mr. Van Vechten, the creation of Gershwin's "Rhapsody in Blue." And about thirteen years before there was anything like an all-Negro revue the ostensible autobiographer tells of Negro comedians at the "Club," asserting that the time would come "when they would compel the public to recognize that they could do something more than grin and cut pigeonwings."

But for most of us the justified prophecy about the American Negro is not sufficient to bring us knocking at the door of this book. A book bearing the title "The Autobiography of an Ex-Colored Man" should have human interest. You don't have to be an advocate of anything to be able to read and enjoy "The Wooings of Jezebel Pettyfer." But you can't expect James Weldon Johnson to be a Haldane Macfall.[4] The Autobiography lacks unity and sustained interest. It

3. Inspired by Sinclair Lewis's 1922 satirical novel of the same name, this term refers to shallow, conformist, materialist-minded businessmen.
4. The complete title of this scandalous novel is as follows: "Being the Personal History of Jehu Sennachrib Dyle, commonly called Masheen Dyle; together with an account of certain things that chanced in the House of the Sorcerer; here set down by Haldane Macfall." Set in the West Indies (Barbados and Jamaica), the novel relates the romántic escapades of its title characters. First published in London in 1898 (by Grant Richards), the novel was banned in the United States for twenty-five years because of its risqué cover and frontispiece, which featured a creole woman nude from the waist up. Knopf reprinted the novel in 1926, *sans* the risqué illustrations, as part of its Blue Jade Series—the same line in which *The Autobiography of an Ex-Coloured Man* was reprinted.

is narrative, tract and bald report in one. Yet the account of the lynching is quite exciting as is the melodramatic shooting of the white woman by her dark paramour, and the discussion in the Pullman smoking car between the Texan and the Northern Civil war veteran is interesting, if elementary. I wish that Mr. Johnson had made more of an imaginative effort picturing the life and state of mind of a Negro *after* he has passed. Mr. Johnson seems to be somewhat perfunctory with his character from the time he makes his great decision. The best parts of "The Autobiography of an Ex-Colored Man" deal with the colored man!

There was no Harlem in those days. When our hero comes to New York he lodges in a house on 27th Street, west of Sixth Avenue. The gambling house, where for a time he supports himself shooting craps, and the "Club," in which his ragtime playing brings him to the attention of the rich and generous patron who takes him to Europe, are nearby. "M New York was limited to ten blocks; the boundaries were Sixth Avenue from 23rd to 33rd Street, with the cross streets one block to the west." Vaudeville performers, sporting men, idlers, jockeys, and gamblers seem to be the sole representatives of the Negro race in our hero's segment of New York. The autobiographer meets many intelligent Negroes resembling the hero of "Nigger Heaven" who desert their serious ambitions and hopes and yield to the seductions of an irresponsible night life, "the gaslight life."

It is in Atlanta that our Negro discovers the race of which he is a member—the lower strata and their dialect. "Lawd a mussy!" "G'wan, man!" "Bless ma soul!" "Look heah, chile!" were not expressions familiar to him. Up in Connecticut, to which his white father had sent him and his mother from the South, he had not been aware of any distinction between him and his white chums until a teacher had taken the trouble to point it out to him. Upon the death of his mother he goes to Atlanta to enroll in the Negro university. On the streets he hears his brothers-in-color:

> "The unkempt appearance, the shambling, slouching gait, and loud talk and laughter of these people aroused in me a feeling of almost repulsion . . . These people talked and laughed without restraint. In fact, the talked straight from their lungs and laughed from the pits of their stomachs . . . I have since learned that the ability to laugh heartily is, in part, the salvation of the American Negro; it does much to keep him from going the way of the Indian."

This suggestion is fruitful for the student of the races. For better or for worse, the Negro is learning other things besides laughter.

ALICE DUNBAR-NELSON

As in a Looking Glass†

When the "Autobiography of an Ex-Colored Man" appeared anonymously some fifteen years ago, the furore that it created was tempered by the feeling that it was either written by a white man, or the work of a Negro who had deliberately bared the secrets of the race to the prying eyes of non-Negroes. Later we found out that while it was pure fiction, yet it might easily have been literal truth, and the passage of years has made us less hyper-sensitive about racial matters. So the re-publication of the "Autobiography," under the name of its author, James Weldon Johnson, by Alfred A. Knopf in the Blue Jade series has caused a recurrence of the old furore, and we re-read the book with increased interest in the light of the present-day glorification of Harlem.

Those of us who are old enough to remember the New York of the days mentioned in the book, when Negro life was down in the Thirties, and there were no cabarets, only night clubs; when Ada Overton Walker[1] was the darling of the race: when jazz was unknown and ragtime was gaining a foothold; when Harlem was a day's journey into the hinterland, will find a renewed interest and delight in the life described in one section of the book. But apart from the purely fictitious tale, or the study of the mental processes of a man who decides to "go over," the autobiography has two distinct claims upon our interest. The tale itself in the light of present-day accomplishment, sounds almost late-Victorian. But the manner of the telling, in its bald, terse cold, almost impersonal clarity reminds one almost involuntarily of Booker T. Washington's "Up from Slavery." There is much of the same style throughout both narratives—the true and fictitious one. So that you know the autobiography is quite what Carl Van Vechten claims for it, in his introduction—"a composite autobiography of the Negro race in modern times." The other claim upon our interest lies in the descriptions which Mr. Johnson has elaborated lately in his "God's Trombones," and the introductions to his two edition of Negro spirituals. Here we find "Singing Johnson" and the great preacher John Brown, whom we have learned

† From the *Washington* (DC) *Eagle*, September 2, 1927. This is an African American newspaper. Reprinted by permission of The Improved Benevolent and Protective Order of Elks of the World. Dunbar-Nelson elaborates on several points raised in the review she published in *Opportunity*; see 324–27 to compare.

1. Dancer, choreographer, singer, and actress (1880–1914); her solo performances and her collaborations with Bert Williams and George Walker (her husband) helped transform early 20th-century black musical theater.

to know from the later books. A vast wealth of unmined material still lies for Mr. Johnson to bring to light, polished and carved as only he knows how.

The big thought of the book lies now as it did fifteen years ago, when the supposed writer recalling his life as a white man says, in the last sentence—"I cannot repress the thought that, after all, I have chosen the lesser part, that I have sold my birthright for a mess of pottage."

[Review of 1927 Edition]†

A much needed reprint is "The Autobiography of an Ex-Colored Man," by James Weldon Johnson, which first appeared anonymously fifteen years ago, and has been out of print for almost as many years. Carl Van Vechten in his introduction acknowledges it to be "an invaluable source-book for the study of negro psychology," and point out a number of features which show the author to have anticipated later developments, especially his remarks on spirituals and ragtime. The hero, who passes the color line, succeeds in presenting, directly or indirectly, the various phases and problems of negro life, and no time could be more propitious than the present for an exposition of this kind. What once may have been a matter of academic curiosity is now a social necessity for those who combine in a like enthusiasm Ethel Waters[1] and Walter White, Paul Robeson and Florence Mills. Perhaps Mr. Johnson will enable some of them to draw distinctions.

DEWEY R. JONES

The Bookshelf: Prose and Verse‡

The fall crop is beginning to arrive. In another two months, according to information, there will be on the market more books by and about black Americans than have appeared in the last decade. What was thought to be a fad that would run its course and go the way of fads, has turned out to be a genuine permanent interest in the subject and especially in the manner in which it is being treated these days.

† From an unsigned review in *The New Yorker*, September 3, 1927. The novel was listed in this magazine's "Books Worth Reading" column from September 17 to November 5, 1927. Ernest Boyd/*The New Yorker*. Reprinted by permission.

1. Ethel Waters (1896–1977), blues singer, stage and screen actress.

‡ From *The Chicago Defender*, September 27, 1927. This is an African American newspaper. Used with the permission of the *Chicago Defender*.

Jean Toomer led the array a few years ago with his "Cain," and because his startling handling of his Georgia Dusk songs he was declared unusual. It was said that he would have no real competition in his particular field for many years to come. But "Cain" had hardly reached its climax before "The Fire in the Flint," "Confusion," Color," "Weary Blues"[1] and numerous other publications followed in rapid succession. Since that time there has been a continuous procession of books on all subjects by and about the Race, and for the most part they have been most cordially received.

But from that group has come little of what can be called masterpieces. "The Fire in the Flint" preached too much, and while it attracted unusual attention for a few months, has gone the way of all cheap melodrama. "Flight" was too pretentious: it was far too heavy and was handled far too consciously to leave the proper taste in one's mouth.[2] While many were surprised at its content, few persons felt that the subject had been adequately handled, when they finally succeeded in wading through the mass of words.

Perhaps coming nearest to having a lasting value were the books of poems by Cullen and Langston Hughes. They at least indicated a talent in the two young poets, coupled with knowledge of what they were trying to do. Eric Walrond automatically finds himself in this class.[3] His stories, I believe, will live as long as stories live. They are new, vibrating and filled with life.

I have commented on the above to classify the two books which represent the vanguard of the fall crop. Although James Weldon Johnson's "Autobiography" was published about 15 years ago, it came off the press anonymously, and Knopf is now exposing for the first time its author. This fact alone, I believe, detracts from the interest in the book. And when one reads it and finds that it is not at all what the title indicates, he is disappointed beyond words.

"The Autobiography" is not of an ex-Colored man at all, but some incidents in near-white Negro psychology. It starts off with a boy whose father is a white man and whose mother is an unusual type of woman, who, because of her race and the Georgia law, could mother a child by a white man but could not marry him. They move to Connecticut, this mother and son, and he does not know that he is not white until he is well along in school. From that point on until within a few pages of the end of the book, it is the Colored man speaking. Then he turns white—and becomes disgusting! He falls

1. Jones refers to novels by Walter F. White, *Fire in the Flint* (1924), and Jessie Redmon Fauset, *There Is Confusion* (1924); and poetry collections by Countee Cullen, *Color* (1925), and Langston Hughes, *The Weary Blues* (1926).
2. Walter White's second novel, *Flight* (1926).
3. Eric Walrond (1898–1966), *Tropic Death* (1926).

in love with a pale, frail, beautiful white girl—and from there to the end of the book Mr. Johnson displays unusual weakness.

The book is incoherent; the narrative lags, and while there are a couple of interesting scenes, the "Autobiography" fails to convince—and does not even hold the interest throughout. I think it would have been far better had the book been published anonymously; this would at least have added to its interest.

"Copper Sun" also falls far short of the mark Mr. Cullen set for himself in "Color."[4] True, he reaches some great heights in artistry in this book, but mediocrity far overbalances these divisions. There are poems in the collection that show that Cullen is a talented person, and one capable of almost anything in his chosen field; there also are numbers that show a straining for effect, and leave one in doubt as to their author. They are not of even quality, either in tone or content.

In his poems of death, and there are many of them, I believe Mr. Cullen shows real artistry. He seems to have spent many hours trying to solve the enigma of the permanency of death, and, although he contradicts himself in more than one instance, seems to have a pretty fair conception—a poet's conception—of the whys and wherefores of it all. His excursions into love themes leave me unconvinced.

But, contrasting with all I have said, is "Confessions."

If for a day joy masters me,
Think not my wounds are healed:
Far deeper than the scars you see.
I keep the roots concealed.

They shall bear blossoms with the fall:
I have their word for this.
Who tends my roots with rains of gall,
And suns of prejudice.

Beautiful, is it not? Simple, direct and pregnant with meaning. This represents the short ones in the book that make it worth while. Nor is there anything wanting in his sonnet, "From the Dark Tower," dedicated to Charles S. Johnson, editor of Opportunity:

We shall not always plant while others reap
The golden increment of bursting fruit,
Not always countenance, abject and mute,
That other men should hold their brothers cheap;
Not everlastingly while others sleep
Shall we beguile their limbs with mellow flute,
Not always bend to some more subtle brute;
We were not made eternally to weep.

4. Cullen, *Copper Sun* (1927).

The night whose sable breast relieves The [*sic*] stark
White stars is no less lovely being dark,
And there are buds that cannot bloom at all
In light, but crumple piteously and fall;
So in the dark we hide the heart that bleeds,
And wait, and tend our agonizing seeds.

"Copper Sun" is beautifully illustrated by Charles Cullen, who, I learn, is no relation to the poet.[5] The illustrations, while meaningless to me, follow accurately the adopted custom for books of contemporary poetry and seem to represent the spirit of the modernist, although Mr. Cullen, the poet, shows a distinct leaning toward English poetry of the last century. Only in rare cases can he be described as a modernist. Taken all in all, "Copper Sun" does not live up to the promises of "Color." While there is a maturity of thought, there also appears to be a dearth of material with which the poet is familiar. However, the book is worth reading, for poetry is not expected to have the same effect upon all those who read and hear it. I recommend that no one be guided by my experience in this case.

ALFRED L. S. WOOD

Autobiography of an Ex-Colored Man[†]

The Blue Jade Library published by Alfred A. Knopf becomes increasingly interesting. The latest title to be added is "The Autobiography of an Ex-Colored Man," by James Weldon Johnson, whose recent "God's Trombones," Negro sermons in verse, is the season's most important contribution to Americana. It is the mission of the Blue Jade Library to given another and more beautiful chance to certain splendid books that have inexplicably failed to attract the notice they deserve on first appearance. The chance is beautiful because of all the lovely books issued from the Knopf presses none is dressed and printed as are those of the Blue Jade. For instance, the book under discussion displays colors of flame, black and gold; the type is Caslon Old Face, set on a linotype.[1] Mr. Knopf with

5. Book illustrator Charles Cullen was not African American. For more on his stunning work with black texts, see Caroline Groeser, "The Case of *Ebony and Topaz*: Racial and Sexual Hybridity in Harlem Renaissance Illustrators," *American Periodicals* 15.1 (2005): 93–98.

† From "Agates and Migs," the *Springfield* (MA) *Union*, September 21, 1927. Reprinted with permission of *The* (MA) *Republican*.

1. Machine used throughout the late nineteenth and twentieth centuries to print books, newspapers, magazines, and posters. The linotype transformed mass media publishing because the technology required fewer typesetters and could cast many pages for printing at a time.

unusual publishing intelligence is doing much for the historic type faces by using them on these Blue Jades and other important books of his lists and printing notes explaining their beauty and historic interest.

"The Autobiography of an Ex-Colored Man" was first issued in 1912. Sherman, French & Co. were the original publishers and, as the introducer Carl Van Vechten notices, the book was long out of print and practically unprocurable. The Autobiography in 1912 was to a greater extent than it is now an unbelievable book. In 1912 Mr. Van Vechten and others who have studied the geography of the place had not discovered Harlem. As a matter of fact, Harlem as it exists today had not come into being. There was nowhere in the country a Negro city and the Negro, his art and his problems, even the problem he presents to the white race, were not taken with the seriousness now given to them. In 1912, most of us were complacently sure that if the Negro "kept his place" there would be no such problem as that of which the South and Northern missionaries to the South were complaining. The Negro then, even more than he is now, was popularly supposed to be a happy-go-lucky clown, of a certain value as an entertainer, but of no great importance in a world obviously made for Caucasians. Sometimes he dignified himself to the estate of annoyance, but generally he was regarded as a sterile race living within the borders of another and tolerant race that permitted him to grab certain crumbs. Of Negro intellectuals white men had heard of Booker T. Washington and a very few, indeed, knew that Dr. DuBois was writing bitter books about what he was pleased to think was the oppression of one people by another. Dr. Washington was supposed to believe that a Negro who had been taught to do certain useful and necessary work for his white protectors was a Negro in a fair way of becoming good and, so, most of those who knew of his existence were in sympathy with Dr. Washington; Dr. DuBois, in so far as he mattered at all, was considered troublemaker.

I do not think that in 1912 there were any great number of persons who considered Negro music any more seriously than as one of the art used by a clown to entertain the people he must entertain. Certainly in that remote time there were few who took social equality as a problem—even those who were rabid in the denunciations of the Negro's imagined pretensions always spoke of social equality as a gift that the white race could give or withhold and that, quite properly, the whites were withholding it and always would. The legend of "passing" has grown up, it seems to me, with the consciousness that Harlem exists and thrives. But Mr. Johnson in his title indicates the plot of his Autobiography. The Negro hero of it, after a series of experiences in which is reflected the thought and experience of Negroes in general in their contact with American civilization, does desert his own people and does officially become a white man, marries a white girl who knows his history and has white children. He lives to regret that he did not devote his life to the music that should have been that life's valid reason and, as might have been expected, contributes no solution to a complication that civilization has tangled both for Negroes and white men.

In the Blue Jade Library of 1927 "The Autobiography of an Ex-Colored Man" comes to a public that understands, sympathizes and is antagonistic to its ideas in a degree that never could have been attained by the public of 1912 to which it was first addressed. Mr. Johnson, measured by the importance of his "God's Trombones," is one of the most gifted of Americans and the assertion is made, as will be noticed, without qualification of color. He is, on the testimony of Trombones, a poet and his contributions to music are now being generally acknowledged. His earlier work, the book being reviewed, contains testimony that Mr. Johnson is, too, a literary craftsman of merit. One needs to know, in this age and in this country, what the Negro thinks of the white man and to endeavor to estimate the rapidly changing thought of white men toward the Negro. The first point of view is obtainable from Mr. Johnson's book; I do not know where one can learn what white men think who have abandoned the theory that Negroes are clowns when they are not worse.

WALLACE THURMAN

Novelist, editor, publisher, playwright Wallace Thurman (1902–1934) writes here with the acerbic, keen wit of the satirist he was during his years in Harlem Renaissance circles. Consequently, this review can be read on multiple levels. First, it offers an unsparing critique of *The Autobiography of an Ex-Colored Man* (near its end). Second, it serves as Thurman's rejoinder to two earlier manifestos on African American literary politics of the 1920s, W. E. B. Du Bois's "Criteria for Negro Art" (*Crisis*, October 1926), and Langston Hughes's "The Negro Artist and the Racial Mountain" (*The Nation*, June 16, 1926). Finally, it clarifies the stakes of Johnson's 1928 essay, "Dilemma of the Negro Artist," published the year following Thurman's review but rarely acknowledged as part of this literary debate (reprinted in this volume).

Nephews of Uncle Remus†

It is too bad that negro literature and literary material have had to be exploited by fad finders and sentimentalists. Too bad that the ballyhoo brigade which fostered the so-called negro art "renaissance" has

† From *The Independent*, September 24, 1927, 296–98.

chosen to cheer and encourage indiscriminately anything which claims a negroid ancestry or kinship. For as the overfed child gags when forced to swallow an extra spoonful of half-sour milk, so will the gullible American public gag when too much of this fervid fetish known as negro art is shoveled into its gaping minds and mouths, and the Afro-American artist will find himself as unchampioned and as unimpressive as he was before Carl Van Vechten commenced caroling of his charms in *Vanity Fair*,[1] and the *Survey Graphic* discovered the "new negro" in 1924. Less so; for even in the prerenaissance days any negro who achieved something in literature was regarded with wonderment even by the emancipated white intellectuals. But now so many negroes have written a book or a story or a poem that the pale-faced public is no longer astonished by such phenomena.

There has, of course, been some compensation. Negroes have become more articulate and more coherent in their cries for social justice, and they have also begun to appreciate the advantages of racial solidarity and individual achievement. But speaking purely of the arts, the results of the renaissance have been sad rather than satisfactory, in that critical standards have been ignored, and the measure of achievement has been racial rather than literary. This is supposed to be valuable in a social way, for it is now current that the works produced by negro artists will form the clauses in a second emancipation proclamation, and that because of the negro artists and their works, the Afro-American will reap new fruits of freedom. But this will be true only inasmuch as the negro artist produces dignified and worth-while work. Quick, tricky, atmospheric bits will be as ephemeral as they are sensational, and sentimental propaganda, unless presented in a style both vigorous and new, will have the effect of bird shot rather than that of shrapnel. Which is to say that the negro will not be benefited by mediocre and ephemeral works, even if they are hailed by well-meaning, but for the moment, simple-minded, white critics as works of genius.

There is a constant controversy being waged as to whether or not there can be in America something specifically known as negro literature. One school says yes, pointing out the fact that there are inherent differences between whites and blacks which will cause the artistic works of the two groups to be distinctly different. The other school contends that there can be no such thing in America as an individual negro literature; that the Afro-American is different from the white American in only one respect, namely, skin color, and that when he writes he will observe the same stylistic conventions and literary traditions.

1. Launched in 1913, this magazine (based in New York City) featured writing on popular culture, current affairs, and fashion. Carl Van Vechten published his reviews of and critical essays on African American arts and modernist aesthetics here in the 1920s.

This latter school seems to have the better of the argument. It is true that anthropologically the American negro is really no negro at all. He retains such an ethnological classification only because there seems to be nothing else to call him. There are probably no pure-blooded negroes in America. The present-day American colored man is, as the Anthropological Department of Columbia University has advanced, neither negro, Caucasian, nor Indian, but a combination of all three with the negroid characteristics tending to dominate.[2] Furthermore, the American negro has absorbed all of the American white man's culture and cultural appurtenances. He uses the same language, attends the same schools, reads the same newspapers and books, lives in the same kind of houses, wears the same kind of clothes, and is no more keenly attuned to the African jungle or any of its æsthetic traditions than the average American white man.

It is hard to see, then, that the negro in America can produce an individual literature. What he produces in the field of letters must be listed as American literature, just as the works of the Scotchman Burns or the Irishman Synge are listed as English literature.[3] The negro author can, by writing of certain race characteristics and institutions, introduce a negro note into American literature, just as Yeats, Colum, A. E., Lady Gregory[4] and others introduced a Celtic note in English literature, but in America this can be done by a white writer as well as by a black one, and there is a possibility of its being done much better by the former, in that he may approach his material with a greater degree of objectivity. For example, no negro has written about his own people as beautifully or as sympathetically as has Du Bose Heyward, the author of "Porgy,"[5] purely because the negro writer, for the most part, has seen fit to view his own people as sociological problems rather than as human beings,

2. Thurman alludes to the work of Columbia University anthropologist Franz Boas (1858–1942), specifically to Boas's theories about the cultural roots of human difference. Boas held that human societies varied from one another not because of biological, anatomical, or physiological characteristics. Rather, according to Boas, social learning shaped differences between societies and their peoples. Foregrounding culture as the driving force defining human identity and behavior, Boas repudiated then-reigning concepts of scientific racism, which asserted the opposite view. He extended this idea into the concept of cultural relativism. Through this concept, Boas rejected claims that societies exist on a single, fixed hierarchical scale (with Western societies perennially at the top). Instead, he argued that societies defined norms, values, and behaviors in their own distinct ways, which, though they might be compared, could not be ranked against one another.
3. Poet Robert Burns (1759–1796) and playwright John Millington Synge (1871–1909).
4. Thurman names more poets and playwrights linked to Irish literary nationalism of the 1920s: W. B. Yeats (1865–1939), Padraic Colum (1881–1972), A. E. (pseudonym for George William Russell, 1867–1935), and Augusta, Lady Gregory (1852–1932).
5. Born in Charleston, South Carolina, Heyward (1885–1940) first published *Porgy* as a novel (1925). Several adaptations followed. Heyward scripted it as a stage play in 1927 (co-authored with his wife, Dorothy). He then collaborated with Ira and George Gershwin to produce the folk opera *Porgy and Bess* in 1935. The opera was adapted as a feature film in 1959.

and has written of little else save the constant racial struggle between whites and blacks. Consequently, he has limited himself and left a great deal of fresh vital material untouched.

It was to be hoped that the renaissance would make the negro writer more aware of the value of the literary material provided by his own people. During this time, Du Bose Heyward wrote "Porgy," Julia Peterkin wrote "Green Thursday" and "Black April,"[6] but as yet no negro novelist has taken a hint from these white writers, let alone tried to surpass them.

The question arises: Must the negro author write entirely of his own people? So many of the young negro writers have asked this and then wailed that they did not wish to be known as *negro* artists, but as *artists.* They seemed to think that by writing of white people they could produce better work and have a less restricted field of endeavor. In trying to escape from a condition their own mental attitude makes more harrowing they forget that every facet of life can be found among negroes, who, being human beings, have all the natural emotional and psychological reactions of other human beings. They live, die, hate, love, and procreate. They dance and sing, play and fight. And if art is the universal expressed in terms of the particular, there is, if he has the talent, just as much chance for the negro author to produce great literature by writing of his own people as if he were to write of Chinese or Laplanders. He will be labeled a *negro* artist, with the emphasis on the negro rather than on the artist, only as he fails to rise above the province of petty propaganda, or fails to find a means of escape from both himself and his environment.

The pioneer work done by Jean Toomer in freeing himself from restrictive racial bonds and letting the artist in him take flight where it will, and the determination with which Langston Hughes went about depicting his people, their rhythms and institutions, make these two appear to be the most important literary figures the renaissance has produced. They, of all the young negro writers, have seemed to be the most objective and the most aware of the æsthetic value of literary material in their race. Their work is distinctive because it contains vestiges of that negro note which will characterize the literature produced by truly talented, sincere negro writers. Neither of them is worried by an inferiority complex which makes him wish to escape his race by not writing of it and at the same time binds him more tightly to the whipping post he

6. Peterkin (1880–1961) published her short story cycle *Green Thursday* with Knopf in 1924; her first full-length novel, *Black April*, was issued by Bobbs-Merrill (Indianapolis) in 1927.

would escape. The trouble with Mr. Toomer is that he has written too little. The trouble with Mr. Hughes is that he has written too much, in that he seems to lack, where his own work is concerned, that discriminating sense of selection which makes the complete artist as critical as he is creative. Urged on by a faddistic interest in the unusual, Mr. Hughes has been excessively prolific, and has exercised little restraint. The result is that his work is uneven to an alarming degree, and makes one fear that soon he will expend all of his spiritual energy in bubbling over in his adolescence rather than conserving himself until he matures. He needs to learn the use of the blue pencil and the waste-paper basket.

Eric Walrond can be classed with Mr. Toomer in that when writing of his own people he treats them objectively and as human beings. His "Tropic Death" was marred only by the writer's inability to master completely his style. He was attempting to forge a new method of expression, to escape, as Jean Toomer escaped, from the staid conventionality of stereotyped prose; and he succeeded to a degree that almost made one overlook those passages which were incoherent or tiresome. Nevertheless, it must be admitted that had his style been less esoteric or more controlled, the subject matter would have been more effective, a large order when one remembers such stories as "The Vampire Bat" and "The Black Pin."

Rudolph Fisher has written one very good short story of negro life in Harlem, and a few more which, while vivid with local color, are weak in other respects. "The City of Refuge," which appeared in the *Atlantic Monthly* almost three years ago, and was later incorporated in "The New Negro," that handbook of the renaissance edited by Alain Locke, was one of the first short stories written by a negro about negroes which did not follow the conventional formula. It told the story of a Southern negro's coming to Harlem, the city of refuge, and of his struggles to adapt himself to a strange and complex environment. Here was drama of a new order, drama and color and life, a story as good as it was unusual. One waits expectantly for Mr. Fisher's first novel.[7]

There are many more negro writers who could be discussed in detail if the space allowed. Zora Neale Hurston is a good story-teller, but an indifferent craftsman. Walter White and Jessie Fauset have produced nothing out of the ordinary, or very good. James Weldon Johnson belongs to the elder generation of negro writers, as his "Autobiography of an Ex-Colored Man," recently reissued by Knopf, will prove. Despite Carl Van Vechten's enthusiastic introduction,

7. Rudolph Fisher (1897–1934)'s first novel appeared a year later, *Walls of Jericho* (1928). Fisher is best known for his second effort, *The Conjure Man Dies* (1932), because it is the first detective novel that features only African American characters.

there seems to be no real reason for reprinting this volume in the Blue Jade Library. It is well written, yes, and the author predicts the popularity of ragtime, but its content seems uninspired and stereotyped. Fifteen years ago it might have been a little more than just a well-written book; today it merely makes one wonder why the author didn't call it the autobiography of a colored man rather than that of an ex-colored man. Mr. Johnson's "God's Trombones" is of a different species. The majesty and eloquence of the sermon poems included therein, especially "Go Down Death," are searing and unforgettable. In these poems Mr. Johnson has been the artist rather than the propagandist, and "God's Trombones" will be remembered long after the "Autobiography" has been forgotten, even by sentimental white folk and Jeremiah-like negroes.

Countee Cullen has published three volumes, "Color," "Copper Sun," and "The Ballad of the Brown Girl," all of which tend to convince the critical investigator that although Mr. Cullen can say things beautifully and impressively, he really has nothing new to say, nor no new way in which to say it. He follows the tradition of a literary poet. His lyrics of love and death are reminiscent of Keats, Housman, and Edna Millay[8], and one gets the impression that Mr. Cullen writes not from his own experience, but from vicarious literary experiences which are not intense enough to be real and vital. His poetry is not an escape from life in the big sense, but from the narrow world in which he has been caged, and from which he seems to hare made no great effort to escape.

Undoubtedly Mr. Cullen has more talent than any of his colored contemporaries. What he lacks is originality of theme and treatment, and the contact with life necessary to have had actual, rather than vicarious, emotional experiences. He is still young, and perhaps when some of the fanfare aroused when it was discovered that a *negro* could write beautiful conventional verse has died down, he will be able to work out his own destiny. He has far to go if only he is given the chance and stimulation.

In a recent issue of *Opportunity*, journal of negro life, there are reviews of two recent books. Both of the reviewers were white poets, both books were by negro poets. The first was of Countee Cullen's "Copper Sun," and in dithyrambic prose the reviewer went to every possible verbal excess in praising the volume. According to him Countee Cullen is *the* thing in American poetry—he equals

8. John Keats (1795–1821), British Romantic-era poet; A. E. Housman (1859–1936), Cambridge University poet and classicist scholar; Edna St. Vincent Millay (1892–1960), American poet best-known for writing sonnets, a genre central to Countee Cullen's work.

Housman and surpasses Edna Millay. There is more such lyric nonsense, all done in good faith, no doubt, but of no value whatsoever either to Mr. Cullen or to the race to which he belongs. The second review, while less turgid and more restrained, was excessive in its praise of "God's Trombones," and in neither piece was there any constructive criticism or intelligent evaluation.

These two reviews are typical of the attitude of a certain class of white critics toward negro writers. Urged on by their desire to do what in their opinion is a "service," they dispense with all intelligence and let their sentimentality run riot. Fortunately, most of the younger negro writers realize this and, as most negroes have always done, are laughing up their sleeves at the antics of their nordic patronizers. It is almost a certainty that Countee Cullen and Langston Hughes know full well that there are perhaps a half dozen young white poets in these United States doing just as good if not better work than they, and who are not being acclaimed by the public or pursued by publishers purely because a dash of color is the style in literary circles today.

If the negro writer is to make any appreciable contribution to American literature it is necessary that he be considered as a sincere artist trying to do dignified work rather than as a highly trained dog doing trick dances in a public square. He is, after all, motivated and controlled by the same forces which motivate and control a white writer, and like him he will be mediocre or good, succeed or fail as his ability deserves. A man's complexion has little to do with his talent. He either has it or has it not, and despite the dictates of spiritually starved white sophisticates genius does not automatically descend upon one because one's grandmother happened to be sold down the river "befo' de wah."

BEN RAY REDMAN

From Old Wine in New Bottles†

"The Autobiography of an Ex-Colored Man" is, as Carl Van Vechten states it to be in his introduction to the narrative, "a remarkable book." First published in 1912, it must have come as a shock to man white readers who found described in it phases of colored society of whose existence they had never dreamed. To-day it holds no revelations for any one who has even the slightest acquaintance with Negro life and literature, but it has lost none of its value as psychological history. Mr. Johnson wrote from so sure and complete a knowledge

† From the *New York Herald Tribune*, October 2, 1927.

that it is difficult to believe in the invention of even the story's smallest detail. The narrative is a trifle spare—a fuller treatment of certain topics and episodes would have not been amiss—but it may be this very sparseness that gives the book verisimilitude. It seems not the work of a professional writer, but that of a man bent upon telling his own story for the sake of his own soul. And it is really that, despite the fact that it is not Mr. Johnson's own story. Writing as a man whose white skin permitted him to mingle naturally with white people and whose African blood made him view the world through the eyes of black people, the author placed himself in a position from which he could view Negro life at once from within and without. For those who are ignorant of cultured Negroes, their aspirations and their accomplishments this book will prove a perfect introduction to an important phase of contemporary life.

CHARLES WILLIS THOMPSON

The Negro Question†

Without doubt there are a great many persons passing for pure Caucasians who have some negro ancestry. There is a superstition that after the mixture of blood reaches the octoroon state[1] sterility ensues, because nobody has ever seen a mixed-blood below the grade of octoroon; or if he has, he simply raises the degree to the sixteenth drop of blood and rests on the same superstition. The reason why nobody sees a negro whiter than an octoroon is that after that stage the individual decides to call himself white and deny all negro "taint," and nobody can prove the contrary.

As for the reason why a sixteenth-drop negro, or even an audacious octoroon, changes from one race to the other, it is simple enough. It is that life in this country is more comfortable for a Caucasian than for a negro and the rewards are greater.

This is a dramatic situation, and Mr. Johnson, well known as an eloquent and powerful writer, has made the most of it in this pretended autobiography—the story of a negro who deliberately changed races. But the theme is even larger. The book, as Mr. Van Vechten says, discusses "pretty nearly every phase of negro life, North and South and even in Europe," and "reads like a composite autobiography of the negro race." It ranges from the half-brute to be found frequently in the South, the factory worker and the Tenderloin sport of New York to the intellectuals.

† From *The New York Times*, October 16, 1927.
1. Term used to designate mixed-race persons as having one-eighth African ancestry.

It is truth in the form of fiction; a study so rushingly written that it has all the fascination of a novel of the highest class. One of its most thought-provoking phases to the white reader is a thing which to this reviewer's knowledge has not been dealt with elsewhere—the fact that while the negro knows what man thinks of him, the white man has no idea of the negro's view of him. Partly, Mr. Johnson thinks, this is due to the negro's ability to mask his feelings so that he can appear to be clowning foolishly while his mind and heart are at their most serious. But that is by no means all of it. There is a real and striking difference, of which the white man gets no glimpse.

To illustrate: Once at Atlantic City the writer was listening to the talk of two negro women. One was describing a white man she had known very well, and she said: "He was a fine man, a splendid man; he was gentle without losing his manliness. Why, he did not seem like a white man; he was almost like a colored man!" She brought it out as if she were paying him the highest compliment imaginable. I wondered what the white man would have thought if he had heard her.

The first part of Mr. Johnson's book deals with his hero as a colored man, North and South. He is a musical genius, and conceives the idea of aiding in the upbringing of his race by devoting his talent to a welding of negro and classical music. To that end he returns from France and renews his studies of his race in the South. His disheartenments and disillusionments follow so fast as to bring him to the conviction that the game is not worth the candle; but what finally decides him to change his race is the lynching by burning of a negro. He is at pains to describe the orderly and what might almost be called the respectable character of the lynchers, which powerfully convinces him that in any demonstration of the claims of his race he is running against a stone wall. He goes North, changes his name, becomes a white man to all appearances, drops his ambitions and his genius and becomes a successful business man.

At this point the reviewer diffidently offers an objection to the thesis of Mr. Johnson, who of course knows more about such cases than I do. I have never seen a lynching, but I have talked with many who have, and they all tell me that the lynchers are the toughs and riff-raff of the community, mostly drunk, led perhaps by a foolish man or half dozen men of education, and that the rest of the intelligent whites remain aloof, either from fear, disgust or indifference. I have seen lynchers after the event, and they verify this description.

At the moment when, in Europe, the hero of the book determines to devote his genius to righting the wrongs of his race through example, a white friend attempts to dissuade him by showing him the futility of it, and utters these striking words:

> Perhaps some day, through study and observation, you will come to see that evil is a force, and, like the physical and chemical forces, we cannot annihilate it; we may only change its form. We light upon one evil and hit it with all the might of our civilization, but only succeed in scattering it into a dozen other forms. We hit slavery through a great war. Did we destroy it? No, we only changed it into hatred between sections of the country; in the South, into political corruption and chicanery, the degradation of the blacks through peonage, unjust laws, unfair and cruel treatment; and the degradation of the whites by their resort to these practices, the paralyzation of the public conscience, and the ever overhanging dread of what the future may bring.
>
> Modern civilization hit ignorance of the masses through the means of popular education. What has it done but turn ignorance into anarchy, socialism, strikes, hatred between poor and rich, and universal discontent? In like manner, modern philanthropy hit at suffering and disease through asylums and hospitals; it prolongs the sufferers' lives, it is true, but is at the same time sending down strains of insanity and weakness into future generations.
>
> My philosophy of life is this: Make yourself as happy as possible, and try to make those happy whose lives come into contact with yours; but to attempt to right the wrongs and ease the sufferings of the world in general is a waste of effort. You had just as well try to bale the Atlantic by pouring the water into the Pacific.

Mr. Johnson's pale-faced pessimist uttered these words prior to 1912 and had no knowledge of what would come of the efforts in the next fifteen years to right the world by prohibited "commercialized vice" and the drinking of liquor. The hero of the book did not agree with him at the moment, but the story, if it can be called such, ends with an unanswered question. Should the hero, as he finally did, have acted on this philosophy and deserted his race to become rich and influential, or should he have stuck to his guns in spite of all the lynchers and gone down to destruction in a heroic effort to uplift those who, in spite of his white skin, were fellow-negroes? It is a question not limited to negroes, and every man, as it is presented to him, must answer it for himself.

Mr. Johnson is so well known a writer that there is no temptation to comment on his style. Still, not to omit anything, let us take this fragment from his hero's first impressions of New York as he steams into the harbor:

> New York City is the most fatally fascinating thing in America. She sits like a great witch at the gate of the country, showing her

> alluring white face and hiding her crooked hands and feet under the folds of her wide garments—constantly enticing thousands from far within, and tempting those who come from across the seas to go no farther.

This is a fit prelude to the hero's immediate but temporary fall into crap-shooting and worse forms of negro dissipation in the New York Forties, in the course of which the author gives more realistic and truthful descriptions than any I recall written by white men. He is as merciless toward his own race as toward the whites.

Strictly speaking, the book is not new. It was published anonymously in 1912 by a forgotten and extinct firm and speedily went out of print. But it was such a true and all-embracing study of the race question from every angle, white and colored both, that the demand for it persisted until Mr. Knopf brought it out of the grave, clad in the beautiful dress one expects from him and often gets.

ALICE DUNBAR NELSON

Alice Dunbar Nelson (1875–1935) elaborates on the brief but insightful analysis she published in the *Washington* (DC) *Eagle* just two months earlier. Here, she develops what is probably the most perceptive review *The Autobiography of an Ex-Colored Man* ever received. A short-story writer and novelist herself, Dunbar-Nelson demonstrates a remarkable appreciation of the novel's publication history, its experimental ambitions, and its cultural commentary all at once. Given the critical frameworks set by Carl van Vechten's introduction to the 1927 edition, Dunbar-Nelson's categories of analysis make for a striking comparison.

Our Book Shelf†

It was in 1912 that the reading public among Negroes and friends of Negroes was shaken to its inner core by the appearance of a book, surely the strangest that had ever been written by or about the Negro. *The Autobiography of an Ex-Colored Man*, published anonymously, evoked wide and varied speculation. Was the author really a Negro? Was it not perhaps some white man, who having observed the phenomenon of the fair colored man, slipped over into the ranks of the Caucasians, was perhaps venting his delicate satire on the American public? Negroes generally believed that the author was "one of ours". There were too many little subtle ear-marks of the man born, bred and nutured in the traditions of the race. No mere white man

† From *Opportunity*, November 1927, 337–38. This African American periodical, published by the National Urban League, was a major venue for black authors during the Harlem Renaissance.

could hope to penetrate into the mysteries of racial psychology. But the wonder died down, as wonders have a fashion of doing, and the book was out of print before the secret of its authorship leaked out and became generally known.

But the memory of the remarkable work clung, and therefore it is felt that Alfred A. Knopf has performed a distinct service to present day literature by bringing out another edition of this delicate satire. For satire it is, couched in the most subtle form. The same sort of satire that Swift perpetrated in *Gulliver's Travels*, bland, lucid, arresting by its very naiveté.[1] Or perhaps the kind of disarming narrative that Defoe writes in his apparent autobiographies, the supreme art of putting oneself into the soul of another, albeit that other has probably only existed in one's imagination.[2]

Carl Van Vechten has written an introduction to this late edition. He acknowledges his indebtedness to the book in making his studies of the Negro, and compares it to Booker Washington's *Up From Slavery* which it rather resembles in manner and diction. Its dispassionate, impersonal air, with complete lack of verbiage, fine writing, hysterics, passion, adjectives or rhetorical involutions does suggest Mr. Washington's style. But as suggested by Mr. Van Vechten, the limitations of *Up From Slavery* are not to be found in the Autobiography.

Fifteen years ago, when the book appeared, there was no Harlem, as we know it now. Negro night life had moved from the Thirties, which are described in the Autobiography, to the Fifties. The early scenes of the book lie in the Thirities, twenty-five years ago, in the hey-dey of George Walker and Cole and Johnson and hansom ccabs and the Floradora sextette[3] and all the rest of the hectic days of the early twentieth century. The child of mysterious parentage, such as the author describes himself in the earlier chapters, was common enough in the South of thirty or forty years ago, but fortunately no more. And for that the race may heave a sigh of relief and thankfulness. Jazz was unknown, but Lottie Collins[4] had glorified rag-time, and the big Negro shows of the time were making it classic. Cabarets were "Clubs" and vice was gilded, not painted. Life was a bubble and froth in the cup of pleasure, but its bubbles were perhaps caused by real champagne, and not by bootleg substitutes.

1. Jonathan Swift (1667–1745) published *Gulliver's Travels* in 1726.
2. Daniel Defoe (1660–1731)'s *Robinson Crusoe* (1719) deceived its early readership by crediting his title character as author of the novel.
3. This British troupe of vaudeville dancers enjoyed a long run at New York City's Casino Theater in 1900 following their star-making performances in "Floradora," an imperialist-themed musical first staged in London (1899).
4. When she toured the United States in 1889, British singer and dancer Lottie Collins (1865–1910) picked up the popular tune and turn of phrase "Ta-ra-ra Boom-de-ray!" and popularized it (with the spectacular flash of can-can high-kicks) on the London stage in 1891.

All this Mr. Johnson has made live in his pages. Somehow you move with him through all his vicissitudes—in the little Connecticut town, among the Spanish speaking cigar-makers, in the beautiful town of Jacksonville (here certainly Mr. Johnson was at home), in the noisome dens of the gambling clubs of New York; in France, in England, and back at home in his own country. He makes you feel his griefs from the very supression of his own emotions. And here is where the sheer art of the book is evident. The author expresses both objectively and subjectively emotions both complex and powerful. He is shaken to the soul by grief, tormented by indecisions, perplexed by grave problems, and you feel it all with him, albeit yon are, at the same time, standing with him on the outside of the emotional area watching the writhings of the nameless individual who acts as protagonist.

Another great claim upon the imagination of the present day reader lies in the musical hints which Mr. Johnson gives of what he was later to elaborate. The "Ex-Coloured Man" was primarily a musician, and it was as a musician that he had hoped to create his career. Hence his interest in the folk-songs of the Negro, and his dismay when he found he must throw over his chosen career if he were to be white. Had he lived now, it would have only served as a whet to his ambition, whether white or black, to write of the music of the Negro. In the book we find precursors of the scholarly and exhaustive introductions to the two books of Negro Spirituals, edited by Mr. Johnson, and to *God's Trombones*. There are glimpses of the classic "Singing Johnson" and "John Brown, the Preacher", now well-known to Mr. Johnson's readers. "The day will come," he avers, "when this slave music will be the most treasured heritage of the American Negro." A bold prophecy, but that day has come, and more than that, for this slave music is the biggest thing in the modern musical world.

The book runs the whole gamut of the life of an American Negro not only twenty-five or thirty years ago, but of today, from the debauched slave woman with her octoroon offspring, to the very latest style in lynchings—which the author describes with so few lines that it seems almost like a dry-point etching, nauseatingly vivid and terse. It describes every variety of American Negro from the crudest field hand to the cultured professional man and their wives in the inner circles of fashionable Washington. In a small space he has epitomized the life and soul of the Negro, as surprisingly true then as now. There have been additions to the charmed circle of the culturally elect, yet the soul of the race is essentially the same. And the lynchings go on as merrily and as vividly, yea, even more so, as ever, so that the thoughtful Negro may still feel "Shame at being identified with a people that could with impunity be treated worse than animals. For certainly the law would restrain and punish the malicious burning alive of animals."

We, who must be always looking for the moral of any story, may rejoice to find it in the last sentence, "I cannot repress the thought that after all, I have chosen the lesser part, that I have sold my birthright for a mess of pottage." For so it must ever be for the man or the woman of any race or nationality whatever, who turns his back upon his own people for his own fancied gain—the canker worm of self-distrust and shame at his own cowardice will eat at his heart until he shall close his eyes upon a deceitful world.

MARY WHITE OVINGTON

In Black and White[†]

The Autobiography of an Ex-Colored Man reads as if it had been written yesterday, but it is a reprint of a book dated 1912. To be sure, there are slight differences—the New York cabaret is a "club" on West Fifty-Third Street instead of a dance hall in Harlem; the new music is ragtime, not jazz; and the young people play progressive euchre[1] instead of bridge. But the Negro moves through the New York world of 1912 as he moves through the streets in 1927. And the problem of race that he faces was the same then as now.

The quiet detachment about the Autobiography made it a matter of speculation when it appeared as to whether it was biography or fiction. Librarians did not know how to classify it, and many were the eager questions asked of Negroes and their friends. The book was anonymous and opened with the statement, "I know that in writing the following pages I am divulging the great secret of my life." A colored man was "passing," and yet he dared to tell his story! After a little, the author became known, his brown face proclaimed that he had not told his own tale. But perhaps it was some one of his friends? Conjecture continued. This reprint dispels any doubt as to the books being fiction. But as Carl Van Vechten, who writes the introduction, says: "It reads like a composite autobiography of the Negro race in the United States in modern times."

† From *Survey Graphic*, November 1, 1927. Mary White Ovington (1865–1951) was one of the white co-founders of the National Association for the Advancement of Colored People and, thus, a colleague of Johnson, who also served as an officer in this organization.

1. Straight euchre is a card game played by four people, in teams of two, where the goal is to bid for high-value cards and trump opponents into losing theirs. In progressive euchre, players constantly change seats but in a predetermined order. Mixing and matching partners stresses the social play of the game, rather than competition. The ex-colored man meets his wife at such an affair; see 108.

The book has at once received a warm welcome. Especially in the South appreciation has been genuine and sincere. Here is a colored man who can see both sides of the question. Who can even feel a certain admiration for the dogged Texan who says to his northern acquaintance: "You might argue from now until hell freezes over, and you might convince me that you're right, but you'll never convince me that I'm wrong." Indeed, he hero of the story is a length defeated by the spirit of the Texan, and leaves his race when he sees the depths of degradation that it must suffer. He marries a white woman, becomes part of the white world—and at the end wonders whether he has not sold his birthright for a mess of pottage.

An engrossing story and a quiet, unprejudiced discussion of the race question. The Jade Library is enriched by this new volume. As Mr. Johnson stands on its shelves he may run sides with Gautier and Goldoni.[2] It's rare company.

James Weldon Johnson, colored, has a more interesting life than anything he can imagine for his hero. We hope that some time he will give it to us to read. In the meanwhile this entertaining novel contains many of his views, thus reflecting the opinion of one of the sanest and at the same time one of the most fearless men in public life today.

NAT J. FERBER

The Book World†

The house of Alfred A. Knopf offers James Weldon Johnson's THE AUTOBIOGRAPHY OF AN EX-COLORED MAN in timely season. In a day when 300,000 negroes overnight displaced in a limited area the City of New York 200,000 whites, one is prone to pause and make inquiry into when and how this was done. Certainly, few were cognizant of the sweeping change, effected without offensive aggression on the one side and protest or reprisal on the other. The author could not treat of this phenomenon in this work, first published in 1912, because the northward march of his people in great numbers is rather recent. But in his poignant story of the white boy in whom there flowed a strain of negro blood, Johnson foretells the change

2. French poet, art critic, and journalist Theophilé Gauthier (1811–1872) toured Spain in 1840. His account of that journey, *Voyage en Espagne* (1845), was translated by Catherine Alison Phillips and reprinted by Knopf as *A Romantic in Spain* (1926). First published in 1787, *The Memoirs of Carlo Goldoni* (an 18th-century Italian playwright and librettist) was translated by John Black and released through Knopf's Blue Jade Library in 1926 as well.

† From the *New York American*, November 9, 1927.

that was to be, the change that has since made long strides. Although its title implies that this work is an autobiography, it is plainly not the story of the life of the author. Rather does this pulsating, throbbing document reveal the outlook of a people through the medium of one man, a fictional character. Through him is revealed an awakening of a people long oppressed, an almost passive revulsion against this oppression which, inevitably, started the race northward.

It is needless to quote from the early history, so well told by the author. The book has been discussed for more than a decade. Only because of the recent interest in the negro and because it was a work that one sought vainly did the present publishers cause its reissue. It is in the latter portions of his story that Mr. Johnson paints the scene that compelled the current exodus, a movement that is rapidly changing the character of New York, Chicago, and other large Northern cities. Political and economic questions aside, there is more than a hint in his scene:

> "It was over before I realized that time had elapsed. Before I could make myself believe that what I saw was really happening, I was looking at a scorched post, a smouldering fire, blackened bones, charred fragments sifting through the coils of chains; and the smell of burnt flesh—human flesh—was in my nostrils."

Despite this harrowing picture, the author can still recall that, man to man, the Southern white, with a degree of justice, claims that he loves the negro more than does the Northern white. He points out why and where this is so.

Many and varied are the phases of negro life and its relation to the dominant white touched upon by this writer. Their places socially at work, at play, in the schools and in politics are treated soberly and with keen discernment. One is struck with the vision of the author as regards developments here. As far back as 1912 he foresaw that instead of a deluge of ragtime based on or—as is more often the case, stolen from—the classics, there might be classics based on old negro folk songs. Here Mr. Johnson anticipated George Gershwin and his Rhapsody in Blue[1] by almost fifteen years. The work throughout is prophetic no less than an absorbing life record. It is valuable, above all, for the candor with which is given the viewpoint of the negro, the attitude of the negro, hitherto denied an attitude toward the white man. A remarkable document is this new addition to the Knopf Blue Jade Library an addition which many will receive with keen interest.

1. See 241, n. 6.

E. H. W.

An Ex-Colored Man†

Although this remarkable revelation of the conditions which a Negro must face in America was written before Harlem existed, it furnishes indirectly an explanation of why a miniature city, with a culture and life of its own, has sprung up beyond the Park.[1] First published anonymously in 1912, the "Autobiography" is a dispassionate statement of the educated Negro's viewpoint. The passing of fifteen years has merely enhanced its value as an interpretation of the Negro problem.

The story, which is probably not wholly autobiographical, introduces one first to a handsome, intelligent little boy in a New England town who learns of his Negro blood through the callous stupidity of a school teacher. That cruel enlightenment altered the universe for him, and precipitated him into his subsequent adventures in the intolerant South, in the Negro gambling dens of New York, and eventually in Europe. There were few phases of Negro life which this young man did not experience, and as the injustice and bitterness of anti-Negro feeling became clear to him, he finally decided to take advantage of his white skin, to desert his race, and to "pass." Without employing either rhetoric or rancor, Mr. Johnson exposes the shameful prejudices which made this "passing" advisable.

Despite the importance of the "Autobiography" as a human and sociological document, its value as a piece of literature is not equally great. In this book, though not in some of his other writings, Mr. Johnson lacks the power to convince one emotionally of the stark, hard truth of the scenes which he presents. He fumbles his climaxes, even when the material offers him superb opportunities. Moreover, he does not distinguish with sufficient clearness between the trivial and the supremely relevant. One could spare much of the long account of the hero's youth, but of the psychological reactions which accompany the phenomenon of "passing" one is told only too little. The "Autobiography" is an excellent, honest piece of work. One wishes that it were even better.

† From *The New Republic*, February 1, 1928, 303–04. The review's author (E. H. W.) may be the critic Edmund Wilson, who worked as an editor at this liberal magazine during the 1920s. Reprinted by permission of the publisher.

1. Central Park, in New York City.

RICHARD DENIS CHARQUES

An Ex-Coloured Man†

First issued anonymously in 1912 when its author, it appears, was United States Consul to Nicaragua, this book, which has since been much sought after, was well worth republication. It is quite fair to describe it as "a classic in negro literature"; few other books throw so clear a light upon the psychological factors in the negro problem in America; and there is probably none which is at the same time so skillful and telling a piece of imaginative writing. Mr. Johnson, who is well-known at the present day as a poet, has a gift of story-telling which is rather rare; he can set down social facts of a serious and disturbing kind with extreme simplicity and, although his sympathies are never in question, without appearing to plead a case. How much of the calm even tone of the narrative is directly owning to the author's experience is beside the point; it is clear that the story could not have been told to greater advantage than Mr. Johnson's objective and dispassionate treatment achieves.

The hero of his imaginative autobiography is a young man of negro origin whose colour safeguards him against the normal handicaps of his race; whose negro strain is a matter of racial consciousness, not of physical appearance. Many Europeans do not realize that, largely as a result of miscegenation, of course, many persons of negro stock in America are often quite fair-skinned; in many cases, indeed, they have none whatever of the physical characteristics of their race and are able to pass as "white." The phenomenon of "passing," as it is called, is more common than is generally recognized; and the peculiar interest of Mr. Johnson's story lies in the sympathy and common sense with which it treats the attitude of the educated negro, not merely to the white man, but to his own race. Perhaps the crux of the social problem for the negro in the United States lies, as the author points out almost in the first few pages of his book, in "a sort of dual personality"; one aspect of him is disclosed only in the freemasonry of his own race.

And this [Mr. Johnson writes] is the dwarfing, warping, distorting influence which operates upon each and every coloured man in the United States. He is forced to take his outlook on all things, not from the view-point of a citizen, or a man, or even a human being, but from the view-point of being a *coloured* man. It is wonderful to me that the race has progressed so broadly as it has, since most of its

† From an unsigned review in *The Times Literary Supplement* (London), March 22, 1928.

thought and all of its activity must run through the narrow neck of this one funnel.

On the subject of "passing" itself Mr. Johnson illustrates the pressure which the sentiment of the country exerts on the race, on their social opportunities and means of livelihood, by advertisements in newspapers for waiters, bell-boys, or elevator men, which read: "Light coloured man wanted." His hero, after many vicissitudes of fortune, in which his love of music largely shapes his career, is still regarded as a white man; but he asks himself at the end whether he has sold his birthright for a mess of pottage. The book is an extremely valuable study of negro psychology, but it is also a genuine human document. Incidentally it is remarkable for its prophetic judgment on the subject of "rag-time" and negro spirituals. The four things which demonstrate, Mr. Johnson writes, the negro's originality and artistic conception are the Uncle Remus stories, the Jubilee songs, rag-time music, and the cakewalk.

Contemporary Reviews: 1948

When New American Library reprinted *The Autobiography of an Ex-Colored Man* as a cheaply priced paperback in 1948, the firm hoped the book would reach a mass audience. However, the novel did not stir the same levels of interest with book reviewers in 1948 as it did in 1912 and 1927.

Reprinted here is the press coverage the novel earned during its first year of re-publication (1948–49). With the exception of a brief citation in the *New York Times*, *ECM* was commented upon primarily by the African American press.[1]

NICK AARON FORD

Here Are the Ten Best Novels by and about Colored People†

Within the past eight years the colored novelist has come of age. Since 1940, four colored Americans have written novels in the best-seller class.[1] Two of them—Frank Yerby and Willard Motley—have won such recognition with stories outside the realm of racial life. (Although Yerby's *Foxes of Harrow* and *The Vixens* have some colored characters, they are primarily stories of white people; while Motley's *Knock on Any Door*, which is still

1. In "Books Published Today," *The New York Times*, June 30, 1948, 23, *ECM* is listed as a nonfiction work. A decade earlier, the *Times* acknowledged that the novel was "purely a work of fiction," to correct its obituary of Johnson; see "Books and Authors," August 7, 1938, 81.

† From *The Baltimore Afro-American*, April 3, 1948, M3. Used with permission from the Afro-American Newspapers Archives and Research Center. Literary scholar Ford (1904–1982) taught at Morgan State College, a historically black institution in Baltimore. For more on his career, see Lawrence P. Jackson, *The Indignant Generation: A Narrative History of African American Writers and Critics, 1934–1960* (Princeton: Princeton University Press, 2011), 334–38.

1. Ford most likely refers to Richard Wright's *Native Son* (1940) and *Black Boy* (1945) and Ann Petry's *The Street* (1946), along with the works he cites by Frank Yerby and Willard Motley, published in 1946, 1947, and 1947, respectively.

among the ten best sellers of the nation, is a story of Italian Americans.)[2]

I have set up two criteria for selecting the ten best novels in the order of their goodness. First, the literary quality of the work must at least be average. Second, the subject matter must be presented in a manner that can contribute to race relations.

Because of the desperate need in our generation to enlist all forms of education and propaganda in the fight for racial equality and brotherhood, I place greater emphasis on the latter criterion.

I know some critics will say I am sacrificing "art for art's sake" to "art for propaganda's sake."[3] I acknowledge their right to disagree. But I stick to my guns.

[Ford discusses his top three choices: *Native Son* (1940), by Richard Wright; *The Street* (1946), by Ann Petry; and *Blood on the Forge* (1941), by William Attaway.]

In fourth place I rank *The Autobiography of an Ex-Colored Man* by James Weldon Johnson. It is written in the first person, and the language is simple and convincing.

The plot is centered around a light-skinned colored man who experiences the prejudices, discrimination, and contemptible treatment that his race is subjected to.

It contrasts with these attitudes the greater respect of European peoples whom the hero encounters in his travels abroad. It emphasizes the talents and achievements of colored people.

By a wise selection of details it builds up a psychological concept which finally drives the hero to his decision to forsake the race and live ever afterwards as a white man. He marries a white woman and vows to give his children the right to happiness which they could not attain as colored Americans.

[Ford goes on to discuss the remaining six novels on his list: Walter White's *Fire in the Flint*; Jessie Fauset's *There Is Confusion*; Arna Bontemps's *Black Thunder*; Rudolph Fisher's *The Walls of Jericho*; W. E. B. Du Bois's *Dark Princess*; and Jessie Fauset's *Comedy, American Style*.][4]

2. Yerby (1916–1991) and Motley (1909–1965) were among several mid-twentieth-century African American novelists who featured white protagonists in their work. For more on this trend, see Arthur P. Davis, "Integration and Race Literature," *Phylon* 17.2 (1956): 141–46; Gene Andrew Jarrett, ed., *African American Literature beyond Race: An Alternative Reader* (New York: New York University Press, 2006); and John Charles Williamson, *Abandoning the Black Hero: Sympathy and Privacy in the Postwar African American White Life Novel* (New Brunswick: Rutgers University Press, 2012).
3. Though Ford's phrasing alludes to the debate sparked by W. E. B. Du Bois's 1926 essay "Criteria for Negro Art," *Crisis* (October 1926): 290–97, his position was no doubt informed by his Ph.D. thesis, The Negro Author's Use of Propaganda in Imaginative Literature" (1945), and by the growing rapport between African American writers and the Communist Party during the 1930s.
4. These works are surprising choices. First published during the 1920s and 1930s, none of them were reprinted during the 1940s, unlike *ECM*.

Book Publisher Honors James Weldon Johnson†

June 17 was James Weldon Johnson day among literary groups throughout the country in a program sponsored by the New American Literary of World Literature, publisher of Penguin Signet books and Pelican Mentor books.

For this observation New American Literary printed a special edition of Johnson's first book. "The Autobiography of an Ex-Colored Man," the first of the "passing" books.

Johnson is remembersd as author of seven books, editor of three and a number of first in several fields. He is best remembered for writing the words to "Lift Every Voice and Sing."

Some of his first were: Negro lawyer admitted to the bar in Jacksoonville, Fla., first to edit a Negro owned daily newspaper, first Negro professor to hold seminars on Negro life at the University of North Carolina in 1927, first field secretary of the NAACP, first Negro executive secretary of the NAACP, first colored visiting professor at New York university and others.

Books written by him include "Along This Way," "St. Peter Relates an Incident," "God's Trombones." "Negro Americans, What Now?" "Fifty Years and Others Poems" and "Black Manhattan."

He edited "The Book of American Negro Poetry," "The Book of American Negro Spirituals" and "The Second Book of Negro Spiritpals."

J. RANDOLPH FISHER

Looks at Books: James W. Johnson Classic Reprinted‡

A reprinting of James Weldon Johnson's "The Autobiography of an Ex-Coloured Man" has appeared as a Pelican Mentor Book (New American Library of World Literature, New York 16, 35 cents). This fictional life-story has long held a prominent place among race relations literature.

Here we see the development of a distinguished poet, musician, scholar, cosmopolite, diplomat, linguist who identifies himself as a

† From *The Atlanta Daily World*, June 22, 1948, 1. Reprinted by permission of the publisher.
‡ From *The Pittsburgh Courier*, September 4, 1948, 13.

polished man of the world. His development into manhood, extraordinary experiences, praiseworthy achievements make perhaps the most fascinating life-story in the literature of the American Negro. Indeed in this respect it is probably surpassed not even by the author's real autobiography ("Along This Way"), which has got for itself a secure place among those books we are wont to designate as classics.

* * *

Reared as a white boy, Mr. Johnson's becoming aware of his being a Negro impresses him indelibly. "Like my first spanking, it is one of the few incidents in my life that I can remember clearly. . . . This is the dwarfing, warping, distorting influence which operates upon each and every colored man in the United States."

This is an admirable account of an individual and a people who have had placed upon them "the brand," because God made them colored. This is a courageous book by a great man.

Savannah, Ga.

J. SAUNDERS REDDING

Book Review†

When The Autobiography of an Ex-Coloured Man was published anonymously in 1912, it had so unusual an approach to the complex of bi-racial living in America that it repelled the very readers it was intended to attract.

Small groups of the intelligentsia speculated on its authorship, and "Who wrote The Autobiography of an Ex-Coloured Man?" became as popular as a guessing game among the elite as "Button, Button?" among the lowly.

The author, who was James Weldon Johnson, had the experience of being introduced to "and talking with one man who tacitly admitted" that he had written the book.

Classic Republished

Reissued in 1927, what reader success the book had was due to timeliness, for the year marked the peak in the Harlem renaissance

† From *The Baltimore Afro-American*, March 12, 1949, B9. Used with permission from the Afro-American Newspapers Archives and Research Center. This review's author was a renowned novelist and major literary critic during the post-World War II decades. For an overview of Redding's career (1906–1988), see Jackson, *Indignant Generation*, Chap. 1.

movement. But the approach, the detached point of view, and even the manner of writing were still unusual in Negro fiction.

Since that time, however, The Autobiography has become a minor classic, and now Pelican Mentor Books has republished it at a price everyone can afford.

Mr. Johnson was certainly not the first colored man to write fiction about colored people.

As a matter of fact, for the stretch of time between 1895 and 1915, writing fiction about colored people seemed to occupy the spare hours of every colored man who had spare hours and as much as a third grade education. What they produced was a monotypical and glorified picture of life that simply did not jibe with their own experience of reality.

Except in so far as the interest of the social scholar is concerned, the result was nothing. Then along came James Weldon Johnson with a dispassionate, unbiased interpretation of what it feels like to be a colored man.

For those who read the book in 1927, it was like getting a cleansing draught of fresh air in a smokefilled room. Curiously enough, reading it now still gives the same sensation.

A Simple Story

The story Mr. Johnson tells is simple and can be outlined in a few words. Told in the first person, it concerns itself with a talented young colored boy who, migrating from Georgia to Connecticut with his mother, tries to make a place in life.

After high school, he goes to Florida, thence back to New York where his musical talent earns him a precarious living. A series of circumstances, including a murder, force him to take a job as traveling companion to an eccentric millionaire. He tours Europe, returns to America, and after a time, going over into the white race, wins renown, security, and a white wife.

He is happy with her and with the children she bears him before her early death. Renown, economic sufficiency, lovely children—what could one want more? But in the end, the hero feels that after all he had "chosen the lesser part," that he had "sold his birthright for a mess of pottage."

The Autobiography of an Ex-Coloured Man is more memorable historically than artistically. Many of its incidents seemed, forced; much of its writing strained and artificial; but its fundamental truth is indisputable. Along the steep road of the development of Negro American fiction. The Autobiography is a milestone.

CRITICISM

ROBERT B. STEPTO

Lost in a Quest: James Weldon Johnson's *The Autobiography of an Ex-Coloured Man*†

Approaching the novel as a "textual event" but resisting the impetus to categorize it as modernist, Robert Stepto examines how *ECM* borrows from and recasts the conventions of African American writing across the nineteenth and early-twentieth centuries. In Stepto's view, *ECM* should be understood as a "generic" narrative—that is, as a text whose literary frameworks are at once grounded in African American expressive culture but are also free-ranging on their own.

> I sat amazed. I had been turning classic music into rag-time, a comparatively easy task; and this man had taken rag-time and made it classic. The thought came across me like a flash—It can be done, why can't I do it? From that moment my mind was made up. I clearly saw the way of carrying out the ambition I had formed when a boy.
> —James Weldon Johnson,
> *The Autobiography of an Ex-Coloured Man*

> A friend told me
> He'd risen above jazz.
> I leave him there.
> —Michael S. Harper, "Alone"‡

By the time our journey through Afro-American narrative literature arrives at Johnson's *The Autobiography of an Ex-Coloured Man*, first published anonymously in 1912, several assumptions about the literature are presumed as given. One is that we have entered a zone called the modern era or modernism, which means of course that *The Autobiography* is a modern or modernistic text. Another is that the term "narrative" has run its course in Afro-American letters and is now obsolete. The implication here is that *The Autobiography*, in part because it is a "modern text," either fits an established generic category—historiography, autobiography, or the novel—or doesn't exist. The third assumption, which in effect rescues the reader from the horns of the dilemma posed by the second, is that there *is* something we can assuredly call an Afro-American novel, and that by Johnson's time it had existed and prospered for at least sixty years since William Wells Brown completed *Clotel; or, The President's Daughter*. The net effect of these assumptions is that,

† From *From Behind the Veil: A Study of Afro-American Narrative* (Urbana: University of Illinois Press, 1979), 95–127.

‡ From *Songlines in Michaeltree: New and Collected Poems*. 2000 Michael S. Harper. Used with permission of the

without bothering to fashion a working definition of literary modernism *in Afro-American letters* (can even one such definition be found in the critical canon?), and without recourse to what Geoffrey Hartman would call the "historical consciousness" of Afro-American narrative forms, *The Autobiography* is conventionally and routinely delivered unto us as a "modern novel," or, more boldly, as a "modern Afro-American novel." In retrospect, the only thing more extraordinary than this conception and delivery is the deliberate nurturing that has been bestowed upon this illusionary child.

In the course of this discussion of *The Autobiography*, and of my subsequent commentaries on texts by Richard Wright and Ralph Ellison, I remain ever mindful of Paul de Man's effective warning that "the question of modernity could . . . be asked of any literature at any time, contemporaneous or not." I will generally avoid using terms such as "modern," "modernism," and "modernity"; however, when such terms are employed, they will refer to a contour in Afro-American literary history that is characterized by textual events which revoice their antecedent narratives, or, in terms closer to the Afro-American *genius loci*, which *respond* to the post-textual *call* of those antedating texts. "Novel" is a more difficult term to establish in a fresh way, partly because it is so encrusted with nebulous definitions and partly because, if we take its etymology seriously, we cannot help being genuinely agitated by the question, "What *is* new?" In the case of *The Autobiography* (and *Invisible Man*, and possibly *Black Boy*) no discerning reader can call the book a novel and in the same breath agree that *Clotel* is also a novel. *The Autobiography* and *Clotel* are textual events of differing orders and differing degrees of newness. Like *Clotel* in its indebtedness to antislavery writings, *The Autobiography* identifies and collects from antedating texts—notably *Up from Slavery* and *The Souls of Black Folk*, but also the slave narratives—those key tropes which form the Afro-American literary tradition. In this way both texts are, as literary events, watersheds in literary history; and insofar as watersheds represent something new, they are new. However, *The Autobiography* differs from *Clotel* in that while *Clotel* is, as Jean Yellin has shown, little more than an anthology of borrowed expressions, *The Autobiography* attempts fresh renderings of its collected tropes in a work independent of an authenticating text. This suggests that *The Autobiography* is a generic narrative far more than it is a primary or ancillary text in an authenticating construction; indeed, that suggestion is bolstered when we recognize that *The Autobiography* is, like the Douglass and Du Bois narratives, a coherent expression of personalized response to systems of signification and symbolic geography occasioned by social structure. Yet when we recall the complete arc of the generic canonical story, culminating so magnificently and so hopefully with literal and figurative expressions of voice, literacy, bloodline, mobility, and personal space within racial-communal space achieved, we realize that Johnson has fashioned a narrative different from those of Douglass and Du Bois. What is telling here is that the Ex-Coloured Man's inability to create and assume a heroic or communal voice is predicated, for the most part, upon his adoption of the public language of a different narrative tradition: namely, that of the authenticating narrative initiated by certain slave narratives, and sophisticated almost singlehandedly by Washington's *Up from Slavery. The Autobiography* is at very least a synthesis of (and hence a watershed in) Afro-American narrative history, in that it fuses aspects of authenticating rhetoric to aspects of generic narrative form.

Here one could stop and ask whether this synthesis and all such syntheses create novels—but to do so is to run the twofold risk of fashioning yet another nebulous definition of the novel, and of ignoring the harder question of whether Johnson's text generates narrative energies that propel it beyond synthesis into a new narrative realm. At the end of this chapter I will attempt an answer to this question, but first I must suggest in what ways *The Autobiography* is a literary event.

Indebtednesses

Since the grand dialectic in *The Autobiography* binds multiple expressions of mobility to multiple expressions of confinement, it is no surprise that certain features of the text are rooted in slave narrative tropes and conventions. In some instances tropes and conventions are simply borrowed; in others—and this is where Johnson begins to fashion something new—aspects of slave narratives are not so much borrowed as improvised upon, much as the Ex-Coloured Man syncopates and "rags" Mendelssohn's "Wedding March." Perhaps the most notable borrowing from the slave narratives is the device of the authenticating preface, written in this instance by Johnson's publisher, Sherman, French and Co., and signed somewhat cryptically (but in capital letters) "THE PUBLISHERS." In slave narratives such prefaces conventionally affirm the former slave's authorship of his tale, make some effort to verify facts within that tale, and, insofar as they mount their own documented indictment of slavery's injustices, compete with the former slave's tale—his personal history—for control of the narrative as a whole. While *The Autobiography*'s "Preface" does not sustain all of these activities, it is nevertheless an authenticating text that seeks to position the tale's narrator in society and to shape the reader's opinion of his story. For example, the startling absence of any commentary about the author may be a rhetorical silence that abets the persona's own well-calculated omissions; it may even be an ingenious stratagem supporting his final posture as "an ordinarily successful white man who has made a little money." (The implication is that, unlike an *ex-slave,* an *ex-coloured man* may thrive without the alms of authorial verification.) But the overwhelming effect of the Ex-Coloured Man's lack of a history, place, name, or referential pronoun in the "Preface" to his life story is that he is portrayed less as a human being than as a fact, or, to borrow language from the "Preface," an integer within an "unascertainable number." Since the focus of the "Preface" is removed from the author, it falls on the reader and what he may "glimpse," "view," and be "initiated" into while reading *The Autobiography.* Predictably enough, despite the Ex-Coloured Man's mobility in both a black and a white world, the publisher is emphatically clear in stating that *all* such glimpses, bird's eye views, and initiations are of or into the black world. Indeed, according to the publisher, the glory of *The Autobiography* is its "composite and proportionate presentation of the entire [Negro] race." At very least, these gentle words to the reader seem to pursue two ancient strategies: to ignore, undercut, or render aberrant the narrative's glimpses, views, and opinions of the white world, while sustaining the integrity and even the social posture of the publisher *vis-à-vis* the tale's author in a manner commonly found in what I've previously called an eclectic or phase-one slave narrative. The "Preface" puts the Ex-Coloured Man in his place by acknowledging his mobility in two worlds, but authenticating the clarity of his vision in only one.

The final touches to this strategy are provided by the most peculiar feature of the "Preface"—its indebtednesses to Du Bois's *The Souls of Black Folk.* That Johnson is struggling with the example of *The Souls* while composing *The Autobiography* is, as I will discuss later, manifest almost to the point of embarrassment. That is to be expected, partly because *The Souls* saw print just four years before Johnson began work on his narrative, but mostly because *The Souls* is a seminal text in Afro-American letters. However, as the following language confirms, the author of the "Preface" (the publisher, if indeed not Johnson himself) cannot perform his task without echoing Du Bois as well:

> It is very likely that the Negroes of the United States have a fairly correct idea of what the white people of the country think of them, for that opinion has for a long time been and is still being constantly stated; but they are themselves more or less a sphinx to the whites. It is curiously interesting and even vitally important to know what are the thoughts of ten millions of them concerning the people among whom they live. In these pages it is as though a veil had been drawn aside: the reader is given a

> view of the inner life of the Negro in America, is initiated into the freemasonry, as it were, of the race.

For the most part, this is the heart of Du Bois's "The Forethought" in *The Souls*—"Leaving, then, the world of the white man, I have stepped within the Veil, raising it that you may view faintly its deeper recesses"—recast in a public rhetoric for matters of race most commonly assigned to the tactical genius of Booker T. Washington. While I doubt that this rather accurate expression of *The Autobiography*'s narrative and rhetorical indebtednesses is an *intended* dimension of the "Preface," it must be there for reasons related to the conscious and unconscious strategies confining the Ex-Coloured Man to his place. Since, for the average reader, the Washingtonian rhetoric unquestionably dominates the Du Boisian allusions, I judge that the strategy here is to create a rhetorical signal assuring that the Ex-Coloured Man, *as* an Ex-Coloured Man, and even as an Ex-Coloured Man thinking Coloured Thoughts, is nevertheless a Coloured Man of "proper spirit." The absurdity of the strategy is matched by that of the conditions creating it—and that is another, albeit a lesser, legacy of the slave narrative canon.

The other legacies appear in the tale itself, and are employed mostly to establish the layers of irony that pervade the text. One such legacy is suggested by the houses where the persona and his mother reside in both Georgia and Connecticut. Although he supposedly has only a "faint recollection" of it, the Ex-Coloured Man describes the Georgia dwelling in some detail:

> I can see in this half vision a little house—I am quite sure it was not a large one—I can remember that flowers grew in the front yard, and that around each bed of flowers was a hedge of vari-coloured glass bottles stuck in the ground neck down. I remember that once, while playing round in the sand, I became curious to know whether or not the bottles grew as the flowers did, and I proceeded to dig them up to find out; the investigation brought me a terrific spanking, which indelibly fixed the incident in my mind.

As the description continues, the focus remains upon exterior features—what is "behind the house," what is "back from the house," what delightful things "grew along the edge of the fence." Given these features, and certain well-calculated references to the "endless territory" of the vegetable garden, sumptuous blackberries, and the "patient cow," it is clear that the narrator is trying to convince the reader that the predominant qualities of this birthplace are pastoral and idyllic. However, this torrent of nearly rhapsodic pastoralism, which adumbrates many later passages in which romantic music is employed to buffer personal assault, must be contextualized in the passage as a *response* to the Ex-Coloured Man's aforementioned *initial* memory—of digging up the glass bottles and his subsequent "terrific" whipping.

As Robert Farris Thompson, the historian of African art, has explained to me, the "planting" of multicolored glass bottles, like the careful positioning of light-giving or light-reflecting objects such as mirrors and automobile headlamps in tombstones in southern black cemeteries, is unquestionably an example of what we've come to call, perhaps too glibly, an African survival in the New World. These objects express the "flash of the spirit," the "spirit embedded in glitter"; they "rephrase" the African (and more specifically, in many instances, Kongo) custom of "inserting mirrors into the walls or pillars of tombs" and of "displaying a mirror embedded in the abdomen" of statues "as a sign of mystic vision." To be sure, the front yard of the Ex-Coloured Man's first home is not a burial ground, but is a ritual space in that it is the place of his birth—a spatial expression of community into which he is born. When the Ex-Coloured Man digs up the bottles—ironically, in order to "know whether or not the bottles grew as the flowers did"—he performs an innocent yet devastating act of assault upon a considerable portion of his heritage. That act prefigures his misdirected attempts to approach, let alone embrace, black American culture, including most obviously his desire to render the "old Southern songs" in "classical form." Such acts, in Thompson's articulation of African values, are "experiments with form at the expense of community." Little wonder, then, that the narrator's mother, in this first of several occasions where she postures as a custodian of those aspects of black culture confronting her son, spanked him so hard that the incident became "indelibly fixed" in his mind.

Unfortunately, while the Ex-Coloured Man remembers the event, he appears, in the course of the narrative, not to have learned from it—or, to put it another way, not to have read or comprehended its semiological meaning. Never do we sense that he knows, finally, *why* he was spanked; and he performs virtually the same transgression against black cultural and spiritual forms when he returns from Europe to uproot the old songs for what are, in effect, experimental purposes. Predictably enough, this second uprooting leads to another "terrific spanking"—namely, the psychological whipping he receives from witnessing the "nigger burning." While in the second instance he retreats to New York City, which is as much the City of Mammon for *The Autobiography* as Atlanta is for Du Bois's *The Souls of Black Folk*, the first instance of transgression, or at least the Ex-Coloured Man's depiction of it, occasions his removal to the interior spaces of the cottages, first in Georgia then in Connecticut, where he and his mother live. Despite the extraordinary mobility upon an international landscape (a mobility which is prompted by his racially ambiguous appearance, facility with several languages, and ease of gaining employment), the Ex-Coloured Man grows distrustful of open spaces, particularly in their American and southern configurations. Instead, he is confident of himself and his abilities only in strictly defined interiors such as parlors, clubs, and drawing rooms; there, usually by means of his musical abilities, he can at least initially control the socially required personal relationships by presenting himself as a man of talent.

All this helps explain why he is most exhilarated by Paris in general and by its outdoor cafés in particular. To be sure, the Ex-Coloured Man portrays Parisians (in contrast to Americans) as being relatively free from race prejudice, but that old bromide hardly does justice to the complexity of his feelings or his situation. Paris is the one landscape he roams without experiencing racial assault (the exception being his encounter with his white father and half-sister at the Opera—but that is an American dilemma brought to Europe). The outdoor cafés represent an exquisite commingling of exterior and interior space; that milieu allows him the excitement of exploring an outdoor territory while controlling, or at least experiencing an illusion of control of, a discrete social setting. The Ex-Coloured Man's love of Paris and its amphibious spaces partially explains his relative ease in Manhattan: for him, as for others, New York is a city of interior spaces. Perhaps because it is an island, even its out-of-doors is more a boundaried space within the reach of benign and malignant human orchestration than it is an "endless territory," especially of the prototypical American persuasion.

But we mustn't lose sight of the similarity between the Ex-Coloured Man's initial retreat into the interiors of his boyhood cottages—from which he seems to emerge only for school, music lessons, and duets of one sort or another with radiant young women—and his final flight to New York. If New York, in all its multiple expressions of gambling, intemperance, and violent miscegenetic relations, is Mammon's city, then the narrator's boyhood homes, replete with the jingle and flash of his absent white father's lucre amid the thick pall of his black mother's woeful circumstance, is Mammon's natal lair. What the narrator recalls most vividly from his Georgia home's interior are those transient accoutrements, those flashes and gleams of shined leather and polished gold, that came and went as his father billowed into and out of his and his mother's lives. These gleaming *objets materiel* stand in bold and horrific relief as Mammon fetishes, when compared to the spirit-in-glitter phrased and rephrased by the multicolored bottles implanted in the yard. Clearly, the Ex-Coloured Man has made a choice when, upon leaving his Georgia birthplace, he accepts his father's gift of a ten-dollar gold piece that is fashioned to a string around his young neck. Despite the obvious allusions here to collars, shackles, and nooses, the Ex-Coloured Man's sole remark (in retrospect, from what we wish to assume is a posture of wisdom and maturity) is: "I have worn that gold piece around my neck the greater part of my life, and still possess it, but more than once I have wished that some other way had been found of attaching it to me besides putting a hole through it."

By the time the Ex-Coloured Man and his mother arrive in Connecticut, his alienation from landscapes (occasioned, one assumes, partly by the terrible spanking in Georgia and partly by his mother's overprotectiveness in the face of her circumstances) is so complete that he can only describe his new home in terms of its interior furnishings: "My mother and I lived together in a little cottage which seemed to me to be fitted up almost luxuriously; there were horse-hair covered chairs in the parlour, and a little square piano; there was a stairway with red carpet on it leading to a half second story; there were pictures on the walls, and a few books in a glass-doored case." Later, after the narrator's father visits the cottage and is overwhelmed by his son's renderings of rhapsodic melodies, this lovely domicile is graced by a new piano of considerable tone and worth. Of this event the narrator remarks, presumably with his Mammon fetish still fast about his neck, "there momentarily crossed my mind a feeling of disappointment that the piano was not a grand." Although he attempts to soften this with a line of pious rhetoric—"The new instrument greatly increased the pleasure of my hours of study and practice at home"—the damage is done. We know that, even in retrospect, the Ex-Coloured Man has not yet comprehended or "read" the events of his personal past.

I have gone on at some length about these homes and how they prefigure other features in *The Autobiography* in order to demonstrate the extent to which Johnson has borrowed a particular legacy from antislavery literature, elaborated upon its implications and potential narrative strategies, and set it in motion within the bounds of his text. The legacy to which I refer is the haunting image of the snug cottage in the clearing. To cite two examples, that cottage is the lure forsaken by Linda Brent (Harriet Jacobs) when she refuses to submit to the lecherous Dr. Flint in *Incidents in the Life of a Slave Girl* (1861), and it is the payment (one hopes only the down payment) received by Henry Bibb's wife near the end of his narrative, once she becomes her master's favored concubine and in that way halts, once and for all, Bibb's valiant forays into slave territory in quest of her deliverance. While the construction of this image in antislavery literature rarely goes beyond the literal assembly of such cottages (after all, one need not cross the portals or light the hearth to envision the moral sore that festers there), Johnson's constructions begin with the cottages not only finished and furnished, but also inhabited, both by the kept woman and by the inevitable issue of her protracted liaison. His purpose is not to expose this once common or tacitly accepted persuasion among males of the South's "best blood," but to accept that persuasion as what Du Bois would call an unvarnished fact of life along the color line and then assign to it, in the course of a fresh narrative, those human complexities that it will undoubtedly bear (and bare), including certain modal expressions of relations between master and slave, their children, and those children's children as well. In this way the Ex-Coloured Man's boyhood homes do not so much echo as recast a primary trope in antislavery literature. If this makes *The Autobiography* a modern text in Afro-American letters, then so be it.

Much the same argument can be brought to a discussion of the various journeys in *The Autobiography.* The antecedent trope for the black mother's and racially ambiguous son's journey north from Georgia, complete with its inland leg to Savannah and sea leg up the Atlantic coast, is William and Ellen Craft's perilous escape from bondage. Moreover, the Ex-Coloured Man's trip south from Atlanta to Jacksonville in the cramped quarters of a Pullman linen closet is clearly an inversion (of nearly grotesque proportions) of Henry "Box" Brown's celebrated crating and shipping of himself north to the City of Brotherly Love. And when the Ex-Coloured Man flees the scene of the "nigger burning' (in which the chaining of the victim to a post occasions, in part, his fear and shame of being shackled to an inferior race), buys a ticket to New York on the "overground" railroad, and, once there, "grows" a disguise and changes his name, his flight is a fresh but skewed expression of every antedating ascent from bondage in the Afro-American canon. The point is not so much that Johnson portrays his narrator as being different, but that he enables us to perceive the fullest dimensions of these differences by juxtaposing certain features of the narrator's character and experiences against a host of canonical images. In every case the self-centered, hermetic, and idiosyncratic qualities of the Ex-Coloured Man's perils and travails present him as being less than heroic. They sustain the heroic proportions of the canonical types and tropes by offering what is, in effect, a negative example of them. Thus *The Autobiography*'s posture in Afro-American letters depends as much upon its implied definition of the hero as upon its explicit study of a non-hero. Indeed, this counterpoint is just as central to the narrative as is that between the expressions of mobility and confinement.

So far I have stressed those features of action and setting that are found both in *The Autobiography* and in antislavery literature, but language must be mentioned as well. While there are a number of points of comparison, including the various biblical allusions, Johnson's use of what I've previously called a rhetoric of omission seems to be the most pertinent here, principally because it fuels the aforementioned contrapuntal machinery of the narrative. In the Douglass *Narrative* of 1845, especially at the beginning of chapter XI, Douglass lends a certain extraordinary credence to the communal and archetypal aspects of his tale and authorial postures by eloquently omitting the details of his escape to freedom; he does not want to "run the hazard of closing the slightest avenue by which a brother slave might clear himself of the chains and fetters of slavery." Through this omission Douglass achieves a full measure of authorial control over his narrative, because he defines a body of knowledge possessed by him and unknown to the ancillary voices (principally those of William Lloyd Garrison and Wendell Phillips) circling within and without his tale. Douglass inaugurates a rhetoric and narrative strategy so powerful in the context of Afro-American literary history, and more specifically still in the context of that history's leitmotif of the quest for authorial control, that it becomes something of a requisite trope for succeeding narratives of its kind. In *The Autobiography* the most notable rhetorical omissions appear at the beginning and end of the narrative. In the first instance, the Ex-Coloured Man is careful not to name the Georgia town where he was born "because there are people still living there who could be connected with this narrative"; in the second, which begins the final chapter, he is most assiduous about being "brief" and "skipping" and "jumping" and providing "meagre details" because he is now thoroughly ensconced in New York, and he dreads the possibility of unraveling his position or that into which his children have been born. This is all effective writing that tends to authenticate the narrator's tale and elicit readers' sympathy for his circumstances, but it doesn't screen the fact that the personal arena of concern to which these rhetorical ploys are brought is not on the same scale of Douglass's. Even though matters of physical, psychic, and social mobility are at stake in both narratives, what the Ex-Coloured Man protects through his strategies is finally too personal and idiosyncratic to sustain significant communal resonances. While Douglass's rhetorical omissions serve to obliterate social structures and race rituals, the Ex-Coloured Man's omissions appear to be designed only for the exploitation of those structures and rituals; on one hand, a race is freed, while on the other, a material world is propped up for the immediate comfort of a racially ambiguous few. The point is not so much that the Ex-Coloured Man comes off again as a less than heroic figure, but that we are aware of his limitations because of the various ways—involving actions and, in this last example, language—in which *The Autobiography* aggressively invites comparison with major antecedent Afro-American texts. Although the comparisons made thus far between *The Autobiography* and certain slave narratives sketch its narrator's character, for a full portrait we must add those shadings and hues provided by the narrative's indebtednesses to *Up from Slavery* and *The Souls of Black Folk*.

In his informative biographical study, *James Weldon Johnson: Black Leader, Black Voice*, Eugene Levy makes the following remarks about *The Autobiography*'s literary indebtednesses:

> Johnson was the first black writer to use the first-person narrative in fiction. He had before him the nonfictional models furnished by Douglass and Washington. As a student at Stanton School he had won a copy of *The Life and Times of Frederick Douglass*, and after reading it he added Douglass to his list of heroes. . . . By 1906, as a friend of Washington, he was also thoroughly familiar with *Up from Slavery*. Both works are written in a simple, straight-forward prose style generally free of rhetorical flourishes; in both, the narrator seems to detach himself from the experiences he describes; and both authors make frequent asides to comment directly on the significance of particular incidents to the American racial situation. It seems clear that *Up from Slavery*, more than any other literary influence, led Johnson to the use of the pseudo-autobiography.

As I have discussed before in the chapter on *Up from Slavery*, the precursing text with which Washington struggled while composing his most famous narrative is none other than the *Life and Times of Frederick Douglass*. That Johnson was apparently influenced by features of both of these texts—texts which already spoke to one another as opposing events in Afro-American literary history—constitutes, I think, a remarkable example of *transitio* and *traditio* in literary history, one that is well worth further study in another context. In this way, Professor Levy's remarks are most helpful; in other ways they are not. At the heart of his opening sentences are problems created by simplistic and limited working definitions of "fiction" and "nonfiction." Obviously, the language there does not allow for what is nonfictional in fiction, or for what is fictional in nonfiction, especially autobiographies. When these complexities of form, content, and authorial posture are taken into account, it is clear that his remarks are rather glib and one dimensional. If we agree that autobiographical statements are, by definition, fictions imposed upon a given personal history (theoretically, a nonfiction) in which what is singularly personal is the author's control over *which* fiction is imposed on his history, then we cannot submit that

Douglass's and Washington's models are nonfictional any more than we can say, given the host of generic, authenticating, and autobiographical narratives antedating *The Autobiography*, that Johnson was "The first black writer to use the first-person narrative in fiction." Since, as Levy notes, Johnson himself admitted in later years that "he had not written [*The Autobiography*] with the *intention* of producing a 'piece of fiction,'" perhaps it is more accurate to say (if indeed we must sustain the enterprise of locating whatever a given black author did first) that Johnson was the first black writer (we can think of) who successfully employed first-person narration in a narrative where nonfiction imposes on fiction far more than fiction (in accord with the models provided most notably by Douglass and Washington) impinges on nonfiction.

Levy's phrase "rhetorical flourishes," in his remarks on Douglass's and Washington's prose styles, is also bothersome, primarily because it is not completely clear what kind of bond is implied between "rhetoric" and "flourish." Surely he does not mean to suggest that the terms are synonymous; that would suggest that if Douglass's and Washington's prose styles are "generally free" of flourishes, they are also devoid of rhetoric—a judgment that is a common mistake of many readers. If, as Levy claims, "*Up from Slavery* . . . led Johnson to the use of the pseudo-autobiography," it is because Johnson came to be as influenced by the example of Washington's rhetoric as by narrative's autobiographical impulses. In both *Up from Slavery* and *The Autobiography*, the narrative balance between participation and observation is skewed toward observation; thus both narrators create what I will term a rhetoric of detachment in their tales. Furthermore, this rhetoric performs much the same function in both narratives: In *Up from Slavery* it combines with the accumulating power of Washington's burgeoning résumé to express the domination of the past by the present; in *The Autobiography* it reveals almost singlehandedly how the unambiguousness of the Ex-Coloured Man's outward posture in the present (he is an ordinary white man who has made a little money, and who plans to remain so) dominates his interpretation of his ambiguous past and controls his actions, if not all of his thoughts, in the present.

On the other hand, whereas Washington's narrator is quite comfortable with, and derives a certain power from, his posture and rhetoric of detachment, this is much less the case for the Ex-Coloured Man. Here we begin to see a fundamental difference between the two narratives, a difference that clarifies the point at which Johnson stopped borrowing from Washington and started creating something new within the Afro-American narrative canon. In *Up from Slavery,* the narrator's posture and rhetoric of detachment serve as literary means to certain specific *extraliterary* ends. Above all, that posture never transcends its status as a strategy or a technique to become a subject, or *the* subject, in *Up from Slavery.* In contrast, the Ex-Coloured Man's posture and rhetoric of detachment are literary means to a literary end: Johnson's exposition of his narrator's character. His posture and rhetoric are a subject in *The Autobiography* not only because the Ex-Coloured Man's character is bound to the language with which he attempts to interpret the past, but also because the only meaningful development in the narrative is the accumulation of events and forces that prompt him to submit to (far more than to choose) the ennui of which his rhetoric is an expression. Just as he builds upon the familiar yet haunting image of the snug cottage in the clearing, an image also found in exposés of the immoralities of male slaveholders, Johnson takes the rhetoric of detachment (of which Washington is the prime practitioner) less as a given than as a thing to be explored, as well as used, in the course of a narrative. And while Washington's example instructs that rhetoric is a powerful mask, Johnson's own considerable imaginative energies lead him to inquire in his narrative whether this mask does not, indeed, affect its wearer as well.

Much of this comes clear when we look at a passage that is heavily indebted to Washington's style of rhetoric but which also, in the end, assumes Johnson's stamp. Such passages abound, but few are more developed or more interesting than the one in which the Ex-Coloured Man remarks on the furor over *Uncle Tom's Cabin:*

> This work of Harriet Beecher Stowe has been the object of much unfavorable criticism. It has been assailed, not only as fiction of the most imaginative sort, but as being a direct misrepresentation. Several successful attempts have lately been made to displace the book from Northern school libraries. Its critics would brush it aside with the remark that there never was a Negro as good as Uncle Tom, nor a slave-holder as bad as Legree. For my part, I was never an admirer of Uncle Tom, nor of his type of goodness; but I believe that there were lots of old Negroes as foolishly good as he; the proof of which is that they knowingly stayed and worked the plantations that furnished sinews for the army which was fighting to keep them enslaved. But in these later years several cases have come to my personal knowledge in which old Negroes have died and left what was a considerable fortune to the descendants of their former masters. I do not think it takes any great stretch of the imagination to believe there was a fairly large class of slave-holders typified in Legree. And we must also remember that the author depicted a number of worthless if not vicious Negroes, and a slave-holder who was as much of a Christian and a gentleman as it was possible for one in his position to be; that she pictured the happy, singing,

> shuffling "darky" as well as the mother wailing for her child sold "down river."

If these excessively balanced remarks are meant to reflect the "perspective" on life in the black and the white worlds that the Ex-Coloured Man supposedly gleaned from reading Stowe's novel, then we need not wonder why he is so tentative and embattled, or why he seems incapable of interpreting or "reading" the significance of most events in his life. His circumstance obviously confirms the theory that one kind of illiteracy breeds another. As far as indebtednesses to Washington are concerned, the most overt example is probably the Ex-Coloured Man's echoing of Washington's "Mars Billy" anecdote and other stories which, in their depiction of slaves and ex-slaves mourning the death of a master or honoring a specific trust, bolster Washington's arguments for southern whites to cast down their buckets amongst the black folk. Washington retells these tales because he has a plan for revitalizing the South in general, and the Black Belt in particular. But when the Ex-Coloured Man pursues a similar vein and remarks on those "old Negroes" who left their fortunes to former masters' living kin, his statement appears gratuitous and, most certainly, bereft of the kind of goal-directedness that underlies Washington's seemingly straightforward commentary.

This issue of story-telling of one form or another as a means to an end continues when we turn to what is really the heart of the matter of Washington's influence—the Ex-Coloured Man's rhetoric of detachment. In the above passage, the narrator first creates the illusion that he has an opinion, that he is willing to debate those who have a contrary view, and that he is about to offer his opinion in a substantial way. Then, after segregating *Uncle Tom's Cabin*'s critics into a class ("Its critics")—which suggests that he has sighted his adversary and is primed for the kill—he bravely launches a salvo with the words, "For my part. . . ." But for reasons having to do exclusively with the Ex-Coloured Man's radical degree of detachment from any cultural base for opinion-making, his salvo has the substance and velocity of a gradeschooler's spitball. We have every reason to expect that a narrator bound by sympathy and bloodline to Afro-America, one who is only too aware of the history of assault upon the race, and who declares (as the Ex-Coloured Man does) that Frederick Douglass is one of his heroes, would take greater issue with his opponents' charge that there never was a slaveholder as bad as Legree than with their claim that there never was a Negro as good at Uncle Tom. But alas—the opposite is true. To be sure, he suggests that "there was a fairly large class of slave-holders typified in Legree"; but this remark is buried between his speculations on "good" Negroes and his acknowledgment, for purposes of fairness and objectivity, of Stowe's depiction of "worthless if not vicious Negroes." One can only assume that part of the Ex-Coloured Man's strategy is to suggest that Stowe's critics are one-sided in their views, and therefore irrational, while he, the narrator, has a balanced view and is thus a reasonable person. He accomplishes this fairly well; but eventually, as the passage's final sentence attests, the seams in his construction expose themselves and, in turn, expose him. Only an exaggerated sense of balance—which is to say, a sense crazily adrift from its moral site and source—could first extract from *Uncle Tom's Cabin* and then champion an illusionary symmetry between the stereotype of the "shuffling 'darky'" and the type of the slave mother whose child has been sold away. Shortly thereafter the Ex-Coloured Man concludes, in a tone calculated to convey his fairmindedness, that "it is [not] claiming too much to say that *Uncle Tom's Cabin* was a fair and truthful panorama of slavery"; but, as we know from the preceding language, he has not fashioned a vigorous and persuasive argument to support that claim. Indeed, more often than not what he cites as evidence of fairness and truthfulness in Stowe's novel are examples of how his own personal and, in some cases, skewed racial reveries balance out on the ledger of his mind.

As these remarks suggest, Johnson has his narrator intone a rhetoric akin to Washington's, but he also has the rhetoric turn back upon its speaker in such a way that his character is exposed as his argument, in all its failings, is advanced. While this new development, occasioned by improvisation upon a seminal linguistic model in a given literary tradition, creates fresh space for *The Autobiography* in Afro-American letters, it does not remove the text from that canon. On the contrary, as far as the Ex-Coloured Man's rhetoric of detachment is concerned, Johnson repeatedly appears to argue that one cannot fully comprehend the devastating aimlessness portrayed when a compromising public tongue becomes a figure's private confessional speech without knowing how Washington, in contrast, employed such a tongue *only* in the public arena and *only* to advance a grand plan for communal uplift.

The last point I wish to make by way of "improving upon" Professor Levy's remarks is that I am astonished at his omission of Du Bois's *The Souls of Black Folk* from his list of literary influences on *The Autobiography*. In reading *The Autobiography*, one must take care not to confuse the Ex-Coloured Man's opinions with Johnson's; but late in the book Johnson probably speaks through his narrator when he declares: "the opportunity of the future Negro novelist and poet [is] to give the country something new and unknown, in depicting the life, the ambitions, the struggles, and the passions of those of their race who are striving to break the narrow limits of traditions. A beginning has already been made in that remarkable book by Dr. Du Bois, *The Souls of Black Folk*." Clearly this is not another aside on the state of Afro-America but an admission of literary indebtedness. At very least, the point is made that *The Souls* influenced Johnson's decision to attempt, a narrative about "something new and unknown"—in this case, an "ex-coloured" man who is probably more of a Du Boisian "weary traveler" than a Douglassonian hero-as-metaphor or a Washingtonian hero-as-authenticator. This particular influence of *The Souls* is readily seen, largely because it is not predicated upon any need to judge the book as a literary form. But the form—or, more precisely, the generic aspirations—of *The Souls* undoubtedly affected Johnson's conception of *The Autobiography*, and his writing of it as well. Obviously, *The Souls* is a first-person narrative with autobiographical impulses; but, more important in terms of the model it offered Johnson, it presents a more overt and radical commingling of nonfiction and fiction than any that can be observed in texts by Douglass and Washington. Indeed, as I will suggest later on, Johnson is virtually incapable of composing those southern episodes in his narrative where nonfictional (social scientific) and fictional (pseudo-autobiographical) threads interweave without specific recourse to Du Bois's antedating volume.

In the parlance of jazz, many of Johnson's opening riffs are improvisations upon Du Bois's basic melody in *The Souls*. Within the first chapter it is established that the Ex-Coloured Man, like Du Bois, was born a few years after the Civil War; that he spent his boyhood in a Connecticut village not unlike Du Bois's Great Barrington, Massachusetts; that, like Du Bois, he knew the "old songs" long before he came to know something of America's rituals along the color line; and that he learned, as did Du Bois, through a seemingly frivolous episode at school that he was black and therefore different, but nevertheless acceptable as a classmate and neighbor on certain, usually unspoken, terms. In both narratives these configurations of setting and experience, entwined with an awakening race consciousness, occasion remarks on the peculiar and debilitating psychology with which American Negroes seem to be afflicted from birth. Here Johnson's debt to Du Bois is so obvious that one first wonders why a footnote is not appended. At the beginning of chapter II, after the Ex-Coloured Man confesses with characteristic overstatement that "that fateful day in school . . . wrought the miracle of my transition from one world into another," adding that "From that time I looked out through other eyes, my thoughts were coloured, my words dictated, my actions limited by one dominating, all-pervading idea," he goes on to explain this condition in these terms:

> And this is the dwarfing, warping, distorting, influence which operates upon each and every coloured man in the United States. He is forced to take his outlook on all things, not from the viewpoint of a citizen, or a man, or even a human being, but from the view-point of a *coloured* man. It is wonderful to me that the race has progressed so broadly as it has, since most of its thought and all of its activity must run through the narrow neck of this one funnel.

Clearly, these words echo DuBois's famous description in *The Souls* of the Negro's "double-consciousness": "It is a peculiar sensation, this double-consciousness, this sense of always looking at one's self through the eyes of others, of measuring one's soul by the tape of a world that looks on in amused contempt and pity." But what are finally more significant than the echoes are the subtle ways in which the Ex-Coloured Man's seemingly unintended revisions of Du Bois's thoughts and language begin to reveal his character.

While Du Bois laments the fact that the American Negro seems psychically bereft of a "true self-consciousness," he never goes so far as to suggest, as does the Ex-Coloured Man, that the Negro's resulting "outlook" is somehow subhuman or inhuman. Furthermore, while Du Bois very deliberately describes a duality accosting the Negro ("One ever feels his two-ness,—an American, a Negro"), the Ex-Coloured Man radically reduces this to a nearly grotesque oneness: "the view-point of a *coloured* man." Finally, unlike Du Bois, who concludes by mining even further the "recesses" of an archetypal soul within the Veil and praising the Negro's "dogged strength" in the face of what is, in effect, an imposed schizophrenia, the Ex-Coloured Man ends with vapid remarks about the race's broad progress—remarks that are as shrill with false cheer as they are devoid of substance and earnestness. Given these points of contact between the pronouncements of Du Bois's and Johnson's narrators, I am willing to credit Johnson with the extraordinary ability to reveal his narrator's character in at least two sophisticated ways at once. On one hand, the Ex-Coloured Man exposes his extreme fear, shame, and utter distaste for things "coloured"—hence, for that considerable part of himself that is black—when he very nearly states that the Negro is not a citizen, a man, or even a human being. This, one might say, is the distinctly literal level of his self-exposure. On the other hand, if we consider the Ex-Coloured Man's remarks to be revisions of Du Bois's ideas—not in the sense of improvements or misreadings for purposes of appropriation and authorial control within the literary tradition, but in the sense of misreadings due to deficiencies of vision and character—then we may say that the Ex-Coloured Man also exposes himself in a virtually figurative way. I have spoken before of the Ex-Coloured Man's chronic inability to "read" the events of his life; here we observe, even more than in the aforementioned passage on *Uncle Tom's Cabin*, his illiteracy *vis-à-vis* a verbal text. In *The Autobiography, The Souls* is the verbal manifestation of the Afro-American *genius loci*. If the Ex-Coloured Man cannot read *The Souls*, then he cannot possibly gain immersion in the soul and spirit of Afro-America. Illiteracy *vis-à-vis* a "master" verbal text is thus a grand trope for displacement from the *genius loci*.

Before we are far into the second chapter of *The Autobiography*, the Ex-Coloured Man's deficiencies of vision and character are almost completely sketched. The rest of the narrative is little more than a nearly deterministic statement of what logically happens to a young man who *never* overcomes a type of illiteracy whenever confronted by either a tribal text (notably, *The Souls*) or context (constructed initially and figuratively by the Georgia yard aglitter with "flashes of spirit"). As an Afro-American narrative type, *The Autobiography* is essentially an aborted immersion narrative. With high expectations and a growing awareness of what he *ought* to be, the Ex-Coloured Man makes two journeys to the South, to regions including his Georgia birthing-ground; but these pilgrimages never become rituals, and the pilgrim never achieves a personal tongue beyond a borrowed public rhetoric. Moreover, immersion and rebirth occur only in the perverse sense that a baptism by the fire of a nigger burning and an ascent to Mammon's city grotesquely complete the shape, if not the substance, of an immersion ritual's narrative arc. With all this in mind, it is not surprising that echoes and revisions of *The Souls* continue in *The Autobiography,* and appear with particular clarity and import in those episodes where the Ex-Coloured Man ventures south. Indeed, in these instances the most effective feature of Johnson's narrative strategy is the comparison he aggressively encourages us to make between Du Bois's questing narrator and his own.

The comparison begins in a major way in chapter IV of *The Autobiography*, where the Ex-Coloured Man draws heavily on Du Bois's narrator's antecedent language (at the beginning of chapter VII of *The Souls*) while describing the Georgia landscape which emerges as he travels south to Atlanta. The parallels—and discrepancies—between these descriptions are so numerous and striking that I shall quote from each at length. *The Souls* reads:

> Out of the North, the train thundered, and we woke to see the crimson soil of Georgia stretching away bare and monotonous right and left. Here and there lay struggling, unlovely villages, and lean men loafed leisurely at the depots; then again

> came the stretch of pines and clay. Yet we did not nod, nor weary of the scene; for this is historic ground. Right across our track, three hundred and sixty years ago, wandered the cavalcade of Hernando de Soto, looking for gold and the Great Sea. . . . Here sits Atlanta, the city of a hundred hills, with something Western, something Southern, and something quite its own, in its busy life. And a little past Atlanta, to the southwest, is the land of the Cherokees, and there, not far from where Sam Hose was crucified, you may stand on a spot which is to-day the centre of the Negro problem,—the centre of those nine million men who are America's dark heritage from slavery and the slave-trade.

The echoing and yet contrasting passage in *The Autobiography* is as follows:

> The farther I got below Washington, the more disappointed I became in the appearance of the country. I peered through the car windows, looking in vain for the luxuriant semi-tropical scenery which I had pictured in my mind. I did not find the grass so green, nor the woods so beautiful, nor the flowers so plentiful, as they were in Connecticut. Instead, the red earth partly covered by tough, scrawny grass, the muddy, straggling roads, the cottages of unpainted pine boards, and the clay-daubed huts imparted a "burnt up" impression. Occasionally we ran through a little white and green village that was like an oasis in a desert.
>
> When I reached Atlanta, my steadily increasing disappointment was not lessened. I found it a big, dull, red town. This dull red colour of that part of the South I was then seeing had much, I think, to do with the extreme depression of my spirits—no public squares, no fountains, dingy streetcars, and, with the exception of three or four principal thoroughfares, unpaved streets. It was raining when I arrived and some of these unpaved streets were absolutely impassable. Wheels sank to the hubs in red mire, and I actually stood for an hour and watched four or five men work to save a mule, which had stepped into a deep sink, from drowning, or, rather, suffocating in the mud. The Atlanta of today is a new city.

The parallels between these two descriptions—in content, diction, syntax, and the symbolic use of the color red—are obvious; however, the discrepancies between the two are, I think, more interesting and to the point. Both men are assaulted by the "crimson soil," but while Du Bois responds to temporary immobility with expansive images of immersion in time and space ("this is historic ground"), the Ex-Coloured Man submits to this immobilizing force and offers embellishing images of his stasis, for which the "impassable" streets of

Atlanta are a vivid expression. These contrasting images of immersion—in history on one hand, and mud on the other—tell us much about each narrator's gut-level response to the South as a culture's ritual ground. They also suggest the true dimensions of their inherited (if not always assumed) postures as questing, articulate heroes. There is no doubt about Du Bois's narrator's strenuous effort to assume the mantle: the landscape is strange and "unlovely," but he can see that it both stretches and straggles (the Ex-Coloured Man dwells only on the "straggling," and appropriates that very term from *The Souls*). Because he can envision the myriad points of a wonderful compass charting territories of race and culture, time and space, he becomes what Richard Wright proclaimed the Afro-American voice should strive to be—a guide to our daily living. In contrast, the Ex-Coloured Man's vast removal from the speech and responsibilities of the articulate hero is best expressed by his anecdote about witnessing the rescue of a mule from a sink of Georgia mud. In the context of *The Autobiography* as a whole, the incident prefigures the terrifying nigger-burning; in both instances the Ex-Coloured Man is not a guide but a bystander—an observer in the most unambiguous sense, who is transfixed and inarticulate before the horror conjured by his momentary yet acute empathy with either victim. As American history and literature both inform us, the suffocating mule and the burning Negro are partners in a centuries-old cultural dialectic that still haunts and punishes us. However, the Ex-Coloured Man cannot see this in his past, for he clearly lacks a fully interpretative or historical mind. His imagination is self-directed and present oriented. When he sees a mule stuck in a muddy road or a terrified black man burning while chained to a post, he can identify with the victim but not see *through* the victim—even in retrospect—to the underlying historical and racial tropes. The Ex-Coloured Man is a seer of surfaces, which helps explain why he becomes a master of disguises, far more than a student of prophecy. In the face of tribal texts and contexts advancing an archetypal protean posture, the Ex-Coloured Man becomes more and more of a chameleon.

While the nearly asphyxiated mule leaves the Ex-Coloured Man speechless and mired in his own psychic mud (so much so that he actually spends an hour studying the dilemma without lending a hand), other features of southern life, including the social and economic classes he observes among the Negroes of Jacksonville and the quality of food and shelter in the Black Belt, prompt a great deal of commentary. One supposes that these passages, appearing principally in chapters V and X, are what the publishers had in mind when they praised *The Autobiography*'s "composite and proportionate presentation of the entire [coloured American] race";

but in truth they are low points in the narrative, where simplistic sociology and thin fictional impulses take turns trying to sustain each other. The most one can say about the narrator's remarks on Jacksonville and the rural Black Belt is that they confirm our suspicions: he is instinctively an elitist for whom lower-class black folk are animal-like, "offensive" and "desperate" or "dull" and "simple," and those in the upper classes are colored yet "refined" and fairly interesting. While in Jacksonville, however, the narrator avoids relegation to either of these classes by falling in with, and in effect becoming, one of the Cuban-American cigar-makers. The resulting narrative thread is bare from the start, but here Johnson probably wants to establish supportive attitudinal bases for several subsequent episodes in his narrator's life. For example, given the Ex-Coloured Man's unsympathetic depiction of the lowest class of Jacksonville Negroes, we should not be startled when he describes the "wretch" who is about to be burned as "a man only in form and stature" with "every sign of degeneracy stamped upon his countenance." In a sense, the Ex-Coloured Man has despised and feared this man ever since he laid eyes on his *type* in Jacksonville years before. Thus, when a twist of his imagination informs him that the world views him, too, as a man only in form and stature—that is, if he announces himself a coloured man—and he flees across the color line to New York, we are meant to understand the full, if perverse, historical dimensions of his shame. Similarly, we are encouraged to make historical connections between the Ex-Coloured Man's initial plunge into racial ambiguity as a bilingual "Cuban" in Florida and his final posture as a white, multilingual businessman in New York, and between his interest in the refined yet racially committed colored upper class and his fear that he has sold his birthright. The threads are there but, as suggested earlier, Johnson does not discover the proper weave.

These problems are not inconsiderable, but they merely shroud the heart of this particular narrative failure which, like Johnson's successes, involves his indebtednesses to Du Bois. To begin with, the Ex-Coloured Man's sociological expositions are not original; his study of Jacksonville's Negro community merely rehashes Du Bois's observations in chapter IX of *The Souls* ("Of the Sons of Master and Man"). In the case of his lament that the best of each race never gain a meaningful or heartfelt communion with each other, he pirates both language and sentiment. Similarly, the Ex-Coloured Man's remarks upon the state of affairs in the Black Belt's rural reaches are clearly indebted to both "Of the Sons of Master and Man" and its preceding chapter, "Of the Quest of the Golden Fleece." All this is nothing new; as I have already suggested, one of Johnson's key narrative strategies is the illumination of his narrator's failings through presentations of his misreadings and non-readings of "tribal" texts and contexts—the former including most obviously and most consistently *The Souls.* What *is* new is that these particular echoes and revisions do not reveal the Ex-Coloured Man in any consummate way, principally because the strategy of playing the Ex-Coloured Man's ambiguous stature off Du Bois's narrator's heroic stature is stunted by the Du Boisian voice's purposely less than heroic posture as a participant-observer social scientist. Once Du Bois's protean voice assumes an objective or scientific posture (a posture that almost masks Du Bois's own ambivalences about southern black life), Johnson can no longer portray the Ex-Coloured Man as simply the inverse of Du Bois's wayfarer. Any suggestion of a powerful, emotional immersion in black life at its cultural fount in the South on the part of the Ex-Coloured Man will dismantle all we've come to know about his character and will render the outcome of the narrative an improbable contradiction. Since the shades of distinction between Du Bois's narrator's "scientific" rhetoric and the public tongue of the Ex-Coloured Man are so mute, Johnson's only recourse within his narrative strategy is to suggest that his narrator is less heroic or archetypal than Du Bois's by having the Ex-Coloured Man be just a little more obsessed with surfaces, and hence more assaulted and shamed by the conditions he observes. But this is not a satisfactory way to construct a fresh narrative out of the shards of a narrative tradition. Johnson's dogged pursuit of his strategy in a situation requiring new narrative approaches ultimately reveals more about his artistic indebtednesses and dependencies than about his central character.

On the other hand, the episode in which the Ex-Coloured Man visits a "big meeting" is also patterned upon incidents and commentary in *The Souls* (see especially Du Bois's chapter X, "Of the Faith of the Fathers"). It offers reassuring evidence that Johnson can interweave nonfictional and fictional threads with great facility when the nonfictional subject matter—here, the interplay of the preacher, the singing leader, and black sacred music—is of greater interest to the Ex-Coloured Man and, one imagines, to Johnson as well. Early in the episode the narrator remarks that he found "a mine of material" for his musical compositions at the big meeting; the rest of his commentary, complete with annotated transcriptions of the words to "master" Sorrow Songs such as "Swing Low" and "Steal Away," bears this out. His use of the word "mine" is telling, because it sustains all that we know of his inherent Mammonism and all that we've come to suspect about how he will view a ritualized manifestation of artistic traditions once he stumbles upon it. The Ex-Coloured Man seeks neither communion nor succor; he comes not to embrace but to extract. The big meeting is, for him, a mine riddled with ore, not a welcome table laden with food for body and soul. Nevertheless, the overall implication of the episode is that the Ex-Coloured Man has been genuinely stirred by both word and song. For this reason his commentary may be described in part as a revision of antedating passages in *The Souls,* a revision that selects portions of "Of the Faith of the Fathers" and "Of the Sorrow Songs" and binds them into a single, abbreviated statement. With this in full view, Johnson's indebtednesses to Du Bois again become abundantly clear. However, Johnson does more than just borrow from Du Bois in this instance, partly because his own special knowledge of preachers, sermons, singing leaders, and song allows him to improve upon Du Bois's earlier commentary, and partly because he is able to capitalize on what I believe to be a lapse in Du Bois's narrative.

To be sure, the Du Boisian voice is marvelously subjective and self-conscious in both a personal and racial sense, in the Sorrow Songs chapter. But in "Of the Faith of the Fathers," where he visits his first campground or revival meeting, he is first and foremost a scientific observer. His initial remarks on "The Preacher, the Music, and the Frenzy" do not immediately advance the narrative's immersion ritual, prompting instead a rather dry and, in many parts of the argument, suspect analysis of Afro-American religious practice, North and South. In light of *The Soul*'s ultimate drive and direction as an immersion narrative, it could be argued that Du Bois should have revised "Of the Faith," as he did so many of the essays that became chapters in his volume, with an eye to enhancing the full import of the revival experience. But he did not, and his narrator remains to the end conspicuously uninvolved and even unmoved. While Johnson begins the big meeting episode with intimations of the Ex-Coloured Man's detachment and paucity of racial and moral sentiment—he first views the meeting as an opportunity to "mine" or "catch the spirit of the Negro in his relatively primitive state"—he ends by taking advantage of Du Bois's lapse and portraying the Ex-Coloured Man as being moved for the first time (save perhaps in those youthful moments when his mother sang and played the old songs) by Afro-American spiritual and creative expressions:

> As I listened to the singing of these songs, the wonder of their production grew upon me more and more. How did the men who originated them manage to do it? The sentiments are easily accounted for; they are mostly taken from the Bible; but the melodies, where did they come from? Some of them so weirdly sweet, and others so wonderfully strong. Take, for instance, "Go down, Moses." I doubt that there is a stronger theme in the whole musical literature of the world. And so many of these songs contain more than mere melody; there is sounded

> in them that elusive undertone, the note in music which is not heard with the ears. I sat often with the tears rolling down my cheeks and my heart melted within me. Any musical person who has never heard a Negro congregation under the spell of religious fervour sing these old songs has missed one of the most thrilling emotions which the human heart may experience. Anyone who without shedding tears can listen to Negroes sing "Nobody knows de trouble I see, Nobody knows but Jesus" must indeed have a heart of stone.

This is Johnson at his best. We are made aware of the Ex-Coloured Man's considerable enthusiasm through an abrupt change in rhetoric; the language here is far more personal than public. However, the more he attempts to wax eloquent, the more he irreparably exposes himself. When, for example, he accounts for the songs' sentiments by stating that "they are mostly taken from the Bible," he again shows himself to be an ahistorically minded seer of surfaces, even though in this instance the surfaces he views are most resonant and metaphorical. To be sure, sentiments in the Sorrow Songs *are* taken almost exclusively from the Bible; but the Ex-Coloured Man never comprehends the singular racial-historical experience that occasioned the adoption of biblical allusion and reference in the first place. He can hear an echo and read a reference, but that is all. The Ex-Coloured Man's embarrassing self-exposure is compounded when he suggests that he has been so terribly moved by his experience because he is a sensitive, "musical person," and that other "musical" persons are missing something if they haven't yet heard Negroes sing the Sorrow Songs. *That* argument is ludicrous to the point of being painful. In sum, while Johnson's object here is clearly to bring his narrator as close to the figurative site of the Afro-American *genius loci* as he will ever come, and hence to buoy him up before the nigger-burning brutally tears him down and sends him fleeing to the City of Mammon, he also reveals that those uplifting emotions and sentiments are skewed and impure. While it is tempting to fault Johnson for being so singleminded in his pursuit of a strategy that plays his narrator off that of an ever-looming prototype, we must finally praise him and thoughtfully consider his achievement. Even more than *The Souls, The Autobiography* forces a rereading of Afro-American literature in order for its wayfaring narrator to come alive, to be heard and seen. And *we* must do the hearing and seeing, since the Ex-Coloured Man is lost in his quest and cannot even hear or see himself.

Anticipations: Race, Music, and Mammon

While *The Autobiography*'s indebtednesses to antecedent texts (especially *Up from Slavery* and *The Souls of Black Folk*) tell us much about how Johnson fashioned "something new and unknown," they tell only a partial story of his narrative's literary past. The rest of the story involves *The Autobiography*'s literary future, and especially its literary present. Only by discovering this literary present may we assume that the narrative achieves enough integrity to begin to predict a literary future. In this regard one feature of *The Autobiography* stands out from the rest: its uncompromising study of race and music in the world of Mammon. This feature constitutes a nearly sacrilegious inversion of those hallowed tropes in Afro-American art which remain responsible for the culture's abiding belief in the essential oneness of its music and tribal integrity. While it certainly can be argued that the feature is to some degree an indebtedness, since it inverts preexisting tropes found in the writings of Dunbar, Du Bois, and others, the quality of the inversion is such that the feature finally must be assigned to a new category, namely, that of "anticipation." In this particular instance, the distinction between an indebtedness and an anticipation is quite specifically that between a literary feature that inverts and one that demystifies a preexisting trope. To be sure, the line between these two activities can be quite fine, but that is part (and probably most) of the point: the line is fine because indebtednesses and anticipations *both* exist in a given text's literary present.

I want to suggest here that *The Autobiography*'s demystification of the "sacred" bond between Afro-America's music and its tribal integrity is not only part of the "something new," creating fresh space for the narrative in Afro-American letters, but also a feature anticipating certain prominent tropes and expressions in the literature to come. Indeed, once the music is heard in Mammon's lair as well as in cultural ritual grounds such as the Black Belt, both the sacred and secular (if not exactly profane) strains in the music and the discrete subcultures enveloping each become artistic subjects, especially in periods such as those following the publication of *The Autobiography,* when there is an interest in a literary social realism. While it can be argued that Johnson "broke the new wood" for subsequent Afro-American (and American) literary ventures, it also can be said that he almost singlehandedly created a great deal of havoc. When Afro-American literary critics in the 1920's (including especially Du Bois) roundly condemned those vivid portraits of Negro America's urban underbelly in the "renaissance" writings of Claude McKay, Langston Hughes, and others, they sustained, albeit from their own point of view, a peculiarly American notion of degeneracy and sordidness which achieves its greatest frenzy in the face of spatial configurations of music, interracial liaison, and intemperance such as the Negro cabaret. In *The Autobiography* the Club where the Ex-Coloured Man is first introduced to ragtime music and "coloured

Bohemia," as well as to his future patron and "the rich widow," inaugurates all such spatial configurations in modern Afro-American letters. It does so because it is not so much a setting as a symbolic space.

The significance of Johnson's invention becomes clear when we not only look forward in literary history to the literature fashioned by Jean Toomer, Langston Hughes, Claude McKay, and Sterling Brown, but also turn back once again to texts by Du Bois and Washington. *The Souls of Black Folk* and *Up from Slavery* are seminal texts in Afro-American letters partly because each contributes to the series of symbolic spaces in the tradition. In the case of the former, there is first and foremost the Black Belt, but also the consummate construction of Du Bois's Atlanta study; in the latter, the chief symbolic space is Tuskegee itself. Coming hard upon the heels of these volumes, *The Autobiography*'s novel and in many ways abrasive assertion is that the Ex-Coloured Man's Club, in all its external and internal complexities, is a compact world unto itself, a world of no less significance and resonance in Afro-American art and life than that readily assigned to Du Bois's and Washington's more agreeable constructions.

While the club is catacomb-like and occasionally a setting for intemperance and violence, it is less an inferno and more an Afro-American ritual ground where responses to oppressing social structures are made and in some measure sustained by "tribal" bonds, as they are in Du Bois's Black Belt. The main floor of the Club is divided into two large rooms. In the back room is the piano that introduces the Ex-Coloured Man to new forms of Afro-American music, and areas for performances, buffets, and dancing. In the parlor, carpets and lace curtains help establish a particular atmosphere and tone, but the significance of the space is most accurately and directly conveyed by the fact that "the walls [are] literally covered with photographs or lithographs of every coloured man in America who [has] ever 'done anything.'" As the Ex-Coloured Man continues his description, we learn that this visual pantheon includes a marvelous array of heroes—athletes, entertainers, and (not surprisingly) Frederick Douglass—that it is as much a new expression of Afro-American heroism as the Club is a fresh symbolic space. The Club's gallery of heroic images transports us back to the single tattered handbill adorning the rough walls of the Negro hut sketched with such eloquence by Du Bois, as well as forward to such recent constructions as Bigger's "gallery" in his quarters at the Daltons' in Wright's *Native Son*, the array of homely treasures in the Harlem eviction episode in Ellison's *Invisible Man,* and the family tree of real and adopted kin in Michael Harper's *Nightmare Begins Responsibility.* At the very least, this journey affords us a nearly prophetic vision of a race's history of response to assault. But in truth, just as "something new and unknown" is launched in Afro-American letters by the radical juxtaposition of Du Bois's study and the Ex-Coloured Man's Club, the full measure of our visionary experience as readers is triggered by the parlor with its gallery, *in communion* with the back room with its matériel for ritual dance and song. Plagued as he is with a particular kind of illiteracy, the Ex-Coloured Man cannot "read" the Club's deep structure, and hence experience the "spiritual race message" and history brimming forth from this highly accoutred and orchestrated vessel. But we are meant to perform this literate act, if for no other reason than to achieve the proper spirit in which to receive certain representatives of the pictured heroes once they enter the Club and, in effect, come to life.

As the Ex-Coloured Man's description of the Club unfolds, he sketches many sporting types, including "the most popular jockey of the day," who earned $12,000 a year but spent "about thirty times that rate." However, his most pertinent remarks regarding aspects of black heroism in Mammon's world involve the entertainers for whom the Club is something of a practice area, audition hall, and guild lodge rolled into one. Of these, the most important are "the younger and brighter men" who often discussed "the time when they could compel the public to recognize that they could do something more than grin and cut pigeon-wings," and especially the minstrel who "whenever he responded to a request to 'do something,' never essayed anything below a reading from Shakspere [*sic*]." Given the topic of discussion that obsessed the younger performers, and the Ex-Coloured Man's remark that the minstrel, in his ambition to be a tragedian, did indeed "play a part in a tragedy," it seems clear that when Johnson composed this passage he thought of well-known poems by his good friend Paul Laurence Dunbar—"The Poet," "We Wear the Mask," and possibly "Sympathy." More to the point, however, is Johnson's particular use of Dunbar's tropes in his own literary work. Whether the lines speak of caged birds singing, jingles in a broken tongue, or of masks and who is the seer and who the seen, the Dunbar poems are finally less concerned with specific *fin de siècle* issues such as the accuracy of Negro dialect and the influence of "plantation" literature than with the abiding crisis involving the Afro-American artist's pursuit of authorial control. When certain Negro performers come to the Club and, in effect, reenact and rephrase Dunbar's expressions, we may say that Johnson clearly establishes two major points involving both his narrator and the most remarkable symbolic space in *The Autobiography*. First, much of what makes the Club a significant Afro-American ritual ground is that it is an intricate space wherein authorial control is not only discussed, but also aggressively pursued. Again the relationship between the Club's parlor and back room figures prominently in

Johnson's strategy: the communion between the two rooms is but a spatial expression of the bond between artful acts in the present and a sense of tradition shaping past, present, and future into a single continuum. In the Club, an Afro-American artist may refine, direct, and hence gain a measure of control over his or her talent through contact with fellow "weary travelers" past and present, known and unknown, gathered around a table or portrayed upon a wall. This, and not the lure of drink, revelry, and the transgression of racial taboos, is the true source of the Club's power and position in the Negro world of Johnson's narrative.

The second point is that once the Ex-Coloured Man becomes a nearly famous ragtime piano player, he also becomes, without really knowing it, one of the many black performers at the Club who must wrestle with questions of authorial control—especially as those questions persistently relate to a sense of self. Given Johnson's construction of this symbolic space, based as it is upon a profound comprehension of Afro-American artistic traditions, one imagines that if the Ex-Coloured Man realized for even a single moment that Frederick Douglass was staring at him from the parlor while he was improvising ingenious rags in the back room, *The Autobiography* could end right then and there. But the point is that the Ex-Coloured Man is a performer without control and, quite probably, out of control. Alienated from the deepest bonds of his race, he learns to play the music without reference to who is "in the other room"—he becomes a musical technician bereft of an artistic soul. It is inevitable that the Ex-Coloured Man will be as much drawn to the white slummers—who appear to appreciate him and his music more than any of his other admirers—as they are attracted to him. Caught as he is in a kind of illiteracy that argues that technique can pass for art, it is also inevitable that the Ex-Coloured Man will unwittingly mistake the modulation and exploitation of race rituals along the color line for proper relations between artist and audience. The disastrous consequences of these mistakes are expressed in the narrative when th Ex-Coloured Man is almost killed in the Club by the wealthy white widow's "other" black lover, and when he is forced to play for his "second" white father for hours on end—often in the middle of the night. In *The Autobiography,* as elsewhere, the most unsettling outward expression of the condition plaguing the Ex-Coloured Man occurs whenever the subtle and potentially honorable bond between artist and audience is grotesquely skewed, and art becomes something transiently novel, amusing, or soporific.

Given the Ex-Coloured Man's nearly obsessive attraction to interiors after he receives the whipping for digging up the "spirit in glitter" in the yard of his birthplace, the greatest of *The Autobiography*'s many ironic touches must be the fact that the essence of black life and song, for which he searches so energetically in the "outdoors" of the Black Belt, was readily available to him earlier, in the confines of the Club's resonating rooms. Had he been in tune with these resonances, not only could he have filled many a notebook; he could also have achieved contact with artistic traditions and concerns which would have focused and directed his compositions in such a way that he would have indeed become, for himself as well as his race, a Negro composer. In this way Johnson's initial construction of the Club seems to be a fresh and assertive configuration, in conflict with more established "tribal tropes" such as the Black Belt. But such is not the case: on the contrary, the Black Belt of *The Autobiography* is not a wasteland devoid of cultural resonances, but the homeland and ritual ground of a preacher extraordinarily named John Brown, and a master-singer known to all as Singing Johnson from whom the Ex-Coloured Man, in his limited way, learns much. Clearly, in Johnson's view, the Ex-Coloured Man could have learned all of what he thinks he ought to know in *either* symbolic territory. What we must see, as students of Afro-American narrative, is that this fresh assertion is part of what places *The Autobiography* on the literary map.

All in all, the hallowed dialectic between race and music which yields the most revered expressions of the Afro-American *genius loci* in much of the literature preceding and following *The Autobiography* is an alien idea for the Ex-Coloured Man—or at least an idea that is subsumed by his personal opinion of what are more pertinent constructions. For him, the modulation and occasional exploitation of America's race rituals are persistently more important than true and honest contact with his race, and so a bond between music and race ritual is seen to be more useful and valuable than one between music and race itself. Since the Ex-Coloured Man is in this way always *upon* the color line, and not truly on either side of it, even in his most joyful moments as a "black" music-maker, Johnson's full and complete nightmare vision of race and music in Mammon's world is ultimately quite clear. As far as Afro-American music is concerned, what distinguishes the heights of Pisgah from the mire of the dusty desert has less to do with genres and traditions (ragtime versus the Sorrow Songs) than with how the music is approached, perceived, and used. When Johnson renders this point by presenting his narrator as being more preoccupied with his white patrons—which is to say, with taboos and materialism—than with the kinfolk, present and portrayed, who constitute his other audience, he transports his narrative into realms never before explored.

If *The Autobiography* is a modern Afro-American text, it is so because tropes such as the Club revoice tropes such as the Black

Belt, and because new territories, including the ambiguous domain between America's black and white world, are finally explored. In my estimation, Johnson's peculiar allegiances to past examples of sociological reportage retard *The Autobiography,* making it ultimately something less than a novel. But given his abiding interest in how fact imposes upon fiction, it is clear that he is up to something different from what Douglass, Washington, and even Du Bois pursue in their autobiographical narratives. For this reason it may be said that *The Autobiography* is on the verge of achieving generic stature—much as its narrator, albeit for very different reasons, is perpetually on the verge of seeing sign and event and himself. In light of Johnson's statement that he was not attempting a novel in the conventional sense of the term, we cannot fault him for almost achieving something that was not his goal. With a steady eye on what had come before in Afro-American letters, Johnson pursued and found both a form and voice that are, if not absolutely new and unknown, very peculiar. The task of *fully* describing and weighing these peculiarities remains before us still.

M. GIULIA FABI

The Mark Within: Parody in James Weldon Johnson's *The Autobiography of an Ex-Coloured Man*†

Where Stepto emphasizes *ECM*'s "generic" relationship to earlier African American texts, M. Giulia Fabi analyzes the novel's "parodic" engagements with nineteenth-century black prose fiction. Paying special attention to Johnson's revisions of racial passing and its tropes, Fabi argues that *ECM*'s narrative strategies inaugurate a self-reflexive awareness about race, on the one hand, and the practice of writing, on the other, such that Johnson's novel transforms how parody itself functions. This innovation becomes a defining hallmark of black modernist fiction writing, Fabi contends.

> The Negro author—the creative author—has arrived. . . . He appears in the lists of the best publishers. He even breaks into the lists of the best-sellers. To the general American public he is a novelty, a strange phenomenon. . . . Well, he *is* a novelty, but he is by

† From *Passing and the Rise of the African American Novel* (Urbana: University of Illinois Press, 2001), 90–105, 159–61.

> no means a new thing. . . . What has happened is that efforts which have been going on for more than a century are being noticed and appreciated at last. (J. W. Johnson, "Dilemma" 477)

Even after all of the major all-but-white characters in *Iola Leroy* have cast their lot with their mothers' people, Harper's narrative disparagement of passing does not relent. If anything, it becomes more insistent and rhetorically tenacious,[1] in indirect recognition both of the exacting implications of the choice of blackness in a segregated society and of how much easier passing has become in a post-Emancipation era of greater mobility and potential loosening of family and community ties.

The danger Harper tries to exorcise becomes fully realized in the fictional autobiography of James Weldon Johnson's Ex-Colored Man, the 1912 descendant of a male line of determined passers that goes back through Chesnutt's John Walden to Webb's Clarence Garie.[2] In contrast with Clarence Garie's eventual exposure and pathetic death, both John Walden and the Ex-Colored Man survive the text's closure. Chesnutt diffuses the threat of his successful passer by progressively withdrawing narrative attention from him, so that by the end of the novel John Walden practically disappears in the background and implicitly into whiteness. Johnson's Ex-Colored Man, on the contrary, remains prominent throughout the text, not only as protagonist but also as narrator, having survived and prospered by his defiance of racial barriers (through passing) and sexual taboos (through intermarriage).

Published when Johnson was forty-one years old and considered by him among his "more serious work" (J. W. Johnson, *Along* 193), *The Autobiography* definitely was a novelty but not a particularly welcome one, at least not initially. Johnson's book was first published anonymously in 1912 by a small Boston house (Sherman, French and Co.) and it enjoyed a less than glamorous reception. *The Autobiography* did not sell well, received few reviews, and was mostly mistaken as a "human document" (*Along* 238).[3] Although Johnson originally intended it as a way of creating interest in his novel, this autobiographical misconception encouraged literal

1. I borrow the notion of "rhetorical tenacity" from Hortense Spillers ("Moving on Down the Line").
2. Chesnutt's decision to name "Clarence" the town where John and Rena Walden pass is an explicit intertextual reference not only to Bulwer-Lytton's *The Last of the Barons* but also to Webb's *The Garies*. Johnson, in turn, evokes Chesnutt's *The House Behind the Cedars* in his own novel by recuperating, for instance, the ironic image of the coin with a hole in it that John Walden gives to his sister (*The House* 174) and that the Ex-Colored Man receives from his white father (*The Autobiography* 6).
3. A notable exception is Jessie Fauset, who in her 1912 review for *The Crisis* describes *The Autobiography* as "a work of fiction founded on hard fact" (38).

readings of the text, and the author eventually came to regret it.[4] It this inauspicious debut links Johnson's novel with most antecedent African American fiction, the popularity it enjoyed after its republication in 1927 highlights the different cultural climate of the Harlem Renaissance. "Beautifully bound and printed" by Alfred A. Knopf (Du Bois, "Browsing Reader" 308), *The Autobiography* underwent a veritable rebirth, as the author's name was finally affixed to the book and Carl Van Vechten's introduction established the generic status of the text "inform[ing] the reader that the story was not the story of [the author's] life" (*Along* 239). In the making of its belated success, the novel's treatment of themes and environments characteristic of the New Negro movement and its interest in folk expressive culture coalesced with Johnson's own greater visibility as the secretary of the National Association for the Advancement of Colored People and with his active participation in the cultural project of the Harlem Renaissance through the publication of three important and groundbreaking anthologies.[5] As Benjamin S. Lawson notes, "Now that his [Johnson's] name could make the novel, the novel could help make Johnson's name" (98).

Fifteen years after its original publication, *The Autobiography* finally entered the canon of African American letters and emerged as the only pre-World War I novel to become "one of the most influential books" of the Harlem Renaissance (Fleming, *James Weldon Johnson* 19). This belated appreciation continued to be informed by an emphasis on the biographical and documentary aspects of the novel[6] and even "those critics who admire[d] the

4. Johnson writes in his autobiography, "When the book [*The Autobiography*] was published . . . most of the reviewers . . . accepted it as a human document. This was a tribute to the writing, for I had done the book with the intention of its being so taken. But, perhaps, it would have been more farsighted had I originally affixed my name to it as a frank piece of fiction" (*Along* 238).

5. Johnson's pioneer anthologies are *The Book of American Negro Poetry* (1922), *The Book of American Negro Spirituals* (1925), and *The Second Book of American Negro Spirituals* (1926).

6. Van Vechten's introduction to the 1927 edition is paradigmatic. Although he clarifies that "*The Autobiography* . . . has little enough to do with Mr. Johnson's own life," he radically qualifies the text's fictiveness by stressing how "it is imbued with . . . his [Johnson's] *views* of the subjects discussed, so that to a person who has no previous knowledge of the author's own history, it reads like a *real* autobiography" (v–vi). To reconcile this biographical emphasis with his previous assertion of the work's fictiveness, Van Vechten expands the documentary focus of *The Autobiography* and argues that "it reads like a composite autobiography of the Negro race" (vi). The emphasis on the nonfictional elements of *The Autobiography* also characterizes much later volumes such as *Three Negro Classics*, edited by John Hope Franklin (1965), and *Early African-American Classics*, edited by Anthony K. Appiah (1990). In both texts, Johnson's is the only novel included in a selection of such nonfiction works as Douglass's *Narrative*, Jacobs's *Incidents*, Washington's *Up from Slavery*, and Du Bois's *Souls of Black Folk*.

novel often [did] so for the wrong reasons" (Fleming, "Irony" 83). Literal readings of the text have long overlooked the consummate artistry of "Mr. Johnson's objective and dispassionate treatment" ("An Ex-Coloured Man" 207) and have consequently effaced the parodic intent that makes *The Autobiography* an unrecognized, sophisticated prototype of avant-garde modernist "self-conscious novels" (Alter 139).[7]

Nineteenth-century African American novels, as I have argued in the previous chapters, in many ways already anticipated the relativistic and self-reflexive sensibility of modernism by portraying and problematizing the dramatically different realities and subject positions of blacks and whites. However, Johnson's pioneer fictional play with both the autobiographical mode and an unreliable first-person narrator[8] is indicative of a new interest in portraying how reality is filtered, recreated, and mystified by individual consciousness. This difference is symptomatic of a larger shift in artistic sensibility: The modernist revolution was already beginning in the first decade of the twentieth century and came to full fruition in the 1920s. For African Americans, full fruition came with the New Negro movement. Also called the Harlem Renaissance, this new cultural climate was influenced by the innovations in philosophy, psychology, physics, and anthropology that are often mentioned with regard to Euro-American modernism but also by the mass migration, urbanization, and class differentiation the black population underwent in the years around World War I and by an unprecedented mainstream fascination with the folk and African roots of African American culture.

Johnson has long been recognized as a "contributor to and preserver of the Afro-American literary tradition, linking the nineteenth century to the Harlem Renaissance" (Kinnamon, "James Weldon Johnson" 168),[9] but only in the last twenty years have scholars discussed how his transitional status stems not only from his early thematic interest in black music and folk expressive culture but also

7. Robert Alter describes twentieth-century self-conscious novels as "deeply concerned with a particular historical moment, with the very nature of historical process, . . . as they deploy their elaborate systems of mirrors to reflect novel and novelist in the act of conjuring with reality" (139–40). The "ontological quandaries" (154), "relativistic" sensibility (157), "tongue-in-cheek narrator" (166), "parody-inventions" (168), and the "impulse of iconoclasm" (177) Alter identifies in the work of such modernist authors as Gide, Joyce, Unamuno, and Woolf also are prominent constitutive features of Johnson's novel.

8. Henry Louis Gates Jr. describes the Ex-Colored Man as "the first flawed character in Afro-American fiction," explaining that this is "the first instance where a character's fate is determined not by environmental forces such as racism but by the choices that he makes" (Introduction, *The Autobiography* xix). His unreliability and the proclaimed autobiographical purpose of his narrative differentiate the Ex-Colored Man from other first-person narrators such as Griggs's Berl Trout and E. A. Johnson's Gilbert Twitchell.

9. See also Bone (48), Kent (29), Sterling Brown (*The Negro* 132), Lawson (98), and Davis (*From the Dark Tower* 30).

from his modernist formal self-awareness.[1] Critics such as Robert Stepto, Lucinda MacKethan, and Valerie Smith point to the ironic relationship between Johnson's simulated autobiography and the tradition of black autobiography and the slave narrative as indispensable to the appreciation of the novel. However, little or no attention has been paid to how *The Autobiography* identifies and collects key tropes from antedating African American novels.[2] Also in this respect *The Autobiography* proves to be a "watershed" (Stepto, *From Behind the Veil* 96). It synthesizes the generic conventions and argumentative strategies of the previous sixty years of African American fiction and also recasts them in parodic ways that foreshadow the modernist concerns of the Harlem Renaissance and the self-reflexivity that characterizes postmodern "metafiction" (Hutcheon, "Historiographic" 3). Through his glaringly unreliable first-person narrator, Johnson parodies previous African American fictional tropes that were an integral part of nineteenth-century black culture, such as the race hero and heroine and the ideal of uplift.

Johnson's parodic manipulation of the African American novelistic tradition and nineteenth-century cultural values ushered in a major change in the use of the trope of passing in black fiction, a change that influenced subsequent twentieth-century treatments of this theme and critical evaluations of nineteenth-century fiction of the color line. In contrast with previous novelists of passing, in *The Autobiography* Johnson presents passing for white as the *result*, rather than the *cause*, of cultural alienation and divided racial loyalties. His emphasis shifts from physical to ideological passing, from whiteness as a mark without to whiteness as a mark within, as his narrator unwittingly reveals his inability to shake off his white supremacist values and prejudices even for the short period when he decides to become a "race hero" and spokesperson for African American culture. *The Autobiography* thus performs the transition from a nineteenth-century concern with race loyalty and the insider's description of black life to a twentieth-century preoccupation with defining a distinctive African American identity. In Johnson's novel parody functions not only as ridiculing but also as reverential

1. In 1980, Joseph Skerrett assessed the currents of criticism on *The Autobiography* in the following terms: "One group, which includes Sterling Brown, Hugh Gloster, David Littlejohn, Stephen Bronz, and Nathan Huggins, feels that Johnson's narrator and his opinions are more or less direct reflections of their author. The other group, whose membership includes Robert Bone, Edward Margolies, Eugenia Collier, Robert Fleming, and Marvin Garrett, argue that Johnson's treatment of his narrator is essentially ironic" (540). Since then, critics have reached a greater agreement about the ironic tone of *The Autobiography*. See Stepto (*From Behind the Veil*), V. Smith (*Self-Discovery*), MacKethan ("*Black Boy*"), Warren ("Troubled"), C. Clarke ("Race"), and Sundquist (*Hammers*).
2. Critics such as Andrews (Introduction, *The Autobiography*) and Sundquist (*Hammers*) have recently mentioned the influence of Stowe, Twain, and Chesnutt on *The Autobiography*, but they have not focused on the consistent intertextuality that enabled Johnson to perform a feat of cultural preservation of antedating African American novels.

imitation: It guarantees the continued existence of the mocked conventions, and it is "the custodian of the artistic legacy" (Hutcheon, *A Theory of Parody* 75). *The Autobiography* is at once a harbinger of the Harlem Renaissance and the last articulation of post-Reconstruction cultural values in new fictional form. It is precisely its dual, Janus-like quality that leads to a new, more complex understanding of the differences and the continuities between Old and New Negro literature.

The plot of *The Autobiography* is an aggregate of the salient and defining topoi of previous novels of passing: the extramarital relationship between a rich white southerner and a devoted but eventually forsaken mulatta, the illegitimate offspring's initial ignorance of his racial background, the ritual trips to the North and to a more prejudice-free Europe, the all-but-white protagonist's decision to reconnect with his cultural roots and the difficulties of such "immersion,"[3] the moral crisis of the passer who falls in love with an unsuspecting white person, and the sense of loneliness and alienation of the passer in a prejudiced white world. It is exactly because of the obvious ways in which "*The Autobiography* aggressively invites comparison with major antecedent Afro-American texts" (Stepto, *From Behind the Veil* 106) that the difference between the Ex-Colored Man's story and previous articulations of the theme of passing becomes so clear. The irony that stems from the contrast between the Ex-Colored Man's experiences and his motivations and rationalizations can be fully appreciated only when *The Autobiography* is read against the previous literary tradition of committed novels of passing. The Ex-Colored Man's mimicry of the race loyalty characteristic of early African American protagonists highlights the opposing ideological frameworks between which he oscillates. His proclaimed loyalty to his "mother's people" (210) is continuously undercut by his admiration for and identification with mainstream white America. When contrasted with the brave trickery or the serious life choices of previous passers, the Ex-Colored Man's oft-noted cowardice, self-commiseration, and superficial comments call attention to his lifelong estrangement from African American culture and foreground his unreliability as a first-person narrator.[4]

This unreliability is one of the formal solutions that insert *The Autobiography* among the harbingers of modernism. It induces a

3. Stepto defines immersion as "a ritualized journey into a symbolic South" (*From Behind the Veil* 167). His eloquent analysis of the parodic quality of *The Autobiography* has influenced my own interpretation of Johnson's text.
4. Several critics note the cowardice, egotism, and ultimate unreliability of Johnson's narrator. See Garrett, Ross, Vauthier, C. Clarke, Andrews (Introduction, *The Autobiography*), and Sundquist (*Hammers*).

consistent metanarrative reflection that is more pervasive and overt but not easier to interpret than Chesnutt's in *The House Behind the Cedars* or than the one occasioned by the hermeneutic clues of earlier African American novels of the color line. Johnson's oblique approach, his parodic exposure of the narrator's contradictions and inconsistencies, underscores the constructedness of the "autobiographical" text and compels readers to become suspicious of smooth surfaces, nonthreatening statements, sentimental situations, and detached objectivity. By "highlight[ing] the narrative process" itself (V. Smith, *Self-Discovery* 45) and heightening the reader's awareness of the Ex-Colored Man's self-interested, defensive interpretive manipulations of his "black" experiences, Johnson situates his audience in a self-consciously cautious posture of reception. This distrust of the narrator mirrors, ironically, the "distrust of the reader" (Stepto, "Distrust" 300) that beguiled nineteenth-century African American authors, who were addressing a double, highly ideologically polarized black and white audience. On one hand, as a result of "directing his irony at the ex-colored man, Johnson attacks a hypothetical white audience" (Ross 199) and undermines in ironic ways superficial interpretations of African American literary and cultural texts. On the other hand, by capitalizing on his induced distrust of the narrator, Johnson provides a hermeneutic tool for interpreting not only his own text but also previous African American fiction.

The profound and parodic differences between Johnson's protagonist and the heroes and heroines of previous novels of passing become clear from the outset of *The Autobiography.* Reared in racial unawareness and assuming himself to be white, the Ex-Colored Man is easily indoctrinated into racial prejudice by other children, and he does not possess the delicacy of mind or the humanitarian bent that makes the similarly unaware Iola Leroy condemn practical instances of discrimination even while supporting the institution of slavery in principle. Johnson's narrator does not reveal any qualms of conscience about running after his black schoolmates and "pelting them with stones" (15) [11][5], nor does he seem to be touched by his mother's heartfelt though vague rebuke. Even the revelation of his mixed racial background fails to engender any deep changes in his outlook or his early identification with whites. In contrast to turn-of-the-century characters such as Iola Leroy, who, upon making this same discovery, embark on a series of learning experiences that are motivated by race loyalty and lead to race consciousness, for Johnson's ex-white picaro "becoming" black is just the first of many temporary metamorphoses. In the course of the novel (which the author considered calling *The*

5. Page numbers in square brackets refer to this Norton Critical Edition—Editor.

Chameleon), the nameless narrator turns into an all-but-native speaker of Spanish, a black gambler, a black ragtime player, a racially indeterminate American expatriate in Europe, and a black musicologist and finally settles for being a white businessperson.

The least successful and most obtrusive of his metamorphoses is as an interpreter of black culture. After having recounted his shock at the revelation of his black ancestry, the protagonist periodically interrupts his narration with lengthy sociological digressions on race. These "didactic" (Levy 134) digressions represent Johnson's most obvious parodic recuperation of the stylistic features of nineteenth-century African American fiction. His proficient mimicry of earlier texts is confirmed indirectly by critical lamentations on the "loose episodic framework" (Vauthier 179) of *The Autobiography* and its "compromised" literary artistry (Kinnamon, "James Weldon Johnson" 174), which sound like belated echoes of similar critiques leveled against Brown, Harper, and Griggs. Rather than "present a problem for a reading of the narrator's portrayal as totally ironic" (Ross 204), the oft-noted accuracy of the Ex-Colored Man's descriptions of black life in different social classes and geographic areas only sharpens the strident contrast with his prejudiced readings of the material he presents. As Fleming notes, the "fact that the narrator's observations of black life in America have been so highly praised by readers and critics adds an element of irony that Johnson may not have foreseen" (*James Weldon Johnson* 35).

The Ex-Colored Man's stereotyped reflections on African America and his never-ending surprise at instances of black artistic skill or social accomplishment glaringly reveal his continued white supremacist allegiances. More subtly and pervasively, his qualities of "unconscious misreader" (Clarke, "Race" 88) emerge from the very tone of his telling, from the deceptively objective detachment against which Johnson warns his readers in his real autobiography. In *Along this Way*, which he wrote partly to correct literal readings of his novel (*Along* 239), Johnson describes in the following terms his own experiences in the "backwoods of Georgia" where the Ex-Colored Man roams only to plunder them culturally: "As I worked with my children in school and met with their parents in the homes, on the farms, and in church, I found myself studying them all with a sympathetic objectivity, as though they were something apart; but in an instant's reflection I could realize that they were me and I was they; that a force stronger than blood made us one" (*Along* 119). This "instant's reflection" escapes the Ex-Colored Man throughout the novel.

By signaling the failure of the narrator's immersion through the contrast between his superficial interpretive tools and the serious and often dramatic situations he confronts every time he plays the black man,[6] Johnson provides an obliquely critical insider's report on the power of mystification of white supremacist ideology. Whether he describes the workings of Du Boisian double consciousness (21–22) [13–14], praises gifted black men (25–26), classifies the "coloured people" of the South on the basis of their socioeconomic status (76–81) [41–44], or reports a debate on race he hears on a train (158–67) [82–87], the Ex-Colored Man's detached sociological tone is accompanied both by a propensity to generalize on the basis of his own personal experiences, which often results in stereotyping, and by expressions of sympathy and apology for the discriminatory behavior of whites. Whereas in previous novels of the color line those digressions constituted thematic and formal sites of resistance that foregrounded the subject position of African Americans, in *The Autobiography* they are turned into spaces for articulating stereotypes and defending white supremacist beliefs.

Notwithstanding his self-proclaimed introduction into "the freemasonry of the race" (74) [40–41], in his retrospective sociological digressions the narrator operates a shift from the past of events narrated, when he was "black," to the present of the writing, when he is "white," which reveals no development of his race consciousness. His continued belief in his juvenile hierarchy of authorities on the race question is transparently ironic and indicative of the ideological blinders through which he (mis)interprets African American life. Although he admits that "Frederick Douglass was enshrined in the place of honour" (46) [26] among his "coloured" heroes, the most significant influence on his supposedly budding race consciousness as an African American derives from another text. He confesses with pride, "*Uncle Tom's Cabin* . . . opened my eyes as to who and what I was and what my country considered me; in fact, it gave me my bearing" (42) [24]. Should the irony of this declaration remain unclear, Johnson's protagonist also praises the objectivity of Stowe's novel echoing plantation tradition representations of African Americans: "We must also remember that the author depicted a number of worthless if not vicious Negroes . . . that she pictured the happy, singing, shuffling 'darky' as well as the mother wailing for her child sold 'down river'" (42) [24].

The appreciation of the author's intertextual parody and of the ironic discrepancy between the Ex-Colored Man's proclaimed ideals

6. The narrator himself discusses his "inability to 'read'" (Stepto, *From Behind the Veil* 114) early in the novel, when he brags about how he invents stories and reproduces tunes instead of reading books and music sheets. Even when he does become a reader at the cigar factory, his skill remains purely technical, and his duties do not require exegetical abilities but "a stock of varied information" (73) [40]. The protagonist's incapacity to read literary or racial texts becomes more obvious as he confronts more complex situations. See Lucinda MacKethan's comments on the difference between language and communication in *The Autobiography*.

and his practices, between his varying masquerades and his unwavering allegiance to the authority of whites, prompts the reader to assume the inquisitive critical pose that the protagonist himself lacks and that proves indispensable in moving beyond parody toward recuperating the political agenda of resistance that *The Autobiography* shares with previous novels of passing. As Stepto suggests, "The Ex-Colored Man's perils and travails . . . sustain the heroic proportions of the canonical types and tropes by offering what is, in effect, *a negative example of them*" (*From Behind the Veil* 104–5, emphasis added). For instance, the narrator's driving opportunism and his attempts to rationalize the lack of racial commitment that will lead to his decision to pass permanently indirectly point and give new life to that notion of "service" (*Along* 122) to the race that dominates pre–World War I African American fiction and that Johnson himself continued to value.[7] Also revealing of the interventionist subtext underlying the novel's irony is the Ex-Colored Man's seeming obliviousness to the contrast between the clear-cut sociological classifications through which he attempts to regulate "race" and especially "blackness" and his own ambiguous racial status. The protagonist's unawareness of this contrast foregrounds the constructedness of racial categories that was more explicitly critiqued in previous novels of passing. Johnson's ironic, newly oblique strategy of consciousness raising indicates his awareness of the changing cultural climate among African Americans and anticipates features of the literary production of the post–World War I writers whom Johnson praises in *The Book of American Negro Poetry* (1922): "The best of them have found an approach to 'race' that is different. Their approach is less direct, less obvious than that of their predecessors, and thereby they have secured a gain in subtlety of power and, probably, in ultimate effectiveness" (6).

The most revealing instance of the ironic discrepancy between the narrator's black experiences and his white supremacist ideology is the lynching that eventually motivates him to pass for white permanently. Protected by the fact that his "identity as a coloured man had not yet become known in the town" (185) [97], the Ex-Colored Man becomes a spectator of ritualistic antiblack violence. In clear parodic contrast with the profound indignation and increased racial commitment that lynchings inspired in previous race heroes and heroines, the Ex-Colored Man's reactions to the spectacle of

7. Johnson writes in *Along This Way*, "Grown older, I occasionally meditate upon the kind of education Atlanta University gave me. . . . The central idea embraced a term that is now almost a butt for laughter—'service.' . . . The ideal constantly held up to us was of education as a means of living, not of making a living. It was impressed upon us that taking a classical course would have an effect of making us better and nobler, and of higher value to those we should have to serve. An odd, old-fashioned, naive conception? Rather" (122).

violence betray no marked sympathy for "the poor wretch" (186) [97] who is burned alive. Although he briefly describes the "transformation of [white] human beings into savage beasts" as "terrible" (186) [97], he spends more time detailing the "degeneracy" of the black victim, "a man only in form and stature" (186) [97]. Even as he witnesses the brutality of the lynching, his comments reveal awe and fearful respect for the power of the murderers and contempt for the victim. His ultimate concern is to reconcile what he has witnessed with his conviction that "Southern whites are in many respects a great people" (189) [99]. Rather than an attempt to avoid stereotyping all southerners as violent racists, the Ex-Colored Man's intention to be fair soon emerges as opportunistic. He tries both to rationalize self-interest out of his subsequent decision to cut himself off from "a people that could with impunity be treated worse than animals" (191) [100] and to minimize his own passive complicity with the organized, communal racial violence of the white society he has decided to join by passing. Within the value system implied by the novel's ironic tone, the significance of the Ex-Colored Man's effort at accommodationist self-deception looms larger than an example of individual cowardice. It becomes metonymical of the broader extratextual reality of institutionalized blindness to the pervasiveness of racial violence.[8]

The lynching occasions in the Ex-Colored Man a veritable reversion to (white) type that is highly parodic of the social Darwinism still popular when Johnson wrote his novel. As the fictional first-person narrator describes his motives for leaving the South and the race, Johnson operates a crucial shift in the use of the passing motif. Unlike his antecedents, the Ex-Colored Man claims that the primary motivation behind his decision to pass is not "discouragement or fear or [the] search for a larger field of action and opportunity" but "shame, unbearable shame" (190–91) [100]. Although this claim offers, characteristically, only a thin disguise for his opportunism, his willingness to interpret the lynching in ways that degrade the victim's people represents the most obvious symptom of the deep-seated white supremacist allegiances that beguile the Ex-Colored Man throughout the text. Johnson's protagonist thus emerges as a thoroughly self-deceiving modernist revision of Webb's Clarence, whose estrangement from and shame of the black community are the result, rather than the cause, of the externally imposed decision to hide his racial identity. Whereas Clarence initially resents passing as contrary to his inclinations and familial affections, the

8. In light of Johnson's own early experience of near lynching (*Along* 165–70), it is hard not to read the emphasis he places on this episode in *The Autobiography* as foreshadowing his later political activism against racial violence.

Ex-Colored Man's eventual decision to pass permanently is little more than the formalization of his continued estrangement from black culture and black life. Despite the Stowe-like, melodramatic tragic mulatto posture with which the Ex-Colored Man closes his narrative, passing is a decision that does not create the psychological torture Webb describes so effectively in relation to Clarence.

The uncharacteristic humility, regret, and critical self-analysis and the characteristic egotism and self-commiseration that dominate the ending of *The Autobiography* constitute the last metamorphosis of the narrator, who presents himself as a failed race hero of tragic proportions. Whereas some critics interpret these closing passages as an indication that the very act of writing leads the narrator to a first level of self-awareness,[9] I read them parodically as the Ex-Colored Man's final effort at self-fashioning that frames *The Autobiography* and disguises how the text itself represents his most successful exploitation of the culture of his mother's people for purposes of self-aggrandizement. The Ex-Colored Man's "fast yellowing manuscripts" are not "the only tangible remnant . . . of a sacrificed talent" (211) [110] but one of the many sentimental images instrumental to the realization of his musical ambition, albeit in a different artistic medium. *The Autobiography* itself opens up a space for the public presentation of his folk musical findings and represents the triumph of his talent as an artist as well as a masquerader. As he had calculated with regard to music, the narrator builds his autobiographical enterprise on the conviction that he has "greater chances of attracting attention as a coloured [writer] than as a white one" (147) [77] and that his personal and sociological digressions enable him "to voice all the joys and sorrows, the hopes and ambitions, of the American Negro, in classical . . . form" (147–48) [77].

It is before the studiedly pathetic ending of *The Autobiography* that Johnson's Ex-Colored Man voices something akin to protest or self-awareness. Finally established as a successful white businessperson, the narrator returns to the more defiant tone of the opening lines of his autobiography, admits that the "anomaly of [his] social position often appealed strongly to [his] sense of humor" (197) [102], and appreciates passing as a "capital joke" (197) [102], as an intrinsic refutation of the racial stereotypes he has invoked in his own narrative. For a brief moment, the text restores the traditional subversive function of the passing motif and comes to constitute the Ex-Colored Man's first act of loyalty toward his mother's people. As narrator, the passer finally declaims what the passer as protagonist never has the courage to utter: "I am a coloured man. Do I not disprove the theory

9. See Fleming (*James Weldon Johnson* 40; "Irony" 96), Faulkner (151), Ross (209–10), Kinnamon ("James Weldon Johnson" 174), and Skerrett (557).

that one drop of Negro blood renders a man unfit?" (197) [102]. As the narrator decentralizes his enjoyment of the disruptive joke to close his narrative on the aforementioned sentimental note, this dual ending mirrors similar double closures in nineteenth-century African American fiction and represents a parodically self-centered equivalent of the covert protest strategies characteristic of earlier novels of passing (e.g., *Clotel* and *The Garies*).

The Autobiography calls attention to the text's constructedness and "the ontological meaning of the act of telling" (V. Smith, *Self-Discovery* 45), and its autobiographical packaging of a fictional text transforms the protagonist's telling of his story into an epistemological exercise for the reader. It also foregrounds in new ways the larger extratextual threat that the theme of passing has always incorporated. In most previous African American novels, the passer's defiance of racial categorizations was only partly contained by the end of the novel by the proud determination to relinquish passing, by emigration, and less often by death. In contrast, the end of *The Autobiography* coincides with the passer's return to his undetected extratextual white existence. In an autobiography the world of the text and of the reader "are . . . in a way permeable" (Vauthier 179), and in Johnson's "autobiographical" tale of passing permeability coincides with the real-life osmosis of the races. When the narrator closes his story and returns to his anonymity as an "ordinarily successful white man" (*The Autobiography* 211) [110], his joke on society, though couched in the language of melodramatic regret, turns into a continued threat to the group identity of the whites among whom he prospers undetected and whose racial privilege has lost some of its glamor because the narrative has foregrounded the "diminished stature of the white man who could have been black" and who could have participated in the "grandeur of black achievement" (Warren, "Troubled" 276).

Given his low level of self-awareness, however, the Ex-Colored Man, unlike previous passers, poses as serious a threat to black as to white group identity. Johnson's novel thus foreshadows the dramatically different ways in which the trope of passing was deployed during and after the Harlem Renaissance. If the very fact of the Ex-Colored Man's success at permanent passing undermines the "whiteness" of whiteness, his own misinterpretations of African American culture and white supremacist allegiances problematize the "blackness" of his blackness. By parodying previous uses of passing to undermine racial stereotypes and represent black culture, Johnson ultimately foregrounds the complex process of articulating the specific cultural and historical grounds on which "to define a black identity within the American cultural context" (Huggins 142). By parodying them, he also preserves increasingly outmoded cultural values that provide a historical perspective crucial to the definition of that very identity.

It is in the ironic interstice Johnson creates between the Ex-Colored Man's "black" experiences and his "white" (supremacist) interpretations, between his proclaimed desire for cultural memory and his de facto cultural amnesia that the crucial issue of the black "racial spirit" lies (Johnson, *The Book of American Negro Poetry* 41). Johnson recuperates and foregrounds the dual valence of Du Bois's widely influential 1903 statement that "The problem of the Twentieth Century is the problem of the color-line" (*The Souls* 41). Du Bois's prophecy obviously referred to the unsolved problem of racial inequality and black-white relations, but it also represented an insider's posing of another problem: how to define the distinctiveness of African American culture without invoking essentialist notions of blackness or prescriptive ideological standpoints, how to strengthen the bonds of race in light of the increasing internal differentiation within the black community.

Johnson's answers to these questions reveal once again the transitional status of his novel, as he looks back to the nineteenth-century values of service and uplift even as he recasts them in new ways. Like previous writers of passing, he moves beyond and ridicules the dominant Darwinian biological essentialism of his age by disintegrating "race" into its sociocultural components through a narrator who is legally black because of his ancestry, phenotypically white, and ideologically a white supremacist. Although the Ex-Colored Man's experiences, more than his explanations, reveal the class, geographic, and cultural differences between African Americans, Johnson situates his criteria for a communal, nonessentialist definition of "racial spirit" in the aspects of black culture his narrator cannot sustain or accept: in the history of resistance to the oppression that makes the Ex-Colored Man flee into whiteness permanently,[1] in the literary tradition his narrator misreads, and in such different cultural artifacts as ragtime and the spirituals, which the Ex-Colored Man cannot appreciate without attempting to recast them in the mold of European art. That the Ex-Colored Man's flight from racial violence proves coterminous with the surrender of his musical ambition indirectly attests to the close connection Johnson establishes between historical and cultural distinctiveness. Two years before *The Autobiography* came to new life at the height of the Harlem Renaissance, in his introduction to *The Book of American Negro Spirituals* (1925) Johnson comments more directly on the

1. Some critics who have recently focused on Johnson's deconstruction of racial categories tend to underestimate his coterminous emphasis on the distinctiveness of black history and culture. See Pisiak, Kawash, and K. Pfeiffer.

issue of cultural specificity in ways that clearly distinguish his notion of racial spirit from simplistic biological essentialism and bring to mind Harper's description of Iola Leroy's process of sociocultural acculturation into blackness: "Carl Van Vechten . . . declared it as his opinion that white singers cannot sing them [the Spirituals]. . . . I think white singers, concert singers, *can* sing Spirituals—if they *feel* them. But to feel them it is necessary to know the truth about their origin and history, to get in touch with the association of ideas that surround them, and to realize something of what they have meant in the experiences of the people who created them" (28–29).

The Autobiography thus culminates the process of shifting the focus of racialist discourse from biology to culture, a process that can be traced back through the post-Reconstruction emphasis on uplift to the first African American novelist's discussion of passing as paradigmatic of the artificiality of racial classifications. In the nineteenth century the emphasis was on redressing stereotypes and arguing the existence of African American culture and the agency of African Americans as subjects. In the 1920s, this order of priorities was reversed, and the focus shifted on analyzing blackness not only in its differences from mainstream culture but also in light of intraracial variations of gender, geographic provenance, class background, sexual preference, shade of color, and education. As the "subtle processes of internal reorganization" of the race (Locke xvii) foregrounded internal divisions and stratifications, passing became an extreme example of how deep such divisions could run but also remained a tool to focus on the ideological and cultural components of blackness. Johnson's parodic re-vision of previous African American fiction of the color line, his focus on whiteness as a mark within as well as without, and his use of passing as a symptom rather than a cause of cultural confusion and existential angst became as characteristic of the Harlem Renaissance as his interest in African American music and the urban scene. Similarly, Johnson's notion of the black racial spirit pioneered later discussions both on the criteria for articulating an African American literary canon and on the centrality of the vernacular to the modernist agenda of the Harlem Renaissance.

During the Harlem Renaissance the emphasis on folk forms was presented as a novelty and constituted a rebellious gesture. The determination to proudly enhance them was predicated in opposition to "the psychology of imitation and implied inferiority" (Locke 4) that supposedly characterized antecedent African American discursive forms. In his groundbreaking 1925 anthology, Locke boldly proclaims, "The Negro to-day wishes to be known for what he is, even in his faults and shortcomings, and scorns a craven and precarious survival at the price of seeming to be what he is not" (11). Although the continued reality of a white-dominated publishing industry and the need for white sponsorship qualified the readability of this uncompromising stance, the unprecedented primitivist vogue of the 1920s made possible a different set of artistic choices, one that sustained the New Negro's agenda of radical novelty and greater outspokenness.

Within this new context, in the 1927 reprint the Ex-Colored Man is reborn with all "his faults and shortcomings" (Locke 11) as a new literary product, if not as a new hero. In his (in)capacity as a narrator, he proves instrumental in advancing the iconoclastic rationale of the New Negro movement because his low level of self-awareness, confused racial loyalties, and emphatic appreciation for all things white provide what became an influential framework for the interpretation of the supposed representational compromises and racial self-hatred of previous African American writers of passing. In the absence of an appreciation of his novel's celebratory parody, Johnson's manipulation of nineteenth-century African American fictional conventions contributed less to a recognition of the strategic maneuvering that historically was practiced by African American writers beguiled by "a double . . . [and] divided audience" (Johnson, "Dilemma" 477) than to their dismissal and patronizing critical neglect. From the vantage point of the Harlem Renaissance programmatic rupture with the very literary tradition Johnson synthesized, the lack of racial spirit that turns a potential African American musician into a white businessperson mirrors and recapitulates the proclaimed dichotomy between Old and New Negro artists.

Yet despite the Ex-Colored Man's retreat from the artistic production of his mother's people, in 1927 Johnson's 1912 presentation of the expressive culture of the folk was received as prophetic of and consistent with the cultural nationalist agenda of the Harlem Renaissance. However, it is worth repeating that the fact that the Ex-Colored Man's statements on black culture have long been taken at face value represents an irony that Johnson may not have anticipated. The Ex-Colored Man in fact constitutes a characteristically "negative" (Stepto, *From Behind the Veil* 104) parodic model for the new kind of cultural spokesperson Johnson envisioned. This becomes most obvious when the Ex-Colored Man tours the South "to catch the spirit of the Negro in his relatively primitive state" (173) [90]. Then he once again demonstrates his alienation from black culture by being surprised at the consummate artistry of black folk musicians and orators. Within the contrapuntal ironic structure of the novel, his reluctant "enthusiasm" (182) [95] is dialogized, and it ultimately enhances the significance of his bewildered recognition of the artistic value of folk creations: "As I listened to the singing of these songs, the wonder of their production grew upon me more and more. How did the men who originated them manage to do it? The sentiments are easily accounted for; they are mostly taken from the Bible; but the melodies, where did they come from?" (181) [94]. Beyond the narrator's culturally uninformed artistic stance lies Johnson's affirmation of the uniqueness of African American artistic contributions, his respect for the "genuine folk stuff" (Johnson, *The Book of American Negro Poetry* 6), and his critique of the hierarchy of literary value that belittles the artistic potential of the folk in their vernacular medium. *The Autobiography* articulates the interest in "the classical sound of Afro-America" that Houston Baker identifies as a distinctive feature of African American modernism (*Modernism* 73).

Johnson's Ex-Colored Man foreshadows the cultural nationalist agenda of the Harlem Renaissance in another, less commented upon sense as well, because his emphasis on the vernacular mother tongue does not result in a comparable interest in the "tongue of the mother" (Gilbert and Gubar 262). The hierarchy of folk artistic authenticity is gendered in the novel, and the narrator seems to reinscribe in distinctively African American terms the modernist distinction Sandra Gilbert and Susan Gubar analyze between the male creators and the female users of language (227–71). In *The Autobiography*, the mother who plays by ear "some old Southern songs" (8) [7] functions as a cultural mediator and vulgarizer by reproducing folk and religious melodies. However, the Ex-Colored Man has to move beyond the mother's "simple accompaniments" (8) [7] to recuperate the complex artistry of the original folk pieces. John Brown and "Singing Johnson," respectively the preacher and the leader of singing he encounters years later at a big meeting in the South, are "a revelation" (175) [91] to the narrator. They emerge as "archetypal" (Carroll 354) cultural figures despite the Ex-Colored Man's characteristically stereotypical comments on their "primitive poetry" (177) [92] and "born" (175) [91] artistic skills. The different degrees of male and female cultural agency become equally clear in the description of the call-and-response pattern of the Spirituals: The congregation, which includes a mass of faceless women, "sings the same lines over and over," whereas the male leader's "memory and ingenuity are taxed to keep the songs going" (180) [94].

Within this gendered economy of the novel, the Ex-Colored Man's eventual rejection of cultural agency by passing "feminizes" him in ways that are reminiscent of Webb's seduced and abandoned Clarence. Clarence's hysteria finds an equivalent in the petulant, self-commiserating tone that dominates *The Autobiography*.[2] The

2. In both cases, the "feminine" nervousness of the protagonists is not portrayed to be naturally inherent in mulattos, as contemporaneous racist discourse maintained, but constitutes the psychological result both of racial discrimination and of the characters' disloyalty to their race.

Ex-Colored Man's short-lived project of immersion and his rhetoric of cultural uplift confirm Johnson's oblique, parodic feminization of the narrator by connecting him with the host of all-but-white race heroines that populated the novels of the Black Woman's Era. This feminization of the narrator in turn reverberates on and genders the contrast between Old and New Negroes. The novelty of the Harlem Renaissance, with its emphasis on the expressive culture of the folk and its aggressively "masculine" affirmation of race pride and self-reliance were predicated on a "feminine" definition of pre–World War I African American literature, which emphasized its gentility, "sentimental appeal," "hyper-sensitiveness," and "'touchy' nerves" (Locke 10).

The appreciation both of Johnson's parodic approach to earlier African American fiction and culture, and of the proclaimed male genealogy of folk art and the vernacular lends important insight into the different set of artistic choices that characterized the supposedly more formally conservative literary output of African American women during the Harlem Renaissance.[3] A case in point is Nella Larsen. On one hand, like Johnson but with a less playful and ultimately more tragic tone, Larsen focuses on ideological as well as physical passing and constructs her novels against the familiar script of the race heroine and the ideal of uplift. By portraying Helga Crane and Irene Redfield, the protagonists respectively of *Quicksand* (1928) and *Passing* (1929), as failed, unhappy Iola Leroys who outlive the fictional happy ending and struggle with the frustrations of marriage and uplift, Larsen highlights how traditional African American cultural scripts fail to prove liberating for female characters. On the other hand, Larsen explicitly discusses the tensions between the problematics of gender and the glorification of the folk in *Quicksand* (1928). Helga Crane's marriage to the "grandiloquent" (118) Reverend Mr. Pleasant Green and her eager, condescendingly naive immersion "in the tiny Alabama town where he was pastor to a scattered and primitive flock" (118) trap her in a victimizing cycle of unwanted pregnancies. Even Zora Neale Hurston, "the outstanding exception" (Wall 155) in terms of female artistic use of the vernacular and folk themes, deals with these tensions in *Their Eyes Were Watching God* (1937), for instance, a novel that details the heroine's struggle to achieve control and assert her creative use of the vernacular in a male-dominated folk environment. The negative reception of her book by critics such as Locke and Wright highlights the gendered politics of folk representation that were already present in *The New Negro* and *The Autobiography*

3. Bone, for instance, includes Nella Larsen and Jessie Fauset among "the rear guard" of novelists who, during the Harlem Renaissance, "lag[ged] behind" (97).

and that would influence so strongly the process of articulation and canonization of the African American literary tradition in the twentieth century.[4]

The Autobiography thus proves to be a precursor not only of the themes and concerns but also of the tensions and omissions that characterized the New Negro movement. The sociocultural changes that gave rise to the Harlem Renaissance altered dramatically African American modes of artistic depiction of race and of the related trope of passing. After World War I, ideological passing, often unredeemed by irony, gained center stage as a symptom of cultural confusion, existential angst, and divided racial loyalties. As a theme, passing continued to be an essential tool to foreground the dynamics of black and white group consciousness; to analyze the distinctive but far from monolithic black cultural identity in light of differences in class, gender, color, sexual preference, education, and geographic provenance; and to explore the shifting boundary between cultural change and cultural estrangement. To reconnect, without simply conflating, the nineteenth-century tradition with the profoundly different uses of the trope of passing by such Harlem Renaissance figures as Jessie Fauset, Nella Larsen, George Schuyler, and Walter White grounds the uniqueness of the African American novelistic tradition in the "changing same" of a people's distinctive sociocultural history (Jones, "The Changing Same" 112).

SIOBHAN B. SOMERVILLE

Double Lives on the Color Line: "Perverse" Desire in *The Autobiography of an Ex-Coloured Man*[†]

The ex-colored man's status in the literary genealogy of the "tragic mulatto" has been a central preoccupation of critics, not least because this lineage featured few men prior to *ECM*'s publication in 1912. Here critic Siobhan B. Somerville turns to the history of sexuality and queer theory to propose a different analysis of the novel's gender politics.

4. On the reception of Hurston's novel, Christian writes, "Locke . . . said the novel was 'folklore fiction at its best,' but asked when Hurston was going 'to come to grips with motive fiction and social document fiction.' Richard Wright called the novel counter-revolutionary and a continuation of the minstrel image" (*Black Women* 62).

† From *Queering the Color Line: Race and the Invention of Homosexuality in American Culture* (Durham: Duke University Press, 2000), 111–30, 208–10.

In his autobiography, *Along This Way,* published in 1933, James Weldon Johnson discusses the two literary lives of his fictional autobiography, *The Autobiography of an Ex-Coloured Man,* which was first published anonymously in 1912 and subsequently reissued in 1927 "affixed" (in Johnson's words) with his identity as the author. Addressing the reception of the book's initial publication, Johnson explains:

> I did get a certain pleasure out of anonymity, that no acknowledged book could have given me. The authorship of the book excited the curiosity of literate colored people, and there was speculation among them as to who the writer might be—to every such group some colored man who had married white, and so coincided with the main point on which the story turned, is known.[1]

Johnson emphasizes his pleasure at witnessing his text "passing" as a "human document": like the (unnamed) ex-coloured man himself, the text circulates anonymously without being clearly marked as "truth" or "fiction." Yet this passage also asserts a key—and, as I will argue, strategic—characterization of the narrative of *The Autobiography of an Ex-Coloured Man:* that the "main point" of the text concerns "some colored man who had married white." For, as I will explore in this chapter, the pursuit of interracial (heterosexual) marriage is hardly the main trajectory of desire in this text. In fact, it is both integral to, and subordinated by, another form of desire figured as "perverse" that shapes the ex-coloured man's narrative, that of male homosexuality. In this way, Johnson's text participates in the uneven transitions occurring in early-twentieth-century American cultural understandings of bodies and desires that I have discussed in previous chapters. Specifically, in *The Autobiography of an Ex-Coloured Man,* the representation of the mulatto body is mediated by the iconography of gender inversion, and interracial heterosexual desire functions in the text as both an analogy to homosexual object choice and a screen through which it can be articulated. As he shuttles between racialized subject positions, the excoloured man is constructed simultaneously as the subject and object of multiple trajectories of desire. The very proximity of these oscillating racialized and sexualized "perversions" is integral to Johnson's fascination with, and critique of, his unnamed protagonist.

"A Pretty Boy": Gender Inversion and the Mulatto Body

A key turning point in most fictional narratives of the tragic mulatto/a figure is the protagonist's confrontation with an epistemological

1. James Weldon Johnson, *Along This Way: The Autobiography of James Weldon Johnson* (1933; reprint; New York: Penguin, 1990), 238.

crisis about her or his racial identity.[2] In American fiction about mulatto/a characters—including, for example, Frances Harper's *Iola Leroy,* Mark Twain's *Pudd'nhead Wilson,* Kate Chopin's "Désirée's Baby," Zora Neale Hurston's *Their Eyes Were Watching God,* and William Faulkner's *Light in August*—the protagonist is unaware of his or her racial identity or assumes herself or himself to be white until some external source of knowledge steps forward to present evidence of her or his African American ancestry. Typically these epistemological and ontological crises are rendered as moments when the subject is interpellated into a racialized position by institutions and their technological apparatuses, such as the school, the law, the hospital, the orphanage, or, in the case of Hurston's Janie, an itinerant photographer.[3] In *The Autobiography of an Ex-Coloured Man,* the scene of recognition occurs in a classroom, when the teacher separates the white students from "the others."[4] When the protagonist, who has never before consciously considered the question of his racial identity, stands with the white children, the teacher excludes him from the group. Given this new "knowledge," the narrator later confronts his own image in a mirror:

> I had often heard people say to my mother: "What a pretty boy you have!" I was accustomed to hear remarks about my beauty; but now, for the first time, I became conscious of it and recognized it. I noticed the ivory whiteness of my skin, the beauty of my mouth, the size and liquid darkness of my eyes, and how the long, black lashes that fringed and shaded them produced an effect that was strangely fascinating even to me. I noticed the softness and glossiness of my dark hair that fell in waves over my temples, making my forehead appear whiter than it really was. How long I stood there gazing at my image I do not know. (17) [12]

As this passage so richly demonstrates, although the narrator initially frames his crisis as one of racial identification, this moment in the narrative coincides with a (somewhat pleasurable) renegotiation of his gender. Where one might expect the narrator to respond to his new knowledge about his African American identity by suddenly recognizing features associated with racial stereotypes, the narrator presents a scene in which he enters instead a new

2. For a discussion of fictional representations of this "crisis experience," see Judith Berzon, *Neither White nor Black: The Mulatto Character in American Fiction* (New York: New York University Press, 1978), 119–39.
3. See Louis Althusser, "Ideology and Ideological State Apparatuses (Notes Towards an Investigation)," in *Lenin and Philosophy and Other Essays,* trans. Ben Brewster (New York: Monthly Review Press, 1971), 121–73.
4. James Weldon Johnson, *The Autobiography of an Ex-Coloured Man* (1912; 1927; reprint, New York: Vintage, 1989), 17 [22]. Hereafter cited in the text. [Page numbers in square brackets refer to this Norton Critical Edition—Editor.]

consciousness of his own "beauty." His description presents a series of contrasts between light and dark: the "ivory whiteness" of his skin and forehead brings out the "liquid darkness" of his eyes, "long, black lashes," and "dark hair." This play between light and dark is itself erotic and the source of the "strangely fascinating" effect on the narrator. Through descriptions such as "fringed and shaded" and his focus on the "softness and glossiness" and "waves" of his hair, the narrator is also distinctly feminized, recalling descriptions of the highly eroticized mulatta of nineteenth-century fiction.[5]

As discussed in the previous chapter, the narrative trajectories of male and female mulatto characters in nineteenth-century fiction differed considerably, with tragedy as the more likely end for a female character. In Charles Chesnutt's *The House Behind the Cedars,* for instance, the very light complexioned character John Warwick successfully passes into the white world (and out of the text). His beautiful sister Rena, however, is exposed in her attempt to pass as white and subsequently dies young, fleeing the attentions of rival suitors into a wilderness that ultimately punishes and destroys her.[6] In a recent discussion of black masculinity and passing narratives, Philip Brian Harper has resituated the meanings of this gendered difference, arguing that "the tragic mulatto has been conceived as a specifically feminine character."[7] In his reading of the "mirror scene" in *The Autobiography of an Ex-Coloured Man,* Harper argues that the feminization of the protagonist calls into question his sexual orientation: "This feminized orientation itself potentially constitutes the protagonist's personal tragedy, indicating a gender identity that is anything but properly masculine, and verging dangerously on a sexual identity that is anything but hetero."[8] I fully agree with Harper's point that Johnson figures the disruption of the narrator's sense of a stable racial identification through a corresponding slippage in gender and sexuality. It may be argued more precisely, too, that rather than simply "feminizing" the narrator, Johnson characterizes him

5. For discussions of the conventional emphasis on the mulatta figure's beauty, see Berzon, *Neither White nor Black,* 99–116; John G. Mencke, *Mulattoes and Race Mixture: American Attitudes and Images, 1865–1918* (Ann Arbor, Mich.: UMI Research Press, 1979), 154–55; and Anna Shannon Elfenbein, *Women on the Color Line: Evolving Stereotypes and the Writings of George Washington Cable, Grace King, Kate Chopin* (Charlottesville: University Press of Virginia, 1989), 1–24. Claudia Tate, among others, has made the important point that these standards of beauty were also associated with upwardly mobile or elite social status within African American culture in the late nineteenth century. See her *Domestic Allegories of Political Desire: The Black Heroine's Text at the Turn of the Century* (New York: Oxford University Press, 1992), 59–64. As I will discuss, this fascination with aristocracy, or at least aristocratic style, also has a hold on the ex-coloured man's erotic attachments.

6. Charles Chesnutt, *The House Behind the Cedars* (1900; reprint, Athens: University of Georgia Press, 1988).

7. Philip Brian Harper, *Are We Not Men? Masculine Anxiety and the Problem of African-American Identity* (New York: Oxford University Press, 1996), 103.

8. Ibid., 110.

through a model of gender inversion. That is, as a "hybrid" racialized subject, symbolically both black and white, the narrator is also gendered "between" male and female, like the bodies of the inverts who were subjected to the taxonomizing gaze of sexologists. In the case of the ex-coloured man, his *own* gaze importantly constructs and internalizes an eroticized version of the mulatto as invert.

Racialized Homoerotics

The gaze through which the narrator so powerfully eroticizes his own biracial body in this early recognition scene also turns on and eroticizes other male bodies throughout the book. Although he does not direct this gaze exclusively at men, as I will show, the narrator's homoerotic attachments hold a much more powerful place in the narrative than do his erotic attachments with women. Johnson's repeated use of these scenes to destabilize the narrator's masculinity is an integral part of the novel's overall project of critiquing racial passing and the narrator's racial naïveté. These homoerotic attachments begin early in the narrative, when the narrator is a child in school, with descriptions of his crushes on two boys, symbolically one white and the other African American. These attachments oscillate between identification and desire. On the one hand, his identifications with the white and black boyhood friends literalize the ex-coloured man's seemingly split identification with white and black culture. On the other hand, these figures are also rendered as objects of the protagonist's nascent homoerotic desire, which will shape his most important adult relationship later in the narrative.

The narrator describes his meeting with his first "staunch friend," a white boy nicknamed "Red Head":

> This friend I bound to me with hooks of steel in a very simple way. He was a big awkward boy with a face full of freckles and a head full of very red hair. . . . I had not been at school many hours before I felt that "Red Head"—as I involuntarily called him—and I were to be friends. I do not doubt that this feeling was strengthened by the fact that I had been quick enough to see that a big, strong boy was a friend to be desired at a public school; and, perhaps, in spite of his dullness, "Red Head" had been able to discern that I could be of service to him. At any rate there was a simultaneous mutual attraction. (11) [9]

This description foregrounds a number of issues that recur in the narrator's relationships with white men later in the novel. Importantly, the "simultaneous mutual attraction" depends explicitly on the relationships of power between the narrator and this boy within the world of the schoolroom. Clearly, as the narrator admits, he was partly attracted to the power that "Red Head" represented: the narrator sees this older boy as a reliable ally and protector against the other boys at school, some of whom, the narrator remembers, "seemed to me like savages" (10) [8], an unself-consciously racialized construction of his own superiority. In return for this protection, the narrator is quite willing to "be of service to him" by coaching Red Head in his academic work, often simply giving his friend the correct answers on exams. As the narrator writes, "through all our school-days, 'Red Head' shared my wit and quickness and I benefited by his strength and dogged faithfulness" (13) [10]. A similar system of patronage and service characterizes the narrator's subsequent relationship to white men, as the narrator foreshadows: "And when I grew to manhood, I found myself freer with elderly white people than with those near my own age" (23) [15].

If the narrator eroticizes the position of power granted to Red Head by means of his white identity, gender, age, and sheer physical bulk, he also eroticizes black male bodies, but in very different ways. At the same time that the narrator bonds with Red Head, he also meets "Shiny," who, he writes, "strongly attracted my attention from the first day I saw him" (14) [10]. The narrator gives great attention to Shiny's physical characteristics:

> His face was as black as night, but shone as though it were polished; he had sparkling eyes, and when he opened his mouth, he displayed glistening white teeth. It struck me at once as appropriate to call him "Shiny Face," or "Shiny Eyes," or "Shiny Teeth," and I spoke of him often by one of these names to the other boys. These terms were finally merged into "Shiny," and that name he answered good-naturedly during the balance of his public school days. (14) [10]

The narrator's description of Shiny unself-consciously draws on popular cultural stereotypes of the black male body, particularly those that had circulated through the conventions of blackface minstrelsy.[9] The narrator constructs Shiny's body as a collection of fetishized parts, fixating on his "polished" face, "sparkling eyes," and "glistening" teeth. Indeed, the narrator expands the imaginative hold of these fetishizations by using them metonymically to name his friend: in the narrator's eyes, his friend's identity becomes synonymous with the "shiny" characteristics on which he fixates. When Shiny makes a speech at grammar school graduation, the narrator again expresses his fascination with his friend's physical presence:

9. See Marlon Riggs's film documentary *Ethnic Notions* (1987) for a survey of these stereotypes in American popular culture.

> He made a striking picture, that thin little black boy standing on the platform, dressed in clothes that did not fit him any too well, his eyes burning with excitement, his shrill, musical voice vibrating in tones of appealing defiance, and his black face alight with such great intelligence and earnestness as to be positively handsome. (44) [25]

In this portrait of Shiny, who later in the novel becomes a professor at a "Negro college," Johnson borrows the tropes of the African American hero, dignified spiritually and physically. In contrast to the narrator, who repeatedly demonstrates his lack of spiritual or physical defiance, Shiny represents a race leader, one whose racial and gender identifications are, not coincidentally, never in question. In this scene, however, the narrator's desire for Shiny takes on the form of a powerful identification with this heroic figure: "I felt leap within me pride that I was coloured; and I began to form wild dreams of bringing glory and honour to the Negro race" (46) [26].

The figure of Shiny resurfaces at a crucial moment in the closing pages of the novel, when the narrator is passing for white, and again his presence has the effect of eliciting the narrator's desire for racial identification. Standing in line at a theater with his white fiancée, who at that point does not know about the narrator's African American ancestry, the narrator spots Shiny in the crowd. Although the ex-coloured man perceives Shiny as a threat to his secret and thus to his potential status as husband to this white woman, Shiny protects him from exposure: "[Shiny] seemed, at a glance, to divine my situation, and let drop no word that would have aroused suspicion as to the truth" (202) [105]. Although Shiny participates in the narrator's passing, this incident has the ironic effect of making the narrator want to reveal his African ancestry to his fiancée. As in the earlier scene, however, so the narrator's identification with Shiny is fleeting and ultimately replaced by his desire, however ashamed, to be an "ordinarily successful white man" (211) [110].

The narrator's early fascinations with Shiny and Red Head prefigure perhaps the central and most powerful erotic relationship in *The Autobiography of an Ex-Coloured Man,* that of the narrator and his patron, a wealthy white man whom the narrator meets while performing as a ragtime pianist in New York. The narrator describes his fascination with this figure on his first encounter with him:

> Among the other white "slummers" there came into the "Club" one night a clean-cut, slender, but athletic-looking man, who would have been taken for a youth had it not been for the tinge of grey about his temples. He was clean-shaven and had regular features, and all of his movements bore the indefinable but unmistakable stamp of culture. He spoke to no one, but sat

> languidly puffing cigarettes and sipping a glass of beer. He was the centre of a great deal of attention; all of the old-timers were wondering who he was. (116) [61]

This eroticized and lone figure gradually focuses his attentions on the narrator and begins a slow seduction of him, leaving a five-dollar tip each time he visits the club. The man, later referred to by the narrator as "my millionaire friend," symbolizes a somewhat sinister version of fin de siècle decadence, a figure of wealth and forbidden sexuality. At a party in the millionaire's home at which the narrator is a hired entertainer, the narrator observes: "The men ranged in appearance from a girlish-looking youth to a big grizzled man whom everybody addressed as 'Judge.' None of the women appeared to be under thirty, but each of them struck me as being handsome. I was not long in finding out that they were all decidedly blasé. Several of the women smoked cigarettes, and with a careless grace which showed they were used to the habit" (118) [62]. This scene suggests the existence of a spectrum of gender and sexual identities that exceed the boundaries of bourgeois norms, a certain outlaw sexuality possible within wealthy social circles at the time.[1] The male figures are thus described in language that exaggerates conventions of femininity ("a girlish-looking youth") and masculinity ("a big grizzled man"). Likewise, the female figures do not conform to standards of middle-class femininity: described as "handsome," they are associated with gender transgression through their accomplished cigarette smoking, a taboo for respectable women at the time and a symbol of sexual freedom.

The relationship of the narrator to his "millionaire" recalls that of both son and lover. The millionaire's position as an admirer of the musical abilities of the ex-coloured man echoes the earlier position of the narrator's white father, described as "a tall, handsome, well-dressed gentleman of perhaps thirty-five," evoking a figure much like the suave patron (32) [19–20]. During one of his father's rare visits, the piano similarly mediates the emotional relationship between father and son:

> My father was so enthusiastic in his praise that he touched my vanity—which was great—and more than that; he displayed

1. Although it is situated in early-twentieth-century American culture rather than Victorian England, the association of this scene with decadence suggests affinities with the kind of aristocratic gay subculture and aesthetics discussed by Eve Kosofsky Sedgwick in a brief overview of the class-inflected parameters of homosocial and homosexual identities. Groups of aristocratic men and small groups of their friends, according to Eve Sedgwick, formed a "genuine subculture, facilitated in the face of an ideologically hostile dominant culture by money, privilege, internationalism, and, for the most part, the ability to command secrecy. . . . Its strongest associations . . . are with effeminacy, transvestitism, promiscuity, prostitution, continental European culture, and the arts." See her *Between Men: English Literature and Male Homosocial Desire* (New York: Columbia University Press, 1985), 173.

> that sincere appreciation which always arouses an artist to his best effort, and too, in an unexplainable manner, makes him feel like shedding tears. I showed my gratitude by playing for him a Chopin waltz with all the feeling that was in me. When I had finished, my mother's eyes were glistening with tears; my father stepped across the room, seized me in his arms, and squeezed me to his breast. I am certain that for that moment he was proud to be my father. (34–35) [20–21]

Both the narrator's father and the millionaire are older male figures who support both emotionally and materially the narrator's efforts to have a musical career. Just as his father rewards his performance with the gift of a new piano, so the millionaire provides him with cash, travel, and a new wardrobe.

At the same time that the relationship between the narrator and his patron is one of son to father, however, it also has associations with a more directly sexual relationship. Robert Stepto has noted that in his portrayal of the narrator's mother as a "kept woman" to a wealthy white man, Johnson borrows and recasts antislavery literature's "haunting image of the snug cottage in the clearing," provided for the slaves who became concubines for their white masters.[2] I suggest that there is also at work here an implicit analogy between the narrator's relationship with the patron and his mother's relationship with his father: both echo the figure of the slave mistress, who is given a minimal amount of financial and material security in exchange for her sexual service to the white master.[3] Through an identification between the narrator and his mother, Johnson foregrounds the ways in which processes of racialization shape and resituate codes of masculinity.

Johnson clearly delineates the racialized hierarchies of ownership and property that define the relationship between the protagonist and the patron, implicitly connecting this instance of patronage with the historical legacy of slavery. The complex interplay of economic power and eroticism between the narrator and his patron becomes increasingly apparent as their "friendship" progresses. Eventually, the millionaire develops an exclusive arrangement with the narrator, and the full dimensions of the patron's economic control are revealed in the narrator's comment that "occasionally he

2. See Robert B. Stepto, "Lost in a Quest: James Weldon Johnson's *The Autobiography of an Ex-Coloured Man*," in *From Behind the Veil: A Study of Afro-American Narrative* (Chicago: University of Illinois Press, 1979), 103.
3. In a reading of *The Autobiography of an Ex-Coloured Man* that also marks the centrality of homoerotic desire in the text, Cheryl Clarke refers to this relationship as one of "homosexual interracial concubinage." See Cheryl Clarke, "Race, Homosocial Desire, and 'Mammon' in *Autobiography of an Ex-Coloured Man*," in *Professions of Desire: Lesbian and Gay Studies in Literature*, ed. George E. Haggerty and Bonnie Zimmerman (New York: Modern Language Association, 1995), 89.

'loaned' me to some of his friends. And, too, I often played for him alone at his apartments" (120) [64]. Although the narrator defends his patron—"Between him and me no suggestion of racial differences had ever come up" (145) [76]—clearly "racial differences" are central to the structure of their relationship.

Johnson implicitly criticizes the protagonist's inability to see the class and racial hierarchies that structure his relationship to his patron, a blindness that implicates the narrator in his own exploitation. After detailing the odd habits of the millionaire, who demands that the narrator play for him alone late at night in his home for hours at a time, the narrator begins to sense that something is askew:

> During such moments this man sitting there so mysteriously silent, almost hid in a cloud of heavy-scented smoke, filled me with a sort of unearthly terror. He seemed to be some grim, mute, but relentless tyrant, possessing over me a supernatural power which he used to drive me on mercilessly to exhaustion. (121) [64]

In this passage, the narrator seems close to articulating and acknowledging the millionaire's underlying sadistic and exploitative powers. Yet he immediately disavows this possibility: "But these feelings came very rarely; besides, he paid me so liberally I could forget much" (121) [64]. And indeed the narrator does forget much, dismissing his earlier portrait of the millionaire as a "grim, mute, but relentless tyrant," and instead insisting that the two men had "a familiar and warm relationship," and that "[the patron] had a decided personal liking for me" (121) [64]. In fact, the narrator seems to idolize this man and his position of power: "On my part, I looked upon him at that time as about all a man could wish to be" (121) [64]. Here the narrator's attempts to convince himself that their relationship is about mutual regard rather than power and money echoes his mother's romantic attachment to his father: "She loved him; more, she worshipped him, and she died firmly believing that he loved her more than any other woman in the world" (43) [25]. Although the narrator casts a skeptical eye on his parents' relationship ("Perhaps she was right. Who knows?" [43] [25]), he is unable to doubt his millionaire's motives.

Although Johnson portrays the narrator as a naive participant in his own economic exploitation, he also characterizes the patron as skillful at securing his own power through its very erasure. Nowhere is this process more apparent than in the scenes in Paris, where the millionaire has brought along the narrator as his "valet." Because they have left New York for Europe quite suddenly, the narrator has few clothes when he arrives in Paris, a situation quickly remedied by the patron: "He bought me the same kind of clothes which he himself wore, and that was the best; and he treated me in every way as he dressed me, as an equal, not as a servant. In fact, I don't think anyone could have guessed that such a relation existed" (130) [68]. The narrator mistakes the superficial appearance of similarity between the two men as evidence of their equal status. Although the narrator never explicitly suggests that their relationship might have a sexual component, his descriptions have all the characteristics of a sexual liaison: "He kept me supplied with money far beyond what ordinary wages would have amounted to. For the first two weeks we were together almost constantly, seeing the sights, sights old to him, but from which he seemed to get new pleasure in showing them to me" (130) [68]. At one point, the narrator seems to go out of his way to deny that their relationship is erotic. During a discussion between the narrator and the millionaire about the ex-coloured man returning to the United States, Johnson writes, "When I had finished [telling him my plans] he put his hand on my shoulder—this was the first physical expression of tender regard he had ever shown me—and look[ed] at me in a big-brotherly way" (144) [75]. The narrator's characterization of their relationship as that of siblings is ironic, after his previous descriptions of inequality and exploitation. His description of the patron's look as "big-brotherly" masks the condescension (and perhaps sexual desire) of the white patron; the narrator wants to remember this gesture as one of benevolence rather than subjugation. Further, it is significant that the narrator interrupts this sentence with the explanation that "this was the first physical expression of tender regard he had ever shown me." This assertion marks a self-conscious disavowal of the powerful eroticism, whether physical or not, that has structured their relationship.

While Johnson depicts the relationship between the narrator and his patron as fraught with inequities, he also implicates the narrator's own acquisitive motivations; in addition to the literal money and possessions he receives, the ex-coloured man gains enormous cultural capital through exposure to Europe. The narrator ends his relationship with the patron by temporarily reidentifying with African American culture when he decides to try to pursue a career as a black composer in the United States (one of Johnson's own successful careers). In this way, he also seems to avert the inevitably tragic end that the patron meets by "leaping into eternity" (143) [75]. Yet Johnson implicitly criticizes the narrator, who, despite his physical departure, remains nostalgically attached to "this peculiar man" and refuses to recognize the racialized discrepancies in power that shaped their relationship. In fact, the narrator elevates the formative effects of the patron on his life: "And so I separated from the man who was, all in all, the best friend I ever had, except my mother, the man who exerted the greatest influence ever brought into my life, except that exerted by my mother. My affection for him was so strong, my recollections of him are so distinct, he was such a peculiar and striking character, that I could easily fill several chapters with reminiscences of him" (148) [77]. Through this effusive and arbitrary resolution to their relationship, Johnson suggests that the narrator's feelings toward the patron exceed the limits of what is representable. With what seems a disingenuous concern for "tiring the reader," the narrator ends his discussion of this "peculiar and striking character."

In his discussion of the text, Harper describes the function of the wealthy patron as ultimately bearing the burden of representing homosexuality and thus relieving the ex-coloured man from such a stigmatizing characterization. He notes that the patron's suicide, his "leap into eternity," removes the threat of homosexuality from the text: "Luckily for the protagonist . . . the relationship that he undertakes that most nearly approximates a homosexual coupling also functions as the means by which the narrative can exorcise this unwholesome element."[4] Yet as I will show in the next section, the narrator's sexuality is not rendered normative through the various heterosexual relationships that he enters. Two forms of taboo desire, incest and interracial sexuality, function as evidence of his perversity and are linked symbolically to the potentially tragic narrative of homosexuality.

Deviant Heterosexuality

Although his relationship with the white patron is arguably the most fully rendered erotic bond in *The Autobiography of an Ex-Coloured Man*, the narrator's attachments are not exclusively homoerotic: The narrator presents brief portraits of girls and women to whom he is attracted: a young musician for whom he is an accompanist, a schoolteacher he meets in Florida, a young girl he believes to be his stepsister, a rich widow he meets in the Club, and his wife. All of his attachments to these women, however eroticized, are aborted in some way beyond the narrator's control, as if they must be expelled from the narrative. For example, despite the narrator's secret rhapsodic infatuation with an older teenage girl, a violinist, the attraction is entirely one-sided, with no possibility that his affection will be returned. Likewise, the narrator's attachment to his first fiancée, "a young school-teacher," with whom he entertains "dreams of matrimonial bliss," is described fleetingly. He introduces her and dismisses her, all in a single sentence, alluding to "another turn in the course of my life [that] brought these dreams to an end" (83)

4. Harper, *Are We Not Men*, 110.

[45]. When the factory in which he works closes, the narrator's visions of middle-class heterosexuality ("marrying the young school-teacher" and "raising a family") are replaced by "a desire like a fever" to return to New York (88) [48]. Importantly, there are racial as well as sexual implications to the narrator's flight: marrying the schoolteacher would have committed the narrator to a permanent identity within a black middle-class community.

The narrator's adult attractions to women are represented as transgressive, fleeting, inevitably tragic, and culturally taboo. In his representation of these relationships, Johnson depicts as dangerous the narrator's attraction to women who (like the white patron), by law and custom, are prohibited objects of sexual desire for black men. But unlike the rendering of the protagonist's attachment to the patron, these relationships are represented as explicitly sexual, thus providing, according to the cultural logic of segregation, a recognizable pattern of deviant sexual object choice. For example, while attending the opera during his trip to Europe, the narrator becomes enchanted by "a beautiful, tender girl" (134) [70]. Recalling this encounter, the narrator describes her as a disembodied presence: "I cannot describe her either as to feature, or colour of her hair, or of her eyes; she was so young, so fair, so ethereal, that I felt to stare at her would be a violation; yet I was distinctly conscious of her beauty" (133–34) [70]. When he realizes that the man accompanying this girl is his own father, the narrator is overwhelmed by the tragic implications of his incestuous desire. Staring at her is indeed a "violation": within the historical context of the early twentieth century, his desire for his white stepsister transgresses cultural prohibitions against both incest and interracial heterosexuality.[5]

Similarly, the narrator presents his brief relationship with the "widow," a wealthy white woman, as transgressive and dangerous. He describes her as "an exceedingly beautiful woman of perhaps thirty-five . . . [who] had glistening copper-coloured hair, very white skin; and eyes very much like Du Maurier's conception of Trilby's 'twin grey stars'" (108) [58]. The widow is one of a group of white women, "regular habituées" of the Club, who have a specifically racialized erotic orientation: they seek out "coloured men" as their sexual companions (108) [58]. The narrator portrays this woman and her exclusive desire for African American men in terms of a femme fatale: when he is warned about her jealous lover, the narrator writes, "the woman was so beautiful that my native gallantry and delicacy would not

5. For an intriguing discussion of historically racialized and sexualized proscriptions against "the right to look," sec Jane Gaines, "White Privilege and Looking Relations: Race and Gender in Feminist Film Theory," *Cultural Critique* 4 (Fall 1986): 59–79.

allow me to repulse her; my finer feelings entirely overcame my judgment" (122) [65]. Their relationship and the woman's life come to a tragic and violent end when her lover murders her. The narrator is haunted by the scene of "that beautiful white throat with the ugly wound. The jet of blood pulsing from it had placed an indelible red stain on my memory" (125) [66]. This murder serves as a brutal punishment for the widow's sexual and racial transgression. Significantly, it is also the catalyst responsible for the narrator's decision to travel to Europe with his white male patron. According to the logic of the narrative, male interracial homoeroticism becomes an antidote to the potentially horrific consequences of interracial heterosexuality, one not entirely unwelcome for the protagonist.

Likewise, the narrator's heterosexual courtship and marriage receive relatively little attention in contrast to the narrative space and intensity devoted to his relationship with the white patron. The first description of the narrator's future wife does not occur until the final chapter of the book: "She was almost tall and quite slender, with lustrous yellow hair and eyes so blue as to appear almost black. She was as white as a lily, and she was dressed in white. Indeed, she seemed to me the most dazzlingly white thing I had ever seen. But it was not her delicate beauty which attracted me most; it was her voice, a voice which made one wonder how tones; of such passionate colour could come from so fragile a body" (198) [103]. This description eroticizes a contrast between, on the one hand, the overwhelming, whiteness of her image and its distinct lack of physical presence (she is "almost tall and quite slender," with a "delicate beauty," and a "fragile . . . body") and, on the other hand, the "passionate colour" of her overpresent voice. Again, as if the narrative cannot sustain interracial heterosexuality, the narrator's wife dies a tragically young death, a death significantly linked to childbirth, seemingly punishing her for the miscegenous results of her sexual behavior. Although the narrator does not describe her death directly, he states that "it was for [their second child, a son] that she gave all; and that is the second sacred sorrow of my life" (209) [109]. Echoing the death of the widow earlier in the novel, the death of the narrator's wife works narratively as retribution for interracial heterosexuality. Although he laments that "her loss to me is irreparable," he also admits that she represented a threat that her death coincidentally removes: "I no longer have the same fear for myself of my secret's being found out" (210) [109]. The death of the narrator's wife removes a threat to his performance not only of whiteness but also of masculinity. Despite their "supremely happy" marriage, her very presence had made the narrator wonder "if she was scrutinizing me, to see if she was looking for anything in me which made me differ from the other men she knew. . . . I began even to wonder if I really was like the men I associated with; if there was not, after all, an indefinable something which marked a difference" (199–200) [104]. The "indefinable something"—the hidden identity that could be rendered as either his mulatto or invert status—is at once racial and sexual.

"Like Van Vechten, Start Inspectin'"

So far this chapter has enacted a primarily textual account of the ways in which questions of mixed-race identity and interracial desire in Johnson's *Autobiography of an Ex-Coloured Man* became enmeshed with those of emerging (and contradictory) cultural understandings of gender inversion and homosexual object choice.[6] Johnson's "cover story" that the text hinged on the narrative of "some colored man who had married white" belied the ways in which his text participated in constructing homosexuality, along with interracial sexuality, as deviant sexual object choice and the "hybrid" mulatto as a figure of gender inversion. In this section, I turn to issues of reading and reception, shifting my focus away from the intersecting constructions of race and sexuality *within* the text, toward the ways in which these issues circulated *around* the text and its publication. In this context, Johnson's 1933 assertion that the narrative of *The Autobiography of an Ex-Coloured Man* pivoted on interracial marriage can be read as a strategic (if unconscious) intervention into potential reinterpretations of the text after its republication in 1927. In its second life, the text was "affixed" with not only Johnson's name but also that of Carl Van Vechten, the white (gay) patron of modernism and the "Harlem Renaissance" who initially suggested to Knopf the text's republication and whose introduction accompanied the text.[7] If Johnson's name signaled the closing of an epistemological gap concerning the text's authorship and genre, the attachment of Van Vechten's persona to the text through his introduction made more palpable the imbrication of interracial and homosexual desire, both among characters within the book and between the text and its various audiences.

And so, fifteen years after the book's first anonymous publication, the 1927 Knopf edition of the *Autobiography* found a new and

6. The title of this section alludes to black lyricist Andy Razaf's 1930 hit song "Go Harlem," quoted in Barry Singer, *Black and Blue: The Life and Lyrics of Andy Razaf* (New York: Schirmer, 1992), 239.
7. I use the term "Harlem Renaissance" loosely here, following the important and enabling critiques of critics such as Hazel Carby and Ann duCille, who have drawn attention to both the problematic periodization and lack of attention to women writers in most characterizations of the "Harlem Renaissance." See Hazel Carby, *Reconstructing Womanhood: The Emergence of the Afro-American Woman Novelist* (New York: Oxford University Press, 1987), 163–75; and Ann duCille, *The Coupling Convention: Sex, Text, and Tradition in Black Women's Fiction* (New York: Oxford University Press, 1993), 82–85.

wider readership that had become familiar with, and eager for, creative work—writing, music, and visual arts—about African American culture beginning in the early 1920s. Van Vechten's introduction to the text was, of course, in keeping with his friendships and promotion of numerous writers and artists during this period, including Countee Cullen, Ronald Firbank, Langston Hughes, Nella Larsen, Rudolph Fisher, and Gertrude Stein, among others. Johnson and Van Vechten met and became close friends in 1924, when Van Vechten first began participating in Harlem's social and artistic circles.[8] As many critics have noted, Van Vechten's motivations for supporting African American cultural production were ambiguous, mixing admiration and savvy literary judgment with colonizing voyeurism and appropriation.

With his introduction to the *Autobiography*, Van Vechten mediated between Johnson and his new audience, a gesture echoing that of nineteenth-century white editors who authenticated slave narratives, such as Lydia Maria Child, who presented Harriet Jacobs's *Incidents in the Life of a Slave Girl*, and William Lloyd Garrison, who provided a preface to Frederick Douglass's narrative.[9] Unlike those introductions, however, which functioned to verify the slave's identity and story as authentic, Van Vechten's introduction had a more complicated purpose in the context of the text's modernist aesthetic. On the one hand, he affirmed the "inauthenticity" of the text, emphasizing that it had "little enough to do with Mr. Johnson's own life" (xxxiii). On the other hand, he verified the accuracy of the experiences that Johnson chronicled, positioning the text as the raw material out of which other representations of African Americans, including his own novel *Nigger Heaven* (1926), could be produced: "When I was writing Nigger Heaven I discovered the Autobiography to be an invaluable source-book for the study of Negro psychology" (xxxv).

Although Van Vechten supported (and appropriated) a broad range of modernist and African American artistic production, his position as a white gay man arguably played a significant part in the circulation and production of these texts. Van Vechten's sexual identity was complex, since he had sexual relationships with both women and men, but homoeroticism and the growth of a more visible gay subculture in 1920s Manhattan (in which he energetically participated) did seem to shape his selection and construction of particular writers and texts. More specifically, by reprinting and attaching

8. Bruce Kellner, *Carl Van Vechten and the Irreverent Decades* (Norman: University of Oklahoma Press, 1968), 197–98.
9. See Harriet A. Jacobs, *Incidents in the Life of a Slave Girl, Written by Herself* (1861; reprint, Cambridge: Harvard University Press, 1987); and *Narrative of the Life of Frederick Douglass, an American Slave, Written by Himself* (1845; reprint. New York: Signet, 1968).

himself to the *Autobiography*, Van Vechten rehearsed prototypically the strategies of queer reading and re-assemblage that would become more explicit in his later life. One of the motivations for republishing the *Autobiography* may have stemmed from the way it had begun to articulate an identity and subculture more recognizable as gay to readers in 1927 than in 1912. In attaching his introduction, Van Vechten staged, whether consciously or not, a position of reading and subjectivity that had as much to do with the sexual as racial subcultures associated with the Harlem Renaissance.

Although Van Vechten's introduction never explicitly identifies himself or the text as "gay" or "queer," it is useful to speculate about his attachments to this particular narrative. It is possible, for instance, to imagine Van Vechten's dual identifications with its characters. In the image of the ex-coloured man's white patron, the "clean-cut, slender, but athletic-looking man [with] . . . a tinge of grey about his temples," the fortyish Van Vechten may have seen an eroticized or idealized version of himself. But he may also have identified with the ex-coloured man—a man who shuttled among the nightclubs and drag balls of Harlem, the downtown world of the white literary industry, and the expatriate modernist salons of Paris—a figure resembling himself. The multiple worlds and identities inhabited by the ex-coloured man may have uncannily echoed, or perhaps provided a map for, Van Vechten's own movement among diverse social circles. A particularly compelling set of caricatures by Mexican artist Miguel Covarrubias also makes explicit the ways in which Van Vechten's identity was mediated by his racial identifications. In a caricature entitled *A Prediction*, Covarrubias represented Van Vechten in blackface. A kind of "ex-coloured man" in reverse, the title—*A Prediction*—suggested that Van Vechten was an imminently coloured man. This image makes explicit the logic of using racial discourse to articulate Van Vechten's sexualized "difference" from normative white culture.[1]

These resonances become more obvious when one takes into account the more than twenty scrapbooks that Van Vechten put together in the mid-1950s, which contained various collages of photographs, mostly of nude men, juxtaposed with texts clipped from newspapers and magazines. One page, for instance, shows a photograph of a young man in a sailor suit, labeled with two captions, "Boy Crazy," and "My Queer." Art historian Jonathan Weinberg has

1. See Eric Lott, *Love and Theft: Blackface Minstrelsy and the American Working Class* (New York: Oxford University Press, 1995), for a useful discussion of the ways in which blackface has circulated historically as a vehicle for white male bohemianism in the United States. Lott suggests that nineteenth-century "blackface stars inaugurated an American tradition of class abdication through gendered cross-racial immersion which persists, in historically differentiated ways, to our own day" (51).

analyzed these "homemade sex books" in detail.[2] As he points out, what makes the scrapbooks compelling is not so much the actual images but the way they provide evidence of Van Vechten's strategies of reading and "writing" images and text as a gay man: "Van Vechten appears to have been scanning the newspapers looking not only for the public naming of homosexuality, but for the way in which same-sex love can only be deduced by reading between the lines."[3] Weinberg explains that the scrapbooks demonstrate the acts of assertive reappropriation at the heart of Van Vechten's processes of queer reading: "He found homosexuality where homosexuality had been suppressed—the crime reports—and he found homosexuality where it was not supposed to be—the tennis court or the wrestling mat."[4]

Given this evidence of Van Vechten's prolific re-production of "mainstream" culture as decidedly queer in the scrapbooks, we might read a similar, though more veiled, process occurring in Van Vechten's earlier promotion of the *Autobiography*. If, as we know, the meaning of a text is produced in acts of reading, then Van Vechten's public performance of his own reading of the *Autobiography* in the introduction to the 1927 edition produced a different text, one that spoke to the presence of a more explicitly gay culture woven into the artistic and social fabric of both the literal and imagined space of Harlem. As historians such as Eric Garber, George Chauncey, and Kevin Mumford have noted, during the 1920s, two neighborhoods in Manhattan—Greenwich Village and Harlem—developed flourishing enclaves of gay culture.[5] Indeed, many of the writers who were central to the Harlem Renaissance movement actively participated in these lesbian and gay cultures.[6] As Henry Louis Gates Jr. has contended, the Harlem Renaissance "was surely as gay as it was black, not that it was exclusively either of these."[7]

2. Jonathan Weinberg, "'Boy Crazy': Carl Van Vechten's Queer Collection," *Yale Journal of Criticism* 7, no. 2 (1994): 25–49.
3. Ibid., 31.
4. Ibid.
5. See Eric Garber, "A Spectacle in Color: the Lesbian and Gay Subculture of Jazz Age Harlem," in *Hidden from History: Reclaiming the Gay and Lesbian Past*, ed. Martin Duberman, Martha Vicinus, and George Chauncey Jr. (New York: Meridian, 1989), 318–31; George Chauncey, *Gay New York: Gender, Urban Culture, and the Making of the Gay Male World, 1890–1940* (New York: Basic Books, 1994), 227–67; and Kevin Mumford, *Interzones: Black/White Sex Districts in Chicago and New York in the Early Twentieth Century* (New York: Columbia University Press, 1997), 73–92.
6. See Garber, "A Spectacle in Color," 326–31; Thadious M. Davis, *Nella Larsen, Novelist of the Harlem Renaissance: A Woman's Life Unveiled* (Baton Rouge: Louisiana State University Press, 1994), 325; and Gloria T. Hull, *Color, Sex, and Poetry: Three Women Writers of the Harlem Renaissance* (Bloomington: Indiana University Press, 1987), 95–97, 136–47.
7. Gates, "The Black Man's Burden," 233.

In *Along This Way*, Johnson admitted that he was writing his "real" autobiography in part to make clear once and for all that *The Autobiography of an Ex-Coloured Man* "was not the story of my life."[8] While Johnson's assertion had a great deal to do with distancing himself from the ex-coloured man's tendencies toward assimilationist racial politics, it may also have been compelled by the questions of sexuality that the text and its circulation raised. Just as the ex-coloured man's narrative offered a space in which to explore forbidden desires to "pass" and "marry white" in a racially segregated culture, so it registered the existence of other forbidden desires, most notably homosexuality. Part of the enduring fascination of readers with the *Autobiography* lies in the ways in which the text mapped culturally taboo sexual desires onto the color line, a relationship that was integral to the literary and artistic landscape of the 1920s.

* * *

CRISTINA L. RUOTOLO

James Weldon Johnson and the Autobiography of an Ex-Colored Musician[†]

Because Johnson's experience as a songwriter clearly informed his characterization of the ex-colored man's piano-playing career, scholars have turned to *ECM* to reconstruct the world of ragtime music in early twentieth-century America.

In this essay, Christina L. Ruotolo departs from a strict musicological account (like that of Edward A. Berlin; see pp. 205–19). She analyzes how music, as much as the narrator's ambiguous physical presence and appearance, redefines the ex-colored man's world as foundationally permeable.[1]

In all the critical attention paid to James Weldon Johnson's *The Autobiography of an Ex-Coloured Man*, surprisingly little has been

8. Johnson, *Along This Way*, 239.

† From *American Literature* 72.2 (June 2000): 249–74.

1. Taking a new approach to *ECM*'s interests in and use of music, critics Katherine Biers and Noelle Morrissette place the novel's compositional history in a "soundscape"—that is, an "aural environment containing noise, silence, and cultures of talk as well as music," to use Morrissette's helpful definition (98)—in order to address how sound (broadly conceived) defined the novel's modernist contexts. See Morrissette, *James Weldon Johnson's Modern Soundscapes*; and Biers, "Syncope Fever: James Weldon Johnson and Black Voice," *Representations* 96 (Fall 2006): 99–125.

directed toward the crucial role of music in the narrator's experience and identity. While music scholars have cited the novel's passages on the origins and significance of ragtime, literary critics seem relatively uninterested in the narrator's principal means of supporting himself, which is also, arguably, his principal means of crossing racial boundaries.[2] Comfortable and capable in both European and African American music, the narrator's musical performances function, more than once, as agents in his "passing" as either "white" or "black"; indeed, his convincing performance of Frédéric Chopin ultimately convinces a "lily white" woman to marry him, while his masterful performances of ragtime make audible a blackness invisible to the eye.[3] But the narrator challenges the "color line" even more dramatically in his repeated efforts to produce music that revises both "black" and "white" musical traditions by sounding an intimate relationship between the two—by performing European music in a style learned from his mother, by "ragging the classics," and finally by composing (or preparing to compose) African American symphonies. Because it occupies the invisible

2. For citations of Johnson's novel by historians of music, see Edward Berlin, *Ragtime: A Musical and Cultural History* (Berkeley and Los Angeles: Univ. of California Press, 1980), 24, 30, 50, 54, 71, and 76; and John Michael Spencer, *The New Negroes and Their Music: The Success of the Harlem Renaissance* (Knoxville: Univ. of Tennessee Press, 1997). Referring to one of Johnson's descriptions of ragtime, Berlin writes, "Although this passage is from a work of fiction, its serious consideration as a historical document is justified" (30). Spencer introduces his study of Harlem Renaissance composers with an account of the ex-colored man's aborted final project to compose classical music based on African American themes. Spencer reads this project as "prophetic" of the symphonies, oratorios, and operas by black composers of the Harlem Renaissance, a focus that, in my view, obscures the novel's relationship to a prior musical moment as well as its implicit critique of the project itself. Jeffrey Melnick's remarkable book, *A Right to Sing the Blues: African Americans, Jews, and American Popular Song* (Cambridge: Harvard Univ. Press, 1999), places Johnson's novel, along with his later writings on popular culture, in the context of early-twentieth-century collaborations between African Americans and Jews in the music industry and Johnson's own interest in African American contributions to "national" culture.

Most other recent scholarship focuses on problems of the narrator's racial (and sexual) identity. Against an earlier strain of criticism that reads the novel as supporting notions of racial authenticity and ultimately regrets the narrator's choice to "sell his birthright for a mess of pottage," recent critics trace ways in which the novel variously challenges the idea of authentic racial identity. The latter notably include Samira Kawash, "The Epistemology of Race: Knowledge, Visiblity, and Passing," in her *Dislocating the Color Line: Identity, Hybridity, and Singularity in African-American Narrative* (Stanford, Calif: Stanford Univ. Press, 1997); Cheryl Clarke, "Race, Homosocial Desire, and 'Mammon' in *Autobiography of an Ex-Colored Man*," in *Professions of Desire: Lesbian and Gay Studies in Literature*, ed. George E. Haggerty and Bonnie Zimmerman (New York: MLA, 1995); Donald C. Goellnicht, "Passing as Autobiography: James Weldon Johnson's *The Autobiography of an Ex-Coloured Man*," *African American Review* 30 (Spring 1906):17–33; and Kathleen Pfeiffer, "Individualism, Success, and American Identity in *The Autobiography of an Ex-Colored Man*," *African American Review* 30 (Fall 1996): 403–19.

3. James Weldon Johnson, *The Autobiography of an Ex-Coloured Man* (New York: Vintage, 1989), 198 [103]. All subsequent references to this novel will be from this edition and will be cited parenthetically in the text. [Page numbers in square brackets refer to this Norton Critical Edition—Editor.]

medium of sound, this "hybrid" musicality promises to distract both the narrator and his audiences from the visual markers of the "color line" and to invite them into an aural experience of racial mixture and ambiguity, of "colors" that are not so clearly mapped onto stable racial identities.

Typically overlooked by recent critics who read this novel as a powerful exposure of the social constructedness of "race," the narrator's musical practices not only challenge the notion of an absolute boundary between white and black but also reveal the limits of this "hybrid" musicality within his social world.[4] Like "passing," music that crosses the color line depends on a perceivable (in this case, audible) "line" between black and white in the very process of defying its authority. Indeed, the novel arguably grounds its otherwise slippery approach to "race" in the audible blackness of certain African American musical practices that ultimately cannot be imitated or reproduced: the ragtime performed by the "natural" player at the "Club," the "call and response" songs performed by "Singing Johnson" and the Southern black congregation, and the Southern melodies sung by the narrator's mother. Johnson presents the value and difference of this music in no uncertain terms. Unlike European music that is fixed on a page, learned by imitation, and performed for paying audiences, African American music, as this novel represents it, involves an entirely different set of rituals and values, as well as different sounds. Spontaneous and improvisatory, involving its audience in call and response, and expressively tied to body and memory, black music occupies a unique position in Johnson's text. The narrator's repeated attempts to bridge these differences—either to unfix European texts by "ragging" them or to transfer the spirit of black music to the notated page—inevitably fail, even as they promise to unsettle American racial ideology. Cast by his European "training" as an inauthentic imitator of or mute audience for black music, and by his white audiences as either imitation white or exotic "other," the narrator repeatedly becomes caught in an inflexible racial binary. From his "ex-colored" and alienated position at the end of the novel, he can only gesture as a silent writer toward a realm of African American sound that, safe from the commodifying, imitating, and fetishizing ears of white America, has been returned to an imagined, if now inaudible, authenticity.

4. Kawash, for example, in her compelling argument that *The Autobiography* denies the possibility of racial authenticity, grounds her idea of identity in Lacanian terms of visibility and vision: "his blackness," she concludes, is "a specular image of the blackness he observes in others" ("The Epistemology of Race," 140). Not once does she mention the place of hearing and musical performance in the novel's racial ideology, which allows her to avoid what I see as the novel's refusal to give up the notion of authenticity even as it recognizes that modern identity is inevitably imitation and copy.

Rather than simply revisit the ongoing debate about *The Autobiography*'s constructions of "race," I would like instead to focus on how this text reflects and engages the racial politics of early-twentieth-century American music. The ex-colored man's various innovations (he claims to be the first to "rag the classics," the first to conceive of classical music based on African American themes) in fact echo the collective innovations of the circle of African American musicians among whom Johnson worked before beginning his novel. Between 1900 and 1906, Johnson, his brother J. Rosamond Johnson, and Bob Cole together wrote popular songs that quickly launched "Cole and Johnson Brothers" as the most successful black songwriters in Broadway musical theater. This songwriting team found themselves at the center of a new community of black composers, songwriters, and performers trained in black musical traditions by family and community, and in European traditions by childhood piano teachers and conservatory educations. Though still highly constrained by the degrading minstrel stereotypes demanded by their predominantly white employers and audiences, these musicians nonetheless recognized their unprecedented opportunity to generate both a new "American" musicality infused with African American sounds and styles and a new American music culture inclusive of African American performers and composers.

To read Johnson's fictional autobiography as largely concerned with the aspirations, achievements, and disappointments of these musicians yields new insights into the text's ambiguous racial discourse and into turn-of-the-century American music. I hope to shift the focus on this novel away from often dehistoricizing questions about the constructedness of identity in order to consider its engagement with a historical moment when the visually policed "color line" was being challenged not only by light-skinned blacks "passing" as white but also by black music straying into the forms, styles, and sounds of "whiteness." Scholarship on early-twentieth-century African American culture has productively identified black musical forms as a site of critical difference from European traditions. But in theorizing the importance of blues and jazz to an emerging black cultural aesthetic and politics, scholars have tended to dismiss—or at least qualify—the turn of the century as a moment when black musicians paid too high a price, gave up too much "authenticity," for entry into a music industry still dominated by the sounds and sights of blackface minstrelsy. Johnson himself would downplay, and even elide, this moment in his career, while later devoting himself to more "authentic" black cultural forms in such projects as the *Books of American Negro Spirituals*. While understandable, this tendency to bracket the turn of the century keeps us from recognizing the degree to which a group of black musicians imagined themselves transforming American music and, more importantly, transforming Americans' perceptions and conceptions of racial difference.

Given the willful forgetting of this moment, it is all the more important that Johnson's fictional reflection on it through the character of the ex-colored man be recognized as such. Johnson began his novel in the midst of making his decision to leave songwriting, and he completed it while working as U.S. Consul in Latin America. While abroad, Johnson continually received letters from his brother and his wife urging him to return to songwriting and to New York. In one, his brother Rosamond reminds him there is "easy money" in vaudeville and insists that "there is no future for you in the consular service compared with your possibilities in putting up some good musical plays."[5] It is not surprising that Johnson's novel dwells on the characters and struggles of the world he had just left behind in a departure he described in his memoir as "an escape."[6] As Joseph T. Skerrett has noted, the ex-colored man similarly "escapes" the New York entertainment scene. Indeed, both Johnson and his narrator "escape" the music industry only to write "autobiographies" preoccupied with it.[7]

"The one true American music"

As an adolescent, Johnson's narrator earns money for college by playing Beethoven's *Pathétique* sonata to a white Connecticut audience; while living in Jacksonville, Florida, he supports himself in part by giving piano lessons that both introduce him to "the best class of colored people" and initiate his "entrance into the race" (74) [40–41]; in New York he supports himself playing ragtime renditions of classics on the piano, a practice that eventually "opened to [him] more doors and made [him] a welcome guest than [his] playing of Beethoven and Chopin could ever have done" (115) [61]; and, after abandoning his idea of composing classical music based on African American themes, he finally persuades a white woman to marry him largely through a convincing performance of Chopin. His versatile musicality allows him to enter both white and black society, and arguably to "pass" as either white or black; it enables

5. Rosamond Johnson to James Weldon Johnson, 10 October 1912, James Weldon Johnson Collection, Box 40, Series III, Folder 11, Beinecke Library, Yale University.
6. In his autobiography, Johnson writes, "The feeling came over me that, in leaving New York, I was not making a sacrifice, but an escape; that I was getting away, if only for a little while, from the feverish flutter of life, to seek a little stillness of the spirit" (James Weldon Johnson, *Along This Way: The Autobiography of James Weldon Johnson* [New York: Viking, 1933], 223).
7. Joseph T. Skerrett Jr. makes this point in "Irony and Symbolic Action in James Weldon Johnson's *The Autobiography of an Ex-Coloured Man*," *American Quarterly* 32 (Winter 1980): 559.

him to earn a better living than he could otherwise imagine. His versatility is crucial to the narrative's capacity to "reveal" the color line with such authority and detail while also revealing the cultural basis of its construction.

Although a lyricist rather than a musician, James Weldon Johnson similarly gained unprecedented social mobility and financial reward by working in the music industry at the turn of the century. While living in Jacksonville during the summer of 1899, working as a high school principal and studying for the Florida Bar exam, Johnson received a royalty check for a song he and his brother, now living in New York, had recently sold. With little hesitation, the thirty-year-old Johnson abandoned the stable professional future he had long worked toward and rushed to join his brother at the black-run Marshall Hotel on New York's West 53rd Street. Johnson attributes his attraction to this community to its emerging status as a "new centre" for black entertainers that, he later would claim even as he wrote himself out of the story, "brought about a revolutionary change in New York artistic life" two decades before the "Harlem Renaissance."[8] Black songwriters, composers, and performers poured into New York around 1900, drawn as Johnson was by a sense of new professional and cultural opportunities.

These opportunities depended on two emergent musical trends in mainstream culture that promised to involve African American music in new definitions of American music in the 1890s and thus provide an entrée for African American musicians.[9] On the one hand, Tin Pan Alley publishers and musical theater producers began to see large profits in the syncopated rhythms of "ragtime," which soon became identified as the first distinctly American popular music; on the other, American composers, eager to define a national style, turned to whatever they could claim as native "folk" traditions, the most distinctive of which, many felt, were the "plantation melodies" of slavery that had been transcribed by nineteenth-century ethnographers and popularized by black college groups like the Fisk Jubilee Singers. Coming out of different, and even opposed, musical spheres, both trends were celebrated as distinctly American and welcome departures from European influence. One eminent critic proclaimed ragtime as "the one true American music," able to express the "American personality" as "no European music can or

8. James Weldon Johnson, *Black Manhattan* (1930; reprint, New York: Knopf, 1991), 118–19.

9. The openings black musicians saw in ragtime and classical music resembled the opening that dialect fiction provided to writers like Charles Chesnutt and Paul Lawrence Dunbar around the same time. In both music and literature, black artists could claim a more authentic voice while recognizing the degree to which they were, in fact, involved in imitating white constructions of authenticity.

possibly could."[1] Similarly, Antonin Dvořák described the "plantation melodies and the slave songs" as "the most potent as well as the most beautiful" examples of "the voice of the people," and the most promising basis for a new national musical style.[2]

The new vogue for both ragtime and classical incorporations of "slave songs" inspired not only enthusiasm but also anxious debate, particularly over the idea that such music expressed a *national* character. Several critics questioned the idea that African American culture could represent anything but its own "foreign" nature. Music critic Rupert Hughes dismissed African American music as "in no sense a national expression" and "as foreign a music as any Tyrolean jodel or Hungarian czardas."[3] Ragtime's critics were even more aggressive, hyperbolically characterizing its syncopated rhythms as "commotion without purpose," or "virulent poison" that would "infect" America's youth with immoral impulses.[4] In their claims to guard the nation against intrusions from outside its boundaries, both the reaction against the slave songs and that against ragtime harbored fears of racial contamination. This is not to say that white defenders of ragtime and "plantation" symphonies necessarily supported equal rights and opportunities for black musicians. The history of ragtime, indeed, is largely a story of white composers and performers taking credit for and profits from music they heard blacks perform and then transcribing it as their own. Nonetheless, the fact that mainstream America began to consider African American music as a possible basis for a national culture created an important opening for a generation of musicians who could themselves transcribe—and thus publish and market—"black" music. W. E. B. DuBois's *Souls of Black Folk* (1903) pays special attention to the new American appropriations of black music in the chapter devoted to the "sorrow songs," which DuBois insists are the "sole American music."[5] As Ronald Radano suggests, DuBois accords music no less than the power to "put into motion a 'transformation' destabilizing the whiteness and oneness of American life."[6] Where white musicians and audiences might have seen novelty and "national" spirit, black musicians and audiences saw an opportunity to redefine the very idea of "American" as applied to music.

1. Hiram Moderwell, "Ragtime," *New Republic*, 16 October 1915, 286.
2. Antonin Dvořák, "Music in America," *Harper's New Monthly Magazine*. February 1895, 430.
3. Rupert Hughes, *Contemporary American Composers* (Boston: L. C. Page, 1900), 22.
4. The first phrase is from Daniel Gregory Mason's *Contemporary Composers* (New York: Macmillan, 1917), 247; the last two are quoted in Berlin, *Ragtime*, 44.
5. W. E. B. DuBois, *The Souls of Black Folk* (New York; Penguin, 1989), 205.
6. Ronald Radano, "Soul Texts and the Blackness of Folk," *Modernism/Modernity* 2 (January 1995): 88.

While most opportunities for black professional musicians opened up in the fields of musical theater and popular song, a handful of black musicians found themselves drawn to and welcomed by institutions of classical music. Harry T. Burleigh, who would become one of the musicians in Johnson's circle, earned a scholarship to the National Conservatory in 1892, where he befriended Dvořák and claims to have influenced the composer's conception of the "slave songs": "I feel sure the composer caught this peculiarity [a flat seventh] of most of the slave songs from some that I sang to him; for he used to stop me and ask if that was the way the slaves sang." Widely held to be the first black composer to incorporate black musical forms in "classical" works, Burleigh considered Dvořák's own use of a "slave song" in his *Symphony of the New World* to be a milestone in music history: "[The 1893 premiere] was the first time in the history of music that a Negro's song had been a major theme in a great symphonic work."[7]

Like Johnson's ex-colored man, Burleigh received training in both African American and European musical traditions, learning spirituals from his mother and grandmother and studying classical voice and piano through the encouragement of his white employers. After moving to New York, Burleigh maintained and combined these paths, composing works based on African American music and performing as singer in, and then director of, the choir at St. George's Episcopal Church (a predominantly white congregation). Burleigh's acceptance into this white community seemed to rest, according to his biographer Ann Simpson, on his mastery of European musical conventions as well as his willingness occasionally to perform "Negro songs." Though he spent many of his evenings with the Johnsons and others at the Marshall Hotel, Burleigh defined himself as definitively outside musical theater, which was clearly the more remunerative route for black musicians; indeed, he was said to have composed popular songs under a pseudonym, thus reaping financial rewards without damaging his emerging reputation as a "serious" musician.[8] Burleigh was most famous for his numerous "art song" and instrumental arrangements of spirituals, and for his settings of African American texts, such as Paul Lawrence Dunbar's "An Antebellum Sermon," all of which worked to carve out a central place for African American traditions within the highbrow forms and venues of "classical" music.

7. Harry T. Burleigh, quoted in Anne Key Simpson, *Hard Trials: The Life and Music of Harry T. Burleigh* (Metuchen, N.J.: Scarecrow, 1990), 15, 14.
8. Like that of the ex-colored man, Burleigh's career was boosted by a wealthy white man's intense interest in his particular musical style. J. Pierpont Morgan, a member of the church, found himself "so immediately and completely smitten" with Burleigh's voice that he hired him for private parties in his home and the homes of his friends (Simpson, *Hard Trials*, 19).

Most of the crowd on West 53rd, however, had moved from the conservatory into musical theater as opportunities arose. Their training in composition and classical styles and forms allowed these musicians to take ownership of and market their songs at a moment when the publication of sheet music was a growing industry closely tied to the growing popularity of Broadway musical theater. While black performers were for the most part constrained to working for little pay in black clubs, a growing number of black musicians with skill in notation and an ear for the mainstream began to find work as both songwriters and performers in white musical theater. Many of these musicians were drawn to New York and to musical theater by the several new all-black variety shows suddenly popular in the late 1890s. By hiring the "best-trained Negro singers and musicians then available," and by diversifying their minstrel repertory with such novelties as a "cakewalk jubilee" and "operatic kaleidoscope," shows like *Oriental America* and *A Trip to Coontown* started a new wave of black musical theater and brought more African American musicians to the attention of white producers, publishers, and audiences.[9]

Rosamond Johnson's early career, as his brother describes it, demonstrates a consistent awareness of his power, as a musician, to bridge the gap between white and black cultures, a power that was dependent on his mastery of and mobility across different musical traditions. After six years of study at the New England Conservatory of Music, Rosamond was hired to perform with *Oriental America* for a year, followed by a brief stint back in Jacksonville, where he returned to "classical" music as choirmaster, teacher, and organist. According to his brother, Rosamond's students' recitals "set a new standard" in Jacksonville musical performance and "started local white music lovers coming to concerts given by colored people." At this time, James, a high school principal, joined Rosamond to write a comic opera in the style of Gilbert and Sullivan, which brought further notice from local whites. Rosamond played through the opera on the piano at a party that James describes as "the first inter-racial artistic party in our experience." In 1899 the brothers took their opera to New York, where they found that their songs, if not the opera as a whole, "seemed to open doors by magic" and very quickly plunged them into the limelight of an increasingly "inter-racial" musical sphere.[1]

9. For more on these shows and the larger contexts of black musical production, see Eileen Southern's *The Music of Black Americans: A History* (New York: Norton, 1983), 293–302; and Johnson, *Black Manhattan*, 94–110. These shows, unlike their "white" counterparts, combined European and African American musical traditions in their programs by typically including opera scenes or arias as one of their "acts."
1. Johnson, *Along This Way*, 150, 149, 147.

Eventually the Johnsons, like most songwriters at this time, were producing songs that "ragged"—that used syncopated rhythms and often depicted black characters in dialect. The popularity of ragtime, like that of plantation music, created a space for black artists who could claim a privileged relationship to the genre. The ragtime of black culture was, of course, already a "hybrid" form, combining the rhythms and harmonies of African American expressive culture with the Euro-American march form. While the "line" between white and black might have been heard within the music as an implied tension between downbeats and syncopated offbeats, it persisted quite dramatically among musicians as a difference between "trained" musicians who wrote down their songs, marketing them as sheet music, and those for whom music remained an oral practice, inseparable from performance. Like their white counterparts, black songwriters seeking mainstream success crossed *this* line by producing notated versions of what had been a vernacular and largely improvised practice. By crossing this line, black musicians expressed their "blackness," if this in fact was their goal, through the print medium of while culture. They were also in a position, whether dark or light-skinned, to pass as white, since their music was now detached from their bodies, Indeed, the Johnsons, whose sheet music often featured a photograph of the white performer who popularized the song rather than the black songwriters, occasionally were presumed to be white, particularly by audiences outside New York.[2] With their songs heard by white audiences and, in the case of "Cole and Johnson Brothers," performed for the most part by white singers, these black songwriters had in effect infiltrated an institution central to the production of racial ideology.

The majority of "rag" songs published during the 1890s and early 1900s were "coon songs," which—like the dialect fiction also popular at this time—"fixed on the page" and in the minds of listeners and readers a very narrow set of stereotyped plantation scenarios and "happy darky" characters. In their many contributions to this genre, Cole and Johnson Brothers might be said to have achieved mainstream success by wearing black masks, just as Jewish performers like Al Jolson and Irving Berlin, according to recent scholars, achieved their success (and their "whiteness") by donning blackface.[3] But the Johnsons saw themselves neither as recuperating some kind

2. In *Along This Way*, Johnson describes his response to a letter in the *Ladies Home Journal* whose writer clearly assumed the Johnsons were white: "I laughed too; but my laughter was tempered by the thought that there was anybody in the country, notwithstanding the locality being Georgia, who, knowing anything at all about them, did not know that Cole and Johnson Brothers were Negroes" (196).
3. See Melnick, *A Right to Sing the Blues*, and Michael Rogin, *Blackface, White Noise: Jewish Immigrants in the Hollywood Melting Pot* (Berkeley and Los Angeles: Univ. of California Press, 1996), 73–120.

of black authenticity nor as simply performing in an inauthentic blackface; instead, they worked quite seriously to transform racial stereotyping from within one of its most popular and powerful media. Their strategies from within were several; indeed, Johnson recalls many heated debates over what degree of assimilation to the white mainstream was desirable. While at least one scholar has identified a pronounced strain of irony and parody in many of the "coon songs" composed by blacks at this time, the Johnsons adhered primarily to the more genteel idea of "elevating" stereotypes from lowbrow to highbrow status, along a scale that Johnson seems entirely to accept.[4] But in accepting this cultural hierarchy, he insists that a more authentic black music, of which the "coon songs" were necessarily inauthentic copies, cannot be judged by the same terms. In acknowledging the "crude, raucous, bawdy, often obscene" qualities of "coon songs," Johnson claims these traits "frequently were excellencies in folk-songs" but "rarely so in conscious imitations." Rather than themselves imitate such "imitations" of "crude" "folk-songs," his team instead tried to transform the genre—based as it was in imitation—with, in Johnson's words, a "higher degree of artistry."[5] The black press celebrated the Johnsons' songs in just these terms; one critic praises their ability to "blend" "the music of the Negro enslaved" with "the intellectual strivings of a newer life, prompted by study of purely classical lore"; this "blend," he continues, bespeaks a "new spirit, peculiarly American."[6] In fact, the Johnsons' music relied less on "the music of the Negro enslaved" than on the minstrel tradition of mainstream white popular culture. Johnson makes clear that "folk-songs" remain something altogether different from the productions of trained musicians, which are in effect combining two imitative traditions—that of minstrelsy and that of artistry.

Indeed, Johnson remained well aware of the degree to which he and his companions were all engaged in some kind of "conscious imitation," whether composing "coon songs" or "art songs." It is this awareness, I will argue, that becomes a central preoccupation of his novel. Johnson's veiled, fictionalized account of this moment in American music gives voice to the efforts of his group—and surely to his own investment as songwriter in their ambitions—while it ultimately represents their efforts to produce "hybrid," newly "American" music as an impossible task within early-twentieth-century American culture. A color line persists, the novel suggests, not only

4. See David Krasner, "Parody and Double Consciousness in the Language of Early Black Musical Theatre," *African American Review* 29 (Summer 1995): 317–23.
5. Johnson, *Along This Way*, 153.
6. R. C. Simmons, "Europe's Reception to Negro Talent," *Colored American Magazine*, November 1905, 635, 639.

in the music industry's ongoing investment in racial stereotypes but also in the very project of "blending" textual and oral traditions. While some critics have noted how *The Autobiography* exposes all identity as a matter of "imitation"—and thus exposes "race" as a learned rather than inherited quality—the novel nonetheless upholds a distinction between original and copy in its refusal to give up the possibility of an authentic black musicality that cannot be incorporated into the mainstream music industry.

"Something they've never had before"

Like Rosamond Johnson and Harry Burleigh, the ex-colored man receives formal "training" as a classical musician, training that prepares him for his ragtime performances as well as for his ambitions as a composer. But Johnson is careful to include in his narrator's youth a different form of training that precedes and shapes his reception of his piano lessons: the distinctly African American style that the ex-colored man hears in his mother's piano playing and singing. "[W]hen she was not sewing" for the white women of the neighborhood and as an alternative to her Sunday practice of playing "hymns from the book," the ex-colored man's mother would sing "old Southern songs"; in the performance of these "she was freer, because she played them by ear" (8) [7]. By setting her "freer" style of singing "by ear" against both her labor and "the book," Johnson suggests a complicity between her white employers and their musical practice, both of which work, however subtly, to keep her in a confined place.

The source of these alternative and freer musical impulses is not explicitly named at this point in the narrative, which precedes the narrator's "racial" consciousness. But Johnson gestures towards an invisible, absent black cultural presence enigmatically coloring the mother's performance and pathos:

> Always on such evenings, when the music was over, my mother would sit with me in her arms, often for a very long time. She would hold me close, softly crooning some old melody without words, all the while gently stroking her face against my head. . . . I can see her now, her great dark eyes looking into the fire, to where? No one knew but her. (8) [7–8]

In imagining her point of reference as private and solitary ("no one knew but her"), the narrator remains unaware of the social context of her musical memory, its basis in a Southern black community that he will encounter for the first time only later in his life, again as an outsider. His own musical impulses, influenced by his mother, will find expression through the instruments, institutions, and genres of the

North, a world, in his experience, predominantly white and middle class. But before taking piano lessons from the local white teacher, Johnson's narrator recalls how he responded to his mother's playing by joining her in a kind of call and response: "I used to stand by her side and often interrupt and annoy her by chiming in with strange harmonies. . . . I remember I had a particular fondness for the black keys" (8) [7]. His "chiming in" not only "interrupts" her playing but carries on an oral tradition whose racial basis is perhaps symbolized by his preference for "black" keys.

The narrator asserts this style learned from his mother at his first piano lesson, where, in response to his teacher's attempt at "pinning [him] down to the notes," he chooses instead "to reproduce the required sounds without the slightest recourse to the written characters" (9) [8]. Similarly eluding convention, the narrator approaches the piano as a "sympathetic, singing instrument," a manner he attributes "to the fact that I did not begin to learn the piano by counting out exercises, but by trying to reproduce the quaint songs which my mother used to sing, with all their pathetic turns and cadences" (26, 27) [17]. Resistant to printed "notes" and to "counting out exercises," the narrator continues an African American musical tradition passed down orally rather than textually and characterized by "pathos" rather than discipline. This effort at infusing European music with his mother's style initiates the narrator's series of efforts to create a new, hybrid musicality, while it also, already, suggests the inherent difficulty in bringing together such fundamentally opposed musical practices. Understood as "natural" rather than disciplined, vocal rather than instrumental, oral rather than textual, and improvisatory rather than composed, his mother's Southern songs invoke a black space of freedom that depends on its difference and separation from white cultural practices.

The color line is also maintained, though in a different way, by the narrator's audiences. While we are aware of the contribution of black musical style to his talents, his white audiences seem capable of hearing his performances only as the commendable but ultimately limited efforts of a black boy to learn the dominant cultural language. Early in the text the narrator's white father offers his only display of emotion toward his son upon hearing him play Frédéric Chopin: "[M]y father stepped across the room, seized me in his arms, and squeezed me to his breast. I am certain that for that moment he was proud to be my father" (35) [21]. This intimacy quickly dissipates, however, as his father returns to his white family and rewards his son's performance with the gift of an upright piano, which, the narrator notes, is "not a grand" (40) [23]. This gift sends a familiar message to the black artist aspiring to succeed in "European" cultural practices: however talented he might be, the pianist will never surpass the level of amateur. Furthermore, by rewarding his son's performance with a gift rather than any sustained supportive relationship, his father underscores what will become an increasingly problematic condition for the ex-colored man's performances: the reward of success in white America is also its cost, as music's expressive value becomes overshadowed and indeed obscured by its exchange value on a market determined by white audiences.

In a black New York "club," the narrator discovers an entirely new style of music that, while nothing like his mother's plaintive songs, seems similarly and more powerfully to express "freedom" from the "required sounds" of European practice. On his first night in New York City, the ex-colored man finds himself "dazzled and dazed" not only by gambling, alcohol, and the "brilliancy" of the nightclub atmosphere, but also by ragtime:

> I stopped talking to listen. It was music of a kind I had never heard before. It was music that demanded physical response, patting of the feet, drumming of the fingers, or nodding of the head in time with the beat. The barbaric harmonies, the audacious resolutions, often consisting of an abrupt jump from one key to another, the intricate rhythms in which the accents fell in the most unexpected places, but in which the beat was never lost, produced a most curious effect. (98–99) [53]

It was this "curious effect"—the music's irresistible and seemingly "barbaric" arousal of the body—that inspired anxious debate and many urgent calls for ragtime's suppression. Through its aggressively syncopated beats and "abrupt" changes of key, ragtime dramatically challenged the rhythmic and harmonic conventions of European music and in so doing "demanded" new ways of hearing—potentially giving black musicians a kind of power over white bodies.

Through his narrator, Johnson underscores the significance of ragtime as a black contribution to American culture in a long passage that has been excerpted more than once in histories of black music. In insisting upon the African American origins of this music (in the year of the novel's publication [1912] ragtime was most associated with Irving Berlin's popular "Alexander's Ragtime Band"), Johnson's narrator casts white ragtime performers as "imitators" and "adulterators" who have stolen both the music and its rewards (99–100) [54]. These imitators, the narrator insists, are doomed to mediocrity by virtue of the very skills that allow them to copy—to write down on paper—what they hear. The pianist in the "Club," on the other hand, achieves the status of originator and rightful owner because he *can't* write his music down; he is untrained in a skill that, according to the narrator, might allow him to better market his music but would destroy its authenticity. The narrator introduces the ragtime pianist as "just a natural musician, never having taken a lesson in his life," whose relation to music is, in other words, entirely unlike his own:

> He had, by ear alone, composed some pieces, several of which he played over for me; each of them was properly proportioned and balanced. I began to wonder what this man with such a lavish natural endowment would have done had he been trained. Perhaps he wouldn't have done anything at all; he might have become, at best, a mediocre imitator of the great masters in what they have already done to a finish, or one of the modern innovators who strive after originality by seeing how cleverly they can dodge about through the rules of harmony and at the same time avoid melody. It is certain that he would not have been so delightful as he was in ragtime. (101–2) [54–55]

This moment theoretically defines an unbridgeable gap between narrator and musician and suggests a "color line" that this novel, with all its subversions of "race," refuses to cross. An essential, if mutable, difference inheres for Johnson between "black" and "white" models of music production: for the rag player, as for the narrator's mother, music remains inseparable from the moment of its performance and from the body of its performer; for the white "imitator," as for the narrator himself, music transcribed into notes on a page becomes detached from its originator and endlessly repeatable anywhere there is a piano and someone who can read music.

As a trained musician himself, the narrator seems inevitably to occupy the deprecated position of white imitator, though Johnson reserves a privileged place for the black imitator who, like his circle at the Marshall Hotel, is in a position to bring "a higher degree of artistry" to black music's place in mainstream American culture.[7]

> Through continually listening to the music at the "Club," and through my own previous training, my natural talent and perseverance, I developed into a remarkable player of ragtime. . . . I brought all my knowledge of classic music to bear and, in so

7. A letter from Rosamond, written just after the publication of *The Autobiography*, indicates the distance James Johnson himself felt from ragtime, having been away from New York for several years. Responding to several songs James had sent him, Rosamond writes: "I don't think that you'll be able to write a *low* class rag song for some time to come as you have not been in touch with the sayings of the day—you may practice on this style by writing words to the tunes of some of the now famous ones. And in that way you'll get the run of the peculiar metre. Your 'Ark' song is a good poem of its kind but it's rather too regular in its construction. Of course there is no need of advice when it comes to lyrics like 'The Awakening.'" Johnson is more at home writing lyrics to songs like "The Awakening"—which is in the style of an "art song" and contains no explicit racial references—than writing a "*low* class rag." See letter dated 29 August 1913, James Weldon Johnson Collection, Box 40, Series III, Folder 12, Beinecke Library, Yale University.

> doing, achieved some novelties which pleased and even astonished my listeners. It was I who first made ragtime transcriptions of familiar classic selections. (114–15) [61]

In producing "ragtime transcriptions of familiar classic selections," the ex-colored man makes no pretense of authenticity but instead utilizes all aspects of his musical background to create something overtly derivative that is also an original fusion of two "racial" traditions. By "ragging the classics" he performs an African American "transformation" of the "required sounds" of European American performance practice and repertoire.

This "novel" performance style also promises him greater financial and social rewards than his classical performances, and Johnson takes great pains to represent his narrator's new relationship to white audiences:

> By mastering ragtime I gained several things: first of all I gained the title of professor. . . . Then, too, I gained the means of earning a rather fair livelihood. . . . Through it I also gained a friend who was the means by which I escaped from this lower world. And, finally, I secured a wedge which has opened to me more doors and made me a welcome guest than my playing of Beethoven and Chopin could ever have done. (115) [61]

This account of ragtime's cultural capital—as it grows to become greater even than that of Beethoven and Chopin—underscores why such classically trained black musicians as Rosamond Johnson would gravitate toward popular music in the 1890s. Moreover, it emphasizes the degree to which white audiences—like the narrator's new millionaire "friend"—seemed to approve of and reward a musical practice that entwined black culture with the more familiar context of the "classics." But while open to the black sounds of this music, the narrator's audience ultimately fixes both performer and music as projections of their seemingly unquenchable desire for novelty. The millionaire who rescues him from the "lower world" of New York black culture hires him to play at private parties in his home and the homes of his friends, all of whom crave, like the millionaire himself, an escape from the ennui of white culture in the consumption of black culture. While his white father responded to—and seemed to require—the narrator's musical suppression of his blackness, the more modern millionaire and his friends, ever in search of "a new sensation" or "a fresh emotion," respond specifically to his musical expressions of blackness (119) [63]. Although it is not stated, one imagines that he becomes a comfortable bridge for this audience between a black culture perhaps too remote and dangerous (as suggested by the slumming white widow's murder by her jealous black lover) and their own more genteel world. Indeed, it is worth noting that the "natural" black musicians in this novel never play for white audiences, who only ever hear "black music" as it is performed—through imitation, transcription, and incorporation into "white" forms—by the narrator himself.

At first, the narrator enjoys his ability to grab his white listeners' attention with ragtime, as he himself had been grabbed upon first hearing it: "It was a pleasure to me to watch the expression of astonishment and delight that grew on the faces of everybody." True to its reputation of "demanding physical response," the narrator's ragtime creates the "curious effect" of leading "the whole company involuntarily and unconsciously [to dance] an impromptu cake-walk" (119–20) [63]. In thus gazing upon the effects of his own musical agency, the ex-colored man witnesses the visually defined "color line" challenged, at least momentarily, through the invisible exchange of sound and hearing. But this apparent power, which culminates in drawing the audience into a black dance form that is itself a parody of white culture, does not alter the fact that he has become a commodity for white consumption, a fact summed up by the millionaire at the end of the party: "Well, I have given them something they've never had before" (120) [63]. The white listener's desire for novelty and sensation, furthermore, reveals itself less as openness to the coupling of black and white sounds than as addiction to "novelty," addiction that requires the performer and his music to represent and maintain their difference from the (white) familiar. In thus becoming an object of obsessive desire, the narrator finds himself trapped in a seemingly endless performance of the same, represented by the private performances he must give his employer. Playing for three or four hours at a time,

> I soon learned that my task was not to be considered finished until he got up from his chair and said: "That will do." . . . At times I became so oppressed with fatigue and sleepiness that it took almost superhuman effort to keep my fingers going; in fact, I believe I sometimes did so while dozing. During such moments this man sitting there so mysteriously silent, almost hid in a cloud of heavy-scented smoke, filled me with a sort of unearthly terror. He seemed to be some grim, mute, but relentless tyrant, possessing over me a supernatural power which he used to drive me on mercilessly to exhaustion. (121) [64]

Johnson thus demonstrates how the "color line" that continues to define and constrain the narrator's music is grounded in both racial ideology and the economic relationship between performer and listener. The successful ragtime pianist experiences a link between commodification and race: as "ragging" acquires commercial value by being offered up for the consumption of white audiences, the critical and historical difference of its "blackness"—its basis in an inimitable and thus "freer" oral culture—becomes inaudible, as does its unsettling of the line between white and black.

The ex-colored man's plan to write classical music based on Negro themes seems at first like a way out of the bind of ragtime, but it ultimately brings into sharp focus the inescapably paradoxical situation of the "trained" black musician. Like all of his preceding musical innovations, this one involves imitation and improvisation. The very idea of making black music "classical" arises when a German musician hears the narrator's own ragtime transcriptions and "develops" them:

> He seated himself at the piano, and, taking the theme of my ragtime, played it through first in straight chords; then varied and developed it through every known musical form. I sat amazed. I had been turning classic music into ragtime, a comparatively easy task; and this man had taken ragtime and made it classic. The thought came across me like a flash—It can be done, why can't I do it? (142) [74]

In following through on this idea, the narrator in effect turns his own hungry ears toward a black music that remains foreign to him, traveling "back into the very heart of the South, to live among the people, and drink my inspiration firsthand" (142) [74]. In perhaps the most ironic moment of this fictional reflection on turn-of-the-century music, Johnson characterizes his narrator's stance toward "the people" as dramatically self-serving and piratical. Indeed, the ex-colored man's relation to black musical traditions seems to become more fraught the more he tries to "imitate" them, reaching an extreme in his assumption that the raw "material" of black music is there for his taking: "I gloated over the immense amount of material I had to work with, not only modern ragtime, but also the old slave songs—material which no one had yet touched" (142–43) [74]. While he granted the "natural" ragtime player the status of originator, he seems here to assume that only the trained musician's "touching" of this material counts, discounting the very Southern "people" whose inspired performances he "drink[s] . . . firsthand." Traveling about various communities, the narrator echoes the work of postbellum ethnographers, "jotting down in my note-book themes and melodies, and trying to catch the spirit of the Negro in his relatively primitive state" (173) [90]. On his last stop, a "big meeting" that promises "a mine of material," he witnesses "Singing Johnson," whose function is to bring the large congregation together in song. With "every ear in the church . . . fixed upon him," Singing Johnson sings out "leading lines" that the congregation responds to in a call and response pattern (178) [93]. In what becomes a prelude to the novel's most dramatic turning point, the narrator's anthropological detachment suddenly breaks down in the overwhelming presence of these sounds and their collective performance:

> As I listened to the singing of these songs, the wonder of their production grew upon me. . . . [S]o many of these songs contain more than mere melody; there is sounded in them that elusive undertone, the note in music which is not heard with the ears. I sat often with the tears rolling down my cheeks and my heart melted within me. Any musical person who has never heard a Negro congregation under the spell of religious fervor sing these old songs has missed one of the most thrilling emotions which the human heart may experience. (181) [94–95]

Echoing Frederick Douglass's claim that no one could hear the slave songs without being moved by them to tears (and to opposing slavery), and anticipating Zora Neale Hurston's insistence that spirituals must be heard in their original contexts to be fully understood, Johnson's narrator here relinquishes his own musical authority—based as it is on the ability to imitate and to notate—to that of the "Negro congregation," whose collective musical expression gives meaning to the particular religious ritual of which they are a central part.[8] It is, in fact, one of the only moments when Johnson's narrator allows his individuality to be submerged in collective experience.

It is also the moment just preceding the narrator's flight from all explicit identification with, and musical expression of, blackness. His plan to transcribe the collective music of the church into classical music forms is interrupted by racial violence; upon witnessing a black man being lynched, the ex-colored man is driven by "shame, unbearable shame" [100] to abandon his black identity, along with his musical project, and to live in New York as a white businessman. What this dramatic narrative turn suggests about the ex-colored man's relationship to music—and Johnson's attitude about his narrator's musical project—remains unclear. I would suggest, however, that Johnson, if not his narrator, ultimately sees no escape from the inherent violence of any musical project that attempts to express "blackness" and "whiteness" together. The narrator's "shame" at being identified with a race subject to the violence of lynchings encompasses, I would argue, a less articulable shame that he himself was involved in "mining" black culture for the acquisition of cultural capital in order to produce art for the eventual consumption by white audiences. After his experience at the "big meeting,"

8. See Frederick Douglass, *Narrative of the Life of an American Slave, Written by Himself* (New York: Penguin, 1986); and Zora Neale Hurston, "Spirituals and Neo-spirituals," originally published in *Negro Anthology, Made by Nancy Cunard, 1931–1933* (London; Nancy Cunard at Wishart, 1934) and reprinted in Zora Neale Hurston, *The Sanctified Church* (Berkeley: Turtle Island, 1981), 79–84.

whose Southern, collective, religious context defines its musical value for him, it is difficult to imagine how he would translate this value into a symphony or oratorio to be performed by professional musicians on a stage before a paying, silent audience, an audience perhaps eager to own and consume the sounds of blackness.

The narrator's abandonment of blackness is punctuated by his ensuing marriage to whiteness, a marriage that once again draws our attention to music's capacity to perform, as well as represent, racial identity. Upon his return to New York, the narrator, now passing as white, and a woman as "white as a lily" (198) [103] fall in love through their "mutual bond of music" (201) [104]—specifically the music of Chopin, which the narrator now performs casually at cocktail parties. While their plan to marry is almost permanently postponed by the narrator's revelation of his racial heritage, the partnership is saved, as it began, with the narrator's performance of Chopin, which ultimately dissolves her resistance to miscegenation by, in effect, dissolving his blackness. Underscoring the emptiness of the urban middle-class white society he is about to join, Johnson's narrator performs one last improvisatory act, altering the "required sounds" of Chopin's piece so that it ends on a major rather than a minor chord, thus signifying in the most hackneyed of harmonic turns a "happy" ending (209) [109]. While this musical act might be taken to signify his ongoing playfulness with both music and racial identity (as one critic has suggested), it seems more an ironic signal of the end of his ambitious and interesting musical experiments in favor of (white) bourgeois convention.[9]

This novel's ending clearly registers, among other things, Johnson's disillusionment with the various projects of turn-of-the-century American music that promised to bring African American music into mainstream American culture. Standing in the way of a truly cross-cultural musical expression, Johnson implies, are obstacles not only of racism but also of an American "culture industry" that reifies racial difference as it depends on the repeatability, marketability, and novelty of its products, separates performer and audience into commodity and consumer, and erases the social history of musical styles and forms. The narrator's efforts to express "blackness" within the dominant forms of white musical expression seem ultimately complicit in the silencing of black culture. Johnson chooses instead, as I have suggested, to preserve the idea of an

9. Kathleen Pfeiffer reads the narrator's improvised "major triad" at the end of the Nocturne as a sign of his continued refusal of racial binarisms, choosing instead a third (i.e., "triadic") position of racial ambiguity. But rather than emphasize the triad (the original Chopin chord is also a triad), Johnson clearly intends to emphasize that it was a *major* as opposed to *minor* harmony. The character (if not the author) thus seems to be reproducing, rather than evading, the conventions of "whiteness," and indeed he plays right into a major/minor binarism.

authentic black music outside the domain of the American culture industry, a music not only expressing its own sounds, rhythms, and melodies but also involving its own social rituals and relations. Thus defined, black music becomes unrepresentable to anyone outside its social economy and thus loses its power to transform the "required sounds" of mainstream white America, while it remains invulnerable to any efforts to "mine" its resources for commercial or cultural gain.

Johnson's decision in 1905 to leave songwriting and turn instead to politics and literature reflected his growing sense of the limits of his work in musical theater: "[B]eing light enough for Broadway," he writes in his memoirs, "was beginning to be, it seemed, a somewhat heavy task."[1] As, perhaps, its novelty wore off, the vogue for black music and musical theater waned considerably in the 1910s, revealing the degree to which Johnson's group depended on the desire of white audiences. In December 1913, after a period of pronounced success in London, Rosamond wrote a letter to his brother about his own efforts to remain optimistic in spite of dramatically changing circumstances:

> I have had a very hard drive of it, and just at the time when it looked like easy sailing—long came the storm. But they haven't licked me yet, they've knocked me down, but they haven't knocked me out. . . . If I keep my health, I am bound to find some work to do, and I am never afraid to tackle it no matter how hard, or embarrassing it may seem I've got to get hold of some real money, and I am willing to work work work and then work some more for it.[2]

Rosamond and others would find work again, of course, in the various new musical venues of 1920s New York, but with a different sense of their relation to both American culture at large and to African American identity in particular. With the growing emphasis on racial authenticity in black cultural production, African American musicians of the 1920s were involved in more racially specific expressive forms and gestures, as, with the birth of "race records" and a growing black urban audience, was the music industry itself.

Indeed, the Johnsons would become partners again in their publication of the *Books of American Negro Spirituals* (1925, 1926), a project that, unlike the ex-colored man's and Harry Burleigh's efforts to work the spirituals into "classic European form," attempted

1. Johnson, *Along This Way*, 222. Johnson left at the moment when his brother and Bob Cole decided to take their most recent shows on tour, which would have meant enduring the racism much more prevalent outside New York (and particularly in the South).
2. Rosamond Johnson to James Weldon Johnson, 29 December 1913, James Weldon Johnson Collection, Box 40, Series III, Folder 12.

to reproduce them "authentically." But in spite of this turn to the preservation of an authentic black culture, Johnson's introduction makes very clear that such a project is itself inherently problematic. Proclaiming their attempt "to recreate around [the spiritual] as completely as we can its true atmosphere," Johnson acknowledges the impossibility of totally recreating the original social context of the spirituals in a textual reproduction, and he emphasizes the failure of European notation to represent adequately the nuances and improvisational performances of this music: "I doubt that it is possible with our present system of notation to make a fixed transcription of these peculiarities that would be absolutely true; for in their very nature they are not susceptible to fixation."[3] By acknowledging their status as "imitators" incapable of thoroughly translating one musical language into another, Johnson thus acknowledges his own difference from those now absent musicians whose music he wishes to preserve while delivering a deeply felt tribute to that different, improvised, oral culture of another moment in black cultural history. (One could argue that this tribute, in consigning this oral culture to an unrecoverable history, also obscures the thriving black music culture of the 1920s.)

In spite of his implicit critique of the racial polities of turn-of-the-century American music, Johnson at moments looked back with definite nostalgia at his stint as songwriter. I would like to close by describing Johnson's notes to a musical play called "Down the Nile," which he clearly intended as a vehicle for reviving the songs written by the "Cole and Johnson Brothers" at the turn of the century. The first and only completed scene describes the household of a famous African American composer, whose "Negro Symphony" has been performed by the National Symphony and who thus embodies what the ex-colored man might have become (Johnson, echoing the allegorical anonymity of his novel's characters, calls him only "Great Colored American Composer"). Through the nostalgic musings of the composer's housekeeper, we learn that this man once wrote popular songs, songs that the housekeeper decidedly prefers to his more recent output: "I'm certainly sorry he's started writing this new-fangled music—no tune to it," she says; "This here Negro Symphony—the only thing Negro about it is the name." The housekeeper is soon joined by the composer's devoted student, who initially scorns her lowbrow taste but quickly finds himself moved by shared memories to sit at the piano and play some of these old songs. The titles Johnson indicates in his manuscript—"Nile—Congo—Bamboo"—refer, in shorthand, to the most famous

3. Introduction to the *Books of American Negro Spirituals* (New York: Viking, 1925), 14, 30.

hits of his songwriting team: "Castle on the Nile," "The Congo Love Song," and "Under the Bamboo Tree."[4]

More explicit than any references in *The Autobiography of an Ex-Coloured Man*, this insertion of his own contributions to musical history attributes their value not to their "higher degree of artistry" but to their popularity with audiences and their lack of any claim to racial authenticity. The play's first scene clearly sides with the housekeeper's preference for tuneful songs over avant-garde symphonies that neither entertain nor seem connected to black experience, even as they claim to speak for it. The housekeeper's nostalgia hearkens back to more than just the songs of her employer; it represents, I would argue, Johnson's own nostalgia for a moment of "trained" black musical production that preceded both the explosion of the more racially defined expressions of the 1920s and the ongoing experiments among classical composers with "black" sounds."[5]

Finally, we should not discount the ex-colored man's last creative project, which is neither the aborted symphony nor his whitened performance of Chopin but rather his writing of his autobiography. The status of writing, as a process of translating the "elusive" spirit into a tangible, marketable, and repeatable artifact, has by the end of Johnson's novel been thoroughly problematized by the narrator's various experiments in cultural synthesis. Indeed, rather than preserving the narrator's "dead ambition" to give voice to his African American heritage, the "yellowing manuscripts" on the novel's final page have themselves, as manuscripts, silenced the very black musicality they claim to preserve. And yet, in acknowledging this cultural cost of his attempts to revise, inspirit, and transform America's musical traditions by way of African American ones, the narrator remains committed to the project of writing and to crossing the "color line" *through* writing that cannot claim to represent—but can nonetheless gesture toward—a black musicality independent of and inaudible to the industries of American music.

4. "Down the Nile," James Weldon Johnson Collection, JWJ MSS 196, Beinecke Library, Yale University.
5. The term "new-fangled" dates this undated fragment to the post-tonal era of musical modernism at the moment when such "New Negro composers" as William Grant Still and Nathianel Dett gained a degree of fame (1920s–1940s) unknown to the earlier generation. For a discussion of these composers, see Spencer, *The New Negroes and Their Music*, and Southern, *The Music of Black Americans*.

James Weldon Johnson's Life and Times: A Chronology†

June 17, 1871	James William Johnson (JWJ) born. With brother, James Rosamond, reared in Jacksonville, Florida, by Helen Louise (Dillet) Johnson and James Johnson.
1884	The Johnson family visits New York City. This trip awakens JWJ's lifelong fascination with Manhattan and urban life.
1885–87	JWJ meets J. Douglas Wetmore, the real-life model for the ex-colored man. Their friendship endures until Wetmore's death (by suicide) in 1930.
1886	JWJ meets Frederick Douglass in Jacksonville. JWJ had won a copy of *The Life and Times of Frederick Douglass* (1881), as a prize from the Stanton School, where he was a high school student in Jacksonville.
1888	JWJ enters Atlanta University's Preparatory Division.
1888–89	JWJ meets physician-surgeon T. O. Summers in Jacksonville. Working as Summers's office assistant, JWJ enjoys mentoring privileges, including a luxury cruise to New York City and rail travel to Washington, DC (spring 1889). Summers likely served as the model for "the Millionaire" in *Autobiography of an Ex-Colored Man* (*ECM*). Summers committed suicide in 1899.
1890	JWJ begins college curriculum at Atlanta University. He meets George A. Towns, who would become a key confidante as JWJ composed *ECM*. The scholarly Towns (who became an English professor at

† This chronology draws from Johnson's autobiography *Along This Way* (*ATW*) and Rudolph P. Byrd's chronology in *The Essential Writings of James Weldon Johnson* (New York: Modern Library, 2008). Byrd, in turn, based his summary on Sondra Kathryn Wilson's compendiums of Johnson's writings. I am indebted to both scholars' foundational work.

Atlanta University) may have been the model for Shiny, an important foil to the novel's narrator.

1891 JWJ spends summer teaching in rural Georgia, an experience that sharpened his resolve to do public service work on behalf of African Americans. This locale likely informed JWJ's descriptions of the Georgia backwoods in the final chapters of *ECM*.

1893 JWJ spends summer working at the Columbian Exposition World's Fair in Chicago, where he meets Frederick Douglass, Ida B. Wells, and Paul Laurence Dunbar.

1894 JWJ graduates as class speaker from Atlanta University and spends the summer touring New England with the school's singing quartet. When he returns to Jacksonville, JWJ is appointed principal at Stanton Preparatory School, his alma mater.

1895 JWJ founds the *Daily American* newspaper, the first daily newspaper owned and published by an African American. Frederick Douglass dies.

1896 The Supreme Court issues its decision in *Plessy v. Ferguson*, which legalizes racial segregation in public facilities.

1896–98 JWJ studies for law career as an apprentice to Jacksonville, Florida, attorney Thomas Ledouth. JWJ passes state bar exam in 1898, the first African American to do so.

1900 JWJ collaborates with brother, Rosamond, to compose "Lift Every Voice and Sing," first performed by Jacksonville schoolchildren to commemorate Abraham Lincoln's birthday. The tune circulates rapidly and becomes renowned as the Negro National Anthem.

1901 JWJ attacked by a mob of National Guard soldiers in Jacksonville. He relocates to New York City. Booker T. Washington publishes *Up from Slavery*.

1903 W. E. B. Du Bois publishes *The Souls of Black Folk*.

1902–10 JWJ launches his musical career in New York City. Joins forces with musician brother, Rosamond, and vaudeville performer-composer Bob Cole to form Johnson Brothers and Cole. The group writes a string of successful "coon songs" whose sheet lyrics become best-sellers and are widely performed on the Broadway stage. JWJ tours the United States

	and Europe, accompanying Rosamond and Cole, who staged the tunes as part of their vaudeville act.
1903–06	JWJ attends literature classes at Columbia University in New York. Studies modern fiction and drama with renowned literary critic Brander Matthews. Begins drafting *ECM* during his studies with Matthews.
1906–10	JWJ's political activities in New York (he was president of the Colored Republican Club) earn favor from Booker T. Washington, who engineers his appointment to the U.S. State Department's Consular Service. JWJ begins his tour of duty in Puerto Cabello, Venezuela, and completes it in Corinto, Nicaragua. He finishes *ECM* while in Latin America.
1909	National Association for the Advancement of Colored People (NAACP) founded.
1910	On a visit home from Nicaragua, JWJ marries Grace Nail in New York City. The couple first met in 1900, on one of JWJ's visits to New York.
1912	*ECM* is published by Sherman, French & Company on or about May 18. JWJ changes name his middle name to "Weldon," because it seemed "more literary," as he explained to George A. Towns.
1914	JWJ resigns from the U.S. Consular Service because he does not win sought-after appointments to France. Returns to the United States. Stays briefly in Jacksonville, then moves again to New York City. Begins writing an editorial column, "Views & Reviews," for the African American–owned and –managed *New York Age* newspaper.
1915	Booker T. Washington dies.
1916	JWJ recruited to join national staff of the NAACP as a field secretary. In this post, he leads the organization's membership drives and anti-lynching protest movement.
1917	JWJ organizes the NAACP's Silent Protest March in New York, held in the midst of the Red Summer riots, an outbreak of racial violence in America's largest cities. This march is the largest and most widely reported anti-lynching demonstration in U.S. history.
1917	JWJ publishes his first volume of verse, *Fifty Years and Other Poems*, with Cornhill Company of Boston.

1919–20 *Half-Century Magazine*, an African American periodical based in Chicago, publishes *ECM* in (near) monthly installments, starting and ending in November of these years.

1920 JWJ promoted to executive director of the NAACP. Continues to foreground black voting rights and antilynching protest during his term in this post. JWJ also publishes a major critique of U.S. military intervention in Haiti for *The Nation*, which begins his public activism in diaspora politics.

1922 JWJ compiles and publishes *The Book of American Negro Poetry*, issued by Harcourt, Brace and Company. He will go on to revise and reissue this anthology multiple times. The anthology exemplifies JWJ's role as a mentor to the new generation of African American poets and writers working during the Harlem Renaissance. In its own right, this book's preface is a classic in African American poetics. Roots of his argument can be traced back to the 1912 edition of *ECM*.

1925 Together with his brother, Rosamond, JWJ edits *The Book of American Negro Spirituals*, issued by Viking Press. Like the preface to the poetry anthology, JWJ's preface on the history and performance aesthetics of singing spirituals becomes a classic analysis. Roots of his argument can be traced back to the 1912 edition of *ECM*.

1927 JWJ publishes *God's Trombones*, with Knopf. The collection's seven poems are written as "sermons in verse." *ECM* is reissued by Knopf on or about August 20, as part of the Blue Jade Series.

1928 *Der Weise Negre* (The white negro: a life between the races), a German-language translation of *ECM*, is published by Frankfurter Societäts-Druckerei of Berlin, by contract with Knopf.

1929 JWJ travels to Kyoto, Japan, on a Rosenwald Fellowship, to attend a conference sponsored by the American Council of the Institute of Pacific Relations. In this context, JWJ claimed he achieved his fullest understanding of "the universality of the race and color problem" (*ATW*, 398).

1930 JWJ resigns as executive director of the NAACP. JWJ publishes *Black Manhattan*, a history of African American community building and performing arts culture in New York City, with Knopf. This

	same year he also publishes a limited edition of his final verse collection, *Saint Peter Relates an Incident of the Resurrection Day*, with Viking. Only two hundred copies were printed, for private circulation.
1931	JWJ accepts the Adam K. Spence Chair of Creative Writing at Fisk University in Nashville, Tennessee. The award makes him the first African American to hold an endowed professorship at a research university in the United States.
1933	JWJ publishes his memoir, *Along This Way*, with Viking.
1934	JWJ joins New York University as a visiting professor, becoming its first African American faculty member. JWJ publishes *Negro Americans, What Now?*, an assessment of (then) contemporary racial politics, with Viking.
1935	JWJ reissues *Saint Peter Relates an Incident* with other selected poems, published for general sales with Viking.
1937	Knopf reissues *ECM* on December 1.
June 26, 1938	JWJ killed in a car accident near Great Barrington, Massachusetts.
1948	New American Library (NAL) publishes a posthumous edition of *ECM* in June. This edition introduces race fiction to NAL's line of mass-marketed paperbacks.
1951	The U.S. State Department considers issuing *ECM* in India and Indonesia as part of a Cold War cultural outreach program to send race literature abroad. Extant evidence does not confirm that this actually occurred. Ironically, the State Department's plan brings the novel back to its 1912 origins, given the vital role that JWJ's diplomatic jobs played in his completion of the first edition.

Selected Bibliography

• indicates works included or excerpted in this Norton Critical Edition

Andrade, Heather Russell. "Revising Critical Judgments of *The Autobiography of an Ex-Colored Man*." *African American Review* 40.2 (Summer 2006): 257–70.

Badaracco, Claire Hoertz. "*The Autobiography of an Ex-Colored Man* by James Weldon Johnson: The 1927 Knopf Edition." *Papers of the Bibliographical Society of America* 96.2 (2002): 279–87.

Baker, Houston A., Jr. "A Forgotten Prototype: *The Autobiography of an Ex-Colored Man* and *Invisible Man*." *Virginia Quarterly Review* 49.3 (Summer 1973): 433–49.

Balter, Ariel. "The Color of Money in *The Autobiography of an Ex-Coloured Man*." *Complicating Constructions: Race, Ethnicity, and Hybridity in American Texts*. Ed. David S. Goldstein and Audrey B. Thacker. Seattle: University of Washington Press, 2007. 48–73.

Barnhart, Bruce. "Chronopolitics and Race, Rag-time and Symphonic Time in *The Autobiography of an Ex-Colored Man*." *African American Review* 40.3 (Fall 2006): 551–69.

Bechtold, Rebeccah. "'Playing with Fire': The Aestheticization of Southern Violence in James Weldon Johnson's *The Autobiography of an Ex-Colored Man*." *Southern Quarterly* 49.1 (Fall 2011): 30–49.

Belluscio, Steven J. "'To Rise Above This Absurd Drama That Others Have Staged': Race Critique and Genre in Chesnutt, Johnson, and Schuyler." *To Be Suddenly White: Literary Realism and Racial Passing*. Columbia: University of Missouri Press, 2006. 132–75.

• Berlin, Edward A. *Ragtime: A Musical and Cultural History*. Berkeley: University of California Press, 1980.

Biers, Katherine. "Syncope Fever: James Weldon Johnson and the Black Voice." *Representations* 96 (Fall 2006): 99–125.

Bombergen, Anne. "Passing Through Europe: Race and National Identity in Weldon Johnson's *Autobiography of an Ex-Colored Man* and James Baldwin's *Giovanni's Room*." *Journal of American Studies of Turkey* 13 (2001): 23–32.

Bone, Robert A. "Novels of the Talented Tenth." *The Negro Novel in America*. Rev. ed. New Haven, CT: Yale University Press, 1965. 45–49.

Brooks, Neil. "On Becoming an Ex-Man: Postmodern Irony and the Extinguishing of Certainties in *The Autobiography of an Ex-Colored Man*." *College Literature* 22.3 (Oct. 1995): 17–29.

———. "'Passing Over': The Passing Novel and America's Inauthentic Narratives of Race." *Fakes and Forgeries*. Ed. Peter Knight and Jonathan Long. Buckingham, Eng.: Cambridge Scholars, 2004. 177–86.

Brown, Sterling A. "Counter-Propaganda—Beginning Realism." *The Negro in American Fiction*. Washington, DC: Associates in Negro Folk Education, 1937. 104–05.

Bruce, Dickson D., Jr. "The Two Worlds of James Weldon Johnson." *Black American Writing from the Nadir, 1877–1915: The Evolution of a Literary Tradition*. Baton Rouge: Louisiana State University Press, 1989. 230–62.

Bryant, Jerry H. "The Limits of the Hero: Chesnutt's *Marrow of Tradition* and Johnson's *Autobiography of an Ex-Colored Man.*" *Victims and Heroes: Racial Violence in the African-American Novel.* Amherst: University of Massachusetts Press, 1997. 105–25.

Byrd, Rudolph P. *The Essential Writings of James Weldon Johnson.* New York: Modern Library, 2008.

Cartwright, Keith. "On James Weldon Johnson's Cigar Factory 'Reader' and the Need for Local Readings in Florida's Contact Zones." *Florida Studies: Proceedings of the 2005 Annual Meeting of the Florida College English Association.* Ed. Steve Glassman, Karen Tolchin, and Steve Brahlek. Newcastle-upon-Tyne, Eng.: Cambridge Scholars, 2006. 123–30.

Clarke, Cheryl. "Race, Homosocial Desire, and 'Mammon' in *Autobiography of an Ex-Coloured Man.*" *Professions of Desire: Lesbian and Gay Studies in Literature.* Ed. George E. Haggerty and Bonnie Zimmerman. New York: Modern Language Association of America, 1995. 84–97.

Collier, Eugenia W. "The Endless Journey of an Ex-Coloured Man." *Phylon* 32.4 (1971): 365–73.

Dexl, Carmen. "Ambiguity and the Ethics of Reading Race and Lynching in James W. Johnson's *The Autobiography of an Ex-Colored Man.*" COPAS 10 (2009).

Dickson-Carr, Darryl. "Precursors: Satire through the Harlem Renaissance, 1900–1940." *African American Satire: The Sacredly Profane Novel.* Columbia: University of Missouri Press, 2001. 38–81.

Dowling, Robert M. "A Marginal Man in Black Bohemia: James Weldon Johnson in the New York Tenderloin." *Post-Bellum, Pre-Harlem: African American Literature and Culture.* Ed. Barbara McCaskill and Caroline Gebhard. New York: New York University Press, 2006. 117–32.

• Fabi, M. Giulia. "The Mark Within: Parody in James Weldon Johnson's *The Autobiography of an Ex-Coloured Man.*" *Passing and the Rise of the African-American Novel.* Urbana: University of Illinois Press, 2001. 90–105.

Faulkner, Howard. "James Weldon Johnson's Portrait of the Artist as Invisible Man." *Black American Literature Forum* 19.4 (Winter 1985): 147–51.

Fleming, Robert E. "Contemporary Themes in Johnson's *Autobiography of an Ex-Colored Man.*" *Negro American Literature Forum* 4.4 (Winter 1970): 120–24.

———. "Irony as Key to Johnson's *Autobiography of an Ex-Colored Man.*" *American Literature* 43.1 (March 1971): 83–96.

———. *James Weldon Johnson.* Boston: Twayne, 1987.

Gallego, Mar. "'On Which Side?' James Weldon Johnson's *Autobiography of an Ex-Colored Man.*" *Revistos de Estudios Norteamericanos* 8 (2001): 33–48.

Garrett, Marvin P. "Early Recollections and Structural Irony in *The Autobiography of an Ex-Colored Man.*" *Critique* 13.3 (Jan. 1971): 5–14.

Gayle, Addison, Jr. "The White Man's Burden." *The Way of the New World: The Black Novel in America.* Garden City, NY: Doubleday, 1975. 91–111.

Gilmore, Michael T. "Politics and the Writer's Career: Two Cases." *Reciprocal Influences: Literary Production, Distribution, and Consumption in America.* Ed. Steven Fink and Susan S. Williams. Columbus: Ohio State University Press, 1999. 199–212.

Gloster, Hugh M. "James Weldon Johnson." *Negro Voices in American Fiction.* Chapel Hill: University of North Carolina Press, 1948. 79–83.

Goellnicht, Donald C. "Passing as Autobiography: James Weldon Johnson's *The Autobiography of an Ex-Colored Man.*" *African American Review* 30.1 (Spring 1996): 17–33.

Goldsby, Jacqueline. "'Keeping the Secret of Authorship': A Critical Look at the 1912 Publication of James Weldon Johnson's *The Autobiography of an Ex-Colored Man.*" *Print Culture in a Diverse America.* Ed. James P. Danky and Wayne A. Wiegand. Urbana: University of Illinois Press, 1998. 244–71.

———. "Lynching's Mass Appeal and the 'Terrible Real': James Weldon Johnson." *A Spectacular Secret: Lynching in American Life and Literature.* Chicago: University of Chicago Press, 2006. 164–213.

Greene, J. Lee. "The Beast-Bridegroom: Johnson's Ex-Coloured Man." *Blacks in Eden: The African-American Novel's First Century*. Charlottesville: University of Virginia Press, 1996. 89–95.

Harper, Philip Brian. "Gender Politics and the 'Passing' Fancy: Black Masculinity as a Societal Problem." *Are We Not Men? Masculine Anxiety and the Problem of African American Identity*. New York: Oxford University Press, 1998. 103–26.

Jackson, Miles M. "Letters to a Friend: Correspondence from James Weldon Johnson to George A. Towns." *Phylon* 29.2 (1968): 182–98.

Japtok, Martin. "Between 'Race' as Construct and 'Race' as Essence: *The Autobiography of an Ex-Coloured Man*." *Southern Literary Journal* 28.2 (Spring 1996): 17–33.

Johnson, James Weldon. *The Selected Writings of James Weldon Johnson: The New York Age Editorials (1914–1923)*. Vol. 1. Ed. Sondra Kathryn Wilson. New York: Oxford University Press, 1995.

———. *The Selected Writings of James Weldon Johnson: Social, Political, and Literary Essays*. Vol. 2. Ed. Sondra Kathryn Wilson. New York: Oxford University Press, 1995.

Jones, Jill Colvin. "Rights and Birthrights: The Mis-Reading of Jacob and Esau and *The Autobiography of an Ex-Colored Man*." *Florida Studies: Proceedings of the 2005 Annual Meeting of the Florida College English Association*. Ed. Steve Glassman, Karen Tolchin, and Steve Brahlek. Newcastle-upon-Tyne, Eng.: Cambridge Scholars, 2006. 51–68.

Kardos, Michael. "Musical and Ideological Synthesis in James Weldon Johnson's *The Autobiography of an Ex-Colored Man*." *Music and Literary Modernism: Critical Essays and Comparative Studies*. Ed. Robert P. McParland. Newcastle-upon-Tyne, Eng.: Cambridge Scholars, 2009. 126–35.

Kawash, Samira. "*The Autobiography of an Ex-Coloured Man*: (Passing for) Black Passing for White." *Passing and the Fictions of Identity*. Ed. Elaine Ginsberg. Durham: Duke University Press, 1996. 59–74.

Kinnamon, Keneth. "Three Black Writers and the Anthologized Canon." *American Literary Realism* 23.3 (Spring 1991): 42–51.

Kostelanetz, Richard. *Politics in the African American Novel: James Weldon Johnson, W. E. B. Du Bois, Richard Wright, and Ralph Ellison*. New York: Greenwood Press, 1991.

Kutzinski, Vera. "Johnson Revises Johnson: *Oxherding Tale* and *The Autobiography of an Ex-Coloured Man*." *Pacific Coast Philology* 23.1–2 (Nov. 1988): 39–46.

Lamothe, Daphne. "Striking Out into the Interior: Travel, Imperialism, and Ethnographic Perspectives in *The Autobiography of an Ex-Colored Man*." *Inventing the New Negro: Narrative, Culture, Ethnography*. Philadelphia: University of Pennsylvania Press, 2008. 69–90.

Lawson, Benjamin Sherwood. "Odysseus's Revenge: The Names on the Title Page of *The Autobiography of an Ex-Coloured Man*." *Southern Literary Journal* 21.2 (Spring 1989): 92–99.

• Levy, Eugene. *James Weldon Johnson: Black Leader, Black Voice*. Chicago: University of Chicago Press, 1973.

MacKethan, Lucinda H. "Black Boy and Ex-Coloured Man: Version and Inversion of the Slave Narrator's Quest for Voice." *CLA Journal* 32.2 (Dec. 1988): 123–47.

Marren, Susan, and Robert Cochran. "Johnson's *The Autobiography of an Ex-Colored Man*." *Explicator* 60.3 (Spring 2002): 147–49.

Mason, Julian. "James Weldon Johnson: A Southern Writer Resists the South." *CLA Journal* 31.2 (Dec. 1987): 154–69.

McCarthy, Timothy Patrick. "Legalizing Cultural Anxieties: Plessy, Race, and Literary Representations of 'Passing' in James Weldon Johnson's *Autobiography of an Ex-Colored Man*." *Griot* 16.1 (Spring 1997): 1–10.

Miskolcze, Robin. "Intertextual Links: Reading *Uncle Tom's Cabin* in James Weldon Johnson's *The Autobiography of an Ex-Colored Man*." *College Literature* 40.1 (Spring 2013): 121–38.

Morgan, Thomas L. "The City as Refuge: Constructing Urban Blackness in Paul Laurence Dunbar's *The Sport of the Gods* and James Weldon Johnson's *The Autobiography of an Ex-Colored Man*." *African American Review* 38.2 (Summer 2004): 213–37.

Morrisette, Noelle. *James Weldon Johnson's Modern Soundscapes*. Iowa City: University of Iowa Press, 2013.

Nielson, Aldon Lynn. "James Weldon Johnson's Impossible Text: *The Autobiography of an Ex-Colored Man*." *Writing Between the Lines: Race and Intertextuality*. Athens: University of Georgia Press, 1994. 172–84.

Nownes, Nicholas L. "Public Acts and Private Utterances in James Weldon Johnson's *The Autobiography of an Ex-Colored Man*." *Southern Studies* 12.1–2 (2005): 63–77.

Oliver, Lawrence J. "Teaching James Weldon Johnson's *The Autobiography of an Ex-Colored Man*." *Teaching the Harlem Renaissance: Course Design and Classroom Strategies*. Ed. Michael Soto. New York: Peter Lang, 2008. 145–52.

O'Sullivan, Maurice J., Jr. "Of Souls and Pottage: James Weldon Johnson's *The Autobiography of an Ex-Coloured Man*." *CLA Journal* 23.1 (Fall 1979): 60–70.

Page, Amanda M. "The Ever-Expanding South: James Weldon Johnson and the Rhetoric of the Global Color Line." *Southern Quarterly* 46.3 (Spring 2009): 26–46.

Payne, Ladell. "Themes and Cadences: James Weldon Johnson's Novel." *Southern Literary Journal* 11.2 (Spring 1979): 43–55.

Pfeiffer, Kathleen. "Individualism, Success, and American Identity in *The Autobiography of an Ex-Colored Man*." *African American Review* 30.3 (Fall 1996): 403–19.

Pisiak, Roxanna. "Irony and Subversion in James Weldon Johnson's *The Autobiography of an Ex-Coloured Man*." *Studies in American Fiction* 21.1 (Spring 1993): 83–96.

Portelli, Alessandro. "The Tragedy and the Joke: James Weldon Johnson's *The Autobiography of an Ex-Coloured Man*." *Looking Back at the Harlem Renaissance*. Ed. Geneviève Fabre and Michel Feith. Bloomington: Indiana University Press, 2001. 143–58.

Powell, Tamara. "Looking toward the Future: Examining the Tangibility of Margins in James Weldon Johnson's *Autobiography of an Ex-Colored Man*." *Publications of the Mississippi Philological Association* (2004): 27–36.

Price, Kenneth M., and Lawrence J. Oliver, eds. *Critical Essays on James Weldon Johnson*. New York: Hall, 1997.

Roberts, Brian Russell. "Passing into Diplomacy: U.S. Consul James Weldon Johnson and *The Autobiography of an Ex-Colored Man*." *Modern Fiction Studies* 56.2 (Summer 2010): 290–316.

Rottenberg, Catherine. "Race and Ethnicity in *The Autobiography of an Ex-Colored Man* and *The Rise of David Levitsky*: The Performative Difference." *MELUS* 29.3–4 (Autumn–Winter 2004): 307–21.

• Ruotolo, Cristina L. "James Weldon Johnson and the Autobiography of an Ex-Colored Musician." *American Literature* 72.2 (June 2000): 249–74.

Russell, Heather. "Race, Citizenship, and Form: James Weldon Johnson's *The Autobiography of an Ex-Colored Man*." *Legba's Crossing: Narratology in the African Atlantic*. Athens: University of Georgia Press, 2009. 29–58.

Schultz, Jennifer L. "Restaging the Racial Contract: James Weldon Johnson's Signatory Strategies." *American Literature* 74.1 (March 2002): 31–58.

Scott, Darieck. "'A Race That Could Be So Dealt With': Terror, Time, and (Black) Power." *Extravagant Abjection: Blackness, Power, and Sexuality in the African American Literary Imagination*. New York: New York University Press, 2010. 95–125.

Sheldon, Glenn. "Doubt and Denial in Johnson's Novel." *MAWA Review* 13.2 (1998): 96–98.

Skerrett, Joseph T., Jr. "Irony and Symbolic Action in James Weldon Johnson's *The Autobiography of an Ex-Coloured Man*." *American Quarterly* 32.5 (Winter 1980): 540–58.

Smith, Valerie A. "Privilege and Evasion in *The Autobiography of an Ex-Colored Man*." *Self-Discovery and Authority in Afro-American Narrative*. Cambridge, MA: Harvard University Press, 1987. 44–64.

• Somerville, Siobhan B. "Double Lives on the Color Line: 'Perverse' Desire in *The Autobiography of an Ex-Colored Man*." *Queering the Color Line: Race and the Invention of Homosexuality in American Culture*. Durham: Duke University Press, 2000. 111–30.

Spaulding, A. Timothy. "The Cultural Matrix of Ragtime in James Weldon Johnson's *The Autobiography of an Ex-Colored Man*." *Genre* 37.2 (2004): 225–44.

Stecopoulos, Harilaos. "Up from Empire: James Weldon Johnson, Latin America, and the Jim Crow South." *Reconstructing the World: Southern Fictions and U.S. Imperialisms, 1898–1976*. Ithaca: Cornell University Press, 2008. 53–76.

• Stepto, Robert B. "Lost in a Quest: James Weldon Johnson's *The Autobiography of an Ex-Colored Man*." *From Behind the Veil: A Study of Afro-American Narrative*. 2nd ed. Urbana: University of Illinois Press, 1991. 95–127.

Sugimori, Masami. "Narrative Order, Racial Hierarchy, and 'White' Discourse in James Weldon Johnson's *The Autobiography of an Ex-Colored Man* and *Along This Way*." *MELUS* 36.3 (Fall 2011): 37–62.

Sundquist, Eric J. "These Old Slave Songs: *The Autobiography of an Ex-Coloured Man*." *The Hammers of Creation: Folk Culture in Modern African-American Fiction*. Athens: University of Georgia Press, 1992. 1–48.

Vauthier, Simone. "The Interplay of Narrative Modes in James Weldon Johnson's *The Autobiography of an Ex-Colored Man*." *Jarbuch fur Amerikastudien* 18 (1973): 173–81.

Wald, Gayle. "Home Again: Racial Negotiations in Modernist African American Passing Narratives." *Crossing the Line: Racial Passing in Twentieth-Century U.S. Literature and Culture*. Durham: Duke University Press, 2000. 25–52.

———. "The Satire of Race in James Weldon Johnson's *Autobiography of an Ex-Colored Man*." *Cross-Addressing: Resistance Literature and Cultural Borders*. Ed. John C. Hawley. Albany: SUNY Series in Postmodern Culture, 1996. 139–55.

Walker, F. Patton. "The Narrator's Editorialist Voice in *The Autobiography of an Ex-Colored Man*." *CLA Journal* 41.1 (Sept. 1997): 70–92.

Wandler, Steven. "'A Negro's Chance': Ontological Luck in *The Autobiography of an Ex-Colored Man*." *African American Review* 42.3–4 (Fall–Winter 2008): 579–94.

Warren, Kenneth W. "Troubled Black Humanity in *The Souls of Black Folk* and *The Autobiography of an Ex-Colored Man*." *The Cambridge Companion to American Realism and Naturalism: Howells to London*. Ed. Donald Pizer. Cambridge, Eng.: Cambridge University Press, 1995. 263–77.

Washington, Salim. "Of Black Bards, Known and Unknown: Music as Racial Metaphor in James Weldon Johnson's *The Autobiography of an Ex-Colored Man*." *Callaloo* 25.1 (Winter 2002): 233–56.

Yarborough, Richard. "The First Person in Afro-American Fiction." In Houston A. Baker, Jr., and Patricia Redmond, eds. *Afro-American Literary Study in the 1990s*. Chicago: University of Chicago Press, 1992. 105–34.